The Earth-Chai Saga

Book One:
Waking the Dragon

J. A. Di Spada

PublishAmerica
Baltimore

First printing

At the specific preference of the author, PublishAmerica allowed this work to remain exactly as the author intended, verbatim, without editorial input.

ISBN: 1-4241-5275-5
PUBLISHED BY PUBLISHAMERICA, LLLP
www.publishamerica.com
Baltimore

Printed in the United States of America

Dedication

This book is dedicated to my wife Ramona, whose encouragement, understanding, and patience made it possible to complete it. And to my daughter Artemis, who's mostly silent, and often rueful, approval meant so much to me as I was writing it.

It is also dedicated to my daughter Gabriella, and my son John Anthony, both of whom I love dearly!

For Barbara
    and Hank

    Thanks for being such a steadfast
friend for Ramona, and for letting
me join in the fun.
                    Best Always,
                    John

            J. A. DiSpada

Acknowledgments

I would like to thank the following authors, Isaac Asimov, Philip K. Dick, Frank Russel, Robert Heinlein, R. A. Salvatore, Andre Norton, Frank Herbert, Greg Bear, Robert Ludlum, J.R.R. Tolkien, Jack Vance, David Morrell, Gordon R. Dickson, E. C. Tub, David Drake, and the many others who are too numerous to name here.

I wish to thank them for the more than fifty years of pleasure in reading and learning they provided this author. They have been my unsuspecting mentors, and I hope they will look kindly on this first effort of mine, wherever they may now be.

I would also like to thank the owners of the, Cornerstone Café, and the Manalapan and Golden Bell diners in Freehold NJ, where most of this book was written. They provided a place to sit and write, and gallons of coffee.

In conclusion, I would like to thank all of the friends, relatives, and complete strangers who, once they found out what I was scribbling, encouraged me to complete this work.

Thank you all!

Table of Contents

Author's Note—Please note that those parts of the conversational portions of this book that are in bold italics are intended to portray telepathic conversations between various characters.

PRELUDE

The piece of space debris was not moving very fast, not fast that is by cosmic standards, a mere tenth light in velocity. Nor was it massive in size either, except for where it was and where it was coming from. More important, of course, was where it was going!

The object came barreling in slightly above the plane of the ecliptic of our sun, from a rather remote spiral arm of another galaxy, a direction that to an Earthman could be called the galactic north.

What made it so dangerous was the density of its mass. In size, it was a little smaller than an earth child's toy marble, about a half-inch in diameter. It was a minute piece of jetsam, flung out eons past as part of the cosmic cataclysm of a sun going nova. It was coming in from the vast empty void between galaxies.

It should not have been there. Or maybe fate was back from it's' holiday

What also made it so dangerous was that its flight path would shortly cause it to interdict that of another object. That object, though, was not a natural one!

Someone had manufactured this object. Moreover, it was inhabited. It, also, should not have been there, as any of the inhabitants of the third planet of this obscure sun would have said had they known of its existence.

Luck, chance, fate, or whatever you care to ascribe to it, was about to change the lives of both the beings inhabiting the object, and almost all of those inhabiting a little known planet of a little known solar system called Earth, and Sol respectively.

It was about to pull many of those inhabiting that small planet, by the boot straps, into the reality existing for the rest of this galaxy and its numerous and extremely varied inhabitants.

It was also about to pull that galaxy and its many and varied inhabitants by their own bootstraps, figuratively speaking, into facing a terrible threat that was on the verge of exploding into their domains.

A threat that if not stopped would place them all into an existence of abject slavery for every being.

CHAPTER ONE
The Happening

The Platform

The observation platform had been permanently fixed in its present orbital position for a relatively short period of time. Short, that is, by the occupants' standards. Only seventy-five revolutions of the primary of the planet that was being observed, which was a comparatively young, and bright, yellow star.

The planet being observed was a beautiful blue green sphere, third out in orbital position of its planetary system and about ninety million miles out from its sun. It had one planetoid-sized satellite that was both airless and lifeless. The inhabitants of that planet were a carbon/oxygen based life form which had reached the atomic stage of development.

The Chai, the being in command of this platform, had just finished the arduous job of repositioning It's observation platform to a new position about three hundred million miles above planetary orbital plane of the solar system, and right in line with the extreme coronal ring where that suns glare was brightest.

The reason for the move was that the inhabitants of the third planet were very near the brink of achieving serious space flight capability. For the past seventy five planetary revolutions around it's' sun the platform had remained hidden from the inhabitants of the third planet by maintaining a position about sixty million miles directly sun ward from the planets rotational axis.

It was a simple ruse, always keeping the sun in their eyes, making it unlikely for it to be seen. However, that would no longer work. The technology being employed on the platform was very advanced by the standards of the people on the third planet but by no means out of reach of their potential for understanding.

That was one of the reasons for moving the platform. They had advanced to the point where they could deduce a great deal just from observation alone. The Chai did not want its' presence known to them just yet.

This species had the disconcerting ability of taking seemingly unrelated bits of information and forming them into working hypotheses, especially where mechanical technology was concerned.

They were advancing at a rate that was phenomenal by the standards of most of the other intelligent species in the galaxy. In the last seventy-five years, they had made technological strides that took most races hundreds, even thousands, of years to achieve. This factor alone would have condoned there being an observer on the platform full time.

There were other reasons, ominous ones, for the Chais' presence as part of a permanent observation effort of this race.

Although, as yet, there were no overt signs here, as there had been in other systems closer to the galactic divide, it was because of this anomaly that there was a possibility of Drel influence affecting this races actions.

The Chai did not think this was so but there was a small possibility that it was. That possibility had to be checked and rechecked, as thoroughly as it was possible to do so, without exposing its own presence. Thus, the need to move the platform to its new location held even more importance than the discovery of it by the indigenes.

The Incident

After making the final telemetry checks on the platforms positioning and orbital stability, and the positioning of its observation drones, the only thing left to do was to raise the fixed position defensive shields. To do that it was necessary to raise the output of the utility fusion core and switch over to it from the interplanetary drive reactor, a process requiring another hour or so's work.

The Chai informed/asked its' present symbiotic partner to commence with this process and visualized for It the precise operating procedure that would be required. The Trine, its present host-partner began the process of shutting down the interplanetary drive core reactors and the drive shields.

These shields operated somewhat like an auger in interplanetary space, moving small slow moving and stationary particles, and other debris, around the hull by means of gravitic wave manipulation, thereby creating a tunnel and taking the ship through the path of least resistance.

Most of space is generally thought of as a void, but it is not empty, especially space within a planetary solar system.

The difference in the shields was simple but mechanically demanding. The drive shields worked on a pulsed, push/pull principle, of alternating waves that moved objects around the ships hull while it was moving.

The fixed position shields worked on a single wave repulsor or pressor beams which are fan shaped and operated in layers of depth and distance with overlapping fields to create an englobement of the platform while in stationary orbit. They also demanded a great deal of power, therefor the requirement for separate power supplies.

The fusion reactor was kept on line at minimum power, simply because it took so long to re-initiate fusion ignition and spool up for power output. As the Trine began spooling up the fusion power for the stationary shields, it also began to initiate the sensor package tied into the shield array. At half power, the sensors had a range of about half a million miles.

As the sensors came on line, every warning light on the control boards came alive all at once, both visually and audibly. Bedlam seemed to break out as every warning klaxon sounded at the same time.

The computer analog began a vocal litany of immanent collision/impact warnings while simultaneously giving time and distance readouts, both visually and audibly also. There was very, very little time left for the platform.

The shields would not be fully up in time to stop whatever was coming as the distance and time to impact warnings dropped off precipitously!

One glance was enough to show this. There might be enough time to get into an escape vehicle, and dubious safety. There was no time left for thinking, only time enough, hopefully, to act and escape certain doom.

Doom with a capital D! Because anything this far out, and big enough to set off every alarm on the platform, meant virtual disaster. The Chai bade the Trine to run for the escape craft.

It did so, with great speed, moving along on six of its eight appendages, using the other two to help guide itself along and around the looping corridors to the escape vehicle hatch. As they entered the long, high ceilinged landing bay, the deck lurched under their/its feet, shivering the whole platform.

They knew this meant that the outermost shields had been breached, and as they ran across the deck it lurched again, more violently, almost throwing the Trine off its stride again, and to the deck. Something extremely hard to do when it was down on all six.

Dust was beginning to rise and swirl about as seams began to open in the buckling deck plates, and fixtures were being shaken loose from the upper superstructure that began to fall about them in a weird dance as the pseudo-gravity began to intermittently cut in and out.

The Trine ran harder. A couple of spreader beams fell from above landing with loud clangs, all too close to the fleeing beings. The deck was pitching and yawing without letup now, and producing loud agonized groaning sounds. The second layer of the shield had been breached.

Every step seeming like miles, the Trine ran all out. Twenty-five, fifteen, five yards, now the escape hatch was up. As they dove through the hatch, the whole platform lurched mightily.

The Trine, just getting up to close the hatch was thrown down again so hard that one of its hind legs was broken.

Needing little urging now from the Chai it climbed up and immediately pulled the hatch shut behind it, dogged it closed. Then it dove into a chute that led to the emergency flight couches in the small control cabin.

As they landed, crash webbing snapped out automatically and held them against the shock absorbing material of the couches.

The last shield was gone!

As soon as the safety webbing locked in place, the escape vehicle was pushed, with tremendous force, out and away from the platform. Looking into a rearview monitor the Chai saw what appeared to be a thin line of fire come through the space that had so recently been occupied by the escape vehicle.

Then it seemed as though the whole platform was collapsing in on one side and trying to come out through the same tiny opening they had just been ejected from.

As the escape ship sped away, tumbling sunward, the fusion reactor overloaded and went critical. It exploded with a tremendous flash, burning out the monitor camera eye on the outside of the little ships' hull.

The shock wave from the fusion reactor explosion, and the secondary explosion of the super heated gases from the atmospheric storage tanks, vaporizing metals and plastics, kicked the small craft in a one-two punch, severely shaking and rattling everything inside it, including its' live occupants.

The end result of all this was that the little craft was sent off at a tangent from its original course to safety. It was now on a course to immanent doom!

As soon as things settled down a bit the Chai sent hundreds of nano-organisms through the Trine's circulatory system to help block off pain, and start rebuilding the now severely mangled rear leg of it's very faithful and brave host being.

As soon as this process was done the Trine reached up and released the webbing restraining them, and began to check the systems that were down and the reasons for them being down.

As it went through this process, it reinitiated systems that had been shut down automatically by the safety devices built into them, and at the same time checking out the backup systems.

The good news was that all of the systems seemed to be working properly, with the exception of the one monitor camera that had been burnt out from the main explosion flash. The bad news was that they were now headed directly into the suns' gravity well!

The Chai

How do you describe a being with seemingly godlike abilities and powers, and is about the size and shape of an oblate (slightly flattened out) Earth softball? Well...

The Chai are a very, very old race. They are prone to be thinkers and seekers of knowledge. In addition, surprisingly enough for this type and size of species seemed to be infected with an equally strong desire to wander and explore.

As said the Chai are old race, with an active history some eight hundred thousand terran years old. The closest physiological description that could be applied to them is that they were semi-gelatinous amoebae-like beings with extremely flexible epidermis's and the ability to create and extrude from their bodies multi-purpose pseudopodia that are used for dexterity and locomotion.

They are capable of living, in reasonable comfort, on worlds with a gravitational pull of up to five gravities earth standard, but are most comfortable in gravitational fields at one and a half to two gravities earth standard.

The Chai race's normal atmospheric composition, like that of humans, is a nitrogen-oxygen based one but they can exist for periods of up to a year in almost any atmosphere that is not acidically caustic. They can also withstand most atmospheric pressures from ten to sixty pounds p.s.i.

Early in their development the Chai had learned to completely control their bodies, and more importantly, how to control and manipulate all of the micro and nano organisms that they were host to. Due mainly to this ability the Chai race became a very long-lived race of beings, the average life span ranging from seventy five hundred to ninety five hundred earth standard years in length. Some, living as long as twelve thousand years.

The Chai were also short-range telepaths and empaths. This was a survival trait that they developed early on in their history. The Chai also had one very great weakness. They were not very mobile. In fact, they were downright slow. This being the case, early in their history, they were very high on the preferred edibles list of the larger predators of their home world. As a matter of fact, almost every predator!!

This factor, more than any other, caused the Chai to develop into a race of symbionts, and in the early stages of their development they were strictly the dominant partner.

As their abilities and intelligence grew, so too grew their philosophic and ethical sense of behavior. They were by no means all sweetness and light. Much trial and error, and the application of hard come-by common sense, proved to them that willing hosts were many times more beneficial to their well being.

As an end result of this their ethics prevented them from using any intelligent being as a host without its willing consent. These hosts usually traded being the transportation and extended manipulators for a specified time period. And in return they received new knowledge and experience that they would not normally have had access to.

They also got perfect health and a longer life span due to the Chai's ability to manipulate and adapt those micro and nano organisms in their systems to filter, clean, repair and improve the hosts bodily systems.

For this reason alone there were several races in the Chai's home part of the galaxy who not only agreed to this exchange, but actually vied for the privilege of being a host for the Chai.

As previously said the Chai were not all sweetness and light. They were the dominant species on three of the planets in their home system. They had strong wills and survival instincts. They were explorers and risk takers.

Knowledge and experience had taught them that value given for value received always paid the highest dividends in loyalty and effort on the part of their hosts and that cooperation, not coercion, worked best.

The Chai preferred carbon based life forms who were oxygen breathers in the ten to twenty psi ratio range as they seemed to be the most flexible and compatible type of life form for them.

The Chai, because of their abilities were extremely efficient energy converters and could live very well on minute amounts of the nutrients and minerals shared from their hosts systems. The Chai were a race of beneficial symbionts.

They interacted with their hosts by reading the hosts DNA imprint. They then adapted some of their own micro and nano organisms to interface with those of the host DNA protein strands and then sent them to train and improve the hosts own organisms performance, thereby improving its hosts life and performance potential. This type of enlightened self interest greatly extended its own survival potential.

About four hundred thousand years ago the Chai were in the outer rim of our galaxy, in the direction of the Andromeda galaxy and ran into another exploration vessel. The race manning this other vessel had crossed the gulf from the Andromeda galaxy to this one. These beings were also a type of symbiotic race that called themselves Drel.

But there was a great difference between these two races. That difference being that the Drel was a parasitic type of symbiot, a type of symbiot that took much and gave very little in return in the relationship. The meeting was a disaster for both races from the very beginning.

Their philosophical, methodological and ethical ideologies were diametrically opposed. They became instant and implacable enemies. The result of that meeting and several more after that escalated into an intergalactic war that lasted for fifty thousand years.

That war devastated both races and their allies, and by the time the Drel was driven back where they had come from and the war ended there were less than ten million Chai left from a galaxy spanning civilization numbering nearly forty nine billion.

Though very long lived the Chai were slow breeders who propagated by the process of parthenogenesis, and seldom produced more than ten offspring in a lifetime. It was also necessary for them to return to their personal home system for them to reproduce because the gestation period for their parthenogenesis took about three hundred years for them to maturate.

Over the last two hundred fifty thousand years the Chai had slowly rebuilt their civilization until there were now close to thirty seven billion Chai again inhabiting the galaxy. They now occupied their home and two nearby, solar systems and held several colonies along with many trading, exploring and repair bases, all within a sixty thousand two hundred fifty light year radius of their home system.

The Chai now operate on two prime imperatives. They still roam and explore. They still maintain a constant watch for any return incursion of the Drel. They have not forgotten. They cannot possibly forget. They dare not forget!!

About fifty thousand years ago, remembering the lack of general cooperation and organization among the then star faring races the Chai, along with the two or three other surviving races from the war with the Drel, agreed upon and initiated a loose but strong alliance for mutual protection and trade. This alliance, commonly called the Union by its' members, eventually metamorphosed into its present form, which translates into The Union or Brotherhood of intelligent Beings.

Any race can apply for and receive membership in this union if it could show three things to another member race willing to sponsor it. The first is intelligence and the ability to control violent tendencies. The second was technological capability, and third, a strong societal/ sociological structure based on ethical behavior acceptable to interspecies relationships.

Membership in the Union had four tiers, Associate member—Pre Space Flight, Junior Member—In System Space Flight, Intermediate Member—Inter System Space Flight (usually the capability to reach its nearest neighboring star system.) And Senior Member—The Attainment of Faster Than Light Space Flight

No non member race was ever interfered with by a Union member, there being only two exceptions to this rule: i.e. one, if a non member race took "unprovoked" aggressive action against a Union member. Two, if aggressive actions between non-member races spilled over into Union space causing a threat to a member race.

The rules which bound the Union together were few but very rigid. They are as follows:

1) Tolerance of all other races

2) Integrity in all dealings with other races

3) Mutually beneficial trading policies

4) All disputes between member races must be arbitrated by a panel of three, selected by lot, from the union membership.

5) Unhesitating mutual defense of any member race by all member races against any aggressor race, member or non member.

Non member races are not excluded from trade with member races, but if they elect to do so they must abide by the first four rules or they will be considered to be hostile aggressors.

The space flight rules evolved to their present state out of necessity because just knowing about space flights possibility does not mean that a race can produce it or manage it. Space flight is something that a race must, and should, evolve into.

At present there are some one hundred ninety four well known and interactive races in our galaxy, one hundred sixty three of which are members of the Union. To date only a moderate portion of our galaxy has been thoroughly explored because it is truly a vast area, and there are estimated to be close to another three to four thousand races that are still unknown to, or uncontacted by the Union.

A very few races, like the Trine, are octopodal vertebrates. The Trine are a very intelligent tool using race, who, for some inexplicable reason of their own, don't care one way or the other about having or not having space flight of their own.

Their one exception to this general feeling is when they are in service to the Chai. They are excellent pilots and navigators. They are also exceedingly good natural botanists. Not surprisingly, they are also an herbivorous species.

They have been acting as hosts for the Chai for many thousands of years now, even vying among themselves for the opportunity of doing so. It has been an extremely good relationship for both races. TuLan Chai came out of his reverie and inspected the repair progress to his Trine.

From the looks of things both he and the Trine would need all of the help they could get.

The Escape

The little escape ship was well and truly caught in this suns gravity well now and it would be long odds indeed if they could get the sturdy little vessel out of it again. TuLan the Chai could feel the pressure building.

The first thing to do now was to establish the longest decaying spiral orbit possible in the very shortest amount of time. Possible—Possible—Possible— Possibilities!

What are the possibilities? ***Stop this,*** TuLan Thought to himself, then ***Panic will hasten entropy, dissolution of being, both yours and your loyal Trines***.

While with a part of his mind TuLan Chai checked upon the progress of the repair work to the Trine's hind member, another part began to extrapolate orbital decay vectors with time-distance and heat resistance quotients. He had the Trine punch the results into the command control computer and crossed his mental fingers.

As the little ship responded the new results began to scroll across the main control monitor screen. He gave a long mental sigh. The rate of decay in the newly established orbit was much better than he had first anticipated. There just might be a decent chance for their survival. Time, even small amounts, was very important, and precious, now!

This slim chance was one taken from the history tapes. Since the drives on this small ship were not strong enough by themselves to escape the gravity well of this sun history would be both teacher and savior. The maneuver, translated from any of the various languages in the galaxy, was called the 'sling shot' effect and was learned at one time or another by every race that achieved star flight.

The idea was to plot a deliberate decay into your course or orbit so that you fell inward towards the body you were trying to escape from. And let its gravity well pull, or whip, your ship around it in a parabolic curve, and as you come out on the far side you applied as much power as possible to break away from its hold on your ship.

Once free you cut your drive unit and let the built up inertia carry you outward while you check, or correct, your course if necessary. After running the figures through his flight computer for the second time TuLans' figures showed that at the present rate of decay they had only one and one half rotations left in this spiral orbit before they must initiate a course change and dive almost directly at the sun.

The timing must be as close to perfect as possible if they were to have some hope that the heat shields would maintain their integrity and keep them alive long enough to achieve escape velocity.

At their present speed and decay rate that would translate into five hundred and four hours local time, three weeks to prepare for the ordeal ahead. It was time.

Everything that could be done had been done. Anything that could move had been tied down or stored away. The new course had

been plotted and re-plotted, then had been programmed and locked into the flight control computer.

The Trine was now completely healed. The only thing bothering It/them now was some mild dehydration due to heat buildup. It would get much, much worse for them over the next eighty hours. As they started their plunge toward the sun all of the external sensor units were withdrawn into the hull to save them from burning up.

If anything went wrong it wouldn't matter now because there wouldn't be enough time left to look into a mirror and kiss yourself goodbye.

Fifteen hours into the plunge and something started to rattle, lightly, and the internal temperature was up ten degrees.

Thirty five hours into the plunge and everything, whatever it was, that could rattle or bang was doing so, very loudly. Internal temperature was now up by twenty five degrees and the coolers were beginning to work hard to maintain a reasonable temperature.

Seventy hours into the plunge now and the whole ship was shaking and rattling. Dust motes danced everywhere. The gravity compensators were straining at maximum and it was almost impossible to move even their eyes for fear that they would be shaken out.

Seventy nine hours plus into it. Every inch of surface or structure vibrated or rattled. Their sight was now blurred and the Trine was already succumbing to heat prostration. The internal temperature had been up by sixty five degrees when the safeties on the cooler unit had burnt out. The dust and heat were making breathing dangerously hard for the Trine.

S L A M. That was the drive unit kicking in.

BLACKNESS!

S I L E N C E !

Beautiful silence! That was the first thing that TuLan Chai became aware of. Silence! The Chai caused a small amount of an adrenaline like substance to pump into the Trines circulatory system and shortly thereafter he helped to guide one of the Trines digital appendages to inject itself with a mild stimulant, then a massive dose of glucose and vitamin complex. He then had to induce, almost force the Trine to ingest liquid slowly so that it would not upchuck it.

Lastly, after the Trine had had enough liquid to slake its thirst he helped to reach out and activate the external sensors, then let it rest. As the vision screens came alive they showed space. Beautiful, empty, black space. They had escaped the suns gravity well and certain death!

A Solution—Maybe

After letting the Trine rest for two hours TuLan bade It eat a couple of the emergency food ration packets which were packed with very rich energy producing nutrients, and to again take as much fluid as It could ingest. He then let it understand that he wished it to rest for another two hours when finished.

When TuLan again roused the Trine the procedure of eating and taking in fluids was repeated, this time letting the Trine take in the fluids at it's own pace. These things were soon completed and the Chai began to send out microbes to check for and to begin any repairs that were necessary to the Trines internal systems.

These necessities completed they began a complete check of all of the ships operational functions and systems. As small as the escape vessel was it was a good little ship. Even firing the motors at full output, as they had had to do to escape the suns gravity well, the little ship had only used ten percent more fuel than anticipated to break free. That might pose a problem later but TuLan did not think so. After running their checks they found that the port side lateral thruster was damaged and inoperable. That seemed to be the total extent of the damage. Everything else seemed to be in good working order. It was a good little ship!

After checking their navigational computer TuLan found that they had been thrown six degrees off course to port and lateral of their pre plotted course. TuLan had the Trine, because of the damaged port thruster, roll the ship with the ventral thrusters one hundred eighty degrees and then fire the starboard lateral thruster to correct the course error, and then roll the ship back again.

The Chai then did some more calculations on the flight computer and estimated that they had ten to twelve weeks local planetary time to try and fully recover.

And to reestablish contact with their observation drones still in deep orbit to locate a safe landing site on the third planet of this system.

The built up inertia would take them well within the planets gravity field before they would have to expend any more fuel for maneuvering and landing purposes.

All seemed to be well with the Chai and the Trine for the time being.

Or was it?

Fate is usually fickle.

And always a trickster!

CHAPTER TWO
It Begins

Planetfall

The planet was both beautiful and an anomaly. It had four major continents, most of which were huge. Several islands that were almost sub-continent sized and many that were just plain large, and a number of small to large archipelago.

The ocean's colors ran from clear and dark blue to the dark gray-green that indicated tremendous depth. The larger land masses also showed large desert areas, indicating the possibility that the seas had once covered those areas, which seemed to be geologically recent in nature, probably within the last ten to twenty thousand local years.

The vegetation ran the gamut of the color spectrum with dark blue-green being the base color, indicating a high percentage of oxygen in the atmosphere. The water to land ratio was in the area of sixty percent water to forty percent land, including the polar ice caps which also seemed to have large continent sized land masses under them. From the recorded data stored in the observation drones the planets crust still seemed to be in a mild state of tectonic flux.

That didn't compute either, because there was minimal volcanic activity and the instrument soundings said that the mantle was stable. On top of that the planet had several highly developed life forms living both on the surface and under its oceans, the predominant one calling itself human or more commonly, Man. Most of this information had been gathered and decrypted from audio and video signals being broadcast on lower range electromagnetic carrier waves used for communications by these beings.

Strangely the most intelligent of these, both the bipeds living on the surface and the aquatic ones living below the water surface were mammalian, warm blooded. Even stranger, their reproductive cycle resulted in live birthing.

Although not unknown among the known races there were only six out of the one hundred ninety four races that were live birthing mammals, two of which were water breathers, three of mixed variations of oxygen and one a methane breather. In most cases warm blooded, live birthing, mammals with as little apparent means of self defense as these bipeds displayed seldom survived to become dominant as a species. Nor did they evolve on a planet with so many widely spaced land masses, and among so many species with obviously superior self defense and attack weapons, fang and claw, as a part of their makeup.

Most oxygen atmosphere planets, when they stabilized, did so by forming two or three world spanning continental land masses which straddled it's equator, with a few islands and archipelagos scattered across a vast world ocean where the water to land ratio averaged seventy five percent water to twenty five percent land.

Odder still was that the predominant humans had only been true tool users for about twenty to twenty five thousand local years. And a historical social civilization for twelve to fifteen thousand local years, keeping accurate written records for only the last five to eight thousand years. Yet here they were with a very technologically advanced, world spanning civilization. A true anomaly, but a beautiful one.

Well, thought the Chai, it would be a minor miracle if they could find a safely remote place to land the ship, and get it down in one piece without being seen. That accomplished, he would find the parts and time to build a sub space emergency transmitter beacon out of the emergency stores from the ships disaster locker.

There were enough emergency rations and species specific nutrient bars to last for three local years, if necessary, in the survival locker. And water would not be a problem. The Chai could survive almost anywhere but the Trine could not. Well thought TuLan, it's time to choose a final, secluded location to land, and he began to run final configurations before laying the new course into the flight computer.

The Chai was surprised! The Chai were not infallible, but neither were they known as error prone beings. It had not run a full security scan of its observation drones technological watch program for a couple of local years. It had been one of the items on his list of things to do just prior to the accident, so it had not anticipated the inhabitants below having such advanced computer technology nor the advanced state of their detection equipment, which had almost allowed them to pick up the ship as it passed over the smaller of northern continents.

one more second would have let them paint the ship with high band sound waves, If the ship had not passed over a huge electromagnetic storm which was forming and beginning to cover the area it had chosen for the landing site, creating an echo picture of the ship and telling the indigenes of its size and speed on their scanning equipment. Their satellites had been relatively easy to avoid because there were so few of them.

Although by stellar standards the ship was very small, used mainly as an escape vehicle and as a planetary explorer it was capable of interplanetary space flight but not interstellar travel. Its drive system was just not powerful enough to create the gravity vortex required to punch a hole into subspace.

The ship, one of the smallest in use in the union, was at least five times as large as anything these humans had in use in their atmosphere, or their fledgling space program. The ship was shaped like an ovoid, flattened on the bottom. It looked something like an earth chickens egg, cut in half lengthwise. It was two hundred fifty feet long tip to tail, one hundred ten feet wide from tip to tip at its central flair and forty feet high at the top of its ventral arch. It was equipped with a photo-plasmic drive for interplanetary use and a gravitic drive for atmospheric planetary use.

As the little ship headed for the apogee of its final orbit before planetfall, the Chai was busy entering minute final adjustments to the flight computers program. It was well pleased with finding that the electromagnetic storm used for escaping detection earlier would be right over the chosen landing site, and could be used again.

The site chosen for landing was just above the confluence of two rivers that fed into the upper portion of a tremendous geological fault that slashed across a quarter of the continent. It then fed into what appeared to be a very large lake created by the humans. The landing site was well watered with large forested tracts surrounding it, and most importantly, it appeared to be quite remote from any large population centers.

Unfortunately for the Chai it was about to make an unprecedented second mistake within a few short local weeks of its first one.

With the sites characteristics in mind the Chai had the Trine run a fast check on its chameleon device, the ships holographic camouflage system, which made the ship appear to be virtually invisible. Unless you knew exactly what to look for you could be standing within twenty feet of the ship and not know it was there. Just to be safe the Chai decided to use the radiation shield screen at its lowest power to defuse any detection device signals directed at it. They would need only one sensor eye since the whole landing procedure would be computer controlled. No matter where it's from a being likes to see what is happening and where it is going.

It was time! The little ship was fast approaching orbital perigee, the closest it would come to the planet and maintain an orbit. The ship was just coasting now, as it came up over the polar ice cap, at a mere fifteen hundred miles per hour. Swinging in over the northern continent the ship was happily humming and clicking to itself as the electromagnetic storm was spotted rushing to meet it. The ship shed more speed. As it came in over the center of the storm it reached perigee nadir almost directly over the landing site at an altitude of one hundred thousand feet.

Inside the ship relays clicked, and a high pitched whining started that quickly rose above most beings audible hearing range. The ship ceased all forward movement relative to the planet as the gravitic drive reached out and grabbed at the planets gravity field. The ships gravity compensators whined a low growl as they fought both the planet and inertia.

The ship fell like a stone dropped down a well. Ninety, eighty, seventy, sixty thousand feet and the gravitic drive whined anew as it reversed pull to push and the gravity compensators whine rose in pitch as they fought the new inertia. Fifty, forty, thirty thousand feet and the ship slowed to a hundred feet a second. The Chai's second mistake was about to manifest itself!

The ship was only a thousand feet above the ground now and had slowed its decent momentum to a sedate two hundred feet per minute. It was at this point that disaster struck. The Chais' second mistake manifested itself. A blinding flash lit up the night around the ship as a truly gigantic bolt of lightning, an electromagnetic discharge, seemed to spear through the ship.

Not finding entry to the ships interior, because of its shields, the huge bolt of energy then completed its circuit by spending itself into the earth below. But the damage was done. A portion of the energy released by the lightning bolt had found the sensor eye circuit node, sending a super concentrated surge of power back along its feeder line.

Since the ships internal power was supplied by the drive coil this is where the surge of power short circuited. The energy discharge from the short circuit over loaded and fried the drives coil, disrupting the gravitic drives repeller field before the safety cutouts could engage.

Inside the ship the safety cutouts had finally closed, automatically switching over to the emergency drive coil even as the main drive coil sputtered to a halt. Even as the main control room lights were fading out the emergency lights were coming up.

Before the Chai realized what it was doing the Trine hit the quick release on their webbing restraints, and leapt from the command control seat into the manual pilot's seat slapping down, as it landed, the manual override release handle.

Grabbing the control yolk with three of its three digit hands it pulled up and back, straining mightily, while with a fourth hand it pushed the power control bar all the way to the stops for full power to the repeller field.

The ship had dropped almost eight hundred feet already. The full power output of the little ships repeller field did a great job. It was a well built ship. It had slowed the rate of decent to a hundred fifty feet a minute, but while dropping the ship had gained forward momentum and there was very little time left. The Trine would not have time to slow both the rate of decent and the forward momentum. It chose the rate of decent. It would not be a soft landing at all.

What saved the little ship from destruction was a marshy backwash formed by a shallow box canyon. The ship came in over the cut in the low cliffs on the side of the river, which kept the marshy floor of the box canyon fed, pulling low scrub pine and brush with it as it cleared the top of the cut by no more than six inches. It did a belly flop into the marshy ground.

Great gouts of water, mud, and vegetation fountained up onto the walls of the little box canyon. The ground heaved, and out thrusts of rock that had withstood centuries of weather and erosion cracked away and fell back into the canyon along with the mud, water and pieces of vegetation.

The ship rocked with the backwash as it settled, still in one piece. Safe! The Trine was not! It was mortally injured from being thrown forward onto the control yolk, because it had not had time to fasten its safety harness. The Trine had saved both the ship and the Chai. The Trine might well be dead within hours from massive internal injuries that the Chai could not help it overcome completely.

The Chai realized that it was still in grave danger, and must ask of the Trine a greater gift of more sacrifice. From its own body it fed a dose of highly concentrated stimulant directly into the Trine's fluid steam. He then guided it across the cabin and down a short corridor to the medical facility and with the last of its strength had the Trine lay itself down inside the automated medical cabinet.

Straining with exhaustion he had the Trine raise its' one uninjured forelimb and press the button marked stabilize.

On the Ground

The Chai had been injured when the ship had plowed into the earth and the Trine was thrown into the control yolk. It had not had time to harden its epidermis (The Chai could harden their skin to rocklike hardness) and the sheath of muscle just below it and now it was bruised and shaken.

It could and would heal itself, and quickly, for the feeling of being injured was new to it and very unpleasant. It had now had more close encounters with death in the last two and a half months than it had experienced in the last two and a half thousand years of its existence. TuLan Chai also knew that he was in very serious trouble.

One of the first things that had been done was to place a distress locator beacon out beyond the orbit of this planets satellite before they had entered its gravity field. They could set the ship's locator pulse broadcaster and crawl into the stasis tank, but that was not TuLan's way, and was risky at best.

The stasis tanks had been designed for preserving animal tissue and vegetation, not living, thinking beings. It was, however, theoretically possible because both plants and animals stored in stasis had been brought out alive and well, and seemingly unharmed.

The Trine was now, after being in the auto-med unit for a week, conscious and aware. What could be done had been done. The Trine knew it was going to die!

For the Chai to ensure its own survival it must ask the Trine to live and endure a great deal of pain on the Chai's behalf for a short time longer. TuLan initiated direct contact with the Trine's mind and felt its' pain being artificially subdued and held at bay. TuLan did not hesitate. He made his request, explaining what needed to be done.

He also, truthfully, expressed his affection and respect for the many years of service and companionship that the Trine had provided him with.

The Trine agreed to his request, saying, what was a little more pain? It would die today or a week from today, but die it knew it would! If living in pain for another week would ensure the Chais' survival, so be it! The only request it made was that the Chai return to 'Trinar', the home world of the Trine, and tell Its' family of the many adventures and the quality of It's service with the Chai, for it was a thing of great pride to be chosen as a Chais' partner.

The Trine was one of the oldest races partnering with the Chai. They had been doing so for close to two hundred thousand years. The Trine were also very much in demand, being hired by many of the other races for planetscaping projects because they were brilliant natural botanists.

TuLan agreed to this readily, for it was little enough for the Trine to ask for its many years of faithful service. TuLan was Anxious now to proceed, having been confined in the med-unit with the Trine for the last week.

TuLan began by creating some fast breeding micro-organisms specifically tailored to help the Trine cope with its pain. And others to help promote the temporary functionality of its damaged organs and muscle tissue.

These TuLan inserted by extruding a hair fine tendril, and injected them directly into the Trine's circulatory system. As these micro-organisms did their work the Trine was able, within three hours, to rise under its own power and exit the medical unit.

They began by making sure that the chameleon camouflage system was still operating properly. It should have automatically come on again as soon as the back up systems had kicked in after the power surge, caused by that tremendous electrical discharge when the storm fused the main panel. It had, and was operating at ninety eight percent of optimum.

They then began collecting, by using the ships sensors and remote probes, samples of air, soil, vegetation, insects and small fauna that had returned to the immediate area after the cataclysm of the ships landing had settled down.

Chemical analysis, microbe and bacteria counts, as well as numerous other tests were completed on all samples for composition and function.

Time was a crucial factor, so extra care was taken with all of the testing procedures. They would, of necessity, be done only once.

From the results of those tests the Chai began to adjust it's metabolism to the planets echo and bio structure. The Chai gave a great mental sigh of relief because the changes necessary were minor and would not require much time because there seemed to be many parallels to it's own biological makeup.

While this testing was ongoing the ships computer was running a language translation program. This was done by scanning all radio and video transmission bands, and at first, it was very slow going because there seemed to be seventy or more languages in use on this planet at the present time. Two to three languages were normal for most planets with advanced cultures.

The computer was saved an electronic headache by comparing audio sounds with some audio video transmissions, using comparative association and repetition. It got very lucky by finding what appeared to be a teaching program.

There seemed to be six major languages in use on a world wide scale. These were called English, Spanish, Chinese, Russian, French and German. Of these English seemed to be the most predominant.

The computer made an English/Trine translation, putting it on a direct inductor wire so it could be fed directly into the Trine's brain while it rested, thus both the Trine and the Chai could use and understand it.

Two planetary rotations, or days, had elapsed and TuLan could feel the strain building within the Trine's body. Time was running very short now.

Several quadrupeds had been located close by but the Chai could not judge their host suitability without being in close proximity. There was also the necessity of a certain level of intelligence present in a host for there to be a viable partnership.

All beings with intelligence radiated an aura that the Chai was particularly sensitive to, but to sense it the Chai must be within approximately twenty five feet of the being to do so.

In dire need the Chai could use a host with a minimum of intelligence for mobility, and because of the remoteness of this location that just might be necessary at this time. They must make an excursion from the ship with the rising of the sun. Time was fleeing for both the Trine and TuLan!

They had made two complete circuits of the box canyon in a widening spiral from the ship and the Trine was tiring quickly. Even though it was being assisted by a miniature gravity nullifier mounted on a harness with a power pack. None of the quadrupeds had been at all suitable. They had animal cunning but very little intelligence.

They would make one more circuit, further out next to the canyon walls, and maybe explore the gap in the walls leading to the river. There had been a faint trace of something there, east of the gap, but no sense of what it was, or a definite direction. They had best get started now for the Chai could sense that the Trine's strength was ebbing quickly and time was fleeing faster and faster.

As they moved into the span of the cut they noticed that it narrowed rapidly, and there seemed to be several fresh falls of rock, most likely caused by the ship's close passage.

They had gone almost three quarters of the way around the canyon again and it was the same as the last time, nothing viable. TuLan was getting very worried now. He did not think the Trine would last much longer.

What was that? Almost instantly the Chais' every sense was alert. There! Further into the defile. There was the aura of a very intelligent mind.

TuLan urged the Trine forward. Wait, it was fading! Hurry! Hurry! It was gone. No, wait, not gone but emanating very lowly, like a being at rest, asleep, or unconscious.

More slowly now, it was close. With this new awareness of the being the Chai had linked itself directly into the Trine's optical receptors. As they moved around a rock outcrop the Chai could feel that it was close now.

TuLan had expected to see one of this planets predominant biped species but there on the floor of the cut was a medium sized quadruped.

There was no mistaking this; the emanations were coming from it. It was all black, heavily muscled, and it had a long tail or appendage. Its' head was large with long pointed ears and a blunt muzzle showing very sharp teeth. It appeared to be stunned and possibly injured. As the Trine/Chai moved up next to the being it opened its eyes.

They were huge and a deep gold in color with a gold hued black vertical slit. The color seemed to swirl, as might molten metal. They Closed.

The Chai gave itself a mental shake as if it had been mesmerized. For an eon or a moment, it didn't know, and then everything snapped back into focus.

They must hurry to the ship for another nullifier unit and harness to transport this being back to the ship.

By the time they had gotten the being fastened into the gravity nullifier harness and pushed and pulled it through the cut, across the marshy ground, up into and through the ships airlock, around corners and along corridors, and finally into the automated medical unit both the Trine and TuLan were exhausted and near collapse.

The last task for the Trine before it could rest was to push three buttons on the med units control panel. Examine, Analyze, and stabilize!

This job had been barely accomplished, before the Trine staggered of to a rest compartment and collapsed.

It was not dead but that specter seemed to be standing very, very near!

The Trine had very little left to give, and time seemed to have grown wings on its already very fleet feet.

The Chai could exist here now!

But could it live here?

The Cat Thing

It was black. All black! Midnight, no moon or stars, black! The kind of black you see when you close yourself into a room with no windows and turn off the lights black!

That was your first impression! Then you might notice that from the tip of each ear grew several thick silvery black hairs, the color of tarnished silver. They were very long, flexible looking, and almost seemed to move with a will of their own.

Then, suddenly, you saw the eyes! They arrested you! Held you! Almost mesmerized you from the first second! They were round, not oval as most cats eyes, and they were huge, like an owl! And they were gold. Not the green gold that most animals eyes reflected, but more the rich yellow of pure, old, twenty four carat gold!

The irises were slitted vertically like normal cats eyes were. If you looked at them closely the color in the pupils seemed to swirl like molten metal in a smelter pot. And, if by chance, they looked at you directly, it was like being raked by twin search lights! When they rested on you, you were sure that they missed absolutely nothing! And you somehow got the impression that they were smiling with some secret wisdom or perhaps an old joke all their own.

When you could pull yourself free of the eyes you noticed that the head was very large and much rounder than normal cats.

The ears were large, long, pointed, and seemed able to swivel, rather than twist like a cats, to front, side and the rear.

The snout was short, almost blunt, and the mouth wide giving it the appearance of a permanent smile. But if you were lucky enough to see it smile, or unfortunate enough to see it snarl, you would see that it had a very formidable set of fangs!

The head was mounted on a somewhat long, almost sinuous, neck that flared into strongly muscled shoulders.

Overall it was deceptively big, four or five times the size of a large Main Coon tabby, or twice the size of a big lynx or bobcat and twice the weight of either. Its' bulk was centered in the wide set of the shoulders and the deep barrel of its chest, which tapered back to its powerful hindquarters. And when it moved it was all grace and spring steel, doing so with a balance that any cat would envy.

Even sitting still it seemed to flow, leaving you with the impression that you just knew it could be up and running full tilt before you could blink your eyes.

It stood close to two feet high at the shoulder, two and a half feet to the top of its head. Its' body was three feet long, nose to hind quarters with another two and a half feet of sinuous tail. Up on its hind quarters it could easily stretch to a height of four and a half feet.

Taking the different parts of its anatomy separately there was something very strange about it, nothing seemed to fit properly. But when taken as a whole the impression was of total rightness. But, there was something very strange about it, almost as if it didn't belong here at all!

There was also something else that was very strange about it. It was sentient, and aware of itself as an individual.

It also had a name that it would answer to, if you knew how to communicate with it. Its' name was 'Balor'. Just recently, Balor, the Cat Thing was running swiftly—

The Cat Thing, Presently

The cat thing was running swiftly through the brush and stunted pine that was so much a part of the land in this part of this continent, heading westward toward the spot where the confluence of two rivers formed a much larger one which rolled southward.

At the point of the confluence these rivers were still in the upper foothills, which were a part of the heavily forested mountain range to the northwest. They then flowed south through land that gradually turned into lush valleys and open prairie land that was a very beautiful part of this continent.

The cat thing moved through the obstacles of brush and small pine with sure footed ease, its night vision almost as good as its day vision. The cat thing had a name but had not thought of it for a long Time. Its' name was Balor.

The river was close now, he could tell, because he could smell alder, which never grew far from water. He would cross both of the rivers before they joined because the water was not as deep and the current less swift there. Then he would cut through the box canyon he knew was there. He would go around the inner base and up a narrow defile at the rear which led straight into the lower mountains where he must turn north into the tall trees, and into the area he believed the object of his search might lie.

As he angled slightly north a jagged streak of lightning forked down about a mile behind him turning everything, temporarily, into stroboscopic black and white. This was followed shortly by a loud crack—abooom as deep rolling thunder echoed across the heavens above him.

Balor had hoped to outrun the storm. He had seen the thunderheads building as he moved swiftly westward, but the storm was quickly rolling in over him now. Thunder and lightning held little worry for him normally, but this storm was in some way different. It held a feeling of strangeness, and foreboding!

Over a small rise, then down, and he splashed into the shallow stone studded rapids of the first of the two rivers. Four strong leaps and he was across and heading up the opposite bank, moving into the low brush and alders lining the opposite bank. Suddenly, it seemed, the rain had caught up with him, was pouring down on him like a waterfall, and matting his beautiful black fur flat to his body.

Another flash of lightning and the growling roar of the thunder coming right behind it. The storm was fully on him now. As he ran, dodging trees and thick stands of lower alder bushes, the growling roar of the thunder continued, seemed to be growing louder, closer. That wasn't right; the sound should have lessened between the peals of thunder.

Ah, there ahead, the bank of the other river. This one he would have to swim but it wasn't that far to the other bank. He knew this spot and he lengthened his stride.

Reaching the near bank he took a mighty leap, rising upwards as he sailed out over the water, reaching fully half of the distance across the river before he began to sink towards the surface of the water again. Without warning the sky seemed to split apart as a blinding actinic blue white flash of light seemed to freeze everything in mid motion like a surreal still life painting.

As he craned his head back, and around, to look back over his shoulder he saw a truly gigantic, many branched, bolt of lightning converging at a point high above and slightly behind him. It balled and coruscated, then uncannily seemed to come straight at him. The bolt of lightning must have been at least ten feet across when it hit the ground at the spot he had just leapt from. Suddenly he was being lifted and pushed through the air, spinning end over end. Then he was falling! He hit the water with a huge splash, legs, and tail and head all akimbo, nearly on the other bank.

He was stunned, nearly to unconsciousness, as he struggled to stand up in the shallow water near the bank where he had landed, coughing and spitting water from it's' mouth. This, as rocks, soil, tree branches and plants fell around him from the explosive contact of the lightning bolt on the other bank.

Looking back at spot he had just leapt from there was nothing but a smoking crater. He shook his head to clear his eyes of mud and water as he began to climb up the bank toward the entrance to the box canyon. As his hearing began to return to normal, what he had thought was thunder now sounded like a rushing freight train, the growling roar rushing right at him. He ran. Flat out, belly to the ground, with all of the amazing strength and speed that his kind was capable of! He ran toward the cut leading into the little box canyon. The thunderous roar was right on top of him now as he entered the cut. The roaring sound shook and vibrated the walls and floor of the cut, sending debris falling down around him as he tried to find some shelter where none was to be had!

Suddenly the earth heaved, jumped up, hitting him in the chest, forcing the air from his already straining lungs and he went down, sprawling onto his stomach, gasping for air. As he finally got his lungs working there was a sharp cracking sound from above. He looked up just in time to see a section of rock break away from the rim of the narrow cut and begin to tumble down toward him.

He moved, feeling like his overstrained limbs were wallowing in molasses, but he was not fast enough. A melon sized piece of stone that broke away from the larger one falling towards him hit him in the neck, just below his skull sending him into utter blackness.

Through the darkness, he didn't know how long he had been here; he heard the sounds of furtive movement close by. He heard it again. He struggled to open his eyes and, finally getting them to slit open, what he did see was blurry and indistinct. He did not realize it then that the only thing he was able to move was his eyes.

As his vision cleared a little more what he saw seemed to be a round furry face with a smallish mouth and large dark eyes. It also seemed to have six legs and two arms attached to a short barreled torso. The lights went out again.

Survival and Accommodation

Now that the Trine didn't have to move around so much it could function much better. It and the Chai had rested for a full planetary rotation. A day it was called by the local inhabitants. Humans, TuLan the Chai corrected itself. He had been going over the language information that had been transferred directly into the Trines mind from the direct induction wire that the computer had made its translation on.

The Trine was now seated at the auto-med units read out console, checking the condition of black furred Quadra-pedal being inside the unit. All of the life monitor readings were stable, based on the life forms tested from this planet.

The med-unit based its' findings on the mean average results of all of the subjects tested and allowed a plus or minus factor for variation. The number of tests were much too numerous to name here and now. But the ones which were most telling, body fluids content, and pressure, and circulatory system pump rhythm, oxygen extraction bellows rhythm and the overall temperature of the body were well within the means already established.

The one difference that could not be checked with any accuracy was the cephalo-electrical impulse reaction, the synaptic system, because they had not been able to test any of the higher intelligence, human, life forms as yet. And that was where the present problem seemed to now be originating.

The beings body was functioning, it was awake, and obviously intelligent because it seemed aware of its condition and the strangeness of its new high tech environmental location. This was being born out by the beings brain electrical activity, or lack of it. The other specimens tested had shown marked panic reactions, spiking the meters, whereas this one appeared to be just observing and waiting.

The problem was that there just did not seem to be any inter-medial response between its' brains electrical impulses and its neural muscular response system. In other words it couldn't/wouldn't move.

More strangely still TuLan could not feel that original aura of intelligence, encountered when they had first found the being. There was intelligence here, well above the minimum he needed, even higher than the Trine average, but not that bright flash he had originality encountered.

The beings physical damage was limited to a large swelling at the juncture of the skull and the spinal extension. The neck, it was called, if the translation was correct. The rest of the body, both musculature and skeletal appeared to be intact.

TuLan could feel the Trine weakening even as he sent a mental plea for it to proceed with the transfer. The Chai needed the Trine alive to make an easy exit. If the Trine died it would go into rictus, a spasming contraction of every muscle and tendon in its body which would stay that way until the dissolution of the body was well under way, making the Chai's exit painful and dangerous.

To make the exit, the Chai worked with the host's body to create a bloodless opening just large enough for the Chai to exit from its resting place in the small pocket created for that purpose. Then aided the hosts' body in closing the wound with out a trace of it having been there. The Trine heaved itself up and they entered the med-unit so the Chai could contact the being with direct mind touch.

As they entered the treatment capsule the beings eyes fastened on and followed the Trines every movement as it approached the table upon which it was stretched out. The Trine placed its lower abdomen upon a stool and leaned forward, placing its upper torso on the table as the golden eyes watched.

With the Trine this close it was easy for TuLan to push out with that part of his mind that made mental contact and communication possible for his kind. Most species were telepathic receivers, could react to and/or respond to thoughts broadcast to them. A very few, like the Chai, could direct their thoughts directly into the minds of others as well as receive them.

As TuLan reached out and felt the mental shape of the beings mind he was totally unprepared for what happened next! Out of nowhere came questions, a virtual barrage of mental speech that stunned him! *WHO/ WHAT ARE YOU? WHY / HOW AM I HELD THUS? WHAT / WHERE IS THIS* **PLACE?** The questions were fired at his stupefied mind in a rapid fire manner. Then reaction set in for TuLan. **SHOCK! WONDER! ELATION! HOPE! FEAR!!**

TuLans mind, in its present state of shock, could only sputter mentally at first. His mind still in a state of wonder, but quickly recovering, TuLan responded mentally saying I *apologize. It was just that I was so surprised to encounter another telepath. We true telepaths are so rare.*

He then continued, this *being is known as TuLan of the Chai.* he projected, then waited for a response. When none came he continued to explain, *we found you injured and without awareness in the entrance to this box canyon. You are inside of our automated medical care unit, which is inside our transport vehicle. It appears that you have suffered an injury to that nerve ganglia which lies between your brains motor and muscular control signaling system. In other words, all of your autonomic systems are working, but you just cannot move.* TuLan concluded.

The cat thing eyed the equipment that it's confined position allowed it to see, then it responded with *From what you have explained, and also from what you have not said, it appears that this injury is not repairable. What will you do with me? A quick and if at all possible, painless death would be preferred.* It finished with a resigned overtone to its thoughts.

Certainly not! TuLan responded somewhat indignantly, *you are an intelligent being, and in any case all that can be done shall be done!* he cried mentally.

Then he continued in a somewhat more subdued tone of thought, saying, *the computer that operates this unit has informed me that the work required to repair the damage to your systems, due to the delicate work required, is beyond its present capacity to perform.*

Yet there does remain one possibility. As time, right now, for me is very limited I would ask you to hold any more questions until I have explained all. If that is acceptable I will proceed. TuLan concluded, and then waited for a response.

The cat thing, with a new note of hope in its response, replied, *a chance to continue existence in a state of renewed wholeness will not be ignored. Please be so kind as to explain.* It finished, as a picture came into TuLan's mind of it sitting back on its haunches, head cocked to one side in an attitude of listening.

TuLan again felt time fleeing on very swift feet. He knew without a doubt that he could work very well with this being but he could not, would not; try to force a joining with it. Not altogether altruistic in his feelings, for survival is a powerful motivator, he also knew that an attempted joining, if forced and resisted strongly, could well kill them both.

He paused for a moment, gathering his thoughts. Then he began, *the being you see before you is not I, TuLan-Chai. It is half of a symbiotic partnership. I, the Chai, am presently emplaced within its' physical structure. Its race is known as the Trine and they have been partnering with the Chai race for a very, very long time. The partnership is a mutually beneficial arrangement. Each gains from the other those things it needs or desires in various ways.*

TuLan paused, and then continued, explaining the Chai's historical development and their ability, developed over an eons long span of time, to create, alter and manipulate micro and nano organisms for their own and their hosts benefit. The Chai, physically limited in size and with an inherent weakness in it mobility capabilities, evolved into and then actively developed symbiosis as a survival mechanism for their race.

He also told of the disastrous war with the "Drel" and the persistent knowledge that they were a serious threat and cause for worry to all of the beings of this galaxy.

And He told of the Union of worlds and its formation. Of the discovery of this planet and the union's long observation due to its unprecedented technological advancement and the nagging fear of possible "Drel" influence and interference at some point in their history.

He told too of moving their observation platform, its destruction by the meteorite and their escape from the station and the suns gravity well. Then he told of the ship being damaged by the massive lightning strike on its landing approach and the resulting semi-controlled crash at this spot.

TuLan paused to take a mental breath, and then continued, *the Trine was mortally wounded during the crash, beyond my ability to effect meaningful repairs. Had I the facilities available aboard the platform both the Trine and your prognosis would be different. Even now the Trines life force ebbs dangerously low. So this now is the possibility, the chance that can be offered. As host to me I believe that with my abilities I may be able to make the repairs necessary. Externally I can do little, as I must be in intimate contact with your physical being to affect repairs or improvements.*

In return for this you offer me physical safety and true mobility. Also, a side effect of a symbiotic partnership with a Chai is that of enjoying a much extended life span. This because as we learn the hosts systems, and we have a natural tendency to repair anything we find wrong, and to improve those systems whenever possible. This is both for gratitude! And survival! A strong healthy host means safety for us. All things being said, I now ask you to accept a partnership with me. Under these circumstances it could be on a very temporary basis if you feel that is necessary. If you decline I will still do all that I can to help you, little as that may be. The situation and circumstances as well as the choices to be made are strange and hard. Your choice must be freely made, for I cannot and will not coerce it.

Here TuLan paused again, letting his words take root. Then he said, *finally, simply, I offer this. I have something to offer you as you have something to offer me in this arrangement. Simply put it is life to each other. The only constraint upon us both is time, for there is very little left for the poor Trine, who is holding on to its life force by a thread, and for there to be a smooth transfer he must be alive. I will now withdraw from contact for a short period to allow you uninterrupted thought.* So saying TuLan withdrew from direct contact with the cat things mind.

A short time later, but for TuLan an eternity, He felt a tentative mental touch, to which he quickly responded with, *what have we? Life?*

The cat thing responded with a question of its own, *How is this process achieved?*

To this TuLan quickly replied, *With the Trines assistance I will cause an opening to occur in its epidermis, both painless and bloodless, through which I (my body) will emerge. I will then extend a very fine tendril which I will insert into your abdominal section to obtain a DNA and tissue sample, from which I will create and alter micro and nano organisms to match those taken. Those organisms I will inject back into your system and those in turn will assist you and me in creating a like opening in your epidermis and subcutaneous fat and muscle layers. After that I will enter the opening, fitting myself in and around the spaces and voids surrounding your internal organs, closing the opening in your abdomen, with you assistance, behind me. The size of my body is quite small and very malleable so you will feel little or no discomfort what so ever.*

After completing this I will extend and insert very hair fine tendrils into your major organs to learn, monitor and possibly improve their performance. Next to last I will insert a tendril into one of your major nerve ganglia to monitor and assist nerve performance. From this contact I will also tap excess nervous energy, this being how I take my sustenance while with my host. Any other trace nutrients necessary to me will be taken from the excesses created by your body. Lastly, I will attach one tendril to the base of your cortical stem so that we may have constant and uninterrupted communication when necessary. Once settled within I will begin diagnosing and repairing the damage to your system. With that last TuLan stopped and figuratively held his mental breath.

Surprisingly the cat things reply was very fast in coming, *I agree to act as host to you for as long as may be mutually beneficial. And with the understanding that after I am repaired your immediate needs and concerns shall be our prime objectives. This agreement comes with four provisos. They are as follows.*

One, that henceforth we shall address each other by our personal being identifiers, yours being TuLan, and I am Balor.

Two, that you absolutely not insert anything into my brainstem.

Three, That having met your most immediate needs and concerns we begin a search for a more suitable host, for I perceive your future need for appendage with more ability for manipulation and dexterity than mine are able to provide.

Four, That upon finding such a host and the completion of a successful transfer, I shall maintain the right to continue or discontinue our association, in whatever manner I decree, without objection and at my own discretion. Then it was the cat things turn to wait for a reply.

At this time TuLan gave little thought to these well thought out provisos, nor to the very short time that it took this being to think of them. They seemed to be fair and harmless in their basic content.

Then with great excitement and relief TuLan gave his consent and agreement to seal the bargain. Immediately TuLan notified the Trine, who by some miracle was both aware and alert.

As the process of exiting his Trine host's body neared completion, TuLan, before breaking contact, sent one last message, *"Your last request shall be honored."*

Then, as the Chai exited the Trines body, it gave one last great sigh, and then died. Once more survival would continue through accommodation. Both beings would be very surprised at how soon those four provisos of their agreement would be met, and the manner in which it would come about.

The human following the western river was heading south, towards the confluence of the two rivers, to investigate a strange—

Survival and Mobility

The transfer had gone as smoothly as it could under the circumstances. With its completion TuLan had spent several hours learning about his hosts body and nervous system, in that intimate way that could only be done by this form of symbiosis.

After making all of the connections he had informed Balor about, excluding the one to Balor's cortex, he spent many more hours studying the damage to the nerves in his neck. And was now ready to speak of them with his new host.

Balor, about the injury to your neck said TuLan, *it is both less and more serious than first thought. The good news I will give you first. The nerve from your brainstem which governs your control of the muscles in your neck and back is severely pinched, thereby blocking any signal sent to those muscles. The result of which you know, you cannot move. As I said, the good news is that there is no apparent damage to the nerve itself.*

And the bad news is? asked Balor, quietly.

The bad news, TuLan replied, *is that the top half of your first vertebra has been crushed. That is the one that is pressing down on and blocking the nerve from functioning properly. The two vertebras directly below are both broken and misaligned, compounding the problem with the pinched nerve. The two directly below those are seriously cracked and will separate if any pressure is put on them, and most likely cause additional nerve blockage. Also, three of the cushioning sacks between those vertebras have ruptured and lost their liquid medium.* he finished with a mental sigh.

Is there a glimmer of hope to be found anywhere within this depressing litany of disaster? asked Balor in a subdued tone.

No hope whatsoever, replied TuLan deadpan, then after a minimal pause, *just the absolute certainty of a complete recovery.* Thereby proving that the Chai race, and TuLan in particular, had a sense of humor. Although in TuLan's case one that seemed to be somewhat macabre.

Giving a great shuddering mental sigh Balor said *I knew that there must be a useful purpose for your existence!*

With a mutual understanding of the contents of these last two statements both TuLan and Balor found themselves facing a situation that neither had anticipated. The humans on this planet had a quaint name for it. They called it Friendship.

TuLan then went on to explain that because of the delicacy of the work and work area he had already set micro-organisms to work producing certain endorphins that would put Balor into a coma-like sleep.

And others to help keep his muscles flaccid while he slept. These to keep him from moving in his sleep and to also prevent his muscles from spasming.

Having already taken samples of blood, tissue and bone composition he also tailored others to start dissolving the bone and tissue of the damaged area of the spinal column. Finally, he was now imprinting on still others a template of the sections that must be rebuilt.

TuLan said, *finally, when you wake you must be very careful because you will be very weak and somewhat uncoordinated. This because everything needed must be taken directly from your/our body."* This last was heard, by Balor, as consciousness fled and a deep soothing darkness replaced it.

Balors' head came up and his great round eyes snapped open. And, even as he became aware, his mind was snapping questions, *WHAT? Where?*

Then he heard words in his mind, *Easy Balor, easy.* and everything came rushing back to him. He lay his head back down as memory washed over him. It was all real. He was still in the ship. As he lifted his head again, slowly this time, the reality of his memory settled in. The proof in his ability to move! To look around!

Softly in his mind TuLan spoke to him, *Easy Balor. Lie here for a while. Practice flexing your muscles and moving your limbs. Slowly, individually, to re-establish your control and equilibrium. That's right, slowly. Now try stretching your whole body.*

A short time later TuLan spoke again, *Balor. You should try to get down off the table now.* And as he was doing so, slowly, for he felt very weak, TuLan said *when your down go to the panel and press the lower button on the left side. Go through, turn right and follow the passageway to the ramp. Go up the ramp to the next level and turn into the second opening on the right. That is the galley. Your body is very weak and it badly needs sustenance. There are energy ration bars there that will work with your metabolism.* And hearing this Balor was immediately aware of his roaring hunger.

Having followed his instructions Balor reached the galley, and following more instruction was soon busy consuming quantities of revitalizing liquid and chewy ration bars without regard to taste.

As he ate, TuLan spoke to him, *you must rest again shortly so your body can absorb these nutrients, and then eat again. Then soon again thereafter to replenish what was used during your therapy.* Then a short hesitation and *your body's absorption rate,* TuLan said, *is now much faster.*

Why, asked Balor, *is that?*

While the repair was being done I also improved your body's system for chemically converting raw materials into nutrients and energy. TuLan said.

Again, said Balor, *why?*

Because, you are physically much stronger now. I tailored micro— organisms to increase the density of your bones, muscles, tendons, and etcetera. When you gain your full strength back again it will be about twice what it was. replied TuLan a little bit smugly.

That, said Balor, *was very considerate of you, but not trying to seem ungrateful, why?*

Because, replied TuLan with a rueful mental smile, *I told you that* **survival and safety is a fetish of mine.** After saying this, TuLan guided Balor to a compartment with a raised platform for sleeping.

After twice more eating and sleeping TuLan began instructing Balor in the ships operation. Much of the operational information could be passed directly from mind to mind but the actual operation required some hands on practice.

As flexible as Balors' paws and claws were, some of the equipment was either too difficult to operate or completely impractical to even try. They required manipulatory digits.

As they progressed they again began to explore the canyon floor and the low cliff tops. TuLan and Balor found that it became easier and easier to work together, with little resistance on either's' part.

They had made several excursions around the canyon, the forested hills just to the north, and short distances up and down the river. Balor had stalked and brought down a couple of small animals, and with great gusto, eating them on the spot saying that he needed the fresh meat in his diet.

TuLan was at first both a little appalled and amazed, but then very pleased, with Balor's eyesight and awareness of his surroundings. He seemed to miss little or nothing as they traveled.

The ship had been down now for a full phase of the planets satellite, or as the locals called it, a month, and they were preparing to make one final excursion to a higher elevation to make sure that the ship could not be seen.

They were in the control room setting the proximity alarms, which would send a signal to a small radio unit that was attached to the harness Balor now wore, when Balor froze into stillness.

He was staring at the screen of the external monitor. TuLan's awareness to danger was immediately aroused by the intensity of Balors' stance. *What?* From TuLan.

There, Balor paused, watching the screen. Then pointing he said, *there along the cliff top, something is moving towards the cut that leads to the canyon.*

Then, as they watched, the object of their attention came into full view. It was one of the bipeds, a human. And it was moving very carefully along the rim of the canyon, heading directly for the trail leading to the cut.

It seemed to be moving with great care, stealthily, keeping to whatever cover was available.

It moved with great skill, from bush to shadow to rocky projection, exposing itself only momentarily as it slipped from cover to cover as if it knew it was being observed. It neared the upper lip of the entrance to the cut and disappeared.

TuLan realized that if he had still been with the Trine that he would not have known that the human was there.

TuLan and Balor agreed almost in unison that they must go out carefully and investigate the human and its reasons for such stealthy movements.

They may not have been as careful as they thought they were!

The Human

The human was a male of the species. A big male, solidly built. At present he was moving swiftly southward. He had been traveling for six days now, coming down out of the upper foothills and canyon country to the north, and was now following a forested trail along the banks of the western river.

He had been camped in a shallow cave on the southwestern wall of a ravine, at the bottom of, and between, two rocky hills, almost small mountains, the night of the big thunderstorm. He had felt strangeness about that storm. That was why he had been standing at the mouth of the cave, watching the play of the lightning.

That was why he had seen the strike of that gigantic lightning bolt. Seen it hit something in mid air, throwing off wild coruscation's of light before grounding itself. Had seen something huge outlined in that flair of brilliance. And, even half blinded by that flash, he still had the impression of something like half an egg, slightly flattened in shape, and even at that distance could tell that it had been very big.

Shortly thereafter he had felt the ground shake under his feet and knew that something very big had cone down and hit the ground. That in itself was a little strange because there were no bases in this region, secret or otherwise. He would have known, or at least have heard about it if there were. He thought it might have gone down in the area of the confluence of the two rivers. He had spent another hour standing in the mouth of the little cave, watching the pyrotechnic display of the lightning before making up his mind to check out his belief that something had gone down. Even as he was rolling himself into his bedding he was planning his route south.

For the last three days he zigzagged back and forth through the forested low hills and gullies, using high spots to help in spotting any crash site. Nothing! Also, there had been no over flights of planes following search patterns. He was beginning to think he had been wrong, the image a mirage.

He was almost down to where he knew there was a fair sized box canyon, at a spot just above the point where the two rivers joined. This little box canyon always had good vegetation and water. Because during flood season the rivers overflowed creating a back flow into the canyon, filling two medium sized water holes and keeping the rest of the floor slightly marshy, making it a good campsite. He would check that out tomorrow, after checking a couple of good sized glades in the low hills behind it. If he found nothing he would head back north.

He spotted the burned area of the lightning strike from a mile upstream and started to pay more attention to the surrounding terrain, moving more slowly now.

It was nearing dusk and at this time of year darkness followed quickly, so he decided to find a campsite and think about how he intended to continue his search for a crash site.

He had just finished climbing the steep wooded slope that led up to the canyons rim about a quarter mile around from where he knew the entrance to the cut was. He was now sitting in the shade with his back against a large boulder set a few feet back from the canyons' inner rim wall, resting and a little disappointed at not finding a crash site.

As he was sitting there he swept his gaze back and down the slope he had just climbed. Then back up, sweeping the entire rim of the little canyon, then down to the rear floor and forward to the entrance cut. As his gaze came to the cut his body tensed then froze, all movement ceasing. He could have been a part of the rock he was leaning against he was so still.

Coming out of the cut, into the canyon, was a very large black cat. A black cat about three quarters the size of a yearling puma. At first he thought it might be a panther, but there weren't any panthers in North America, except in zoos. And if it were a wild panther it wouldn't be this far north. This was not its' kind of climate.

He carefully eased a small telescope that he always carried from his jacket pocket and slowly brought it up to his eye. The cats' image zoomed into clarity. As he watched it move across the short open space on the canyon floor to the brush and trees he hissed an in drawn breath. It was beautiful! It didn't trot like most animals but seemed to glide across the ground, its' movement was so smooth.

Another, hissing, in drawn breath as he realized that the cat was wearing some kind of harness. As it neared the brush and scrub, on the canyon floor, it did something very odd. It stopped and seemed to search the canyons rim with a quick glance, like it knew he was up here somewhere, then took three quick steps into the brush and disappeared from sight. That was wrong! He should have been able to follow its progress further into the brushy undergrowth, especially since it was black.

This was very odd. He could not see a thing moving. Not even the brush moving or shaking as it moved through it. Another thing he noticed, there were no birds or small animals anywhere, now that he was looking. This was definitely worth looking into.

Looking at his watch he saw that it was three thirty, about three hours before dark, plenty of time to work his way around to the cut and down onto the canyons floor. There was something else strange about this place, when he looked too long at the brush down there where the cat disappeared; his eyes kept wanting to slide away from it. It was like they were trying to see around something not visible. Well, he would just have to be careful and use all of his considerable skill in doing so.

He slowly closed the small telescope, keeping the glass pointed down to keep it from giving a reflecting flash in the sunlight, and pocketed it. Then he slid back around the boulder, out of sight of the canyon floor. His training enhanced sense of caution not withstanding, he had an eerie sense of watching eyes.

As he moved along the trail to that part leading down to the cut he took advantage of every piece of cover available.

He darted from boulder to bush, crawling across slight depressions and trying to keep himself below the skyline of the rim, while always trying to keep the cats point of entry into the brush in sight.

Finally he was just five yards from the trailhead leading down. As he looked around he began to notice brush with bent or broken branches, some partially uprooted, all bent in the same direction, the canyon. There was the stump of a pine near the rim, its eight inch bole snapped off just a foot above its partially exposed roots. The splintered break was still white, meaning it had happened very recently.

Now, looking into the canyon, he noticed damp spots and mud clinging to the inner walls, indicating the impact of a large object within the canyon itself.

The canyon was about three hundred yards across yet there was no crater nor any other signs of something impacting within the canyon other than the wet muddy walls. But it was also obvious that something very big had come across this rim, very close to touching it.

He scanned the area around him again. It was time to move. He lifted himself out of the depression he had been lying in and moved silently across the stony ground. As he reached the trailhead, where the path began to slope down he looked over the edge of the rim.

Nothing moved. Good. As he stepped out onto the ledge itself, where the path began to slope downward, a prickling feeling began at the base of his spine. And the small hairs at the back of his neck rose as a cold knot started to form in the pit of his stomach! Every sign of immanent danger he had ever experienced seemed to coalesce at once! He snapped his head around to look over his shoulder, behind him!

And there it was! Or one just like it. It was sitting there just five feet from him. The thought flitted giddily through his mind that, being this close to him, it seemed much, much larger. It was just sitting there, looking at him. And those eyes! Huge, golden, and he could feel himself beginning to fall into them.

Somewhere he could hear that primal part of his mind screaming at him, danger! Run! Danger!

He shook his head violently, desperately, to break that spell. His right arm came up, reaching across to the left arm pack strap, his right hand closing around the handle of the ten inch, wickedly pointed, SAS commando fighting knife strapped hilt down to the shoulder strap.

The knife came free, his hand moving down and slightly forward with the wicked tip up in a knife fighters grip as he spun completely around facing the big cat as he dropped into a crouched fighting stance.

As fast as he had moved, his speed a blur of motion, the cat moved even faster still. One second it was just sitting there watching him, the next it was standing three feet closer reaching out with a paw, and without touching him, slapping the knife with incredible force, sending it spinning out over the canyon.

Pulling his eyes away from the spinning knife he saw the cat take another half step closer.

Swiftly stepping back to gain some room between the cat and himself he realized, too late, that there was nothing there for his foot to come down on.

As he toppled backward he began to tumble, arms pinwheeling frantically, for balanced that just wouldn't come.

Tumbling downward, he hit two projecting outcrops of rock, breaking his fall somewhat. He hit the floor of the cut on his back, pain flooding all through him.

Looking up through pain glazed eyes he saw those two golden orbs, in that round midnight black face, staring down at him. And he was amazed, because he could swear that there was a look of sorrow in them.

Then…

Nothing!

CHAPTER THREE
Earthbound

The Man

His full name was John Longknife Dirk. But no one who actually knew him called him that. Those few who did know his name just called him Dirk.

His ancestry was Scottish, American Indian and Italian. The mother was Italian, the father more Apache Indian than Scottish, but the name had somehow held on for over a hundred years or more. That didn't really matter either. He was who he was.

He was a big man, without appearing to be. That was until he stood in front of or next to you. Then you noticed and felt the presence of overall size.

He stood six feet one and one half inches in his stocking feet, and weighed in at two hundred twenty five pounds, little of which was fat.

He was very well muscled but not in an overly obvious way. He had amazing strength in his hands, arms and shoulders. His hands were big and capable looking, big knuckled and thick fingered, yet you got the impression that they were capable of great dexterity.

He had a soft olive complexion with a light coppery overtone to it. His hair was a very dark brown, almost black, and just beginning to gray at the temples.

The most arresting feature about John dirk was his eyes. They were gray, the dark stormy gray of the North Sea during an arctic tempest. Their look was normally reserved and somewhat withdrawn, but when angry they could pin you down like an insect on a board. And you could see in them the potential for violence, being fiercely held in check by an iron will.

If you were looking you might notice that he didn't walk like most people but seemed to move from place to place with a curious gliding step, the result of many years of training in the martial arts. His other movements were also, when noticed, smooth and economical, with little wasted motion. Most people, if confronted, would quickly realize that Dirk was a very dangerous man. One of the wolves among the sheep!

Dirk had lived most of his life with his paternal grandfather, since the age of eight, having been left there by his mother when she gone to the city to find work. His father had died two years earlier from a fall while working on a high rise construction project in that same city. He was ten years old when he found out that his mother had been killed by a hit and run driver shortly after leaving him with his grandfather.

For nine years he lived well with his grandfather, who was a part time author writing booklets on Indian folklore, but earned most of his income as a fishing and hunting guide. His grandfather taught him many things of importance, but most importantly he taught him self reliance.

Years was forced to drop out due to a lack of funds. Thinking to earn enough money to finish school he enlisted in the army. He was wrong. He found in it a true at seventeen he entered a local college on a partial scholarship. After two vocations, he was a natural and took to the training like a fish to water, ultimately opting for paratrooper and ranger training.

His career in the regular army was short but impressive. While serving two tours of duty in Southeast Asia he earned two purple hearts, for wounds received, and both the bronze and silver stars. Rising quickly through the ranks he received a battlefield commission near the end of his second tour. Returning stateside he decided to make the military his career. And being well liked by his superiors he was quickly seconded to OCS on his re-enlistment, which, by graduating would make his rank permanent.

Dirk was a quick study. He not only completed the officer candidate training at the top of his class, he completed and received his BA by the end of that same year. At the beginning of the second year of that enlistment he was promoted again, to the rank of first lieutenant. At this point he made a critical decision. He decided to enter military intelligence, was accepted, and transferred to begin his new training. He didn't know it then, or even soon after, that he was being very closely watched.

The people watching him were part of a very secret, and seldom mentioned branch of the defense intelligence agency. This branch worked in close cooperation with many other agencies, both domestic and foreign. They carefully picked their candidates, taking them from all of the special training units and all branches of the military. The work was military espionage and counters espionage as well as counter terrorism. The joint missions with other agencies were what were euphemistically called 'wet' or 'black' operations, or just plain 'black ops'.

Upon completing his new courses, again graduating in the top ten percent of his class, he was cautiously approached, then inducted into this agency. Upon being accepted all of his records, both military and civil, were gathered up and put under special seal. He virtually disappeared from the system. He became one of the Shadow People.

It was now eleven years later and he was a much wiser, if sadly disappointed person. It seemed that the work he was doing had gone from a necessity for perpetrating an ideal to the ideal of self perpetuation.

He was a major now, often exercising the authority of a general. He was thirty four years old now, pushing thirty five, and he was very tired. He also had a very important decision to make. That was why, at the present moment, he was loading the last of the supplies he had just purchased into the old surplus jeep out behind the general store of this little two light town.

He was known here as an occasional visitor who liked to tramp the wilds hereabouts. What they didn't know, and neither did anyone else, was that he owned a thousand acres of prime forest and grazing land in the upper foothills. Land which he had purchased very quietly, a parcel at a time and over the years that he had been coming up here.

He had used every technique he had ever learned to protect and preserve his identity and privacy. His last enlistment was about up, so he had taken the sixty days of accumulated leave time he had coming to come out here to make up his mind about what his future was to be.

As he finished lashing his backpack to the roll frame he stiffened imperceptibly, as he first felt, then heard, the quiet footsteps approaching. He turned smoothly, to see one of his very few friends, Bill Tate, coming towards him across the dusty parking lot.

Bill was one of the few men left in the unit who had come into the unit at the same time as he had.

"Bill" Dirk greeted him softly.

"Dirk" Bill replied just as quietly.

"The general send you?" Dirk asked.

"Partly, and partly on my own." Bill said, then "you've been real quiet lately. Something I can help with? "He asked softly, concern for his friend in his eyes.

"Old story Bill. I think its time to quit. Things have changed a lot, not all for the good. I need time away to make up my mind." Dirk finished, speaking just as softly.

"The old man said to tell you to talk to him before you make anything final." said Bill, then "that's it."

"That's fair enough." said Dirk.

Bill put out his hand and as Dirk put out his own, took it and shook it once, giving it a gentle squeeze as a close friend will. Turning to leave he said quietly "walk softly my friend."

"And carry a big gun." Dirk replied, finishing the units' private motto.

Dirk turned and climbed into his jeep, started it with a roar and headed out of town and into open country, his eyes already seeking the forested hills and restful solitude. Unfortunately, or fortunately, for him that wasn't to be all he would find.

Serendipity and fate were about to reach out and touch him.

Soon!

Then to Now

As Dirk drove along, jouncing over ruts and stones, he followed one of the seldom used and mostly unknown, to anyone but himself, tracks leading onto his property from the rear. He decided to pull the jeep into one of the blinds that he had discretely erected, in many different locations, over the years to check his back trail. This was one of the things he did out pure habit to ensure his privacy.

He also used them to observe the profusion of animal life that abounded on his property. He had set a salt lick close by this one as he had the others scattered throughout his thousand acre retreat. On each visit he would walk a circuit of the property, adding to, or replacing the salt blocks as necessary.

Since he had brought along a fresh supply of the blocks this trip he decided to replace this one before going on up to the snug little cabin he had built himself. It was tucked close up to, almost under a large craggy up thrusting outcrop of rock, on the edge of his property where it butted up to the feet of the sky reaching mountains to the north.

It would take three days for him to make a complete circuit of the blinds. So doing this one now would save him some of the time he knew he would need, as he hashed out the answers to the questions that were bothering him.

Having decided to do as many of the blinds as he could today, with the daylight left to him. He had made good time on the rutted tracks leading to most them. As he pulled his jeep into the entrance to a deep, narrow, ravine which led to a small glade about five hundred yards up this track. He pulled over and stopped, because the ravine grew to narrow to pass through, shut the motor off and climbed out.

He went to the rear and removing a salt block hefted it to his shoulder and carried it up to the glade. He only had two spots left to do now and as he came back up to the jeep he looked up at the sky, then his watch. It was only four fifteen in the afternoon but seemed later, almost dusk, and getting dark fast. This was because of the black thunderheads that had been piling up for the last couple of hours.

Knowing he wouldn't make it to the cabin before the storm broke tonight he decided to camp here for the night in a shallow cave, about twelve feet up the side of the ravine wall. He would have a comfortable place to sleep and be able to keep dry at the same time.

Thinking of the rain to come he began gathering dry branches and brush, throwing it up onto the ledge at the small caves mouth. This done he pulled his loaded backpack, a warm lightweight sleeping bag, and a waterproof tarp off the back of the jeep. The tarp he threw over the jeep and tied it to the frame, thereby making the interior of the jeep weather proof.

Carrying the backpack and sleeping bag he climbed up the face of the ravine wall, using hand and foot holds he'd cut there years before, and threw them into the mouth of the cave.

Upon reaching the ravine floor again he noticed that it was getting colder. So he peeled off the light over shirt he was wearing and, lifting a corner of the tarp, exchanged it for a heavier jacket he had stored there.

He replaced the tarp, and shrugging into the jacket made sure it hung loose from the ten millimeter colt that hung, butt down, from the shoulder holster he wore under his left arm.

He seldom went anywhere without it. And never out here where there were some very nasty razor backs (wild pigs) with long, very sharp, tusks that could lay open a hand or leg with little provocation and less effort.

He walked back up the ravine to the glade to get another armload of firewood, to make sure he had enough for the night, and was almost back to the jeep when the first fat drops of rain began falling. By the time he had climbed, with his load of wood, up and into the cave he was drenched and the rain was a steady, pounding downpour.

He quickly shed his dripping jacket and built a fire, setting it as far back from the opening as he could, both to keep the wind driven rain off it and to get as much reflected heat as possible. He then removed a small metal tri-pod and pot from his pack, set it up over the fire and added water from his canteen to boil for coffee.

Next he pulled a box of field rations from the pack and sat back, frowning at it with distaste, and began to eat while he waited for his water to boil.

Finished eating, he sat drinking his coffee, as he lit one of the three cigarettes he allowed himself each day, staring out into the darkness, watching the play of lightning as the storm intensified. The longer he sat there the more he began to feel a sense of uneasiness, thinking to himself, ***something's not right.*** And as the center of the storm moved closer to him so did the feeling of unease.

Getting up he moved to the mouth of the cave, and standing there, he flipped the stub of the cigarette up and out, watching it arc and disappear into the rain.

A cannonade of thunder cracked and rumbled, seeming to rush right towards him, reverberating inside the small cave. Then, still rumbling, it receded very slowly.

All at once he knew what was bothering him. It was that background rumbling he had thought was part of the thunder, but it had been too steady and the sound had been increasing steadily. The pyrotechnic display increased as the lightning flashed from all parts of the heavens. Blackness! Silence for a few seconds.

Then that persistent rumble again. Receding somewhat now. Lightning again. Now its arms were flickering all over the sky. Then they were coalescing at one point, the sky lighting up with an awesome actinic flash as they came together.

The coruscating light from the almost continuous flashes seemed to be combining into one gigantic bolt of lightning that seemed to reach straight down to touch the earth. Another huge flash of light, this one the red and orange of a fiery explosion.

He stood there, all motion frozen! For in the after image of that last flash was the outline of something. Something very big for him to be able to see it from this far away. The ground shook slightly under his feet. Whatever it was it had gone down and it must have been big for him to feel it here. He did some fast calculating in his head and said to himself, *bout eighty miles away, I'd guess* and *all rough terrain too.*

This was beginning to seem odder and odder. What he thought he'd seen was bigger than anything he knew of that the military had, the B-fifty two not withstanding, and there were no bases in the area, secret or otherwise. This, he, of all people would know.

Still, it could be one of ours, he muttered to himself, and *something I haven't heard about yet.* He thought it might have gone down somewhere in the vicinity of the confluence of the two rivers, give or take a little. He decided that he was going to investigate this.

He would have to go in on foot because there were no roads, not even tracks he could get the jeep through without going a long way out of the way. It would all be up and down hill travel, most or all through thickly forested area. Five, maybe six days travel on foot for sure.

It had been three days now since he had started quartering back and forth, the sixth since he had begun this trek, and much of it up and down in these lower foothills, looking for the crash site. He had been working his way south and west towards that fair sized marshy bottomed, box canyon just above the confluence of the two rivers. Six days travel in all and he had turned up nothing.

He decided he would make one more sweep, using the two highest hills, just ahead, to check most of the small valleys and glades around and between them for any signs of a crash. It was on this, the sixth day, that he spotted the place where that huge lightning bolt struck the ground.

He saw it just after reaching the summit of the second hill. A large area, almost round, of torn and broken tree limbs hanging by their splintered ends, with uprooted trees and underbrush within an area of scorched earth.

The spot was on the long point of land between the rivers, just opposite that little box canyon.

Reaching the spot, about mid morning, he checked the surrounding area and had found nothing but the strike spot. He decided that, since he was here, he would check out the box canyon, just on principle. As he reached the top of the outer canyon wall, hot and sweaty from the climb, he decided to take a short rest.

Putting thought to action he found a good sized boulder set a few feet back from the inner rim wall with a nice patch of shade under it. As he sat in the shade with his back against the boulder he was, he knew, about a quarter mile from the entrance to the cut leading into the canyon.

Sitting there, idly gazing around the floor of the canyon while he rested, his line of sight swung past the inner entrance to the cut and that's when he saw it.

A black cat, big as a yearling puma, trotting towards the center of the canyon. He froze all movement, for a moment, then very carefully reached up to his breast pocket and removed a small brass telescope and, extending it, brought it to his eye. Very odd he thought. The only black cats of that size that he'd ever heard of weren't ever found this far north.

This, he said to himself, *is just too odd to pass up.* As he watched it move across the open ground towards the brushy area in the center of the canyon his hand clenched on the tube of the telescope as he thought in shock, *that damn cat is wearing some kind of harness. One with tools on it too!*

As he sat watching the cat cross the open ground it almost seemed to be gliding across the ground rather than trotting like most animals did. As it entered the brush it seemed to disappear from one step to the next. That was odd too; he should have been able to see some movement in the brush.

Fascinated, he decided that he just had to investigate this, and matching deed to thought he got up and began moving, with all the skill in stealth learned in many years in his profession, he moved towards the trail he knew led down to the entrance of the cut leading into the canyon.

Finally, after moving from cover to cover with great care, he was at the head of the path leading down to the cut—

The Cat That Killed Me

The hair on the back of his neck stiffened and rose! His head snapped around to look behind him and he froze, staring into two huge golden eyes. There the cat sat, not five feet from him. Just sitting there. Watching him! Unable to stop, he was being drawn right into those molten, golden eyes.

Somewhere in the primal recesses of his mind he heard a scream, and broke contact with a violent shake of his head. Instinctively his right hand flashed across his chest to the left pack strap coming away filled with the ten inch, wickedly pointed, SAS fighting knife from the sheath taped there, hilt down, combat style.

He spun around, knees bent, knife held low and point up, feet apart in a knife fighters stance, all in one coordinated blur of movement to face the cat and those huge golden eyes.

He saw now, facing it, that those eyes that were set in a large round skull covered in shining black fur, with long pointed ears, and a blunt muzzled largish mouth, which strangely, seemed to be smiling at him.

All of these things he noticed as time, as it so often seemed to do under extreme stress conditions, began to dilate for him, stretching into infinite sequences of observation and action.

As fast as Dirk had moved, as fast as his speeded up perceptions had seemed to slow time and movement the cat moved faster, with incredible speed.

One second it was sitting and watching him and the next it was three feet closer, standing with one paw reaching out, and without touching him, slapped the knife, with incredible force, out of his hand, sending it spinning out over the rim to the canyon floor below.

Reacting, Dirk was already shifting his stance and stepping back to put some space between them. Realization came, at the same time he completed the move, that there was nothing but space there for his foot to come down on.

As he toppled backwards, pin-wheeling his arms for non existent balance, two inconsequential thoughts flitted through his mind. ***OH! SHIT!***

As he began to tumble backwards, the wall of the cut spinning past his eyes, he completed one revolution before he bounced off of the remainder of the rock spur that had crushed the cat things neck earlier that month.

He hit the floor of the cut with stunning force, the air driven from his lungs, and an explosion of light behind his eyes as pain instantly racked his body.

He had landed on his back, arms and legs akimbo. He had also found the remnants of the sheared off pine from the top of the rim. One of its sharp ended, broken, branches was protruding up through his abdomen, his blood welling up and out around it in time with his slowly fading heart beat.

With great effort he opened his eyes, and looking up, saw through the building haze of terrible pain those great golden eyes staring back at him over the ledge at the top of the wall of the cut.

Oddly he thought he saw an expression of deep sadness in those eyes as they blinked, once, slowly, at him.

Then he saw nothing but blackness as his eyelids slid slowly down over his eyes. He had one last semi coherent thought before the darkness took him completely.

I'M—DEAD!

Interlude

He seemed to be hearing voices, yet that couldn't be. He had fallen to his death and his body lay on the floor of a cleft in one of the river cliffs, somewhere in the middle of a mostly unexplored wilderness area.

Maybe I'm not really dead! he thought to himself. It seemed to be a strange thought because he appeared to be floating in a soft velvety blackness, totally alone. Aroused now, he began to notice a difference in his surroundings and his awareness of it. There was a difference in the blackness about him and that difference was up. Yes up! That felt right to him. He sensed that awareness was up and he wanted to rise up to it.

Thought seemed to initiate action as he felt himself rising. As he rose he began to notice that the difference was in the color of the blackness around him. Above him the color was turning to red and seemed to be moving, roiling angrily, like the surface of a stormy ocean seen from below.

Floating upwards he thought he heard voices, faintly, as if at a great distance. Nearing the angry red, surging and rolling above him, he became frightened because he somehow knew that to enter there he would find pure and utter agony. He slowed himself, coming to a floating halt, just below the angry red surface.

The voices were clearer now, but disembodied, as he seemed to be. There were two of them, he was sure of it now. The words started to make sense to him as he listened.

I have seen members of this species injured before, said voice number one, and *"this one is mortally injured, near death."*

You are undoubtedly right, said voice number two, Then, *but life force remains. We will do what we can for it.*

How will we get it to the ship? Voice one again, and, *it is very badly broken, and see there, that piece of tree branch has penetrated completely through its torso.*

First, we go back to the ship for a small nullgrav cargo sled. When we return with it, we use its lifting tines to raise its body from the ground. Said voice two fading somewhat, and, *after raising the body you can then use the small laser cutter on your harness to cut away the branch, as close to the body as can safely be.*

The voices seemed to recede and he was alone again, floating, in the blackness just below the surface of the angry redness roiling above him. The voices, he suddenly noticed, were back and the angry redness above seemed closer.

He recognized voice two, *it's good, and a bare inch still protrudes; now reverse the tines and lower it to the bed of the sled.*

Then voice one, *it's very big. Will the sled clear those large rocks at the entrance?*

With maximum lift it should just clear them. Voice two again, and *we'll take it through the cargo entry. There's an entry from the bay to the auto-med unit. It is even larger than the Trine but should just fit onto the lower auto-med shelf.*

Voice one, *if we get it there alive you mean.*

Voice two, *then let us proceed with some haste then.*

The sled was moved across the open area and into the hold, surprisingly without a single bump, for the cat thing was not used to walking on only its two hind legs. And it was also panting from trying to control both momentum and direction with muscles new to the task.

They had lined the sled up with the med-units slide out tray and were shifting the body onto the shelf when Balor said, *quickly, it is losing fluid at a much faster rate now!* Dirk's awareness recognized this as voice number one.

The body now on the shelf voice number two said, *well enough. The unit is programmed with the parameter readings I obtained while studying this species. If any one factor will now save this being it will be the readings taken while we were moving it here. They will provide the comparisons that the unit would take valuable time to establish. Time that is now at a premium.*

This was all said as Balor moved around the unit pressing the buttons marked diagnose and stabilize.

Dirk did not hear any of this as he was being moved from the sled to the tray because the angry red roiling descended upon him to explode, in the tenuous state of consciousness he had achieved, with rending searing pain.

Then there was nothing, as he sank back into the soothing blackness.

And peace.

For a while.

For neither fate nor serendipity had taken their hands from him yet!

CHAPTER FOUR
Introductions

Introduction to Terror, Then Hope

The savagely tearing redness had receded now to a point that was still close, still threatening, waiting.

With that knowledge also came the realization that somehow, in someway, he still existed. He did not know how to explain it, but he knew that it was so.

Also the voices were back. Only now they were like a radio broadcast, with the volume turned very low. He also understood, somehow, that he was the topic of their conversation. Straining, mentally, they became clearer, louder.

Its circulatory pump rhythm has stabilized but is still very weak, said the voice he had begun to call voice one, remembering it from some time before.

Then came the one he remembered as voice two, *the med-unit has analyzed and produced a solution that is safe for it and is now feeding it directly into its circulatory system to replace fluid loss. But the loss itself must be stemmed for this procedure to do more than delay its expiration.*

The body temperature has also been stabilized, voice one again. But is higher than the bio-meter reading says it should be. This probably means that infection is beginning.

I must make contact with it directly, said voice two, *physically, as you know, to effect any change in this beings condition. its chemistry is well within my capabilities to manipulate but without continuous monitoring, adjustment and reinforcement, that which I can do will be transitory at best, because the shock to its systems will put them beyond my ability to repair.*

So, The voice continued, *I will do the minimum at once, to buy us some small amount of time, by manufacturing and supplying it with a micro-organism to at least delay the spread of bacterial infection. This will not be much and will only assist its own antibodies.*

Then let us proceed at once, Said voice one, sounding almost exasperated, *before it is too late to save it!*

After what seemed a long/short while later the angry redness appeared to retreat a little further from him. And as that pressure eased, so to eased the feeling of being compressed into a small, tight, little ball.

With this relief the velvet blackness began to soothe him so he closed his eyes, mentally, thinking to rest.

Without realizing when it had started he began to hear words again. This bothered him, had been bothering him, because the words seemed to be inside of him, inside of his head. The words came again, the volume building, until the meaning of the words was clear to him. He was really frightened now!

Human being…Human being! You must respond if we are to help you! Do you hear/understand us?

He was badly frightened now. He was sure now that the voices were inside of his mind. He had heard of telepathy, of some of the experiments, but he had never, ever, expected to encounter it personally. How could something be inside of his mind?

He retreated slightly within himself. It came again. He retreated further into himself, terror of the unknown beginning to yammer within his mind. This was wrong! They didn't belong in here, inside his mind! He knew this!

He curled in tighter around himself, pulling the velvet blackness tighter, closer to himself.

This is most strange. " said TuLan. ***I perceive its awareness of us yet it retreats.***
What is strange? stated Balor.

The strangeness, it fears what it does not know, replied TuLan in a tone both clinical and fascinated, ***"goes beyond that basic premise. I will explain quickly. Thus we may gain some insight into promoting real contact.***

First, you are correct! It fears, no, it manifests a degree of terror of some invasion of that part of it that recognizes self. Yet at the same time it is aware of the method being used to communicate with it as a part of its mind has begun to analyze that method and the import of that to it personally. Here TuLan paused.

Consider, he continued, There are normally three basic functional levels of the mind. The instinctive or autonomic, which monitors the bodies daily operations, including those semi-conscious operations like walking and breathing etc. and only draws awareness to the next conscious level when something goes wrong. The only thing that is truly exclusive to the instinctive level is the fight/flight—act/react response to direct stimuli, which in higher thinking beings can be, with training, overridden. Stated TuLan didactically, then continuing in the same lecturing manner

The conscious level of the mind generally collects, separates and interprets direct stimuli and provides associative integration for the comparison of

known/unknown quanta to supply itself with a viable hypothesis or rational thought. Particular to this level, also, is its ability to ask itself speculative questions of a non specific, non linear nature. Or 'What if?' . All of this and more, including speech form, active memory, command to action and the execution of those thoughts. TuLan paused again, seeming to take a mental breath.

Tied very closely to the conscious level, he continued again, *is the sub conscious level. Although not as well understood as the conscious mind it is basically agreed that this level is the repository of both active and passive memory and operates very much like a computer with multi function operational programming.*

It gathers the information from all four source spectrums, visual, audible, empirical thought and speculative hypothesis, sorting and storing it for retrieval at need. It has one other faculty that is little understood if at all, and that is intuitive reasoning. That is it is able to, seemingly, take unrelated bits of information, interpret them, integrate them and present the results to the conscious mind in an empirical format.

TuLan took a mental breath and plunged on saying, *now here is the really strange part. While trying to initiate contact I had to penetrate both the autonomic and the conscious levels, and simultaneously try to maintain control of the repairs I had begun, while both were completely inundated by systemic shock and pain response. The Id or ego, as expected, had retreated to the comparative safety of unconsciousness via the sub-conscious level. When I penetrated this level and tried to make contact, it rejected me and retreated to what appears to be another level below that one. A level that, though not unheard of, I was totally unaware of or prepared for because it was not to be expected in this species.*

TuLan went on with, *the Chai, because of our particular survival traits and abilities have long been aware of this fourth level of awareness. It is quite rare in all species, most having only the common three levels which are almost universal to all known intelligent beings. From the ones of great intelligence to those just above idiot level. Yes, this is quite strange,* he concluded.

The absence of the voice and the soothing effect of the velvety blackness began to relax some of the straining tenseness from Dirk. He began to uncoil from his mental fetal position. He oriented himself by locating the angry red cloud, which seemed to be, far above yet still very close. Waiting. Deadly!

He did not know exactly where he was but the impression of it was familiar, of always having been there. Of himself. Too, he felt that feeling of gibbering terror which had caused him to flee here but somehow he was holding it away. At arms length so to speak.

Slowly he became aware of it. The voice, calling to him again. He tensed himself to flee again but sensing something different, waited. Somehow he sensed no threat from it this time. He would listen for a moment…

Out of Terror, Into Hope

As TuLan explained what would be necessary to Balor, so too he tried to express the sense, the feeling that was growing within his mind about the importance of this particular being.

Balor, as I explained to you my race will not impose itself upon another. What I am about to try may seem a contradiction to that statement. There are a few exceptions to it, very few. This is now, I think, a necessary one.

Firstly, if I do not make contact with this being there will be no way that I can help it. It will die!

Second, for the reasons I have explained of its mental retreat, I must, must have physical contact with its mind to reach it.

Third, for reasons that I do not fully understand yet I feel a growing importance in direct connection with this being to both of us. So I ask you now, will you freely assist me in what I have to do? TuLan finished, his tone showing excitement, fear, and pleading all at once.

Balor, sitting rock still now, watched the human form laying on the treatment tray, noting the sharp odor of its perspiration and its labored breathing replied, *since our association began I have learned many new things, and am continuing a life which might well have ceased but for you. So far, in our bargain, I have received much beyond what was promised. Your motives, admittedly, are not altogether altruistic, yet I have not found you to be a liar. What must be done and how do we begin?*

You must, like the Trine before you, position yourself on the tray as close to the humans body as possible. Your neck and chest as close to its head, as you can do so comfortably, because it may take some time. Together we will cause a minute opening in your throat to occur through which I will extend a tendril to penetrate the human's brain. Using the cut on its temple as an entry point I will be able to make a connection.

The time factor will involve causing the involuntarily separation of its tissues to gain entry without creating further damage or shock to its systems.

Pausing for a few second of thought He then continued, *remember that once positioned you must remain completely still for the duration. Now we must make sure its' body is well sedated before we begin.*

And yes, to answer your unasked question, this being would make an excellent host if it would agree, but I think that if it does that I will sorely miss your direct presence.

So they began and things proceeded as TuLan had described them, each event going smoothly. The tendril TuLan extended entering the human's brain through the cut in its temple.

After establishing this direct physical contact, and searching with mental fingers, TuLan found that portion which handled communications functions located at that ethereal point just between the conscious and the sub-conscious levels, effectively bypassing the autonomic level altogether.

He found, as he had expected, the entire area littered with both sedatives and pain messages. He then, using the direct physical contact, pushed part of his mind in past the subliminal terror emotions and again called out to the human's center of awareness.

Human——Human please! You must respond or there is no way for us to help you! Then TuLan waited a space of heart beats before trying again, *human, please respond! Without your active participation we cannot prevent your dissolution. Your death!* The, after another few heart beats, TuLan heard a faint response.

Who are you? What are you doing here? This is not your place!

With immense relief TuLan responded, *we are the parts of the being you perceived just before you fell off the cliff.*

The black cat with the huge golden eyes?!! the thought, in startled wonderment, came to him.

Yes! At present I am part of that being, and to forestall a flood of questions he could feel building TuLan continued, *you were very seriously injured as a result of your fall. It had not been our intent to cause you injury, only to prevent harm to ourselves from your weapon. Now, we are trying to help you but have done all that we can without your assistance.* he finished.

Through all of this Dirk still felt no sense of threat, so he drifted closer as he shot more questions, *where is my body then? How seriously am I injured? What do you mean when you say 'we'?* he finished in a rush.

TuLan delayed answering these questions, feeling the pressure of time, saying instead, *we brought you here to our facility and stabilized your bodily functions, but fear that we cannot maintain them much longer.*

He paused for a few heartbeats then continued, *to help you further your active participation is necessary. Please! Come up from that well. All will be explained to you. Hurry please, time we need passes all too quickly!* he also finished in a rush.

Feeling no sense of threat whatsoever now, but still wary, Dirk let his awareness rise. As he was rising he felt himself passing through some kind of barrier, intangible but there none the less, and found himself confronting another presence.

Still he felt no sense of threat from it, only a feeling of worry which seemed to surround it like a cloud. Rose up until he was, figuratively, face to face with it.

The Explanation

As he drifted slightly closer to the essence of the others presence it spoke to him again, saying, *human, I profoundly thank you for coming up here to meet me, for maintaining contact while you were down below there was a great strain on me.*

To which Dirk responded, *who are you and where is here?*

My personal identifier, came the disembodied voice, *is TuLan of the Chai and here is in your mind, as I see you already have a suspicion.*

If that's so, Dirk replied, *what are you doing in here, and just how are we talking?*

The first, said TuLan, *I have already stated, and if you agree I will explain further. The second is a form of mind to mind communication, your name for it I believe is telepathy, which I see you already perceive.*

Are you reading my mind!? questioned Dirk, retreating somewhat.

Not at all, reassured TuLan hastily, *some of your thoughts do leak around a sort of stop/go shield but that is all. The thoughts that I receive, other than those that leak past this shield, are those you push past the shield yourself and are directed at me.*

That part behind the shield is the Id or ego, the private part of yourself that you identify as being you. He explained, then went on saying, *invading your personal self is something which my species would not do. It is against our ethics of conduct because it is held that the self is sacred to each individual."* Then added, *I would like to know, if you please, your personal identifier as it would make conversation much easier.*

My name, said Dirk, *if I take your meaning correctly, is John Dirk but if you like you can just call me Dirk.*

Well then Dirk, there is much to explain to you and time presses ever harder as it passes. If you would hold most of your questions until you have my explanation it will most likely answer many of them and save much needed time. said TuLan with some urgency in his manner.

This is all new to me, said Dirk, *but I do sense your urgency, so I agree to hold my questions and listen. Please begin.*

As TuLan began his explanations the imput from the translation program kicked in causing him to start using terms and idioms easily understandable to Dirk, and his speech, too, became less stilted in manner.

He began the explanation saying, *after you fell, even though we tried to stop you from falling, over the cliff edge, and may I say that you move very fast for one of your species, it took Balor and I several of your seconds to reach you where you had landed on the tree in the floor of the cut.*

TuLan was rushing his speech now but couldn't stop himself as he continued, *to forestall confusion and questions I will explain that Balor is the name of the being, the cat thing as you describe him, which forms the other half of our partnership. Due to circumstances, which I'll explain later, we operate as a single entity.*

Here he paused to take a mental breath, then, *now to continue. Upon reaching you we found that you had sustained several severe injuries. Three of your four limbs were broken and you had received a nasty blow to your head, causing a very bad concussion. But most serious of all, you had fallen upon the splintered point of an up thrusting branch of a tree knocked into the cut by the close passage of my ship as it landed.*

Pausing again as he felt the questions forming TuLan interjected *Please Wait! All will be explained later.* Continuing with his explanation he said, *that branch penetrated your lower back and came out through your abdomen, causing much damage to your internal organs,* here TuLan paused, taking a mental breath, to let Dirk absorb some of what he had said.

We were able, he continued, *to lift you, after cutting away the larger portion of the branch, by using a device brought from my ship. Using this same device we transported your body to the ship and placed it within another device called an automated medical unit, where it now is. This unit was able to stabilize your life functions and to produce a type of plasma, compatible to you, to replace some of your lost and leaking body fluid. Blood, I believe you call it.*

From the way your telling it, interrupted Dirk, *that's not the worst of it. Just what is the bottom line here?*

The bottom line here, TuLan went on, *as you so aptly put it, is as follows. Your injuries are systemic, involved in and interfering with several of your bodies life processes, and being complicated by the invasion of that foreign object, the branch, and bacteria the unit cannot identify as yet. The auto-med unit has, as I said, temporarily stabilized your condition but cannot maintain it for a much longer period of time. This is due mainly to a lack of an intimate knowledge of your physiology and it's beneficial organisms.*

Here TuLan paused momentarily, then continued, *your body is losing the fight for it's existence, it's life. The angry red cloud you perceive, roiling above us, is the manifestation of the pain and shock your body is experiencing.*

And, *the med unit cannot maintain you in this state much longer.*

For moments after TuLan had stopped Dirk waited for him to continue, then said, *that's not all of it, there appears to be an option left to you, yet you hesitate to present it. Why ?*

Of course, said TuLan, *you are correct, and astute. That is why I came in here to find you. I hesitate because these are not the conditions under which I would choose to make you this offer, your option.*

My dilemma, he went on, *is that you should, by all rights, be in a position to make this choice completely freely, accept or reject, without adverse conditions pressing you to it. Note this though, no matter what your choice we will continue all our efforts to save you. Yet again honesty requires that I not offer any false hopes, for your situation is grave. Do you wish to hear my offer?*

My grandfather said many times, snapped Dirk, *that while life remains there is always hope. If it really is a choice I will make it freely. Let's hear your offer!*

Well enough then, said TuLan, *I offer you a full and very long life! But of course there are, as in most cases, strings attached!*

I expected as much. Said Dirk softly, *please continue. As you have so often repeated, time passes and presses!*

Just so, yet there is much to be explained, much you must truly understand, for your response could concern more than just yourself, TuLan stated enigmatically.

Who else might my life or death concern ?" asked Dirk crossly. *You still speak in riddles. Come to the point, if there is one.*

Please, your forbearance is...

The Offer

...forbearance is needed. I will begin and continue to the finish if you will listen for a little longer!

Time still passes. Dirk now stated flatly.

As you say." TuLan said, and began to talk in a hurry. *First, to answer your last question, the answer to it is me. The reason for this you will very soon understand."* said TuLan in a now subdued tone. *"But before that you must know who and what I am and where I come from to understand why this is so.*

He then began to tell Dirk the story of his species and of himself. Of the Union of Races, and their galactic civilization. Of the Drel wars that had devastated and almost ended it, and their long climb back from that near disaster. Lastly he explained the techniques his race had developed for survival and mobility, in graphic detail, leaving nothing out

In objective time this narrative took an hour or two. Subjectively it seemed to take many hours more than that. When he stopped speaking the sound of the silence between them seemed somehow quite loud.

TuLan waited patiently for a period but there was no response from Dirk, so he began to ask a question. At which point Dirk signaled him to *"wait"* as he continued to ponder what he had been told.

Presently Dirk signaled for TuLans' attention and said, *TuLan, you have told me a great deal. Much of it amazing, much of it also at least surmised at by my own people's scientists and philosophers. I have said little of my own background but it is one that demands that I ask you the following questions.*

One: *What have you not told me ?*

Two: *Why did you move your space platform to begin with ?*

Three: *Why were you here to observe us in the first place ?*

Four: *Did your long observation of us have anything to do with your not contacting us, which is, as you've said, contrary to your policy with most other intelligent races?*

TuLan paused for long moments, considering his next words, before going on with the conversation, knowing unerringly without knowing how he knew, that this would be the turning point for both of them. Putting aside all reservations he went on!

Dirk, said TuLan gravely, *once more I must ask, do you accept the offer I made you and the advantages that go with it? Of a very prolonged life, excellent health and vastly improved strength and endurance for your body? Will you accept, knowing that part of the price for these advantages is acting as my host, and the method of that hosting?*

He paused, hesitant, then went on, *will you, can you, accept those conditions for a period of time that we will both agree on? Here he paused for a breath, then continued, Please wait for a short period before answering, to consider this also. The process, because of the nature of your injuries, will be long and, I'm afraid, quite painful at times during your recovery. This also I promise as part of our agreement, that I will change or alter nothing without your knowledge or permission. The only exception being those things which may become immediately and absolutely necessary during the transfer and initial healing period.* And here again he paused, for a short time, allowing Dirk to digest what he had said so far.

After the pause TuLan said, "*Dirk, time is growing shorter so I will ask you to accept the answers I give you now, to your last questions, at face value for the time being. You are an astute listener and observer, paying as much attention to things unsaid as those said, and my respect grows for you by the moment.*"

The answer to your first question is that you are correct, I have not told you everything, but the omission was by choice and had nothing to do with deception. The reasons for my being here to observe your people and planet are more of a personal nature than an official one. My relationship with the officialdom of the Union governing body is that of a free-lance seeker of facts. You see, I am considered by many to be, and am by nature, an overly curious individual.

I have been known to take on commissions deemed boring, or even distasteful, by some others. By doing thus I gain some measure of semi official standing and am allowed some latitude in the course of my personal inquiries, gaining me access to records and information not readily available to everyone. Often because of the nature those inquiries and the seriousness of my approach in seeking answers some have gone so far as to label my efforts as fanatical. Happily though, the results of those efforts produce direct, complete and correct information.

After taking a short pause, TuLan went on, *to answer your second question, the reason for moving the observation platform is quite simple. Your space exploration, although still in its infancy and somewhat haphazard, has progressed to the point where the improving quality of your sensing and detection technology would have eventually allowed its discovery.*

Answering your third question, he said, *the reason for your being under observation was twofold. The first part is that all newly discovered races are observed for a period of time, a hundred or so of your years, to determine the impact that contact might have on them. Or, if contact should be delayed, pending a time when they might achieve more stability for themselves.*

Part two, which also answers question four, is that I, having done the original observation, extended the observation period on my own authority because I found far to many anomalies in your technological, historical and philosophical growth. Because of them, I had serious concerns that your people were being interfered with by an outside and not friendly source.

In addition, *I would very much like to discuss those reasons with you at a later time, if there is to be one My particular fanatical bent, or in your own vernacular my hang up, is based on my investigations of several other races and the results I obtained. Results which, when coupled with what I believe I have discovered here, have lead me to the conclusion that the Drel have returned to this universe. The evidence of this I would also like your opinion on. If my suspicions are correct your planet and its people are in very grave danger indeed!* TuLan finished with a sigh.

TuLan waited several beats then said to Dirk; *I would like to clarify one point for you, before you ask it. You're probably wondering why I would leave my present host to host with you. The answer is in three parts the first two being both simple and direct in nature. The third is a little more complex. They are as follows.*

One, TuLan explained, *I offer you this because I have had a direct involvement in the reason for your present condition.*

Two," He said, *is that although Balor is as fine a being as I have met, having amazing intelligence and ability in combination, he lacks the one ability that you so abundantly possess. Appendages that are capable of manipulative dexterity.*

Third and last, TuLan concluded, *is since our first encounter I have had a growing conviction that our futures were somehow destined to be very closely entwined, each with the others. Do not ask me to explain this feeling for my race has seldom, if ever, even acknowledged the remote possibility of the idea of fate.*

Dirk was so quiet for so long that TuLan began to fidget mentally. Suddenly Dirk said, *so be it!* And *I have one or two provisos, if acceptable?*

What really surprised TuLan, after hearing them, was their similarity to those that Balor had made!

Acceptance and Life

So be it! said Dirk, and *"But I do have one or two provisos if acceptable?"*
TuLan let out a long mental sigh, then said, *State them.* Then he waited.

The provisions that Dirk quoted were surprising only in their similarity to those quoted by Balor, with the exception of one. That one being…

…And the final provision is this. As I had already been planning to make a change in my life, of course not expecting one of this magnitude, it will be necessary for me to travel back north to pick up my jeep and equipment. That, so I can get into an urban area where I can contact those for whom I work. I must do this so that I can tender my resignation. This may take some time and must be done with great care, for I am employed by the military arm of the governing body of this continent. This must be accomplished as soon as I am physically able.

TuLan had no objections to any of the provisions and said so. Then he said, *I must withdraw for a short period to work with Balor to prepare for the transfer. As soon as we are ready I will return and work with you to help you prepare for accepting me. When that is complete, I will immediately begin the repairs that are necessary to make you whole again.*

I must warn you that in the condition you are in the process will take some time to accomplish. Balor will monitor the med-unit as it manages the care and feeding of your unconscious body for the duration.

I must also warn you, again, that even with that care you will most likely be extremely weak upon awakening, so plan now to accept at least fifteen to twenty days in recovery before you begin to recover your strength. So saying, TuLan made his exit.

After TuLan had left his mind Dirk lay wondering at the odd sense of aloneness, he felt. It was so very strange to be feeling this way after so many years of striving to achieve this very condition in himself. Strange too, after so short a time together, was his sense of loss in missing TuLan, otherworldly being or not.

He also thought to himself, in some wonder, that he was laying here very close to death and very soon now, he was to be whole again, better even, in a month or less. It would have taken all of his own peoples combined medical expertise a year or more, if at all, to heal him.

As he lay there, drifting in the velvety black darkness, he sensed above him that roiling red cloud that seemed angrier than ever, and he sent a thought up at it, almost as if to appease it. *Not today brother, not today.*

TuLan returned as promised and with great skill and care guided Dirk into and through the transfer of TuLan from the body of Balor into his own.

It had begun! *Dirk! Dirk! You must come up now!* He heard TuLans' voice calling faintly, from a long, long way off.

As his awareness began to return the first thing that he noticed was that the angry red cloud was gone, and far above him there was the faint glow of light. The second was that he was rising, faster and faster, towards it.

His eyes snapped open! Or, at least that's what they tried to do. Then he felt something rasping across his cheek forcing him to finally open his eyes all the way, to be confronted by two, great, golden orbs staring right into his own!

What he said was *MGMPH!?* What he thought was *Balor?* He heard, from somewhere in his mind, a deep mirthful chuckle as the tongue rasped across his now heavily bearded face one last time. Then those great golden eyes and Balor were gone from his sight.

He turned his head and felt creaky muscles protest, sharply, and from that same part of his mind that had come, he somehow knew, Balors' chuckle he heard TuLan say, *Dirk, you must take in liquid and some solid forms of nutrition. Balor brings sugared water and energy bars for that purpose.*

TuLan paused here to make sure he was understood, then said, *you must do this slowly, taking in as much as you can hold down. This must be repeated every two hours for the next twenty four hours. After that you must start to exercise by flexing the muscles in your arms and legs and, in a day or so, you must begin moving them about.*

Dirk said aloud, *how long?* with a groan.

Thirty one rotations, or days. TuLan thought in reply, understanding the meaning of the question.

Dirk groaned again, then said, *long time!* Then, *I've got to learn not to do this or people will think I've gone round the bend.*

Again, understanding that Dirk referred to answering him aloud, TuLans' thought came right on the heels of another of those mental chuckles from Balor, *You will master the technique very quickly with practice. Drink now and eat a little. Then flex arms and leg muscles. Then rest, lightly this time.*

And so began the genesis of John Longknife Dirk! And so too the genesis of TuLan the Chai!

TuLan, after mapping and studying almost every cell in Dirk's body, began the repairs and improvements which he had promised.

He also began to learn a great deal about this human, this man Dirk, who he would be so dependent on for the foreseeable future.

But little, at this time, did TuLan Chai realize to what a powerful personality and unflagging ally he had attached himself.

The future held many surprises for this pair!

TuLan and Dirk would form, and they would maintain, a relationship that would last for a long, long time.

The humans called this type of relationship a friendship, a term that TuLan did not yet quite understand.

But he, TuLan, would learn about friendship. Learn about the many wonderful things that are brought to such a relationship.

And he would also learn all that it could cost, as well!

CHAPTER FIVE
Genesis, New Beginnings

Conversations on a Trip

Dirk was sitting on a log, outside the ship, going over in his mind the time elapsed since this adventure had begun for him. He was also practicing speaking telepathically with TuLan without audibleising. *Lets see now,* he said, *two days placing salt, six days getting here on foot, three days finding this place, thirty one days in the med unit, four days recovering from that, and now you say you want me to spend another eight to ten days exercising and practicing. Practicing what?*

TuLan's voice, and it was as distinct as an audible sound Dirk realized, spoke in Dirk's mind, quietly *Dirk, there is one thing that I have not yet told you.*

What, said Dirk, *haven't you told me yet? Come to think of it, you have been unusually quiet for the last couple of days. Ok! Out with it.*

It should only take two days to reach your property now; three if you take it very easy as you go. said TuLan, voice still quiet.

That's crazy!" Dirk sputtered, *it took me six days hard travel to get here! And that's knowing how to travel in the wild.*

Dirk, look at the log we're sitting on. How much do you think it weighs?

Dirk stood up and gave the log a good look. *About three fifty—four hundred pounds.* he said.

Please, lift this end of the log. TuLan instructed.

Bending his knees, Dirk squatted, and flexing his leg, back and shoulder muscles heaved upward on the end of the heavy log. And promptly fell on his backside, as the log flipped up and away from him, end over end. *Holy shit!* he exclaimed, stunned.

As an individual I may not be as much of an altruist as I might wish to be. said TuLan, then *while you were recovering in the med-unit I initiated a process in your body that has increased the strength in all of your bones, sinuses and muscles by a factor of two and a half to three times what was normal for your race. I am sorry I had to spring this on you like this. But I did say that survival is a fetish of my race. I hope that you are not displeased with me?* he finished ruefully.

As he sat there, still somewhat stunned, Dirk again heard that throaty chuckle in his mind, then *He pulled that same thing on me. How do you think I got behind you so easily and so quietly?* Balor sent.

Still sitting where he had landed, Dirk sent back, *I had a sneaking suspicion you could talk, Balor.*

Balor replied in a somewhat pontifical manner, *all beings that are aware of self can talk Dirk. It is most often a question of learning how to listen.* This last almost had the flavor of a smirk. And, *and when there is need!* he ended, and he was gone again.

Dirk spent the next seven days learning to control his newfound and swiftly increasing strength, and a good part of each night learning about the ship, its equipment and it's operation. By coincidence he discovered that his minds awareness seemed to be much sharper, and his hearing and eyesight much improved too. Also he found that he needed less sleep.

On the fifty fifth day he was up early, preparing for the trek north. Feeling a tingle of amusement in his mind, which he had quickly learned was Balors' personal aura, he turned to face that beautiful catlike being as it projected it's thoughts to him, *I would accompany you north to see this land you prize so highly.?* Balor said/asked.

Dirk looked, for a long moment, into those large golden eyes, then said, *Balor, though little has seemed to pass between us I would like to consider you a friend. There is much that could possibly be said but it comes down to a thing of simplicity.*

Dirk paused for a second then went on, *That simple thing is this, when you are behind me I feel no discomfort, and for a man such as myself that is a rare thing indeed! We humans have a thing, an understanding with those we consider true friends. Therefore, having said as much, I will share it with you now. Balor, I would like to consider you my friend. And, as my friend what I have is yours for as long as you may need it.* he concluded, real warmth in his eyes emphasizing the feeling in his thoughts, for he realized that this was exactly how he felt.

Balor his huge golden eyes swirling like molten metal for a moment as they regarded Dirk, suddenly stepped back and was gone. Dirk was to find out, many times over the years, the quality of the friendship that he had struck that morning,

As they moved north that first day, he retraced his earlier passage south, Dirk was still trying to completely accept and adjust to his improved strength. And also amazed at the pace he had set and maintained, as evening brought them to the campsite he had made on his third nights travel south. They had covered as much distance in one day as it had taken him tree to traverse before.

As he was building a compact campfire within a ring of stones Balor stepped out, wraithlike, from the darkness. He dropped two fat rabbits down beside Dirk saying, *you are ruining my image by developing in me a taste for cooked meat!* so saying he lay down a few feet from the fire, waiting for dinner to be prepared.

Dirk, smiling to himself, rejoined with, *And you're going to make a nervous wreck out of me the way you keep appearing and disappearing!*

On the evening of the second day, they entered the ravine where Dirk had spent the night weathering the fateful storm that had started him on his present course. As he reached the jeep he pulled the built up wind blown brush away, pulled the tarp off and threw it and his pack into the back.

He jumped into the driver's seat and inserting the key started it up, surprised that it had started on the first try. He called to Balor to join him for the ride to the small cabin where they would overnight before starting the trip to the city.

He received that deep chuckle and, *no thanks, a being could get hurt riding in that contraption.*

Upon reaching the cabin the jeep was quickly unloaded and the supplies stored away. From the cold room, cut into the rock under the rear of the cabin, Dirk brought a small slab of dried venison, which he cut into medium sized chunks.

He then gathered small dried potatoes, wild onions, dried carrots and peas, and several dried herbs. All of these, along with the meat from his cold room, and a gallon of water, he threw into an iron pot hanging on an angle brace in the fireplace.

Taking dried wood from a box beside the fireplace he quickly laid a fire under the pot. Soon thereafter, as the mixture in the pot began to simmer, a very tempting aroma began to fill the little cabin. Smelling this he added some more wild spices, then dropped a lid on the pot to let them cook into his stew completely.

This done he went to the bunk in the back of the room and shook out the blankets neatly folded there, then made up the bunk. That finished, he admitted to TuLan that he was really tired. They would eat and sleep, to rise for an early start in the morning.

He went out to the front of the cabin and sent a thought/call to Balor, asking if he wanted to join them in eating. Not receiving an answer he turned back to the cabin, only to see Balor sitting in the doorway looking at him with that cat smile of his.

Balor finally said to him, *Thanks. Nice place you have here. I think I see why you prize it so much. I will stay here and watch for you while you are gone.* So saying he turned and went inside, lying down by the fire, waiting to eat with his friends.

Early the next morning, just after dawn, Dirk set out in the jeep for the city. It would be a long, three day, drive and he was anxious to be on his way. Too, he had many things on his mind which he wished to talk with TuLan about. Four hours of hard driving brought him out onto a decent secondary road.

As the necessity of strict attention to his driving eased Dirk began to talk with TuLan, saying, *If we are to find out if there is any evidence of these people, The Drel, being here there are things that must be done very soon.*

Continuing, he said, *to be at all effective we are going to need a well trained organization, with some experienced people for both field work and leadership. From the things you have told me, so far, most of your work to locate any of these people was done through and by long range observation.*

This is quite true. Replied TuLan, *the method that I developed was to first detect, then locate, areas and eras of specific trend repetitions. Then by matching those trends, against similarities of known incursions from past records I have kept, I can narrow down my locus of search and verify or clear a suspected area.*

Also, Dirk interjected, *you have mentioned several times before that my people, humans, are an anomaly. I don't quite seem to grasp your meaning. Please explain it to me again. This time try just presenting the things or items that you consider to be anomalous. That might help to clarify things for me.*

Well enough, said TuLan, *but let me begin with the, to me, most glaring examples. Although, I admit, it might be an exception it really stands out for me. Here it is then. Most civilizations, and I'm speaking planetary here, have a recorded history which has achieved a completely stable base by the time it was in its fifth or sixth millenium of record keeping, and maintains a true linearity in that record. Once that linearity is achieved, it remains stable, barring planetary catastrophe, for the foreseeable future. Even if that civilization has not covered the entire planet.* Without realizing it TuLan had dropped into a lecturing tone of thought.

He went on after taking a mental breath, *your race has only been keeping a truly linear record of its history for the last four to five millenium, and that's stretching the term linear. Yet you have pocket histories that have been recorded, dating as far back as twenty thousand years. Each with many dissimilarities as opposed to similarities in all the important aspects. Aspects such as language, philosophy, art, and religion.*

And more oddly still most of those had very large discrepancies in the level of the basic technologies they were able to achieve in their timeframes. This then is the anomaly that glares out at me. In comparison most civilizations who have managed to maintain a steadily recorded history for a thousand years do not simply cease to exist!

Here TuLan paused, then continued. *Your species is, admittedly, a most contentious and warlike one but this is not a true rarity among the traits of all the other species in the galaxy. There are several that, were the conditions egregious enough, could match or even exceed, your own in their capacity for ferocity.*

The major difference is, for most other species that in their overall histories warfare on any large scale is the exception rather than the rule. In the last five thousand years that your species has been recording, spastically, its history there has been only one true constant throughout. There has been a war, of major proportions, constantly in progress on some part of your world.

What makes this such an anomaly, even excluding the broken lineage of your histories, is that almost universally your greatest philosophies are diametrically opposed to these actions! No matter in what way they have been stated the net result is that they eschew war in favor of conciliation, tolerance, peace and learning. Nowhere else in the known galaxy have these factors been the exception rather than the rule of the norm!

Dirk, as he drove, was silent for some moments as he digested what had been said, then said, *I can see, using the background that you provide, how you might come to that conclusion. But those alone cannot be the only reasons you have for your suspicions to be so strong in regard to my people and planet.*

They are not," said TuLan, *if you take them separately. But putting them together they form, for me, a signpost which says to me, in large letters, follow this trail-follow this trail!* And the discussion went on as they drove south and east onto better and larger roadways, until they were finally driving on a major highway. In this manner they drove until they decided to stop for the night.

Feeling very tired after driving, with few breaks in between, for ten and a half hours, and still recovering from his ordeal, Dirk just ate a quick meal at a local diner and went to bed at the motel they had stopped at. Leaving further discussions for the next days driving.

The next morning after a hearty breakfast, they were on the road early again. And, after driving for almost an hour in silence Dirk spoke to TuLan, *I can see, and even concede, most of your points for using disparity to norm as a yardstick.*

A yardstick whose measure is enough to cause concern for the initiation of an investigation of a species to determine if an outside influence is affecting its progress, but unless you have something further to lock it up it won't hold water in the end. Knowing you, now, as I do there has to be something more concrete, specific, to cause you the concern I can detect that you feel.

Dirk, said TuLan, *I had hoped to have more time to bring up and discuss these things, mainly because some of my information is, seemingly, somewhat amorphous. Could even be considered to be conjecture by those without my personal experience and background to balance it against. But before going into those there are a couple of things we need to talk about, mainly, because it is important for you to understand 'timeframe' and its relationship to the subject matter and myself, and now you.*

Here TuLan paused, as if he were collecting his thoughts, then went on, *although I gave you a good idea about most of the races in the union, and a basic history of my own, I did not relate much to individual or personal topics concerning them. I did, I remember, tell you that we, my people, were a long lived race by most standards, did I not? Do you have any idea of exactly how long we live?*

I originally thought it was about two or three hundred years, said Dirk, *but from the way that you've been talking I would now say it was a thousand years."* He finished with some wonder in his voice!

Dirk, began TuLan with some trepidation in his tone, *There is no other way to tell you this, but it is something that you must know, so here it is.*

After a short pause TuLan plunged on, *the average life span of my race is seven and a half to nine and a half thousand of your years, and I am almost twenty five hundred of your years old. I reached full adulthood some twelve hundred years ago and finished, what for us, is my advanced education over seven hundred of your earth years ago. I am in what you might call, here on earth, my early middle age. The oldest recorded age of one of my race was almost twelve thousand five hundred of your years, and there is some evidence that our life spans are lengthening.*

Dirk was so stunned that he almost swerved the jeep off the road, but quickly regained control, then decided to pull off anyway, for a few minutes, to recover his wobbly equilibrium. After some few minutes, and after he had regained some control of his whirling thoughts, TuLan went on again.

Just after you had chosen to partner with me, I'm sure you'll remember, I told you that you could expect to live a long and healthy life. If I remember correctly the average life span of your species at this point is about eighty years and, with reasonable care, one hundred years is not unheard of. Is that fairly accurate? He asked.

That's just about right on the money. said Dirk, his thoughts still a little shaky, and wondering where this was going.

Dirk, since the repairs and modifications I made to your body and systems, barring death caused by an accident or violence, you should live anywhere from six to eight hundred of your years, much longer if I am still with you. I told you, we do not take our obligations to our partners lightly, TuLan finished, projecting a smile with these thought/words.

If Dirk had been stunned before, he would have fallen down now, if he had not already been sitting down.

His breath caught, seeming to freeze the movement of his lungs, his pulse rate climbed erratically and sweat broke out on the palms of his hands!

Slowly, and with a tremendous effort, he willed his body to relax bringing his systems gradually back under control. He expelled the air, frozen in his lungs, in a long whoosh, saying,

Whew! You really know how to spring a surprise on a guy!

Perspective Adjustment

It was necessary for you to know this, for you to grasp the scope of the things I will tell you, from my perspective. said TuLan.

Bearing in mind what you have just told me there is no way that my perspective can remain unchanged. said Dirk, still somewhat shakily.

If you are ready to listen/see my perspective I will endeavor to give it to you in a nutshell. said TuLan, somewhat didactically, preparing himself for a long explanation.

I am, metaphorically speaking, all ears. Said Dirk dryly, also preparing himself to listen closely to what TuLan had to say.

We, started TuLan, *meaning the Union, have been observing your planet since it was discovered, by a disabled freighter, some four hundred of your years ago. Until about eighty years ago most of the observation was done by a satellite set in a geo-synchronous orbit, about eighteen million miles out. Eighty years ago, for specific reasons that I will go into later, I took over to provide personal observation, bringing in my own platform. A couple of months ago I decided to move it further out, because of the advances you had made in your detection equipment and the progress of your space program. The result of that move you know. The overall reasons for my being here I will now tell you.* TuLan paused, waiting for any comments.

About eighty five years ago," he continued, *" we were going over the information collected from your satellite and the pattern we saw developing both startled and worried us. The thing that we saw was that virtually one third of your planet was embroiled in open warfare. That was bad enough, but what really worried us was the leaps that you were making technologically. It was decided then that an on site observer was a real necessity because passive collection of information was no longer feasible. It was now very important to gain an understanding of you as a people and to closely watch your development, both technological and philosophical.*

Our rules, and ethics, forbid interference with the self determination of non member species. If you decided to destroy yourselves, well that was your choice. We would mourn the loss of an intelligent species, but that would/ could be all. As it was our fears were sound.

About fifty years ago you were yet again embroiled in world wide warfare of such proportions that it encompassed more than two thirds of your planet. The thing that really worried us at that point was what might happen when you moved out into space, as the direction of your technology must eventually lead you to do.

A short pause, then, *and even then you would be left to your own ways and means until, as you must, you discovered the method of faster than light travel. Then sooner or later, if the pattern of your behavior didn't change and mature, action might have to be taken.* TuLan paused again.

I am familiar with the periods that you were speaking of and agree that they were no part of our best, said Dirk, And I also recognized the implied threat at the end of your statement. he finished flatly.

Dirk, listen to me! TulAn pleaded, *I told you that these were issues of perspective as much as of content. In the past eighty years, let alone the past eight hundred, your history has been a skein of paradoxes! On one hand you espouse that all merit respect and freedom, and with the other you are fastening chains on people and selling them as slaves!*

You develop and build an entire organization to provide medical aid and health education, free, all over your world. Then your best medical researchers spend vast time and effort to develop the worst and most virulent diseases' that are conceivable to you. Your religious leaders preach peace and tolerance, yet will come to blows over differences of interpretation of the same text.

TuLan finished passionately. *You will cold bloodedly shoot or maim an enemy soldier, then pick him up and carry him miles to an aid station. Your political leaders will negotiate for months, even years to achieve a peace treaty, then seek or even invent reasons to break them and cause another conflict. Your entire history is a contradiction in terms and rationality. Your one, 'ONE', saving grace as a species is that you always seem to be looking ahead, by some action or deed, to some magnificent goal that you haven't quite yet been able to define. Dirk, put yourself in our position, if possible, and view it from our perspective. How would you answer our question?*

That you perceive us all to clearly, said Dirk sourly, *and not well at all.* Dirk said with some chagrin, then *I must think before commenting further,* and with that drove on in silence for the rest of the afternoon. That evening was a repeat of the one before. A quick meal and early to bed.

The next morning, after getting on the road and driving for a short while, Dirk said to TuLan, *I hope that you were not offended by my silence. Your assessment was all too accurate for my immediate comfort, and I reacted from a conscience already burdened with personal knowledge of some of the things about which you speak.* Dirk said somberly.

As I have already told you I was a member of an organization designed to avert or interdict many of the baser conditions you have been describing. He began slowly now.

Then he went on more rapidly, *the reason I had decided to resign from it was that it seemed as if its purpose had changed from one of preventing excesses to one of instigating them. This aside, a question remains. Why did you stop? You have yet more to tell which, I think, you believe has a direct and important bearing!*

You are truly as astute as I first thought. TuLan said with some warmth, "*It is true. The rest of what I have to tell you are the parts that I must relate as conjecture and supposition, for there are no specifics as yet, only parallels.*

Go ahead then. said Dirk as he settled into a more comfortable position to both listen and drive.

Since the beginning of your last century," TuLan began somberly, *your world and its people have experienced two wars in which almost your entire race was involved. And at least a dozen more that could be considered major, or very close to it. Of those, all, with the exception of the one about fifty years ago seem to have been driven by greed rather than ideology. You are currently experiencing an onslaught of terrorism, a thing I might add, that is almost but not quite unique to your species, and it is being perpetrated more frequently and on larger and larger scales.*

And most of your governing bodies seem to be acting in a manner contrary to their stated goals. Dirk, all of these chains of events, plus the alarmingly fast development of your technology has a parallel. 'Two' as a matter of fact!

They are both now nothing but lifeless cinders circling their respective suns'. On both of those planets, the actions of the inhabitants were similar to those of your own. Our suspicions were aroused as the actions of your people began to parallel those of planets lost in our distant past.

There was a definite similarity to those who had succumbed to incursions by the Drel long ago. In both of those cases, because we weren't sure and it had been such a long time since the Drel had been heard from, by the time our suspicions were seriously aroused it was to late to stop it. They, like yourselves, were located far out in the outer reaches of the populated galaxy, where little oversight was maintained.

TuLan took a quick mental breath and plunged on, *By the time help was sent for, and came, it was too late. Investigations were made but no conclusive proof could be obtained from the remains. Your planet is the third, showing similar signs, in less than two thousand years. The statistical probability of three occurrences, with particulars so closely paralleling the previous two, and in such a short period of time is so small as to not exist!*

There is only one other period when these paralleling situations occurred with any regularity. It was some three hundred and seventy or eighty thousand years ago and was one of the main causes of the war fought between the Union and the Drel. That war lasted almost fifty thousand years and devastated both combatants, completely destroying many planets and races in the process. Here TuLan paused momentarily, then continued.

We know of these parallels because one of our oldest allies, and the second oldest race in the Union, invented a method of transferring and storing thoughts directly onto wire filament tapes. This method is the same principal that our translation program works on. I also have a copy of that information for you to read/hear when you are ready to do so. Now you know just about everything. There are a few more items, but they can wait for a while. More importantly, if my suspicions are correct, and I believe that they are, your planet and its people are in terribly grave danger! TuLan finished, very tired now.

This was the meat of the conversation on this last day of travel to the city. The whole of it contained a great deal of background information and detail which consumed most of the time that was spent driving.

As they entered the outskirts of the city and headed for the apartment Dirk kept for the times when he was here, he said, "Let me digest what you have told me overnight. Then, tomorrow, after I hand in my resignation papers we can go over it and also some questions that I have. And some ideas too."

Dirk stopped to eat dinner at a restaurant close to the apartment then went straight there. As he exited the elevator into the vestibule, which was also for his exclusive use, Dirk checked the telltales that he always set upon leaving, to make sure that no one had entered while he was away. Finding them as he had left them went on into the apartment proper.

After showering, and laying out clothes and the papers that he would need the next day he settled back on his bed, picked up the remote control and turned on his television. He tuned it to the local late news program so he could watch it before going to sleep.

After watching the news program he turned the set off and lay back on his bed, where he lay awake for long hours, thinking things over.

CHAPTER SIX
Allies, New Friends and Old

Out in the Cold

Despite his tiredness, he lay awake into the late hours of the night but even so Dirk was up early, feeling refreshed, and ready to get started. He made himself a quick breakfast of juice, toast, eggs and a pot of coffee. After eating he cleared the table and sat down with his third cup of coffee and the resignation papers that he had taken from a drawer the night before. The drawer where they had lain for the last three months while he tried to make up his mind. He began to quickly fill in all of the blanks and signing on the appropriate lines with a sense of determination.

Having made up his mind he didn't want to waste any time getting on to the new life that he had been planning last night. Because it felt very, very, good to have a real sense of purpose. One that he could believe in. One with a real goal to work towards again. Also, He wasn't kidding himself about this new life, it would be very dangerous. But he had been there before, too!

These thoughts in mind he showered again, shaved, and dressed quickly in the clothes he had laid out the night before, and gathering his papers went down to get his car out of his garage and put the jeep in its place.

He drove across town to the commercial district and, reaching his destination, pulled into the small parking lot of a medium sized red brick building. One of the many similar looking three story, and somewhat rundown, buildings typical of the area. The sign over the door said Braxton Sales Co. It was the regional headquarters for his groups operations.

He locked his car and, as he moved towards the building, took out his special 'I. D.' card. He entered the building through an unobtrusive side entrance. Once inside he waited for the door to close completely, then turned right and went down a short corridor to a small elevator and entered it. When the door closed he put his card into a slot on the control panel, waited for a green light to show, then pressed the button for the third floor.

As the car began to move upward a video camera, mounted near the ceiling, whirred as it turned and focused directly on him. A second or two later a pleasant female voice came out of hidden speakers in the ceiling saying, "Hi Dirk. Did you get all of the kinks out on that nice, long "vacation?" The voice belonged to one of the very able security people who kept a close watch on all points of entry and exits to this building.

"I guess that would be a fair way to describe it." he replied with a smile, "Is Bill Tate in or out?" dirk asked. "No. OK. When he comes in ask him to see me if I'm still here, or have him call me tonight at home if not. Right now I'm going into section thirty for a while." he finished as the car stopped and the doors opened.

As he entered the section thirty office he smiled at the captain sitting behind the single desk.

He was an ex field operative who, due to a wound that put a stop to that phase of his work, was now pasturing in this office. Dirk handed him the papers he had filled out so early this morning.

Section thirty was so named because retirement was mandatory after thirty years of service. If you lasted that long! Most didn't, lasting only ten to twenty years on average, because this agency and the kind of work done within it created a high attrition rate. Dirk had been here just under twenty years, and was considered, to be, one of the very best at this work.

As he was handing the papers to the captain he said "I'd like these to take effect immediately Jim. I've still got five days leave coming so I'll take them while you process those, then I'll come in to sign the final forms when you're ready. Ok?"

With a look of surprise on his face the captain looked up from the papers Dirk had dropped on his desk saying, "I don't understand? The general thought you were going to extend for one more tour. Did you speak to him yet?"

"It wouldn't do any good. I've thought this out very carefully over the last two months and my decision is final. Please check those over for me and let me know if everything is ok. I'll be going to weapons and I.D. to turn in my side arm and cards, then to operations to turn in any outstanding paperwork I may still have that's unprocessed. I'll check in with you before I leave the building. Thanks Jim."

Later, as he was going from one office to another, he heard his name called and, turning in the direction of the voice, he saw Bill Tate coming towards him. "Lo Bill. I got in pretty late last night or I would have called you."

"Heard you dropped your papers this morning." Bill said, "you sure about this thing you're doing, Dirk?"

"First thing I've been completely sure about for a long, long time, Bill."

"If you say so, I'll take your word for it." Bill said. Then taking a casual, but guarded, look around he continued, saying, "Listen, there's something funny going on around here. I don't know exactly what it is yet but something just doesn't feel right around here any more. You know the feeling I mean!" he said, looking directly into Dirks eyes. Then "I can't talk right now but I'll catch up with you soon!"

Dirks eyes widened slightly, but that was the only sign he made in recognition of Bills meaning.

In their private code Bill had said, 'Watch your back!' Now, with understanding that a serious situation existed here, he said in return,

"Ok, the next time you've got an evening free, call me and we'll put away a few beers and I'll bring you up to date." Which meant, 'Contact me as soon as your clear. It's very important that we talk. Much to tell!'

"Ok. I'll call you the first free time I get." So saying Bill continued on his way to the ops planning office.

With a slight frown on his face Dirk continued on to the other end of the building to pay his respects to the general, and to inform him of his decision.

Taking a left turn, and five steps down a short hallway brought him to a door marked 'Adjutant'. He rapped once, smartly, entered and came to rigid attention, saying, "Major Dirk to see the general if he has the time sir."

The adjutant was a lieutenant colonel. Tall, heavy set, and balding, with dark eyes that stared flatly past a nose that had been broken more than once. He looked up at Dirk with a frown and said, "I spoke to the general a few minutes ago. He's been delayed in Washington until late tonight, and I can tell you this, he's not a happy camper! He is both upset and disappointed that you didn't speak to him before putting in your papers. He is not taking it well at all!"

"I'm sorry, sir," Dirk said, "that he feels that way about it, but it was my decision to make, and it's final."

"I'm sorry, too, that you feel that way Dirk, but as you say it is your decision to make. Alright, check back in at the end of the week for final debrief and severance formalities. Dismissed!" The officer said crisply.

"O-eight hundred Friday good sir?"

"That will be fine Dirk. It's a shame, really, you were one of our best. But, done is done." Looking down again, at the papers on his desk, he dismissed Dirk from his thoughts, a busy man already moving on to the next item on his agenda.

As Dirk exited the office and started up the short hall he saw two men, who he did not recognize, passing in the cross hall in front of him, both involved in a low voiced but animated conversation. As he crossed the hall behind their retreating backs he felt a sensation like hairs rising on the back of his neck, only this was felt in his mind. *What was that all about?* he silently asked TuLan.

One of those men was either wearing a 'Drell' or had just been in close contact with one. We must get out of here now, before it becomes aware of me, and you! Said TuLan fervently.

Are you sure? How can you tell? I didn't notice anything odd about them except I didn't know either of them, nor had I seen them here before.

Now there is reason," said TuLan, *for your friends feeling of not rightness. Let us depart this place quickly! If they are here, openly, in a place you have said is secret, things are indeed serious, and far further along than I had feared!*

All right. We'll go back to the apartment and go over a few things, and then lay some plans. But wait! Now that I think of it, that's not such a good idea after all. To many people know about that place. Maybe we should just take what I need and head back to the cabin until some things can be put in order.

As he went back through the security section dirk relinquished his pass to the duty officer before entering the elevator and going down to the parking lot.

While unlocking his car, dirk, without seeming to, looked over the top of it and up at the third floor windows, There, his nose almost pressing the glass, was one of the new faces staring down at him.

As he got into the car warning bells were going off in the back of his mind, and he felt that prickling sensation along his spine which had so often warned him of trouble to come. He exited the parking lot and drove quickly through the streets, and because of that premonition of danger he employed the skills he had learned so well to check and see if he were being followed. Unable to detect anyone following, he headed for his apartment.

Reaching his apartment, he parked on a side street and walked around to his garage. There he checked his security trips, making sure that they remained untouched, then entered his apartment building by the rear entrance, checking his trips there as well. Finding no tampering he entered the apartment proper and quickly began changing his clothes from his suit to blue jeans, boots, and a flannel shirt.

This done he then went over to a cleverly designed custom made wall unit and, reaching in, pressed a hidden panel that released a lock with a barely audible click. The center of the wall unit rolled out to expose the hidden closet behind it.

He entered and, having turned in his service issued weapon, took down from its peg his customized, ten millimeter colt automatic and the specially designed shoulder holster rig. Donning this he felt slightly more comfortable in being able to handle any trouble that might come his way now. He went to the kitchen and fixed himself a quick sandwich and some coffee while detailing the steps he wanted to take in his preparations for leaving.

Done eating he began those steps immediately by going back into his hidden closet carrying a briefcase. Into the briefcase, he began by putting several complete sets of alternate identity papers, including passports, driver's licenses, and valid concealed weapons permits. He was fairly certain that these identities were 'cold' or unknown to anyone but himself because he had collected them piece by piece over a number of years.

Into the case he also put two spare automatic handguns with spare clips of ammunition for each. To these things he added several file folders with lists of names for active and semi-active agents along with other information sources.

Some of those lists were from different agencies. Both domestic and foreign, giving contact methods and codes for each. All this he took, plus some files he kept on agents he had personally worked with, or across, in the field.

He closed his case, went out, closing the secret panel as he went and set the booby trap on it with a smile of satisfaction.

Next he went to his bedroom, opened his wall safe and withdrew two cellular phones, neither of which were traceable to him personally. And twenty thousand dollars in cash and another twenty thousand in bearer bonds. These items he also added to those in his case. Next he packed two small, soft, suitcases with clothing and toilet articles.

All of these preparations, including his quick meal, had taken a scant hour so he took another quick look around, checking to make sure he had taken everything he might need or want.

As he completed this task he let a sad little smile cross his face, feeling that he would not see this place again. He would miss it. He had been comfortable here.

It was now about an hour before dark so he sat down in a comfortable chair and began to converse telepathically with TuLan. Asking many questions about the Drel. And what he/they might expect to run into with them.

After many questions and answers Dirk finally said, *one thing is sure, to make any headway at all we'll have to set up some type of organization. The scope of what you have described to me says that they have one up and running already. If you were correct, earlier today, they have already penetrated very deeply into a very secret and sensitive part of this government!*

To this last TuLan replied, *the sensation that I was feeling in that office today, from those men, is not one I would be likely to mistake! Even after all of this time it is exactly as the rememberers have described it! Also, what you said about the need for an organization makes a great deal of sense, because what I feared is now truly a reality in the worst way. Your world and the freedom of its people are surely at stake now!*

Looking out of the window dirk saw that it was now full dark and said, *It's time to get started.* He picked up the bags and as he moved to the door the phone began to ring.

Dirk waited for the answering machine to pick up so he could screen the caller. It did so, saying this is four one five one, please leave your message after the tone. As the tone sounded the caller started without preamble, "If you're there, don't answer."

A long overdue favor was just paid to me he thought. The voice went on, "There is a detain order out on me, and a detain or terminate order out on you! Get out now! I'll contact you again where we last spoke on your vacation, within forty eight hours from eight p.m. this day. I'm going under now. I don't think that they know where you took that vacation, but watch your six! Good luck!"

The sound of the answering machine stopping was loud in the silence that followed.

Dirk quickly ejected the tape from the machine and replaced it with a blank one as he thought at TuLan, *Could they know already?*

If they even suspect, TuLan thought back, *it is the kind of action that the Drel would take. Too, if I sensed them, they, by this action, sensed me or at least that you had some contact with me.*

Dirk, moving swiftly now with his three bags, left the apartment. After setting the trip on a booby trap he locked the door.

He moved quickly down the rear stairs, bypassing the rear entrance, went to an almost unseen side exit and carefully went out. Screened from the front entrance and the street by trees he had planted for shade, he scanned the street for observers.

Seeing none he moved quickly through the trees to the garage and his jeep. He quietly opened the door and, throwing his bags in the rear, jumped in the front and started the jeep without turning on the lights.

He scanned the street again, then sped out into the night, saying to TuLan, *Well, we're really out in the cold now!*

Friends And Allies

About a block away from his apartment Dirk turned on his driving lights and, keeping in mind his friends warning message, drove a zigzag course through the city just to be sure he was not being followed.

On the long drive away from the city Dirk again spent many hours in discussion with TuLan about the Drel, the problems that they could foresee, and also the probability of more that they couldn't foresee.

They also talked a good deal about the numerous, if not major, advantages that could be gained by implementing a lot of the Chai technology, along with some of the very newest of his own peoples discoveries. Dirk felt that by cross combining some of them he could put them to some unorthodox and unique uses, uses that neither race had thought of, in their coming campaign.

After some five hours of driving Dirk pulled off the main highway onto a secondary highway, explaining to TuLan, *Bills' message said he would contact me within two days of his message at the small town nearest my property. There's only one way to make sure that I'm there in time. We'll rent a small plane and be there in another ten hours. No one will pay any attention to the plane because so many out that way use them to go anywhere that's more than four hours in driving time away. Also, he may be traveling fast and not be able to wait around for me to get there.*

At a small airport he entered a mid sized hanger located near the control tower. Dirk rented a small single engine bush plane, using one of his alternate identities and leaving a good sized cash deposit. The formalities completed, they were soon in the air. Once again he was heading north and west.

As he flew through the crystal clear moonlit air above the clouds Dirk broached the subject of the potentials of some of the Chai technology again, and what he thought might be done with it. Saying, *What we really need is some sort of distinct advantage that the other side won't be expecting. The thing that fascinates me is that chameleon cloaking device that you use to hide your ship with. If that could be adapted to personal use it could give us the advantage that we're looking for.*

TuLan, radiating the warmth of a smile in Dirks mind said, *That is one of the reasons why I was so interested in your people. You look at something and see ten applications for it, where we might only have seen three. It is an excellent idea, but that unit uses a great deal of power. You would need a truck to carry the power source for it.*

First, Dirk said, *"look at the size of your ship, by your standards only a small one! It is used only as a lander or an escape ship you say!*

After a quick mental breath he went on, *well, it's as big as our Saturn Rocket and the Mir space station combined, and has a hundred, a thousand times the power output!*

Second, even if this is so, and from what I've seen of your equipment, I think that we're ahead of your people on computer technology. Right now we have lap top, or miniature, computers that have a standard capacity of handling a couple of billion bytes of information. And that seems to be almost doubling every year or two.

This is mainly due to our advances in micro-miniaturization, laser technology and the development of fiber optics for information transmittal. Third, if it could be understood at all by some of our whiz kid engineers it can be miniaturized by them. And in a sub audible he said to himself, *"and I think I know just who to set on it.*

But! TuLan mentally spluttered, *that would take the entire output of several different industries to make any usable units, let alone the time needed for study and trials.*

That, said Dirk, *is where my knowledge of my planet, my people, and how they work comes in. We'll break the information down into component parts and have them built to specs by many smaller companies.*

This type of conversation went on, over the hours in flight, for most of the trip. Each learning from it.

Dirk landed the small plane at a landing field some thirty miles south and east of their destination, arranging for refueling, maintenance, and storage with the field owner. He also made a deal with the owner to rent a four by four vehicle from him for several weeks, at a good price for both of them. After loading his luggage into the big 'Blazer' he headed for the small town near the road leading out to his property. Two hours later he pulled into the parking area at the rear of the little general store.

Dirk went into the store to speak with to owner with whom he had, over the years, forged a grudging but strong friendship based on mutual respect and few questions asked or answered. The man knew that Dirk worked for the government but not in which branch, nor in what capacity. Dirk told him that he had quit his job for his own reasons and that the people he had worked for were not to happy with him about it.

Also, because he liked the man, he told him that if some of them came around looking for him, asking questions about him, to just tell them the following. That he had been through and gone on up into the hills as he usually did. And not to get any further involved because there could possibly be some danger involved to him if he did.

Then, making it seem almost as if it were an afterthought, he told the man that there was one exception to this, the man who had been out to see him a couple of months ago. Did the store owner remember him? Good, he would see that man only, and would appreciate it if someone could notify him if he came looking for him.

Dirk knew that the owner knew who he was talking about because he missed very little that went on around here. Dirk then thanked the man, saying also that he would be staying at the Truckers Rest, a local motel up the road a mile or so, for a day or two before heading out.

Before leaving Dirk made arrangements for a large order of staple goods to be delivered, to a spot that both men knew on a small side road close to his property, and paid for them in advance with cash.

It was close to one o'clock so he ate lunch at the local cafe in town, then went to the Truckers Rest Motel.

As he was checking in the owner looked up at him and said very quietly, ***Don't you worry none Mr. Dirk, Abner called and gave me the word! Won't nobody be disturbin you, ceptin your friend when he gets here, like you asked.***" giving Dirk a toothy smile, went on, *"Abner says yer a friend of his, so anythin you need you jest ask!*

Dirk thanked the man, then paid him for two days in advance. When he received his change Dirk laid another five-dollar bill on the counter saying, *I certainly do appreciate all of your kindness Mr. Jessup, and would you please have a beer or two on me.*

After leaving the office and retrieving his bags he went to his room, and during the short walk there, shook his head and smiled to himself in appreciation of these quiet, simple people. In his room now he dropped his bags on a rest put there for that purpose. Sat down on the bed, put the spare pillow on top of the other one and leaned back, just then realizing how tired he actually was.

Phutt! Phutt! Dirk came wide awake, his body instinctually moving, as he rolled off the bed to the floor, drawing his automatic from its shoulder holster as he did so. As he hit the floor, his wild movement from the bed caused the small lamp on the night table next to the bed to topple off and crash to the floor, going out as it hit.

In the brief moment before the light went out he saw the starred hole in the pane of glass of his rooms front window. As he crouched behind the bed, his heart pounding wildly, he listened intently for any sounds that would give him more information. Then he heard a muttered curse, bitten off before it could become a complete sound, and a loud thud as of something heavy hitting the ground right outside his window.

Again, the muffled sound of a silenced weapon being fired. Then again, and a deep groan, then silence. He moved very cautiously to the corner of the window shade, and pushing it very slowly aside, peered out.

He could see very little because his line of sight was partially blocked by the windowsill itself. Outside, someone had gone to the trouble of putting out the pole and wall nightlights that normally burned in the parking area and along the unit walls.

The only light available was from the motel sign, a hundred yards away, and that light reflected from those few windows still showing a light.

As his eyesight adjusted to the darkness he scanned as far to either side as he could, using the technique he had learned in his early army training for spotting things at night. This technique was accomplished by flicking his eyes from point to point rather than letting them rest on any one point for any length of time.

Still seeing nothing he moved over to the door, reached up, and gripping the knob firmly, turned it slowly and silently until he felt the latch release.

Still holding the knob tightly, in the open position, he gathered his legs under himself for a spring through the door when he pulled it open.

Just as he was ready to pull the door open and spring out into the darkness he thought he heard a whispered call. When it came again he was sure. Someone was softly calling out his name as they stealthily shifted position from place to place.

As the whispered call was repeated once again he recognized the callers voice so he eased the door open a crack and called out softly, "Bill?" then waited.

Just as he was about to call out again he heard from much closer, "I'm coming in low from your the right on three!" Dirk counted backward, to himself, softly and just as he reached one his friend Bill came around the corner of the building across from him.

He was moving quickly and low to the ground as he came, stumbling once and righting himself as he came up against the wall beside the door just as Dirk pulled it open. As Dirk stepped through the doorway he saw the body laying face down on the walkway just under his window.

"Nice work!" he said to Bill as he came fully out of his room, holstering his automatic slowly.

"Not to hard." Bill said, "He was outlined against the light from your window." He paused for a shuddering breath, then, "Dirk, I think I might need a little help. My first shot wasn't fatal. He winged me pretty good in the side before I could put him down permanently!"

As Dirk spun around to face his friend, Bill began to slide down the wall he was leaning against, leaving a smudged red stain as he went down. Dirk reached out and, grabbing him, half carried him inside his room. Laying him on the bed, he pulled open his friends' jacket and shirt to see how badly he was wounded.

The entry wound was just above the left hip, in the abdomen, and exited just above the hip in the back. Both the entry and exit points were welling dark red blood with each beat of Bills heart.

Dirk laid his friend gently back down on the bed. Then turned and grabbed one of his bags, pulled out two clean white tee shirts and a spare belt, then turned back to Bill saying, "It went clean through but it looks like it hit something important inside. I have to bind it to stop the bleeding and it's going to hurt like hell." That's all I can do until I get rid of that body outside. Then I'll get you some real help.

Bill just grimaced and nodded. Dirk folded each shirt into squares and pressed one over each wound, then fastened them in place with the belt. He then covered his friend with a blanket.

J. A. DI SPADA

While all of this was going on, TuLan had been very patiently waiting to speak with him. Now, outside, as Dirk bent to turn over the body of the one Bill had shot he spoke quietly in Dirks mind, *you were reacting even as I called you. I'm sorry that I did not sense that one sooner!* he said in a tone that went from admiration to sheepishness.

Soon enough, said Dirk, then, *this is one of those men from the office. What I want to know is how they found us so quickly?"* Dirk asked as he rifled the mans' pockets for any identification or other information.

Finished with this he lifted the body over his shoulder in a fireman's carry and walked to the rear of the Blazer, rolled down the window, and tossed the body into the cargo area. *We'll dump this trash in a gully on the way out of town. I'm worried about Bills wound. I really don't want to leave any tracks by going to a doctor. They'd want to know to much about a gunshot wound. Is there anything you can do for him?"*

I cannot do anything for him here. TuLan replied, *I could, possibly, do something for him if we can get him to your cabin alive. Stop the internal bleeding temporarily, but if the wound is as serious as you believe it to be we really need to get him to the ship to do any lasting good. Is there a way to make him unconscious for a time?* TuLAn asked.

I have some morphine syrettes in my med kit, said Dirk, *that should keep him pretty much out of it until we reach the cabin.*

Then, *let us move quickly, for there is the sense of the Drel about that one you put in the back of the vehicle."* said TuLan with some distaste.

With that Dirk went back to his room. He got out two of the morphine syrettes and injected Bill with them. Then carefully carried him out to the rear seat of the Blazer and lay him across the seat, covering him with the blanket. He went back for his bags and, before leaving, straightened up the room as much as possible.

Back at the Blazer, he threw his bags onto the floor in the front passenger side. He went around to the passenger side, got in and started the truck.

Then, heading east, drove out of the small town to find a place to dump the body, and create a bit of misdirection, before heading west again towards his property and cabin.

Dirk had to stop about half way to the cabin to give Bill another shot because he was moaning so much from the pain. Checking his makeshift dressings, he found them both soaked with dark blood. Seeing this he said to TuLan, *I hope we can get him there soon enough, I'd hate like hell to lose such a good friend.*

Put your hand over there on his neck, over the main artery, said TuLan, *I will check his pulse rate and temperature through your touch.*

Dirk did as he was instructed. TuLan said, *his pulse rate is a little thready, but strong, and he is running a fever.*

But that is better than shock, the injections you gave him prevented that from going to far. He is strong and should make it that far safely.

Close to three hours later Dirk pulled up in front of his cabin. It was still dark outside but dawn was very near as Dirk went into the cabin to light lanterns and prepare his bunk for Bill.

While Dirk was busy doing things in the cabin that TuLan couldn't help with he sent out a questing thought. As Dirk was coming down the steps, heading for the Blazer to get Bill, his eyes were busy scanning the nearby woods. He was both relieved and pleased to see a large pair of golden orbs coming at him at a fast pace.

Doing as he had learned to do Dirk pushed a thought outwards towards Balor, expressing his relief and pleasure at seeing his friend and immediately received one of the same nature in return, followed closely by question, *Trouble?*

Yes! Replied Dirk and TuLan together. Then Dirk said, *TuLan, please explain while I get Bill into the cabin."* Then as Dirk busied himself moving Bill TuLan brought Balor up to date on events.

After hearing the explanation Balor said, *in that case I will stay out here to keep watch on things while you go and help your friend.* And with that he disappeared into the woods as the rosy tints of dawn appeared on the eastern horizon. Then seemingly only minutes later daylight sprang into being as the sun jumped above the mountain tops.

Dirk, after getting Bill settled in the bunk, and knowing what was necessary, settled himself as comfortably as possible next to him and began to help TuLan by relaxing as completely as he could. TuLan soon had a small opening made, just large enough, for one of his tendril-like pseudo-pods to extend itself out and into one of Bills wound openings. An hour and a half later the tendril retracted and the opening in Dirks abdomen closed as if it had never existed.

TuLan said in Dirks mind, *I have caused his body to manufacture some extra strong coagulants to stop the internal bleeding and also stimulated the production of antibodies to halt the infection. What I could do was only a stopgap, because several of his internal organs have been decimated by the passage of that projectile. If we are to save him we really must get him to the ship as soon as we can. He will waken in a few hours, feeling much better, but as you know that is a false recovery and will not last for long. You must try to keep him quiet and rested for the trip to the ship.* Then expressing a mental yawn TuLan said, *that was very taxing on my strength. I must rest for a time.* and with that promptly disappeared from Dirks consciousness.

Dirk, also very tired from holding still for so long, and from driving most of the night, closed his eyes for some much needed rest.

Balor's Gift

After sleeping for a few hours Dirk was up and about again just after first light because he had always been an early riser. He had changed the dressing on Bills hip and eaten a quick breakfast of biscuits and coffee. Now, feeling the need to move about, he went out of the cabin and down the trail to the woods through which they had come early this morning. As he walked he thought to himself that he would never cease to be amazed at the beauty and serenity of this small piece of the world that he had made his own.

He turned off the twin ruts of the rough track road that led directly to the cabin and headed up a path leading to the crest of a low ridge. One that overlooked the entire fan shaped valley that held his cabin retreat.

From the top of the ridge he would have a good view of the entire valley. As he quietly moved through the undergrowth and trees he was wondering where Balor might be, and was startled, as the thought came to him with a slight chuckle in it. *I am to your rear and just to your right. You move very softly for a two legs.* was Balor's comment as he showed himself.

You will do that to me, won't you? Dirk thought back to him, ruefully. Then, *did you enjoy your rest here my friend?*

Yes. This is a good place, friend Dirk, well chosen." said Balor, *the animals show little fear of your presence.*

Yes. Here, at the least, we coexist in peace." said Dirk as they broke out onto the crest of the ridge. As they stood looking out over the valley Dirk went on, **"But just now it is very quiet in the area, almost to quiet for this season and time of day.** Dirk mused.

I have noticed this also. said Balor, *there is, I think, something moving this way that does not belong,* and with that Balor changed the subject. *Does your companion fare well?* He asked.

Thanks to TuLan the bleeding has been stopped, but he feels strongly that we must get him to the ship to do him any lasting good. We had planned to rest here for a couple of days to let him regain some strength, then head south. Will you travel with us again, my friend?" Dirk asked his friend with warmth.

I think I will. Interesting things seem to happen around you! Balor teased with some warmth.

Come to the cabin in a while and I'll fix you some of that salt pork you strangely have become so fond of. said Dirk with a smirk. He sent a picture of Balor sitting with a knife and fork in his paws, and a bib around his neck. *You're a very strange cat!* As he looked around to see what effect his picture had had he realized that he was standing alone.

94

As he was looking around a thought came into his mind with an echo of laughter to it, youu *are right,* Balors' thought came, amused, *a very strange cat indeed.*

As Dirk headed back to the cabin to prepare the promised meal, and to wake Bill, he sent a thought to TuLan, *there are a few things that need to be discussed with Bill, concerning us, and I also want to find out what led up to the other night?!*

Dirk, said TuLan in a somewhat pensive tone, *there is something I have to tell you before you speak to your friend again.*

"What's wrong?" asked Dirk, the worry obvious in his tone. *Was the wound much more serious than we thought at first?*

It's not that. said TuLan gently. *I only know one way to tell you this,"* he said with some reticence, *your friend has a very advanced case of what your medical people call cancer in his lower intestinal tract. I found it there when I was working to stop his bleeding the other night. The only reason he was still on his feet was because he was already loaded to a dangerous level with pain killers. The carcinoma are already well advanced and spread throughout his system.*

Dirk was dumbfounded, as he said, *he never let on to me, not even once. But I should have known something was up when I noticed him taking pain pills he said were for an old wound where a bone was nicked. Is there anything, anything at all that we can do for him?*

That, said TuLan, *is why it is so important for us to get him to the ship where we can stabilize him, and he can be treated as necessary. I fear that if we don't get him there within the next five or six days there will be little that can be done for him because of the extra complications caused by the shock from his wound!* he finished anxiously!

At this point in the conversation Dirk was almost at the front door of the cabin when he heard the clicking sound of a weapons hammer being drawn back to full cock position. He instantly flattened himself against the wall beside the door and called out softly, "It's me Bill, ease off!"

"Figured it might be," said Bill weakly, "but I wasn't gonna take any chances on it not being you either. Come on in."

As Dirk entered he saw Bill sitting on the edge of the bunk, one arm braced stiffly on it to prop himself up. The other hand, holding the gun, hanging loosely at his side, the gun barrel almost touching the floor.

"Let me help you get dressed," Dirk said, "then I'll move you out into the sunlight to sit while I fix some food for you. After that we can talk some things out."

As he helped Bill to get dressed he gave him a couple of heavy duty pain killers along with some water from a bucket he had brought in from the spring behind the cabin earlier.

After Bill had finished dressing he helped him to move out to a spot in front of the cabin where a split log chair sat in the sunlight. Bill sank down on this with a sigh of relief, saying to Dirk, "I'm not very hungry but some coffee would go down real good."

Dirk, looking at him hard said, "You'll eat. To get where we're going you'll need all of the strength you have, plus some. Don't ask questions now," said Dirk, seeing the expression forming on Bills face, "just soak up some of this beautiful sunlight until the food's ready." After he finished saying this he abruptly turned and went inside.

A short while later, when he was just about ready to serve the food, he heard Bill gasp, and then, "Oh holy shit! Dirk, you better come out here! And you better bring a gun with you!" He also heard Balors chuckle in his mind!

He came out of the cabin door with a plate piled high with slices of cooked salt pork in his hand to a tableau scene. Bill was sitting stiffly as far back against the chair back as could get, staring at Balor, who was sitting calmly about five feet in front of him.

With a flick of his eyes in Dirks direction, Bill asked, "Where's that gun? Why is it just sitting there staring at me? And why do I get the impression that that thing is smiling at me?" he finished his questions with a gulp!

"Possibly," said Dirk, "it's because he is." And, as he walked up to Balor and set the plate down in front of him, "Relax Bill! He happens to be a good friend of mine. Bill, meet Balor!" Dirk said to his incredulous friend.

As Balor started, daintily, to eat the strips of meat Bill looked on with the expression of a man for whom things had started to move to fast. As he watched Balor eat, Bills almost inaudible whisper was just loud enough to hear, "God, but that thing's beautiful!"

I, said Balor in Dirks mind, with a smirk in his tone, *like your friend. He has excellent taste!*

Whereupon Dirk sat back against a stump and started to laugh as the tension began to ease all around. With this also came a feeling that things would work out.

"What's so damn funny?" Demanded Bill, frowning.

"Balor thinks that you have good taste." said Dirk as he tried to subdue his continuing mirth.

Balor, now finished with his meal, was again looking directly at Bill, and licking his whiskers. And Bill, beginning to look decidedly uncomfortable again, said, "what do you mean by, Balor thinks?"

"There have been a lot of changes in my life since the last time we had a chance to talk at any length, and more in the last two months since I saw you last. I have a great deal to tell you my friend." Replied Dirk.

Bill, his eyes now locked with Balors', could just manage to get out in a voice only a little over a whisper, "He could hypnotize you with those eyes!"

"Yes, he could." Said Dirk, deadpan, then, "I'll get you some food and then while you're eating I'll tell you a story. One that you may have to work at believing!"

Without another word Dirk got up and went into the cabin, and when he returned it was with two plates heaped with steaming food. Before Bill could say anything Dirk said "Eat! All of it! No arguments at all!" as he set the plate down on his lap and handed him a knife and fork.

Suiting action to his own words Dirk sat down on the ground in front of Bill and began eating with a concentration that brooked no argument at all.

Dirk finished eating quickly, took his plate inside, then returned to sit in front of Bill again. He began to talk, telling him of his discontent with the outfit they worked for, his disappointment in the apparent changes in it's stated goals, and his decision to end his connection to it by resigning from it.

He told Bill of the strange things that had happened after their last meeting in the parking lot behind the little general store, which had led to him following a hunch and heading south. It took about an hour to tell that much of the story because he wanted to make sure that Bill understood what was to come as he continued the narrative. But, right now he could see that Bill's eyes were beginning to droop with exhaustion, so he told him to sleep right there in the sunshine for an hour or two, then he would continue with his tale.

As Bill's eyes closed in sleep Dirk was already in deep conversation with TuLan, who was saying, *do you think it wise to tell so much to your friend?*

To which Dirk replied, *I know that you feel somewhat uncomfortable with others knowing about your existence, but if we are to get the people we need you will just have to have trust in my judgement. Especially concerning matters where we are dealing with humans! I wouldn't say anything about you to someone that I didn't trust. Aside from the fact that this man is my best friend, he saved our lives not so very long ago, and deserves to know the whole truth about the way things stand!* Dirk finished firmly.

As the conversation continued Dirk was busy cleaning up the dishes from the meal, checking the dressing on Bill's hip, and beginning to prepare the things that they would need for the trip south.

Noticing that Balor was not in evidence, both Dirk and TuLan sent a questing thought to him. The reply, when it came was both direct and succinct. *Listen to your host TuLan! He knows what must be done for the present, and knows the people of his own planet, for all of your studies, better than you. More importantly, as allies you must learn to trust each other completely!* and he was abruptly gone again from their awareness.

Within the privacy of his own mind TuLan was a little concerned with the comment that Balor had just made, and with something else about Dirk. His concern with Dirk was more surprise than anything else. Simply because he had never had a host that was so individually forceful and so mentally strong before.

With this thought came the realization that there would, in the future, be many things to be learned about his present host. He had a prescient feeling that some of them might not be too pleasant for him.

His concern with Balors' statement was a question. Why had Balor said 'his own planet' instead of 'his planet'? He abruptly pulled his awareness back to what Dirk was saying as he realized that he had almost missed what was being said.

Dirk was saying, *do you think that there is anything that you can do for Bills' cancer if we can get him to the ship in the time frame you gave me?*

Pausing to consider his answer, TuLan replied, *this disease is not unknown among some of the other races. So the answer is yes, I believe that he can be cured of the cancerous growths eating away at his intestines. But it will take some time to cure it completely, and it will be somewhat painful for your friend.*

TuLan was totally unprepared for the wave of pure gratitude that washed over him from Dirk's mind. It was at this precise moment that TuLan got the beginnings of his first real understanding of what these earthlings meant by true friendship.

It was not that he did not understand the concept. He had many acquaintances among the other races. It was just that his closest relationships had always been with his other hosts, and perforce had been kept on a professional level.

He did remember a certain fondness he had had for several of his previous hosts, but there was nowhere near the level of raw emotion that Dirk expressed for his friend. He admitted to himself that there was a great deal, indeed that he must learn about not only his host, but his species in general.

These conversations, the musings, the questions, answers, and more questions, and the chores that Dirk was doing in preparation for heading south took about two hours.

Making one of his periodic checks Dirk found that Bill was awake again, so he finished what he was doing and went outside to continue his story, taking a large mug of coffee with him for Bill. As soon as he was sure that Bill was fully awake he began to talk again, telling him of all that had happened.

He talked steadily for three and a half hours, with few breaks in between. And as he told the story he watched the expressions on Bill's face run the gamut of changes from skepticism, to wonder, to pure disbelief, and back to wonder again.

As he finished his narration the sun was just beginning to drop below the western peaks. At this point he said to Bill, "I want you to hold any judgements and questions you have until we reach our destination south of here. It will be much easier for you to see and think clearly then. I also want you to think about this, I know about your cancer!" He finished with an unreadable expression on his face.

"But," spluttered Bill, "no one but my own doctor and I could know that!" he finished in confusion.

Looking at his friend, his gaze steady and intent, Dirk said, "Bill, you've known me for ten years, or more, and you would have good reason to know how strong I am, or am not." Still gazing at his friend steadily, and without saying another word, Dirk bent down and, without seeming to strain, lifted Bill and the heavy split log chair up to chest height and carried them both into the cabin.

Bill, as he and the chair were set down next to the bunk, was left completely speechless as Dirk walked away without a word. That chair, thought a completely astonished Bill, must weigh at least sixty pounds, and he still weighed at least about two hundred pounds, from his original two hundred forty pounds before the advent of the cancer.

Looking wonderingly at Dirk he thought to himself, he just lifted and carried close to three hundred pounds like it was only a ten pound sack, and without a sign of strain.

Dirk came back with a tumbler of water, a pain killer, and an extra blanket, because it was starting to get chilly now that the sun was gone. Setting these things aside he bent, and still with no sign of strain lifted Bill out of the chair and gently placed him on the bunk. He then handed him the tumbler and pain pill, took the tumbler back when Bill finished and covered him with the blanket.

Bill just stared at his long time friend, wide eyed and speechless. Dirk, still not saying anything, just looked at him with a smile and walked over to the fireplace, where he had already laid a fire. Sat down in a chair next to it where he picked up a book from its' arm and began to read.

Bill lay back on his pillow and closed his eyes, his mind in a whirl of thought, as he tried to comprehend it all.

About an hour later Dirk got up and walked over to the bunk and, looking down at his friend, saw that he was still awake. Looking at him with that strange smile, he said, "Get some sleep. We leave tomorrow at first light. I'll be back in an hour or so. I'm going out for a walk, and to talk with Balor."

Bill's mind, as he watched Dirk walk out, was stunned again as the import of what Dirks words meant sank in. Sometime later Dirk came back in, checked to make sure that Bill was still covered, then went over to bank the fire for the night before bedding down on a sleeping bag in front of the fireplace himself.

Some few hours later both men were jerked out of sleep, as they both came rolling up with weapons in their hands frantically searching for a target. They had been pulled from sleep by the sound of a big cats enraged yowl echoing through the woods around the cabin. Then two quick shots, followed a short time later by a piercing scream from a throat constricted with terror and pain. Then, sudden silence in the night again!

Dirk was up and moving cat quiet across the cabin to a cabinet from which he took a large powerful flashlight. Just as quietly he moved to the cabin door and, easing it open, slipped out and stepped immediately to one side of the opening. Staying in the shadow of the cabin wall, where the scant moonlight didn't penetrate, he scanned the surrounding terrain, as he let his eyes adjust to the moon and starlight.

From close by he felt a familiar touch in his mind, *friend Dirk, I met the one that was disturbing the wildlife. It was creeping very quietly towards the cabin. It was also armed with a long gun.*

And as Balor paused Dirk said, *"So I heard."* as he turned to face those glowing eyes.

Balor continued, *it carried another! For both, life has ceased.* he finished with a shudder of revulsion, and satisfaction in his thoughts. Then, *please follow me to the place of its' death, for there is something you and TuLan should see.* As they listened to this both Dirk's and Toulon's thoughts seemed to freeze for a second or two, then, *how far out?* Dirk asked. And *"Did you sense any others?*

About a hundred and twenty of my body lengths. Balor replied. And, *no!*

If this is what we think it is Bill needs to see it also." Dirk said, and turning, called for Bill to join them.

As Bill, limping, joined them Dirk shielded the light with his shirt before turning it on and then kept it pointed at the ground to keep it from ruining both Balor's and their night sight.

The body, when they reached it, was not a good thing to see. The mans throat had been torn out by razor sharp claws. The mans' jacket was humped slightly at the top of the spine, and the jacket itself was slashed to ribbons and soaked with blood.

A few yards away from the body lay an M-16 combat rifle, equipped with a starlight night scope. Picking this up dirk walked back to the body as TuLan said to him, *we must be sure of this. Pull the clothing away from the area of the spine.* he finished with a slight tremble in his mental voice.

Kneeling beside the body Dirk began to peel the shredded cloth away. As he lifted a large piece away he let it fall as he quickly sat back on his haunches, his breath hissing out loudly, nearly matching Bill's loud hiss of in drawn breath. TuLan's hiss was mental, but just as loud to Dirk, and full of loathing.

There, attached to the mans spine, was an elongated star shaped thing, about a foot in length. It was a mottled gray and dirty yellow in color. The skin of the mans back was slightly puckered where the points of the star penetrated his back along the spine.

"What is it?" asked Bill, an unconcealed loathing in his voice.

"Drel" said Dirk disgustedly, matching TuLan's mental statement and sentiment exactly.

"Now," Bill said, "it begins to make sense. Do you remember that I told you things were becoming very odd around the unit? It makes sense now! This is one of the new men that was recently assigned to the unit!"

Turning to face Balor Dirk said both mentally and aloud, *Balor my friend, not only have you saved our bacon, but you have saved us a great deal of time and trouble in trying to get the proof of these things for the record. We now have two witnesses to their existence.*

Balor, with that smile that was both mental and physical, replied, as he walked up to Bill where he was sitting against a tree bole and put his paw on his shoulder, *it was what was needed. What else are friends for?*

Bill's eyes snapped open with a look of frightened shock, and wonder, in them as Balor continued, *this friend of yours, if you will allow it, will also be one of mine!* He then moved into the woods saying, to Dirk only, as he departed, *I will check to make sure that this one was alone!*

As he moved off he looked directly at Bill and winked one eye as he disappeared, leaving Bill sitting there with his mouth hanging open. Bill looked at Dirk and asked, "Did I really just hear what I thought I heard?"

As he was coming back to himself he looked over at Dirk, who was laughing quietly to himself. Then Dirk looked at him and said with a perfectly straight face, "Yes! And you can consider yourself singularly honored." then, "Stay here for a few moments while I get the camera and flash to record this."

He came back a few moments later with the camera and a shovel. After photographing the body and it's rider he buried them both in a shallow grave.

Then he helped a still somewhat stupefied Bill back to the cabin, and more of some much needed sleep. As he helped Bill to lay back in the bunk he said, "On the trip south we will have much more to talk about."

Bill just lay there with a bemused look of wonder shining in his eyes!

A Gift for a Friend

Dirk, Bill, TuLan, and Balor had been moving south for three days now, traveling mostly on the secondary roads, stopping only to eat and sleep for a couple of hours at each break so that they could keep up a steady pace and cover the distance more quickly.

They were towing a small trailer, made from the rear end of a short bed pickup truck, used occasionally when Dirk had loads larger than he could pile into the jeep. They had stopped to pick up the rather large order of supplies Dirk had ordered, and the store owner had delivered and stored as promised. The big blazer made towing the heavy load even easier.

Bill was riding shotgun in the second large and comfortable bucket seat, almost fully reclined now, and Balor was sprawled across the rear seat, his large golden eyes closed, and seemingly asleep. They had been talking for almost every minute of the time spent driving, Bill asking every question he could think of. Dirk often silent for moments before answering, when he was consulting with TuLan, then answering his friend as fully as was possible.

Finally Dirk said "Bill, there are some things that I want to say to you now that you know most of the story and have seen some of the proof at first hand."

"OK" said Bill, "You have my undivided and captive attention!"

"Funny man." Dirk said with a smile, "Here goes then. If you remember, when we talked in the parking lot at the store just before I went into the outback, I told you that I had been giving serious thought to quitting you gave me a message from the general. 'To talk to him before I decided anything final."

"Actually, at that point, I had pretty much already made up my mind, but wanted to be alone to give it one more good going over. The real reason I was quitting was because, over the years, the goals had changed and that in turn had begun to prostitute the ideal for which I had committed myself. I know it probably sounds a bit corny, but I actually believed in what I was doing when I started out in the outfit. I think you did too! Since the events leading up to, and including, the change in myself I think that I've recaptured that feeling, that ideal, only on a much larger scale. Now I won't be doing those things for my country alone anymore, I'll be doing them for my world. Because my world, not just my country, is how I must look at things now. I'd like for you to have that belief back again too. What I want, what I'd like, is for you to join me in what I'm about to do as my second in command. Well my friend, what do you think?"

"Dirk" Bill started slowly, his voice sounding the troubling thoughts he was dealing with, "You are one of the very few men whose word I would accept without any reservations whatsoever. I've known you for almost twelve years and have been in some very hairy situations with you."

"And I've been with other good men but trust none of them completely, as I do you, with my life! If you say that this is a good and right thing, you should know without asking, that I'm with you all the way. But I wouldn't be of much good to you for much longer than six months."

"The reason for that you already know. My cancer. That's what I was gong to tell you about when you came back to the outfit. I've kept it hidden for the last eighteen months, with pain killers, but it has been getting worse progressively for the last few months. But I'm with you for as long as I can think clearly."

"There should be time to find and train someone to take over for me in the time I have left." he finished, with an unspoken sadness he tried to keep out of his voice, and a look pure longing in his eyes. Longing to continue that which he'd trained for and become one of the best at throughout most of his adult life, and didn't believe he'd live to see.

Dirk was very quiet for a few long minutes before he said, his face very serious but with a hint of a smile lighting his eyes, "Well Bill. I'm sorry that you feel that you want to get out of this new thing so fast, considering that we had just begun it."

Bill, both angry and hurt, was spluttering as he tried to talk. He finally got control of his voice, saying in utter consternation, "What's the matter with you? You don't really think I want to die, do you?"

"I'm sorry Bill, I thought you just weren't interested in working with me again." but Dirk couldn't hold his face straight any longer and let a huge smile take over his features as he said, "But since you put it that way, I'll just have to make sure that you live to be a very old dirty old man."

Bill, now both furious and very confused, just sat looking at Dirk, waiting.

Dirk, still smiling widely, said "Bill, I couldn't and wouldn't bring this up before because I did not want to influence your decision in any way before I told you this. You put your life on the line for our friendship, and most assuredly saved my life and quite inadvertently TuLan's as well. We are both grateful, and I would have told you this no matter what your answer had been, although I was pretty sure of what it would be. I have been talking this over with TuLan for the last three days, so here it is. TuLan is sure that, with your active help, he can completely cure your cancer! There are a couple of other things involved, but that is the main thing on the menu."

Bill just looked at him for a moment, stunned surprise on his face! Then he said, "I can't take to many more of your surprises for a while. I need to rest for a little bit." and as he turned in his seat, to face the window, Dirk saw the silent tears that began to form in the corners of his eyes as the hope of life rekindled in him.

Balors' thought came to him then, confusion evident in it, as he said, *why was it necessary to anger him when you offered hope?*

Balor my friend, came Dirk's quiet reply, *man is a very strange species, even to himself. Bill had given up his hope, his drive to live, and accepted death as inevitable, final. Man as a species will continue to fight on, even without hope, for an idea, or an ideal.*

But as long as he has hope he becomes unconquerable. The anger that I brought out in Bill was to make him want to fight on, even for a short time, want to live. I know him well. He is my friend, and for that I am fortunate and grateful, and will do what I must to preserve that friendship and life.

Here he paused for a moment, then continued, *in the last two short months I have had my life saved and renewed, my Ideals reawakened, gained two new friends, and regained an old one. This my friend, to a man like me, is a rare treasure. After all, it is not every day that a man can give back the gift of life to a friend!* With that said he waited but only felt a warm resonance coming into his mind from Balor. When Dirk looked over his shoulder at him there almost seemed to be a look of chagrin in his large golden eyes.

About an hour later Bill turned to him and said simply "Please explain."

So Dirk began to explain about the ship and the auto-medical unit. How it would be used to take care of him while TuLan worked his magic on his body. He paused briefly, then said "There is for you one very hard part. I know how hard it is because I had to make the same decision. That part is letting TuLan, at least part of him, enter your body, willingly.

Willingly, because, for him to do what is necessary he will have to have your very active help. This will be both trying and painful for both of us because I will have to be laying down next to you for most of that treatment time. TuLan will not come out of my body completely but will extend part of himself into you. That is what you must accept, that seeming invasion of your body. But please believe me, that is not the case at all. We hope that you will accept this gift from us."

"There are," said Bill, his eyes bright and steady now, "only two things that I can respond to that with. One, because it is you who is saying that the help is real and that I can trust it, I will do so without question. And two, I will do whatever is necessary to live long enough to see my son grow into manhood."

"Good enough, we'll be at the ship this time tomorrow." said Dirk, and "In the meantime get as much rest as you can until then."

"Dirk, can you tell me what it's like, talking with someone in your mind? I know that I heard Balor. At least I think I did, and it scared the shit out of me when he did that to me." said Bill somewhat hesitantly, fearfully.

"It is strange, wonderful, and even a little scary, all at the same time, and because you can use both verbal and pictorial expression it is much clearer than speech alone can ever be. Too, I think that I can sense a little fear in your tone, possibly about having your thoughts invaded. Don't worry about that because TuLan would just not do that without your permission."

"What is your friend TuLan like?" asked Bill.

"When you meet him in your mind, soon, why don't you ask him? I'm sure that he will be glad to show you whatever you want to know." said Dirk, showing a sympathetic smile to him.

The next day they crossed the river at a shallow ford a couple of miles upstream from the small box canyon. As they pulled up onto the bank, balor said to Dirk, *I will go ahead to check the area about the canyon and ship. I will remain and meet you at the cut, or return, as necessary.* As he finished saying this he jumped across the seat and out the door Dirk was holding open for him.

"Hey! Where's he going?" asked Bill in surprise.

"He's going to check out the area around the site where the ship is." said Dirk, then "It's all four wheeling from here on. There are no roads, not even tracks through most of this."

Three hours later they pulled up on the small shingle beach in front of the cut leading into the box canyon. Having already discussed the need for getting the supplies into the ship and stored away as soon as possible Dirk was looking forward to having a little fun with Bill. As they climbed stiffly out of the blazer Dirk said to Bill "Follow me up through this cut and I'll show you the ship."

As Dirk turned and moved off into the cuts entrance Bill was right on his heels, a look of eager anticipation on his face. Moving into the cut proper, Dirk heard/ felt Balors' chuckle in his mind, then, *naughty man!* and another of those eldritch chuckles. As they came out of the cut and into the canyon Bill stopped suddenly and blurted out "What ship?"

Dirk, smiling broadly now, just said "Stay close and follow me." and moved into the canyon following the memorized path. .

Bill, following a few feet behind him stopped suddenly, his hand coming up as if to rub his eyes, as the outline of Dirks' image first began to waver and then disappeared completely from sight.

After standing there for a moment or two he said "Ok. I'll bite, where the hell are you Dirk?"

Dirk's disembodied voice, coming from a few feet in front of him, was saying "Come straight forward about fifteen steps."

Bill moved forward cautiously, the required number of steps, then gasped as the true size of the object in front of him finally registered. "How'd they do that?" he asked in an awed voice, almost a whisper, then "God, that thing is huge!"

"I hate to tell you this buddy but this, as their ships go, is a very small ship. This one is basically an interplanetary runabout and planetary landing vessel." said Dirk with some awe still in his own voice. "Ok," he continued, "while you've still got some strength left in you, you can help me move the supplies and equipment into the ship."

"But that will take us at least twenty trips apiece!" said Bill in a tone of dismay.

"Nope, just one apiece." said Dirk with a knowing smile as he walked along the hull to a point where he knew there was a concealed access panel.

He stopped, put his hand flat to the surface and pressing in and twisting at the same time released a small control box which dropped out and down just to his right. Stepping in front of it he began pressing buttons on the surface within. Then, as he finished, a large door silently swung out and up, then retracted into the hull exposing a large cargo bay with much strange equipment stored all around its perimeter.

Dirk walked into the bay and over to a spot where several low railed platforms about four feet by six feet were sitting. Each had what appeared to be guide bars, front and rear, and a control panel built into the deck housing just below the front guide bar.

Dirk walked directly to the first platform in line and, bending down, began to press the buttons on the control panel. As he finished a low whining hum started, quickly rising in pitch until it disappeared, and the platform silently rose from the deck to a height of three feet, where it stopped, floating in the air and swaying slightly with the movement.

He went to the next one in line and repeated the process, saying as he worked "These cargo carriers work by negating the gravitic attraction between themselves and whatever they are sitting on, or anti-gravity, as we say it. The repulsion field builds until they lift to the height you see now and can maintain it carrying a load of about two and a half tons. The only thing you have to be very careful about is pushing or pulling them to fast, because of the inertia." So saying he began to carefully maneuver one of them out of the bay. Bill was quick to follow his example.

"Ok, just a little to your left." said Dirk, as they finished maneuvering the heavily laden sleds back into the cargo bay and into their parking slots. "Now, just pull that small lever down slowly, it's the field limiter control." he instructed.

The sleds gently sank to the deck. When they were sitting solidly on the deck again Dirk said "Now press that blue button there, at the bottom of the panel." As they did so the high pitched whining sound became audible again, reversed itself, spooling back down the scale to silence again.

"Just leave everything on the sleds, I'll unload them and store everything away later. Let's go up to the galley. TuLan wants me to start filling you up with some extra rich energy ration bars to build up your strength for your recovery process. I'll give you the three penny tour on the way up." He finished.

It had been five weeks now since they had completed the treatments begun on Bill's cancer. Bill, sweating lightly from jogging around the inner perimeter of the canyon, was coming up the ramp of the personnel entrance to the ship where Dirk was sitting, making some notes on a pad.

Stopping next to him Bill said "It's so good to have a tomorrow to look forward to. I feel great!" Dirk smiled up at him, shook his head, and went back to making his notes.

An hour or so later Dirk was sitting in the galley with hot coffee, after a lunch prepared by Bill, and was still going over his notes as Bill sat down next to him.

Dirk looked over at him and said "That was great, Bill, thanks. Now it's time to put on your thinking cap because we have a lot to think about and some hard decisions to make. But, before I go into that, you should know, the last tests that TuLan made on you came out completely negative. I thought this news might make your day!" he finished as he watched the smile light both Bill's face and eyes.

Letting his own smile slip a little, he continued "TuLan also says that you need about two more weeks for your system to complete the integration of the new antigens he created to produce the correct antibodies for keeping the cancer from reforming. He also says that you need to practice your coordination exercises more often, you fell twice this week by moving to fast when you're turning, and to exercise your new strength more to smooth out the jumping in your muscles."

"Now, the reason for your thinking cap. I want you to try and remember every person that we have ever worked with who you think might be of use to us for this new venture. Make a list of them, go through it a couple of times, and cross out those you think might be questionable or the least bit unreliable."

"If you can complete that over the next couple of days it will coincide with my own plans to head out for a few days to make some calls and to get some info verification I need to finish rounding out my own plans before sitting down with you to hash them out and finalize them."

"How long do you expect to be gone?" asked Bill.

"Three or four days if things go smoothly, a week if I have trouble finding out what I need to know."

"You're not going to leave that cat thing here, are you?" asked Bill with some little apprehension.

"First," said Dirk, a little asperity showing in his voice, "his name is Balor and second, Balor does pretty much as he wants to do! Third, I really don't understand why you seem to fear him so much."

And, of course, at that precise moment Balor appeared, as if by magic, next to Dirk, his large golden eyes looking directly at Bill, his mouth seeming to smile. And, true to form, Bill started, almost jumping from his seat. "That's why! He seems to pop up out of thin air! It gives me the willies!"

Dirk smiled as he heard Balor chuckle and said, "He is very much like us, you know. The most loyal of friends and the worst kind of enemy." at which point Balor asked Dirk to ask Bill to kneel down so that he could bespeak him, which Dirk did.

Bill knelt down and Balor came over to him, and putting his forehead against Bill's said in his mind, *friend Bill, If I startle you I apologize, it is really unintentional and only the way that I am accustomed to moving about. You should not fear me, for you are my friends closest friend and therefore my friend in turn. This thing I thought you should know from me.*

And, with that, Balor gave Bill one long lick with his sandpaper tongue and was gone again, as if by magic, leaving a very distinct chuckle echoing in his mind. Bill just sat back on his butt and stared at the point where Balor had disappeared, then said "Well I'll be damned, and double damned!"

"Probably." said Dirk as he stood up and started his preparations for leaving. He turned back and said "Take care of yourself properly while I'm gone. When I get back you and TuLan and I have a great deal of very serious planning to do, so get your brain well rested." and with that he was gone, almost as fast as Balor had gone.

He left the ship about two hours later.

CHAPTER SEVEN
Organization

The Foundation

Although it was not apparent to anyone else Dirk and TuLan had been talking to each other nearly every waking moment for the last three months. During one of those conversations Dirk had learned about a piece of TuLan's equipment that could trace an electronic signal back to it's source. And for what he had in mind it was the perfect tool to help him begin acquiring the team that he wanted to put together. It was the only piece of hard equipment he had left the ship with, along with his weapon, money, and the I.D. papers for his alternate personas from his cache.

The 'Tracker', as he had dubbed it, was about the size of one of the large older lap top computers and weighed not much more. Using his own knowledge of computers and TuLan's insightful instruction he had drawn up a design for an interface unit which would allow it to be used with human equipment.

It had taken, much to his chagrin, almost two full days to find, and drive out on, a decent secondary road that connected to a main highway. Upon reaching the highway they headed for the nearest town with an airport.

After reaching the airport Dirk, having already decided where he wanted to work from, chartered a plane for a flight directly to Tulsa, Oklahoma. There he had hired a suite at the Marriott Executive Hotel in the name of Mr. Harris, one of his alternate personas. At the same time asking the hotel to have a new rental car waiting for him at the airport when he landed.

He arrived at the hotel a couple of hours later, checked himself in, and went straight up to his suite. Once the bellman had left he picked up the room phone and asked the switchboard operator to put him through to the Marriott executive offices in San Francisco. He asked the operator there to connect him with Ted Price, an executive with whom Dirk had done business several times in the past.

When Price came on the line Dirk introduced himself as Mr. Harris, and did Mr. Price remember him? Good. He was staying at the Executive Tulsa and had to be there for a period of two weeks to a month and needed some special considerations for his stay. Could this be arranged?

Ted Price, knowing that Mr. Harris was somewhat eccentric also knew that he paid his bills on time, some of them quite hefty, and without question. Mr. Price was quick to respond with his assurances that whatever he needed would be taken care of immediately. Mr. Harris said wonderful, and would he be so kind as to inform that nice assistant manager, Mr. Wells, of the hotels' intentions to cooperate.

And, could he fax that to him as soon as possible, because Mr. Harris' people would start arriving very soon. Yes, it would be done right away, Mr. Price assured him.

Done with the call Dirk sat down at the desk in the sitting room and began to write out instructions for the hotel staff.

He also informed them of his need for the suites to either side of his and the one directly below him, and the one directly above as well. He knew what the fax would say—Give Mr. Harris whatever he asks for—so he didn't worry about whether any of those suites were presently occupied or not. He sealed the envelope and set it aside for the moment.

He then called down to the front desk for a bonded courier and when he arrived sent the plans for the interface unit out to a firm he had dealt with several times in the past. Along with the plans he sent a check for ten thousand dollars and the promise of ten thousand more in cash if he could have the unit within the next eight hours. This finished he moved on to the next item on his list, his time frame.

Seeing now that he would have to drastically alter it he took the remaining cellular phone he had brought along from his apartment out of his bag and proceeded to call Bill to bring him up to date with his new estimated time frame of one month. After speaking with Bill for a few minutes, and checking that he was doing the things recommended for him by TuLan, he hung up feeling better, knowing that his friend was doing well.

Picking up the envelope with the written instructions for the hotel he went down to the hotel desk and gave it to the desk clerk to place in the assistant managers box. He then went to a nearby exclusive men's shop and ordered two new suits, sports coats, slacks, and all of the other items he would need for a new wardrobe befitting the president of a major company.

With the fittings completed he asked that they be delivered to his suite at the hotel as soon as they were ready, and could they please use all haste, as it seemed that the airline had misplaced his luggage. He changed into one of the sports coats, pair of slacks, shirt and shoes from his order. Next he went to a computer store and ordered a top of the line laptop computer. And a full range, high capacity P.C., both already loaded with the specific programs he wanted, along with modems and a fax machine and printer, to be delivered to his suite at the hotel.

Back at the hotel now he began making calls. One to a stationer, ordering general office supplies. Another to a private firm to install three separate phone lines that would completely bypass the hotel switchboard, and would they do it immediately? Cost was not a problem. Yes the hotel would cooperate. Thank you very much. He then ordered and ate a light lunch.

These things, and his lunch, completed he went out to see a local man he knew, who was the head of a very prestigious security firm.

Arriving at the mans offices he presented his card to the receptionist and after a short conversation on her phone he was politely shown to a well appointed waiting room.

After a few short moments the man's personal, executive secretary came in saying that she was sorry that he'd had to wait so long, and would he please come with her, the man would see him immediately. As she led him into the mans office he came out from behind his large desk with his hand extended, saying "It's very good to see you again Mr. Harris. How can we serve your needs this time?"

"It's nice to see you again George. You know that I always feel better knowing that you have things in hand." said Dirk/ Harris.

George Meade knew that Mr. Harris was a very close and personal friend of the owner of Protek Services, the company he ran for the mysterious man whom he had never met. A man who had hired him at an excellent salary and very nice perks, with only one directive, 'Run it like it was your own!' and he had, very successfully.

He said, as he guided Dirk to a seat, "That's always good to hear from you sir. If you will let me know your needs I will see to them personally."

"That's very kind of you George." said Dirk/Harris as he thought again of what a stroke of luck it had been in following his gut instinct, hiring George six years ago. What George Meade did not know, of course, was that Dirk/Harris was his very mysterious employer. "Ok George, it's a big list. First of all, for personal coverage, I will want Davis and Colfax. Possible?"

"They are on something else right now but I'll have them reassigned to you within the next twenty four hours. Will that be satisfactory?" asked George.

"Excellent!" said Dirk, and "Here's the rest of it. I'll want the best you have for this one. The time factor is uncertain but figure it at a month. Ok?" and, as George smiled and nodded, Dirk continued "I'll want two teams of ten men each for internal and external security. Each team will be broken down into two man teams working six-hour shifts around the clock, with the extra team working as floaters. Then I want four armed couriers, weapons licensed for public transport, and two of your best commo men for anti—bugging sweeps every four hours."

"Lastly, I want three of your best computer and communications men to work one shift in three, every twenty-four hours. All of your men are to be equipped with discrete radios with secure channels. All of the operatives will occupy the suites to either side and below mine at the Marriott Executive at all times, and George, every man you send must be licensed and armed. Standard rates plus ten percent and a flat rate bonus on completion for both the men and the company. Good enough?"

"Oh! I almost forgot two things. I need two of your best pilots and helicopters on call for twelve-hour shifts each. Same rates and bonuses. I know it generally goes without saying, but on this one I must stress it again. This is a no questions, just do it job! Can you deal with that without any problems?"

"Certainly Sir." said George Meade as he busily typed commands into the computer on his desk, waited for a moment to see the information coming onto his terminal screen, then "Your men will start arriving within the hour. A Mr.Tony Ebbets will be the team leader until Davis and Colefax get there tomorrow morning. One of the pilots, and a helicopter will be on the Marriott roof pad within two hours, the other will be available within four hours. Mr. Ebbets, a very seasoned operative, will choose the men for this operation himself. Will that be satisfactory Sir?"

"As I said before George, I always feel much better knowing that you have things in hand." as he rose to shake hands with his unsuspecting employee.

As he was ushered out of the office Dirk was much relieved to know that his primary security concerns were now in professional hands, as he was expecting some kind of reaction from the local and regional powers, and soon. Also, some kind of look see by the national agencies. You just couldn't talk to as many people in the intelligence game as he was planning to without provoking some kind of reaction from them.

He went directly back to his hotel and, upon entering his suite, found that his new cloths had been delivered already. Looking about, he was a little surprised to see that not only had his computer and other equipment been delivered, but that the hotel had moved a desk into the room and the equipment had been installed already.

He smiled a little sadly to himself as he thought of what the disparity in peoples perceptions and actions were when one was thought to have money. And as opposed to what they were when one was thought not to have it. The suits and other clothes, along with the computer and other equipment had been delivered to him and the hotel had signed for it. All as a matter of course!

Still shaking his head he went over to the phone and called room service and ordered himself a large steak dinner, then went in to take a shower. As he showered he tried to relax because he knew that from the next day on he would have little time to relax and enjoy anything for quite a while.

As he was drying himself after his shower the phone rang. Answering it he listened for a moment, smiling to himself, to the somewhat flustered assistant manager as he requested information about the rough looking platoon of men that were in the hotel lobby demanding immediate access to him! "Please sir, What would you like me to do with them?"

Dirk replied, saying "Mr. Wells, is it? Good. Mr. Wells, there should be two envelopes in your box at the desk there. Be so kind as to get them, Please." As he waited Dirk felt some small amount of sympathy for the man, knowing that his troubles had just begun.

When he came back on the line Dirk said "You have both of them? Fine. Now, one of those envelopes, the one that is not sealed, should be addressed to you personally. If you would be kind enough to read it, it will, essentially, tell you what to do with all haste, whatever is in the other sealed one. Is this not the case?"

Getting an answer in the affirmative he went on, "Good. Do you recognize the signature? Again good. Is the second envelope still sealed? Very good."

"Is Mr. Ebbets at the desk with you? Fine. Please show him that the envelope is still sealed, and then I would consider it a personal favor if you could expedite the instructions within it as rapidly as you are able to.

Thank you very much Mr. Wells. Oh! One other thing, would you please double the order I just gave to room service, then ask Mr. Ebbets to tell his second to take over, and would he be kind enough to join me for dinner?"

Dirk did not normally go in for this kind of show. But he was fully aware of the importance of quickly establishing a good rapport with the men who would be watching his back, and the backs of those he would be calling in. Besides, he was curious to find out what kind of man Tony Ebbets was.

Tony Ebbets turned out to be a slender man, of average weight and height, and completely average looks. An almost classically nondescript person. A man who could step into a small crowd and completely disappear.

He came into the room, introduced himself, shook hands crisply and said he would be delighted to join Dirk for dinner.

Yes Dirk thought, as he looked at him, he was very nondescript. Until you looked into his eyes! They told you two things if you knew what you were looking for. First, that he was a careful, thoughtful man. He was also a killer! Dirk knew right away that he had a very professional man here.

After laying out his basic requirements over dinner, and they had finished eating, Dirk poured coffee for both of them. As Dirk turned to hand Tony his cup he said, "I've just made up my mind about something! I don't feel that I need question your abilities, so, henceforth, if you have no objections, you will be third in command of all of the security arrangements, subject to orders from Davis and Colefax. And myself, of course. Also, I think it only fair to tell you a little more about what's going on, before you accept." Looking directly into the mans eyes Dirk finished with "Do you want to hear more?"

Ebbets, his eyes now seeming like two chips of flint, looked hard into Dirks for a long, long moment. Then a fire seemed to kindle somewhere far back in his eyes as he answered simply, quietly. "Yes."

"Well enough." said Dirk, "Just so you understand the parameters completely, I'll brief you and you can brief Davis and Colefax, with one proviso. That being that you ask the same questions and give the same information that I'm giving you."

And as Ebbets nodded Dirk continued, "Here is the first part. This is a new game. It is non national. But it is unilateral in scope. We will start it here in the U.S., then expand it outwards as we go on. Eventually it will be worldwide. It is dangerous, and has already been deadly. This you must tell them before you accept an answer from them! This will save me a lot of time later. And now, do you still want the job?"

The fire in Ebbets eyes was now a steady glow as he answered simply "Yes."

"Good. If I Ask you again it will be for a permanent position. Will you consider that also?" At his nod Dirk went on to tell him about what he was doing here and now, trying to contact and bring in specialized operatives who were well known to him or those about which he knew about by reputation.

He told him a lot without telling him about the Chai or the Drel. Just describing the danger to themselves from an unnamed opposition, and possibly from intrusive local and national agencies.

The next afternoon, after testing the security of the newly installed telephone lines, and the computer techs having reconfigured the setup of the computers and tied them into two of the phone lines Davis and Colefax arrived. They shook Dirks hand warmly, saying how good it was to be working with him again.

Dirk spent five minutes in greeting them and some small talk, then told them that Ebbets had already been briefed and would brief them, then would bring them back to give their answers. They left with Ebbets, both men with curiosity written all over their faces.

A half hour later they were back, and being the kind of men they were gave simple 'Yes' answers. Dirk then sat down with them for another half hour, first admonishing them to bring their men up to speed on the potential dangers, ruefully explaining to these men that he didn't distrust their abilities, he just liked being careful while he had the time to be. He then worked with them to help set up an operating outline and routine so these things could be put into motion.

Two days later Dirk and his team were ready to start. The first call he wanted to put through was going to be one of the most important ones he would make. He went into the spare bedroom, now being used as his communications center, and asked Davis, who was on duty then, when was the last time the room had been swept. And was told fifteen minutes ago. Dirk went and got the new interface from the locked closet in his bedroom and returned to the communications center with it.

He asked the techs on duty to cut in the anti-surveillance equipment they had installed, then asked Davis to clear the room except for himself and to also call Colefax into the room. He then proceeded to install his special interface between the phone lines and the computer. Just as he was finishing up Colefax stepped into the room, a question on his face. Since Colefax was also one of the best men around on computers Dirk began to explain his equipment.

What it did and how to work the program he had had installed with it. By the time he was finished both Davis and Colefax were looking at Dirk with some wonder on their faces, as this type of technology was totally new to both of them. Dirk went over the programs operation a couple of more times with Colefax and when he said he was ready turned and told Davis to stay inside the room, lock the door, and tell the outside man that no one was come in until notified differently by Davis.

This done he proceeded to punch out a number while reading from a book he took from his attaché case. The phone on the other end rang four times before being answered by a pleasant feminine voice saying the last four digits of the number and "Whom do you wish to speak with please?"

"Mr. Lester Please. Tell him it's Longknife." said Dirk.

There was a slight pause as if she were checking a list, which she was, then "Very well, please hold on for a moment."

As he waited Dirk indicated to Colefax to start running the program. As numbers started to run up one of the smaller screens map sections began to flash on the main monitor, which was tied into a modem on the locators interface. As Dirk watched this progression on the monitor he heard several clicks in his receiver then a deep basso voice said "Is that you Dirk?"

"Who the hell else would have the balls to call you on a very unlisted number, Bad Boy?" answered Dirk dryly.

"I wish you wouldn't call me that." said the rich basso voice plaintively, but with a chuckle also in it.

"Just letting you know it's me." said Dirk with an answering chuckle in his voice. The voice turned somewhat wary, asking "This line secure from your end Dirk?"

"As secure as I can make it from where I am at present." said Dirk as he looked at the section of map flashing on the screen, then, "Listen Jimmy I have a few thing I'd like to tell you, but first, just to emphasize a point, would you like me to tell you where you are right now?"

Suddenly there was a very cold silence on the other end of the line, then "There are only two people who know where I am, and both of them are here with me! Explain what you just said Dirk!"

"Jimmy, I know where you are, and I'm about a thousand miles from you right now."

"I repeat, Dirk. No one knows where I am but those two, so how can you know?" said the deep voice, now with ice in it.

"Jimmy, I'm going to tell you where you are in a minute. You know me for a long time, and you also know that I must have a very good reason for coming on to you like this! Are we together so far?" said Dirk in a calming voice.

"Go on." was the cautious reply.

"Ok. I'm going to give you a street name and a state. No numbers, no towns, and the meat of your setup. Will that convince you to give me ten more minutes of serious listening time?" said Dirk in a flat professional voice he knew the other would recognize.

"If you can do that I'll have to listen, won't I?" said the other in the same tone of voice.

"Ok. You are on Henshaw Street, in Oregon. You are using two blind forwarding lines and a main trunk bypass. That's general. I can get more specific if you like!" Dirk said very flatly.

There was a long, dead silence on the other end of the line. Then came a simple flat *"Talk."*

"All right. This is from God to you. One, I no longer have any connection to my previous associates. Actually I think that they're a little peeved at me! Two, There is a new game on, and it's already gone deadly! Three, I used a new piece of equipment I came into possession of to get your attention, because I'm now recruiting and I want, need, you to join me in this. I need a first rate planner and strategist to be my second. I'd like it to be you." said Dirk quietly.

"What kind of new game?" was the response.

"Jimmy, we need to discuss this in person, face to face. There is evidence to support claims but I need you here to do it. By the way, Bill Tate is already in and playing. I can give you a number sequence if you want to confirm it. I'll also provide you with security, if that would make you feel better."

"Dirk, like you said, I know you for a long time and I also know the value of your word. Give me a name and send a team. I'll be there tomorrow afternoon. One question. What's this worth?"

"Would having your belief in something worth fighting for returned to you be worth it?" said Dirk with some feeling.

"I'll see you tomorrow, now give me that name." and after Dirk gave it the line went dead.

Dirk turned to Rick Davis and said "Call the agency and get another four man team. Pick them yourself and put Ebbets in charge. Have the agency charter a jet for the trip out and back, and have one of the helicopters pick them up at the airport to bring them here. Keep it tight, ok.

Then copying the address and phone number from the bottom of the screen he handed it to Davis, saying "Have Tony go to this address, but he's to call ahead before going in. They are to bring this man back here to me, safe and in one piece."

Davis took the address and phone number from Dirk, and smiling moved off to set things in motion. He was smiling because he really liked it when things were moving.

As Davis turned away to get things going Dirk turned back to Colefax with a smile of his own on his face, because he knew how lucky he was to have this caliber of men with him.

Building Blocks

The next afternoon a knock sounded on the door of Dirk's combination sitting room—bedroom. "Come." he said to the closed door.

Colefax stuck his head into the room and said "The chopper will be on the roof pad in fifteen minutes. The package is safe and secure."

"Thank you. I'll be right out." said Dirk.

A few minutes later Jimmy Lester was led into the suite by Dirk's men. As he came fully into the room Dirk came across the room to meet him, his hand extended, saying "It's been a while Jimmy, I'm really glad you decided to come."

"It has been at that. I am glad I came too, if for no other reason than to say hello in person, and to see you operate again. I'm very impressed with what I've seen so far."

"This is only temporary." said Dirk, pleased anyway with his friends compliment, "We have a great deal to go over and time is not one of my greatest assets right now. So I'm sure that you will forgive me if I temporarily skip a few of the social graces for a short while. Also the physical stuff I could bring was very limited so you'll have to take a lot on faith until I can show you the rest of it." said Dirk.

He turned to face Colefax, saying " This mean looking desperado is Ron Colefax. He's head of operational security for our group. Ron, say hello to Jimmy Lester better known as Bad Boy, and B.B. to his friends."

"Pleased to meet you." said Colefax, extending his hand, and "I've heard some interesting things about you over the years." he finished with a smile.

"Jeez Dirk, I wish you wouldn't call me that." said Jimmy as he shook hands with Ron.

"Ok," said Dirk, clapping his hands once, "Ron will order any refreshments you might want from room service so order something, and please order another pot of coffee for us too Ron. I have a lot to tell you so get ready to listen." said Dirk turning again to Ron Colefax and nodding.

Turning to Mr. Davis he said "This is Rick Davis. He's head of site security." As Rick and Jimmy shook hands he continued to Rick, "I'd like you to speak to the management and tell them that we would now like to exercise the option we had earlier discussed with them.

As soon as they acknowledge that I want you to clear the floor below us, this floor, and the roof. Secure them with our people only. Call for more men if you need them, but only men you know and trust."

He paused for a moment, then "Rick, I've known you and Ron for a while and I know your backgrounds even better."

Here he paused again as he saw both men's eyes widen slightly, then continued "You see, you actually do work for me. I am the mysterious owner of the security company."

He paused again but got the reaction that he was expecting, that of both men looking at him, waiting for whatever came next. "I've grown to trust you, and your judgement. I said earlier that I might ask you to come in deeper. Well, I want you to stay and hear what I have to tell my friend. The only proviso is that, If you decide not to come in all of the way, whatever you hear in this room stays in this room. I'll accept your words on it." he finished, looking expectantly at the two men, waiting for their answers.

Jimmy Lester stood there, looking on interestedly, saying softly "This is getting more interesting by the minute!"

Davis and Colefax looked at each other for a long moment, then turned to face Dirk and simply nodded.

"Good enough." said Dirk. Then, after hesitating for a moment, asked "One question first. What do you think of Tony Ebbets?"

Both men smiled in unison, then Colefax said "We were thinking of asking you to include him." he finished, chuckling to himself.

"Excellent" said Dirk, pleased with the outcome and the confirmation of his own good judgement. "please ask him to join us while you set those other things in motion. Also Rick, besides the five of us I don't want anyone within twenty five feet of either side of this suite, and none directly below or above it. How long?"

Davis spoke quietly to Colefax for a moment then said "Fifteen minutes, including the refreshments." and left to see to things. Almost fifteen minutes later he walked back into the suite, following Colefax, and accompanied by Tony Ebbets. As he looked at Dirk he said " Done and secure."

Dirk motioned them all to seats, then said "All of you are professionals and know how to listen, but, because time is such a factor and I have so much to tell you I want to make sure that I have your total attention!" He stopped for a moment, to scan the faces of those seated around him, and they in turn, their interest and questions evident, looked back. He continued "Tony, Rick, how much do you think that marble coffee table weighs? he asked, looking at the two.

The men questioned spoke quietly together for a moment then Tony replied "It probably weighs somewhere around three hundred pounds."

Dirk walked over to it, and bending down, gripped it by one leg and stood up lifting it to waist height.

Then he proceeded to lift it almost to touch the ceiling before gently lowering it to the floor again. All without spilling one drop from the several full coffee cups set around the edge, and he was still holding it with only one hand.

As he stood back up he scanned their faces and was pleased with the looks he found there as he said "Now! Now that I have your complete, and undivided attention I'll tell you a story!"

And he told them. Telling them almost everything, leaving out only what he and TuLan felt could safely be left out for a later time, because they were trained to pick up on things that didn't ring true.

The telling took several hours, with Dirk letting them break in occasionally with questions he knew they would need the preliminary answers to now. They would need those answers now because they were all intelligent and careful men, and putting them off would quickly alienate them to their new cause.

The telling moments were, besides his first amazing display of strength, when he produced the photographs and showed them the Drel, still attached to the spine of the dead agent. And also after he had opened the back of his special tracing unit and shown them the obvious alien manufacture of it to them.

Around midnight Dirk called a halt, for sandwiches and coffee. After everyone was on their second cup he said "Gentlemen, I've told you and shown you everything that I can for now. This is a deadly serious situation, and if it hasn't already sunk in it will shortly. What is going down supersedes any nationalistic concerns that any of you might now hold."

"As you know I'm not a man given to crying wolf. I am also realistic and know when to ask for help. What is in front of us for the future is going to require the best people we can gather, no matter where they are from, and an effort that will almost certainly exceed one hundred percent. And whatever we do will have to be done as quietly as possible."

"The reason for that," He went on, "is simply because we don't know how deeply the opposition has penetrated our, and the other, governmental infrastructures. The organization that we are now starting to build will be comprised of people we know and trust, and some others that, because of their established reputations, should be trustworthy. Any others will be those we can check out and verify for ourselves."

He looked around at them, then went on 'Make no mistake about it, it is not just a country, any country, we are trying to protect! It's our home, our planet! Earth! As screwed up as it can be at times, it is ours and I think that it's worth fighting for!"

He finished this last with more passion than he realized he had intended letting show as he looked around himself at faces that were now very grim and determined. And seeing those grim expressions he said "By the looks on your faces I take it that your answers to my next question is yes, so I'll ask it bluntly. Are you in or out?"

He peered around, receiving nods or muted yes'. He was looking at some of the most determined faces he had ever looked upon. "That's settled then. I know that you all have some questions that you are champing at the bit to ask! But please bear with me for a little bit longer." he said.

Then "All right, it's after midnight and I want each of you to get at least six hours of sleep tonight because I want you all fresh tomorrow morning. We will meet back here at eight A.M. and I'll answer what questions you have had a chance to sleep on. And then we'll get started."

Turning to Lester he said "Jimmy, you can use the bedroom next to mine for tonight, then I'll get you a suite next to this one. It was a very somber group of men that dispersed to get some much needed rest that night.

At eight A. M. the next morning the four men arrived promptly for the meeting, and as Dirk looked at them he saw the same look of determination in each set of eyes and face. But now, as he had hoped, after resting it had melded with the professionalism that each of these men had developed over years of strife and experience.

More importantly still, he saw that which had been missing the night before. He saw in their calm professional eyes that glint of eagerness that only the belief in the rightness of your actions can put there.

These were hard and deadly men who had, over the years, lost their naivete. And now, with the veil that separates polite society from the grimmer aspects of reality removed, had only their personal integrity and deadly skills to sustain them.

Now it seemed as if each had found some personal fountain which had refilled in some measure the belief they had thought trickled away and lost along with their youth. It showed in their eyes, even Dirk's. Now they had in their eyes something that said life was really worth living fully for. And possibly giving their lives for too!

Looking at these men Dirk knew that now he truly had the nexus of a strong and resilient foundation. Now the fight for his home could begin in earnest. And in his mind he felt TuLan respond to the satisfaction he was feeling.

Strangely, because TuLan did not seem to catch it, he thought he heard, very faintly, the echo of a very familiar chuckle. And, as he prepared to build an organization on his new foundation, he pondered briefly then and many times thereafter, that faint echo of laughter, because Balor was many hundreds of miles away.

It was at this point that he began to think that his tie to Balor was far more important than it had, at first, seemed.

Dirk gave himself a mental shrug and shake thinking, enough of this, it's now time to begin building. "All right gentlemen!" He said, his voice strong with new resolution "let's get to work!"

Building Blocks Too

After answering a few more last minute questions generated from the night before Dirk got up in front of his newly founded team to speak.

"Since last night I have been in touch with one of our allies, and we think that you need a little more information!" And being the type of men that they were they shut up to listen. "I get the impression from some of your questions that some of you might think that this may be a long drawn out fight."

"The answer to that question even I don't know for sure, but from the information that I do have that is exactly what I think! The information that I'm going to give you now is more like non-information, or a pre-briefing to prepare for receiving information. It's in no way due to a lack of trust in all of you. It's because the information I'll be giving you should, because of it's very nature, be taken in smaller bites so you can digest it properly." Dirk paused for a moment gathering his thoughts.

Looking up, he saw that all eyes were fixed intently on him. He went on, saying "Look, it's taken me three months to understand what I've learned so far, and I'm still learning more each day. The benefit you have is that I'm here to interpret a lot of what you will need to learn. Over the next few days, weeks, and months you can expect to have your lives and thoughts rattled time and again as you learn the things you need to know. Things you need to know about the enemy, as well as things about our new allies."

"You will also have to learn about the new assets we will have to work with, and the true size of the task we are about to take on."

He paused again, looking at each face, to see if the gravity of what he was saying was taking hold and was pleased with the looks of concentration he met there. "We will have some distinct advantages over our contemporaries with some of the new equipment we will be receiving from our new allies, and even more as we develop new approaches and uses for them. We will also have a few disadvantages because of the enemy we will be facing. To offset that somewhat our ally has said that our race is one of the most inventive and tenacious he has ever encountered. From him that means a lot."

Looking around at the smiles on their faces in response to his statements from our allies' he smiled grimly to himself, knowing that his next words were going to be a real wake up call for these men.

"The first major shock I have for you is a real lulu." he said, seeing the faces return to watchful attentiveness," Our ally comes from a race that has a recorded history somewhat over six hundred fifty thousand Earth years old." he finished, smiling openly now at their stunned expressions.

"Listen up!" Dirk said quietly, knowing that they would now strain for every word.

"They are neither godlike nor omnipotent! They are people. They think, feel, invent and hurt like people! They just look a little bit different. Well, a lot different in many cases, and have been around a while longer than we have." he finished softly, at the same time hearing a strangled snort of laughter in his mind as TuLan tried to stifle his mirth at his gross understatement. It was, he felt, very important that they begin to understand that they could no longer think of themselves as being the center of everything, but rather as a part of everything.

The statement he had just made was part of that awakening. "No questions now," he said, seeing the beginnings of new questions forming. "There's too much to do, and we must get started now! I'll tell you more soon."

And, as he looked around, Dirk could see them trying to shake off the shock of being told of the existence a race so old, and bring their minds back to the present.

"Jimmy," started Dirk in a businesslike tone of voice, "You've got the hardest job to start! I've already made a list of names for the people I want you to find, and contact. The names I have there are for the right people but I want you to go over it and from it make two more lists, one for additions and the other for deletions, and give me comments on both." Dirk paused as he watched Jimmy's eyes scan down the list and Glance up, looking his question, at him.

"Listen up! " he said somewhat loudly to make sure he had their attention, "I want one thing to be perfectly clear from here forward. The thing that will have to go by the wayside from now on is misplaced nationalism. You men are very good but there are a lot of other very good people out there in other places who are in pretty much the same place you were in yesterday. This planet is their home also! Always remember that, in the future when you have to deal with them! It's their home too. Do any of you have a problem dealing with that?"

Each in turn scanned the list and, after a moments thought, shook their head in the negative or gave a quiet "no".

"I know that after so many years of trying to do some of these people in that it will be hard to work and act like brothers with them. But I feel in my gut that before this is over we will wish that we had a lot more of them than we're likely to get to come in with us. Trust will be earned on both sides in this thing we're about to do, so make trying to get along one of your priorities." he finished, then continued to Jimmy, "The list Jimmy, can do?"

Jimmy looked thoughtful for a moment, then said "I know where, and how, to get in touch with a of a couple of those on the list, and a couple more that aren't on it. It will take three, four days for those. And maybe a couple or three days for the rest. Except for the Russian. I'll probably need help with that one. More importantly, we need more and better comm gear, except for your toy, than we've got now."

"Fine," said Dirk " order what you need, but do it quietly. Money is not a problem yet, but don't waste it either."

Then he looked at Rick Davis and said, "Rick, you've got the most experience, so your going to put together a team and run field security. Make a list of who, what, and how much. Give it to Jim so that you can work out the details together." Looking now at Colefax he said, " Ron, you've also got a tough one to start out with! First, you're going to have to play leap frog to help Rick and Jim as they need you."

"And, at the same time, I want you to put together a site operations security team. When we're ready to begin operations that will be your main job. It's going to be a big one so pick your people with care as they will have to be in the know almost from the start."

Turning at last to face Tony Ebbets Dirk said, "Both Rick and Ron speak very highly of you, so of course, I'm going to give you the dirtiest job. At first you will be with Jimmy, as his right hand and protector, until Rick and Ron have something set up. Take a team you feel comfortable with, about four men I should think, until they don't positively need you anymore."

"Then I want you to start planning for, and setting in motion, a set up for internal security. When you have that set up, your word, as far as internal security matters are concerned will be law! The only exception to that might be an override by one of the other six of us, but that will be the exception not the rule. Don't abuse it! Can do?"

Tony sputtered a little, saying "But, but I'll need——"

Dirk broke in saying "These two outlaws said you could do the job. Can you!?"

Tony's jaw snapped shut, "Yes Sir!"

"All right." said Dirk, and "Last business before you get started on your chores. I think that we have about two weeks, plus or minus, before noses start to twitch in our direction. I want you three, Tony, Rick and Ron to get together and have an exit set up for us to disappear with a one hour notice. You know the drill, full fallbacks and cutouts"

Tony spoke up quickly, "A moment ago you said the other six of us. Counting myself and Bill Tate I still only count six of us. Who's the seventh?"

The others looked on interestedly, recognizing Tony's point, as Dirk replied with a smile, "Good catch Tony. The seventh members' name is Balor. He's a bit odd so you'll have to wait until you meet him to understand about him. Besides, I doubt if you could stop him if you wanted to. He said showing a secretive smile to them.

Then "Enough of that! I'll only confuse you by saying things like that about him. You will 'definitely understand' once you meet him. That will be soon enough so just remember, he's a friend!" finished Dirk, smiling to himself even more broadly. This last, much to pondering glances.

Two weeks later they were all again gathered back in the suite. And Jimmy 'Bad Boy' Lester had a definite, self satisfied, Cheshire smile on his rugged face as he said to Dirk, "It looks like your hunch will pay off big. Just how did you know that Carmella would bite so quickly Dirk?"

"What was her response when you said you were looking for Dieter?" Asked Dirk, smiling.

Jimmy snorted a laugh as he mimicked the phony Latino accent Carmella so often affected. " Wha choo wan with tha secon rate bank teller for. He don know beans!"

Then he laughed again before continuing, "I did as you told me and said there was a new game afoot, and that she was being considered for a place on the team. Then she asked 'what new game?' Then I said that I probably shouldn't talk to her about it anyway because there was no profit in it, but they needed someone really good. Then, also as you instructed, I told her that it was going to be to dangerous for a nice girl like her. Her reply was short and to the point, 'Call me back in ten minutes', and the line went dead. Jesus Dirk, you could feel the sizzle over the wires! Anyway, I called her back after the ten minutes was up and you could hear her still swearing from across the room as she came to the phone. Well, she ended up saying, 'if it was that big they needed the best,' and 'she needed a vacation anyway.'" Jimmy finished, his 'Bad Boy' grin still in place.

"Ok." said Dirk, "What's the bad news?"

"We had to drop a couple of Federales as we were bringing he across the Mexican border." said Jimmy, the smile completely gone from his face now." Seems they felt rather proprietary about keeping her there. She'll be here in about three hours." he finished.

"Does she know about me yet?" Asked Dirk.

"Not yet." Jimmy said, smiling again.

Just then Ron Colefax put his hand up to his ear where his mini-transceiver was seated, almost invisibly. He listened for a moment, then walked over to Rick Davis and spoke quietly to him for a minute before leaving the room quickly.

Rick turned to Dirk and Jimmy and said, "We just picked up a sniffer! We've got him cooling his heels in an empty room. We'll know from who soon."

"All right," said Dirk, "have our own people start packing everything up. I want to be out of here, without a trace, by midnight. Then go down and squeeze that sniffer dry, and after you're finished with him, leave him in the room asleep while we leave. Do it quietly. "

Dirk went over to his briefcase and, after rummaging inside it for a moment, took out a small address book. He rifled the pages for a few seconds before finding what he wanted, then wrote something on a small pad on the table next to the case. This he tore off and, reaching into the case again, took out a ring of keys.

Both of these he quickly brought back across the room and handed them to Rick Davis saying, "This is the location of a small building complex I own in St. Louis. Send Tony down ahead of us to open things up and set up some security. You know the drill Rick, move the men in twos and threes over a couple of days."

A quick pause for thought, then "After the men are in you can follow with whatever equipment you and Tony decide you need. There are four buildings and three large sheds plus a ten bay garage. The main building is a four story office building, the top two floors of which have already been converted into one room efficiency apartments with half baths in each. House the men on the second floor, two to a room. The top floor, for now, is for guests."

"This building also has a two story basement and sub basement. You can set up a communications center in the sub basement for the time being. Once you're settled in you and Tony can set up some hard security and perimeter systems. If you need more men bring them in, just make sure they're vetted right, ok?" With a tight smile and a curt nod Rick turned to leave when Dirk said "One more thing. Ron, Jimmy and two men will stay with me. Ok. go!" With that Rick nodded again and left at a fast walk.

Dirk then turned to Jimmy Lester and said, with a tight smile on his face, " Pick up Carmella and bring her to our alternate airport. I'll be waiting for you there at one a.m., no later than one fifteen." Then seeing the look Jimmy was giving him said, I know, I know. Take two men with you and take her out to buy some clothes, then take her out to dinner." Looking at Jimmy's continuing sour look Dirk said, barely choking down a guffaw of laughter, "Go on. Get out of here."

Dirk really needed some time to sit and think while listening to some music. So, suiting action to thought, he walked to his case and took a tape of Mozart's symphony number nineteen, walked to the stereo and jacked it into the tape player.

As he lowered himself to the edge of the sofas' seat he was thinking that because of the events of an hour or so ago this place was no longer usable for his needs. He had hoped that he might get four to six days use out of this place but his premonition had been correct. Things were beginning to hot up. And quickly.

He eased back against the cushions, letting some of the tension ease out of his neck and shoulders. Letting the melody of the symphony wash over him as the music began to fill the room, he began to think and plan his next moves. Now, besides the ship, St Louis was his only real fallback position so he would have to set some serious misdirection in motion. With this in mind he made some notes on the pad laying on the coffee table in front of him.

As he finished his notes another thought struck him so he got up, went to his brief case, withdrew his remaining unregistered cell phone and dialed the number to the one he had left with Bill Tate at the ship. Bill answered on the third ring.

"Bill, how much money do you have set aside? And can I borrow it for a while? " Dirk asked.

There was only the hum of the carrier as Bill thought for a moment, then "About half a million counting my stocks," and, "If you need it it's yours. Uh, Dirk, should I ask why?" he asked curiously.

"I want to let 'Chickie' play with it for a while to set up a front for us, and as a cash source." said Dirk.

"Are you crazy!? She's still after your blood for the way you closed down that operation she was running for that dissident faction in Saudi Arabia."

"She doesn't know it yet." said Dirk, smiling ruefully to himself, and "I'll figure a way to let her know as soon as I can. For now 'Bad Boy' is fronting it for me." he finished quietly.

"Wel-l-l. At least I'll know that my money is being handled by one of the best there is." Bill said grumpily.

"Bill." said Dirk quietly, causing the other to listen attentively, "As we had been expecting we caught a sniffer. We just didn't expect it so soon, so it might just be a coincidence. We don't know who yet, but he's being wrung out now. Just to play it safe we're moving out to the fallback position in St. Louis. I should be able to come and get you out of there in about two weeks, if you want? Is everything alright there? And you?"

"I'm fine now," snorted Bill "but the way that cat Balor moves around like a ghost still scares the bejesus out of me!" he finished fervently.

"Ok," said Dirk" When I come out I'll have some friends with me. Please ask Balor not to scare them shitless when we get there." he finished with a laugh as he cut the connection.

He had been pacing as he talked. Now finished with the phone he sat back down and began to think about Carmella 'Chickie' Martinez, running her stats through his mind like an ops. File.

Name—Carmella Maria Martinez
Nationality—Colombian (expatriate)
Current Status—American Citizen (Naturalized)

Description Follows:

Age—32 DOB—11 January 1966
Height—5ft—5in. Weight—125 lbs.
Color Hair—Dk. Brown Color Eyes—Hazel
Education—High School Graduate—Graduated top 5% of Class
College—Wharton School of Business—Graduated top 3% of Class
Degrees—International Banking & Finance—Accounting Business Management
Specialties—International Banking and Arbitrage
Special notices—Subject is known to be expert and deadly with any type of handgun!
Observations—Subject is known for having a proverbial Latin temper but in many circles is dubbed the 'Ice Queen' when it comes to her work in the financial arena.

Subject is considered to be extremely knowledgeable and competent by those who have worked with or around her.

Subject is considered to be very well connected worldwide, on both sides of the law, and with many of the various intelligence agencies.!!!!

As these bits of information, which he knew by heart, ran through his mind Dirk thought of what was not there in the file. One of the items he most vividly remembered was from an incident that happened a couple of years ago.

One of her clients, a shadowy figure who specialized in securing financing for terrorists groups, had reneged on paying her commission. So she had rigged his accounts to not only pay double her commission but for the balance of the accounts to dump into different charities as they were accessed. And she did the same thing to the accounts of his current terrorist clients.

Only with them she set it up so that when they tried to make transfers for arms payments the money was dumped into the favorite charities of their intended targets. From what he understood, the backer and the terrorist group had found some very deep holes to crawl into, in fear of both each other and the gulled, angry, and very dangerous, arms dealers.

Those dealing with her in the legal business arena had learned that she was a force to be reckoned with, and respected for her abilities. Those on the other side of legal knew enough to deal straight and leave her alone.

Dealing as a freelancer she had acquired a very diverse client list and knew a great deal about many of their operations and set ups. But she had never, to anyone's knowledge, been known to divulge any information concerning any of her other clients to anyone. In a few short years she had achieved the two aspects of a heavy hitter. Fear and respect!

The last time Dirk had run into her had been when his team had been assigned to terminate a group of Arab businessmen who were posing as terrorists, threatening to use a nuclear devise to blow up one of the major oil fields belonging to one of the middle eastern countries friendly to the U.S. This in an effort to affect world oil prices in their favor.

Dirk had found out, at the last moment, that she had not been involved in that part of their operation. So he had pulled her out of their headquarters, the only one left alive, and kept her handcuffed for two days. And blindfolded for four days. During that period, after removing the handcuffs, she had been told to perform her toilet and to eat without touching the blindfold. If she removed it they would have no alternative to killing her.

It was two days after that, when they were sure that they were in the clear, that they dropped her with her luggage at an airport V.I.P. entrance. Still blindfolded. They drove off as she was removing it, her fury evident in every movement.

Dirk found out later that she had spent a year, and called in many markers, trying to find out that he had been the team leader on that mission. The only reason that she had not been able to get at him was because of his job. He officially did not exist.

After thinking about it for a while longer Dirk admitted that she was the one he needed, and wanted, for the new team. That accepted, he decided that the only way to handle the situation would be to drop her right into the middle of everything, making her a part of the top echelon.

This so that she had to sink or swim with the rest of them. He felt sure that she would be a good swimmer. He also felt that this would go a long way in defusing her feelings of personal animosity.

That decided he moved on, giving some additional thought to what would be of concern to their immediate needs. Satisfied with his conclusions on that matter he moved on to reviewing the list of people he hoped to acquire.

At the end of that train of thought was the name of one person in particular whom he hoped would join them, mainly because of some modifications he thought might be possible to some of the equipment on TuLans' ship.

A short while later, the soothing strains of the beautiful piano concerto washing over him as he let his mind rest, he felt a questing touch from TuLan at his conscious mind.

Earlier on, after long discussions, Dirk had allowed TuLan to establish a permanent contact link with Dirks' conscious mind, the reasons for this link being twofold. First, it allowed TuLan visual contact with Dirks world, seeing it as Dirk saw it without interrupting whatever Dirk might be doing at the time.

Second, it allowed each instant contact with the other at necessity by metaphorically opening a window, as two people who lived across an alley from each other might to have a serious, if needed, talk or just to chat. And as it turned out it was a very comfortable arrangement for both of them over the years.

This arrangement, perforce, meant that while TuLan was observing through Dirks' eyes he also was privy to the surface thoughts in Dirks' mind and vice versa. This also was by mutual agreement allowing each to see things from the others perspective and learning something of the manner in which the other arrived at that perspective.

It was at this point that TuLan said, *I am constantly amazed at the working of your mind Dirk! I watch in amazed consternation as you seem to gather large amounts of seemingly unrelated information, Submerge it into your subconscious mind, all but seem to forget it for a time. And then you open yourself to your subconscious again and up float these almost complete concepts. Ones that I would not even think of unless I had a specific need to, and then, as you revue them, make even more improvements on them. One of those improvements being the way you conceived to miniaturize the array for the chameleon devise and then power it with a battery from one of the small cargo-haulers.* TuLan finished, with open admiration in his tone.

Dirk, as he replied, sent a feeling of warmth in reply to the appreciation the other was so openly displaying and sent *I also have some other ideas.* and he proceeded to show them to TuLan

After reviewing the visual representations Dirk sent, and asking a couple of pointed questions TuLan said, with even more admiration than before, *truly, if anyone can accomplish these things, I believe you will be the one to do it! The one that really fascinates me here is using the antigravity compensator harnesses as a means of personal transportation!*

It is something that was there before us all this time and we never considered doing. It is truly ingenious! TuLan finished, a little awe in his manner.

Again accepting the praise Dirk said, *you agree with my basic plan outlines then?*

Yes. said TuLan, *"But I think you had better keep your prototype development confined to the ship for the time being to limit any losses that might occur. And another thing, though you haven't seen it yet, there is a good sized workshop area in another one of the holds that you can use.*

Surprised, Dirk said, *but TuLan! That solves many problems for us quickly, leaving only the one of controlling the traffic in the area of the ship. And I think I know how to handle that one.*

And his mind spun off into several alternative possibilities almost simultaneously. Thus again surprising TuLan with these humans versatility, as he watched his host throw up almost complete plans, hold them side by side, then pick and pull at them as he improved them or discarded them as impractical.

All too soon Colefax knocked on Dirks' door, stuck his head in and said quietly, "Everything else is packed, time to do yours' sir. Also, we cracked that sniffers' shell. He's from N.S.A. (National Security Agency).

It seems that they had an intermittent watch on Protec and when all of the top men got called in for one job it piqued their curiosity. We picked him up and spotted his backup before they could penetrate our security.

When we leave here they won't have anything but a question mark to follow. I am sorry about leaving that much. I would have liked to have left it completely clean.

"Don't worry about it." said Dirk, "I'm just surprised it didn't happen sooner with the amount of traffic we've been creating. You and two of your men are here with me. Tell your clean up crew to leave just enough around to misdirect anyone towards Houston, then scram. We will be going to the alternate airfield I told you about shortly. Can you still fly a twin engine jet?" Dirk asked, Smiling.

Colefax just answered with a huge smile of his own and nodded. Dirk asked, "Ok if I take your right seat?" As Dirk shrugged into his jacket and packed his briefcase Colefax answered with, "It would be my honor sir!"

Their exit from the hotel went almost totally unnoticed. One curious pair of eyes did however note the late hour departure of a helicopter as it lifted from the roof helipad. And followed it for a while, noting that it headed for the western side of the airport where most of the southern flights were boarded. The attractive middle aged woman the eyes belonged to was also wondering what was taking her partner so long in getting back from checking the hotel lobby for signs of the heavyweights from Protec.

They had been sent to find out who those men had been sent to meet but had had little luck so far. As these thoughts were going through her head Dirks' people were quietly filtering out of the city and heading for St. Louis.

At one forty five that morning Jimmy Lester was leading Carmella Martinez up the stairs of a twin engine executive jet that was sitting on a private parking ramp with its engines idling. As soon as she had been buckled into a seat it began to move out onto the apron and then onto the taxiway, there to wait for takeoff clearance. Within a short time the powerful little jet began to move again.

It picked up speed rapidly, then almost effortlessly it sprang into the early morning sky. When the plane steadied Jimmy got up from his seat and went to the phone mounted on the forward bulkhead between the cabin and the pilots compartment. Pulling it out of its cradle he spoke quietly into the mouthpiece, "You up front there Dirk?"

"In the right seat." The answer came, then "How's our girl doing back there Jimmy?"

"A little tipsy. A lot interested." Replied Jimmy, a smile in his voice.

"Very good." Said Dirk, and "There is a change in plans. After you hang up come forward and get my cell phone. In the next hour both Rick and Tony will be calling on it to check in. I'll tell you the rest up here but before you come up go back and tell her that we'll be in the air for about five hours so she should try and get some sleep. Ok?"

"Gotcha." Said jimmy, and as he hung up the phone he was thinking to himself, 'This is starting to get real interesting.'

As he began to move back along the aisle he was thinking that the Dirk he remembered had an arresting personality. Dirks' personality now was absolutely commanding.

Also, since he had become involved in this, he had actually begun to feel good about what he was doing, and more to the point, good about himself again!

Jimmy entered the flight control cabin and locked the door behind him, then sat down in the pull down flight navigators seat. "Ok. What's up boss?" he said with a smile, and in an aside "Hi Ron. Smooth lift off."

Ron turned his head to look at him "I see she let you get back in one piece." he said, his face deadpan, and "But since you're here and whole it's good to see you too." Ron slowly turned his face to Dirk and they both guffawed.

"Same here." Said Dirk, still smiling, then "Ok. Here it is. I've decided that we have to go to the ship sooner than I had originally planed."

Jimmy's face mirrored his surprise, as did Rons' as he looked over at them both.

"This is necessary Jimmy, Ron." Dirk Said in quiet earnest. "I have the feeling that we don't have the time to run the standard set up. I think that for a while we're gong to have to play catch up and dodgem at the same time. The only real advantage we have right now is that the opposition doesn't know what we know, or even better, what we may have."

"It's imperative that our top people know, without a doubt, exactly what we're up against. Then, as quickly as possible, our seconds need to be brought up to speed. Once you see for yourself you'll understand just how deadly our enemy is, and there will be no doubt left as to what we will lose if we don't start fighting back now!" he finished, with the same quiet earnestness.

After a short pause Jimmy asked "What about Carmella?"

In a flat, strictly business tone of voice, Dirk answered "She's in or she's out. No waffling! You can tell her everything except where we're going. You can even tell her that I'm running this thing, but not that I'm on the plane. Tell her we're going to meet me and be shown proof positive, but make it clear to her, she makes up her mind as to whether she's in or out before we get where we're going. She's been told enough to make a decision. She has twenty four hours to make her decision, no more. I hate to admit it but we need her badly Jimmy! Convince her!"

"Do my best." Jimmy replied soberly.

"Good enough." And, "We'll lay over one day in Houston to complete the misdirection, then we're heading north to this location. "Dirk said, pointing to a spot on the map he was holding.

Then, "When Rick and Tony call in tell them about the change in plans, to put their seconds in charge, and to meet us at that location two days from now. Nothing else! Understood?"

"Got it." Jimmy said.

"Good. After that try to get some rest. You look like you could use it."

As Dirk, after Jimmy left, sat thinking, the lights from the instruments reflecting off his eyes, Ron leaned half over and asked quietly "It's that bad Dirk?"

"Ron," Said Dirk with a weary sigh, "what you've heard up to now doesn't cover nearly the half of it! I know quite a lot right now but there is a lot more that I don't know, that we need to know. That's the part that scares me. Not knowing the things I need to know so we can fight these things effectively."

Sitting back, reflecting again, Dirk was thinking that with Carmella covering as their invisible front it would just possibly give him the time and the money to finish building something that might give Earth half a chance at surviving what he felt was coming.

At that point Dirk felt TuLans' questing touch at his mind, and then his thoughts came, *though I was surprised at your change of plans I completely agree with you. I too have a bad feeling for the near future.*

Dirks thoughts came slowly in reply, *I think I've begun to get a feel for you and your friends in the Galactic Union. To me, and to most of my kind, war is a dirty, and vicious thing. But, once we are moved to a point where we believe we must fight, my kind seems to take an almost perverse pleasure in the fighting!*

And this war, I fear, is one where there will be no quarter asked for or given. I can only hope that you will have the same feelings for us when this is over. You haven't seen our dark side at first hand yet.

There can be no appreciation of light without the contrast of darkness. TuLan quipped.

TuLan would come to rue the flippancy of that remark as time wore on!

Carmella 'Chickie' Martinez

They were flying north at about 30,000 feet in another executive jet that Dirk had rented. They were now about an hour out from an airport that Dirk had chosen specifically because it was the home of a friend of his who ran a helicopter service out of it. And it's runway was long enough to accommodate this executive jet. Also, Dirks' friend had done some things for him in the past without asking too many questions.

Dirk was again in the co pilots seat, but now he was much more relaxed, the muscles in his neck and shoulders having eased out since Jimmy had told him that Carmella had accepted the challenge.

She had thrown only two temper tantrums! The first after hearing what Jimmy had to tell her, refusing to believe his story. Then changing her mind as she sat facing the man, looking into his implacably cold eyes, and seeing the rigid, stone hard, expression on his face. She knew this man, and his reputation. He had a reputation as a jokester but not one as a liar!

The second explosion of her temper came when she found out that this was Dirks' operation. Her expression was so murderous that he actually got up and took a step away from her. She calmed down quickly though when he stepped back up to her, reached down and lifted her easily from her seat, and brought her face to within six inches of his own, saying to her in one of the coldest voices she had ever heard "In or Out?!"

Then "You can give me your answer anytime in the next twelve hours." After which he set her back in her seat very gently and walked back to his own seat near the front of the plane. She knew that he would not say another word to her until she had made up her mind. It was one of the scariest things that had ever happened to her!

During this whole episode her inner mind had been working furiously on two separate levels. The fight or flight level scrambled to find a way to get away, for she recognized that she was truly afraid of this man. She knew for certain, from her own excellent sources, that this was not a man to mess with. Like Dirk he was a stone killer when he had to be, and wouldn't hesitate once he thought killing was necessary.

The more rational portion of that level of her mind was now really intrigued by the possibilities that his story presented. The list of people that she'd been told were already on board was an impressive one because they were some of the best in the world when it came to 'black bag' operations.

Some she knew personally. Some she knew by reputation, and the one that were not on board yet but were being actively sought for recruitment were also in the same category.

Her mind worked furiously as she watched his retreating back. With a deep mental sigh of surrender to the forces that drove her to take on jobs that seemed hopeless or impossible she took three quick steps after him saying in a subdued, yet still defiant, voice, "Jimmy.

When he had turned to face her she said "I'm in, damn you. You and Dirk both!" Whereupon she turned, head high and shoulders back, and walked stiffly back to her seat, where she sat down with an audible 'Hrumph'.

She sat there stiffly, the cold look on her face masking the pensive questions about what kind of challenges, danger, and/or excitement this new venture might bring.

Dirk, with his cell phone now returned, called Bill Tate to inform him of their change of plans, asking him to do several things in preparation for their arrival tomorrow.

After completing the arrival arrangements between them Bill said to Dirk, "Damnedest thing! Balor has been gone for three or four days now. About an hour before you called he showed up and plopped himself down in that chair you always sit in, just like he was expecting you to walk in the door. That cat is very strange!"

Saying he would see to the arrangements Bill broke the connection.

As Dirk sat smiling to himself at Bills' comments he jerked slightly as he felt/ heard, in that part of his mind that only Balor seemed able to reach, an echoing chuckle, and, *welcome back brother!*

And then it was gone! A sudden thought occurred to him at that moment. *It's odd that TuLan never seems to hear Balor when he speaks to me on a private level.* He would have to think about that when he had some spare time.

Looking over from the pilots seat, Ron asked "Everything all right boss?"

"Yeah. Better than just all right." Dirk said, his tone of voice musing.

Paul Denton and the Man

At that moment, fifteen hundred miles away, and deep inside the pentagon, sat a man wearing a rumpled gray pinstripe suit and a blue button down collar shirt with a tie. The tie was loosened and the shirt was open at the collar.

The man sat behind a massive desk that was littered with papers and file folders with red stripes running diagonally across them, indicating that their contents were secret!

The office was big. So was the rumpled man occupying it. The man was the section chief of a very 'hush-hush' intelligence unit. His normal demeanor was one of calmness. But not at this moment!

At this moment he was not very calm. He was snarling at one of his chief aides, "God Damn it! People don't just vanish! They leave traces, trails that can be followed."

His aide, one Paul Denton by name, looking just as rumpled, said "Chief. We found a trace. It led us to Houston. From there we could find absolutely nothing! The two sources we had monitoring them have pulled their heads in and have disappeared also!"

And, "Chief, I'll tell you two things I'd bet my life on. One is, this thing looks like the tip of an iceberg to me. Whatever it is it's very Big! That's Big with a capital 'B'! And two, The people involved appear to be the cream of the crop of professionals. Here's what we've got so far."

Pausing for a moment to glance at his notes and marshal his meager information, the aide went on "One. After three years without a peep Jimmy 'Bad Boy' Lester surfaces in a small city in Oregon, gets on a commercial flight, and promptly disappears right after it lands! He went under again without a trace."

"Two. We catch those two parts of traffic from 'Bad Boy' intimating a new game is starting. Nothing else! Just that one telltale that gave us those two key words. 'New Game'"

"Three. One of our floaters, placed in a highly rated security firm called 'Protec' informs us that three top people, all highly rated as 'professional operatives' have been called in for a special job. One of them, Tony Ebbets by name, was a top hitter. They, all three, have gone under without a trace."

"And four. I just found out a little while ago that Carmella Martinez had a private meet with someone a couple of days ago. Two hours later she dropped out of an operation she was running in Mexico City, and after dropping a couple of Federales went completely under also."

He paused again, then "I don't have any idea what's going on but, like I said, I'll bet it's Big. With a capital 'B'!

His chief sat there looking at him, the dark circles under his weary eyes making exclamation marks to his many unanswered questions.

He said "All right Denton, find out what's going on. Use whatever resources you have to. Follow your hunches. Just produce answers for me before I start getting questions I need those answers for. You know we won't be the only ones looking at this. I just want to be the one with some answers."

Denton left his superiors office mumbling something to the effect that if he didn't get some sleep soon he would end up looking worse than his boss did on his good days.

George Casey—a Matter of Transportation

The twin engine executive jet swept in and touched down on the tarmac gently, hardly raising a puff of smoke as the tires gripped the runway. It rolled to the end of the runway, turned off onto the approach way strip and then onto the service way.

The small jet now rolled slowly along past hangars and service workshops until it came to rest in front of a hangar with several helicopters sitting in front of it. The doors were pulled open and the jet moved slowly into the hangar.

The doors closed quickly behind it as it came to a complete stop, the engines spooling down, in front of a big 'Huey' troop carrier still painted in the traditional military mottled olive drab and black colors.

As the door/ramp for the steps dropped down into place a slender, brown haired man with a short graying beard was coming up to the plane from where he had just completed securing the hangar doors.

As he reached the plane Jimmy Lester was coming down the steps with his hand held out, saying "It's been a long time Casey. Looks like your doing OK for yourself."

"Jimmy, nice to see you," he said taking his hand, a smile of welcome on his lined face. "Yeah. Things were real good for a while but they're a little tight right now." He continued, the lines in his face deepening as the worry behind them showed itself. And "Dirk with you?" he queried.

"Yeah. He's in the cockpit. He wants you to come up there while the rest of us deplane." Jimmy replied.

Casey entered the plane and as he moved towards the pilots cabin eyed the beautiful brunette who looked like she had just awakened. She was looking out of one of the port windows with open curiosity on her face. As he passed her he let out a low, almost inaudible, whistle of appreciation.

As she swung her face to him she let it break into a wide smile to let him know that she appreciated the compliment.

As Casey entered the control cabin another man slid out past him, and, going straight to the woman he began to help her gather her things to deplane. Casey's' eyes widened slightly as the man stopped, looked at the woman, then spoke quietly but forcefully to her, holding out his hand.

She looked at him with a stubborn expression on her face for a few seconds, then reached under her loose fitting shirt and removed a small .380 caliber automatic pistol, which she handed to him reluctantly.

Then his view was cut off by the closing door. He turned to face the pilots seats and was face to face with Dirk, who was sitting in the co-pilots seat. A huge, warm, grin broke out on his face as he reached out to grasp the hands extended to him by Dirk.

He shook both of them warmly. These men did not have to speak. Their eyes spoke volumes to each other!

Dirk spoke first "Casey, it's good to see you. And thanks for the help on such short notice." To which Casey replied simply "Any time. Any place. All you gotta do is ask. You know that Dirk!"

"Look Casey," Dirk went on, "we're on a tight time frame here because of some last minute changes we had to make. I'll tell you about it in a second, but first I need to ask you something."

Dirk paused for a moment, already knowing the answer to the question he was about to ask, then went on "Look old friend, answer me one question without getting your short hairs up. How bad is your business hurting?" he finished.

A little angry, but knowing his friend wouldn't ask something like that without good reason Casey answered slowly, frowning. "About one hundred fifty thousand, more or less."

"OK Casey," Dirk smiled at his friend. "Here's what's going on. There is a new game going on. It's big! Very! It's gone hard already. And I want and need you with me. Very Badly! But it's a two part commitment. I need to know if you want in before I can tell you any more!"

"Dammit Dirk," said Casey still frowning, "When have I ever said no to you?"

There was a soft knock at the cabin door and Ron Colefax stepped into the now crowded cabin as Dirk continued. "Casey, this is so big that we'll be running foreign agents, from all blocks, with our own. You Still want in?"

Casey, a small knot of excitement beginning to grow inside of him answered flatly. "Yes!"

"Good!" And "Casey, this is Ron Colefax." As the two men shook hands Dirk went on. "Ron, please tell Jimmy to fill Casey in."

"Casey, after Jimmy fills you in on the basics you can still opt out before final commitment. If you accept come back up to the cockpit and I'll break it out even more for you. Also, if you accept, you'll be going with us tomorrow night. Oh, one more thing. There will be two more men coming in by tomorrow afternoon. OK. Go talk to Jimmy. I'll wait here for you."

About forty five minutes later Casey reentered the compartment, slightly round eyed. He asked "This is for real, Dirk?"

Dirk just looked at him and nodded, then asked "In?"

Casey, still round eyed, but now with a glint in his eyes said "In!"

"That's Great!" Beamed Dirk, "And of course you'll be in charge of all transportation. Here's what I want right now! You're going to sell us your operation. That will take care of your immediate cash problems."

Then, "But you'll still run the show! Then, when this is all over everything will revert back to you, or your heirs. Good enough?" Dirk finished with a smile.

Casey just nodded, a little taken aback with the speed of things, but he had a big grin on his face again.

"Fine," said Dirk, "You can work out the details with the lady who was in the cabin as you came in. Her name, by the way, is Carmella 'Chickie' Martinez."

"That 'Chicky' Martinez?" Casey whistled, as he remembered his brashness. And his scrotum tightened as he thought of her reputation with a hand gun.

Dirk turned to Ron, who had returned and was sitting patiently in the copilots' seat, "Ron, would you help out Jimmy with getting our people over and checked into the motel by the airport entrance road. It's OK. Casey told them to expect some incognitos tonight. The story is that we're some heavy duty investors on our way to a hush-hush meeting in Canada."

"Right," Ron said, "and he probably covered it as a hot contract of in and out for himself to cover this activity."

"On the money!" dirk said. And, "What time are Rick and Tony expected in tomorrow?"

"Between ten and eleven AM." Replied Ron.

"Good. Please ask Jimmy to pick me up here in about two hours. I want you and every one else to get at least six hours sleep before we leave after dark tomorrow night. There are only seven of us going out. You, Rick, Tony, Chicky, Jimmy, and Casey."

Then, holding up a finger to make sure he had the mans undivided attention "One more thing Ron, and I'm depending on you for this! NO WEAPONS! Of any kind! That's imperative! You'll see to that?" dirk finished, looking directly into Rons' eyes.

"Yes!" Replied Ron, "But that is only six. Where will you be?"

"I'm going out in that small 'Bell Ranger' later tonight to set up a safe landing area. I already gave Casey a course, time, and frequency for contact. I'll contact and guide you in when you're near.

"But!" protested Ron, "You won't have any backup."

"Don't worry about it Ron. Other than you I'll have the best backup possible!" and Dirk would say no more about it.

Ron Colefax was a professional. He let it go. Dirk continued, "Bear with me. In about twenty four hours you will know and understand a lot more than you do now. Just promise me that you will keep an open mind about the things that you are about to learn. That's all I'll ask of you!"

Ron left to do what dirk had asked him to do, tired, but feeling better than he had in years. It had been a long time since he had worked, with the exception of Rick Davis and Tony Ebbets, with anyone of Dirks' caliber.

Testimonial to that was the quality people Dirk was bringing in. Had already brought in, in such a short period of time. The man seemed to be a magnet for quality professionals. Even those who didn't particularly like him seemed to be drawn to, and want, to work with him.

Shortly after everyone had left and the hangar was once again quiet Dirk went into the passenger cabin, reclined a seat, and stretched out on it to get a couple of hours of sleep. About an hour before dawn he awoke, sat up with a groan, and began to rub the sleep from his eyes. As he stood up he groaned again and started rubbing his lower back to ease the kinks caused by sleeping in that narrow chair.

He left the plane and went out to the Bell ranger helicopter sitting on the tarmac in front of the hangar. After a quick pre-flight check, and a call to the small control tower for flight clearance he took off, heading slightly north and west.

About three hours later he pulled one of the cell phones from a pocket and called Bill Tate. As usual, Bill answered promptly. He asked where Dirk was, and Dirk told him that he was about fifteen or so minutes out in a Bell Ranger 'copter. Bill told him that he had located two very good landing spots, both within a mile of the box canyon. Both with good cover close by.

Then, describing the smaller one, he told Dirk he would meet him there. A short while later Dirk was on the ground, and Bill was stepping out from under some near by trees.

As they came together, and after a quick embrace, Dirk stepped back and gave Bill an appraising look, thinking that bill looked better now than he had for the last five years. Bill helped Dirk camouflage the 'copter with brush and vines he had already cut for that purpose, then led him to the other landing site he had picked.

Dirk, nodding his approval, said "They'll be coming in about two hours before dawn tomorrow morning, in a sikorski nighthawk. Do we have something to use for markers?" And Bill replied that he had found six flares in his jeep.

"Good!" said Dirk, Is everything else ready?"

"Everything. I'm even getting to like that damn cat! But I still think that it gets a perverse pleasure out of scaring the hell out of me every once and a while!" Bill said, feigning anger.

As they headed for the canyon entrance Dirk clapped a friendly hand on Bills' shoulder, chuckling, while dirk sent out a questing thought. *Is that true Balor?*

Dirk heard that welcome chuckle in his mind, then, *only partly.* Then a feeling of warmth suffused his mind as Balor sent *Welcome Brother! I will come soon.*

They continued on into the canyon to see to last minute details, Dirk filling Bill in on everything that had taken place over the last three weeks.

The hours passed swiftly as they worked to get everything ready. Then they both turned in to get some much needed rest before the arrival of the big sikorski before dawn the next morning.

A half hour before the estimated arrival time they set out, Dirk to the Ranger, and its' radio, Bill to mark the landing site with the flares from Dirk's jeep.

The big sikorski came drifted along just above treetop level, its' vanes clattering, it suddenly seemed to hesitate, its' nose rearing up as if startled, then it leveled and settled quickly but gently to the ground.

As it touched down its' wheels hardly seemed to bend a blade of grass or break a twig of the dry brush. As the rotor vanes slowed the whine of its' turbine engines rose briefly, then began to disappear as the engine spooled down to a stop.

After the noise of the engines stopped the silence was shattering for a few moments. Soon a door in the side of the fuselage opened inward, figures began to emerge.

As the first reached the ground a figure detached itself from the shadows under the trees and joined those already on the ground.

The silence was broken by, "As I live and breath, 'Bad Boy' Jimmy Lester!" said Bill Tate, smiling into the darkness, only his teeth and eyes showing.

"I wish you wouldn't call me that!" said Jimmy, as he turned to face the voice, "You guys will never, it seems, let me live that down. Bill, it's nice to see you again." He said, extending his hand.

Bill gripped his hand hard, letting him know that the feeling was mutual. As the others began to descend from the big 'copters' body, Bill said to jimmy "Keep them here, tight to the clearing. We have a friend out there, a true ghost, and we don't want any heart attacks before we even begin to get going on this thing!"

"He's that bad?" Jimmy asked, looking the question, knowing, yet not understanding the warning completely. As he looked into Bills' eyes he said "I think I'm almost afraid to know." He finished.

As the pre-dawn light began to glow in the east, its' light reflecting off the bottoms of the light cloud cover in pale golden splashes, Bill got his charges in tow and began to lead them to the entrance to the canyon. Dirk was already waiting for them within.

The five men and one woman followed closely, heeding the warning passed on by Jimmy. None of these people had any idea of what they were about to learn. Each would have to deal with whatever it was in their own way. One thing was certain though. All were in for some startling surprises.

CHAPTER EIGHT
Surprises, Integration, Cohesion

The Ship

They entered the cut entrance to the canyon, having to step around sharp projections, over fallen rocks and tree limbs as they progressed. Then they were through and into the canyon proper. They saw small and mid sized trees, a lot of low brushwood, and the ground was a little damp and spongy.

About one hundred twenty five feet in front of them, unseen behind the chameleon screen, stood Dirk. The light now coming over the rim of the canyon wall highlighting the half smile on his face as he waited for Bills' cue to emerge.

They all looked around again, seeking whatever it was that they might have missed at first glance, noting little of any significance from their first impression.

Jimmy Lester, a frown growing on his face, and looking around again said to Bill, "Alright, where is this great big surprise we have been waiting for?"

"I think you will find out soon enough." Bill Said, a sly smile breaking out on his face. While looking at the spot where Dirk should become visible he saw a slight flicker. He said, "Just keep looking at the center of the canyon!"

As their eyes focused where directed Dirk walked forward, becoming visible to them. This act was accompanied by the hisses of several indrawn breaths. These people were very astute and grasped very quickly what the revelation of this technology could mean to them in their upcoming battles

As Dirk walked up to the group he smiled at the understanding he saw in their eyes, and their admiration for the impact his theatrics had produced.

As they gathered around him he said, "Now you really begin to believe what you have been told. But the reality won't hit you until you have been given the whole ten cent tour we've set up for you."

"Please, all of you, hold your questions until we sit down for a short conference we'll have after the tour is done, and after we eat. Then you can ask and I'll tell you all that I can. I also want to give you some of my thoughts. So please follow Bill and myself. Stay close to us until you get used to the chameleon device. The effect will cease after you get about ten feet inside its outer perimeter. With that he turned and led off. Bill, following, said, "Follow me."

The group passed into and through the screening effects of the chameleon device, and as they emerged into the inner unaffected area, their eyes grew even rounder with wonder at the sight before them.

The ship was a wondrous sight, even sitting so low to the ground, its' landing struts barely able to keep its' belly six inches above the marshy ground of the canyon. By human standards it was huge! It was about forty yards (120 ft.) wide by almost a hundred yards (300 ft.) long, and nearly twenty yards (60 ft.) high. For the moment its' size was overwhelming! Awesome!

The ships' skin was the color of age darkened bronze, the areas of the open holds and entry port were bright spots against its' dark mass. Its' lines were clearly designed for functionality, yet they were clean and graceful none the less for a thing so large.

As the group stood there gazing at the ship Dirk dropped another bombshell on them. Knowing as he did so that he must make them accept and understand how much they were going to have to learn and adapt to as part of this new core group of his.

That they must learn and accept the fact that they were not the center of the universe, just a small part of a very large community. And that there were some very, very big and bad people out there who might not take kindly to their meddling in matters that they considered private.

Dirk dropped the bombshell by saying, "This is one of their smallest space going ships, used mainly as a planetary lander and solar system transport. Their regular space ships are fifty to one hundred times bigger than the size of this one!"

One of the group said, awe in his voice, "You're kidding!" And "That thing is at least three times the size of our biggest space vehicle!"

"None the less," replied Dirk, "That is the case. Let's go inside now." Then they were given a preliminary introduction to some of the technology of their new, other worldly allies.

At first they were overcome because, with the exception of bill and himself, they all had retained some degree of skepticism concerning his story about the aliens. As new wonders were presented, again and again, their faces turned grim as the truth of the story and reality converged!

And that grimness turned to stone resolve as the photographs of the dead agent, with his alien rider were produced and shown around to the entire group. The alien riders' nature and general intent were also explained.

After Dirk had taken them throughout the entire small ship, describing and explaining its' functions as well as he could, he and Bill took the group to the galley for a meal. One prepared by the auto-chef which Bill had finally learned to program. After that they talked far into the night, finishing up near dawn. Dirk assigned them all sleeping compartments saying they could begin again after some much needed sleep and thinking time.

Core Formations

A few hours later they were at it again, asking questions, making suggestions, and asking more questions. Questions that had a habit of raising even more questions. Questions that could not possibly be answered at this time.

Now Dirk was pleased, because they were beginning to think and act as part of a whole instead of as individuals. This was a crux point for them because they were professionals who were, each and every one of them, highly competent individuals used to operating on that basis. This was the beginning of their melding into a whole.

For them to have half a chance at surviving this it would be necessary for these people, and many more like them, to subsume themselves and their egos for a common goal. And work not only for a goal in common but to work towards that goal together as one race, one species!

And they must do so for one reason only. The survival of Mankind! This would be hard for each of them, for it would mean that they must learn to accept survival as a group effort instead of an individual one.

These were talented, intelligent, and very hard people, and it would not be easy. But, from the set looks on the faces around him he was feeling less and less doubt that it could, would be done.

Shortly, Dirk knew, they would start planning for a very uncertain future.

Later, alone, reviewing the gist of what had been brought up, and out so far, Dirk was trying to determine when, and how, to tell them the rest of the story about the Chai.

And the new relationship he had with them as well as their method of interacting with others. It would not be easy, and, the circumstances would have to be right. Of this much he was certain.

He was also certain, perforce, that it would have to be soon!

Revelations and Direction

It was eight a.m. and Dirk was still tired. He had, after his thoughts had begun to chase each other around the inside of his skull, gotten little sleep. Having gone to bed late he now felt like a too often rung out dish rag.

He took a cold shower to get himself completely awake because he had scheduled a nine a.m. meeting to start some short and intermediate term planning. Planning that he hoped, some of which, they would be able to implement quickly and effectively.

These people were self starting, competent, and hard as nails. They were used to working in structured environments that gave their efforts direction and purpose. This he would try to establish for them this morning.

As they began to arrive in the galley-lounge, settling themselves in with coffee, or whatever, he settled himself in as well, listening to their small talk to gauge their frame of mind.

As he listened, a small smile played at the corners of his mouth, the only indication of his personal pleasure in the correctness in the choice of his people. A short time later he called their attention back to the business at hand.

He opened the session saying, "OK gang, listen up!" waited a moment for their full attention, then "There are still a lot things yet that you need to know!"

"First, Though you have assimilated a lot in a very short time period there is still a lot more you need to know about. Because of the present circumstances we are constrained for time and I can't give it all to you right now. But I will get it to you soon. I promised you that you wouldn't have to work in the dark, and I meant it! Right now we have some people waiting for us in St. Louis, and a new organization to set up in a very short period of time."

Dirk paused to gather his thoughts, Then. "You're here because you're among the very best there are at what you do, and you haven't forgotten how to care about what you do and who you are. You, and a few more people I want you to find and persuade to join us, are going to become the nucleus of a new organization for the protection of our planet and our race. We will also be the major force in the way that these things are done and run!"

"We, all of us, will be facing two enemies in the beginning. The first will be the established power bases. We will be going in the faces of the existing intelligence services, and you all know how territorial they are. At best they will try to absorb us and take over control. The worst case scenario will be that they will try to stop us dead in our tracks. We have some serious advantages, but do not underestimate them! As all of you know they have some very, very, good people."

"The second enemy is the new one. The one you were introduced to the other night via the photo's you were shown. That enemy is the truly deadly one. That enemy doesn't give one wit for our petty squabbles, but it will try to use them against us."

"One of its' best tactics is to cause as much divisiveness as possible so we will end up fighting each other, and forget about them. This will not happen because we know they exist, and what they are! So here is what I have in mind. And after I lay it out for you, you can kick it around, then we will decide on what actions to take first."

Dirk stopped, waiting for a few moments and watching their faces as what he had said began to sink in.

Although he hadn't told them that much he had given them a focus point, as he had planned on doing before he had started explaining things the way he saw them. That focus point was collecting people that they needed to fill out their nucleus, and to fill other positions in their new, fledgling, organization.

From the looks on their faces the wheels were already beginning to turn with purpose. He cleared his throat to let them know that he was ready to continue, "This is the way I see it!"…

"First, I want 'Chicky' to set up a front company for us, in her own inimitable fashion. You know what's needed for this type of operation, 'Chicky', so I won't belabor the point. But there are two things you do need to know about for all of our sakes."

"One: People know that you've dropped out, so you've got to do everything from deep cover. No ties to you or us."

"Two: We are going to need money. A lot of money for this to work! Right now we only have about a million and a half in cash for you to play with. But I may be able to get you another million within a month. This part of the operation is in your hands. You run it in whatever manner you think is right. Where money is concerned you are the go to Guru!"

Dirk paused, thinking, then "Actually, there is a third item that you may be able to help with. We need to acquire a small, but good, hi-tech electronics firm. Can you do it?" Dirk stopped, waiting for her answer.

For a moment or two, as he watched her, she had a far away look in her eyes, and when they cleared she looked up at him with a small, satisfied, cat smile on her face. She nodded emphatically. So he went on to the next item on his mental list.

"Rick. Since you will be handling field and operational security I want you to keep working with Jimmy. You and he together can put together three or four teams of the best people available if you pool your knowledge."

"Also, work with Ron to clear the people he wants to keep for our own use. One thing! Make sure you keep Tony up to date on all of your people, so there will be no cross ups with internal security!"

"Your teams will be very important to us in the near future, so if there is anything you need please see Bill or Carmella to get it. Can Do?"

At Rick's' nod he went to the next item. "Ron, the same goes for you as well. Pick your people and clear them through Tony. You've got some good people now, but you're going to need more, and soon. So go over your lists again. OK on that?"

At a nod from him, he went on to Tony.

"Tony, We've been over your particular problem of people, so do what you need to do. I will have more info for you about additional sites in a couple of days. The same goes for you as Ron and Rick. If you need something that you can't get for yourself see Bill or Carmella."

"One very important item, I want you to pick ten of the very best men on your list for this site! Remember, everything must be kept very low key here for a couple of months until a final disposition can be made for it."

"I want you to make this site as tight as a misers you know what within a two mile perimeter. Use sono-sensors and infrared trip sensors on the farthest perimeters. We have some very interesting sensors here on the ship that can be adapted for your use also. For equipment see Jimmy, Carmella or Bill. Can do?"

Tony just smiled, so Dirk went on again.

"Jimmy, I need you to find two more people for me. You know both of them so that should help you in finding them. I want, and need, them as fast as possible. The first is Jerry Burke, AKA to most of the rest of you as G. 'Whiz' Burke. I want him here ASAP! We have some equipment here that can, and needs to be, modified for our own use."

"I also want him to work with Bill to develop some new, and very nasty, toys for us to entertain the opposition with. As you all know, he is one of the best, if not the best, people around with 'elint' (electronic intelligence) and counter measures equipment. I think that with him here we will have a very large advantage going into any situation."

"The other person I need you to find is John Crow. He will be very hard to find, and even harder to contact. But, I do have a contact name for you. And Jimmy, I don't have to remind you to be very careful how you approach him! I want you to give this top priority! Can you do it within seventy two hours?"

At Jimmy's "I'll try my best." Dirk nodded and turned to Casey.

"Casey, stand up and let everyone take a good look at you please." As Casey complied, Dirk said "Casey will head up our 'covert' and 'ultra covert' transportation for all operations personally, and transportation in general. He will also be working with G. 'whiz' to develop some surprises for the opposition. Casey, did you speak to Carmella as I asked you to?" At Casey's nod he continued.

"OK people, go through the ship again. Ask questions, and write them down. And think innovative thoughts! We'll have a couple of days before heading out to our new headquarters in St. Louis, and I'd like some of that innovative thought as input in writing before we leave."

Dirk stood there, thinking for half a minute then said, "I want you to stay with me for a minute Jimmy, Rick, Casey. The rest of you get started."

And, turning to the three named, said "Meet me in my cabin in about half an hour. I'll have some special information and instructions for you then!"

He then turned, walking quickly, and went out of the lounge, and on out of the ship. He continued, passing through the entrance to the canyon, and on until he was following a faint path through the woods along the river.

Dirk and TuLan, Conversations in Innovative Thought

As he walked along the path, and as TuLan had taught him to do, Dirk made the mental effort that enabled him to have direct mental contact with TuLan, to the fore part of his consciousness.

He said, *I need to know a couple of things right now TuLan, one of them being this. Can any of our people learn directly from the teaching machine I remember seeing in your memories when we melded?*

TuLan gave a mental start, again surprised at the acuity of the mind of his host, *what do you need that machine for Dirk?* Letting some of his surprise show to his host. *That machine can be extremely dangerous if it is used improperly!* he finished.

Dirk's reply, after a momentary pause, was again a surprise to TuLan. Because it showed a great deal of forethought for both the present and the future in its' content, *as you can see, from the thoughts I am showing you, I am bringing in an expert in the electronics field. I want him to study your ship and it' equipment in the hope of developing some new equipment for our group.*

That equipment, most of it, will be radical by our earth standards. We could use some of the equipment from the ship, but the real problem with that is that that equipment is irreplaceable. I think that if we could use our own equipment, upgrading and modifying it by adding some of the features from your equipment it would save some time trying to train someone to use it.

And if a unit were lost, or destroyed, it could be replaced. But to do that, my man needs an understanding of some of the principals which make your equipment work, so he can apply them to our equipment without destroying yours. He will also be able to innovate, creating things that neither you nor I can think of right now, Dirk finished in a rush.

Yes Dirk. The machine can be modified for human use, but it will take several hours to do so. But also a warning! That machine can be very dangerous to the user if they stay under its influence for too long, or improperly use it. It could overload the mind and burn out the users' brain! We must make absolutely certain that whoever uses it abides by very strict rules. Are we in agreement on this point? Dirk readily agreed, and so doing turned his steps back towards the ship.

Meanwhile, TuLan was mulling over all of the ramifications that being with his new host was bringing home to him.

He was amazed at the single minded drive that his host was capable of bringing to bear on any task, and at the shear amount of thought and detail he seemed to be able to process in such short periods of time. Already he had thought out a course of action and put into motion a plan that would have taken his own race years to implement.

There were two matters that were bothering TuLan about his host. Matters that he had never run into before, or even heard of for that matter, in any of the other compatible host species. The first was that his host seemed to have an area of his mind that TuLan could not penetrate. This was something he must give a great deal of thought to and investigate more thoroughly. The second was even more disturbing, if that were possible, than the first. His host seemed to have the ability to communicate with the cat thing on a plane, or level that was completely blank to him.

He must give this much thought! He felt that the answers would be very important in the future! He didn't know how right his feeling was!

CHAPTER NINE
Needs and Acquisitions

Needs

Sitting in Dirk's cabin, awaiting his return, Jimmy Lester was thinking about the strange, very strange, events of the last couple of days.

He knew and trusted Dirk without reservation, but he had never seen him so alive, so purposeful, in all the years he'd known him. For that matter, he thought, he had not felt this good himself in far too long a time. That is until just recently. At that moment the door opened and Dirk walked in, followed by Rick and Casey.

As the door closed Dirk asked them to sit, doing so himself. After looking up at the cabin ceiling for a moment, he started by saying, "Jimmy, I need John Crow very badly to set up a very tough extraction, I need him, and the people he can bring in, and his covert contacts to pull off this extraction. This is something I know. I only have one dubious contact for him! I say dubious because I don't think he will contact her."

"What I don't know is why he went under so deeply. What I do know is how to get word to him, but that's all. It's going to take every trick you know to find him if he doesn't want to surface.

That's why I'm putting Casey at your disposal for this, and giving you Rick and five of his best men to get this done. As well as whatever assets you yourself choose to employ. You'll probably need them all!"

"The contacts name is Amy McCoy. She is the daughter of one of his best friends who was killed on a black 'ops' mission a few years ago, and he has been looking out for her every since then. She is an attorney in NYC and I'll give you her number before you leave. You will give her a message for him, and it must be stated exactly as I tell it to you. The message is 'The hawk is stooping-urgent-urgent-urgent! The message means that I really need his help. It's from a code we used a few years ago."

"Contact her every twenty four hours at a pre-arranged time for any reply. When you make contact set up a pick up and bring him here, to the ship, not to

St. Louis. I'll be back here by then, in about four days to meet you, and set some other things in motion." Dirk finished

"I need John Crow," he said, looking directly at the three of them for a full thirty seconds, "Because I'm going to try and bring Yuri Garov in on this!"

He sat there looking at their stunned faces. Stunned because everyone even remotely connected to this line of work knew who the famed head of Soviet Counter Intelligence was!

His was one of the most feared, and respected, names in all of the various intelligence services because he always seemed to be at least three moves ahead of everyone else, and had spoiled many operations all over the world.

"Are you Crazy!!" said Jimmy heatedly, "He swore that he would break both of your arms, and legs, after that 'op' you pulled in Kuwait, leaving him with egg on his face!"

"I have two good reasons," said Dirk calmly, to believe that he might just take my offer."

"First: I heard, about a couple of months ago, that his own people seemed to be extremely pissed at him for some as yet unknown reason."

"Second: I think that he might like to meet me as much as I'd like to meet him!"

Dirk sat musing for a moment before saying, "Listen to me Jimmy, Rick, Casey. We are facing an enemy who doesn't give a lick about our petty squabbles, vendettas, or political preferences or differences. That enemy will use all of those to divide and conquer us, as well as the weapons he may have that we know nothing about!"

"We must, must, begin to seek out and enlist the best and brightest from former allies and foes alike, and learn to work with them in a united front. As one people! Or our cause is doomed to a long, slow death!"

"As far as I'm concerned, if we can get Yuri Garov to work with us we will have one of the worlds most brilliant and talented tactical planners on our team! And, as sure as I would hate to have to face him again, I truly believe that we are going to need his help!"

So saying, Dirk brought the meeting to an end, asking all of them to move as quickly and carefully as possible to accomplish the task before them.

The next morning as the people in this new and excited group began to move out to start working on their assigned tasks there was a look of renewal in their eyes.

And also a definite spring to their steps.

John Crow

John Crow was very angry man at the moment, and also a little confused. He had been dodging two different tails for the last week, and now it appeared that a third one was trying to pick him up.

The first one, he was sure, belonged to some very angry members of Chilean Military Intelligence. Their anger arising from his having spirited a member of their general staff out of their country, under their very noses. The defecting general had information for sale that could compromise some long term operations that were just beginning to bear fruit for them.

The other tail was from one of his own governments' agencies. He was used to this one because the part time surveillance had begun five years ago after he had gone freelance. It did not bother him much because it was intermittent, and the agents being used were a clumsy lot. But this new one seemed different!

This third, and newest, one was the most worrisome of the lot because he was being very careful not to tip the other two to his presence, while not trying to hide his presence from Crow! It was almost like he would like to make contact with Crow without the others knowing about him.

This might tie in with the strange message he had gotten from his very private message drop this morning. It read 'Someone you know and trust wants to speak with you. Set time, date, place. Your drop, and a telephone number for a simple yes or no reply. He had left a response with his drop contact, 'more info on friends' ID! Same contact.' And it was almost time to call his contact.

John Crow knew a great many people. He also trusted very, very, few of them. Whoever was attempting to contact him was either trying to set a deliberate trap, or it was someone he did know who was being very security conscious.

John Crow, at the age of thirty five, stood six feet one inches tall and weighed in at two hundred twenty five pounds. And little, if any of that, was given over to fat. He had a light reddish brown complexion that had been much darkened by long exposure to the sun and elements and his hair was as black as the feathers of his namesake, though now showing some gray at the temples.

He was slim in the hips and deceptively wide in the shoulders. His mode of dress generally hid the fact of his tremendous upper body strength. His facial features were somewhat rugged, but not in a coarse manner. His most arresting feature, however, were the cool gray eyes that seemed to take in everything at once.

His personality was quiet, almost reserved, the eyes often expressing sadness at what life had so far shown him. But those same eyes could freeze you in place when he was angry.

He was normally a quiet spoken man, with a light baritone voice that, when he chose to use it, could literally terrify you with the volume of sound it could produce.

He moved with a curiously gliding gait that was the result of many years training in the various forms of martial arts.

Crow was an ex-captain in the army. He had served two tours of duty in the South East Asian conflict and, just prior to going freelance, had worked for several years for the CIA special ops' division. Now, as a freelance agent, he worked doing high risk penetrations and extractions for his own, and other, free world government and private agencies.

John Crow was a very dangerous man whose skills commanded very high fees, and the respect of those he dealt with. Both friend and foe alike!

John Crow was also, at present, an angry man! He was angry for two reasons, the first of which was the Chileans. They seemed to want to rough him up, or even make a hit on him for the loss of face, and tactical position, he had caused them over losing their general. Not 'cricket' at all!

The other was the report he had in his pocket. It was from his personal doctor, and was the results from his last checkup. The doctor wanted him to come in for a complete blood workup because it appeared that he was developing some form of kidney disorder.

John Crow was an angry man. He was also afraid! Afraid of the loss of use of this wonderful machine that was his body which had served him so well for all of these years.

He was also afraid of a long, lingering death! And too, the helpless state leading up to it! Yes, he was very angry! But he also held onto the deepest hope that the doctor was wrong. He needed something to do to take his mind off of that type of dead end thinking.

He decided to find out who it was that he knew and trusted. Having made his decision, he began the moves necessary to lose the people who were following him. He lost the clumsy one in the first thirty minutes. The Chilean was better.

He lost the Chilean by popping in and out of the several entrances and exits of a department store. It was time to move to a pay phone with some seclusion. The third one was still with him but he couldn't spot him yet because of the crowded streets. He decided to head for the downtown bus station to make his call.

He entered the bus station by its' main entrance and began slipping in and out of the lines of people waiting to buy tickets or to board their buses, hoping to catch a glimpse of the third follower.

Finally, he went to the telephone kiosk in the rear center of the huge room. From it he could make his call, while having a clear view of the entire room. As he dialed the number given to him he swept the room again, but still couldn't spot the third man, who he felt to be nearby.

On the third ring the phone was answered, a voice that he felt he should know asking, "Do we meet?" Before answering Crow asked, "Is there a message for me?"

There was the slightest pause before the voice, he thought he should know, answered immediately, "The hawk is stooping! Urgent! Urgent! Urgent!"

Hearing this Crow immediately said, "Call my contact at eight AM sharp!"

The voice said, "Good." Then, "By the way, look about fifteen yards over your left shoulder!" and the line went dead.

As he looked where he had been bidden, the third man stepped out from behind some lockers and nodded to him, then turned, and putting away a cell phone left the building.

Crow thought that he should know this man, after seeing his face clearly just now. But if he did he hadn't seen him for many years.

Crow nodded to himself in appreciation of the other mans skill, thinking to himself that this was getting more interesting by the minute. He had not heard that phrase for almost five years, but knew exactly what it meant, and who it was from.

Jimmy Lester walked out of the bus station feeling very pleased with himself. He was also very thankful to Rick Davis for the two men he had loaned him. Jimmy was well versed in surveillance work, and even with the two extra men he had been hard pressed to keep up with Crow. The man moved like a shadow, and twice as fast!

It was pure luck, for jimmy, that his DEA contact had known about the Chilean affair. And even more so, for him, that he had known about some 'attaches' (military Intel. Types) who had converged on Atlanta for unspecified reasons.

If it hadn't been for the clumsy DIA agent stumbling all over the place, like a mad bull in a china shop, he might never have spotted Crow.

The phone call just ended had capped off three days of very intensive and strenuous work. Now he had to answer the email he had gotten from G. 'whiz' Burke, and, knowing Burke, if he was being restrained from leaving after completing a contract, he was likely to extricate himself forcefully, and explosively!

As he stepped into the car waiting for him at the curb he said to the driver "Tim, call Arnie on your handset and tell him that we will pick him up behind the station." Then "Let's get back to the hotel and get some lunch. By the way, to both of you a very well done."

After their first real sit down meal in more than a week Jimmy and his men were going over what they thought might lie in their immediate future.

Jimmy was saying, "I figure three more days here to tie up any loose ends on this part of the 'op'."

"Tim, after lunch, give Casey a call. Let him know that we will need transport out of here to Boston by ten AM Saturday, and that we will need the pilot to stay on standby for one or two days up there before returning to home plate. I'd like a positive confirmation on that before eight PM. OK?"

Turning to the other man he said, "Ernie, I think it might be a good idea to change the model and color of our rental car. Let's not get sloppy just when things are starting to go our way." Both men gave him rueful smiles, remembering the last three days of hectic activity.

Back in their suite now, Jimmy was pulling his laptop computer from its' case, and saying to Tim, "I'll be online for at least two hours composing and sending email to our other quarry if you need me for anything." Tim left to make his calls.

Necessities

After setting up the small laptop and connecting the phone line Jimmy sat for a few minutes thinking about the email he had sent to G 'whiz' Burke two days ago, and the response he had gotten back almost immediately.

The original message had gone thus;

Bad Boy seeks whiz kid.

New game is afoot!

New players and old friends!

Much ado about something new!

Do you want to play?

The reply had come back in scarcely half an hour and read thus;

Whiz kid for Bad Boy.

Whose game is it, and where do we play?

Some old friends would be welcome right now!

I think so!?

Jimmy's next message had to be to the point, and it also had to demand a yes or no answer, so he began to type;

Bad Boy wants the whiz kid!

Old friends are good friends!

Grand Game! Lots of new gizmos!!

IN OR OUT? ONE TIME QUERRY!

Jimmy studied the message for a minute or two then clicked on the 'send' button and sat back to await an answer, knowing that Burke would now be looking for this next message.

As he began the tedium of waiting his mind began to range back over the past short weeks that had passed since this astonishing adventure had begun with that phone call on a line he thought to be completely secure.

The momentum and surprises had been staccato like, and had not let up one little bit. Now he was having the time of his life! He had not felt so alive, and worthwhile, in far to long a time! As this last thought was going through his mind the computer beeped, letting him know that he had incoming mail. Sure enough the message was from G. 'whiz' Burke.

As jimmy scrolled down the message his face broke into a wider and wider grin as he congratulated himself on using the right key words, 'new game' and 'new gizmos' in his last message. Those key words were as unresistable a lure for Burke as they were for most of those who plied the intelligence field.

The incoming message also confirmed what he had learned from his own information sources;

Whiz kid to Bad Boy.

Am always interested in new games and new toys!

Present nest is very confining!

Old friends help in learning to fly would be most appreciated!!

I want to play! I want to play! I want to play!!!

Jimmy, resettling himself at the keyboard, thought for a moment then began to type;

Bad Boy to Whiz kid.

Your application to play is accepted!

Stay in your nest, and get some rest.

Momma Bird will do her best.

As he hit the send button Jimmy was already planning his moves to pick up the brilliant but sometimes errant G. 'Whiz' Burke. The key to scooping up Burke from his present predicament was basically very simple.

The people G. 'Whiz' was presently doing his work for were not nice people at all. At this time they had him installing anti bugging devices and programs on their computers and communications lines. It seems that they were siphoning several million dollars out of several retirement funds under their control and diverting it into offshore accounts. And didn't want any heat from any of the various law enforcement agencies that might have jurisdiction over them. Therefore Jimmy thought he could use a revolving door scam to extricate the 'Whiz' from his present predicament.

This scam, when done properly, was simple, but very effective to disappear someone. By using real or fake law officers the target was picked up for questioning. Brought to, and into an official building, then right back out the rear or garage entrance, and taken to whatever destination or pickup point was set up for them.

So thinking, Jimmy suited thought to action, setting up an internet fax link to a close friend, who also happened to be an FBI agent. Said agent, it also happened, owed Jimmy a very large favor. In spades! The fax read;

BB to agent David Price.

FBI Headquarters, Boston Mass.

There is a game afoot.

Urgent! Contact me soonest!

Usual methods.

Clicking on the send button, Jimmy prepared to wait for an answer, knowing that this type of message would be gotten to his friend as quickly as possible. The people at the 'Bureau' weren't exactly sure of who he was, just that he had been helpful to them several times in the past. They had tried, once, to trace him, but he had pulled his head in and completely disappeared. Those actions had caused them to fumble a case that he had been helping with by supplying them with directional leads.

It had been particularly rankling to both parties because the case involved child pornography. They had not, to the best of his knowledge, tried to find out who he was since then. Just accepting, gratefully, the help when it came because his information was always pinpoint accurate.

Jimmy did not like the 'Bureau', or any other form of 'Big Brother' type of government for that matter. He, however, did see the need for a centralized police authority for a country as big as his was. But he also felt that they were way too intrusive, and wielded much too much generalized power for such a central authority. The temptation to abuse that much authority and power was, all too often, converted from temptation to reality.

Almost all of the bureaucracies and agencies abused their power and authority, bypassing the checks and balances set in place to protect the citizenry. They did this by writing into their operational bylaws the right to institute and use phrases like 'secret', 'need to know', and 'national security'. Jimmy was one person who refused to accept most of those abuses by learning how to sidestep most of them.

The sad part was that so many really good people, trying to do a good job, accepted these abuses as a necessary evil to accomplishing their work. Well, when they did this, who was looking out for the little guy? He wanted to know this because, when confronted by the might of a whole government, every individual was a little guy!

"Enough wool gathering!" Jimmy chided himself, "Get on with the task at hand." He returned his thoughts to getting both Crow and Burke back to the ship, quickly and quietly.

The real problem was making a face to face contact with Crow, and without an audience. Those Chilean 'intel' types were nasty customers, and didn't take being foiled well at all. On impulse Jimmy picked up the phone and dialed a number he seldom used. When it was answered he asked for 'Jack'. The quick response was "Wait one."

A moment later a gruff voice asked "Who are you, and what do you want?" Using a code established years before Jimmy answered "It's BB, and I'm at bat!" The gruff voice softened perceptibly as it responded with, "It's been a long time BB! How can I help?"

I need two pea shooters, non lethal, fast acting sleep agents, in Atlanta by tomorrow afternoon! Can you do it?" Jimmy asked.

After another short pause the gruff voice asked, "Personal or impersonal?"

"Impersonal" Jimmy said quickly, and "Over night express would do nicely." and "Usual method of payment?"

The gruff voice on the other end said, "Give me the address. You'll have them by three p.m. your time. By the way, there's no charge for this one. I owe you big time for that help with my sister!"

After giving the required information Jimmy Said, "Thank you." Then, "What are friends for?"

"To few real ones left in this world!" the gruff voice said with real feeling, and the line went dead. Jimmy sat back smiling, for he now knew exactly how he would get Crow out and leave a message for the Chileans at the same time.

Within minutes of completing his last call the cell phone he always kept in his jacket pocket chirped. As he flipped it open the screen lit up with the 'page' function icon flashing, and a number below that. The number had a Boston Mass. area code. That was fast, he thought to himself as he began dialing the number. When the phone was answered he asked, "David, are you sure this line is secure?"

Getting a confirmation he went right into the subject of his needs, explaining the situation and what he wanted from his friend. He ended with, "You owe me at least one big favor David. Normally I wouldn't call it in like this but time is short, and you being the real deal, would make it work more smoothly. Can you do it?"

"You know damned well I'll do it for you BB!" David Price replied with some little passion coloring his words. And, "I owe you more than one big favor, and I was wondering how I would ever be able to pay them back."

"Will this cause you any heat with your people?" Jimmy asked, real concern in his voice.

"Not as far as doing something for you is concerned. Your information is so good that we can usually walk those cases right through the court." The FBI agent said, deep respect for his unknown mentor showing in his reply.

So Jimmy gave him the place to pick up G. 'Whiz' Burke. The timing for the pickup. And the location where the delivery was to be made. After pausing for a moments thought Jimmy said, "I may have something very good for you, so keep a look out for a message from me. It may come in a very short time."

With a little puzzlement in his voice the FBI agent said he would tell those who forwarded his messages that anything coming in from BB would be given top priority.

"Thank you David. I really appreciate you." Jimmy said, and hung up. He was thinking that David Price would be a major asset in the future. He would in the future, also remember thinking that thought, and be extremely glad of his good judgement!

Gerry 'G. Whiz' Burke

Gerry, 'G. Whiz', Burke screwed up his very Irish face in a huge white smile. Now there was a second very good reason his present employers would not try to disappear him! The first was they were afraid that he could crash the new system that he had just completed building for them, even without being there to do so.

Now, if he were just a little better at money management, he would not have found it necessary to take on this job in the first place. He'd had a bad feeling about it from the beginning, but the money was really needed, and just too good to pass up. Now his employers, despite his reputation for never disclosing anything about any of his clients, were too nervous to let him walk away from them.

But not letting him walk was a big mistake on their part, because once he became sure that they weren't going to play fair he had programmed into their system a couple of very nasty surprises. And once they had brought him to where they were now holding him he had let them know about them in no uncertain terms.

He was being held in an executive apartment, converted from an office, in one of the complex of buildings they owned, while they frantically searched for the time bombs he had programmed into their system.

Fat chance they had of finding them! He was one of the best in the world when it came to computers. They should have let him walk! Even as much as he had come to dislike them and what they were doing, he wouldn't have said anything about them.

These were not nice people at all. Not only were they skimming millions from their own employees pension fund, they were also skimming millions from several others that they managed. Even a state employees pension fund!

They were banking the money in offshore accounts that were untraceable to them, and the irony was that they were using the system he had designed and programmed to do it.

The system he had built was originally designed to prohibit external access to the company's networking and communications lines. While checking the systems operation, he had discovered a programming fluke that allowed them to transfer funds out without the transfer being traceable back to the system. He had caught on to them when they told him not to bother trying to fix it.

It was at this point that he began running some closer checks on them and their associates. He didn't like what he found! They were a nasty lot, and it appeared that a couple of earlier programmers had come up missing after working for them. The second reason was the last email he had gotten from Jimmy 'Bad Boy' Lester, just before they had brought him here. He particularly liked the last two lines of 'Bad Boys' email;

Stay in your nest, and get some rest!

Momma bird will do her best!

He felt much better knowing that Jimmy apparently knew who his captors were and where he was being held. One of the things that intrigued him about their email conversations was the reference to a new game being afoot. He had not heard one word about any new games from anyone, in or out of his network of contacts. And he had some very good contacts.

Two things though, the term new players could mean almost anything. But 'Old Friends' meant that some of the players were people he most likely knew personally and trusted, or were people he had worked with in the past and could most likely trust.

One thing was for sure though, if Jimmy Lester were playing in this game personally, it was a very big game indeed. He was intrigued also by the phrase 'lots of new gizmos'. That was a phrase calculated to draw him in, he knew, and it had certainly done its' job well! He had committed himself to something he had absolutely no knowledge of whatsoever. He must really be getting old!

Gerry Burke A.K.A. G. 'Whiz' burke was a multi faceted anomaly to most of those who knew him, and to those who knew about him. He had been a fully trusted member of the IRA at the age of fifteen, and one of the very few men to ever walk away from them at the age of twenty two. The reason for his departure, it was reported at the time, given to his superiors was this statement; "I'll have no more to do with an outfit given to the wanton killing of innocents, no matter what the reason!"

He was an ex-patriot Irishman who was now an American citizen. Burke was, in appearance, what most people thought an Irishman looked like. With ruddy complexioned skin and hair that was the red-orange that was called carrot top. Now at the age of thirty eight he stood six feet tall and weighed in at one hundred ninety pounds.

As said, Burke was an anomaly! A deadly and efficient killer at the age of fifteen, he was also a self taught genius in the fields of electronics, and anything to do with computers. He had never been formally tested to judge his capabilities, but those in the know, and those who'd had the opportunity to work with him, usually went away with a smile and scratching their heads in wonderment!

Gerry had been very pleased to hear from Jimmy Lester, especially under his present circumstances. Of the many associates and contacts that Gerry had, Jimmy 'Bad Boy' Lester was one of the two that Gerry would even consider calling a friend.

The other, John Dirk, he had not heard from in at least two years. He felt an affinity to Jimmy Lester because he, like himself, was a disaffected patriot who did not want to do the dirty work for the 'so called' politicians any more.

He had known, of course, that Jimmy had pulled his head in and gone completely under for a while. But it was real news to him that Jimmy had tied up with anyone for a new game. He hadn't heard one peep from any of his contacts about a new game starting, and he should have!

And this game had to be a big one, if Jimmy 'Bad Boy' Lester were directly involved in it. Also, he couldn't figure out who the 'old friends, were that Jimmy had referred to were. Because most, or all, of the people he knew who were players were either sitting in deep cover or were tied up with one or the other of the governmental agencies. And to top it all off 'Bad Boy' had used his own natural curiosity to get to him, too. He had used the 'new gadgets and gizmos' hook perfectly, and hooked him good!

This was strange, too, because there weren't many new gadgets or gizmos around that he wasn't familiar with or at least aware of. Well, no matter what kind of new game he had gotten himself into it couldn't be any worse than the situation he was in now. Could it?

Knowing that however 'Bad Boy' intended to get him out it would be, in the least very interesting. So, to pass some of the time, he began setting up a sub routine on his laptop computer, which he had forced them to let him keep.

This so he could periodically check in with the system he had built for them to keep it from crashing, as he had told them it would do if he didn't keep checking in with it.

This sub routine program he would download to the main system program, using the backdoor access he had planted in the main program. This new sub routine aplet would hide itself inside the transfer routine his employers were using to steal millions from their employees pension fund. And would, the next time they transferred funds out, automatically transfer all of the stolen money back into the pension fund accounts.

Plus anything else they might have put into those hidden accounts. That would teach them to threaten G. 'Whiz' Burke!

Little did he know at that time that that was the least of his erstwhile employers worries, because 'Bad Boy' had already set them up for a fall from his end!

John Crow

Things were definitely getting interesting thought John Crow to himself as he watched the man leave the bus station through one of the side exits. More so because he realized that he knew the face belonging to the man. As Crow moved out of the station himself, going in the opposite direction, he was pushing his mind to supply a name to the face. Moving back through the city he put the question of the face/name on a back burner. He was now paying particular attention to possible leading tails, being well aware that it was sometimes easier to follow someone with a two person team that stayed just a little ahead of the quarry.

A good leading tail team would be hard to spot so he used the simple technique of doubling back a couple of time to see if he could trip up anyone using such a team. This technique was used to catch someone suddenly stopping and reversing course. He was also paying close attention to his back trail. Thankfully, he arrived back at his apartment without further incident.

Crow had taken a quick shower and was preparing a meager meal of plain yogurt and a salad. The only thing he seemed able to keep down lately. Suddenly he said, to himself, in a very chagrined tone, "Well I'll be dammed!" The name that went with the face was Jimmy Lester. It was no wonder that he was so good.

With this realization, of putting a name to the face, he felt a minor flood of relief! He had, many years ago, worked with 'Bad Boy' Lester, and more recently worked across a couple of his operations. Nothing that he knew, or had ever heard about the man said that he couldn't be trusted if he gave his word on something, so he must really know whoever wanted to talk to him. But someone Crow trusted? That would be hard, because there were very, very, few of those alive today who were still playing at the intelligence game these days!

After finishing his meal, having to choke down the yogurt which he really detested, but ate anyway because he needed the protein, he decided to check the email account he used with his doctor. Just to see if the doctor had left any more information about what was ailing him. After entering his personal password he did find a message waiting for him from the doctor. Almost with a feeling of dread he opened the message and began to read.

What Crow read was both a relief, and chilling, at the same time. It seemed that while he was in Africa a couple of years ago he had picked up a type of bacteria that had settled in his lower intestine. This was the cause of his continued tiredness and general malaise. It would, the message went on, if not treated soon become very serious, and completely physically debilitating!

The real problem was that the treatment for this bug was a long drawn out process, which might require up to eighteen months to completely eradicate the bacteria from his system. The information stopped there, with a request for him to contact the doctor soonest to set up an appointment to start treatment. Well, the news wasn't as bad as he had expected! He erased the message and cleared the screen. He finished by exiting the mail program and shutting down his laptop computer.

Crow decided to get a good night's sleep, then in the morning find out who it was that wanted to talk to him. Who it was that he knew and trusted!? That code phrase was a very old one, and known only by eight people. Three of those, he knew, were dead. He would find this out before making any final decisions on what he would do.

At eight-o-five the next morning Crow called his drop number, using a cutout number he had installed himself, and found the information for his meeting with 'Bad Boy' there waiting for him. The meeting was set for five thirty that afternoon, in the middle of the city park, near the rowing pond. What was oddly pleasing was the message attached to the end of the meeting instructions. It said, 'Don't worry about your two friends from 'C'. They will be dealt with! Relax and enjoy your walk in the park. Don't worry about the local boy either!' the message ended cryptically.

Later that day, after taking care of several personal and general errands, he was making his preparations for the meeting early this evening. As he was doing so he was smiling to himself as he thought "I'm really going to enjoy watching this show!"

It was four thirty p.m. and Crow was nearing the southern entrance to the park. He was thinking to himself as he moved along that to anyone with any knowledge in trade craft, that he and the entourage following him must look like a parade. He was sure of the two Chileans, and the other local one, and he could almost feel, but not see, 'Bad Boy' and his people, because he would not be alone for this. Not out there!

As he moved into the park proper the hairs on the back of his neck rose. This was his finely tuned sense of danger, something he had developed and learned to listen to over many years, and which was seldom wrong, made him feel that he was completely surrounded now. He began to move more cautiously now, checking the positions of his followers more closely.

Scanning serepticiously to his left he spotted one of the Chileans, standing near a tree with some leafy bushes growing next to them, looking directly at him. As he watched the man suddenly stiffened, then slid bonelessly to the ground, unconscious or dead, he couldn't tell from where he was about a hundred feet away.

As he continued to watch the bushes parted and a man he did not know stepped out, bent down and lifted the Chilean to a sitting position against the tree. He placed something into the fallen mans hand, turned and gave Crow a brief smile, then disappeared back into the bushes. The whole incident had taken less than twenty or thirty seconds.

Crow quickly swung back around to where he thought the other Chilean agent would be, to check his reaction to his partners predicament. That worthy, standing half behind a boulder, was also slumping to the ground as Crows' eyes found him. As he watched, another man repeated the actions of the one who had dropped the first Chilean agent, propping him up against the boulder and placing something in his hand before disappearing as the first man had done.

Almost with anticipation now, Crow swung to the direction he knew the local man would be coming from. Sure enough, as that agent started to step out from a copse of trees he had been threading his way through, he stiffened, and began to slip to the ground silently. Even as he did so another man stepped out behind him, and, catching him at the last moment he eased him into a half carry and dragged him back into the trees. Again, something was pressed into the victim's hand, the hand closed over it, and the man who had caught him looked around quickly and melted quietly back into the trees.

Nodding to himself, Crow thought, 'these are some very professional people.' Crow continued on to the location for his meeting, feeling much better than he had in several weeks.

Although he did not drop his guard one iota, even though those who had concerned him the most were out of the picture, Crow now felt that he was moving along in a circle of relative security. He could still feel 'BB' out there somewhere nearby, and his sense of immanent danger had changed to one of watchful wariness.

As he approached the rendezvous point he spotted 'BB' coming to it at an oblique angle to his own. 'BB' had a self satisfied smile, almost a Cheshire grin, on his face as he approached. As they came together 'Bad Boy' Jimmy Lester extended his hand to Crow saying, "Well, it has been a long time John Crow, but it's good to see you again!"

Extending his own hand in greeting Crow said, "It's good to see you too Jimmy. Been so long that I almost didn't recognize you the other day in the bus station." At this point both men's smiles warmed appreciably with remembrance of shared moments of utter terror, and the elated relief at the absence of that terror.

Sobering slightly Jimmy said, "Not to worry now. The three that were following you are out of it, and their backups are sleeping peacefully in their cars just outside of the park. They'll all wake up in about eighteen hours, well rested, but with terrible headaches. It is to be hoped that we will be able to agree on some things and be long gone before they even wake up!"

"I know you Jimmy. We've got some history together." Crow said slowly, "But don't you think that before we talk about going anywhere you should speak about just who it is that I know and trust?" he finished with iron finality in his voice!

At this the smile returned to Jimmy's face, even wider if possible, than the one he had had on it before, as he said quite matter of factly, "John Dirk!" Then, "He's started a new game and he wants you to come out and play!"

At the mention of his long time friends name all of the tension of moments before drained out of him, as a fond smile re-lit his own features. But being the professional he was Crow said, "All right Jimmy, tell me all about it."

"And that, John Crow, is as much as I'm able to tell you about it at this point. Or, at least, until you answer a question in the right manner for me! But before I can ask, or you can answer, the question you must swear that you will never discuss or relate anything I've told or may tell you, outside of our group. It is vitally important to keep this secret! As I said before, this game has already gone hard! Will you swear to hold all you hear secret?" Jimmy finished, his own eyes now hard and cold.

"I will." Crow stated simply.

"OK. Here's the question. Do you want in on this new game we're playing?" Jimmy asked, his expression and voice both deadpan.

His eyes squinting slightly as he thought, John Crow mused to himself at the oddity of his profession. Calling their trade, espionage and counter espionage, a game. It was it was a game that could turn lethal with little or no warning. He went over quickly, in his mind, the already long list of names of those who had already signed on for this one. Not only was the list impressive, he knew, or knew of, many on that list. All very good people, and very talented. Finally, looking up into Jimmy's waiting eyes, he simply nodded, once, his assent.

At this Jimmy reached into his jacket pocket and withdrew a cellular phone, punched a pre-set number, and handed the phone to Crow, saying to him "Dirk said that you were to call him directly if your answer were yes."

As Crow put the cellular phone to his ear Jimmy walked a few paces away to give him some privacy.

Denton, More Puzzlement

Ten days later, and a thousand miles away, in that same basement office in the pentagon Denton was, this time, sitting in the only other chair in his chief's office. He was idly drumming his fingers on a large stack of file folders in his lap while he was awaiting the return of his boss.

Dentons' tired face did, now, really resemble that of his boss, having acquired those same dark rings around his eyes from too much reading and too little sleep. As his boss walked briskly into the office Denton looked up at him.

"Denton, you look like hell!" his boss said as he dropped heavily, tiredly, into the swivel chair behind his desk, and "I hope that what you have to tell me isn't as bad as the way you look!"

Nodding grimly, Denton placed the stack of file on the corner of his chief's desk, saying "I had a hunch that this thing was big, chief. I just didn't have any idea of how big it could be!" Nodding at the stack of files He said, "You're not going to like this! Not one little bit!" Denton finished flatly.

Looking at his aide with some concern, seeing the dark rings around his eyes and the worry lines etched into his normally smooth forehead, his chief said "Wait. I'll order some coffee and sandwiches before we start." To this Denton nodded his grateful thanks.

After the coffee and food had been delivered and set out the underling who had done so left quickly at a nod from the chief. Some minutes later Denton, his mouth still half full of the ham and cheese sandwich he had chosen said "Something very strange is going on here chief. While I was checking to see what the other agencies might know about some hush-hush 'op' being set up, using independents, the people at DIA nearly took my head off."

He waited a second to be sure the implications of that last took effect, then, "They wanted to know if we had co-opted two of their top men. That was strange enough, because we can't co-opt anyone without going through channels. Stranger still is that I got word that two of their top men, John Dirk and Bill Tate, have dropped out and gone completely under! Not only that! It seems that one of their in house sweepers has disappeared without a trace." Denton paused to take a breath and a long swallow of his now cooling coffee.

Looking at Denton, frowning, the chief said "Why do I get the feeling that there is a lot more to tell yet. "And, from the look on your face, I just know that I'm not going to like any of it at all." He finished, his frown etching the lines in his face even deeper.

"I really didn't think too much about it until it hit me right between the eyes!" Then Denton went on, after swallowing the last of his sandwich and a last sip of coffee. "The thing that hit me so hard, after I had done some cross referencing, was that every one of those who have gone under recently know each other! And have history together."

"Is there any question of offshore intervention?" the big man asked harshly.

"None that I can find. And here is the part that you're really not going to like. One of our own ex-ops, who went freelance about three years ago, just dropped out and went under without a trace! After a possible meeting with Jimmy Lester!" Denton finished in a rush.

"Please tell me it's not who I'm thinking it is." The man behind the desk said, wearily.

"You hit it the first try, boss. John Crow! Here's what I have to date on this part. You'll remember that, as a courtesy, we put a couple of our local people in Cleveland on Crows' tail because of that op he pulled off in Chile. Bringing that Chilean general over to us, and saving us from wearing a lot of egg on our faces from that bungled op we ran with the CIA." After a gulp of air Denton rushed on, "Our men had picked up three Chilean Mil. Intel. Types, who were all over Crows backside. Well, we were just about to pick them up and send them packing when Crow made a beeline for that big park they have there. So our men decided to back off and see what was up."

Denton paused for a breath again, and, seeing the inquiring look on his boss's face, went on quickly. "Boss, within three minutes of Crow entering that park both of the Chileans and our own man, all following Crow on foot, were taken out and put to sleep with tranquilizer darts.

Both of the chase car drivers, ours and theirs, were put to sleep in the same manner. The only reason we know who Crow met was because we also had a man trailing him from the front. When he lost contact he doubled back and, apparently, caught the last part of his meeting with Lester!"

At his boss' impatient look he rushed on, "He saw Lester hand Crow a cell phone, Crow speak for a minute and give the phone back. They then left the park by different directions. Our man lost Crow shortly after that."

"The only reason our third man didn't get bagged was because he always carries a pair of those mini binoculars and he spotted Lesters' security detail before they spotted him. He said that Lester had at least six men in that detail, and they were all top rate pros." Denton stopped to let his boss absorb all he had said.

The big man behind the desk, his face now furrowed more deeply than ever with worry lines, sat with his head propped up on his fists, thinking.

Then, as if struck by a sudden thought, his head snapped up and he said, "Tell me the rest of it!"

"OK. Here's the scary part." Denton hurried to comply "All of the agents were knocked out with a fast acting Hydrochloride based sleep agent. Very, very sophisticated! Our lab people are still trying to break it down. Each of the men knocked out had a slip of paper tucked into their hands. What was printed on them was really scary when you stop to think about it!"

He waited for a heartbeat for effect, then blurted "They read, 'One free pass. No more will be issued!' Denton paused, a look of deep concern on his own weary face.

Then he finished with, "That tells me one thing boss. These people are telling us that they are willing to play very seriously in the future. And, We've been warned!"

The chief sat there looking at/through Denton as he mused to himself aloud. "The elusive Mr. Harris. 'Bad Boy' Lester. 'Chicky' Martinez from Mexico. Two heavy duty black ops types from DIA Tate and Dirk. Three or four known freelance intel. heavies. And now John Crow. And an overt warning to stay out of their sand box! Damn it Denton, That is one power house list!"

The big man paused for a moment, looking off into some private place before saying, "Denton, I want you to back off of this for a little while, so I can ask some questions at the highest echelons. I want you just to keep your finger on things, nothing more. Understood?"

At Dentons' nod of ascent, He heaved his rumpled bulk out of his chair and strode out of the office

A few hours later, while in a very hushed conversation with his 'Chief of Intelligence Operation, Western Hemisphere, the big mans cell phone chirped, the one with his very private number.

Excusing himself he reached into his breast pocket and brought out the phone. He flipped it open and brought it to his mouth and ear, saying "This better be very important Denton!"

A very subdued Denton said, "I just got word from one of our FBI contacts. They just pulled a pick up and switch in Boston. The party concerned was one of those names on our 'A' list, one Gerry 'G. Whiz' Burke."

Now Denton said, almost dreading having to do so, "It was done as a favor to one of their best sources of information. The contact name/sign for this source was none other than 'BB'

The only thing Denton heard, Just before the line went dead, was "Shit!"

A 'Whiz' in the Bag

The FBI Agents came flooding into the buildings lobby entrance, from seemingly nowhere, in what appeared to be an unending stream that split into smaller streamlets as they rushed past the reception desk, the agents taking different directions as might a small rivulet moving around objects in it's path on its' journey towards some distant sea.

Three of the first agents into the building went straight to the reception desk, laying down an official looking document. They then proceeded to disarm the security agent there and shut down the switchboard, also removing the walkie-talkies from the rest of the security personnel in the lobby. Still others went directly to the bank of elevators, two man teams taking control of each one as the doors opened to disgorge its' passengers.

Yet more teams went to the stairwells, taking up positions beside each door. There were also three and four man teams taking control of the garage and service entrances and exits.

A particularly large team, twelve men, loaded aboard the two penthouse elevators and, as those cars rose swiftly, headed for the location of the real targets of this raid.

As the cars reached their destination on the thirty second floor the two elevator doors opened almost simultaneously, the black clad and helmeted agents moving quickly to take covering positions in the elevator lobbies, and at the cross hall junctions.

Two of the agents went swiftly to the receptionists desk at the far side of the lobby. One handed the woman sitting there, with a very surprised look on her attractive face, an arrest warrant for one Gerald Burke, along with a search and seizure warrant for the premises these offices occupied. They also cautioned her not to use the phone!

As soon as she read the warrants she was gently removed from her station, to be replaced by one of the agents. This all took less than one minute to occur. As soon as this agent was in place at the reception desk the others moved off in several directions to take complete control of their objective. The largest team, four men led by agent Jim Price, went straight to the executive office at the end of the long main hall and, brushing past the secretary, walked into the CEO's office.

The short, portly man sitting behind the large desk began to splutter as the four armed, black clad men strode into his office "Wha-Who are you? And what are you doing in my office?"

Agent Price dropped both the search and arrest warrants on the mans desk, waiting silently as he read them. Looking up from the papers the man said, "I don't know any Gerald Burke, or any other Burkes for that matter!"

"Are you sure of that statement?" agent Price asked coldly.

"Of course I am!" the portly man stated indignantly.

Turning to his men Price said, "OK. Check that door at the back of the office."

As his agents move to comply the man jumped up from his desk shouting, "Here, you can't go in there!"

Ignoring him the agents went to the door and tried to open it. Turning back to Price the lead agent said "Locked." Price turned to the portly man and asked coldly "do you have the key to that door?"

The man said flatly "NO!" and, "I want one of our attorneys in here! Now!"

"Good enough." Price aid. Then turning to his man at the door he said, "Break it down!" Turning to one of the other agents he said, "Place him under arrest for obstruction! And get him out of here."

Since the door opened inward, towards the agents, one of them removed a three foot pry bar from the satchel he was carrying, slid the flat end into the space between the door and the frame, just above the lock. And, with the help of another agent pried the lock out of its' socket, letting the door swing open.

As the door swung open the agents outside saw two things in the room now revealed. The first was a tall, well built, man with flame red hair standing in the middle of the room. The second was that the room was crammed with computer equipment that was performing some type of operation.

Looking in at the red haired man standing there Price said, "Gerald Burke. My name is Price. I'm with the FBI. And I have a warrant for your arrest." With this last one of the agents stepped forward and placed handcuffs on Gerry Burkes' wrist's.

Turning to the other agents Price said, "I want this office and that computer room sealed. I want all of these discs and tapes seized, bagged, and sealed."

Turning back to face Burke he said to the agent holding him "I'll take Burke down and transport him. You wait here with the other one until the tech guys get here, then transport him to HQ." With that he turned and headed for the door, Burke in tow.

Price took Burke down to the street where he seated him in a waiting car, then walked around to the other side and got in beside him, telling the waiting driver to take them to the federal building garage. As they rode through the city Price gave Burke a long and appraising look. He finally said "You are a very lucky man to have the kind of friends you do! This is not the kind of thing we do every day, or for just anyone!"

Having said this, and as they were pulling into the Federal building underground garage, he reached across and unfastened the handcuffs from Burkes wrists.

Now paying attention to where they were going Price directed the driver to the next lower level of the garage, and to a spot next to a nondescript, dark colored, sedan parked off by itself.

As they pulled up to it Price said, "Your friend is waiting for you over there. Tell him that I hope everything is well, and that I hope to hear from him soon."

As Burke got out and walked to the waiting sedan the one he had arrived in backed out and pulled away, neither occupant looking back as it drove away.

As he neared the nondescript sedan the door opened and a smiling Jimmy 'Bad Boy' Lester motioned him to get in. After seating himself next to Lester and shaking his hand warmly, the sedan pulled out and left the garage by another exit, promptly losing itself in the city's traffic.

As they rode along through the city streets Jimmy reached into his jacket pocket and pulled out a cell phone. He punched in a number, and after listening for a moment said "I have the 'whiz kid'" Then he snapped the phone shut and put it back into his pocket.

Jimmy looked at G. 'Whiz' Burke, and before that worthy could say one word, said to him, "No questions until we get to where we are going!" He then sat back in the seat and wouldn't say another word until they reached their alternate transportation.

Garov

To look at him you couldn't tell that Yuri Garov was sweating! He didn't have any moisture on his face or neck or palms. He had not been running, exercising, or working heavily. He was thinking! In outward appearance, he was working at this desk, calmly going through the stack of papers in front of him.

The subject of his thoughts was what he was sweating about! They had laid a very neat trap for him, and this time he wasn't at all sure that he could get out of this one. He had eluded many traps over the years, both from the rival intelligence services he had contended with, and from his rivals in his own service. But this one was different! It not only came from within his own service, it came from the top echelons of that service. It seemed that the 'Chairman' of the KGB had finally found a way to get rid of him. Permanently!

Yuri Garov was one of those men whose appearance belied the man beneath completely. At the age of thirty eight Garov stood five feet seven inches tall and weighed in at two hundred forty pounds. He was built like the proverbial fireplug! He had straight, dark brown hair that was usually long enough to fall forward across his wide forehead and partially obscure his always sleepy looking yellow brown eyes. Eyes that, contrary to appearance, missed little of anything.

His face, with somewhat swarthy looking skin, had a broad forehead and high cheekbones, with deep set eyes that were couched in slightly epicanthic lids, giving him the look of a peasant from the northern steppes region of Russia. In looking at him the only word that came to mind when trying to describe him was 'stolid'. Or possibly 'plodding'. Stolid and plodding! Though he worked extremely hard to maintain that appearance, it was about as far from the truth of Colonel Yuri Garov as it was possible to get!

Garov, at the age of nineteen, and with two years in the Russian army was spotted by an astute superior officer who had him tested, and then sponsored him to the Frunz Academy, the Russian equivalent of West Point.

At the academy, tested again, he was found to possess a mind with an IQ in excess of one hundred fifty. There, even having to catch up with the other students, he excelled under the new curriculum.

Graduating in three years, he was co-opted by the KGB to attend classes at the 'Little America compound', the non existent school for spies trained to operate in the western Hemisphere. Not only did he graduate in the upper ten percent of his class, he also mastered, in three short years, four additional languages.

He now spoke five languages fluently, English, Spanish, German, French, and Arabic, besides his own native Russian.

He did well at each of his postings, rising steadily in rank until reaching his present position as head of the ultra secret special, or 'wet' operations group. Even today, with Russia being only a shadow of the former USSR, this group, for those in the know, was feared and respected! Yuri Garov, for a man in his position, only had one major drawback. He was a passionate patriot and a scrupulously honest man, who could not abide stupidity In those he worked with. Especially in those who were in positions of high authority. Those whose orders cost the lives of his people due to their short sightedness or the outright stupidity of those giving the orders.

Having had to carry out these types of orders once too often Garov had done the, for him or anyone in his position, unthinkable! He had spoken out openly! Had done so after losing three good agents, one dead and two in prison for life, on the orders of the then KGB chief to terminate an operation in progress early without regard for their extraction. The early shutdown had exposed the operation unnecessarily and he had lost the three men as they were performing a hastily put together delaying action so the rest of the operational team could get out.

The terrible part of that whole mess was that if the team had been left alone they would have been able to shut down the operation quietly and exited the country with the intelligence they had already gathered.

The early, and messy, shut down had cost them the lives of three good and dedicated men, and the intelligence they were gathering. Speaking out had made him a very powerful enemy!

Now Garov was paying! He had been paying for the past several months, under a subtle but constant attack from within his agency, the last incident of which had nearly gotten him shot. The problem he was facing now was even worse. A contact he had helped several times in the past had tipped him that evidence was being planted in several places that would make him look guilty of treason!

Garov was now thoroughly convinced that it was time to exit the country he loved for a place outside of it, anyplace outside of it, where he might at least have a fighting chance to stay alive.

He knew, for a fact, that he wouldn't be able to stay here for much longer. His contemporaries, as disjointed as the workings of the internal agencies of the former and once great USSR had become, were still far too efficient at their work for any least little bit of error on his part.

Crow, Old Friends, and Big Medicine

The phone rang four times before it was answered. The voice, well known to Crow, was strong and vibrant as it said, "Yes."

"Hello, half breed." Said Crow by way of a greeting. "I hear that you are setting up a new game, and you want me to come play with you!" he finished, warmth coming into his voice and words as the past came rushing back to him, bringing mostly good memories.

"There are few men I'd rather have at my back!" came the warm reply "Even if you are a good for nothing Indian." Dirk said, with a laugh of pure pleasure in his voice.

"My sentiments exactly!" said Crow, the infectious laugh entering his own voice. Then, his voice sobering, Crow asked "This the straight skinny? You're starting a new game and you really need me?"

"Straight skinny!" stated Dirk, and "The game has already started. And it's gone hard, too!" he finished, his voice flat now.

Crow, never one to pull his punches, especially when it involved his own participation, or performance, said, "I think I'd really like to play, especially with the people you're putting together. But there are some complications." He paused for a few short seconds, then "Medical!" he finished. His voice a little pensive, waiting.

"How serious?" was the immediate response, Dirks' concern obvious.

"Doc says it's a bug I picked up in the mid east. It's in my lower intestinal tract. He says it could be terminal if something's not done about it soon." Crow replied, the tone of his voice neutral now.

There was a long pause, as if Dirk were conferring with someone in the background, then "John, will you come see me for a couple of days?"

"You're asking. I'll come." Crow replied to this, the puzzlement obvious in his voice, "However, the doc said that this can't be put of for too long!"

"My source says that it can probably be taken care of in less than a week. Besides, it's the least I can do for an old friend. Forget the game for now. We'll talk about it after the problem has been taken care of. You'll come then?" Dirk finished. The warmth very evident in his voice again.

Somewhat stunned by this completely unexpected turn of events, and knowing that Dirk was not prone to making wild statements, Crow replied simply, quietly "I'll come."

"Good! Jimmy is also picking up G. 'whiz' Burke, so the two of you can come out together. Please put Jimmy on the line for a minute."

After speaking for a couple of minutes Jimmy flipped the phone shut, ending the call. He then took out another phone, flipped it open and pressed a pre-selected number and waited for an answer. When he got one he said simply "We're moving to the Crows' nest." And flipped that closed also, ending that call.

To Crow he said "we're covered to move now. I've got four men flanking, and one is sitting on your place. It's clear or he would have let me know by now. We have to hurry a little because I've got to pick up Gerry Burke tomorrow morning in Boston. I have a friend in the FBI there who is going to do a grab and switch on him for me, then we'll fly out of BIA to a smaller field before heading west to St. Louis."

"After we get to St. Louis you and the 'whiz' will transfer to a twin engine prop job and be taken to a location where you will then transfer to a chopper and be taken to Dirks' location. By the way, an old friend of yours' is now handling all of our transport needs. His name is Casey. I thought you might like to know that. Do you need any longer than one day to clear yourself for traveling?" Jimmy finished up.

Impressed in spite of himself, knowing how professional Jimmy and the rest of his people were, Crow replied that he could be ready within three hours time. Crow hesitated for a moment before asking Jimmy if he minded him tagging along on the pick up of Burke. "Not at all. I'd enjoy the company." Jimmy told him.

Crow was pleased at this answer for several reasons. Foremost of them being he would, he was sure, be able to learn a little more about what was really going on. Secondly, he would find out more about who the players were in this new game. He was also feeling much better because he was sure now that, judging by what he had seen so far, most or all of the people involved in this were real professionals.

As they parted, to exit the park from different directions, neither they nor their flankers noticed the man standing just inside a small copse of trees a couple hundred yards away. The man was watching them with great interest through a small, opera sized, pair of binoculars.

CHAPTER TEN
Meeting New Friends,
and Other Things

Balor, Thoughts and Memories

Balor was having the time of his life! He liked most of the two legs that had come to the ship with his packmate Dirk. Dirks' 'nearfriend' Tate was very funny! But, he still wasn't sure about the being that Dirk now carried about in a cavity in his body!

Balor, through his people, knew much about other races and the worlds that they lived on. He also understood the pure instinct for survival that had caused the 'Chai' to save, first himself and then Dirk. His reservation was that he was not sure yet if that being understood the obligation of the 'packmate'! The bonding that 'Must be' for honors' sake.

Balors' race was old, and if he understood the Chais' method of reckoning, much older even than the Chai. Balors' people, the 'Elonee', had first come to this planet as 'Brethren' and companions to the 'Alan Tau', another race of two legs, when there were still huge saurians roaming the wide plains and jungle valleys of this planet.

The Alan Tau had been scientists and explorers when they had landed on the home world of the Elonee, and after several decades of getting to know each other they had made the 'Pact of the Brethren' with his people. Thus, by this pact, the two races would be bound together for all time.

The Alan Tau had asked the Elonee to go star faring with them because, like the Alan Tau the Elonee were telepathic. And because the natural senses of the Elonee were much sharper than those of the Alan Tau, who used machines to do much of what the Elonee' senses did naturally. The Alan Tau were an honorable people who adhered rigidly to the pact, always courteous and fair in their dealings with his people for generations almost uncountable.

Remembering the lore of his people Balor was again amazed at just how old his people were, because by the standards of most races life spans his people lived a very, very long time. His people had been star faring with the Alan Tau for two hundred thousand generations when his own Sept had begun it obligatory service with the Alan Tau.

That had been about three hundred fifty generations ago, just before his people had landed on this planet with the Alan Tau. Balor was of the three hundred fortieth generation of Elonee on this planet, and as his people reckoned time, in earth years, each generation was about five hundred years. That would make Balor about the same age as TuLan Chai, and by his peoples reckoning Balor was barely into adulthood!

Enough 'Oglit' scratching! He had been trying, mostly unsuccessfully, to trace the scent of one of those others who made it necessary to guard the ship so closely. The scent was so faint that he sometimes thought it was just a bad memory from the one he had killed at Dirks' refuge far to the north of here.

He was only able to catch faint whiffs of it on rare occasions, but was unable to track it to its' source. He would continue to search! If his sense of smell was not lying to him, and it seldom if ever did, there was one here who, if not one of those others, was one who associated with them.

He had been, for some time now, wondering if he should tell his pack brother Dirk, or his nearfriend Tate, about this thing. Well, he would wait for a while longer to see if he could find it.

As he ranged the canyon and hills around it he was again thinking about the fun he was having with his packbrother Dirk, and the other two legs he associated with. For his packbrother Dirk he felt a very close bond, almost as that felt for a littermate, because from the very first contact with him he had felt a kinship of spirit, a quality of quiet certitude and strength, and a terrible and tenacious will to life.

He recognized, as he came to know Dirk, an unbendable loyalty to those he called friends. And also, there was the knowledge that Dirk, like his own kind, was and would be a terrible warrior to face. One who, if he believed in what he was doing or seriously wronged, would keep coming at his enemy until he was dead or his enemy defeated.

Balors' people were not unfamiliar with the concept of group conflict, or war as it was called here. They had been embroiled in a couple of wars far in their past. Because of his peoples long lives there were never so many of them that they could afford as a race to wage large scale wars. This was a lesson that was hard learned for them because they were naturally a very competitive people.

In their distant past, according to legend, there had been a war between disputing factions so devastating that it had nearly wiped his people from the face of their planet. It had taken hundreds of generations to recover from that conflict.

But, being the competitive people they were, they had to develop an outlet. To do this they developed a ritualized form of combat to settle their disputes.

This ritualized combat was now for only those directly involved in a dispute. It was no game! The combat was often serious enough to cause injury, or on rare occasions death. It had been from that time of recovery from devastation that it was decreed by unanimous consent that unless the race itself were threatened only those directly involved in a dispute would fight.

Thus his race had flourished, developing into superb warrior-philosophers. Their philosophy developed because of their innate abilities as telepaths, which enabled them to exchange ideas and new concepts in a manner generally not possible to those limited to speech only.

They became aware of other races in their galaxy as some of their strongest philosopher-telepaths began to pick up stray thoughts from star farers passing close to their planet, broadening their perspectives immensely.

Dirk was very much like his own people in this respect, Balor thought. He was a ferocious warrior, and a very deep thinker as well. Thinking thus Balor realized another reason he had been so taken with Dirk. It was because he was so much like the litter brother he had lost a long time ago. It was a strange concept these two legs had, called loneliness. But Balor recognized its' affect in himself.

Out of the more than two hundred of his brother and sister packmates directly descended from those who had landed on this planet few more than one hundred remained. Many of those who now survived were, like himself, twenty first, twenty second, or twenty third generation, Eeolai—Elonee who were born on this planet. World wide there were slightly less than sixty thousand Elonee in existence.

And of those remaining only ten in each hundred were true adults, and another thirty in each thousand advanced adults. The rest were, like himself, young adults or the fifteen hundred or so who were considered to still be children. The rest had died of natural calamities or at the hands of the two legs, 'Humans' they called themselves, who had become the dominant species on this planet.

Balor knew that much of his knowledge of his peoples history, and a good deal of their doings here with the Alan Tau was incomplete, and would remain so until he could return to the pack enclave. But he did seem to remember some bits about the Alan Taus' early experiments on the early forebears of this race when they were still living in tree nests and caves. And still moving about on all fours for the most part. It seemed that the Alan Tau had been trying to raise the reasoning capabilities of those small semi-bipeds of so long ago.

He often wondered if those experiments had had anything to do with their rapid rise to the dominant species on this planet. He didn't know exactly what those experiments were but remembered that they were done because those hominids seemed to possess, or were developing, the rudiments of telepathy. He did know that he had run across several excellent telepaths in his wanderings, but they had been insane or on the verge of insanity because they didn't' understand it or were too superstitious to try understanding it.

Dirk was the second natural telepath that Balor had had congress with, and the first true friend he had ever had among the two legs. The first had been a young girl child he had met when the two legs had first started coming here from across the big ocean to the east, and started establishing their colonies. That one had been stoned to death as a witch, because she had developed the bad habit of audibleizing her conversations with him.

There had been several others over the years. Many of them from the red skinned people who had migrated to this land from the far west over the ice bridges in the north near the planetary axis. They had been called 'Shamans and medicine men' by their people and had been, at best, only partial telepaths, needing the drugs from different plants and fungi to enhance their meager abilities.

Dirk, Balor could tell, was descended from those people. He could taste-sense the similarity in the structure of his mind. Also, there was the same reverence and respect for the land and life forms of this world within him.

Again, as he move swiftly through the heavily wooded hills surrounding the box canyon, Balor chided himself for 'Oglit' scratching. But it was hard not to because most of those now in residence in and around the Chai ship were very interesting two legs who brought up similarities to events in his past.

Most of them were very good in the wilderness, able to move quickly and quietly through the underbrush and trees, their eyes sharp and observing. Also their ears and noses seemed to be more attuned to their environment than most of their breed. And almost all of them exuded an odor that Balor was well familiar with. That odor was of the class of those who were hunters and warriors. This odor was the same with all in that class who he had known over the long years.

Besides Dirk, who was special to him, Balor liked the one whose mind identified itself as Tate, of all of the others here, best of all. Their ability to communicate with each other was, over time, slowly improving but still required some form of physical contact.

The Tate one still jumped when Balor appeared, seemingly out of nowhere, near him but he seemed to have accepted that as just Balors' way. Musing, Balor had to admit to himself that he did seem to get some perverse pleasure in doing so.

Balor, for a change, was having a good time. But he knew that he must soon leave this new and fascinating group of two legs he was fast coming to like, and even admire, for they were much different from the last ones he had had full contact with.

But, he must soon leave them for his place of solitude and quiet. A place that gave him some shielding from the ever present half thought pressure that all of the two legs seemed to radiate on a random basis. Once there he could very painstakingly, and with great effort and concentration, send to the 'enclave' that he had found what they had several years ago told him to watch for. An 'Alien' thought pattern.

And not just one! He had found two! Alien to both those native to this world, and to those of his own kind. The elders would take the news of the Chai, and the ship, well. He would also send a loud warning about the others. The ones he had had an instant repulsion to! They would need to know of those as soon as possible!

His attention must have been focussed on that elusive scent because of his train of thought, because, all of a sudden, there it was! As he lifted his head into the soft breeze the scent grew stronger, causing the hair on his neck and along his spine to lift in warning. And those fine tendrils at the tips of his ears to almost whip back and forth in anger.

He began to quarter back and forth into the breeze, following the scent as it came to him intermittently. Without realizing it his lips had pulled back, exposing his razor sharp teeth, and a low angry rumbling had started deep in his chest and throat, as he steadily moved closer to that foul scent!

The Gathering, and Balor's Catch

John Crow was dead tired, his stomach was in turmoil from the fast food he had eaten for the last three meals, and the pills the doctor had given him were only helping marginally. He had been travelling for two and a half days now without letup, by car, by plane, and by helicopter. That helicopter was now roaring over the heavily wooded hills somewhere, as far as he could tell, in the middle northwest part of the country.

The direction of travel seemed to be southward, into the wild mid range mountainous country south of the Dakota Badlands, near the Montana border. If he was right it was area of the country he was familiar with because many of his extended family members were members of the tribes who called these parts home. John Crows' ethnic background was Dakota Sioux.

At this moment he was not only tired he was really irritated. His irritation was aimed at his red haired travelling companion. It seemed like the man had not stopped talking since he had been picked up in the garage of the Federal building in Boston two and a half days ago. He wasn't really that angry at the man because he understood that part of his incessant chatter was an expression of relief from his previous predicament. The rest of it was a not too well concealed attempt to draw information out of Crow about their destination.

The pilot broke into these thoughts saying over the intercom in their headphones that they were about ten minutes out from touchdown. And that they should be ready to deplane quickly as he would be taking off again as soon as they were on the ground and clear of the rotors.

As Crow acknowledged this he realized a strange thing, that it was quiet in the cabin now. Looking across at his companion he saw that the man now had his face pressed to the small window in the door next to his seat. Looking out his own window now he spotted a fair sized river in the near distance, the sun glinting off of its' surface as they neared it. He couldn't see any type of base setup, or even a campsite, but he was sure something was there or the pilot wouldn't be setting down in a wilderness like this, without even a sign of a road.

He was not disappointed, for, as the helicopter started to descend towards a small clearing in the trees he spotted two men step out from concealment, one carrying a set of guide on paddles, and the other an automatic rifle. Seeing this very limited exposure Crows' opinion of the quality Dirks' operation and people went up another notch.

Crow and Burke each grabbed the single bag they had been allowed to bring and, with the urging of the pilot, made a hasty exit as soon as the crafts skids touched the ground. They ran towards the men standing near the tree line, in a half crouch to stay clear of the rotors that were still spinning at a high rate of speed. No sooner had they cleared the rotors than the pilot increased their speed and lifted off, only clearing the surrounding trees by inches.

Bringing his eyes back to his surroundings, Crow saw a man step from his concealment in the closely growing trees and underbrush. The man put out his hand saying, "It's good to see you again John!"

It took a minute for the face to produce a name, but when it did, Crow who was smiling himself now replied "As I live and breath! is that really you Bill?"

"It's me. And I'm honored that you would remember me after so many years." Bill said, shaking Crows' hand warmly. Then turning, and extending his hand, said "Mr. Burke, I'm Bill Tate and I'm glad you could come out here to join us on such short notice."

Gerry Burke, his freckled face screwed up in some confusion said, "I'm glad to be here. I think? But where are all the wonderful gadgets 'BB' mentioned? All I see are a lot of trees and hills!"

"They are about half an hours walk from here, and if you and Mr. Crow"— Bill stopped talking as Crow interrupted him. "Bill, please call me John! We do have some history, don't we?"

Bill, the formality leaving his voice, answered "Yes. We do! OK." He then continued where he had left off, "As I was saying, if you and John will follow me I think you will be very surprised at what I have to show you, and pleased as well. John, Dirk said to tell you that he will join you later tonight when he returns. Now, if you both will follow me." So saying Bill turned an led them back along the faint path through the trees, the two men with him following as a rear guard.

As Burke and Crow were turning to follow Bill, there came from across the clearing, a scream. A scream ripped from a terrified throat, as a man scrambled from his concealment in the trees and underbrush there. He turned to run and stumbled, falling to his knees, his hands flying out in front of him to help regain his balance and feet. His head was turned almost completely around looking over his shoulder as he tried to get back to his feet. Before he could completely regain his feet he was hit square in the back by a snarling, hissing, totally enraged black cat almost as big as a full grown panther.

This apparition arched its' back as it sank long, razor sharp claws into the downed mans shoulders and hips! Its' head, somehow large for its' body, and attached to a neck that seemed long and sinuous, snapped back, then forward, driving its' now exposed long glistening white fangs into the mans spine. Causing the man to arch backwards almost in half.

Almost as quickly as it had attacked the big cat sprang away again to land a few feet from the downed man. Still facing the man on the ground the beautiful, but obviously furious cat, was snarling, almost it seemed, in utter disgust.

Crow saw all of this, as if in slow motion, as his body spun around to follow the direction of his head.

At the doomed mans shout the men in Bills' group spun around almost as one, the rear two raised their weapons and trained them on the big cat, ready to fire, when Bill Tate yelled, "Hold your fire! That's Balor!" as he began to sprint across the clearing towards the fallen man and cat.

Stunned, Crow watched as Bill, reaching the cats side knelt beside it and put his arm across the cats still furiously quivering shoulders. And then he leaned forward putting his head very close to the cats!

Crow shuddered, remembering those big teeth sinking into the downed mans spine. To Crows' amazement the big cat turned his oversized head and look directly at Bill.

At that moment Crow could almost swear that he felt something pass between them. Suddenly the cats head snapped around, looking straight at Crow, and Crow found himself transfixed by its' brilliant golden gaze! Then it returned its' attention to the fallen man, leaving, strangely, a feeling of longing to be near this magnificent creature.

The moment bill put his arm on Balors' shoulder he heard him saying, *it is one of the ones like we caught near Dirks' retreat. One of the disgusting ones who carry the others on their backs! I will not abide them near us! I have been trying to catch this one for three suns now, and just came upon its nasty scent an hour ago. It was strong enough this time to follow it here.* It was at this moment that the fallen mans shuddering ceased abruptly, and he became still in death.

A moment later the others came up to the two. Bill turned to the two guards and told them, "Radio the ship and have some men come out here and bring this piece of garbage back to the ship"

Turning to Crow and Burke he said, "I'm sorry about this. It seems we've caught an infiltrator. I don't know how he got past our screening process, But I will find out!" he finished, deadly intent in his voice.

Crow was looking at Balor, who was now sitting on his haunches fastidiously cleaning himself. He began to see the differences from what he at first thought to be a panther, but before he could say anything Bill took his arm and led him closer to the big cat. He said "Kneel down", and as he did so Bill put his hand on the beautiful creatures shoulder. Controlling his trepidation Crow forced himself to relax. The big cat turned his head and looked straight into Crows eyes, freezing him in place!

This time Crow was certain they were talking to each other, for those huge eyes changed, seeming now to radiate warmth towards Bill and himself. The big cat stood up, without breaking the contact of their hands on its' shoulders, and turned itself to face them both.

Still frozen in place by those eyes Crow began to feel something like an itching somewhere at the back of his mind. All of a sudden he heard-felt what seemed like a chuckle. Then, in his head or just inside his ears, he wasn't sure which, he heard something, faintly at first and then much stronger. They were words, but words that he could feel! They were saying,

I am pleased to meet you John Crow. For you, like the Tate one here, are a friend to my brother Dirk! It is good also that, like Dirk, you are kin to the people who were first in this land. I see in you a likeness to those who were once brothers to my kind! I welcome you to our number. With that the big beautiful cat stepped forward and gave his cheek a rasping lick before it disappeared into the trees.

Dumbfounded, Crow sank back on his backside, barely catching himself with his hands before he went flat on his back, there to stare at the point where the cat had disappeared into the trees.

He was stunned to his core, as old tribal legends and lore flooded into his mind! A hundred tales he had heard as a boy, of the revered ones who had walked with his distant ancestors as brothers.

Tales of the shadow people who appeared as cats and talked to the greatest of the old shamans came vividly back to him. John Crow was shaken to the very core of his being, yet at the same time a great joy was spreading in him to know that the legends of his people were true.

He was shaken from his reverie as Bill Tate's words broke through to him "He really makes a strong first impression on you, Doesn't he?"

And from Gerry Burke, who was standing to the side and completely ignorant of what had transpired, "What's going on here Crow? I thought that big cat was going to take a bite out of you too! Why are you looking so nonplussed my new friend?"

"Crow just got introduced to one of the top members of our group." Bill replied, with a huge smile on his face.

"That cat's a member of the group?!" Burke squeaked, looking shaken and confused.

"He is! And I would be very respectful to him in the future if I were you!" said Crow, a huge grin breaking out on his own face.

Bill turned to the man he had told to radio ahead earlier and asked if the men he had requested were on their way? He was told yes, and that Tony Ebbets was with them.

At the mention of that name Johns' head snapped up and around to look at Bill! He asked "Tony Ebbets? He works for Protec? That the same man?"

"Yes. Why?" asked Bill.

"I know him. And if he's working with your group you're taking on some of the biggest heavyweights in the game. You people really weren't kidding when you said it was a whole new game, and it was big! Tony's a stone hard man, and he is not known for going in for small issues!" John finished, his eyes introspective, in deep thought.

Garov

Yuri Garov was both surprised and confused, two conditions that he was not used to. For a man like Garov admitting this to himself spoke volumes for the man, and he didn't like it one little bit! He had worked for many years to train his mind to receive and handle new information and situations in a manner that usually excluded these elements from his thought processes.

But there it was sitting on the coffee table in front of him, staring back at him. He was at present sitting in the living area of the small three room apartment he kept as his personal safe house. It had taken him nearly four years to make this place a total secret from everything that might possibly be even remotely connected to him. Until today he had felt as safe in this apartment as it was possible to feel in this country.

He knew that his thoughts were drifting, but he just couldn't help it at this moment. It was there, staring up at him! The message he was looking at, the one lying on the coffee table, had stunned his sensibilities! It wasn't the message itself that stunned him, although it in itself was a huge surprise, it was the fact that it had been slipped under the door of this apartment! This apartment! The one that he would have sworn that couldn't be connected to him.

With an almost physical effort he gave himself a mental shake and forced himself to concentrate on the message itself. It was hand written in Cyrillic, using a close and careful script. But he could tell from the paper and envelope that it had traveled a long distance, from the western hemisphere, to get here to him. The message read;

Dear Yuri,
I know that you will be very surprised at receiving this message, and even more surprised at the place it was delivered to. I sincerely hope that you are! Because it has cost me a great deal of money, and every favor that I had owed to me over there to find out where to have it delivered so it could not be intercepted by anyone. This message is in two parts. It is part personal, and part offer. If you believe that you are not in a situation where you might consider an offer you should stop reading and burn the entire contents of the envelope at once. If the opposite is true, and you decide to accept the offer, I will consider it an honor having you owe me one!
Best Regards
Bad Boy

As he finished reading this first page some of his apprehension eased away, for he recognized the name at the bottom of the page. Although he had never met Jimmy 'Bad Boy' Lester personally he knew him very well by reputation. And he had also crossed paths with him several time in the past, and the experience had been both challenging and frustrating.

He also understood, now, how this place had been found. 'Bad Boy' Lester was probably one of the best ferrets ever to enter the intelligence game, and would be one of the very few who could have done it.

The only other westerner who might have been able to do it was John Dirk. And he would have really enjoyed meeting that man because Dirk was one of the very few in the world who had come even close to putting some serious dents in his operations.

His curiosity completely piqued now, and ruefully considering the situation he was in at work, Yuri broke the tape seal holding the second portion of the message closed and began to read. And, as he started reading his eyes again became round, as the surprise he thought he had managed began to take an emotional hold of him again.

This message read;

Dear Yuri,

In the past we were, perhaps, the best of foes doing what we did to the best of our abilities. In the present things are changing, and I would hope, if the information I have gathered is correct that I could lend a helping hand to someone for whom I have a great deal of respect and admiration as an honorable man. And foe. For the future I would hope that my former foe might become, if not a friend, at the least a valued ally.

There is a great deal of information that I believe you should have, but due to the limitations of this letter that information will have to wait until we can meet to be conveyed. I say meet because, with your consent, I would like very much to assist you in extricating yourself from your present difficulties. If you would like, out of Russia!

I can tell you this much, however. There is a new game in play. It is big! It is bigger than anything you or I may have ever anticipated playing in! Its' scope, I believe, is worldwide and has gone hard over here already. The enemy is inimical, seemingly well entrenched in places of high security, and is a danger to us all, without regard to national boundaries or politics.

We are building a new team. A very large one, with many former enemies who have seen and understand, and are now staunch allies. You are very high on the list of those we are seeking to join us, and I would consider it a privilege and an honor to count you as an ally and a member of our team! Yuri, I cannot overemphasize the danger we face!

If you would like our help, take the coin in this envelope and go to the Pravda seller at the Moskow Central tube station and ask for the twenty fifth edition. If the seller says to you that he does not have that edition, but he will get it for you, give him the coin. He will give you a telephone number. Use it!

Yuri, the help is whether you decide to join us or not! My personal hope is that you will use it and also join us. Best of luck whatever you decide.

Your former foe.

John Dirk.

Yuri Garov sat very still, the only visible effects of the letter he had just finished reading was in the slight trembling of the thick fingers of the strong hands holding the now half crumpled letter.

Yuri had often wondered at the depth of the hidden feelings of respect and caring he held for a man who he had never met, and had considered an enemy.

He understood now, able to look at those feelings in the light of day, that they were an unconscious but sure recognition of someone who was very much like himself. Dirk, also, was a man who cared about what he was doing and always did it to the best of his abilities. A man who respected the abilities of others, even his avowed enemies.

Yuri Garov, in a very uncharacteristic manner, made a snap decision to use the coin. He very much wanted to meet this man who for so long had been his foe, and now, for unspecified reasons, would be his friend.

Yuri also believed that the help would be there, even if he decided he didn't want any part of this new game. Besides, if he didn't like what he found he could always break the mans arms and legs as he had promised to do a few years ago.

G. 'Whiz' Is Gold

Gerry 'G Whiz' Burke was in seventh, or eighth, heaven. He did not care which, as long as he could stay here! When they told him there were lots of new gizmos it had been a total understatement! What he had been shown here, at this remote site, was so far beyond his expectations that he never wanted to leave here. Yes, G. 'Whiz' Burke was, for him, in a place very much like what he might have dreamed of as heaven!

The devices on this ship were well beyond the pale of any current knowledge base that he was aware of, and he was aware of almost anything that was new in the technology sector. Gerry was, besides being a resourceful and innovative inventor in his own right, especially where electronics were concerned, he was probably one of the very best computer hackers in the world today. So, there wasn't much information that he couldn't access if really wanted to badly enough.

He had been going through the ship for three days nonstop now, and he was like a kid turned loose in a candy store. He went from one device to the next, as his mind devoured every scrap of information it could glean, his wonder and amazement shining in his hungry eyes, not stopping to eat or sleep unless forced to.

He was sprawled, now, in one of the control room command chairs on the bridge of the small ship. He marveled at that term, because this 'small ship', overall, was bigger than a small helicopter aircraft carrier. This chair was just one more item he mentally added to the growing catalogue of items that had his mind in a turmoil of speculation about their potential uses with his own technology.

When he had first come onto the bridge he had been tired from his constant exploration, and was only looking for a quiet place to sit and think. Seeing the chair as that respite, he had gratefully plopped himself into it. To his utter surprise the chair had responded to his weight by immediately beginning to mold itself to the contours of his body! His surprise caused him to stiffen his spine and lean forward to get back out of it quickly. The chair had responded by hardening its' surface and began to assist exit by both lifting and pushing his backside up and out, almost spilling him onto the deck.

After getting control of his heartbeat he began to examine the chair very closely. The frame and base were of some type of metal, but the padded back and seat cushion were made of some type of gray-green spongy material. Examining the chair closely, he found a clear, almost invisible, plastic like tube rising out of the deck close to the base of the chair, and disappearing into the gray-green spongy material. As he was looking at it some type of fluid passed through the tube and into the spongy mass.

Very curious now he pressed his hand into the spongy mass, and sure enough the thing immediately began to mold itself to the form of his hand.

As he pressed his hand in with more force the material gave some more, but with greater resistance. It also gave off a slightly pungent, but not at all unpleasant odor. With wonder Burke realized that the spongy part of the chair was organic, and alive!

With this revelation his curiosity was now fully aroused again and he began to explore the entire bridge in earnest, especially the controls and the computers. This included opening access panels and crawling as far as possible into them to examine their working areas. Four hours of this had completely exhausted him, so he crawled back into the control command chair and let it conform to the shape of his body. His mind was in a whirlwind of thought as he let himself go into his favorite thinking mode, a half trance half sleep state. He stayed that way for several hours, the chair holding him comfortably in its' soothing embrace.

He woke up slowly, rubbing his eyes to rid them of the grit of sleep. As he came to full wakefulness you could see, if you looked into his eyes, that he was still thinking furiously. This was nothing new for him. For he had learned long ago to let his subconscious mind do the heavy correlative thinking while he was in a resting mode. So that when he came fully awake he could start putting all of those thoughts in some form of working order. He sat there in that comfortable chair for another hour thinking furiously, before hunger and thirst drove him in search of the galley.

Taking a tray he selected his food from the dispensers, then sat down at an unoccupied table. Looking down at his plate at the greenish colored substance that tasted just like scrambled eggs he shook his head, then started to eat. The thick, dark, liquid in his cup that passed here for coffee was actually quite good, and had a nice kick to it. But what passed for toast needed a lot of work yet.

Within a few minutes of sitting down Bill Tate left the group he was talking to and came over and sat down across from him, asking as he did so how Gerry was doing with his explorations. Gerry, looking up for a moment from his meal, said it was going fine. But there were also lines of puzzlement creasing his forehead as he said, "Bill, there's something a little strange about the way most of this equipment operates."

Before Bill could ask what he meant Gerry went on, "The conceptual and applied technology is first rate, and it's beyond what we have even in the thinking stages right now. Yet most of the control mechanisms are almost primitive by comparison to the technology itself." He finished plaintively.

"Gerry," said Bill tensely, as if he had been waiting, or even hoping, for something like this, "how closely have you been inspecting these things, and do you understand how they work?"

Gerry thought for a moment before answering then said "Yeah, most of it. In general principle anyway."

At this answer Bills' eyes squinted slightly and the look in them hardened perceptively, then he said "Gerry, please stay seated right where you are for a few minutes, while I make two calls!"

So saying he pulled his walkie-talkie from its' belt clip and said quietly, urgently, into it "Ron!" Getting a quick response he went on "I need two men in the galley right away, and you also. So put your second in command for a while. Copy?" Holding the hand held unit a little way from his ear both men heard the crisp response, "Copy! One minute."

Bill then took out the cell phone that gave him direct contact with Dirk and pressed one button on its' face. A very short wait, then he said, 'Dirk. I think you need to get back here as soon as you can! It seems that your hunch about G. 'Whiz' was right on the money, as usual. How long will you be?"

As he was listening to the answer Ron Colefax came hurrying into the galley with two of his men close behind him, and came straight to the table. At that point Bill said into the phone, "OK. I'll expect you in two to three hours. For that time I'll put him under condition yellow until you get here and we can go over what we discussed earlier." Finished, he flipped the phone shut and put it away.

Turning to face the waiting Ron he said quietly, but forcefully "This man," pointing to Gerry, "until you hear otherwise from Dirk or me, has two bodyguards on a twenty four-seven basis! No One, I repeat No One, gets within five feet of him unless they were personally cleared by you or myself! Is that clear?"

Looking a little surprised Ron answered in the affirmative and, turning to his men said a few quiet words. The men then positioned themselves on either side of Gerry, who was now looking a little bit confused, and a little more frightened.

Seeing the look on Gerry's face bill quickly said. "This is only a temporary measure Gerry, but it's necessary until we can discuss what you told me with Dirk. He'll be here in a few hours and we can decide on a few things then. Please be patient until then."

Looking relieved, Gerry went back to his now cold substitute coffee and eggs. Which weren't that bad either. After you got used to that greenish color.

Turning back to Ron, Bill took him a little off to the side and asked him, "Do you remember when we were planning on who we wanted to bring into this thing?"

At Rons' nod he continued, "Do you remember why Gerry was picked over so many others?"

Continuing again at Rons' second nod, "Well, it seems that we were right on the money. Gerry thinks that he understands a lot about the ships basic technology and working principles. That much, in just three days poking around!" The significance of what he had just said reflected in the tone of his voice.

Colefaxs' eyes grew round as the implications of what he had just been told sank in. Nodding his understanding, he said quietly "It's covered," then, "how much leeway should I give him?"

"Anywhere he wants to go in the ship or the canyon until Dirk gets back." Bill said just as quietly.

"I'm going out to see if I can find Balor. I haven't seen him since Burke and Crow came in, and the incident at the clearing." Bill finished with that subtle reminder.

Ron just nodded somberly as he left.

Denton

Paul Denton was beginning to get very irritated, and that irritation was now ready to explode into anger! That he was getting angry caused him to worry, because anger was not normally part of his makeup. In almost every description that had ever been applied to himself the words 'calm' and 'very professional' were invariably a part of the description always given. And that was how he always thought of himself.

Denton was part of an elite class of investigator-agents in a super classified agency of the government that found, or found out about, things for many of the other secret agency's and the president. There were very few of them, because they were of that rare breed of men whose great joy in work was finding the unfindable, solving the unsolvable. If the term secret had a defining correlation, this agency would be it.

They had been given a great deal of power and authority over most of the other secret agency's, and in many instances over the military. There was a designated name for the agency, but no one ever used it. For those who knew about their existence they were just referred to as the ferrets, because knowing about their existence was on a need to know basis. Yet their services were always in great demand. Denton was a member of this group, and he was considered one their best.

Right now Dentons' worrisome anger was being caused by the very limited cooperation he was getting from the 'black ops' unit that John Dirk had, up until a few short weeks ago, been a member of. Denton had received, after putting in a request for any information available on him, only a standard unit personnel file, a copy of his military 201 file, and a copy of the retirement papers he had recently filed. All requests for further information had produced only 'no further information available' responses. And the same thing had happened with requests concerning Bill Tate, a known long time friend of Dirk's.

When he had tried to exert some of his authority there he had been met with nothing but a stony silence. So he tried to approach it from the other end by going to 'Protec Services' to ask some questions about some of the other names on his list. All he got for his trouble there was a polite but firm 'We don't care what government agency you're from. We don't give out any information on our clients or our operatives unless you can prove to us clearly that they have broken the law. Period! Good afternoon.'

This second rebuff he could understand, and felt that he could work around it. But the first one, from another government agency, had been almost openly hostile!

As for the other names on his list, he had a great deal of very good background information on them already. But they too seemed to have fallen off the face of the earth. He knew what that meant, they had gone to ground in very deep cover. And each and every one of them seemed to have left a blank trail to follow.

But that had to be wrong, because even the best of them left some kind of a trail that could be followed. He must be looking in the wrong places! He would go to the FBI agent, Price, and see what he could shake loose there. Having made that decision he felt a renewed sense of purpose, and the anger that had been building retreated somewhat into the background of his thoughts.

During this dialogue with himself he had been driving from his home, in Alexandria, Virginia, to his office in the Pentagon, just outside of DC. Proper. Having made that decision he made another one, he would stop at the next place he found and replace the coffee in his travel mug, because it had gone cold during his reverie. Denton thoroughly detested cold coffee.

After refilling his coffee mug at a local 7-11 Denton resumed his trip to his office, now paying more attention to his surroundings. Glancing into his rearview mirror, because that sixth sense that all good field agents developed told him to, he confirmed what his subconscious attention had been noticing for the last forty five minutes. He came to the unassailable conclusion that he had picked up a tail.

Being tailed bothered him a lot, because the cover used was such a good one. It showed him as a lower level bureaucrat in the Pentagons office of billing and procurement, giving no one a reason to follow him! As he glanced in the rearview mirror again he reconfirmed the identity of the offending vehicle.

It was the nondescript, four or five year old, light blue sedan about two cars back, in the right hand lane. The same one he had noticed, for most of his trip, last night on his way home. The same vehicle that had turned off at the exit before his own.

Denton quickly jotted down the description and license plate number of the vehicle, on the pad he kept on the console next to his seat. Not that he thought it would do him much good. If they were any good, or from some other agency and seriously interested in him, that vehicle would most likely be registered to someone who lived in the same area he did.

Paying no more attention to the vehicle following him Denton continued his trip to his office, turning off the parkway at the special exit for employees of the Pentagon.

As he pulled into the parking lot he came to another unassailable conclusion. He would now have to ask the chief for some extra help.

Things were getting far too complicated too fast for him to manage with just the two assistants he now had!

Dirk, Balor, and TuLan

Dirk, who had gone back to the motel near the small airfield, was just finishing a call with his people in St. Louis when he felt the familiar touch in his mind. He hung up the phone and sat back in his chair, relaxing.

As he did so he felt the familiar touch again, stronger this time, words and pictures began to come clearly now. *You learn quickly my brother, reaching outward to receive my sending, to make our speaking clearer.* Said Balor in his mind, his seemingly perpetual chuckle, which Dirk thought gave him such a personal quality, echoing warmly in the background of his mind.

TuLan, instantly aware that Dirk was communicating with Balor, again wondered at his ability to do so without him being able to overhear. As much, and hard, as he had tried he could still not reach that part of Dirks' mind. It was almost as if it were being done on a higher frequency than he could reach, even being as closely attached to Dirk's mind as he was.

It worried him because it had never happened to him with any of the other symbiotic relationships he'd had previously. It was doubly strange because they seemed able to exclude him from their telepathic conversations at will. Well, this was not the time to bring this subject up, so he would wait to see what was up.

All of a sudden, Dirks' introspection was shattered, *TuLan! You must hear this news!* as Dirks' thoughts crashed into his mind, as if the barriers there did not exist. *Balor has just caught, and killed, another man who was carrying a 'Drel' rider! The bad part is that it was one of the new guards who were brought to the ship! So it now seems that we are going to have to improve our screening methods!*

Welcome my friend. TuLan sent through the channel opened for him in Dirks' mind.

Welcome star friend. Came back from Balor, in the semi formal manner of speech they seemed to have developed with their first communications with each other.

How did this come about? asked TuLan, some small amount of anxiety leaking into the question.

As Balor related his story both TuLan and Dirk listened with barely restrained impatience as questions begging immediate answers popped into their minds. Balor forestalled those with, *that is all that I know.*

Balor then said to Dirk, in that range he knew TuLan could not reach, *there are several things I must tell you my brother. First, the two men you were waiting for arrived just before that incident occurred. They are now both safely with our friend Tate.*

Balor paused for a few seconds, then, *the cold one,* Dirk knew he meant Tony Ebbets, *took the foul one I killed to the ship and has stored it in the cold storage unit. Our friend Tate has told him to have all of the men checked physically, by what he calls 'strip searching', to make sure that there are no others of that kind in our ranks. This is, I believe, being done even as we speak."* and here Balor paused for almost a full minute before continuing.

Dirk, now sensitive to Balor, held himself silent, waiting. *Second,* Balor finally continued, *I have met the one called Crow. He is, like yourself, a descendent of the first people to walk in this land, and he is also descended from a long line of the old 'Shamans'. This I saw in his mind when I gave him the old greeting of the people. He, like the Tate one, is a true and good friend to you, and will also be welcomed by me to our friendship/brotherhood if that is your wish! He is also, like you, a natural receiver of thought, though not such a strong sender, for I did not have to have contact to have communication with him, as the Tate one erroneously thought he must.* Balor finished, this time with his normal chuckle.

As they had in John Crow, these words evoked in Dirk memories of the old tales, told to him by his grandfather over the campfires of their many hunting and fishing trips, of the sacred ones. The demigods who had spoken without words to the great shamans and wise ones, and had appeared to them in the form of great black cats, and other animals. Balors' words, and his memories of the old tales, would create many, many more questions than answers in the years to come.

Dirks' attention was snapped back to the present by Balors; next words, *friend Dirk, I sought you out to tell you that I must leave you for a length of time, for there is a thing that I must do. To do this task I must travel far to the north and west of where the ship is located. It is, for me, many risings of the sun in travel time, even as quickly as I go in my manner. The location is in the high places of the area that you call Canada.*

Can I aid you in this thing you must do, my friend? Dirk interjected.

Thank you my brother, but this is a thing I alone must do. Balor replied warmly.

How long do you think you will gone?" Asked Dirk, and, *for your company will be sorely missed, my brother!"*

As I shall miss you, my brother. Balor replied, his thoughts filling Dirk with a sense of comradeship and warmth the likes of which he had never known in his entire life. This feeling was unlike those he had for those he knew were his close friends, the very few he had, they were much deeper.

They were all enveloping, conveying things so often incapable of being expressed by words alone. He did know though that, since he had made friends with Balor his feelings of friendship for Bill had deepened perceptibly.

The meter of Balors' thoughts changed abruptly as his almost hesitant thoughts now came to him. *Dirk, a thing happened at the time I took the man down who carried the foul thing on his back. At the moment I took him down I believe that my claws penetrated the thing riding him, and just for a moment, I perceived a thought pattern very alien to anything I have ever known, even Tulans'! From that contact I got the impression of two large groups of these things. One on the eastern coast of this land, and another one, far to the east across the great ocean.*

Balor paused, mentally shuddering in remembrance of that contact, before continuing, *I am not entirely sure how accurate my impressions were. For that thing was very strong, and there were other impressions there that I will not even attempt to remember. I felt that this might be of some importance to you so I recalled the moment of contact. Even doing that much makes my insides feel like there are worms crawling around in them! That was the last thing I had to tell you before I got out of range. I will contact you again upon my return, in about thirty five or forty planetary revolutions. Farewell my brother, until we are again on the same path!* and, with that, Balors thoughts blinked out like a light being shut off!

After only a couple of short weeks Dirk would be feeling a sense of loss due to Balors' absence! He would also know, with a certainty he couldn't quite understand, that as long as Balor was on this earth dirk would be able to sense his presence.

For he would learn, too, that the friendship he had formed with this alien being in such a short period of time, and who he still knew very little about, would last far into his future. And that of his entire race!

Dirk, mindful of the being he now carried around within his body, was quick to open a thought channel to him and tactfully bring him up to date on most of what Balor had told him. Both of their thoughts were grim as the reason for these intrusions became evident. Their worst fears had now been confirmed! There was a major physical intrusion by the 'Drell' on Dirks planet.

Worse yet, they seemed to have established a strong foothold on two of the major continents. This was bad news indeed for TuLan, and made it more important than ever for him to get a long message off to the 'Union Council', advising them of the deep incursion into 'Union' territory.

Both TuLan and Dirk were worried about this situation. Dirk was worried mostly about his own people first, which TuLan could well understand. But TuLan would not underrate this humans ability to see the far reaching effects that would come from the 'Drells' invasion of his planet, as he expressed his long range fears to his new symbiotic partner openly.

Dirk, I know that this news is very upsetting for you, and that you feel repelled by what the 'Drel' do to your people as they use them. Yet, there is a fear that I must express to you now!

I will first paraphrase this fear in the following manner. Since we have become joined I have learned/found something that I had not previously known/understood in quite the same manner as I do now. That thing is the meaning your people put on your term friendship!

Pausing, as if to gather his thoughts, TuLan continued, *for me, before this, the closest meaning for it would have been 'not an enemy' or 'not inimical to me. What I have learned about your meaning for this term, since joining with you, has expanded the meaning for me by leaps and bounds of understanding. And I feel that you and I have, to some not too small a degree, developed such a relationship. Am I wrong in this assessment of our overall relationship?*

Dirk did not hesitate in answering, *not at all wrong! Excluding the help you are giving, and the personal benefits you have bestowed on me, I do not think that I could continue to act as your host if we had not developed such a relationship!* He said fervently, Bluntly letting TuLan see the truth of his statements in his mind.

TuLan went on now, somewhat emboldened, *I am most pleased, and very relieved to know this, for you are a most unusual being! So, here is my fear. As you know I have been studying your planet, personally, for close to a century of your time now. I have seen what you, as a race, can do when you are driven to the point of a killing war! I do not know of many species who are as tenacious and ferocious as is yours when you perceive a threat, and I would not want the 'Union' to have to face your people in such a manner!*

TuLan paused for a few seconds to marshal his thoughts, then, *I say this for two reasons. First, I do not want to think of the kind of damage facing a foe like your people would inflict on it. And second, after learning so much more about you and your people, at first hand through you, I do not want to think about what might happen to them!*

Dirk, if the 'Union' were to feel that your people are too much of a threat?—Well, there are weapons that your people haven't even conceived of yet! Weapons so powerful that they could turn your planet into nothing more than a cinder! If Pushed, they might think that the only way to preserve their own peace and freedom would be to use one of them on your planet.

Do not forget what I told you of our history. We fought a war that took us to the brink of extinction, and this would never be allowed to come near to happening again. TuLan finished heavily, with a graveness in his mental tone of voice that chilled Dirk to the very marrow of his bones.

After taking a very deep mental breath, TuLan continued, *that is why it is so important to get a message to them. Not only to warn them that the 'Drel' have returned to this galaxy. But to get from them some of the help that will enable us to fight the 'Drel' with some chance of eventually getting them off of your planet! Dirk, the 'Drel' are cold, immoral, and exceedingly greedy, caring little or nothing for the planets and races they ravage in pursuit to expand and conquer. But, they are not a stupid species! Else why would they sneak into this galaxy again through a tiny solar system, in one of the farthest reaches of a huge spiral arm, of this galaxy!* TuLan finished heatedly, earnestly.

Dirk was silent for a long time, shutting Tulan out of his thoughts while he marshaled them. In that, TuLan thought that his honesty had been taken as a threat, as well as a plea. He was indirectly right. Opening his mind to TuLan again, Dirk spoke, *TuLan, for your honesty and sincerity, if for no other reason, you have shown me that you have grasped what our concept of friendship means to us. But there is something that I don't think you quite understand, or fully appreciate as yet, and that is this. The 'Drel', in their manner of contact and use of my people, have made a mistake. A mistake I don't think they even know they have made. A mistake for which they have no understanding at all of what that mistake will cost them!*

'This last was stated in such a calm and determined manner that it sent shivers through TuLans' mind, for he saw clearly in that instant, what it could truly mean to have these people as implacable enemies. And for reasons he could not now identify, it terrified him to the core of his being!

A moment or two passed, then Dirk said, *well, at least we know where we stand now. So we'll just have to adjust our planning for it accordingly. Anyway, on to other things. That last call was from Bill Tate. He said that our whiz kid, Gerry Burke, has all kinds of ideas about your technology. And how we might integrate some of it with our own for our mutual benefit. Funny thing though, he seems to think that your computers are really primitive!*

Dirk paused for a moment to enjoy one of TuLans' rare expressions of nonplussed chagrin, before continuing. *So, we'll have to go back to the ship to work out what we need to do with his ideas first, along with some ideas I've been thinking about myself.* And he proceeded to show TuLan some mental pictures of those ideas.

Final Steps, First Stage

A short while later, while making final preparations to return to the ship, the cellular phone that he used sparingly to lessen the chance of it being trace monitored beeped loudly for attention. He crossed the room to answer it, surprised that he was getting another call on it so soon. He picked it up, flipping it open as he did so, and said "Yes!"

"Sorry Dirk," said Jimmy Lesters' voice "but this couldn't wait! The problem is one of time lag. We just got an answer from the 'Bear', and he was, as we expected, cautiously amenable to opening some serious dialogue with us. He's waiting for our response as we speak! I have about twelve hours to get back to him. How do you want to proceed?"

"That's OK Jimmy. Did you get any more intel On his situation?"

"Yeah. It's serious!"

"Do you think that he can hold out for a month? Do you think we can get a clean cell phone to him over there?" Dirk said, his mind racing.

Pausing to think before he spoke, Jimmy finally said "If he's real careful he can probably hold out that long. Getting him a clean cell phone should pose no serious problems. I know the people we're using over there personally. Top notch! All ex KGB."

"OK." Said Dirk, still thinking furiously "have your people pick up a matched pair of off market phones. Deliver one to him, and send the other one on ahead to St. Louis where you can pick it up on your way back to the ship. Yes, I want you to go there as soon as you're done there. Send this message with the 'Bears' phone, 'We are very aware of your situation, but need three to four weeks to set things up. Three weeks from the day he gets the phone he is to use the auto dial feature, pressing 0+one! He's to call on the twenty first day, at ten p.m. sharp, his time. He will receive his extraction instructions within forty eight hours of making that call. Then he is to keep the phone with him at all times after that, so that when it beeps he will know to go to the extraction point. He is an old hand at this Jimmy, so he'll be where he's supposed to be, when he's supposed to be. End the message with a good luck from both of us, OK!?"

"Got it!" said Jimmy, thinking that it was good to be working with real professionals again, and "It's going into the pipe in five!"

"Jimmy!" said Dirk crisply, "I know how competent your are, but use a little extra kid glove on this one. I have a gut feeling we're going to need this one a lot in the not so distant future." His voice turning grim, as his racing mind continued to fit pieces into the present, and near future, puzzle.

After hanging up he sat thinking for a few moments, before calling inwards *TuLan?*

Within seconds, it seemed, he felt TuLans' mental aura melding with his own as the response came, as both a reply and a question. *Dirk?!*

Dirk wasn't really sure of how the process worked in his mind yet, but he knew that he was becoming more adept at recognizing when TuLan was trying to get his attention. As well as how he had to shape his own thoughts to get TuLans' attention. He had gotten into the habit of picturing TuLans' mental aura, and picturing the shape of an arrow with a message tied around it, which he mentally shot/aimed at that aura.

In the beginning it had taken a lot of conscious effort, but now it was done almost automatically. The thought of speaking only with his mind was new enough to him to still be a little daunting at times. Mainly because a mental conversation was so much more complete, giving vent to a trilogy of sensory inputs like, verbal/thought words, picture/sound, and emotional overtones to enhance and amplify all.

And overshadowing the wonder of being able to communicate in such a concise manner was the Speed with which a whole conversation could be held. A conversation that, once he became comfortable with this mode of communication, would have taken a half hour could be started, dialogued, and completed in a tenth of that time, and with greater understanding for both, or all, participants.

One thing he was sure of was that since he had started speaking telepathically with TuLan and Balor both the speed at which he thought, and the overall conciseness of his completed thoughts had improved dramatically! *"Yes."* Dirk thought to himself, Both the speed and the quality of his thinking had improved to the point where he sometimes now felt a little impatient as he waited for others to see what was already perfectly clear to him.

To emphasize this it was not more than a few short seconds before he responded to TuLans reply to his call *There are a couple of things that you and I must give some serious thought to. We can do that on the trip back to the ship. The first is this. We must devise a means of identifying the 'Drel' mounted humans. And it will have to be a mechanical means, so the members of our teams, besides you, myself, and Balor can have some sense of security. I have a couple of ideas—"* and here he projected pictures of some mechanical devices to TuLan, explaining at the same time how they worked. *But, I would really appreciate some input from you about any improvements you can think of to add to these concepts.*

Dirk paused for a few seconds to let TuLan absorb the mass of information he had just sent him. Then *The second item is weapons. From what you have told me we are nowhere close to being in parity with the potential weapons that might potentially be brought to bear against us in any direct conflict. If my reasoning is on track, and I believe it is, what we need is something that will give us an edge. Something that can be designed to either disable or kill. In this area, and at this time, I believe that you have some expertise that we lack, and can use!*

That is true. Stated TuLan momentarily.

I don't want to discuss this now, TuLan. I just want you to give it some thought during the trip back to the ship! Also, when we get there I would like you to pay close attention to what Gerry Burke has to say about his thoughts after going through the ship. Will you do that?

I'll be happy to help in any way I can. I also think you're right about those 'Drel' ridden intruders. Them trying to find you, and I presume me, twice in such a short period of time means that there is probably a large colony of them here somewhere, and more than likely more than one colony of them. And that they are aware, or partially aware, of your activities, and that they at least suspect that a member of the 'Union' is present on this planet! With this last TuLan withdrew himself from Dirks' awareness.

Dirk stepped out of the motel room to speak quietly to the man sitting a few feet away from his door. The man, part of dirk's security detail, was dressed unobtrusively in jeans, plaid shirt, and quilted over shirt that blended in with this area. "Please tell the pilot that I'd like to head back to the main base within the next half hour, and ask your men to be ready to leave for the chopper in twenty minutes."

Dirk then stepped back into the room to finish his own packing. He had not disappeared through the door before the man was speaking into his hand held radio, giving instructions to his men.

Finished packing, Dirk had one last thing to do before leaving the motel, so he headed for the motel office reviewing what Casey had told him about the motel owner as he walked. The man was an ex army 'Ranger' and a Vietnam vet. Casey had said that he had spoken to the man already, on Dirk's behalf, and the man seemed willing to listen to what Dirk wanted to offer.

The owner, Tim Jordan by name, was five feet ten inches tall, weighed one hundred sixty five pounds, and at the age of sixty one was still in great shape. Entering the office, Dirk extended his hand as he introduced himself. Looking at the man he was very aware of the calm, watchful, blue eyes that took in every movement with little conscious effort. Shaking Dirks' hand Jordan told him to come on into the kitchen in the back, where they could have some coffee while they talked.

"Casey said you might have an offer to make me! He also said you were on the up and up. Casey and me, we served together through the 'Tet' offensive, so I know his word is good!" As he Said this last he handed a cup of strong smelling black coffee to Dirk. Then, "So, what's on your mind?"

Without giving too much away, Dirk explained that he and his people were running a private operation, making sure the man understood that it was in defense of this country. Explaining also, that because of its' nature, they might have to butt heads with some of our own agency's. If he decided to cooperate Casey would fill in all of the details he needed to know after he had been vetted.

"So." Dirk went on, "Here's the deal. We need a way station here, near the airport, so our people coming in and going out can have a safe place to stop. What we want from you are two things!"

"First we want you to sell us your motel. After the op is over the ownership reverts back to you again, with no payback against the purchase price. We can't afford to haggle, so the offer is one hundred grand, paid up front!"

"By the way, something I know that Casey doesn't. I know that you also own the entire airport through a couple of dummy corporations. The offer for that is five hundred grand! Same terms for that too." He finished, a small smile quirking his lips.

Those calm, penetrating blue eyes, studied him for a minute or so before Jordan, unperturbed by Dirks' disclosures, said "And the second part is?"

Dirks' smile broadened and warmed as he said to the man across the kitchen table from him, "Assuming you accept the first part of our offer, we want you to stay on and manage both places for us. And to run the security for them with the men we send you!"

Those calm blue eyes warmed suddenly with the broad smile that broke across that stern visage, as the man said, "Damn! Casey said you'd cut right to the chase. And be fair about it to boot! Done, and Done! Casey was right, you don't play no BS Games. It'll be good to be doing something useful again, instead of playing businessman! When do I start?"

"Now. Welcome aboard!" said Dirk, his smile now matching the one on the mans' face. "My people will settle with you within a week. I'll have Casey contact you tomorrow to start working out the details, and send you a couple of men to help out until we can get you a full detail. Or, if you know any men who you can personally vouch for and you might want to do security work, give their names to the men we send and we'll get them vetted quickly for you. I have to leave now, but I'll speak to you on my way back through here in a week or so."

As Dirk headed for the car waiting to take him and his men to the helicopter he felt a large weight lift from his shoulders. He now had a safe access point to bring his people in and out from the ship!

Garov, Travel Plans

It had been three and a half weeks since Garov had used the cell phone provided to him by the Pravda vendor at the news kiosk in the Metro station. Three and a half nerve wrenching weeks since he had put his fate into someone else's hands, and he had never felt more uncomfortable or more helplessly exposed in his entire adult life.

The helpless feeling was because he could feel the net his enemies had cast around him pulling him closer and closer to the trap they had set for him. The trap that, if allowed to close, would in the end result in his death!

At this very moment he was sitting at the desk in the small office his rank still afforded him, thinking these thoughts. Wondering for the thousandth time if he should contact the few men he knew he could trust, to let them know he was leaving. He shook his head, minutely, negating that thought, recognizing the danger in doing something like that before he was well on his way.

To anyone watching, Garov appeared, outwardly, to be calmly sitting at his desk reading the reports stacked in front of him. Inwardly his intestines felt as if they were frozen. Something was about to happen! He could feel it from the short furtive looks his coworkers were casting his way when they thought he wasn't looking. His blood felt like it was turning to ice in his veins.

Suddenly his sphincter clenched so tightly he thought he would never be able to use his backside again! Garov was so well schooled that nothing of this showed outwardly. The cause was the cell phone he had been carrying since it had been given to him by the Pravda vendor three and a half weeks ago! It had been set for silent operation and was now vibrating insistently in its' clip holder at his waist.

Garov calmly stood up, marked his spot and closed the cover on the yellow striped secret file he had been reading. He put it into his center desk drawer and locked it before stepping into the very small lavatory in his office. After the door was securely closed and locked he removed the phone from its' belt clip and put it to his ear, saying only, "Da."

The voice that answered that one syllable was flat and neutral. It began to give him instructions in a measured cadence designed to let him absorb everything said without the need for repetition or embellishment from the speaker.

The voice said "Select only those papers you think might be of some importance or value in the future. Also take or destroy anything that might give the slightest lead to your apartment. It is close to lunchtime, so leave as you normally do for your meal. But! Whatever you do, be out of your office before one p.m. because that is when you are slated to be picked up for questioning! The trap is closing Yuri, and the plan is for you not to survive it! So follow the next instructions very carefully."

The flat voice paused for only a second before continuing. "Go to your regular spot for your noon meal, and eat it as you normally would. Then, when you leave, instead of turning left on Lenin Prospect you are to turn right and walk exactly one and one half blocks. At that point there will be a dark blue Zil sedan, with darkened windows, parked at the curb. Get into it immediately. Someone will give you further instructions from there on. Please Yuri, do as you are asked without question. Good luck!" The line went dead, only the silence of the broken connection echoing in the ether now.

With a sigh Garov flipped the phone shut and replaced it in its' holder at his waist. Without hurry now he flushed the commode and ran some water over his hands from the tiny sink in the corner of the small cubicle. Taking a paper towel he opened the door and came out of the cubicle wiping his hands. Throwing the used towel into the wastebasket next to his desk he glanced down at his wrist watch. Nodding to himself, he picked up some papers and a file and slipped them into the open briefcase on his desk, closing and locking it.

As he made his way through the large open office with its' many partially enclosed desk spaces, to the street exit, he felt that every pair of eyes in the place were boring into his back! Once on the street he turned right, walking briskly, to the small restaurant two and a half blocks away on Lenin Prospect.

He spotted the two men following him in the first block he walked, but they stayed about a half block back. They were both very inept, he thought to himself as he reached the restaurant and entered. He seated himself at his regular table, feigning his ignorance of their presence.

As he sat waiting for his lunch of Borsht and Black bread he noticed a fine sheen of sweat on his palms. As he rubbed them dry on his napkin he thought to himself, "So this is what it feels like!" as he realized how so many others must have felt as he closed in on them. It was definitely not a pleasant feeling! He finished his meal quickly, and in his usual manner dropped money on the table as he left.

Knowing the training of the two following him he knew that, expecting him to head back to his office, they would now follow him from the front, almost as if leading him. He turned left, as they expected him to, and let them get almost a full block ahead of him before he abruptly turned and strode off in the opposite direction.

His two tails, in their complacency, thinking the lamb would be easily led to the slaughter, went almost another half block before realizing their quarry was gone. In their panic they began to run back the way they had come, their eyes searching the busy street frantically.

Suddenly one of the two whistled to the other, pointing ahead. There he was almost two blocks ahead of them. As they trotted to catch up with him he stopped next to a large blue Zil sedan, leaned down and pulled the door open, and got in pulling the door shut behind him!

But the big sedan did not pull away immediately. As the two men, now sweating heavily, raced up to within fifteen feet of the auto they drew their issue Chekov automatic pistols. Just then the sedan lurched away from the curb. Both men skidded to a halt and, leveling their weapons, yelled halt, as loudly as they could. Pedestrians on the street, seeing this, scattered in all directions, as the two advanced more cautiously on the now stopped vehicle, their weapons still leveled at it.

The two had taken no more than five cautious steps nearer the big car when there was a blinding flash. The car blew up with a tremendous roar, throwing both men and several pedestrians to the ground. The car lifted itself off of the ground and flipped over on its' back, before crashing back to the ground in a huge ball of flame.

One of the men was almost decapitated as one of the vehicles doors came zipping past his head, to land several hundred feet away. As the men picked themselves up off the ground debris from the explosion, and several nearby trees, was raining down all around them, and the sound from the explosion was still echoing between the nearby buildings. There was glass and metal debris for a couple of hundred yards in every direction.

One of the men, as he approached the furiously burning wreck was ineffectually wiping at a cut on his cheek, caused by flying glass. He looked down at what was left of the car and saw a part of a leg and foot sticking out from behind the door that hadn't been blown off. The other man, wincing from a cut on his hand, was raising a hand held radio to his lips, preparing to report the terminal change in their superiors plans.

A hundred yards away, and twenty five feet below the surface of the street, Garov was running as fast as he could through a huge storm drain tunnel, as the sound of the explosion reverberated along the tunnels walls.

Garov was surrounded by four men carrying flashlights, who were all dressed in dark clothing and armed with what looked like Mac 10 machine pistols. They ran quietly, hardly making a sound or splash in the residue from the last rain a couple of days ago. As they approached a much larger cross tunnel they put out their flashlights.

The lead man flattened himself to the tunnel wall and cautiously peered into the cross tunnel, turned back and made a hand signal to the man beside Garov. This man stepped even closer to Garov and whispered into his ear, "We must cross the park above using this cross tunnel. It has many open grates that can be seen into with the light from above. We must make absolutely no noise now, so please remove your shoes and carry them. We have a truck waiting on the other side of the park. Just watch the lead man for any signals as we move, and all should go well." The man finished, turning back to the front.

Garov touched his arm and whispered, "I must get to my hidden apartment! There are papers and files there I must retrieve!" he finished urgently.

The man turned back to face him fully and said in a hushed voice, a small smile playing at the corners of his mouth, "We cleaned out that place twenty minutes after you left it three days ago." Garovs' eyes widened as the man went on, "Everything is in the truck waiting for us across the park, including the contents of that cleverly hidden safe behind the medicine chest." The man, his smile wide now, finished.

Then, "Come, we go now. There is someone waiting for you at the truck!" So saying the man turned and moved silently ahead into the cross tunnel.

Garov, his mind a little numbed, but admiring, removed his shoes quickly and followed.

The eight hundred yard run through the tunnel was almost anti-climatic. They ran, dashing through the bars of light from the sun shining through the open grillwork above in surrealistic rectangles along the tunnel's length. Their breath rasping in their throats from both fear and exertion.

But, in the end there was only the ghost of perceived pursuit and the empty silence to greet them at the other end. The silence, in this case, meant safety, and a chance to rest.

Garov who, at the age of thirty eight, was in excellent physical condition. He let his chest swell a little with pride as he noticed that he was not panting nearly as hard as a couple of his younger companions were from the long run. A small smile played at his lips as he allowed himself to remember other times and places, where his physical shape had been made fun of, even jeered at.

That had happened much to the detriment of those who had done the jeering, as the true nature of his squat, fireplug body ended up on the top of the pile. Its' true power and agility not apparent until he moved with lightening fast reflexes to defend himself, or go on the offensive. Yes, he had always taken very good care of his body, and it had performed exceedingly well once again.

Again his superbly trained reflexes came into play as his attention was abruptly brought back to the present. He didn't even twitch as the team leader spoke almost directly into his ear in a quiet, but firm, voice. "The exit we will use is about twenty yards ahead. It will be the most dangerous part of your escape because we are exposed the most as we exit the tunnel. The van will be within five meters of the manhole cover, which is in the middle of the street. Our only advantage is that this is a residential street, and normally quiet at this time of day." The man paused a second before asking, "Are you armed?"

Garov turned to face the man and answered flatly "Of course!"

"Well enough." Then a little hesitantly, "Please, if we are intercepted on the street just flatten yourself to the ground, and let my people take care of it. Do not use your weapon unless there is no other choice! Will you do that for me?"

Garov looked at the man for a moment, seeing that he was indeed a professional, before he said simply, "Yes."

The man gave him a piercing look for a moment, then "I must assume then that you are carrying a Makarov ten point three millimeter semi automatic pistol. You are quite famous for your accuracy with that cannon, you know. May I see it please?" he asked with a genuine smile of approval breaking across his stern features.

Garov was just a little apprehensive at this request, but just the same reached under his jacket and removed the weapon from his shoulder holster and handed it to the man, but first.

As he took the beautifully maintained weapon from Garov, he half turned and called softly to another of the team members to join them. As that worthy joined them he handed Garovs' weapon to him and said "Give me the spare." The man stuffed Garovs' weapon under his belt, then quickly shucked his compact, almost flat. Backpack and removed a weapon identical to the ones carried by all of the team members. This he handed to the team leader, and quickly placed Garovs' weapon in the pack in place of the one removed.

This done, the team leader nodded back along the way they had come, and the team member trotted back along the tunnel, stopping just short of the last grill opening. There he flattened himself against the wall in the shadows and became almost invisible. He was now the rear guard for the group.

As Garov turned back to the team leader to protest being disarmed in this way, that one spoke first "Please forgive my little subterfuge, but I had to do it exactly the way the operations head specified. Please let me explain." The man paused until Garov gave a reluctant nod to continue. At Garovs' nod he showed a small smile of relief and began to speak.

"First, my name is Tony Ebbets, and on this mission I am second in command to Jimmy Lester, who is waiting in one of the vans above. By giving up your weapon you confirmed your willingness to comply with our arrangements, thereby letting us go on with our primary plans to get you out of the country and to a meeting with Mr. Dirk. If you had not given up your weapon we would still, using our alternative plans, have gotten you out, as promised, and placed you in a safe house, telling you to wait for further contact. Having told you this much my instructions are to give you one of our weapons and instruct you in its' use."

Garov started to break in, almost sputtering at the thought that he needed instruction in the use of any type of handgun! It was at this point that the realization of just who this man was hit him, his name finally registering in his brain!

Tony Ebbets was one of the deadliest hitters in the game. He was also considered to be one of the best people available for deep penetration extractions, and personal protection!

Garov, his face flushing with chagrin, snapped his mouth shut, now understanding that there must be something very new, and different, about this weapon. Taking a deep controlling breath, and letting a small apologetic smile cross his lips said quietly, "I am sorry. Please continue with your instruction."

Ebbets continued in a quiet voice, letting nothing show reflecting the faux pas. He handed Garov the dull black, surprisingly heavy, handgun, saying "This is a new, first generation, lab tested prototype weapon. It is a semi automatic plasma pulse emitter. It fires a phased plasma pulse carrying a short duration, high intensity, electrical charge designed to short circuit the electrical impulses that control muscular action. It was designed to be non lethal, unless the target has a weak heart, or is hit directly in the head, but we are working on a variation with a full lethal setting. It has a cyclic rate of fire of one pulse per second. It operates on two very small, high voltage batteries. There are, however, two drawbacks to this weapon! One: the weapon can, because of the types of batteries we are using, only be fired twenty times at full effectiveness. Two: on dark cloudy days, or at night, the charges trajectory can be seen because of causal discharge."

Taking a breath Tony went on again. "Its' biggest advantage is that at thirty yards, twenty eight meters or so, it is totally, deadly, accurate! If you can see your target, or any major portion of it, you can hit it! It also has an effective stopping range of eighty yards, about seventy two meters. If there is anything else you want to know about it you will have to talk to our tech people. By the way, you probably know, or know about, the head of our tech section. His name is Gerry, G.'whiz', Burke!" Tony finished, a compassionate smile on his lips for the dumbfounded look of open amazement on Garovs' face.

The look of amazement was not misplaced, because Garov was always up to speed on new weapon development, and he had not even heard a whisper of anything like this.

Tony, his face now serious again said, "Please take good care of that, because you now possess one of only twenty in existence!"

Garov looked up into the now friendly face of the team leader, his admiration for these people growing by the minute. Thinking to himself, "Either these people are totally naive, or I have been very, very wrong about them!"

Ebbets, reaching out to touch his arm, interrupted Garovs' thoughts by saying "I have a personal message for you, from Mr. Dirk. Shall I give it to you now?"

Garov looked again at the mans' face, which had now gone back to its' seemingly more natural neutral, almost solemn expression, replying "Da. Please do."

Ebbets' eyes drifted slightly up and to the left, as if this would help bring back the exact words and inflections as they were originally spoken.

"Yuri Yurivitch. Once my enemy, and soon to be my colleague, and hopefully, a new friend. Jimmy Lester and Tony Ebbets and his men are among the best there are! They have one mission. To get you out of there and safely to me!"

"On a personal note, I want you to know that I, and others you know personally or by reputation, have rediscovered that there are still things that are worth believing in and living or dying for. That you have agreed to come and listen to us has given all heart to face the trials that we see coming! Be careful in your journey to us my friend, for you are wanted and needed among us." Finished, Ebbets eyes came back forward to focus on Garovs' face.

"Thank you Mr. Ebbets." Garov said as he turned half away, trying to order his thoughts. He had, he knew, always seemed to feel an affinity for this man

Dirk! This man who in the past was his nemesis. This man, who by chance of birth had been his enemy, not his brother! At this very moment Garov did something that was totally contrary to his nature, and all of his training. He accepted an occurrence as a statement of fate, something he had never before believed in.

This man Dirk. This former enemy, would become his closest ally, and dearest friend. Garov knew this now without question or reservation. The reason that this was so odd to him was that he, Yuri Garov, would not, could not accept anything as fickle as fate! Yet it had just dealt him one of its' capricious hands!

At the muted, almost inaudible, sound of a low whistle Garovs' head snapped around to face Tony Ebbets. Breaking for him that new, and troubling, line of thought. Within seconds, and as if out of nowhere, the team members glided silently up to the team leader, waiting silently for his orders. Tony Ebbets began speaking to them in a voice that was urgent, yet barely above a whisper.

"Alright. It's time to move. Take special note of this! Mr. Garov, besides being the objective of our mission, is from this moment on a member of this team! Remember this, absolutely no one gets left behind, dead or alive! Dennis, you and Alex will go up and secure the exit point. Two clicks on the whisperphone if it's clear, one if not. Once you see it's clear, switch to channel 'C' and give two clicks to let team two in the vans know that we're on our way out. It's almost full dark now, so one of you two switch on your NVGs. OK, everybody got it? —Good! Let's keep it tight now. OK. Go!" he finished, and those professional shadows began to move silently up the tunnel to the exit ladder.

As they moved, Yuri Garov, for perhaps the first time in his often very dangerous life, felt that he was going where he belonged. To meet the one thing he wasn't sure anymore that he didn't believe in. Fate! Unbeknownst to Yuri Garov that fickle and capricious thing referred to as fate had a few very interesting surprises left in store for him!

Taking his arm to stop him, Ebbets pulled something from inside his jacket pocket, and holding it out to Garov said, "please put your shoes back on. We will be climbing up to the street, and you will need your shoes on." The object was a dry pair of socks.

Garov sat propped against the wall of the tunnel and quickly removed the cold wet socks he had almost forgotten he was wearing, replacing them with the thoughtfully provided warm, dry ones. And, as fast as possible, slipped on his shoes and tied them. "How odd," he thought, "that such a small, thoughtful, gesture could make such a large impression." He finished that thought in grateful acknowledgement and acceptance.

Ebbets put his hand to his earpiece for a second, then quietly said "We Go!" The he motioned Garov to follow him as he stepped off up the tunnel.

At the ladder tube one of the men showed Garov the ladder rungs going up with a muted flashlight, and whispered in his ear "Twenty five rungs to the top. When you come out, role to the left and flatten yourself. OK?" The man shined the light just high enough to see Garovs' mouth, as Garov, nodding said "Da. Yes." With that he climbed swiftly up the ladder.

As Garov came up out of the manhole, remembering his 'Spetsnaz' training, rolled to the left even before his feet had cleared the opening. He came out of the roll lying flat to the ground, about two meters from the manhole, his eyes already scanning his surroundings for anything that looked out of place or dangerous. By the time his eyes came back to the manhole the last two men were already pushing the manhole cover back into place.

The five men lay on the street silently, their almost invisible dark clothed bodies flattened to the streets surface, their eyes searching in all directions for any signs of trouble. All was silent, and nothing was moving.

No sooner had Dennis and Alex risen to a low crouch, and begun to move across the wide avenue towards a dark box van parked at the curb, when two pair of bright headlights came on. They were about twenty or thirty yards on either side of their position when three men jumped out of each vehicle, dressed in traditional KGB uniforms.

One, in the peaked cap of an officer, brought a small bullhorn to his mouth and shouted, in both Russian and English "Stay where you are, do not move! Drop your weapons! Resistance is useless!" while the rest of them spread out to block the street off completely.

The men in a crouch froze in mid step, the others still flat on the ground froze as well. The officer spoke again, "I repeat. Drop your weapons, or my men will open fire!" This made it clear to the team that they wanted to take them alive, and prisoner.

This tableau held for ten eternal seconds, and the officer had just clicked the trigger on the bullhorn to speak again. When, from the dark behind their vehicles, small, bright stars appeared and raced at blinding speed towards their KGB ambushers.

The officer and the man to his right were hit in the side, the man to the officers left in the back. They fell to the ground, writhing, and flapping their arms and feet against the pavement, before becoming still. Garov and the team opened up on the other three. It was over in less than five seconds.

Out of the dark, on the officers side of the vehicle, cautiously walked Jimmy Lester and another man, and from its' other side came two more, approaching just as cautiously. 'Bad Boy' Lester stopped beside the fallen officer, looked down, and made a hand sign. Ebbets, next to Garov, rose to his feet and, motioning for Garov to follow him, went to join Lester.

Standing next to the officer, who was laying on his face, Jimmy Lester pointed down at him. Coming closer, both men looked down at the man laying face down on the street, Garov not seeing at first what he was showing them. Then the area under the coat, over the officers' spine, began to writhe violently. Both men took an involuntary half step backwards, Jimmy aimed his weapon and fired point blank into it.

Garovs' eyes widened in shock, not understanding such an action from a man of Lesters' character. He opened his mouth to protest, then, thinking better of it snapped it shut, remembering that these men had just saved him from certain death. He looked up at Jimmy Lester, his question plain in his eyes, as he waited for some explanation.

Jimmy looked somberly into his eyes for a long moment, then knelt down next to the body, pulling a razor sharp commando knife from his boot as he did so. Grabbing the collar of the officers' coat and shirt he began to slit both open. When he had cut them completely through and pulled them apart, exposing the officers spine, he looked up at Garov.

He said to him, in a deadly calm tone of voice that sent goose bumps racing over Garovs' skin. "There, my new friend, is the enemy of our people, both yours and mine! Look long and well, and never forget! And hope that you never have to get this close to a live one, because I doubt you will survive it.

Dirk says they are here to take this world away from us, and use us for riding and food animals!" he paused for a few seconds, then went on in an even grimmer tone, "This is what we are fighting!"

Bending down and grabbing a fist full of grass and dirt, and lifting it to the level of Garovs' eyes Jimmy said forcefully, "This! This is what we are fighting for. Our planet! Our home!!!!! Do you understand now? Do you see what we face if we do not start fighting now? Together! Lester finished with a shudder, the grim lines in his face looked to be chiseled there permanently.

Garov was a very strong man, both physically and mentally, but the sight of the still smoking gray-green thing still attached to the hapless officers spine caused his gorge to rise in his throat, and he had to turn and step away for a moment to regain control of himself as time seemed to slow everything around him.

When he had done so he turned back to Jimmy and said in a cold and professional voice "I See!! Tell me, how do you think they knew we were here?" As he voiced this question time seemed to speed up to normal.

The other team members had placed the other bodies into the jeep on the far side, and ran it into the park at an angle, tipping it over on its' side. This dumped the unconscious bodies out and away in a limp sprawl.

Others of the team ran to the two men who had been with the officer and carried their unconscious bodies to a nearby lamppost whose light was out, like so many others in this area. They carefully laid them down on either side of it. The officer was picked up and, the men carefully avoiding the mass on his back, and placed in the drivers' seat of the nearby jeep. One of the men, on Ebbets order, removed an incendiary device from his gear pouch and placed it on the floor under the officers' seat.

Another was placed by its' magnetic clamp to the fuel tank Then the jeep was lined up with the lamppost. This done, all but one of the men raced to the now open rear doors of the box van and jumped in.

As Garov seated himself on the floor with the rest of the men Jimmy reached down and removed the briefcase he had been carrying since he had left his office from his hand. Taking a small device from his pocket, Jimmy ran it over the surface of the case. As it passed over the handle a ruby light lit up on the devices surface and Jimmy said, "I thought so!"

Reaching over to a side compartment, he pulled out a sack, and holding it out to Garov asked him to empty the contents of the case into it. Running the device over the contents just to be sure, and getting no response, he said to Tony, "Toss that into the first open truck you can that is going in the opposite direction."

The van pulled up next to the now idling jeep, and the man waiting there lifted the now heavy officers' leg and placed the foot on the accelerator. He put the jeep in gear and the now racing motor caused it to surge forward to slam into the lamppost.

The man now pulled hard on the two wires he had attached to the pins on the incendiary devices and, running to the van, jumped in, closing the doors as he did so.

As the van sped away there was a loud whump, and a bright flash of light that penetrated the small cracks around the rear doors. A few seconds later there was a loud explosion as the fuel tank exploded and the entire vehicle was completely engulfed in the flames of the furiously burning fuel.

In an aside, over his shoulder, Jimmy Lester said to them that there was a fifty-fifty chance that they would accept the accident scenario. But, even if they didn't it would give them enough time to get out of the city and to their exit point.

Garov sat, his back braced against the swaying side of the van as it made its' way through the city, thinking of the gruesome sight of that thing attached to that poor, brave, officers spine. From a couple of comments he had overheard that officer no longer owned a will of his own. As he was thinking these thoughts, he made his commitment to never rest again until every last one of those things on earth was dead and gone!

At the time of this vow Garov had no idea at all that to keep it he would have to spend the length of several men's long lifetimes to keep it. What would completely amaze him was the very real possibility that he might be able to live long enough to see that vow kept.

As the van sped through the dark night Garov, leaning against the swaying side of the van, and, with nothing else to do now was beginning to succumb to the after action lethargy. A condition that was normal to men like himself, and all of those who walked the thin line between life and death.

As his eyelids began to droop he could overhear part of the conversation between Jimmy Lester and Tony Ebbets, coming from the drivers compartment. Jimmy was saying,

"Right after we heard the two clicks of your signal those two jeeps pulled up and parked at either end of the block, and turned out their lights. No one got out. They just sat there. As your guys came out of the manholes they came to life. So we slipped out the side door of the van on the curb side, and we surrounded em—

That was the last of the conversation that Garov heard as his eyelids closed completely.

Denton

Very 'Special Agent' Paul Denton allowed himself only one luxury, and it was the only luxury that he had not paid for out of his own pocket! It had been paid for completely out of the funds allocated to the super secret agency he worked for and absolutely no one begrudged it to him. As a matter of fact he had been asked many times before, on his long climb to his present position, to take a little more than he had. He had always refused, saying that what he had was enough.

That luxury was his office, located within the agency complex which was in one of the third sub-basements of the Pentagon. His office was an oasis of beauty and comfort in a desert of functionality. His office was completely sound proof, and once you stepped through and closed the door the constant clacking, beeping, and warbling of machines, computers, and telephones was instantly gone, and you found yourself in a sea of blissful calm.

His office was, for the area allotted his agency, a very large space. It was almost twenty feet by twenty feet, and only slightly smaller than that of the agency's director. It was very well appointed with a huge ell shaped mahogany desk backing into one corner facing the entry door. The desk sported two built in and one desktop computers. Behind the desk was a long ell shaped countertop sitting on several three drawer filing cabinets and a large safe, which was located in the center of the ell.

Atop this counter were various types of communications equipment and other computer peripherals, along with stacks of printer paper and standard computer printouts. The filing cabinets below were all lockable, and the safe in the center, behind it's fake cabinet door fascia, required two combinations to open it.

In the opposite corner to the desk was an attractive corner hutch used as a combination bar and library. A few feet in front of this, sitting on a beautifully woven oriental rug was sofa flanked by two high backed wing chairs, and a wooden glass topped coffee table finished this comfortable ensemble.

Built into a third corner, and viewable from both desk and sofa area, was a large screen TV, the bottom part of which was a compact kitchenette unit. The carpet on the floor was brown, with beige toned highlights. The walls and ceiling were painted in soft pastels, and all of the rooms lighting, except for that on the desk, was from indirect sources. A very comfortable space indeed!

At this moment, and in these very comfortable surroundings, very special agent Paul Denton was anything but comfortable. In fact he wanted to yell to let out some of the tension that had been building in him. He had been in his office for a little over four hours now, and sitting on his normally immaculate desk were the contents of three files, spread out in seeming disarray before him. These files had been between the coffee table and the desk several times already this morning. The movement had not done anything to help his mind with the contents of the files.

He was sitting behind the desk again, deep worry lines not normally a part of his makeup, etched into his cheeks and forehead as he reread the contents for the umpteenth time today. Making a final decision he picked up the plain black telephone handset from its' cradle, hidden from view on the inside well wall of the desk, and waited for it to be answered. That phone called only one number. His boss! When it was answered he spoke without hesitation, "Chief, can I buy you a cup of coffee?"

After listening for a few seconds he replied, "I'd prefer it at my place if you don't mind!" Listening for a few more seconds he finished with "Fine. In about ten minutes then." And he hung up. Pressing a button on his regular phone console he said "Annie. Would you be kind enough to make a full pot of that famous Jamaican coffee of yours for me right away. The 'Chief' is coming for a chat!" Listening to her reply he said, "you're right! The brandy is probably a good idea too. Thanks."

As he sat waiting for his boss he scanned the contents of the three files once again. The first was a single page, hand written. It was a list of names, quite long now, that had been growing for the last three months at an alarming rate. It was a list that comprised some of the best, most talented and lethal people known to the intelligence community today. And having all of these people on one list was a very scary proposition.

The second file was a number of notes, written to him by his boss, about the answers he had gotten from the heads of other agency's to his questions concerning the possibilities of any secret operations being set up by them in this country. He badly needed clarification about some of those answers.

The third file was the most disturbing to him! Its' contents was from one of his oldest, best, and most reliable sources in Russia. It concerned the disappearance of one of their top KGB people, and the spotting of one of the people on his first files list, at the time of the disappearance. He was hoping against hope that it was pure coincidence, but knew in his gut it was not!

Just then there was a soft knock, and the door opened as Annie walked in carrying a tray laden with coffee pot, cups and saucers, and a bottle of 'Cardinal Mendoza' brandy. She went to the coffee table, set the things out neatly and nodding to him walked out, as he smiled his thanks to her retreating back. She really deserves a grade and pay raise, he thought to himself. 'She knows me better than I know myself! Have we really been together for fifteen years already?' he marveled inwardly.

Looking at his watch Denton got up and moved towards the door Annie had just left by a moment ago. Just as he reached for the knob, there was a sharp rap from the other side and the knob began to turn—

Denton and the Chief

As Dentons' fingers reached for the knob it turned and the door swung inwards, followed by the short, rotund, but still muscular form of his boss as he stepped into the room, closing the door firmly behind himself, saying as he did so, "I told Annie not to let anything disturb us for at least an hour!"

So saying, he stepped past Denton, going to his customary spot at one end of the sofa, where he proceeded to make himself comfortable after placing a small stack of files on the coffee table. Leaning forward he poured two cups of coffee from the pot there and added a generous dollop of the fine brandy to each cup.

The two things that made Denton and his boss such a good team was, one: both men were extraordinarily good at the integration and extrapolation of bits of seemingly unrelated information, and posing it to each other in a way that was complementary to the parallel direction of the others' thoughts.

This ability had been quickly recognized by his boss, early in their relationship and nurtured and mentored to the state it existed in today, like some gruff old mother bear. Some said that they could almost read each others thoughts. The second: was an almost instant liking, each for other, that had grown over the years via a deep and abiding respect for each others abilities and intuition.

Not knowing these two one might think that they were a completely disparate duo, the one usually frowning and gruff, and the other generally smiling and friendly. But to those in the know they were well respected, and even feared.

This was because they ran one of the intelligence communities most secret agencies, and even though it had less than fifty full time employees and agents, it could, at need of proven necessity, take command of an entire segment of the FBI. Or even a whole division of the armed forces of this country by presidential authority. Their charter and funding were so secret that only those in the highest echelons of the government knew for sure that they existed.

Appearances aside, Denton and his boss were cut from the same bolt of cloth. Both men were patriots of the passionate kind. Both were seasoned veterans of difficult wars, and both were highly intelligent, self reliant, and motivated. They were both loving fathers and husbands, and generally decent men. And both, at need, could be totally ruthless. And both of these men took their jobs, with the power and authority that went with them, very seriously indeed.

So, when these men were worried or disturbed about something, those in power that they reported to had cause to listen carefully to them. They were also not the kind of men to bring small problems to the briefing table, or shirk giving the tough answers to any of those hard problems.

As Denton sat down in one of the wing chairs across from his boss at the coffee table, he lay his three files down in front of him. Both men could see the disturbed nature of the other.

"All right, just how bad is it?" the chief asked him without any preamble.

"It's getting pretty bad! Start with this. These are the ones that I'm sure of so far." Denton said, handing the single sheet with the list of names on it to his boss.

As he watched his boss read down the list of names he saw the mans' frown deepen, and his eyebrows rise, and as he finished reading the list, his eyes go slightly out of focus for a minute. This was a typical indication that he was correlating those names with some other bits of information he had picked up somewhere along the way.

As his eyes refocused, the man said "A strange thing happened about the same time Dirk put in his papers for retirement. Defense intelligence black ops lost two men, about a week apart. The strange part is that both men were listed as undercover domestically. And the reports on their loss are suspiciously very thin!"

He paused, thinking for a moment, "Both were new men, transferred in recently, and neither had been, according to their records, vetted by that unit. That is very strange, even for defense intelligence, don't you think?" He asked, then, briskly "What's next?"

"That last may have something to do with that snub you got from Defense when you asked them if there was anything odd going on in their 'domestic' bailiwick, according to your notes anyway. That may also be why State, Naval, and CIA have all been so closed mouth lately. It seems that none of them like losing track of people, especially ones they've had some dealings with in the past! Again, according to your notes, and most of whom are on that list!"

The chief just sat there looking at him, waiting, then nodded at him to continue. Without a word Denton handed him the report from his Russian contact.

As he read this file it seemed that his boss's eyebrows were trying to climb right up his forehead. As he closed the file shut he snapped, "Why didn't you tell me about this before?!"

"I just received that a couple of hours ago." Denton said, a little aggrieved that the man thought he was holding things back. "That's why I called you for this meeting! If we're thinking the same thing, and I think we are, we're going to have to take this higher up before going very much further with it, considering what that report indicates!"

Thinking for a moment the big man asked, "Can your man tie 'Bad Boy' into this one hundred percent?"

"He said he was ninety eight percent certain that it was 'Bad Boy' he spotted. It was from fifty feet away and the area was crowded. He's been over there for eleven years and he's never been off yet."

"It does have all of the earmarks of one of 'Bad Boys' ops, doesn't it?" said the chief thoughtfully.

"Chief, I think that the report is accurate. If so, and if Garov is joining this new secret op, Its' gone international already and we still haven't got a clue as to what's involved besides some of the best people in the world seem to be major players in it. On top of that we don't have enough men or money, or authorization to take it on fully right now!" Here Denton paused, seeing the agreement on his chief's face.

Just then there was a sharp tap on the door. It opened a second later and a troubled looking Annie stepped inside, holding a sheet of paper with a diagonal red stripe running from corner to corner on it. Without a word she walked directly to Denton and handed it to him, then stood waiting while he read it.

The sheet also had, in large bold letters across the top, the words **Urgent! Urgent! Urgent!** As he finished reading Denton, very uncharacteristically swore. **Holy Shit!!**

"What is it?" the boss asked impatiently.

"It's from my contact in Russia," Denton hurried on, "and he took a big chance in sending this out to me! It says that the KGB has put a complete lid on everything having to do with Garovs' disappearance! He says that five men who were sent to pick up Garov were found unconscious on the street with no knowledge of what happened to them other than they saw some bright flashes coming out of the dark at them. The officer with them was found in one of the vehicles burnt to a crisp. The really odd part is that his uniform jacket and tunic were slit up the back, and on his back, on either side of his spine he had small puncture wounds, and one large one at the base of his skull over the spine."

"Even odder, the doctor who performed the autopsy has vanished! The only reason we have this intel is that the doctor was a friend of my contact and sent him a copy of the autopsy report, unknown to anyone else. The only other thing my man says is that the unconscious men all felt that they had been shot at." Denton paused for a breath, then "Shit!! All this! And now a new type of weapon too?!"

With very somber eyes Denton's boss looked up at Annie, let out a soulful sigh, and said "Annie, please call the Presidents office and make a private appointment for Mr. Denton and myself at his earliest convenience." And after a short pause, "Please speak to the man personally and emphasize the terms 'earliest' and 'private'. Thank you." He said, already dismissing her from his thoughts.

Turning back to Denton he said, "As of now everything having the slightest thing to do with this is classified priority one black!"

"And no one but ourselves, Annie and my Martha, and the case agents you assign are to have any contact with this information for any reason whatsoever! Do you understand?" he barked, his face and eyes grim.

The man who had lasted for nearly forty years, longer than any other before him in this position, stood and walked slowly to the door, his wide shoulders now somewhat dropped and tensed, bringing to Denton's mind a picture of 'Samson' carrying the world.

Turning back to Denton before stepping through he said, "Combine all of our files, yours and mine, and put everything into a secure transportation case. I believe we will have an appointment at the White House within the hour." And left for his own office.

Denton hastened to comply, there being a lot of paper that had been accumulated since the first warnings had come to his notice. A couple of quick in house calls brought the two men he had been using on this matter quickly to his office, where he passed on the new security status of their work.

A short forty five minutes later, as he was putting the last of the files into the security transport case, and true to his boss's prediction, Annie stepped into his office to say, "The President will see you and 'The Man' in one hour in his private office in the White House."

Denton, musing to himself as he prepared to leave for this important appointment, wondered if, in a rare bout of second guessing, he really wanted the weight of the load his boss now carried. A sharp shake of his head dismissed these thoughts. After all, he had willingly sought his apprenticeship with his brilliant and intuitive boss, and taken on, even more willingly, his role as the mans' protégé and heir apparent.

He would accept the responsibility and whatever weight came with the power and authority he had achieved. Besides, he was doing what he totally enjoyed doing.

Thinking these thoughts as he left his office to join his boss for their appointment he had little forewarning just how heavy carrying that load could, and would, become for all of them.

Balor's Cave Refuge

Balor had been traveling steadily for a week now, and the cave he was heading for, his refuge for many years, was still about two days hard travel away, and he was beginning to feel the effects of the fast pace he had been maintaining for the last week and a half.

Hunger was also beginning to gnaw at him as his stomach growled for the fifth or sixth time in the last hour. He had killed and eaten a fair sized deer about three days ago, eating as much as he could hold. Now he must stop to rest and eat again.

His present position put him in the upper reaches of the lower Canadian Rocky Mountains, a couple thousand feet below the ever present snowline, and traveling just inside the upper tree line. At this time of year, late summer, and in this area, the hunting should still be pretty good. And sure enough, within half an hour he had caught and eaten three fat rabbits.

He might have, under other circumstances, stayed and hunted another rabbit but the urge to reach his cave and contact the 'Enclave' was growing stronger with each passing hour.

The information he had accrued, and the incidents that had happened over the past few months were, he knew, of vast importance to the remnants of his people! He also believed, strongly, that the information he could now provide would quite possibly cause the elders to call for a full 'Enclave' gathering.

That, if it were to happen, would be wonderful for he had not seen any of his litter siblings for many tens of decades. Yes, he had occasionally farspoken one or another of them as his travels had brought him within range of one of them if they happened to be in the right area of their patrol sectors to have a few moments of conversation. The talk was usually limited in scope because farspeaking required the output of a great deal of energy.

The only times farspeaking could be done for any length of time was when it was done from one of the special places, such as his cave, which seemed to act as an amplifier for sending/receiving his/their thoughts.

As those thoughts were running through his mind Balor realized that those thoughts had done something else. They had made him realize that for the last two days he had been feeling something, in that part of his mind he knew he used for communicating mind to mind, like an itch.

Moreover, it was getting intermittently stronger the closer he got to his cave. If he didn't know better he would almost swear that this itch had the flavor of his brother Dirks' thoughts, but that seemed impossible for he was many hundreds of miles away and the twolegs did not have the mind strength for such farspeaking!

He gave himself a mental shake of the head, concentrating on where he put his paws as his long, lithe body smoothly ate up the miles he had still to go.

Some while, and many, many, miles later he broke out of a very large copse of mountain Birch into a vast mountain valley, still covered with shoulder high, for him, grass and late summer flowers. Seeing this he lengthened his strides, knowing that he was now on the last leg of his journey. Across this valley, and through the narrow pass at the other end and he would be within minutes of his cave.

As he approached a shallow cut leading down into the vast bowl of this valley a hot jolt, like a red hot poker fresh from the fire, slashed across his extended awareness of his mind, causing him to come to a jarring halt and drop down to his belly, well out of sight in the tall grass.

Only one thing would cause his extended awareness to react like that! He had been spotted by a very large predator. Balor was not afraid of anything he might meet out here, but he had learned a healthy respect for many of the larger predators of these far northern reaches.

As he scanned with both his mind and his eyes he sensed that, whatever it was, it was waiting for him just on the lower side of this cut. Moving through the tall grass with just the barest whisper of sound he headed for the low bank on the right side of the shallow cut. As he inched up and over onto the top of the low bank of the cut, he peered cautiously over and down the inner side, and gave a long mental sigh. *This is going to be a rough one!* he thought to himself.

There! Crouched on a low narrow ledge, just inside the cut, was a huge mountain cat! The real grand daddy of all mountain cats it seemed. It must have been seven and a half feet from the tip of its' scarred gray black muzzle to the white tip of its' slowly lashing tail. It was big and powerful, standing nearly three feet tall at it's hunched, powerful looking shoulders, and it must weigh nearly two hundred twenty pounds.

Balor rose to his full height, only three quarters of that of the big cat below him, then sat down. Then he calmly wrapped his long tail around his forefeet. Looking down at the magnificent creature below him he coughed politely to get its' attention.

At the sound of Balors' polite cough the huge cat sprang almost five feet straight up into the air, twisting its' head around this way and that, trying to find the source of the noise. The twisting motion of its' head caused it to begin arching over backward, and with that amazing ability all cats possess, twisted its' body around so that it landed on all fours when it hit the ground.

When it landed it spun in a circle, hissing and spitting a challenge. As it calmed a little it spun in a circle again, now issuing a deep rumbling challenge from deep in its' chest, as it tested the air for its' still unseen challenger.

Again Balor coughed politely. The huge cat spun half around again, its' large head now coming up to face him, its' two and a half inch fangs exposed as its' lips pulled back in a snarl.

Balor could see that this was truly an old cat that was still able to protect its' territory, as attested to by the many scars on its' muzzle, neck, and shoulders. The big cat took a half step backwards, crouching, and gave a coughing roar that would have frozen anything else in fear.

As Balor sat looking down at that magnificent creature, his own huge golden eyes meeting directly those green gold ones, he was careful not to make any sudden or overt moves with any part of his body. As a matter of fact the only thing moving were those silk thread tendrils at the tips of his ears.

Those tendrils were super sensitive neuro-detectors, able to detect the minute neuro-electrical charges still attached to the different dander's and pheromones released by a body. And by testing the strength of these charges he could tell a great deal about the emotional state and intent of that body. Such as now! The big cat was releasing energy in a pattern that said it was still in the indecisive state of 'Fight or flight'.

As Balor sat there, making no threatening moves, the big cat calmed enough to test the air again for his scent. The grizzled old warrior cat, scenting no fear from Balor, decided on caution and backed a few more steps away, putting the safety of more distance between them.

Sensing the uncertainty in the big cats basically simple mind Balor composed and directed a thought/sense of calmness/non threat, that he had developed over many years, and that he found, when there was time, to be very effective. As he felt the calmness begin to spread further, taking a firmer hold in the huge cats mind and the turmoil there declining, the raised fur on its' ruff began to lay flat again.

Finally the big cat backed a few more steps away before turning and trotting off through the tall grass in the opposite direction to Balors' line of march. Before he completely disappeared into the tall grass the big cat turned its' massive scarred muzzle once more towards Balor to give him a last defiant snarl.

As the huge animals tail finally disappeared from sight Balor let out a deep mental breath, admitting to himself that if it had come to a fight it might have been a close thing with such a seasoned veteran. Taking a deep breath, and a last look in the direction taken by the big cat, Balor continued on his journey.

Barring any further delays he would be at his cave in a few more hours, where he could rest and prepare himself for the high demands of the farspeaking. As he trotted along he felt the barest hint of a thought, more like a memory than a real contact, tickle his awareness. It seemed to be saying, *fare you well my brother.*

And it seemed to come from Dirk!

Balor shook himself mentally, and picked up his pace, because he thought that must just be wishful thinking.

CHAPTER ELEVEN
Interludes

Dirk

Dirk had been working non stop now for sixteen out of every twenty four hours for the last two months. The machine of his primary new team was now actually beginning to operate as one. This, in such a short time span, was a little surprising to him. Mainly because they were such a disparate group, with as diverse a montage of individual characteristics as could be found in any group of people.

All were very talented individuals, each in their own right and specialty, yet these same specialties almost always dictated that they worked best alone. He felt sure that this new cohesion was due in large part to the efforts of Bill Tate, always a first class organizer. Not once did he give a thought to the fact that all had come because he had called out to them!

At this moment Dirk was, so far as anyone could tell, in the deep REM cycle of the five hours of sleep he had enforced on himself, and recommended for all of the other team members. He had done this knowing that a tired operative was prone to making mistakes, and mistakes in this business were often fatal. So, Dirk was asleep and dreaming, or so he would have thought were he able to observe himself at this moment.

His dream was about Balor, traveling somewhere far in the north, in very mountainous country. He, Dirk, was in his dream reaching out with his mind to wish his friend good hunting. At another point he seemed to be witnessing a confrontation between Balor and a huge mountain cat. This encounter appeared to have ended well for he thought he heard the echoes of Balors distinctive chuckle in his mind.

Dirk started awake at this then eased back down, some part of his mind wondering how this could be, for Balor was many hundreds of miles away to the north, much too far away for Dirk to be able to contact. Wasn't He?

As Dirk dropped back into deeper sleep another was wondering the same thing.

TuLan Chai

TuLan the Chai was exhausted mentally! This exhaustion was from being in an almost continuous state of amazement at these technologically primitive people, or so he had fist thought them.

TuLan was also learning a lesson that these people had been learning the hard way over the past five or six thousand years by their meager technological capabilities. 'Good Intelligence' is rarely gained at long distance!

As TuLan rested, for him similar to but different from Dirks' sleep periods, he let his mind roam over the many items that were causing his continuing state of amazement.

First and foremost of those was his 'lucky' encounter, an earth term whose only parallel in his own language was 'the uncertainty of ill or favorable potentials', with his present host, Dirk. His host had an extremely complex mind. A mind not only extremely complex, but one that had areas that were impenetrable to his probing.

This was a very rare occurrence for one of TuLans' race, for the necessities involved in becoming almost totally one with the host being required virtually constant mental contact. His host also seemed to be a magnet, drawing to himself on his word alone some of the most talented people TuLan could have ever conceived of and made themselves available to him.

And the way not only his host, but those he had drawn to him, handled information and problem solving, as well as the way that they were able to work together, was completely new to him. They seemed, even as disparate as their education, experience, and backgrounds were, able to weave and meld themselves into a single cohesive whole to solve any given problem set before them. The way each would take a piece of any given problem and gnaw on it mentally until it gave up some form of useful information, then bringing it back to the group to reintegrate it into a part of an overall picture of a working solution was truly awesome.

And their ability to extrapolate whole concept images from very small, and even diverse, bits of information was really scary! This was something he should keep well in mind for the future.

What bothered TuLan the most though was Balor. TuLan knew without a doubt, after being hosted by Dirk, that Balor was an alien to these people and to this planet! One of the ways he knew this for sure was the small amount of DNA comparison he had been able to do from Balor after his temporary hosting right after the crash of his ship on this planet. And another way was by the flavor/pattern of Balors' thoughts. Both Dirk and Balor had been able to accept the ship and his alien origin.

Dirk because of his ability to extrapolate the meeting of different races from different planets. Balor because he had seen it, or knew about it, before this.

Balor was also a powerful telepath, able it seemed, to block TuLan from any part of his mind at will, and even some parts of his mind quite unconsciously.

There was one other thing about both Balor and Dirk. Both seemed able to communicate telepathically with each other on a wave or band that he just couldn't reach or penetrate, no matter how hard he tried. And that really was very unusual, considering that he had been closely host bonded to each.

Those thoughts, and others, were drifting across the surface of his mind as he lay resting in the small cavity, shaped something like a hammock, he occupied in Dirks' body, at the same time taking the small amounts of trace elements he needed from Dirk's blood.

Along with these other thoughts was the subject of the Drel's presence on this planet. Before his crash on this planet he had harbored a strong sense of concern about this. His concern was now turning to a sense of strong alarm, considering that two of them had now been found in the close proximity of Dirk and his friends.

This was, after all, the primary reason for his being in this solar system and observation of this planet. It was the perfect type of planet for the Drel to try to penetrate back into this part of this galaxy. What was strange, if the Drel were here in some force, was that the technology of these people, 'Humans' they called themselves, was of their own devising. Also, how much of this apparent penetration had something to do with the current explosion in knowledge these people were going through. That knowledge, and its' directly relevant technology, were expanding at an alarming rate. But, also, after his experience with Dirk, and some of the other people he had brought in, he was beginning to expect the unexpected.

One thing that he was positively and absolutely sure of, even at this early stage of his relationship with these Earthlings, these 'Human' beings, was that he would be totally and abjectly terrified of having them as an enemy!

He had never in his long, long life met or experienced the kind of fury and hatred that all, each and every one, of those he had come into contact with, either directly or through his relationship with Dirk, had emanated when told what the Drel had planned for their planet and people. It was an aura, so strong at times that he actually had to shield his mind from it, that was terrible to behold! Yes, these people would be a totally implacable enemy!

And yet, on the whole, he knew from his contact with Dirk that they seemed to be a friendly and caring people. Although a young race they were, he was learning, a people capable of deep thought and deep moral convictions.

Jimmy 'Bad Boy' Lester

It had been two weeks now since they had left Russia, and since the incident on the night of the extraction. They had been traveling almost constantly and had not had any problems at any of the various transfer points they used. Jimmy 'Bad Boy' Lester trusted the people he was using to get them to his jump off point in Baton Rouge, Louisiana.

They were consummate smugglers, and had never, to the best of his knowledge, been interdicted, or even questioned, by any police agency. He had maintained a very profitable relationship with them for many years that was based on two simple, but strictly adhered to, principles. 'Ask no unnecessary questions and always pay on time'!

Even 'Bad Boy' Didn't know the exact route that they had used to get them out! At present they were 'Supernumerary' passengers on a coastal freighter, and would be in port within another eight hours.

Ordinarily Jimmy would have split up the teams and taken commercial transports back to St. Louis, their primary destination, but Dirk had been very specific about staying completely low profile while getting back to the US. And he had been one hundred percent right. Before boarding he had checked in with headquarters in St. Louis, and had been told that all of the main and secondary ports of entry were now under heightened observation.

In Baton Rouge the teams would disappear into the city, and the next morning re-converge at one of the busy river docks, where a large river tugboat would be waiting to take them inconspicuously upriver to St. Louis and a private dock abutting their headquarters property.

Standing in the fantail of the powerful little freighter, his hip propped against the rail, Jimmy lit one of the little cigars he rarely allowed himself. He felt a little of the tension that had been building up over the last two weeks begin to ebb slowly away as he puffed contentedly on the small cheroot. The soft breeze carried the muted sound of the powerful twin diesel engines that pushed the little freighter as it plowed across the Gulf of Mexico.

His eyes drank in the beauty of the starlit night sky, and the vee of the wake, effervescing in the moonlight as it spread out behind the ship. He held this peaceful beauty ever so tightly to himself for a short while, knowing that with the dawn all of the tension and danger would come crashing back down around him. "The terrible part about all of it was," he thought to himself, "that he was a danger junky. And he loved it!"

With these thoughts his mind turned to his charge, Garov, and his personal surprise at finding the man so different from what he knew about him. "He really shouldn't be so surprised," he ruefully mused to himself, "because the dry facts seldom held the weight of real flesh!"

Except for those first few hectic minutes when his men had been surprised as they came up out of the manhole, and the ensuing short, but lethal, fire fight Garov had been quiet and a little reserved. During that episode he had noticed Garov react with speed and decisiveness, almost melding with the rest of the team.

The only real benefit from the encounter had been when Garov had seen the Drel attached to the officers spine, at first hand and not from photographs. He had seen the mans' dark complexion pale visibly when the Drel had been explained completely to him.

Later, after leaving the van at a predetermined location, and walking for a half hour through the pitch black woods while being guided by one of the half seen smugglers, they reached a small clearing where they were to be picked up. In the clearing, waiting for them, was a huge black painted 'Sikorsky' helicopter, its oversized vanes just clearing the surrounding trees. They had jumped aboard and were quickly airborne.

Once aloft Garov had gotten up and come across the large cargo bay, and stopping in front of him, reaching into the briefcase he still carried removed the weapon that had been given to him, holding it out to Jimmy. As he looked first at the weapon, then up at Garov and Jimmy smiled and shook his head 'no'.

Because Garov repeated that simple gesture that said 'I put myself completely in your hands' Jimmy smiled again, saying "Please keep it. It's your weapon now." And, with a surprised look on his face, Garov thanked him and returned to his seat, where he entered into a conversation with the team member sitting there.

Garov had behaved in this manner throughout the entire trip. Attentive to instructions, doing what was asked of him and remaining generally quiet and unobtrusive. Whenever there was a conversation where he joined in his speech was quiet and cultured, highlighting his obvious intelligence.

During this trip, and until he was cleared as one of them, the team withheld any judgement concerning him, for two good reasons. First, and most obvious, was the fact that he had not outrightly committed himself to the group. Second was his reputation, known by all of these very talented experienced men. No matter that he had been a foe for many years, these men held him at the same level of esteem that Tony Ebbets, Bad Boy, Dirk, and John Crow were held in. They were not afraid of him! They just respected his intelligence and ability.

Jimmy, finished with his cigar, tossed the but in a high arc out over the ships wake, watching the red glow until it disappeared. He faced about, turning his steps to the teams cabins. It was time to lay out the mechanics for the final leg of their trip for the team and their guest.

As Jimmy walked along the passageway to their cabins he mused to himself that he would probably end up liking this quiet thoughtful man. And, having met him, was beginning to understand why Dirk had gone to so much trouble to get him to join them.

"Enough," he said, shaking himself "we still have to get to St. Louis!"

John Crow

John Crow was sitting very still, with his back propped up against a good sized boulder atop one of the wooded hills an hour or So's fast walk from the box canyon where so much was going on now.

Both his mind and life were now, after only a few short weeks, in a new and different kind of turmoil than he was used to. Yet, as he sat there thinking about what had happened to him in this short span of time, he felt more peace within himself than he had known in many years.

One thing that helped bring that peace to his mind was that his friend Dirk had not changed over the years. He had, if anything, become even more of a magnetic personality, drawing to himself many resourceful and very talented people, making them feel that what they did was important and worth doing. And what they did for him they always did well! It was a real comfort to know that there were still some things that you could still count on in this world.

Dirk had returned, as he had promised, on the night of Crows' very eventful arrival. And, after talking with both Dirk and Bill Tate for nearly twelve hours non stop, he had finally agreed to let TuLan, and the ships' automated 'med unit' treat his ailment. Within twenty four hours of that treatment his pain had almost completely disappeared, and after a week he felt as good as he had ten years ago!

But his mind still shied away from that experience. He knew that he would eventually have to deal with those memories, but now, even a month afterwards, it was still not the right time. Those memories still smacked of the science fiction stories that had so enthralled him as a boy. No, there would be time later to deal with them, it was enough now just to admit that they had happened!

The ship now, was another story, one that had a completely fascinating hold on him. He spent at least five hours a day exploring its' mysteries, finding that he didn't even mind the time he had to share his explorations in its' bowels with G. 'Whiz' Burke. Burke, he found out quickly, was truly a genius when it came to figuring out systems operations, or improvising something else from something he found in them. Truth to tell, he had actually learned a lot from him! But the thing that had brought him here, to this hilltop, was his encounter with that

227

strange and beautiful black cat. Balor. The memory of that encounter was still bright and fresh in his mind.

The mention, by Balor, of Balors' peoples relationship with his ancestors had brought memories flooding back to his mind of the stories handed down by both his father and grandfather. Stories that were old, as old as his peoples' memories of this land. The idea that they were not just fables and story lessons had shaken him to his core. His mind now darted hither and thither, seeking to remember those stories and the truths he now knew they held for him. If he were smart enough to understand them!

His grandfather, great grandfather, and great-great grandfather, all three, had been 'Shamans' of the Lacota Sioux Nation. All had been fervent believers in the ancient lore and legends of his people and their history, and all had been respected among the high councils of the Sioux and many other tribes.

He remembered, again, as he sat with his back propped against the boulder, the early fall sunlight warming his head and shoulders, memories coming back as if it were only last week, those many days his grandfather had spent in helping him to prepare for his ordeal into manhood. The days spent in physical preparation, and the cleansing sessions in the sweat lodge, and the fasting to prepare his mind. And the many long nights spent listening to and learning the lore and history of his people. Among one of those had been the legend about one of his great grandfathers, ten generations removed. He had been one of the great ones, a wise and revered 'Shaman' known as 'One who walked with the old ones'.

As the story went he had, at some point, left the tribe to live in a huge cave in the nearby mountains. From that point on, whenever he was seen in one of the villages or walking in the mountains, he was always in the company of a huge, and beautiful, black cat. Such as those that were spoken of in the legends of the people.

The cat was said to have eyes the color of the sun, and, if it were to look at a man it could freeze him into immobility, or if angered send him running into the wilderness gibbering and foaming at the mouth. And this great 'Shaman' relative always seemed to know where the closest herds of Buffalo were, or where the fattest Elk were to be found in a hard winter. He knew also what plants could be used to fight strange illnesses and infections.

And the story also went that this great 'Shaman' was often heard conversing with this strange and wonderful companion in a manner like that of two men talking. The legend also went that this 'Shaman' had lived the span of years of three normal men.

Then one day the 'Shaman was gone. And for many moons thereafter, the story went, there was heard in those mountains a terrible keening yowling, as if something were mourning a great loss. And for as long as this went on the people were hard pressed to find game within hearing of that cry.

His grandfather had said that he, John Crow, was directly descended from that great 'Shaman' and that he too held the potential for great power within himself, if he could find it. Shortly after being told this legend young John Crow was sent on his vision quest and ordeal.

The ordeal had been a hard one, requiring him to count coup on a large black bear, which he had done with great skill and effort. His quest for his vision had also been successful, but harder still. It had taken six days, with little water and even less food, before his vision had come to him on the sixth night with the fullness of the moon.

He barely made it back to the village, and the shamans smoke lodge before he passed out. To the shaman and the elders he told of his vision of a crow which had come to him and spoken of his future. It had told him that he would become a feared and respected warrior, but that his greatest battles and victories would be fought in strange and far places. He very shortly thereafter took the name of 'Crow'.

What he never told the elders or the shaman was that the crow that had spoken in his vision had done so in a totally strange language, which he had understood completely, yet there had been no words spoken aloud in that conversation. Now, since his encounter with Balor, all of those deeply buried memories had come bubbling and rushing to the surface, clamoring for attention.

After learning what he had over the last few weeks he was sure that his decision to join in this new game was the right one for him. It had been so long since he had worked with people who had no apathy about the right or wrong of what they were doing that his soul felt genuinely refreshed.

"Yes!" he said aloud to himself, "I am truly committed to this thing!"

With this frank affirmation his reservations evaporated, and his spirits lifted, his mind already busy with the plans for the things he knew he could do to help right now.

Carmella 'Chickie' Martinez

'Chickie' Martinez was having an absolute ball. She was having the time of her life doing the one thing that she knew she did better than almost anyone else in the world. She was manipulating and making money. Not only was she doing this well, she was actually providing the necessary funding for an entire organization that looked like it was set to grow by leaps and bounds.

She was also doing it from scratch, starting with very little capital that she was making grow fast enough to stay ahead of the demands she was sure would soon be put upon it. The two million she had been given initially had been parleyed into ten million in cash and credits in a little less than two weeks.

She had done most of this by accessing the 'international float' and piggy backing on some interesting short term partially balanced loans, and by participating in some quick turnover, high return, 'short' position options contracts in the international currency market.

Three weeks into her dealings dirk had given her control of three companies, and several pieces of very valuable commercial real estate properties, which brought the combined total of what she now controlled to slightly over sixty million dollars.

She had just spent five million of that completing an RTO (reverse takeover) of a small, but excellent, electronics and computer chip manufacturing firm that specialized in new and experimental applications. That takeover had gone smoothly because the firm was 'closely held' (not traded publicly)and, it seemed, the owners were almost relieved when presented with the facts of the takeover.

They had given little opposition to exchanging nearly eight million in debt (that she had purchased at a discount of five million) for eighty percent of the company's stock and outright control, and secured positions for them in the new management structure. They would also retain twenty percent of the company stock, but would have to sign away their voting rights to it.

And they were elated when told that the new owners would also inject an additional two million in working capital into the firm. The only thing they were not happy about was the new secrecy agreements they would have to sign if they decided to stay on. They were talented and very knowledgeable people, they just had very little business sense.

She also intended to use this company to acquire another local light manufacturing firm, located not far from this one. It was also 'closely held', and in financial trouble. She also intended to use her two new converts to aid in closing this deal quickly and quietly.

She had spent an additional two million acquiring control of a startup software development firm that was doing phenomenal work in leading edge applications and interface development.

Once these acquisitions had been accomplished and firmed up, another three weeks, she reached out to people she had worked with in the past who knew the rules and were willing to work on a 'need to know' basis. They were highly qualified in management and finance, and knew how to produce results. These people also knew that in working with her they would never be left out to dry if things went south.

They also knew that they would all profit from their association with her, as most of them had in the past. The one thing that they all knew without a doubt was that crossing her could mean a sudden death to their chosen careers. And for those that really knew her it could mean sudden death for them literally. Every one of them understood that crossing her was a very dangerous thing to do!

As far as dealing with the anger where her feeling about Dirk were concerned she had decided to let that anger go. In doing so she had realized that most of that anger was generated from the break up of their short, but very torrid, love affair. Besides, she didn't see very much of him because setting up this new organization required him to be everywhere at once all of the time.

One thing she really appreciated about Dirk was that he had brought up nothing at all about the past, not even a hint. He had, after having Jimmy Lester explain what was going on, come to her and asked her two questions. "Do you want to play?" and "Can you do it?"

At her affirmative answers he had promptly turned over to her a little over two million dollars in cash. And, within a couple of weeks of her trip to that strange and marvelous space ship, had also turned over to her control of several profitable companies and some extremely valuable commercial real estate. Most of these she was using for leverage (loans) for working capital.

But two of them, ideally located stores in New York City, she was going to sell outright and use the proceeds to acquire a medium heavy manufacturing company that specialized in hard to acquire and produce metal alloys. This company would be used to produce repair parts for the ship, and other specialized items they were already beginning to see would be needed.

One of the other pieces, a nice brownstone located on the upper west side of Manhattan, she told him should be kept for use as a safe house and alternate command and control center. She also told him that she wanted to bring in a few key people she felt would be needed. To this he had quietly responded with, "This part of the operation is completely in your control, just have them vetted by Tony Ebbets before telling them anything." She really appreciated the way Dirk ran things.

If a person said they needed or could do something he gave them the wherewithal and information they needed, and the authority to act on it. This given, he only expected results! Or a valid and unquestionable reason for not getting them!

She seemed to be being surprised every day, although she knew she shouldn't be, by the quality of the people who were being attracted and recruited into this operation.

Dirk, she knew, was a veritable magnet, always attracting and drawing the very best people available wherever he went. And those who knew him, or knew about him, knew that good people were the hardest commodity there was to come by in this business. They knew without doubt that they could trust him. Chickie had also adjusted her thinking about this new game. She had been told what it was, and that it had already turned hard (deadly). This she could readily believe because of the caliber of people who had already come on board. The list of those people read like the who's who of the worlds most deadly and dangerous.

Besides Dirk and Bill Tate the crew already boasted three of the deadliest people she had ever heard of. They were—Jimmy 'Bad Boy' Lester, Tony Ebbets, and, probably the most deadly of all, John Crow!

And if the rumor mill was at all accurate they were about to add a fourth to that list. Yuri Garov, the Russian KGB head of dirty tricks.

Not only were these men and women, herself and another she had heard was being approached, deadly in the extreme they were highly intelligent, resourceful operatives able to operate well individually or collectively, as in this case, a real force to be reckoned with.

All of this aside, she was having more fun than she had had in many years, setting up and securing a steady flow of source capital, and supply sources through interlocking companies, false front companies, and off shore holding companies.

'Chickie' Martinez prided herself on being one of the very best in the world at what she did, and, having accepted this position, would not let Dirk or any of the other team members down on her watch!

Paul Denton

Paul Denton was really pissed off! And a pissed off Paul Denton was a very dangerous man! Just recently he had brought in a couple of his agency's auxiliary men to help him find out who it was in the blue sedan that had been tailing him for the last five weeks on an intermittent basis.

When they had forced the sedan over to the side of a country road that Denton had led it out to the driver had jumped out and started to run across an open field. When the men in the chase car had started to follow the man he had opened fire on them with a small automatic weapon, wounding one man and sending the other scrambling for cover as he escaped.

If Denton had had any questions before this about his feelings that his question were stirring things up they were gone now. When Denton had gotten himself turned around and back to the scene the man who had scrambled for cover had gotten his companion back to their car and was giving him first aid for his wound. After helping with the wounded man, he called for an ambulance.

Denton and the unwounded man searched his tails car and found just about what they expected. Nothing. Nothing traceable that would lead them to anyone or any agency, national or foreign. Even the plates came up stolen, as the car probably would also.

This last incident was just the icing on the cake he was having so much trouble eating. His gut instinct told him that something very big was going on, and down, and for some reason he couldn't understand he was just barely missing the one detail that would put him into the picture that wouldn't quite come into focus for him.

This situation was getting way out of hand, and he would have to do something about it soon.

Garov

The trip up the Mississippi River had been a scenic but completely uneventful one for the team and their charge. Garov had never seen this part of America before, just read about it. The sheer size of this river and the beauty of the land along its' banks was done little justice by the dry words written about it.

The bustle of activity in the small towns and cities they passed on that trip reflected the hopes he clung to for his own abused and beleaguered homeland, the people robust and brawling towards some bright future, not care worn and dull eyed as still far too many were today.

A short day and a half ago he had been driven through the streets of a huge city that sprawled on either side of this river, and it had been at some places there two or three miles wide. Here, almost a thousand miles up the length this river it was still nearly a mile wide.

They had turned towards a complex of buildings on the western shore and were approaching a section of waterfront that was heavily industrialized. They were, he was told, coming into the city of St. Louis, in the state of Missouri. On the eastern bank, they also told him, was the city of East St. Louis, in the state of Illinois.

After the boat docked he was taken into what appeared to be a mid sized factory building. Upon entering he was completely surprised to find himself in something resembling a very well appointed bachelor officers quarters building. Once within he was taken up two floors and guided to a large and comfortable sitting room/ bedroom combination with its' own bathroom and shower.

His guide, after letting him in said that he was expected and he could shower and change as soon as he liked. The guide also went on to say that there was a fresh change of clothes in the closet, along with new shoes, and fresh undergarments in the chest of drawers on the opposite wall. His guide then handed him the key to the room and a couple of pages with the floor plans for the building, and telling him that after he showered and changed Mr. Lester would be pleased to meet him in the fourth floor cafeteria for some lunch.

Also, if he wished to speak to Mr. Lester before they met he could do so by dialing two zero one seven on the phone sitting on the small desk near the wing chair. If he needed anything else he could reach someone to assist him by dialing nine. "Oh, one last thing," his guide said just before leaving, "please don't leave the building unless escorted by someone from security. Your security pass has been made up, but has not been processed as yet. It will be ready for you by nine A.M. tomorrow morning. You are being issued a priority five pass, the highest we have, and you can then go anywhere you like." And he was gone, quietly shutting the door behind him.

Garov was not quite sure how he felt about the limited freedom he momentarily had. If he took the man at his word that condition would end in the morning, and he did understand the need for security. What he did know from observing, and the quality of the people he had met so far, was that security here was as good as anything that he could have set up

Out of curiosity he opened the closet door. Inside he found two very nice sports coats, two pair of nicely pressed slacks, one brown and one black, and two very nice dress shirts. One white and one pale yellow. And two pair of shoes. One pair black lace up dress shoes and one pair of brown casual loafers. They were placed neatly on the floor under the clothing.

On the back of the closet door were hung six very nice ties. Crossing the room and opening the drawers in the chest of he found several pair of neatly folded shorts, white tee shirts, and several pair of colored and white socks. In other drawers he found more dress shirts and several attractive polo shirts. These people were as thorough as they appeared to be He was impressed in spite of himself. And he was quite sure that everything would fit perfectly.

On impulse he walked over to the phone on the small desk and dialed the number given to him for 'Bad Boy' Lester. It rang several times before being picked up, the now familiar voice of Jimmy Lester answering curtly, "Yes." He said into the mouthpiece "It's Garov. I'll meet you in the cafeteria in one hour if that is acceptable to you." After hearing Jimmy say "Good." He hung up.

Turning, he headed for the bathroom shedding clothes as he went. He felt a sense of relief as each sweaty, travel stained item was removed and dropped along the way. He entered the bathroom almost with a sense of urgency, wanting to wash away not only the grime accumulated from so much constant travel and too seldom washing, but also the stench of the fear and tension he felt was like a coating on his body accumulated over the last few months. For some reason, as yet unknown to himself, he felt that now was as good a time and place to begin his new life.

As he entered the, to him, large bathroom he was very pleasantly surprised to find a complete set of toiletries. Including, as he preferred, a straight razor for shaving.

As he stepped into the hot shower, the steam billowing out around him as he shut the shower door behind him, a small smile played at the corners of his mouth as he thought to himself, "I think I will enjoy working with my new comrades a great deal."

With this he let the warmth from the steam and hot water envelop his very weary mind and body.

Bill Tate

Bill Tate lay in his bunk, eyes closed against the soft glow of the night light that always burned in all of the sleeping cabins on this ship, trying unsuccessfully to get to sleep because the next day promised to be another hard one, like so many had been recently. His lack of success was due to image after image parading itself across the visual display part of his mind, and along with these images new thoughts were being generated to aggravate his tired mind further. He knew what was going on in his mind, he just wasn't sure he knew how to cope with it all.

The crux of his dilemma came from the wonderful gift he had received from Dirk and TuLan. He had been almost completely resigned to dying within a couple of years from the disease that had been eating away at his body, but now thanks to Dirk and TuLan, he stood a very good chance of outliving both his children and his grandchildren, and therein lay his dilemma.

He didn't know if he wanted to outlive them, or if it was right to! These thoughts had been plaguing him every since the impact of Dirks' statement about him living about another century to a century and a half started him thinking about the perversity of chance occurrence in ones life. His thoughts in this vein were starting to go round and round in his head.

If Dirk had not seen TuLans' ship come down. If Balor had not been there to help TuLan. If Balor/TuLan had not caught Dirk spying on the ship and almost killed him by accident. If Dirk had not agreed to host TuLan. If he had not followed Dirk to that motel and saved his life. If Dirk and TuLan had not saved his own life.

If his world was not being invaded in such an insidious manner. And, after finding the resolve to accept and live his gift of renewed life, putting himself directly back into harms way again to jeopardize it. This last, he knew, was only part of his own personal ethical and moral code. But, none the less, it was having an impact on his thoughts.

Another factor in his thinking was his elevation to his position in this new organization, as head of logistics. He wasn't sure if he was ready for that much power, or worry! His new position gave him almost total control of every asset they had, including this marvelous ship, and who got how much of what, and when! Coupled with everything else was a slight feeling of resentment at now being excluded from field work. He knew that his resentment was unfounded, but it was there just the same.

His resentment was mollified to a large extent by the bright side that his new position brought. That was the fact that he was now working very closely with 'Chickie' Martinez, for whom he was developing a big schoolboyish crush. This situation really surprised him because he had had little interest in women since his divorce five years ago. It was also a situation that he would have to handle carefully, especially if her responses to his somewhat shy overtures continued to be positive, and not just wish fulfillment on his part.

Too, there was the fact that this was definitely not the best environment to try beginning a relationship in, as ones life expectancy under these circumstances could be quite short. This was an unfortunate reality that must be kept in mind at all times now.

As his mind began to relax a little with these pleasant thoughts another image floated across the surface of his minds eye. It was of a beautiful midnight black creature, with huge eyes of molten gold, that moved with all of the grace of every cat that had ever lived. And that strange and wonderful creature called him its' friend! This great and wonderful creature, that could kill almost at the speed of thought, and that seemed to take a perverse pleasure in scaring the shit out of him at times, had called him friend.

Bill Tate was not a standoffish person. He was just reserved in whom he entrusted with his own friendship. So, his responses to Balors' stated friendship were, to say the least, somewhat confused and reticent. Yet he had no doubt of the truthfulness of Balors' professed friendship, for that great creature communicated mind to mind.

Thinking back Bill remembered that first terror filled moment, on his part, of their first meeting. Of Dirk urging him to put his shaking hand on the great cats head. And of the shock, wonder, and awe he felt as that almost whimsical voice said in his mind, *I welcome you, friend of my brother Dirk! My brother has said that you are as one with him, so you and I shall be friends also!*

And since that time their communication had become easier, sometimes his being within a foot of him was enough to let Bill receive those thoughts. And the fear he had nearly frozen him into immobility at first was almost completely gone now.

There was also the playful way in which Balor seemed to appear from nowhere and scaring him silly at times, and the echo of a chuckle in his mind as Balor apologized for doing so. Bill felt no animosity towards Balors' playfulness when he did this for he felt no disrespect from him in his thoughts. Just a sense of playful mirth in that warm chuckle of his.

Also, Bill really thought that Balor was just as intelligent, if not more so, than most of the people he knew. He wasn't quite sure just why he thought this way, but he had an innate feeling that he was right. There was something strange about Balor. He fitted in with his surroundings, yet he really didn't belong here at all! No matter with all of that. Balor was his friend, and he missed him! He was looking forward to his return to the base camp. And that would be soon he hoped. With those last pleasant thoughts Bills' mind finally drifted into exhausted sleep.

Bill didn't, and couldn't, know it yet but he would learn to cherish those half sleepless nights and thoughts in the years to come. For he would be a central figure as the group that was being put together now to fight a savage war to save his own people, their planet, and their very future. Not just their own, nut the future of many more peoples and planets in this galaxy.

Tony Ebbets

Tony Ebbets was, in appearance, not a very impressive or imposing figure. This appearance was, however, exceedingly deceptive! He is, and was recognized by those whose business it was to know such things, one of the deadliest human beings alive!

He was an extremely well trained and educated KILLER! He was a professional killer, not a sociopath! One of the very best in the world, ranked up there with the two dozen or so intelligence professionals such as John Dirk, 'Bad Boy' Jimmy Lester, John Crow, and Yuri Garov, who were recognized as those who were the best there were. And, until just recently he had also become a sadly disillusioned and very skeptical patriot. That is he was, until he met John Dirk for the first time face to face, and found himself in his present circumstances.

His present circumstances not withstanding, his skepticism was still intact. But the dark pall that had been shedding its' darkness on his mind and soul seemed to be lifting, letting the natural patriotism that was the driving force of his life reassert itself. Tony Ebbets was a believer! One of those rare individuals who could, and would, give his heart and soul to what he believed in.

And until just recently his beliefs' had been rather badly battered by the political landscape he had been living in. What had changed for him was his viewpoint and how he looked at it. It had been transformed from one of national proportions to one of worldview proportions. What he understood right now was that there were still some things he could believe in.

That was why he had gladly accepted the mission, after the reasons and conditions had been explained to him, along with Jimmy Lester to extract Yuri Garov from Russia, where he apparently was in danger from his own people. Dirk had said that they really needed him for the fight that was brewing, so he had helped in getting him out and safely here.

Tony, who would be the first to admit it, thought of himself as a very simple man stuck with living in a conversely complex world. The truth was that he was a very complex man with a first rate mind that liked to live in a very simple manner. He was a better than average planner and a brilliant executor of those plans because he was able to integrate changes in them that worked as necessity demanded.

Tony's greatest strength, and greatest weakness, was his loyalty. To his friends, and his causes. The number of friends he had were naturally, because of what he did, few in number. And his ability to believe in causes, until just recently, was severely battered. Battered because over the years he had seen too many of his contemporaries fall by the wayside after breaking themselves on the hard rocks of insensitivity and the callous and wasteful disregard of those in positions of power who sent others out into harms way.

He understood the necessity, at crucial times, of sending people into situations where death was the almost certain outcome. He had done so more than once himself! He had just lost faith in a system wherein those who gave those orders felt themselves to be above the consequences of their actions. He had not completely lost his ability to believe, but he had lost his blind youthful faith in the quality and competence of those in positions of power who were giving those orders. So, after much very careful planning, he had resigned from his agency. After some hard testing of his resolve, and finding it firm, that agency had finally left him alone to go his own way. He was a hard and resourceful man, and they did not want him as an enemy.

After working haphazardly at freelancing for a time in his stock and trade he finally, through an introduction, taken a position with Protec Security Services where he found, to his surprise, several of his former associates working. They were all as disillusioned with their previous situations as he had been. Things had been going along, sometimes interesting and sometimes not. Then entered John Dirk!

Things had begun to change when their boss, who unbeknownst to them worked for Dirk, said that the elite team was needed on a rush basis for a high risk, low profile, job in the local area. The senior team leaders, Ron Colefax and Rick Davis, were immediately sent out with most of the company's best men. It was not known that Dirk was the client until Ron Colefax, who had worked with him once, had recognized him.

Tony had been very surprised when the boss had pulled him in off a high profile and well paying client at the request of Ron and Rick to join their team. When introduced to Dirk he had recognized him immediately, and was very pleased to learn that both Ron and Rick thought so highly of him.

After being interviewed in a rapid fire question and answer manner, and being scrutinized by a pair of the most penetrating and knowing eyes he had ever encountered, he was put in the third position of command of the security team. The next surprise, although it shouldn't have been one to him, was that Dirk owned the company he worked for. This man really knew how to get things going. Within twenty four hours they had set up one of the best security screens he had seen in a long time.

Then he had been put in charge of a team of his own and sent out to escort another one of the best known names in the intelligence field to a meeting with Dirk. Within another twenty four hours all of the team leaders, and those others who had been brought in, were completely committed to Dirk and his mission, the new game. A new game that was bigger than anything that any of them had ever envisioned themselves being involved in.

Which brought him back to the present! He had just arrived in St. Louis, about a half a day ahead of the rest of the extraction team, their new headquarters and command center. After logging his mission brief, and checking on the security measures he had set in motion before leaving, he went up to his own room to shower and shave. This was where his present remembrances had been taking place.

Mentally shaking, and chiding, himself for woolgathering he directed his thoughts to the present. His latest surprise was his almost instant liking for the man they had extracted, the Russian, Garov.

Much of that, he believed, might stem from their mutual and courteous respect, acknowledged initially by a long searching look and then by a curt nod of approval for each other.

That look and curt nod had happened again during a chance encounter on the fantail of the freighter during the last leg of the long trip back as they were entering the harbor at New Orleans. Both men appraising the performance of the other during the last few days.

The Russian had that look, the look of a real professional as most of them did in the intelligence game who had been there and done that. The look was something one acquired, if one lived through it, over the years and miles put on ones mind and body.

The look that made them a kind of breed apart! And if this one lived up to his reputation he would be an extremely formidable foe for anyone to have to face. Tony hoped so, because if this new game was anything at all like Dirk had said it was they were going to need the very best that could be gotten before this whole thing was over.

Tony little realized at that moment how prophetic his seemingly random and roaming thoughts would turn out to be!

G. 'Whiz' Burke

To say that he had been scared 'shitless' on that eventful day just a few weeks ago while talking to Bill Tate, in the galley of that marvelous machine everyone just referred to as the ship, would be a totally asinine understatement!

His fright had started after answering a couple of seemingly innocuous questions put to him by Bill Tate as they sat together. Upon answering them that worthy had immediately called Ron Colefax, the head of all site security for this operation. Upon Ron's arrival Bill had told Ron to put two men on him and not to let anyone talk to him, or let anyone within five feet of him, without his or Dirk's specific approval beforehand. At that moment Gerry Burke felt he had good reason to be frightened. He had been in quite a few tight spots in his life, especially during his time with the IRA, but few of them had gotten to him like that simple order from out of the blue from someone he knew and was supposed to be working with.

The reason for his scare was that he knew, or knew about, most of these people who were here or were rumored to be coming in to join this new outfit. Each and every one was a professional who had earned his or her deadly reputation working in or around the intelligence field. They were hardened men and women who had excelled in a hard and deadly game.

The fact that he had misunderstood the order and its' intent had had little to do with the terror he had felt at that moment. His fear had been set aside a few moments later when he learned that those measures were to protect him, and his recently acquired knowledge about the ship and some of its' operating systems, and was brought on by the incident that had occurred at the landing site on his arrival here. Things had been moving very fast then and he hadn't understood, at the time, who the enemy was or how their security had been partially penetrated so early on.

Now, sitting at his shiny new desk in his shiny new lab located in their St. Louis complex, with all of the shiny new equipment he had begged and pleaded for surrounding him, his thoughts kept returning to that incident in the clearing. He still didn't understand what that huge, beautiful, and strange black cat had to do with the crew, only that it was held in some kind of reverence by many of the top people.

One thing that did impress him about that incident was Crows' reaction to the cat. He knew Crows' reputation very well, and respected and admired his abilities almost as much as he did Dirks'. So, if they said that that 'tabby' was one of the big Indians he would just go along with it!

After his meeting with Dirk that night on the ship he had promised them results if he could have the equipment he wanted. And he had given them results too. Like that bulky plasma rifle, converting it into a basically non lethal hand held pistol which used the plasma charge, a much smaller one than the original one the rifle fired to be sure, as a vehicle to deliver an electrical charge rather than the reverse it had been originally set up to do. And adjusting it to use the much better high output miniature batteries that were made right here on earth rather than those huge things that it used before.

And he had another dozen ideas he wanted to move forward with, but had been told that working on upgrading the control room computers was much more important right now. This brought up another subject that, truth to tell, frightened him a little more than he really wanted to admit to himself right now. It was about the learning/teaching machine on the ship that he had been introduced to by Dirk.

Dirk had told him, in no uncertain terms, that that machine could be extremely dangerous because it had not been designed for use with human minds and might possibly fry the human users brain if misused. Therein lay the problem. That was exactly how it worked. It linked itself directly with the users' mind to teach or instruct. Dirk wanted him to try and figure out a way to adapt it for human users.

Another thing that bothered him was how Dirk and Bill Tate knew so much about what equipment was on the ship, and what that equipment did. Where were they getting their information? With a mental shrug he told himself not to worry about that right now because he wasn't going to let his own fears get the better of himself and keep him from learning as much as he possibly could about that marvelous ship and all that it contained!

Gerry 'G. Whiz' Burke was also a bit of a health nut, as those who were interested in preserving their health were often referred to, and for one who was in this business it was also an anomaly, and one of the things very high on his list of things to learn was how that automated medical units worked. He also firmly believed that a healthy body went a long way in promoting a healthy and productive mind. And understanding the auto-med's workings would not only enhance and benefit his own health but that of the rest of the crews as well.

This last thought, as he began his preparations for a return trip to the ship, would turn out to be totally prophetic! And would, in many ways, go a long way in aiding what would be a long and bitterly fought war. A war that would change the futures and destinies of more people on more worlds than the people of earth now dreamed existed.

And if Gerry Burke had any idea of just how long this war, that he now thought of as only another operation, would last and that he would live to see the end of it he might just give his participation in it some serious second thoughts. That he would outlive his great, great grand children, if he ever had any, would completely sober his present enthusiasm to learn more about the ship, the people who made it, and where they came from.

Colefax and Davis

Colefax and Davis were like two peas culled from the same pod. You seldom if ever heard ones name without mention of the others'. They were both large men, topping six feet, and burly of build. And yet, because of their training, either would be hard to spot in a crowd.

They were both hard men, very well trained, and easily capable of killing without remorse if necessary. Colefax, at forty nine, was the older of the two. Davis was forty seven. They had been working together for close to twenty years. So long that they seemed able to read each others mind. So well that they seemed to be the hand and fingers of the same hand. And each had complete and total trust in the other! They worked so well together that they were often thought of as one person, and for all intents and purposes many seemed to forget who was who.

They were observant and methodical operatives, and to say the very least they were very good at their tradecraft. They had, after getting to know each other early on, worked together as a team throughout most of their intelligence service lives.

Both, after many years of service, were exasperated and saddened by the growing inter-service rivalries and bickering that often led to not sharing important information a sister service could use or needed, which in turn led to poor decision making based on faulty or incomplete knowledge.

This situation all to often caused an agent to blow his or her cover on an operation, or ultimately to lose their lives. These conditions, when a serious offer was presented, was causative to their joint decision to resign from the agency for which they were working and take up lucrative positions in the private sector. This was how the ended up working for 'Protec' Services, and also where, and how, they met Dirk!

Protec, and indirectly at the time Dirk, was very pleased to acquire two such well-trained and resourceful men. And the other men, once they found out where these two had gone, who came out of service to work with them. The extra bonus that they brought 'Protec' Services, and Dirk, was the extensive list of contacts who were well placed in several countries around the world.

That list would come in very handy in the future for this fledgling crews ability to access information and resources that would allow them to maintain operations in the years to come.

Colefax and Davis were patriots in the old fashioned way. They loved their country, but loved what it stood for much, much more. Both men, each without a moments hesitation, would have given their lives willingly to preserve those mores.

But when politics and greed began to take the place of those fundamentals that made up the philosophic basis on which they were founded, so changed their willingness to follow without question the orders issued by those politicians.

When Dirks' offer to join him was made there was little need for a long debate between them because of several factors. One of those factors was that they both knew, or knew of, the man and the mans' reputation. It wasn't earned lightly.

Another important factor was that having worked for him previously, although not knowing that it was him they were working for at the time, they both knew that when they asked a question they would get straight forward information in his answers. And, most importantly at this point in time, his fight was based on the principals they both held as their own.

The major difference was that this fight was on a much larger scale than anything they had ever conceived of being a part of! This fight was for the freedom of their race and their world. This, they both agreed to wholeheartedly, was something worth committing themselves to without reservation. And they both knew the value of having your belief in yourself and the rightness of your actions to be unquestionably right in both heart and mind. For these men it was a fresh breath of air in a life that had made a wrong turn along their road.

Neither of these men, at this point, had any idea how very long those lives and the new road they had embarked upon would be! They would also find that people were people, no matter what form of skin or appearance they wore, and that the temptation to wish a problem away rather than face it when it reared its' head was galactic in scope, not just a condition of their own small corner of reality.

Nor did either man even dream of what their contributions would mean for each one individually, for they were destined for that thing that they detested at this time. They were to become 'Politicians'! The difference would be in the kind of politician they were destined to become. For these two were destined to walk the high road of greatness, leaving very large footprints indeed to fill for those who would, or could, follow them!

This was not something that either would actively seek, but it was something that each would not run from when it needed to be done!

The Drel

It's complete designation, or name, was 'Deng Jem Om Lut Gur Drel Gaz', and this designation told all other of its' kind all that was needed to know of its' background, rank, and name. If it were translated to the audible sound waves that the primaries of this miserable planet used to communicate with, instead of the wonderfully clear thought images of its' own kind, it would sound something like; Deng = Dang - Jem = Jam - Lut = Lute - Gur = Gore - Drel = Drel - Gaz = Gass.

The Chai would argue this because they considered the Drel to be very limited telepaths. The range of their thought projection capability was only about a quarter mile maximum in earth terms, whereas the Chai could project over several miles under the right conditions. And they projected on a very low band that limited their ability to encompass large scale concepts in their entirety. This, the Chai believed, caused their communications to be very long and unwieldy.

Translated the designation would impart the following information to another of its' kind;

Deng = Planet of origin—Home world.

Jem = Location of the individuals' home district on that planet.

Om = Birth generation of the individual within its' sept, or family.

Lut = Individuals' standing, or rank, within that sept or family.

Gur = The individuals' sept or family name.

Drel = Its' race. Properly stated it is Ahn Drel. Translated meaning is 'Those who rule'

Gaz = The individuals personal identifier in its' sept or family. The individuals name

Its' home world was, to it, a wonderful place of hot steaming marshes, and even hotter dense jungles. And it hated this planet! For one of its' kind this planet was like living in an ice house on an ice bound planet circling a dead star. And Gaz, its' personal identifier/name, wanted more than any other thing for its' sept to finish its' tour of duty on this hell planet and go home to Deng, its' home planet.

Gazs' race was re-entering this galaxy for what was, he understood, the second time. It was called 'Gis 'tog uss lal'(pronounced geese toog oose lall)or 'The place of many suns.' The first time had been many thousands of 'mek-ah' ago, or many thousands of generations ago. If he understood his history correctly his race had come here thousands of 'mek-ah' ago and had encountered another very advanced star faring race almost immediately upon coming out of stardrive mode from the last planet in this galaxy they had subjugated for their own needs.

That race had also been telepathic, but very hard to communicate with because they thought on a very high band and their thoughts sped like the wind in a 'Gom' storm (hurricane).

For some reason he did not understand conflict had quickly broken out between them. This should not have happened, because his race was, as he interpreted the history, more than willing to share the spoils to be found here with them.

That conflict had expanded into a war between their two galaxy's, and had lasted for many thousands of years, decimating both sides equally. He assumed that was why the sept leaders were moving so cautiously and secretively in their efforts to subjugate this race. The normal manner of subjugation was to go in and capture an area and convert the local inhabitants in that area into usable steeds, then spread out area by area until the whole planet was under their control.

This was only the second planet in this galaxy that the Drel had begun to take over. The first, one that the elder sept leaders had thought would be ideal for their needs, had turned out to be a poor choice because the inhabitants had been only marginally intelligent, making them useful only as steeds for those on the lowest rungs of any sept.

For a steed to be of practical use to the Drel it must be of reasonably high intelligence to allow its' Drel rider/masters to raid its' mind for useful technological and other information. This technology and other information would then be implemented in plundering the subjugated races planet for much needed raw materials and food stuffs to be sent back to the home galaxy where rebuilding the race, and the need to conquer new races for steeds had depleted almost everything needed to keep his race healthy. That and the burgeoning populations on those planets clamoring for more steeds for those who were rising in the ranks of their septs on all of those planets.

I seemed like that was the whole purpose of the majority of all who had leapt out into space again, sending more raw materials to feed more steeds, to build more ships, to send more raw materials to feed more steeds, into the mists of infinity.

Well, enough of these thoughts. Gaz, on the successful completion of his assigned task of finding the whereabouts, or disposition, of three of the missing members of the 'lit' (a ten unit team) unit sent to investigate a possible incursion from spaceside by an unknown source would be able to return to the much warmer southern hemisphere of this miserable planet. The trouble was that he was having little success for his efforts.

A big part of his problem was that these steeds were very hard to break, and once broken were hard to control. The better ones, that is. They tended to fight control long after they should have by the standards set by the past experience with other races.

The probable landing site had been narrowed down to a relatively small portion of northern central part of a continent the indigenes called America. Finding the intruding craft quickly would secure a promotion that would lift his status within his sept, and also raise him in standing within the command council for this world.

Such a promotion would bring with it an elevation in the level of his education. Thus expanding his abilities to a point commensurate with his new rank standing and responsibilities. It would also put him in a position to choose a new steed. The one he now had, he was sorry to admit, had been sorely used by him for many planetary revolutions, days he remembered the inhabitants called them, and it was in serious need of rest and care.

That thought must be put aside for the moment because it was time for him to check in with his controlling authority, and that meant that he would be communicating second hand, as it were, by the need to use one of the mechanical means these steeds had devised. He despised the incompleteness of this method, but understood that importing more of the specially bred steeds used for long distance communication by his kind was hard on the available supply.

Those already here were used solely by the elder sept councilors. The real problem with these mechanical means was that everything had to be translated twice. Once by the sender and once by the receiver. Then it was necessary to judge if the message was clear in the translation, unlike the clear and precise imaging and meaning in mind to mind speak communication.

As the device was answered by the controlling watch officer at the other end Gaz began his report, which was necessarily short, stating that he had some worry because there was no trace whatever of the three units that had gone missing. He was told in return that there was some concern by the elders of some form of organized resistance going on. This was because another unit on the other side of the planet had also ceased to exist.

This concern came about because trace burns were discovered at the base of the steeds control stem not consistent with those from the chemical fire it had been at first thought to have perished in. That steed, at the time of its' demise, had been on a mission to pick up a high level steed for processing! And the potential steed had completely vanished, as had the two potential steeds who had been under surveillance preparatory to their pickup in his own area of investigation. The council was beginning to fear organized resistance because this made a total of four unanswered disappearances in far too short a time period.

Upon deciphering this information, through the images the words created in its' steeds mind, Gaz made a snap decision and informed his control officer that he would direct his steed to return to central control so that he could study all information related to this new problem at first hand.

It was also necessary to return due to his steeds deteriorating condition. This last, surprisingly, was agreed to by his superior without argument. Gaz ended the call and directed his steed to prepare to return to the population center where one of their bases were located on the continent called Europe.

Gazs' steed, as was usual lately, balked imaging to him tiredness and hunger. Gaz, through its' control stem, caused the steeds body to release a flow of the chemical the inhabitants called adrenaline into its' circulatory system, giving the steed a false sense of renewed energy to prod it into compliance.

At the same time promising the steed rest and nutrition when they arrived at their destination. It was, Gaz could sense, very close to complete exhaustion.

Gaz really disliked the bipedal inhabitants of this planet as steeds, although he had gotten one of the stronger ones of this species, because they constantly fought at being controlled. Sometimes they even went berserk, injuring or killing the rider, the steed, or both. They were physically weaker than many of the other races conquered and used by his people, but it had to be admitted that they had wonderful dexterity in the use of their upper appendages.

They also had weaker vision capabilities in the upper and lower infra red frequencies, but that was offset by their marvelous superiority of depth perception in the range they did use.

Gaz had, unknown to himself, been selected by his superiors for rapid elevation in standing and education within his sept. This was because he had shown the initiative and persistence required of those needed to fill positions in the rapidly diminishing group of candidates available to take on positions of leadership, and eventually council status.

The high council, on Drel, had decreed the rapid advancement of any who showed potential for possible council status. This was deemed necessary to replace those lost to the alarmingly high rate of attrition in the council ranks due to 'burn out' caused by the tremendous pressure and work load at that level of authority. Those replacement losses were also due to the Drel high councils' habit of removing those who did not perform at the level of its' expectations. Removal was quick, and mortally permanent!

Another reason for being selected for quick advancement was Gazs' often expressed opinion, and overheard by his immediate superiors, to its' sept mates that this race would be trouble to the Drel because of their general resistance to control. Something that the controlling council for the expeditionary conquest force for this planet had learned early on, and what only a very few of the officers and soldiers in this force had recognized on their own.

What was not spoken of below sub council level was the anomaly this race presented to the expeditionary force command council. The anomaly was that the basis of resistance was stronger in the upper middle and lower central positions of education and authority rather than, as had been the Drel experience, the reverse of this.

This was one of the main reasons that their takeover timetable had had to be put on hold indefinitely, and also the reason why, after almost an entire planetary revolution around its' primary, ninety percent of the soldiers and officers were still stacked like cordwood in the 'cryo' sleep wells of the three exploratory ships that had put down on this planet, let alone those still in 'Cryo' sleep in the mother ship parked out beyond the orbit of this solar systems huge gas giant.

The normal Drel procedures for beginning a planetary takeover was to put a fair number of officers and soldiers into a sparsely populated area, capture and control as many lower and mid upper level inhabitants as was possible in a short time without arousing undue suspicion, then spread that control ever outwards in a continuously expanding circle by taking control of the essential services that were needed to keep any social structure operating.

Their first experience with these beings on this level had been both a shocking and sobering one for the council leaders! The overall level of resistance to being tamed as steeds was unheard of in their experience, and had caused them much concern.

These beings were unruly, recalcitrant to extremes, and often went, when controlled too closely, into a berserk rage against the riders that usually resulted in the injury or death of the steed and the rider both. This experience had been so contrary to the way in which things normally went that their operations had had to be put on hold before they had even properly begun.

The Drel had not conquered and maintained control over two hundred solar systems and thirty some planets by giving up easily! So, the council had pulled back and consolidated its' control over a much smaller area, then begun the work of finding an answer to this anomaly.

One of the first discoveries made was that by using a much lesser degree of control than was customary, or even what might have seemed to be prudent, on these steeds the resistance factor was much reduced. Another interesting factor learned that had been linked to the lessening of control was that there was a much higher success rate within the upper middle and upper echelon authority base. That faction was called, by them, their political faction. And those individuals operating within it were called 'politicians'.

Their success level within this faction had risen to almost sixty percent within their, admittedly limited, sphere of control. And, due to the lessons they had learned, they had begun to set up satellite groups outside of that sphere that were beginning to show some real signs of progress.

The real problem the Drel expeditionary force faced was getting their operations back onto a realistically workable timetable because the main Drel takeover fleet was now only four local years behind them.

One of the things that the expeditionary command council had learned about this species was that if the takeover were discovered, before the expeditionary forces could take over control of essential services to stop it, was that the now fractious groups, countries they called themselves, would unite and fight such an attempt bitterly.

This would further disrupt their timetable and divert resources that were much needed on other Drel worlds.

The military council representatives were not worried about the outcome of such a fight, if it occurred, at this species present technology level, but if it did occur it brought up another problem that was becoming more evident and serious the more they learned about this race.

That problem was this species apparent penchant for performing technological wizardry! And the expeditionary command council was very decidedly split on what this could mean for the Drel! Half thought that this trait could be a great boon for the Drel. Those siding with the military faction on the council viewed it as potentially being the harbinger of their worst nightmare come true

The problem was that if this species scientists thought that something were even remotely possible they worried that idea like one of the parasitic things they called pet dogs, which the Drel detested because they seemed able to detect anyone that was a Drel steed, did a bone until the problem were solved. The advances made on the design and performance of their computers was one example.

In twenty short local years their computers, and the range of their performance, had improved to such a level that they were almost as good as the ones that the Drel use on their ships. And they were much more compact than were those were. If any of the wild, uncontrolled, steeds ever got their hands on some of the weapons the Drel controlled the command council did not even want to think of what might happen!

Although the Drel had had to fight for the control of some of the planets and solar systems in the recent past that they now controlled they had not come upon a species that fought with the ferocity that was displayed by this species even as it fought those of its' own kind. There was serious concern among the councilors about this because this species had come close to annihilating itself in a conflagration a few short, by Drel standards, years in their past by introducing the use of atomic weapons into a conflict that encompassed the entire globe.

By Drel standards they had been crude and filthy weapons that contaminated large populated areas and even larger productive areas. Though, admittedly, they might have had some limited tactical effect if used properly against the Drel, they would not be enough to stop the invasion and takeover. No, the councilors real concern was that if that ferocity and technological ingenuity were ever focused on an outside foe that foes' supposed superiority might not be enough to contain this species!

Now, to add to the councils' present concerns, there was the strange disappearance, and suspected demise, of three of their best trained field units on one continent, and the demise of one of their officers on another one on the other side of the globe!

Not only those losses were alarming! It now seemed that the one that had died in a place called Russia, where they had been making excellent headway, it now seemed likely that that unit had been killed with a weapon that the command council had not even had a suspicion of this species possessing.

It also seemed that it was a near certainty that there was now some form of organized resistance either being developed or already formed and active on this planet. Their suspicions were now aroused because several of the potential steeds that had been tagged by their satellite teams as strong candidates for breaking and taming had very mysteriously disappeared. And they had done so without a trace!

Yes. They were fairly certain that this was the case. And it was better to know this now, while they could do something about it without the necessity of open conflict.

And it was one of the reasons that Gazs' superior had given him no argument at all about returning to the Drel headquarters to learn all that was available to the council. It was true that he was marked for rapid advancement that superior thought to itself, but he had better be able to produce results or he would end up like so many before him. His superior was just glad that he himself was not on the fast track list. He was older and wiser in the ways of the councils' habits!

And to top off all of these other problems the council was now positive that there had been an incursion on this planet by an unknown extra planetary vehicle. One thing that the council was sure of was that this vehicle was not one of their own.

This incident was cause for very serious concern because this species was not yet capable of practical interplanetary travel. And not knowing where it came from, or who it belonged to, was giving some of the oldest members of the council cause to recall to mind some of the tales about their long, long ago fought war on their first attempt to enter this galaxy. Yes! This incident was cause for very serious concern indeed!

What the Drels' governing expeditionary command council could not possibly know was just how right their concerns would turn out to be!

About all of their concerns!

CHAPTER TWELVE
Chabov, Osov, and Innovations

Chabov

Admiral Dimetri Chabov, Supreme Commander of Strategic Rocket Forces, and now also, since the break up of the former Soviet Union, Director of Space Operations for the new Democratic Government of Russia, was seated in the top tier of the control room. He was smiling and well pleased with himself as he watched the successful liftoff of the newly redesigned and refitted Cherbelinski rocket lift the payload section of the housing for the second truly multi-national space station into the star filled night sky over mother Russia.

He was well pleased with himself because this liftoff had almost not occurred. And without his badgering and pleading, even begging where necessary, it might not have. His superiors were very well aware by now that Chabov was an ardently and persuasive advocate for Russia's' continued participation in the international space program. Arguing with great zeal that for Russia to not meet its' obligation to the joint venture would cause great harm to their country.

Failure to perform would mean not only the loss of the billions of rubles already invested to date, it would cause her to lose her credibility with the rest of the world as a major world technological power in that rapidly expanding area. God alone knew that he had had an uphill fight getting rid of the paper shufflers, and the outright incompetents, over the last five long years in an effort to keep his forces intact and the space program alive! Yes, he had reason to smile at this achievement!

When not being battered by his zealous passion most of Chabovs' military peers and governmental superiors liked him well enough. Most who knew him well enough, or knew enough about him, respected him as a brilliant tactician and a very good commander. These opinions were attested to by the loyalty shown by the bulk of his already much reduced rocket forces, and the training and readiness those troops maintained. And compound that by the fact that his troops had not had a full payday in almost a year now, and still maintained the lowest desertion rate in all of the military services.

Those in power usually ended up giving into, and giving him, more than they really wanted to realizing that it would be foolish and wasteful to lose such a productive workhorse. And even worse to possibly alienate him, turning him into a powerful and dangerous foe! Yes, even in the new Democratic Republic of Russia, those in power knew that to stay in power it was always wise to have a good relationship with the military. And to all too many, Dimetri Chabov was the epitome, and the heart of the military in today's Russia!

Chabov, at only fifty four, was extremely young to hold his rank and command, most at his rank level being in their late sixties or early seventies. The man had been handed nothing in his rise within the ranks, and unlike many of his contemporaries he had earned each promotion and advancement on merit.

Chabov had been seconded to, and graduated from, the famed 'Frunz' Academy among the top ten percent of his class. His meteoric rise through the ranks was not all a chance recognition of his abilities, especially not in a system that was rife with patronage, although recognition of them did play an important part.

Two additional factors were also in play. First, he was considered to be a brilliant analytical tactician, and welcome wherever his assignments took him. As such he quickly, even before graduating, had a phenomenal grasp of the political/military power structure, using it often to his advantage.

Second, he had two secret weapons, totally unknown to most of his superiors, in the form of two of the classmates he had formed very close friendships with at the Frunz academy. One was a colonel in the upper echelons of the KGB. The other, also a colonel, was the executive officer to the chief of staff for the 'Spetsnaz', the army's special operations troops who are similar to the special forces of the United States Army. They had maintained their friendship for over thirty years, helping each other where and when they could. With the information they traded each had a generally good idea of which way the winds of power were blowing.

The smile stayed on his mouth, but left his eyes, as the sights and sounds of the control room mingled with these thoughts. But a very private part of his mind kept returning to the very disturbing message he had received from Yuri Garov, his KGB friend, a few days ago. Not only was the message itself disturbing, the manner in which it had been delivered was completely outside of the channels they had establish for contact many years ago.

The message had been very cleverly disguised as one of the stories on the second page of the Washington Post, which was delivered to his residence each morning by courier from the train station. It was one of the few luxuries he allowed himself, outside of the normal perks of his rank, and he justified it as a means of staying abreast of what the west was up to.

The caption, translated into Russian, was the code phrase they used for their messages of importance to each other, and also indicated the code base to be used according to the wording of the phrase. No! There was no doubt that the message was from Yuri. The only problem was that Yuri had, in a somewhat spectacular manner, disappeared from the streets of Moscow almost six months ago! Now, six months later a very neatly and cleverly done message had been placed in and delivered with his paper. It smacked of some of the capabilities the western intelligence services, and their way of doing things. And the content of the message was very disturbing to him.

The message said that he had joined some operation being run from the west, but he had not defected. The operation was to prevent not only the takeover of the west, but of mother Russia as well. And the message also reminded him that he, Yuri, was not one to run off chasing shadows! That was the part that really bothered Dimetri. His friend Yuri, a very methodical man, was not the kind to do such a thing.

And, if what he said were true, why had he heard nothing of this from his own well placed sources? No, he could not doubt his friend after thirty years of trust and friendship, so there must be something to what he had said. The message also said to check their alternate message drop. There would be a letter and an information package left there for him.

It also said that he was to take extraordinary precautions because the letter and information was in plain form and could not only hurt him if he were caught with it, but it could also hurt the people he was now working with and the agents they had in place. The information provided would, Yuri assured him, be very, very, disturbing and revealing.

Dimetri, intrigued now, and more disturbed than ever at the same time, decided to make arrangements to pick up the package as soon as was possible. Giving the matter some additional thought he decided that he wanted some input from their other friend, Osov.

So decided he penned a message in their code, sealed it into a security envelope, and this morning before the launch he had given it to a captain of the special detachment of Spetsnaz guarding this facility. This captain, one that Osov trusted, would make sure that Osov got the message quickly, and as quietly as possible.

The message asked Osov to meet him at the small flat above the club that the three of them secretly owned in two days time, and that he was to let the captain know if he would be able to make the meeting on such short notice.

The excitement of the successful launch was beginning to wind down a little now so Chabov told his adjutant to take over for him and monitor the balance of the flight, and the orbital positioning of the vehicle. Also that he was to be notified immediately by cell phone if any problems arose. He was returning to headquarters, and would be there for the rest of the day to clean up his desk, He would then be taking two days of well earned leave.

In his car now, a beautiful Zil limousine, his personal aide and driver, a captain whom he had saved from courts martial and disgrace over a stupid indiscretion when he was a green sub lieutenant, and a man he trusted implicitly, asked, "Where to Admiral?". The man was astute, sensing that something of great importance was on the mind of his savior and mentor.

Meeting the eyes of his trusted man in the rearview mirror, a look of understanding passed between them wordlessly, and he gave him the address, then said almost without necessity, "Use caution Yevgeny, Use caution!"

Yevgeny put the automobile in gear and pulled smoothly away from the curb, as he wondered to himself what new and dangerous adventure they were about to embark on.

He was absolutely sure of one thing. Whatever it was, with this powerful and intelligent man who he had willingly served for the last ten years, it would most certainly be interesting!

One thing that Yevgeny could not possibly conceive of was just how far from home his loyalty to this man would take him!

Osov

Peoter Semyonovitch Osov was a full colonel who was soon slated to be promoted to the rank of General. He was a proud man, and was proud of his accomplishments over the last thirty years, as well he should be.

He stood six foot four inches tall and weighed in at two hundred fifty two pounds of still hard muscle. He was fifty five years old but didn't look it, except for the gray that had begun to be pronounced at his temples. He was now the titular commander of all Spetsnaz forces of the New Democratic Republic of Russia for the northern sector of Russia. This promotion would confirm his position as commander.

Osov was an exemplary officer, graduating in the upper percentile of his class at the famed Frunz Academy. He was considered by his peers and superiors alike to be a first rate strategist, as had been proven by his combat tours in Afghanistan, and several other small brush war encounters. Encounters where his tactics had saved the lives of many of his men, and won several important battles in one of his countries most ill conceived military actions, much like the Americans' military exploits in Viet Nam.

His tactics, unconventional much of the time, had him dropping in on a surprised and unsuspecting enemy, like a hawk out of the sky, especially when he was expected to be elsewhere. Hence came the fond nickname that was given to him by very loyal troops. 'The Peregrine'.

Just as important at times as his abilities, and more political in nature, were his two friends, classmates from his time at the Frunz Academy, who always said the right things to the right people about him. If pushed by his peers to describe himself in this environment he would reply that he was an idealistic realist, with a strong belief that rank should be earned, not bestowed. Osov, with no family left alive, was devoted to the military, but like all before him he had wisely learned that even the military had its own form of politics.

So he took what help came from his friends, maintaining the basic belief that you couldn't change things without being in a position to do so. As a commander he did what he could, instilling in his men a sense of pride and loyalty to each other, and giving them the best training and equipment possible so that they would have a fair chance of surviving in combat. And by setting an example by his actions at all times!

The message from Dimetri was very much out of character, giving him cause for concern both due to its' manner of delivery, and not their normal manner of contact, and because he wanted to meet on such short notice. Not that he couldn't do it! Being the commanding officer did have a number of advantages, but for covering his actions for something like this was something he liked to have well planned.

The officer who had carried the message was one that both Chabov and Osov trusted. He had been placed in close proximity to Dimetri so that he would have an emergency means of contact, and help if he needed it, so the request for his presence must be important! Doubly so if Yuri Garov was involved!

Yuri had disappeared from the streets of Moscow in a rather dramatic manner some six months ago, not to be seen or heard from since. The story going around was that he had had help from the west. There were other stories going around but they were only repeated in careful whispers by their tellers, who were said to be always looking over their shoulders while doing so.

The Meeting at the Club

Upon entering the small jazz club just off Nicolai Prospect, an area between the more commercial section of downtown Moscow and the beginnings of the predominantly residential sections of the city, Osov stopped just inside the door to let his eyes adjust to the dim lighting inside the clubs small main room. They adjusted quickly as they had been trained to.

He immediately recognized Chabovs' aide leaning against the end of the small bar, near the hall that led to the clubs one bathroom and the stairs that led to the small flat above the club. Looking indirectly at the man as he walked across the small room towards the bar he saw him nod to him imperceptibly. Twice. One nod meant that Chabov was already in the flat above, waiting. The second nod meant that it was clear for him to go up himself. Nodding politely to the man as he passed Osov went right up to the flat, using his own key to enter.

The flat, two small bedrooms, a small kitchen, bathroom, and combined dining and living room, was where all of their face to face meetings took place. And it was as secure from prying eyes and ears as Yuri Garov, their KGB counterpart, could make it. Chabov was seated at the round dining table with the rooms one table lamp set in the middle of it, alternately looking at photographs that were spread out by his left hand and reading from a sheaf of papers in his right hand.

As Osov entered, he looked up with a smile on his face, saying "Peoter. As always it's good to see you in person again. I would love to sit and talk of inconsequentials for a while, but there is much here that we need to study and discuss!" But he did lay down the papers to shake his friends hand.

Turning half away he rummaged among some of the papers until he found the ones he wanted and, turning back, said as he handed them to Osov, "Here, sit down and start with this first."

The papers, as it turned out, were a letter to Chabov from Yuri Garov, hand written in his very precise script. After a friendly opening, and asking after both Chabov and himself, the letter got right down to nuts and bolts, telling of his escape from Moscow with the help of some freelance western agents. Agents who, he said, had not only known of his trouble with his own agency, and their intended plans for him, but who had also saved him from a trap set for him after someone had attached a locator transponder beacon on his clothing.

It went on to explain that he had been recruited to join a coalition of some of the best soldiers and intelligence agents in the world to fight a threat not only to the west but one that threatened Mother Russia and the rest of the world! After he had been shown proof, undeniable proof, he had willingly, eagerly, joined those brave men and women in this fight. Some of that proof, the parts he could send, was in the material contained in this package, and it must be handled very carefully because if the wrong people found them with it they would be killed, or even worse, taken over by this new enemy. He had included as much as he could to help his comrades understand his actions, and to underscore what he was about to ask of them.

Osov looked up from his reading to find that his friend Chabov had again anticipated him, holding out one of the photos from the pile on the table to him. The photograph was an enlargement, a little grainy from the process, but its' content was still clearly and mercilessly graphic. As he stood there studying it an involuntary shudder shook his body. With fingers that trembled slightly Osovs' eyes went back to the letter.It went on to say that this group, in which he now held a top level position, and one of the reasons he was able to get this letter to them, believed that they would have a long, hard, fight on their hands! They also believed, because they had found out about this early, and because of the top flight people they had been able to enlist so far, that they had a fair chance of eventually winning this fight. There was also, he said, a list of some of these people, many of whom would be known to his friends, included with the materials he had sent.

And again, as his eyes came up from the letter, Chabov was holding out a sheet of paper to him. As he scanned the list his eyebrows lifted and a low whistle escaped his lips. Looking at Chabov directly now, he said "If this is true, and I have little reason to doubt Yuri, it is quite impressive! And brings cause for serious worry!" he finished, a frown creasing his face.

Chabov, excitement now beginning to creep into his voice, and a gleam to light his normally calm eyes, said "If you think that is impressive just read the rest of the next segment of the letter!"

Osov turned his eyes back to the letter and continued to read. It continued with, 'My friends. Our group has also, it seems, made contact with an alien race! One that, at this point, appears to be quite friendly to our own. It has, as of this writing, turned over to the care of our group an operational spacecraft. That's' right Dimetri, knowing of your love for anything concerning outer space, I said a working spacecraft!'

I cannot tell you everything at this point, but I can tell you that we have come into some very advanced technology that we are presently in the process of reverse engineering and adapting for our own uses. There is so very much to tell you, and so little time to do so, and the space in this package is too limited, so I will close with this until we are able to speak face to face." Osov went back over the letter, making sure he had gained all he could from what he had read so far, then read on.

First, and most importantly, we would like for you and Peotre to join us! If you will consider this please contact me soon. I have included a secure cellular phone in the package. I has only one channel which is fed through a privately owned antenna and satellite. Use it sparingly!

Second, we are setting up a new secret base of operations in northern Canada. I know Peotre, and I know how loyal his troops are. We would very much like for him to send a detachment of them here to work with our own to help in providing security. If you decides to join us that will be of prime importance. The arrangements for transportation can then be made at this end.

Third, after digesting this information, and judging the true strength of our friendship, it will be imperative that we arrange for a face to face meeting. I most fervently hope that you will meet with us, and let your own eyes judge the truth! I know that you will be able to see it. When they do we must make immediate plans for both of your extractions!

Lastly, because of our own security concerns, the documents you have received have all been coated with a chemical compound! Knowing you both I estimated the time it would take you to absorb the information in the package. The contents will begin to dissolve within ninety minutes of the time the seal is broken and they are exposed to the air. The cell phones' electronics will begin to dissolve within ninety six hours of hitting the air, or if they are tampered with. I am truly sorry about these precautions, but I must. I sincerely hope that you will contact us soon!

Your eternal friend, Yuri.

With that last sentence read Osov looked up at Chabov. They nodded at each other almost in unison, and with a professional and experienced methodology began to pore over the documents and photographs, committing their contents to memory. Little breath was wasted on conversation! There would be time for that later!

From East, to West, to Center

The big 'Hind' gunship was flying 'nap of the earth' over terrain that was becoming more forested and mountainous by the minute. It had crossed the border from Poland into the Russian Urals several minutes ago and the jerking, swaying, dipping, and climbing movements of the big helicopter was, it seemed now, the most dangerous part of the trip so far.

Yuri Garov wasn't bothered by this, and felt little sense of danger at this point. The only discomfort he felt was at a spot just below his right shoulder blade, where part of the jump seat he was strapped into was pressing against it. His pilot was one of the best he had ever flown with, the big ungainly gun ship responding to his every movement as if it were an extension of himself. What was so surprising was that the pilot was an American!

No, the real danger would come, if it did, as they approached the small mountain village of Pritna, another twenty miles further across the border from their present position. That's where any trap that had been set would be sprung. Hence the heavily armed gun ship! Garov did not believe that there would be a trap, but he had not lasted this long by not being a careful man. His message had said he would arrive by helicopter, it had not specified what kind of helicopter! And, if he knew his friends, they too would have some backup. Probably at least a platoon of Osovs' best Spetsnaz troops.

The pilot looked over his shoulder and, seeing that Garov was looking at him, held up three fingers to indicate three minutes to arrival. At Garovs' nod he turned back to his flying. Three minutes to target.

There was a light sheen of sweat on Garovs' forehead, the only sign of any nervousness on his part. They had not been able to find out why that thing, and its' troops, had been waiting for them the night of his escape from Moscow, so Garov had wanted to be prepared this time. The fact that they had not been able to find out anything at all was what was causing his nervousness now. Garov was a man who liked surprises only slightly less than the thought of a bad case of gonorrhea.

That was also why he had positioned his friends in such a way that he could radio the final meeting location instructions, and they could reach any one of half a dozen places in the same amount of time. He had radioed the location of their jump off point only minutes before taking of from the base in western Poland. It wasn't perfect, but it made it that much harder for any such trap to be set.

Besides, he hadn't gotten any type of warning from his, as his new Americans were fond of saying, 'Ace in the hole'. His ace was a man he had placed in the village more than a month ago. He didn't think the man had been spotted or compromised. He was a native of that village.

Osov had just finished checking the placement of the squad of men he had brought as security, men hand picked by himself, and returned to the mountain jeep that he had come down here in. He told his driver to go back to where Chabov was waiting. As the jeep pulled up next to his friend, and co-conspirator, he took another nervous glance at his wristwatch. "Two minutes to eta."

The location for the meeting sight, about a half mile outside the small village of Pritna, had been radioed to them only a short half hour before, and as he turned to face him Chabov said softly, "Our friend Yuri is as cautious as always. We should, under the circumstances, be grateful for that."

Looking at his friend with a somewhat troubled expression Osov said, as though someone might be listening, "Dimetri, my men and I have been through the village and the landing area twice, and all seems as it should, yet I can't shake the feeling that we are being watched!"

Chabov replied calmly, "Again, knowing our friend Yuri, he probably has a spotter well hidden somewhere in the area. I would!"

Osov said nothing more, just nodded his agreement. At the quiet, but distinctive sound, both men became instantly alert, looking around for its' source. Without warning the huge "Hind' gun ship was upon them, lifting itself over the brow of the low ridge at the other side of the field they were parked on the edge of.

The huge helicopter cleared the tops of the trees on the inner side of the low ridge by only inches. It moved towards them, its' engines still in stealth whisper mode, and seemed to leap at them as it covered the few hundred meters to their position. Flaring almost to a stall scant meters in front of them, kicking up a whirlwind of debris from the lately harvested field, the huge ship lowered itself like a leaf settling to the ground after falling from a tree, touching gently down on its' landing wheels.

The pilot spooled his engines down quickly, in combat manner. As he was doing so the side cargo door was pulled open. In that opening was outlined the unmistakable fireplug frame of their friend Yuri Garov. He jumped from the bay to the ground, half bending as he landed even though it wasn't necessary with as much ground clearance as the rotors on the big airship had, and moved quickly to join his friends.

Seeing that it was truly his friends he held out both arms to greet each of them in turn, giving each a true Russian bear hug of welcome. Looking both men in the eyes he said a heartfelt "Well met my friends, my brothers!" Each responded in kind. Their greetings over, Osov said pointedly "Yuri, I have a platoon of hand picked men placed about for security. Shall I bring them in closer?"

Garov, looking first at Chabov, said "Dimetri, you have made the arrangements as we discussed? You have four days that you can be out of general contact without undue questions being asked?"

At Chabovs' nod he turned to his friend Osov and said "Yes peotre, bring them in, and load a squad of them onto the helicopter. You can bring them along as your personal security, because I know that it will make your suspicious heart feel better. And peotre! Tell them to move carefully, and to sling their weapons!" This last brought a frown to Peotre's face, and a barked laugh from Dimetri Chabov.

At their questioning look he said, as he removed a small handheld radio from his jacket pocket, "They are surrounded by about thirty men, all with automatic

J. A. DI SPADA

weapons!" he finished, a small rueful smile playing at the corners of his mouth. "It's just my paranoia, you know." He said, and gave a short bark of a laughter himself. He then raised the radio to his mouth and spoke a few quiet words into it. Turning back to them he said "My men here saw you setting up and had some friends come out in ways only they know to keep an eye on you. He radioed me five minutes ago. I told him not to do anything, just watch. After all, you were just being sensible!

Looking a little sheepish Osov raised his own radio and called his men in, singling out one squad to go directly to the helicopter and load up. "And for gods sake sling your weapons, and keep them that way!" he growled. The reply was crisp, but questioning. Osov snapped "your surrounded you idiot! And none of you spotted a thing! Move it!" Osov looked back at his friends, saying "Lieutenant Bulenko and his men are, under most circumstances, very good. Just no real experience." He finished a little sadly.

Both of the other men nodded knowingly, and Garov, deciding to show some compassion for his friend relented, saying "Peotre. My man out there is Malasovski. You seconded him to me ten years ago to keep him from being shot. I never did thank you properly for that!"

Osov looked at his friend Garov, and being the proud man that he was would not acknowledge the face saving information. The gratitude was, however, in his eyes as he nodded. Calling Lt. Bulenko again, he told him to have the rest of the men set up a camp at the lower end of the small valley they were in, and that there were special rations in the supply truck for them, including a case of vodka. They were not to leave the valley for any reason, and that he would return in three days time.

The men had finished loading into the big helicopters' cargo/troop bay so Garov motioned for his two friends to board also. He then motioned for the pilot to begin spooling up his engines. Bringing the small radio to his lips and pressing the send key, he said "Andrei, you kept a couple of men with you?"

The radio sputtered, then "Da komrad colonel."

"Excellent Andrei. After we have gone come and get the jeeps. Take them and hide them well. On the morning of the fourth day from now bring them back here."

He paused a second as he removed an envelop from his inner pocket and laid it on the seat of the nearest jeep, then went on "And Andrei, there is an envelop here on the seat of this jeep for you. Take half of what is there for your own needs, and distribute the rest among the villagers, with my thanks for their help. Stay on schedule monitoring your radio as we arranged. When things are set I will bring you out to join me in the west. Stay well my friend!"

262

Putting the radio in his jacket, he turned and ran for the helicopter whose rotors were now spinning at close to take off speed. And, as he ran, he promised himself again that he would not desert a man who had been more than loyal to him for over ten years. That he would not do!

As he strapped himself back into his seat Garov stuck his head through the flight compartment hatchway and said loud enough to be heard over the clattering of the huge rotors "Buckle up and hang on! It will be nap of the earth flying until we cross into Poland." He then turned back to confer with his pilot.

An hour and some minutes later the big helicopter drifted down between two heavily wooded hills, again its' engines put into whisper mode, and flared to a hover, then landing. The pilot did this without showing a light other than the almost unseen instrument glow reflected from the pilots night vision goggles.

Garov, being assured the pilot would be there to take the men back, went into the cargo/troop bay through the flight deck hatch. There he instructed the commanders squad to take everything and, showing no light, debark and go to the second truck waiting behind the helicopter and load up for a short ride. Osov and Chabov he invited into the back of the sedan parked in front of the truck. Once inside he instructed the driver to go. Looking at his two friends in the rear seat he said quietly, "Rest now. The drive is about two hours more. We will talk once we are in the air again." He then turned to face front and laid his head back on the headrest.

Two hours fifteen minutes later they were pulling into the commercial entrance to a medium sized airport on the outskirts of a small city. The sedan and truck drove up to and into the hanger of an American private air cargo firm, the hanger doors closing even before the vehicle came to a halt. As they exited the sedan, and the men in the truck began climbing down with their gear, Chabov commented, "Excellent Yuri, but are we to fly out in a couple of these small planes?"

Garov smiled, but said nothing, as he motioned them to follow him. He stepped off towards a large dark doorway at the side of the hanger. He walked quickly through this door ahead of them and, as they followed him through it, there were several sharp clicks and an array of lights high overhead came on to reveal a shiny seven-o-seven Jetliner taking up most of the available hanger. When they looked at him Garov said, "This plane, when it enters US airspace will report returning dead head (empty) after delivering a very valuable cargo of art work to be sold at auction here. The only passengers will be the somewhat large contingent of guards sent for protection. The original men will wait here to return on the plane which brings you back."

After a quick breath he went on, "Don't worry about the protection company or the air freight company. We own both and they are legitimate. Please board," the lights were coming on in the plane even as he spoke. "And make yourself comfortable in the forward passenger cabin. Ahem! Peotre, would you have your men go through those boxes sitting over there and pick out what will be necessary for each of them of civilian clothing in them, then have them go to the rear cabin and change."

"Also, please have them store their equipment in the crates they will find in the cargo hold directly behind their cabin. I'm afraid the choice of clothing is not the best but the best I could do on short notice. I must make a few final arrangements then I will join you again."

His friends nodded, smiles playing at the corners of their mouths in recognition of how thorough this man always was, and stepped off to do as he had bidden them. Meanwhile Yuri had already turned back to the large door through which they had entered.

Three hours into the flight the three friends had brought each other up to speed on what had been happening with each other. It was at this point in the conversation that Garov was saying, "so you will understand that I can tell you no more of our operation! But once you see our evidence at first hand I believe you will be wholeheartedly willing to join with us to fight this threat!"

Smiling now he said, "The people that you would be working with know your histories and reputations well, and are eager to meet with, and hopeful to be working with, you." He paused for a moment knowing what the next question would be when it came.

"Yuri, do we know these men, and will we meet them after viewing your evidence?" Chabov asked for them both.

"If your reaction is anything like mine was, I believe that you will. Do not forget the incident I told you about happening in Moscow. We have one of the creatures on ice. Enough my friends. I've already said more than I should have. One other thing though. Peotre, I believe you might like to meet the man responsible for failing our operation in Madagascar. Yes?"

Peotre Osov turned startled eyes on his friends, "You mean Dirk! John Dirk!?" he asked incredulously.

"Yes. That's the one. He is working for our operation. Uh. Actually, he is running it!"

Chabov and Osov looked at each other with startled eyes, Chabov remembering the stories Osov had told him of this almost ghostlike man.

Both men were now mentally reassessing their reservations in their minds. They coupled with that the apparent and complete commitment of their friend, who had been a sworn enemy of Dirks, and the quality of people who were being drawn into this clandestine movement began to take on some real shape. And shaping up into something much larger than they had at first thought.

When they surveyed the evidence, and joined the movement themselves, as Garov knew they would, they were in for many surprises as to who was being called, and joining.

Eleven hours, and one fuel stop later in New York, the mid-sized seven-o-seven came down on an airstrip somewhere in the center part of the American Continent.

They were tired and stiff from so many hours in the air but they were quickly hustled into one of the famous American 'Huey' helicopters, being told their men would be cared for at the Airfield. The flight lasted another two hours before they landed in a vast forested area.

They were led through the cut to the blind canyon, and past the effects of the chameleon device. There both men had to deal with their first bout of awe. They were shown the rest of the evidence.

They were convinced. They committed themselves. And Peotre Osov met his Ghost like enemy who would become one of his closest Friends.

Innovation

"I see you've stopped muttering about the forest and the trees" said Dirk, as the group fumbled about a little taking their seats around the conference table, to G'Whiz.

"I thought I was going to be able to live that down" said G.'Whiz' Burke a little truculently, but smiling self deprecatingly just the same, knowing the ribbing wasn't serious. The rest of the people at the table laughed quietly at the good natured by-play.

Dirks' smile was one of self satisfaction in seeing that his simple play to release a little tension from these five people had worked. That tension was caused by having to face an enemy about whom you had limited information and even less understanding.

"OK people! Gerry called this meeting for a specific reason. Let's come to order for his report." The noise of scraping chairs, conversation and paper rustling died away as their attention focused on the head of the table where Dirk and Gerry Burke were seated, the faces of those in attendance expectant now.

"OK Gerry, you've got a captive audience now. Let's hear what you've got to say!" Dirk said turning the meeting over to him.

Gerry stood up and walked to the door, twisted the knob to make sure it was locked, then came back to stand behind his chair, looked at the group for a moment, seemingly studying each face, before he began to speak.

"As you know, and in direct relation to Dirks ribbing, I was having trouble seeing some of the trees for the forest. What that translates to is that because of the amount of new, or lateral, technology I found myself with I was being deluged with information. The vast amount of new information which I let limit my sight of the individual aspects of that information. What that means is that for a while I couldn't see the trees for the forest." Gerry said ruefully. Everyone at the table dutifully chuckled, clearly understanding the previous reference now. Each face now looked back clearly ready to hear something important.

"After the arrival of Felix Ortiz, whom most of you have met, some logging was done and he provided some serious insight to my problem. That insight was that the computer set up on this ship uses three separate languages. One for life support and related operations, one for mechanical and maintenance operations and a third used by the command and control master computer. That wouldn't have been so bad but, what wasn't guessed until recently was that there was a fourth computer system. This system was slaved to the command system, but its sole function was to act as a passive demand only unit. That demand only function was to interpret between the three separate systems when they needed to communicate." Gerry paused for a moment as he saw the implication of what he was saying sink in.

During the short pause Dirk was urgently communicating with Tulan internally. *Tulan. Why did you never mention this matter of the computers to me?*

Tulan, embarrassment evident in his tone as he replied said, *it just never occurred to me. The ship is built that way because those component functions are built by several different races, then assembled at a central construction point. It did not occur to me because it has been that way for as long as can be remembered. Just something that is. Something no one ever thinks about consciously.* He finished introspectively.

I understand, Dirk sent back and, *but it is something that should be kept in mind for the future.* He finished this just as Gerry continued.

"The end result." Continued Gerry "is that we now have almost total access to the entire ship. And because of that we have learned a great deal." Again Gerry paused for a moment, and as he continued, he was now sporting a very self satisfies smile which promised revelations to come.

"One of the most important things we have learned is that this ship seems to have some sort of Galactic Encyclopedia installed as part of a survival library! Another important discovery is that each of the maintenance control computers seems to have a complete technical library installed as part of its legacy memory."

Gerry paused again, walking around, to see that the import of this revelation was lost on no one here. The room was so quiet you could hear each individual breathing, and all eyes were fastened on him like butchers hooks in sides of beef.

The grin on his face seemed to get broader as he said "Let me ask you a question. What, for us, is the greatest aspect of this ship, excluding the ship as a whole?"

"The auto-med. Unit!" said one. "The anti-grav lift sled!" said someone else. "The galley's food processor!" exclaimed another, and there were several loud guffaws as they all remembered several mishaps that occurred in the very beginning before they had learned to program it properly for human edible foods.

"The chameleon cloaking device!" said Dirk quietly, and the group returned to serious thought, several of them nodding their agreement. "After all, it's hard to find what you cant see!" he finished.

"Well, you're all right!" said G. Whiz, still grinning. "We were tinkering around in the lab workshop, after getting access to those tech libraries, and we think we came up with something we think will give us an edge on staying alive!" He paused yet again, now displaying a wide smile of self satisfaction, looking at them expectantly.

"Well, if it's so dammed important where the hell is it?" snapped Bill Tate, and, "We're short handed, overworked, and too tired to play games right now Gerry! If you've got something to show us just bring it in and show it to us!" he finished tiredly, others in the group nodding agreement with that sentiment.

With a hurt look now on his face, the grin almost completely gone, he said slowly "OK Felix, turn it off now."

For a few seconds all eyes looked at him with a quizzical expression, for Felix Ortiz had not attended this meeting. Then, behind him, near the front of the room and near the door, there was a slight shimmer, a flicker, and there stood Felix where nothing and no one had stood before! He was wearing a heavy backpack and a harness with odd looking attachments all over it.

"Well I'll be damned!" muttered Bill Tate, and "I take it all back Gerry! You can waste my time like this any time you damn well please!" he finished fervently, as murmurs of apology and approval came from the rest of the group.

"Nice work Gerry!" said Dirk, as he heard TuLan exclaim in his mind, *I did not believe that was possible! I know that the scientists that developed that system have been working on it for centuries to reduce it to a portable model. The power requirements have always been too high for a portable power source.* Dirk voiced this next aloud "How Gerry?" This demand was instantly repeated by all, most notably by David and Sheila Hull, the physicists.

"To make a long story short," Gerry began, raising his voice to be heard above the hum of animated conversation> And the entire room instantly became silent, waiting, as be went on in a normal tone of voice, which never the less began to express his own rising excitement.

"I was very interested in this device from the very beginning." Gerry launched into his description for his now rapt listeners. "We were downloading a translated version of its' tech specks, and I happened to notice some of the general operational diagrams. They reminded me of some of the older TV studio camera layouts, you know, the way that everything used to be hard wired to everything else. Well, there was one exception, a blue line, that went to all of the output points. These came out of a large box that turned out to be a holographic image projector."

Seeing that they were totally intent on his words now, he went on "That main projector was sending fragmented images to the mini projectors that are mounted around the entire circumference, top, and bottom, of the entire ship. Those mini projectors have a dual function. They are both cameras and image projectors! That main projector was sending a picture to the surface projectors of whatever was on the exact opposite side of the ship from it. In other words, you saw whatever was on the other side of the ship from wherever you were standing, and it was projected in multiple layers to give a true three 'D' picture!"

He stopped. He took a deep breath. He smiled brightly as he looked at his captivated audience before going on. "Wellll—keeping the story short," and he smiled even more brightly to the exaggerated groans this brought forth, "with the help of a lot of electronic parts sent by Carmella, and the schematics from the ships specs, we recreated the system in miniature. The breakthrough came in two parts! You've got to understand that the boys who thought this gizmo up were very, very sharp! But their electronics, as opposed to ours, are almost primitive by comparison. This brings me back to that blue line on the diagrams!"

"It turned out to be some form of flexible crystal, with a non reflective coating on it. Actually it was more like a type of fiber optic cable. The problem, we noticed after examining it, was that when you look at the ship closely while cloaked you notice some occasional distortions. This is because the crystal, like any crystal, is refractive, allowing light to distort. They did an amazing job with it, using what they did."

With a self satisfied smile he went on, "But again, compared to the fiber optics we have developed the net results are close to primitive. I think the key is that because of the way they build things size, weight, and material don't seem to be a factor for them, so there isn't much need for innovation!" he paused again to be sure that his information was sinking in, and another deep breath before going on.

"Anyway, it turns out that they were using a mainframe computer to do what one of our laptops can do quite easily, with a couple of gigs to spare. Secondly, it was a combination of the quality of our fiber optics and how much signal we can compress into a hair fine filament, and the fact that our digital cameras and transmitters are, amazingly enough, light years ahead of anything they were using in the ship! Put those schematics together with out computers and fiber optics, and our penchant for miniaturizing almost everything and it is, as they say, 'The fat lady sang for us'! He finished this last with a wide smile on his face.

After a short round of applause, and a few 'damn good shows, Gerry' he held up his hand. Everyone instantly quieted again. "There are," he began more slowly now, "still a couple of bugs in the unit. One of which is that we still can't move around very fast with it without losing some of the reality field integrity. It's pretty slow right now, only about eighty steps per minute, not even a fast walk. The other bug is in the portable power pack! We are only getting about a full hours use from that with full integrity. We hope to get a full three hours use with the new high compression miniature batteries, the kind that we're using for our astronauts space suits, that we've asked 'Blackjack Jones' to bring with him when he comes in."

He took a gulp of air and rushed on, "We also think that, if we can get our hands on a couple, we can maintain integrity at a hundred fifty steps per minute by using the new high speed digital cameras that 'Kodak' came up with for the company just recently. We want those because they can do multiple imaging segmenting as an internal function!"

"I don't know if you have to get that fancy," said John Crow "the way you have it right now I could walk right into the White House without being seen!"

"Hold that thought!" Dirk broke in, then to Gerry "Get in touch with Carmella and tell her you have priority on this! Tell her to get you whatever you need as fast as she can."

Jimmy Lester piped in with, "I could really use a couple of those units with me when I leave tomorrow to go in and get Garov!" he finished with feeling.

Looking at Jimmy Gerry said, "I don't have any of those that I can give you right now, but I do have something that you might like to take with you when you go." All of a sudden the room went silent again, and every pair of eyes were fastened on him again!

"Two miracles in one day!" said bill Tate in an undertone, and "The man will be a saint before he leaves this room!" Then he too shut up and prepared to listen!

"Dirk, do you remember those funny looking rifles we found in the armory behind the control room? The ones that turned out to be a type of plasma projector?" At Dirks' nod he went on, "Wellll-," and there was another good natured groan from the group that died quickly, "without going into too much detail again, it turns out that they were fairly simple mechanisms. It would suffice it to say that we were able to miniaturize them!" At this last there was a distinct gasp from those in the room.

Gerry, seeing them urging him to continue with their eyes, smiled brightly and went on, "They are a little heavy, but they can be hand held now, and can be set to be non lethal!" There was another gasp, because everyone there had seen what one of those bolts had done to a small tree it had been fired at, but Gerry rushed on.

"We did that by reversing the firing process. Instead of using the electric charge it issued as the accelerator for the plasma charge, we made the plasma charge the carrier for an electric charge by reducing the matter content of the plasma ball, thereby making the electric charge both the accelerator and the delivered weapon! This was done by using the electric charge as a containment field and the tiny plasma ball as a delivery vehicle for that charge. The tiny plasma particle, once ignited, retains just enough mass to follow a trajectory, while being maintained by the electric charge field. The charge field knocks whatever or whoever it hits silly. The plasma particle, now spent, simply dissipates. The only drawback is that the trajectory can be traced at night, or on a very cloudy day." He fell silent, waiting for their reaction.

While every eye in the room looked at him with awe someone in the room muttered just loud enough to be hears, "Jesus Gerry! You're going to give us all a headache if you don't start giving us a little detail on these things you come up with!" There were several loud guffaws at this, just enough to let the group relax a little from trying to follow Gerrys' non technical description of his latest bombshell innovation.

After it died down Dirk said, "What's the other drawback? I could hear it in your voice."

"You're right," Gerry said "I really need a bunch of those high compression batteries that Blackjack is bringing! We can only get three shots out of the ones we're using now. Those things use a lot of juice every time they're fired!"

"OK." Dirk said, turning to Jimmy Lester, "How many of those batteries can Blackjack get his hands on at one time?"

"As many as he needs. His company does a lot of testing for NASA's special projects." Jimmy replied.

"Alright, tell him to bring as many of them as he can get his hands on quickly, and to order as many more as he can without it beginning to look suspicious. Also, put off leaving for a week! I want you and your team to have every advantage you can get when you go in there!" Dirk finished briskly.

"Got it." Jimmy said, then turning to Gerry, he said "I'll take a two dozen of those Gerry!"

"You can have twenty of them. With those batteries you should be able to get eighteen to twenty shots out of them, but you'll have to bench test them first to be sure."

"Good enough!" Jimmy said, and, "I'll have Blackjack here with the batteries in three days."

"I'm afraid that's all I have for you right now, Dirk" Gerry said.

"That's more than good enough" Dirk said with feeling.

Bill Tate piped in with, "It's no damn wonder they call him "G Whiz", and now he's a bloody saint to boot!" he finished good naturedly, as the rest of the group gathered around him to congratulate him on work well done.

CHAPTER THIRTEEN
Interludes

Lt. General Carl Miles

Carl Miles, Lieutenant General, United States Army, at age sixty seven was now retired. He had spent the last forty years doing the one thing he loved doing most. Being a soldier! He hadn't wanted to retire, but because of army regulations he had been forced to.

Carl Miles had had two great loves in his life. The second was the army. The first, and greatest, was his wife Jennifer. Carl and Jennifer had had what was often thought of as a fairy tale romance, and it had lasted for forty four years.

They had been sweethearts since they had met in the eighth grade, lovers in college, and had not been apart since. Now they were! Jennifer had died just five months ago from an unsuspected, and rare, heart disease. Now Carl, and his life, were operating on automatic, for he now felt that there was a large black hole where once there had been light and sanity.

Carl had plunged himself into his work since her death, often working twenty hours a day, trying desperately to fill the gap that existed in it now. His work was his only other love in life, for he and Jennifer had never been blessed with children of their own. Carl was a Lt. General in the U.s. Army, now retired, and while still on active duty he and Jennifer had often marveled, after finding out that she was unable to have children, that all of the men and women under his command thought of themselves as their children. After all, it was his, and her, job to look after them and teach them all that they could.

And they had treated them all as their offspring! He was hard and demanding when necessary, but always with caring and understanding. That caring and understanding had always been returned threefold, because those men and women who might be asked to pay the ultimate price wanted very much to know that those who might ask them to pay that price cared about what happened to them.

Now that was gone now too! He had been ordered, out of the clear blue it seemed, by the head of the joint chiefs of staff to retire as per regulations, instead of finishing out this final tour of duty as was normal. That had come a scant thirty days ago, and it seemed like the paperwork had flown through the system like a rocket. Now, Lt. General Carl Miles, retired, was sitting here in this dark room, in this dark house with the light his Jenny had always brought to it now fled from it like a thief in the night.

He was sitting in his study, nursing the last of a very large bourbon that he had poured himself an hour, or a day, ago and looking somberly back and forth between the last picture he and Jenny had taken together, and the nine millimeter service automatic laying on the desk in front of him. As he sipped the bourbon slowly his fingers toyed with the pistol, turning it slowly round and round on the desk.

"That would be a terrible waste general!" a quiet voice said out of the darkness, abruptly breaking into his dark reverie, causing him to snap his head around and reach out and turn on the desk lamp. Feeling almost as if he were in some sort of waking dream his eyes scanned the room for the intruder, but they found no one.

Turning back to the desk, thinking that he had dreamt the whole incident, or that his conscience had been rebuking him, he once again looked between the picture and the pistol. But the pistol was now gone! The hair at the base of his scull rose, almost with a life of its' own, and the muscles in his neck, back, and shoulders tensed painfully. This could not possibly be happening! Could it?

Jenny is gone. But there are others now that need your help very badly!" The same quiet voice said out of nowhere. Spinning around in his chair again, his eyes searched the small comfortable room frantically, but still found nothing. In a voice that was close to breaking he stammered "Who? Where are you?" while at the same time his mind, even through the turmoil he was feeling, was trying to tell him that there was something very familiar about the voice.

"I am a friend from your past general, and I came here to ask you for your help. From the looks of things I got here just in the nick if time to prevent a terrible waste!" said the quiet, somehow familiar voice, some passion now pushing at the edges of it.

The familiarity taken in using his first name focused his attention, reinforcing in him the idea that he should remember the voice, and the man behind it. If he could just see him! "Damn it," he said in a voice that was a rough half whisper, to himself, "I know that voice, if I could just put a face to it!"

Stop this! he was now thinking furiously to himself. He was a soldier, he berated himself, trained to think and pull myriad facts together under bad conditions! But this situation was really spooky, and his so recent state of mind was still having its' effect on him. But the voice was having its' intended effect on the man. It was making him angry, making him want to think clearly!

The voice said, from another place in the room now "I'm going to do for you what you did for a green shavetail lieutenant twenty years ago when you told him to cut his losses and save his men for another fight, on another day! I learned more from you in that five minute talk with you on the radio than I ever did in O.C.S." The voice went silent, waiting for the memory to come back to the man. And the memory came flooding back! They were in combat. A place and moment in hell. A place and situation that left little hope of surviving it!

The memories came flooding back, the brutal emotion of them reflected in his eyes like pictures on a movie screen. He was a company commander, just promoted to full captain, with six months in country in a war that nobody would ever hear about.

He had just come back to the command bunker on orders from the battalion commander because the exec. had been killed while checking the line. They were under heavy attack by mortar and RPG rounds, as well as a hell of a lot of automatic small arms fire! He was still in the ell shaped blast suppressor part of the bunker entrance when the RPG round came in through the gun port, blowing the CO in half and wounding the new exec badly.

He picked himself up off the floor of the short tunnel, where the blast had thrown him, and rushed into the bunker to find the remains of the CO and the wounded new exec. That man motioned to him weakly to come near. As he bent down next to the man he whispered to him "You're in command now!" before he passed out.

He had now been in command for fifteen minutes, and everything was going to hell in a hand basket! Everything that could go wrong seemed to be doing so! He had lost a good third of the men in his new command, wounded or dead! Now he was on the radio with a green 'gung ho' shavetail lieutenant in a forward position, telling him to cut his losses and run like hell back to the firebase. And he had to do it in a calm voice that said he was in command and in control, when what he wanted was to scream at him that he needed him to get his ass back here to fill in the gaps in the line until the huey gunships he had called for could get here!

"My God! Is that you Dirk? And if it is, where the hell are you?" Anger, and hope, were now taking the place of the morose thoughts of just a few moments before, as some of what had first been said to him began to penetrate the fast disappearing fog that had been creeping over his mind.

"Yes Carl, It's me. Will you listen to what I have to tell you with an open mind, and then decide if you want your gun back?"

Sitting up straight in his chair now, he was trying to keep his feelings hidden behind an impassive front. But he knew that his feelings of guilt, anger, shame, and defiance were parading across his face like they were on parade. His reply, when it came, was, "Repeat what you said when you first spoke!" This last was said with the snap in his tone that was used to command men, and getting results from it!

"I said, general, that the action you were contemplating would be a terrible waste! And, although Jenny was gone now, there are people who could really use your help. In fact, need it very badly! Will you hear me out?" the calm voice said, this time from yet another point in the room.

All thoughts of causing his own demise were gone from his mind now. They had been shunted aside by the keen analytical mind that had brought this man to the position of commanding whole armies. His mind was racing now as questions, answers, and more questions flashed past his minds eye. The voice is moving, how? Speakers? Possibly. My movements are being watched! How? Cameras? I know that voice for sure! Could it really be him? Then, like a dam bursting, the knowledge was there before him! "Dirk? John Dirk! That really is you! And how the hell are you speaking to me, colonel? Do you have my house bugged?"

"Yes, it's me Carl. And no, your house is not bugged. I checked before deciding to approach you this way. I'm right here with you! I just wanted to be sure that I had your undivided attention! Also, I am no longer a colonel. Like you I'm retired. I'm here to ask you for your help. We have a big, with a capital 'B', problem, and it's not just a problem that concerns this country I'm talking about! Will you hear me out?" And again the voice had moved.

General Carl Miles did not trust and respect many of the men he had had to work with over the years completely, but John Dirk was high on the list of those he did! If he said there was a serious problem, there was a serious problem! He was not a man to cry wolf! "I'll listen John, but how the hell are you doing that voice trick?" he said, his eyes still searching the room.

"It's part of the proof I brought to convince you with." The voice said, now directly in front of him. Then there was a shimmer in the air, and the form of the well known man was standing in front of him!

When the shock had worn off a little all the general could splutter was, "How in damnation did you do that?"

"If you'll offer me a drink of that very fine bourbon your having," Dirk said, now with a warm smile on his face, and in his voice, as he reached out to shake the hand of one of the few men he liked as much as he admired, "I'll start from the beginning, and tell you the whole story.

"Yes! Yes, of course." Carl miles said, getting up and crossing to the small bar built into the bookcase opposite his desk. "Please sit down John. That was one hell of an entrance you made!" he said, pausing to add ice to the glass he had taken down. Coming back he handed the glass to Dirk, and picking up the bottle from the desk poured him a very healthy shot. Looking at his own glass on the desk he poured another one for himself as well, saying, "From the look on your face I'd say I'm probably going to need this!" so saying he eased himself back down into his desk chair, his face now attentive.

Dirk began to explain. Three and a half hours later, and a pot of coffee that they had moved into the kitchen to make and have, Dirk was saying, "And this backpack on the table here is one of the innovative modifications we made from the main unit that the ship uses to hide its' existence from prying eyes"

After looking over a list that Dirk had prepared at the table he burned it. General Miles was very impressed by the quality of the people on that list, recognizing many of the names from his two year stint with military intelligence at the Pentagon. Looking Dirk straight in the eyes he said in a level tone, "Look Dirk, I'll grant you that I put a lot of faith in the messenger for the truth of the message, but I'd like to see some of the hard evidence you have. Such as this thing attached to the mans spine, and this ship you speak of so often."

"God alone knows that I haven't got the slightest idea of how your people devised that cloaking device, but I suppose it's possible to make one with all of the technological advances we've made lately." He paused for a couple of seconds, looking a little sideways at Dirk. Then said "But, If I'm going to commit myself to this thing, I have to convince myself by seeing and touching the hard evidence with my own two hands and eyes!"

"Fair enough," dirk replied crisply "when can you be ready to leave for the ship?

The man turned startled eyes to him, not expecting to have to make his decision here and now, and said, "Any time you want. When do you suggest we go?"

"How about right now!" dirk said quickly, a little smile playing at the corners of his lips as he saw Carls' eyes widen even further in his surprise.

The only thing the man could say was "OK!"

Dirk rushed on, not wanting to lose his momentum, "You should only pack an overnight bag. Two changes of clothes should do it. I'd suggest they be jeans and flannel shirts, and warm socks and boots."

He paused for a few seconds himself, as a mischievous grin broke across his features now, "I'll notify the protection team I have waiting outside that we'll be ready to leave in about a half hour!"

So saying he turned towards the door, but stopped, turning his head back to the general, the grin still in place, and said, "you don't think it will take you any longer than that to get packed, do you?"

Lieutenant Valasovic

"Lt. Valasovic!" The voice of major Kukov roared in the headphones of the lieutenant's headset, "You are not paying attention to your asset placements. They are spread too far apart to repel any kind of determined counter attack by the opposition. Do you intend to lose half of your troops due to poor planning?!"

"Sir," the cool voice of Lt. Valasovic came back to him in the darkened command/observation bunker perched on the side of a hill overlooking the training area, "My men are moving into the area according to our plans. Our intelligence tell us that the tactic being employed by these rebels gives us the advantage under the present circumstances. We are moving into the area under controlled advance march"

The result of the exercise was that Lt. Valasovics' troops sustained minimal terminal casualties while inflicting maximum casualties on the adversary forces. This result came about because the lieutenant had clandestinely moved four expert snipers onto the high ground overlooking the exercise area the night before under the cover of darkness and a steady downpour of rain.

Some hours later, in the training compound conference room, major Kukov had asked Lt. Valasovic to remain after the exercise debriefing session was completed. The room empty now, Lt. Valasovic waited pensively as major kukov paced back and forth at the head of the conference table. His head was down, chin resting almost on his broad chest, apparently very deep in thought.

Valasovics' mind had been drifting, tiredly going over every aspect of the recently completed exercise, trying to discern the reason for this peremptory order to remain. A muted 'Humph', and then a just barely audible, "Da!" snapped the lieutenants attention back to the present, and this room. "Lt. Valasovic, why did you join 'Spetsnaz' when you could have been attending the 'Frunz' Academy right now?" Kukov asked, the normal ring of command gone from his voice now.

"Sir?" replied the lieutenant, the question obvious in the somewhat hesitant answer.

"Answer the question Lt.! Do not hesitate, or try to discern the reason I am asking it at this time." The gruff voice ordered in a not unfriendly manner the Lt. Was not accustomed to.

"Sir. I joined 'Spetsnaz' because they are the best in the world at what they do sir!" Valasovic snapped the answer.

"Da. Da. That is the prescribed answer. Now tell me the true reason that you joined, lieutenant!" major Kukov said sharply, now looking directly into the lieutenants eyes.

"Sir, 'Spetsnaz' is the only group in our military trained to operate under any and all conditions," the lieutenant said, voice strong and vibrant with conviction "and soon our space program will require us to begin a colonization program, and I want to be part of that sir!"

"Do you now?" said the major, a small smile playing at the corners of his normally stern lips.

"Yes sir, I do!" the lieutenant replied, rising to stand at rigid attention to reinforce the sentiment of the response.

Still with the faint trace of the smile at the corners of his mouth the major snapped, "What makes you think, lieutenant, that you have, to coin a quaint American phrase, a snowballs chance in hell of ever attaining that goal. How do you dare to reach that high after rejecting a chance to attend the 'Frunz'?"

Somewhat taken aback by this line of questioning, the lieutenant decided to be completely truthful in answering this last, "Sir. I will succeed for two reasons. First, I have had the best instructor in the military to teach me. Second, I will succeed because I want to. Sir!"

"Don't try to butter my bread lieutenant." The major said, turning his face away to hide the grin spreading across his craggy features.

Resigned now to whatever might come the lieutenant said earnestly, "It's true sir. I paid the placement officer two hundred rubles to be assigned to your classes!" This said, the lieutenant remained at rigid attention, waiting for the ax to fall.

The next words the lieutenant heard were dumbfounding, so out of place were they. "At ease lieutenant. Sit down and relax."

"Sir?" The startled lieutenant asked. This was very much out of the ordinary, having anticipated a dressing down for using tactics that were well outside the expected guidelines.

If his previous words had dumbfounding the following ones left the lieutenant dumbstruck! "Sit down Katrina, please. By the way, I've known about that bribe since the day you offered it! The captain has been with me for many years, and reported it to me immediately after he assigned you to me!"

All of the strength gone from her legs now Lieutenant Katrina Valasovic, the only woman officer to have ever been accepted to the 'Spetsnaz' advanced officer training program in it's history, sank bonelessly into the chair behind her.

"Lieutenant, let me tell you of something interesting that happened just a few days ago."

"I was notified by messenger that I have been promoted to full Colonel, and will shortly be assigned to the tactical warfare school as a senior staff instructor." The major, now colonel, paused a moment for thought, and the lieutenant interjected, "Congratulations Sir!"

"For the remainder of this conversation you will call me 'Alexie', and I'm not sure that congratulations are in order yet because I was not scheduled for a promotion review until next year. There have been some strange things happening lately, but I digress, back to why you are here."

After another short pause to order his thoughts he went on quickly now, "A few days ago I received a call from a very old friend of mine. He asked me if I had any bright young officers that I might consider forwarding to him. This, normally, would not be a strange request from a high ranking officer, but my friend is Admiral Dimetri Chabov, commander of the Strategic Rocket Forces and Space Operations Command. What is strange is that he could have his pick of any officer he wanted, but he specifically asked me for a recommendation! This tells me two things. He trusts my judgment. And he is worried about something!"

"Now, my friend tells me he has this problem, and he needs my help with it in this manner! Therefore lieutenant, I have decided to forward your name to Admiral Chabov as my recommendation. That is, if that is all right with you?"

The young lieutenant sat still for a stunned few seconds before recovering her composure enough to stammer, "Me sir? Why me? When would I have to leave, sir?"

"Yes, you Katrina! And the reason is because I have seldom had the opportunity to teach someone who is so willing to learn what has taken me so long, and cost me so much, to learn! If you accept, your posting will be immediate and you will leave within the week, but do not give me your answer before giving it a little thought. There is, however, a caveat to this! You must give me your answer before leaving this room!! There are also some additional things I think you should know before making a final decision. Shall I go on?"

Katarina Valasovic, lieutenant, special operations forces, and the first woman to have ever been admitted to them, looked deeply into the now openly frank eyes of her teacher, and unbeknownst to him until this day her self proclaimed mentor, seeking some further clue to help her make her decision.

She found nothing there that she did not expect to find. There was only the bright blue eyes openly asking her to do as she had been trained to do, think it through. After a short moments hesitation she said simply, "Da. Please do."

Her mentor began to tell her all that he knew. An hour later, as he was coming to the end he was saying, "So you see, because Dimetri is who and what he is, and because our friendship spans some thirty years, I respect and trust him. He is not one to cry wolf, nor one to ask for help without good cause. My personal recommendation to you would be to accept the posting, even though I would hate to lose such a good officer."

He breathed deeply in, then let the air sigh out before continuing, "I had hoped to keep you here as an instructor, but, You answered my first question to you honestly knowing that it could affect you career. So, I will be just as honest with you. If you accept the posting, and do well with Dimetri, your career will be assured in the field you say you want to go into."

A wave of real affection rushed over her, far exceeding the respect she already held for this gruff man who hid so well the deep care he had for those under his tutelage, as she said the words he knew she would say, "Sir, Alexie. I would be proud to accept this posting. And I will do my best to show your friend how well you train your officers!" She was more than rewarded for this answer by the bright pride glowing in the mans eyes as he answered simply in reply "Da. Very good!"

Then he said, "you will not, unfortunately, be here for your graduation, but do not fear. Your records will show that you graduated with honors from all of your instructors. And this is, after all, nothing but the truth!"

The man paused for a long few seconds as an impish smile expanded across his craggy features, then said, "You will immediately begin packing your gear. As soon as you are ready you will report to the headquarters building to pick up your orders and transportation vouchers."

He paused again, leaning down to remove something from his briefcase, the smile on his face even broader than before, if possible, as he said, "I am proud to inform you that as of the moment you accepted this assignment you have been 'breveted' to the rank of major, which I am sure will be made permanent when you reach your new posting!" he finished, chuckling at the completely stunned look on her very attractive face.

"I do not know what to say Alexie! I could not have dreamt of such a thing!" she stammered.

"Do not say anything about it Katrina Valasovic. I told my friend that you were one of my best, and that he had better treat you properly. This was his way of assuring me that he would. Just do me, and the academy proudly is all that I will ask of you."

He said this last as he pinned her new insignias of rank onto the shoulder boards of her uniform. Done, he stepped back and beamed proudly at her.

Major Alexie Kukov would die not too long after this, one of the early casualties in this, as yet undeclared, war for his beloved homeland and his planet.

But he was already a hero to one young and bright eyed, but very competent, brevet major who would, if he had lived, made him more than proud of what he had wrought!

Denton, the File and the Letter

The special courier with the file he had been waiting for, for ten days now, was waiting for him to sign for its' delivery when he arrived. He had been unwilling to accept his secretary's signature for file and had waited for over an hour, flatly rejecting her attempts to leave it with her, telling her that if they did not want him to wait they could go through the whole process of requesting it again! Eyeing the black and yellow striped security sealing band on the file she shrugged and gave in, bringing him a cup of coffee while he waited.

Luckily for Denton he had arrived just as the courier was getting ready to leave. Denton thought he knew all of the special couriers, but new ones did come on board occasionally. Denton walked into his office, asking the man to please wait for one more moment, nodding to his secretary to come in with him for a moment. After answering several mundane questions about calls and messages he asked why the man had insisted on waiting for him.

"I don't know any more than you do, other than he said something about special instructions attached to the file, and that you had to sign for it personally." She said. Then she opened the door and motioned the courier in. After he entered she closed the door quietly behind her as she left.

Coming up to stand in front of his desk the courier said "May I see your ID card please sir?"

A little taken aback Denton removed it from his lapel pocket and handed it, clip and all, to the man who scrutinized it carefully before nodding to himself and handing it back to him. The man then removed one of the new imprint forms from an inner pocket and said brusquely, but politely, "Please sign this, and include the last four numbers of your ID number. Then imprint your thumb in the circle. As soon as that is done I can explain the special instructions attached to this file to you sir."

A little mystified by all of this, but doing as instructed Denton finished by pressing his thumb firmly in the indicated circle. The man tore off a copy of the form and handed it to him, folding the rest neatly and placing it carefully in his inner pocket.

Now looking at Denton intently the man began to speak in a low but clear voice, "Sir. I am instructed to inform you of the following, making sure that you understand each item as I finish it! Is there anything that is not clear so far?" At Dentons' negative shake of his head the man said, "Please acknowledge verbally, sir"

"No. Please continue." Denton said, becoming a little exasperated.

He placed the file on the desk in front of Denton, his fingers resting on it as if to hold it in place. Leaning forward slightly he went on, "Sir, as you can see there is a sealed envelop attached to this folder, just above the security seal. This envelop should be carefully removed and its' contents read before the security seal is broken on this folder. Are these instructions clear to you?"

Now more mystified than ever Denton nodded and said, "Yes." aloud and nodded at the same time.

Then the man went on, more briskly now, carefully lifting the back flap of the folder and showing it to Denton he said, "Also, as you can see, there is another envelop attached to the inner side of the back flap of the folder. When you have completed reading the contents of the folder you should secure it, and then immediately read the contents of the second envelop! Are those instructions clear to you sir?"

Denton was beginning to become frustrated with all of this but held himself in check, knowing where this file came from. "Yes, they are clear." He said a little sharply, some of his frustration coming through in spite of his self imposed control.

"Then, if you don't mind," the man said with a tight smile on his face, "or need anything else from me, I'll return to my duties." At Dentons nod the man turned on his heel and left, closing the door quietly behind himself.

"Now I wonder what all of that rigmarole was all about?" Denton said, half aloud, to himself as he began to carefully remove the first envelop from the front jacket of the folder. Taking a letter opener he slit the envelop open with the care he had been instructed to use, and removed what he could now see were two closely typed pages of print. Unfolding them he sat back in his comfortable chair and began to read. As he read his eyebrows rose higher and higher with each sentence, until he thought they would pass his hairline altogether! The letter read;

Dear Mr. Denton;

The fact that you are now reading this letter means that you, and your boss, can be trusted! The information you requested, and thought you would be getting in this file, remains unavailable to you at this time. So please, for your own safety, stop trying to obtain it or you will bring unwelcome attention to yourself and those you work with.

You are probably asking yourself at this moment, who the hell we are? The answer to that is very simple. We are the people you are having so much trouble locating, or finding out anything more than we want you to about us.

We are also responsible for the surveillance you are under. You have been being surveilled for the last several months now, and had we not wanted you to know it, you would never have spotted one of our chase cars the way you did! We do apologize for your men's injuries! By the way, that surveillance vehicle was one of your own!

The reason for the surveillance on you was to make sure that the waters you were stirring up had not brought undue attention to be drawn to yourself. It should please you to know that your back trail has been clear for the last two months, but we cannot continue to cover it for you, so take that good news also as a warning to take care in what you do in the future. But I digress. Back to this file!

This file has multiple purposes, and the information it contains has come at a high cost to us. Because of this, reading its' contents could end up costing you dearly also. The information it contains will, we believe, take you to a point of total rejection of what it has to say. But after reviewing the material carefully, we think you will come to believe it completely.

At this point I must tell you two things that might make your life a little easier. First, this file is set to self destruct once the security seal is broken. And, the file itself cannot be accessed without breaking the security seal. You will have twenty four hours to examine the material it contains before the treated paper begins a chemical reaction that will reduce it to ashes. Please do not try to stop this process as you might be seriously injured in attempting to do so.

If, after you have digested the material, you find it necessary to retain a copy we suggest you use a digital camera to copy it, one with a removable data storage cell such as a firestick. If you do copy the file guard the data cell very carefully. Being found with the information it contains will put you in mortal danger! And, anytime you access the data use a CPU that is not networked, and has no WAP capabilities installed!

I'm sure that once you view the data contents you will understand why! You should contact your boss, using all of the secure precautions available to you, and go over the material in this packet with him as soon as possible!

Second, I suggest that once you have reviewed the files materials you contact your boss, using the most secure methods, and go over the material with him. At the time of that meeting, keeping in mind the twenty four hour time limit, there is a message we would appreciate you to forwarding to him. The message is— 'There are, to the best of our knowledge at this point in time, only two people we know of that can be completely trusted by the both of you! President Samuel McCarthy, and General Carl Miles, retired. Once he reviews this material he will understand completely.

Now for the gut punch! Paul, our country and our whole world is under attack! If this sounds like an alarmist statement to you, just think about who we are! The attack we are under is at present moving forward covertly and cautiously, but the tempo will pick up as their foothold expands. The enemy is vicious and insidious, and the cost to humanity will be, we fear, a terrible one before this is all over.

Please believe also that all is not lost, for due to fate and luck we have acquired new and valuable allies for the fight to come. We also have, including you and your boss we hope, brought together some of the best people this world has ever produced to carry this fight to the enemy! The sad part is that all too many of those we will have to fight, through no fault of their own, will be human. This last you will understand after reading the file.

In closing, I would ask you to take notice of the envelop the courier brought to your attention that is attached to the inside of the back flap of this folder. I'm asking you not to open it until you and your boss have reviewed the contents of the file material together. Then open it and read it together. You are an honorable man, and I believe you will do as we ask in this matter. Believe me, it is important!

I'm sure that this has all taken you a little aback, as it did me when I first learned about these things. Just keep your powder dry brother!

Your Friend In Arms
Jimmy 'Bad Boy' Lester'

Paul Denton had had many strange things happen to him during his many years in the agency, but this letter and what it might mean topped everything in his experience. He sat, leaning as far back as his chair would allow, looking at the file on his desk, the pages of the letter laying loosely in his lap. His thoughts were ranging far and near as he tried to take in the scope of the meaning the letter left open to him.

Abruptly sitting upright in the chair, he reached out and punched the secure intercom button for his secretary. When she answered he said brusquely, "Mary, where is the boss right now?"

He's up on the hill," she replied calmly, ignoring his brusqueness. "In one of those committee meetings."

"Please get him on his cell phone for me. The one he doesn't turn off for anybody or anything!" he said more calmly, not missing her silent rebuke. "And Mary, use the scrambler!"

Somewhat surprised, because nothing but the most important calls were run though it, she replied, "Right away sir!"

Two minutes later she said over his intercom, "He's on line four, and he's hot!"

Pushing the button for line four Denton heard the chirps and clicks as the scrambler synced itself with his phone. As he started to speak he was cut of by his boss' voice speaking in a low controlled tone of fury, "This damn well better be the fucking end of the world Denton!"

His boss swore so seldom that Denton knew without doubt that the senate committee must have been grilling him pretty hard.

Composing himself Denton said very calmly, "I need to see you in your office right now, sir." And he cut the connection on him.

Denton knew his boss, and knew that he would understand that he didn't want to talk on the phone, even scrambled. Hanging up on one or the other was a device that they had devised to tell the other that it was critically important, and to take extraordinary precautions.

Taking a deep breath Denton picked up the letter and envelop, then reached, almost with trepidation, for the folder bound with the black and yellow security stripe laying on his desk. Gathering this to himself he bent down and opened a drawer in his desk, and removed a compact digital camera. With these items he left his office to wait for his boss in that worthy's office.

Dentons' boss came back the few steps he had taken away from the witness table to take his call and reseated himself. He calmly began to gather up the papers spread out in front of him and put them neatly back into his briefcase.

Looking up at the two tiered gallery of seated men and women in front of him with his piercing brown eyed stare he said, "I apologize Senators for the interruption, but an incident has occurred that requires my personal attention, and I must leave immediately. I will call the chairman's office to reschedule a time that is convenient to this committee to continue this hearing. Thank you all for your indulgence." So saying he left the committee room.

Most men would have paid dearly for such an action. But not this one. He had survived five presidents, and many of their peers. He was a very powerful man who most of them knew very little about.

The one thing that those who had been around for a while did know was that it could be very dangerous to one's career to push him too hard. Besides, though abrupt, he had been very polite to make himself available at their next convenience, hadn't he?

Denton and His Boss, Turning Points

Dentons' boss was saying, as he came through his office door like a runaway freight train, "Martha, put two armed guards on this door, Now! And I don't want to be disturbed for anything unless I ask for something. Is that clear!?"

Martha, the big mans' secretary for more than thirty five years, took his brusque tone of voice with the aplomb of her long relationship with him, knowing that something very important was going on, "Yes sir. Do you want one or two pots of coffee with your brandy?" she said with a knowing smile playing at the corners of her delicate mouth.

That stopped his mad juggernaut rush towards his desk in mid stride. He turned to face her, the stormy expression clearing from his own visage, a smile breaking across his face, "You know me much too well Martha. Yes, two pots would be much appreciated. Thank you." He said in a much more civil tone.

"Ten minutes." She said, smiling as she turned to do his bidding, closing the door to his office quietly behind his back as he entered and she left.

As he removed his coat he turned back to face Denton, who was sitting on the sofa, the contents of a file folder spread out across the surface of the coffee table in front of him. The stormy expression had returned to his face as he said, "I meant what I said about the end of the world Denton. I had those senators ready to increase our funding by half again as much for the next year!"

As he stood there looking at Denton he realized that he had done something completely uncharacteristic of himself. He had missed two key facts as he had barreled into his office! The first was that Denton was busily photographing the contents of the file spread out before him. That was odd enough in itself to cause questions! The second thing he had missed was that his young protégé was wearing the gravest expression he had ever seen on his face in all the years they had been working together. And now that he was really looking, Dentons' normally healthy tan complexion was almost gray in color.

Paul Denton had been working for him for over fifteen years now. He was brave, smart, and intuitive. And most importantly, he was loyal. He had been wounded twice in the line of duty, but always maintaining his cool and finishing the job professionally. Pausing to gather himself, the big man said, "I'm sorry Paul. I know you wouldn't use that code unless you really thought it was necessary. What have you got there?" as he seated himself in a chair on the other side of the coffee table.

Barely slowing the pace of his photography Denton reached to the corner of the table and lifted two closely typed pages, which he handed to his boss. As the great man read his eyebrows also began to climb up his forehead. He read the letter twice. Finished with the second reading he asked, "Where did this come from?"

"That's the scary part boss! I called records, and they said that the file had been delivered at seven thirty this morning. And that they have a signed receipt for the delivery. I then checked with the security courier DO., and he told me that they had no one with the name I gave them on their duty roster!"

"What do you make of the message for me?" his boss asked in a quiet voice.

With a grave look Denton said "Judging by what I've seen in this folder boss, I would say that it should be taken very, very seriously!"

Leaning back in his chair for a moment, then sitting upright again and leaning forward, Dentons boss reached across the table and pressed the intercom button for his secretary, "Martha, please get me the President on the blue phone."

Her response followed him across the room as he got up and went to his own desk and sat down in his chair, "Yes sir. Oh, the guards are in place now."

Picking up the direct line phone from a drawer he put the handset to his ear. There was a short pause, then, "Good afternoon Sir. We've had a package delivered from someone who has been a 'Bad Boy.' He stopped speaking and listened for a moment, then hung up the phone, a thoughtful look on his face.

Reseating himself across from Denton, he leaned forward, elbows on his knees, and spoke quietly, "His exact words were, 'Study the package! I'll contact you later! Thank you for that information." and he hung up on me.

The two men looked at each other across the paper strewn table top, each knowing now that this was to be taken very seriously indeed!"

"All right then, let's get to work on this pile. Pass me the stuff that you have already photographed." Dentons boss said briskly, all professional business now.

Admiral Timothy Berg

Properly speaking, Timothy Berg was Admiral Timothy Berg, Vice Chairman, Joint Chief's of Staff, U.S. military forces. Timothy Berg was having one hell of a day. As a matter of fact Admiral Timothy Berg had been having one hell of a day for the last month.

Berg had been an ace fighter pilot with eight confirmed kills to his credit, and because of a shrapnel wound he had received in the first Gulf war he could not fly any more. He was the proud holder of the navy cross and a distinguished service medal, along with two purple hearts and a chest full of other fruit salad. Tim had come to the navy from the marines, finding his true calling there, and had graduated the naval war college near the top of this class. This, and his marine background, had brought him two things. Fast promotions, and many of the dirtier jobs that needed doing. Which he did without complaint and well.

Admiral Timothy Berg did not like uncertainty in any shape or form. That was why he had turned out to be such a good tactical operations planner. Yet here he was in a sea of uncertainty. And that uncertainty had been caused by the president himself! The president was a man he had known, and liked, and trusted for twenty five years, since he had met him as a junior senator on the armed forces committee. And now he had thrown the monkey wrench of uncertainty into his life!

About a month ago he had been summoned from his office in the pentagon to the 'White house' for a personal interview with the president. When he had arrived he had been met at the entrance by two of the presidents security detail and asked to step into an anteroom, where he had been patted down very thoroughly. Especially about the back and shoulders. And his briefcase had been searched just as competently. He had then been led through several back corridors to the 'Oval Office' where he had been asked to wait, being told that the president would join him momentarily.

A few moments later the man entered from his private office. Berg looked at the well known features, noticing the newer care worn lines that had been added to them. The man looked at him, his smile radiating his inner strength, held out his hand to grip his own in warm greeting, saying "Tim, I apologize for the short notice, but I have so little time these days. Will you forgive me?", and meaning it! But behind the warm greeting he could sense weariness, and wariness! That was something that had never been present in their other meetings!

Berg could see that the man had been under a lot of stress, and probably still was, from the dark circles under his eyes and the deep furrowed lines around his eyes and forehead. He looked noticeably tired, which was unusual for this energetic man.

"Tim, come over here and lets' sit on the sofas, and let me get you a cup of coffee. Black, right?" he said, heading for the coffee service on the credenza at one side of the rooms seating area.

Sitting down with cup and saucer in hand, after the president had, Berg leaned slightly forward and asked, "What's this all about Mr. President, Sam?" seeking knowledge from both his professional and personal relationship with the man.

The man sat looking at him with those tired eyes for a moment, then leaned forward himself to speak in a low earnest voice, "Tim. We've known each other for a long time now, and during my two terms as president I've asked you to take on some tough, and dirty, jobs. You've done them without question or complaint. And very successfully too, I might add!

Leaning back the president paused, then, nodding to himself as if some inner decision had been reached, leaned forward again and looking directly into his eyes said, "I believe that after all these years we've developed a strong working relationship based on mutual trust and respect for each other. Am I far off on my assessment Tim?"

"I'd say that was a pretty fair assessment Sam. If it weren't some of the things you've asked me to do might not have gotten done without that foundation! Don't get me wrong, Sam. I'm a soldier, and I understand the prerequisites inherent in following those orders. But I'm an officer, and I understand the responsibility that goes with being one."

Berg paused just long enough to let a slight smile crinkle the corners of his eyes and mouth as he went on, "But I'm happy to say that you've never given me an order that might be questionable without giving me your reasons for giving it." Now the smile disappeared as he asked "Are you going to give me an order now that you think I might not follow?"

"Not on your life!" the president snapped, then his voice softened somewhat as he went on "but I do need to know how much credit your trust in me is worth?" he finished, his face deadpan now.

Admiral Timothy Berg had no idea where this was going, but he did know that for as long as he had known, and had been dealing with, this man he had never lied to or tried to mislead him in any way. His answer was given with a tight smile and a self affirming nod, "I would say that your credit is in pretty good standing. It is with me anyway."

"Thank you Tim. Now I'm going to ask you to stretch that trust, possibly to the breaking point!" Seeing the look in the admirals eyes he rushed on, "A few short months ago a situation was brought to my attention that will drastically affect the security of this country, and quite possibly the whole world! At the very least it will change our world view forever!"

As Berg was about to interrupt, questions and the demand for an explanation were warring on his face for preeminence, and the mans tense posture told Berg that this man was talking to him seriously. This was not a statement you made to a soldier lightly! The president held up his hand and barked, "Wait! Let me finish what I have to tell you!"

With the look of thunder clouds gathering in his eyes Berg said, "Go on!"

"Tim, I know you want answers to these claims. But I simply can't give them all to you at this moment! I can't give them to you because there are far too many things in play, and the situation is in total flux!" Pausing for a quick breath he went on "This is where I'm going to strain your trust to the breaking point!"

Berg was now leaning back on the sofa, the coffee in his hands now forgotten, his visage stony, demanding information that would keep him from breaking the trust of their long relationship.

It was a full minute, all the while looking into the admirals eyes, before the president went on, "I happen to know that your name is up for the Joint Chief's Chairman's position." This statement brought a questioning look from the admiral, one asking where this was going.

The president settled forward, elbows on his knees now as he spoke, his voice quiet and earnest, "Counter to that I have a job that I want you to take on. A job that will demand every resource that you can bring to bear on it, and challenge every talent you have acquired or developed over the years! If you decide to take it on you will, I can assure you, be working with some of the most talented and intelligent people in the world. If you take this job you will wield more authority than I do now! And to top it all off, you will learn things that will strain your credulity to near breaking at the very least!"

The president, seeing that the cold look had now been replaced by one of reserved interest, got up and took the forgotten cup from the admirals hand and went to the credenza to replace it, and his own, with two hot cups of coffee. Bringing them back to the coffee table he began to speak again, "That, admiral, was the carrot! What I'm about to tell you now is the stick! Outside of you and I you are never to speak of this matter to anyone who you are not sure of being a party to it. Now, should I continue?"

If he hadn't known this man for so long his answer might have been different, but he had, so he said, "I'm still sitting here drinking your coffee Mr. President." He had used his title to let him know that he still had reservations.

"This is what I want, no, need from you. First, in about two or three days you will receive an invitation to attend a technology conference in Toronto, Canada. I want you to accept, and take a ten day leave to do so."

"Second, you will travel by commercial transport, arrangements for which will already have been made for your trip. You will be picked up in transit by a security detail. Please follow their instructions without question, as they will be there for your protection!" At this last the admiral's look became stormy again, but the man held up his hand in a placating gesture and rushed on, "As I said Tim, this part is the stick. You had better realize something right now. I, and the other people involved in this, many of whom I think you would know, or at least recognize their names, are not involved in this because we need something more on our plates!" he snapped, then he went on in a calmer tone, "As I was saying, they will be there to protect you, and if this weren't so deadly serious we wouldn't bother, so take it for its' worth! Once you are registered at your hotel someone will take your place and you will be taken to a secret base, which even I don't know the location of."

"Once you arrive there you will be shown many things to prove what I have said to you is true beyond doubt. You will also be given the parameters for a new type of force we want you to develop and run. You will, I'm sure, be very surprised at who some of the people you will meet there are, and this, I think, will go further than anything to show you how serious we think this threat is."

"And last, You will be given the choice of opting out, which I doubt very much you will do! If you do opt out, you will be sworn to secrecy and your word will be accepted. You see, I trust you, and your word, implicitly! If you accept,

I want you to announce your intent to retire from the service when you return. If you are asked why you can say that you were made an offer too good to turn down." He was done. But now, where there had been a tired man doing a hard job, there was a man who was determined to keep his oath, who would not give up. He finished with a simple question, plea, "Will you go?"

Admiral Timothy Berg had not felt this much uncertainty in his thirty years of service to his country. Oddly enough, even with so many questions he had wanted to ask still unanswered, he had given his word to the president. To top everything else off he had just received his airline tickets to Toronto for this so called conference. And now he was sure that someone had been following him for the last few days. All of this had been going through his mind as he drove along the outer loop of the Washinton expressway towards his home in Bethesda, Md. Looking in his rear view mirror he saw the same car that had been there for the last three days. Suddenly his cell phone began to chirp. Irritated, he picked it up off the center console of the GMC Yukon, his personal vehicle, which he preferred driving, and flipping it open he snapped, "Berg here!"

"Admiral Berg. My name is Ebbets. I'm the head of your security detail, and I'm in the sedan two cars behind you! I thought it was time to introduce myself. I know that you are aware that you have been being followed for the last week, but actually we have been here for the last three weeks! I apologize if you have been a little worried about that, but we just wanted to make sure that no one else has been doing so. By the way, the car in front of you is also one of ours!" There was a short pause, then, "We will make our presence openly known to you once we get to Toronto. Until then just do everything as you normally do it. We'll be here if you need us! I also have a message from Mr. McCarthy. He sends his greetings, and says he will see you in three weeks." With that the line went dead. Looking in his rearview mirror he saw the sedan drop back, then disappear in the heavy traffic.

"Son of a bitch!" Timothy Berg said aloud, those words expressing both his pent up anger and relief. He was definitely not used to this type of cat and mouse game. It had been much too long since he had played it!

On the afternoon of the second day after that call he was boarding an Air Canada 'seven fifty seven' for his flight to Toronto. Three hours and fifteen minutes later the plane had touched down and taxied up to a roundel, and a debarkation tube run out to it. As he was leaving the plane one of the very attractive flight attendants touched his arm, saying, "Mr. Berg, Would you follow me please?" and she turned and led him to another door a short distance away. This led to a set of stairs that led downwards. As they descended she said "There is a VIP vehicle waiting for you on the tarmac below." As he came out into the sunlight, squinting to see in the sudden brightness, he saw a black sedan sitting a few feet away, two men standing by the near side doors. As he approached one of the men turned to face him and, extending his hand as he stepped towards him said, "Admiral Berg, my name is Tony Ebbets."

Turning he opened the rear door and waited while the admiral entered, then climbed in next to him. As soon as they were seated the sedan pulled away. Tony Ebbets reached into an inner pocket of his suit coat and removed a fat envelop, saying as he handed it to him, "The President asked me to give this to you." And, "We will be taking off again in about fifteen minutes in our own jet" Nine minutes later they pulled up to a small, fast looking, ten passenger Executive Gulfsrteam business jet, sitting on the on ramp approach way, its' engines already turning over at idle, its' door/ramp down and waiting for them to board. Fifteen minutes and a few seconds later they were in the air. They had initially headed due west at about twenty five thousand feet, but now timothy Berg could see that they had dropped down and were heading into what seemed to be a small private airport. He was wrong! The small jet screamed over the runway and kept right on going, heading in a northerly direction now, flying nap of the earth. This lasted for another twenty minutes. Looking out the window next to his seat he could see a very big range of mountains off the left wing, then realized that they were flying well below many of the peaks around them.

Suddenly the small jet banked left, between two peaks, and they were now heading towards that range, following a very big valley that seemed to lead right to them. Five minutes later the small jet set down on a well concealed runway that he doubted could be seen from the air. Ten minutes after that he was inside a cavern complex of truly huge proportions, heading for a small cluster of buildings just inside its' entrance. As they came up to them a man came out to greet them. He was tall and well built, with hair that was just beginning to gray at the temples. And he had the most piercing eyes Timothy Berg had ever encountered. He stretched out his hand as he came up, saying, "Admiral Berg, my name is John Dirk, and it is a real pleasure to meet you sir."

Dirk and Felix, Preparations

Dirk was sitting at the large paper littered desk in the largest room on the top floor of the St. Louis complex. That room doubled as both office and conference room. It had also been, on far too many occasions, the place where he was likely to wake up in the morning. Today was an unusual day for him because he had only two things on his plate to deal with. Actually three, but the third item was more of a pleasure than a chore.

It was six thirty in the morning now and his first appointment wasn't until ten thirty. He had four precious hours to himself, hours he needed to go over many things in his mind. Many of the items he would go over would be of concern to the core group meeting at five p.m. this evening, items that needed final decisions made concerning them.

His first meeting was with Felix Ortiz. Acquiring that man had been one of the premier achievements of his fledgling movement. Felix was an anomaly. He was a self proclaimed technocrat, but he was a technocrat with a huge difference. He was a walking encyclopedia of both current, and new cutting edge technology. He actually knew what he was talking about! Even more important than that Felix was a hands on expediter. He was one of those rare people who could visualize concepts, his own or those of others, and turn them into working realities! And the only reason they had been able to get Felix was due to the efforts of 'G. Whiz' Burke, their resident 'mad scientist'.

Gerry had said to him, "Look Dirk, give me a security team and let me handle it." When he came back he had Felix in tow, signed on and completely committed. When they were alone Dirk had asked him how he had done it, considering the fact that the man was making double digit millions where he was. Displaying his 'cat that ate the bird' grin Gerry had said that he had asked him if he would be interested in building an interstellar space ship.

"He told me not to pull his chain, so I showed him one of our plasma pulse weapons! After that he wouldn't let me out of his sight until I signed him on!"

Gerry paused, then his grin got even bigger, if that were possible, and said "Dirk, this guy is a gold mine! He knows every single technician in every field that's worth a damn. And on top of that there isn't a one of them that won't jump at the chance to come to work for him at the wiggle of his little finger!" he finished, almost out of breath now. And that had been an understatement! They were now getting, in ones and twos, and tens the finest scientists and technicians in the world. As a matter of fact they were coming in so fast that it was becoming both a security problem, and hard to house them all. The security issue was another item for tonight's discussion!

Thank god that they had Carmella! She had set up a dozen shell corporations to cover the hiring of so many so that it wouldn't draw too much attention to their activities. She had also bought two medium sized apartment buildings to help house them. She was another one of their treasures, acquiring companies and materials almost before those asking for them could finish writing out their lists for her. Dirk had known she was good, he just hadn't understood how good!

But the most astonishing thing that had been achieved since signing Felix on five short months ago was that they now had working drawings for Earth's first interstellar space craft! Incredibly it had been only eleven months since Dirks' first encounter with TuLan and his ship, and only seven months since the core group had decided that they must begin designing an earth built ship.

For two months Felix had spent nearly every waking moment in the teaching machine on TuLans' ship. Now, in five short months, Felix had filled in so many holes, so fast, that it had made all of their heads spin with the speed of his understanding of new concepts and the way he had of making things happen. Felix was not an idea man, but he sure knew how to make things happen once he understood what was needed! Now all they had to do was find a secure place to build and test it, and Felix had beaten them to the answer to that one too! He told them it had to be done in the Canadian Rockies because there was a blind spot at the polar axis. It seemed that there was a large area of that part of the Rocky Mountains in Canada that had a blind spot to both radar and satellite observation due to position and gravitational distortion effects.

Going over in his mind many of the things that had led to their present circumstances he knew that what was required were dramatic changes in their policies and procedures. They needed now both a new centralized operations and production location that was well hidden from view, and a decentralized operational methodology that would give both tight control and flexibility. Dirks' mind flitted back and forth between the problems he faced and the strategies he was developing, pushing and pulling at them until he thought they were what he needed, or wanted.

Dirk was, like Felix Ortiz, an expediter extraordinair. He was able to plan for immediate needs, and contingencies, on multiple levels while at the same time dealing with the overall operational picture on a daily basis. He well knew that the resistance movements' ability to change direction in mid stride, while maintaining its' focus for the end result, would be one of the factors that would determine whether they won or lost this, as yet, undeclared war! A light tapping on his door snapped him back to awareness of his surroundings.

He had, without conscious effort, slipped into a very restful light trance as he was mulling his problems. "Come." He called, and Felix Ortiz strode into the room, a pensive look pinching his eyes as he said softly, "Hullo, Dirk."

Without preamble he stated in a flat and somewhat plaintive voice, "Dirk, there's no way in hell we can build that ship here! There's still too much that will have to be outsourced to keep a lid on it!" he said as he threw himself into one of the chairs in front of Dirks' paper littered desk.

"I know Felix. That's why I asked you to come see me. I have a plan I've been working on ever since you told me we should build our own ships." Dirk replied calmly, and, "I wanted to run most of it by you and get your input before moving ahead with it full tilt." He finished, watching the other man closely. This because Felix, with all of his good traits and talent, was a worrier.

"That's great news Dirk! What do you have in mind?" he asked eagerly, interest and relief warring for dominance on his expressive facial features.

Felix Ortiz had worked with many high powered men in his meteoric rise in the technology field, and he respected few of them. Dirk was very high on the list of those he did! Very few of them understood what it took to do his job right. Dirk did! When Dirk had something to say, Felix would shut up and listen!

"There are three things," Dirk began "that led to the formation of this plan, and each one in and of itself would have eventually led us to it. But because of the enemy we are facing, and the uncertainty that that enemy brings to the fight, we are going to have to do our planning on multi tiered levels."

"Those three things are," and Dirk began to tick them off on his fingers as he spoke "One: although our facilities here in St. Louis are fairly extensive and well camouflaged there are a number of problems arising that I can only see getting worse as time goes on. One of those problems is already straining our capacities. And that problem is partially your fault!"

Seeing the protestations building on his face Dirk held up his hand to forestall him, saying, "It's not your fault directly, Felix," Dirk said quickly to ease the mans mind, "it's just that I had no idea how many talented people would come so quickly when you put out the call. The numbers are beginning to strain our facilities, and affect our ability to maintain the necessary security! You know how serious the situation is, or you wouldn't have stayed!"

"I know Dirk." Was the now quiet reply.

"The second thing is," Dirk continued "that we need a secure site to build our ships and get them off planet to test them. I'm going to tell you something that very few people know right now. I've had a meeting with the president, and he is now on board with us! He has a close personal friend that owns a huge tract of land in the Canadian Rockies. Almost exactly in the area you told us to look in! And there just happens to be a huge cavern complex in those mountains he owns, large enough to, he says, build a dozen aircraft carriers at once."

Dirk was smiling widely now as he finished with, "Do you think you can set those caverns up to build our ships there?"

"I don't see why not! There are only two immediate questions that will make any difference there. Power, and logistics. Do you have any ideas in that area?" Excitement creeping into his voice as he began thinking, planning.

"Yes," said Dirk, sober again, "we'll set it up as a second effort mining operation. There used to be an active gold mine there once, so it won't seem out of place. As far as power is concerned, I think I can get my hands on a small, portable, nuclear reactor power generator, but we'll have to bury it very deep to keep it from leaving a detectable footprint."

"That's perfect!" Felix warbled as his enthusiasm threatened to break the bonds trying to hold it in check. "And we can use a lot of any recovered gold to plate electronic contacts and switches. Save a ton of money on outsourcing that way! We can also improve security by using our own people for end user deliveries." He was practically gushing now, he was getting so excited.

"That brings up the third item." Dirk broke into his enthusiasm roughly to bring him back to the present needs, "There is no way we can maintain our security as the size of our organization grows here on earth! The only real solution is to move a large portion of it off planet!"

This got Felixs' attention immediately, and he began to pay very close attention to what Dirk had to say as he went on, "To that end I have some information that needs to be checked out as soon as you can contact one or two of our astronomers. We do have astronomers, don't we Felix?"

Seeing the red coloring come to the mans face Dirk went quickly on, knowing he now had the mans mind centered on their present problems, "That info has to be checked out by the time our first ship is ready to test fly. It's about a couple of planets in a solar system about fifteen hundred light years out to the galactic north of our own system."

"If my information is good we can set up one base on one of them. A base closer in would be just too dangerous to effectively deal with, I think." Dirk finished saying to Felix, whose face now wore a stunned expression.

Seeing that expression Dirk now said very forcefully, "Listen Felix, you, and the rest of our people are going to have to start thinking in 'galactic' terms, instead of 'solar ones! As I tried to explain to you before, there are many races and civilizations populating our galaxy, and we are going to learn damned fast how to live and work with many of them!"

Dirk was letting himself get a little hot on purpose, trying to emphasize just how important what he was saying was. He took a gulp of air and went on, "Look Felix, we are going to need those peoples help." At another startled look Dirk nodded, both to himself, and to Felix "Yes Felix, no matter what they may look like to us they will be people!"

Now Felix had an ashamed look contorting his features. Dirk wanted to ease up a little on him, but he also wanted him, and the rest, to start thinking about these things, so he said, "Don't feel too bad about this, just keep it in mind, OK? None of us are really prepared for what's coming. I'll tell you this much though, from what I've been able to learn from TuLan, I think that they are very much going to need our help too!" Dirk finished, his passion coloring his own words now.

"I know," Felix said sheepishly, his expression now that of a lost puppy, eyes almost frantically seeking the comfort of the known, "but knowing something in an intellectual way is so different from the reality! And the only alien we have seen so far is the one we are fighting. And that makes it more like a living nightmare than anything else!"

He took a few seconds for thought then said, "It would help us all a lot more if there were some flesh and blood aliens to deal with on a one to one basis. If that were possible our adjustment to there being galactic societies would come a lot faster!" He finished, still looking a little hangdog.

"I'm aware of that Felix, but for the time being I'm counting on you to spearhead the effort to get our people adjusted to the idea. Just knowing for certain that that is what we can expect to find out there will help us all when that transition to the altered reality becomes our reality in truth! I know you have a lot on your plate to deal with right now, but can I count on your help with this?"

"I swore," Felix began slowly, "when I signed on that I would do every thing I could to help. But since I signed on you have given me the opportunity to learn so much more than I ever dreamed was possible to do in my lifetime that I feel that I have done very little to help our cause so far. Of course you can count on me to help in any way that you ask of me!" Felix blurted these last words out, the passion of a true knowledge seeker coloring them.

"Thank you Felix." Dirk said with real warmth in his tone, "You have no idea how much hearing you say that helps me!

Looking at the man somberly, until he could see that he was becoming a little uncomfortable, Dirk finally said, "There is another reason for asking you to come to see me today. After discussing you with the group it was decided, and they all concurred, that you are to become a full member of our core group. There is much to be done, and much you don't know yet, so get together with the others every chance you get so you can be brought up to speed on everything. You are now to be our 'Director of Earth/Alien Technology Integration efforts. That means that you will also be required to attend all full meetings of the core group!" he finished, smiling now.

Felix was actually blushing now, in both pleased embarrassment, and the pleasure of having his efforts recognized, as he said, "Thank you."

"I want you to choose a second in charge for yourself, because there is another situation I am going to need your help with. We are planning a meeting with most of the people we have been able to clear through the security process we developed.

Many of them are high ranking government officials or world leaders, and we need your planning skills to pull it off!"

"One thing you need to keep in mind about this meeting," Dirks' tone was cold now, "is that we don't have the time, and I don't have the patience, to deal with the political wrangling or positioning that is bound to occur during it! They must all understand from the outset that this is a military type of operation, and that power and authority comes from us and flows outward to those who join our effort. All who join us will be expected to operate at their maximum at what they are best at for the resistance movement. And political BS will not be tolerated when the prize is our freedom, no, survival, as a species!" Dirk finished harshly!

Holding up his hand to forestall comment yet Dirk went on, "We believe that the operations we are going to need will have to be set up as stand alone commercial operations that are capable of being self sustaining, and that we will need at least five such bases of operation! They will also have to be run under a military type governance to maintain necessary control and discipline."

He paused just long enough to take a long breath, motioning Felix to wait before continuing, "What I want is for you, with whatever help you need from the others, to design a general plan of operation for these bases for presentation at this meeting. Also include in your plan the concept of operating from five separate primary base locations that will be producing defensive and offensive material."

Then Dirk dropped his bombshell, "And build a ship that's ready for test flight?!" he finished, a sly grin replacing his stern look of only moments before. "And, that those bases will be 'planetary locations', because we will want to decentralize for security and survival reasons! That's why I told you I wanted the information on those two solar systems checked out asap. Do you think that you and the others can put together a feasible plan in six to eight months time?"

"Dirk!" Felix began heatedly, "The planning is not a real problem. Any fourth year ROTC Lt. With half an MBA could do a decent jib of it. But how in hell am I supposed to build one of those ships in only eight months? The cost alone would be staggering, let alone the materials acquisitioning and testing for them that would be needed!" he came to a halt, his face flushed.

"How much do you estimate the cost would run?" Dirk asked him calmly.

It was amazing to see the change in the mans demeanor as he went into his professional mode, Dirk thought, as he began his answer, "At a conservative estimate I would say it would be in the area of a hundred billion dollars, and I do mean conservative!" Felix stated emphatically.

"Felix," Dirk said soothingly, "money, in this case, is not a problem. With the new resources that have been added from some of the new members, and what Carmella has been able to generate from it and our other funds that problem, thankfully, has become a minor one. And, after laying so many extra things on your plate I have some good news for you." Dirk said with a smile.

"That's good to hear." Felix said, but his expression said he was waiting for another shoe to fall!

"As we speak," Dirk went on "Much of the hull plating you designed is being fabricated to the specs you set, and it is also being stealth coated, which you didn't specify. At the same time most, or all, of the computers you specked, and their backups are being built and shipped north."

Felixs' mouth started to drop open, but Dirk hurried on, "Wait! There's more! To top everything off three separate companies, that we own, are in the process of building the 'Null Grav' generators and the 'Interstellar Drive' components for the ships drive and power systems.!" He finished with a wide smile now.

"But! How? When?" Felix stammered, and "I didn't know we had anywhere near those capabilities!"

"You do now!" and "That's why we're making you a full member of the core group. You've earned it! And we badly need your abilities! Now, do you think you can do it in that time?" asked Dirk, still smiling. Glad for a change that he had something to smile about.

"It's a big job, but I'll get it done for you. And that's a promise I intend to keep!" Felix said with total conviction in his voice.

After telling Felix that that was all for now, and he was heading for the door, there was another tap on it and Jimmy 'Bad Boy' Lester strode in. He had a broad smile creasing his dark features, his white teeth flashed in his dark face as he nodded to Felix as he passed him.

Dirk and Jimmy 'Bad Boy' Lester, Preparations

"What have you got for me Jimmy?" Dirk asked, smiling a greeting in return, "From your grin I hope I can assume it's some good news for a change?" he said, his face sobering again

"Yeah boss. I just heard from Yuri. He said to tell you that Chabov and Osov are both in."

"That is good news, Jimmy. Anything else from Yuri?"

"Yeah, he said to tell you that Chabov is forwarding a special package to you in regards to the conversation you had just before he left. Is that anything I should know about?"

"As a matter of fact it is Jimmy. Yuri suggested that we start training a special unit to augment the ships regular flight crews. 'Space Marines'!" he said, a grin breaking out at the look on Jimmys' face.

"Damn! I knew you had a good reason for bringing that guy in. That's a great idea! I don't know if I would have thought of it myself." Jimmy said, evident respect for Yuri in his voice.

"That's part of the reason I asked you to stop by before the meeting tonight. That package is a very special young officer from the 'Spetsnaz' school. Supposedly one of the best and brightest they have produced in years. By the way, that young officer is a woman Jimmy!" he said, a half smile playing at his mouth.

"You're kidding, right?" Jimmy blurted, and "I didn't know that they let women into that outfit!"

"They have for about the last two years. She's the first one to finish the course. At the top of her class, too!" Dirk said, serious again, then, "This is what I want you to do before she gets here. Get with Tony Ebbets and set up a temporary, secure, training area about two miles from the canyon. There's a pretty good sized cave about two miles north, if I remember correctly, that might do. I'll draw a map for you."

"As Jimmy started to reply Dirk said, "hang on a minute, there's more." Thinking for a minute before continuing, he finally said, "We are being sent some very special troops from all over. Navy Seals from admiral Berg, Army Rangers from General Miles contacts through the president, as well as 'Spetsnaz' from chabov, and Osov too. Also SAS forces from Ian Sinclair in Canada."

Pausing, looking at Jimmy gravely, Dirk went on more slowly now "Jimmy. This has got to remain as black as you and Tony can make it stay, even from most of our own people! Those first few hundred will eventually make up the officer corps and cadre for the follow on troops! So here is how I want you to handle the basics. Get together with Tony and the package and work out the rest after that."

Again Dirk paused for thought, then "Set up a safe marshalling area for processing those men and women in, say within an hours travel of one of your main transport hubs. As your people bring them in tell them to make sure of two things. First: that they are all volunteers and that they do have a choice as to whether they continue to be so. And yes, they get a choice Jimmy. You got one didn't you?!" He snapped at Jimmys' look.

Then, "I'm sorry Jimmy, that was uncalled for! You care for your men more than anyone I know of!"

Dirk went on more calmly "Second: and make this very clear to each individual, that a certain amount of ribbing will be tolerated at those that may decide not to continue, but any more than that and the perpetrators will be shot! They have to value having that choice above all else, because they will be going into this without knowing who or what they will end up facing." Dirk finished, finality in his voice.

"That's pretty harsh boss!" Jimmy said, his eyes getting rounder, larger, as the implications set in.

"Don't you dare go soft on me Jimmy Lester! This is not a kindergarten exercise. It's the real deal, for the whole ball of wax!" Dirk said vehemently, frowning up at his long time friend.

"I'm sorry boss! I know your right. The rules are totally different on this one. I'll take care of it." Jimmy said in a subdued, somber, voice.

"One thing more Jimmy. That special package will be their commanding officer!" Dirk said in a milder tone.

"Boy, are those guys going to like that one!" Jimmy said, smiling at the thought.

"I just hope that they can keep up with her! I hear that she's hell on wheels!" Dirk said, smiling himself now.

"OK. Next order of business." He said briskly now, glad to have that part over with.

Dirk went on quickly now "I'm going to lay out a plan at the meeting of the core group tonight. I'm going to give you part of it now because I want you to get it jump started for me. Just give me a minute to order my thoughts so I can give you some perspective on it."

After a couple of minutes of intense concentration Dirk began to outline the plan for Jimmy. "So you see Jimmy, since Felix got the Hull's to come on board we have made advances I wouldn't have thought to be possible a year ago! We now have working design drawings for the first earth built interstellar space ship!"

"All of our tech people agree that we can build it, just not now, and especially not at this site, as big as it is. There's still a lot they don't know yet! And I've only given Felix half of all of what we've been able to do so far. And that just before you arrived!"

"Knowing you Dirk, you've already got a solution ready. What do you have in mind?"

"To see the whole picture you've got to look at two things. First: As you know our fledgling organization is growing by leaps and bounds. Much faster than even I thought it could!"

"And, you're probably aware that we already have more than three thousand people working for or with us, and more are coming in every day. Our security is good, but our infrastructure is almost at the breaking point! And we have to do something about it now, before it begins to collapse on us!"

He paused for a breath, then "To that end this is what I think is needed. First, We have to concentrate on getting our ships built. That's right, I said ships!" Dirk said at the others look.

"I think eight is a good number to start with. Four heavily armed cruisers, two lightly armed cargo ships, and two troop/passenger vessels with medium armament!" he said, with a cat bird smile on his face. A smile that was in no way intended for mirth, as anyone who knew him well at all could attest to.

"To enable us to do this the president has brought Ian Sinclair on board. He's the head of RCMP intelligence, and his family owns huge tracts of land in the mountains of northern Alberta Province. Thousands of square miles of it! He is going to give us the use of one of his played out gold mines up there."

Dirk flashed a smile that said the best was yet to come "What very few people alive knows is that there is a huge cavern complex that was later discovered in that mine by his grandchildren!"

"That complex, he says, is even bigger than the Carlsbad complex, and it won't take a tremendous amount of work to give us completely open access to them from the main mine entrance! We're going to front its' use as a second effort mining operation, as a cover for the traffic it will create. We're going to build the ships there!!"

"Wow! Said Jimmy, his eyes alight with excitement at the thoughts Dirks' words generated. "You never did go in for half measures, did you?"

"We don't have time for half measures!" Dirk snapped.

Then, his tone easing somewhat, he went on "That brings me to the second part of the solution. This is where I'm going to need your help the most because you and Bill Tate are the best at ops organization, and will be the 'go to' guys on this." He finished with a sly smile.

Seeing that smile Jimmy knew that a particularly tough job was coming, and he was sure it was something that would probably scare the bejesus out of him! "Uh Oh. Whatever you've got in mind for me I'm sure that I'm not going to like it one little bit!" he said, as trepidation crept into his voice.

Knowing his friend Dirk smiled widely at his feigned worry. Jimmy always jumped at the chance to do something new. Something that no one else had done yet.

Well, he had a very big surprise for him! "Jimmy, I want you to second all of your duties to Bill Tate. Bring him up to speed on everything you've been doing. Because, in about seven or eight months you're going to have to disappear for a couple of months!" Dirk paused to check his reaction.

Jimmy just looked at him, real suspicion beginning to surface in his eyes. "Just what do you have in mind for me Dirk? You're doin an awful lot of pussy footing around this thing, and it's not like you!" he said tightly.

"Blackjack Jones," Dirk started, still smirking "says that he can have the first ship ready to fly in about seven and a half months, and your going to co-command that ship with him! You're going out with him to find me two suitable sites on other planets for new bases for our operations!"

Jimmy just stared at him for a couple of heartbeats, then "But I don't know didely squat about flying a space ship!" he exclaimed.

"No, you don't. But you know how to deal with people, and how to solve problems while on your feet. You're also very savvy when it comes to technology, at understanding how it works."

"You'll also know what we're looking for, what we'll need, and first hand knowledge is worth a thousand pictures when it comes to making those choices!" Dirk said, guffawing with laughter at the others look.

He quickly sobered though, saying "Jimmy, that's the real solution to our problems. And you know we have to limit our exposure here! You know how hard it is to get any solid intel on the others, Jesus, what we've been able to get so far will only fill a small notebook! We've got to diversify to ensure our survival! We need those bases, and you're going to find them for me!!" he said harshly, finality in his tone.

"On top of that," he said in a milder tone "you'll be taking the package with you, whose name by the way is Katrina Valasovic, and a couple dozen of her best new men for experience, and to develop new training procedures in a hurry."

"Don't screw around out there Jimmy! You're too valuable to me as a friend, and first rate planner, and expediter!"

Grinning now he said "And 'G Whiz' will be going along too, to evaluate how everything works. Take care of him because he's already earned his keep and weight in gold to boot! I expect he'll do it several times more before this is all over, too!"

"Damn it Dirk, the next thing you know you'll want me to carry around one of those things you've got inside of you!" Jimmy said only half seriously, as the import of where he was about to go really began to impact his senses.

"You don't know how close you are to the truth' dirk thought to himself, then he said aloud "Do me a favor and look outside the door to see if Crow is here yet, will you? And Jimmy, this is strictly need to know! All the way! Yes?"

"Yes!" he said, as he looked out the now open door. "Yeah, he's here now."

"Ask him to come in." and "Get started with Bill Tate as soon as possible on that other thing. The sooner you transfer things over to him, the better for you, OK?" Dirk finished, his mind already leaping ahead to John Crow.

Dirk and John Crow, Preparations

As Crow walked into the room Dirk rose to meet him, hand outstretched in welcome, "John, It's good to see you back. How was your trip?" he asked, shaking his hand warmly.

"Not bad Dirk." Not one to waste words Crow went right to the reason for his being here "I located seven of the nine men I was looking for. Two of the four that came in with me you know, Latham and Mullens, are being in processed as we speak. The other three will be drifting in over the next couple of days." Crow summed up, a small satisfied smile crossing his ruggedly handsome face.

"Something very interesting occurred while I was talking to them." He went on at Dirks questioning look, "They were all, to a man, telling me in one way or another that they are getting some very strange feedback from their contacts in eastern Europe and North Africa. Some saying that their contacts aren't responding to any contact efforts at all. It's begun, like you said it would, and its beginning to spread fast." He finished, worry lines now replacing the smile of moments before.

"You've just answered the question I was going to ask." Dirk said, a frown now replacing his own smile.

"John," Dirk began slowly "I've got a job for you, and because you're primarily a field operative, you're not going to like it much! But the truth is the job is so important that I need you to handle it personally!"

"You know I signed on for whatever comes Dirk, but what could be so important? You've got many of the most talented people in the world signed on with us now, which means that you have your pick of the best available!" Crow said, many unasked questions in his tone of voice.

"John, what you don't know yet is that several factors have come together that make several other actions on our part necessary now. One of the most important of those factors is that we are capable of building our own interstellar space ships now! To do that we need a completely new base of operations, one that is as secure as we can humanly make it. Your specialty, as I recall, was finding ways into secure facilities, was it not?" Dirk paused to let the challenge sink in.

"You know damn well it was," Crow replied "And you weren't too bad at that either, as I recall." He said, as the challenge began to take root.

"Well then John, who better to choose to set up a new base with extraordinary security requirements than someone who successfully specialized in breaking into them?" Dirk grinned, knowing he had him now.

"Well, when you put it that way—." Crow grinned around a frown he couldn't hold onto.

"I thought you'd see it my way." Dirk said, laying his hand on his friends shoulder. "And you won't have to worry about the actual building of the base, because you'll have all of the help you could need. You will be co-commander with general Carl miles. But where security is concerned your word will be the law. Even to, and including, extreme measures!"

"Damn! You sure you want me to go that far?" Crow asked soberly now.

"John. Let me make this perfectly clear to you! At that base we are going to build and test the first eight, yes I said eight, man made interstellar space ships! They will be the first ships of the new Earth Space Fleet. And nothing, I repeat, nothing is going to interfere with or stop us from doing so!" Dirk responded, leaving no room for any type of misunderstanding about what he had said, or meant, "That's how important this job is John!" he finished coldly.

"OK. Consider it done!" Crow said simply, the hook of the challenge now firmly set. "Where's this new base going to be located?"

"This is the part you're going to like John. It's an old mine site that's located in the northern Canadian Rockies. We're going to reopen it as a second effort recovery operation, as a cover for our operations." Dirk said, smiling again now.

"There's an even better part to your assignment John. Besides being the best penetration specialist I've ever known, you're a first rate spook commando. As soon as you're satisfied with your security arrangements for the new base I want you to choose a first rate second to take your place there. He will only answer to you, General miles, myself, and Tony Ebbets. And he will operate under the same guidelines I set out for you. So choose him, or her, carefully!"

"Then I want you to find, and train, a two hundred fifty man unit of spook commandos for special ops. In this you are also to find and choose a first rate second, who will then handle the general training and management under your guidance. You and he will then pick four unit leaders and four non-coms to lead the four sub units that will comprise the whole force.

Each sub unit will be comprised of one officer, one noncom, and twelve special ops commandos. I guess you'd better start with about a four hundred men and winnow it down to the two hundred fifty you want to keep. Can you handle all of that?" Dirk asked, smiling broadly, knowing this was something Crow would jump at.

"You bet I can! How soon can I start picking men? Are there any special training requirements?" Crow chortled, eagerness to begin in his speech and stance.

"You can start making your plans and your preliminary choices in men right away, but there is a fair amount of information you're going to need for this. I'll get it together for you within a couple of days, OK?"

"That's fine Dirk. Will there be any problem getting the equipment I'll need for this unit?

"No, but there is one thing that you should keep in mind for this unit." Dirk said, a sly smile on his face now.

"Shit! I knew there had to be a 'but' in this deal somewhere. What is it that I don't want to know, Dirk?"

"Your new unit will, in the near future, be cross training with a contingent of our new Space Marines!" Dirk said deadpan.

"Huh? What Space Marines?" Crow gaped.

Dirk guffawed openly now at the astonished look his little bombshell had produced. "I said that there was some info you would need to work up your final plans!" Dirk said, still chuckling.

"Damn it Dirk, you're enjoying this much too much!" Crow said through a false look of resentment.

"I know it John, but I have this feeling that there won't be much time for enjoyment in the very near future!" Dirk responded flatly, sadly.

"Look John, that's all I can give you for now. I'll have a little more for you at the meeting tonight. OK?"

"That's fine Dirk. Look, try to get a little rest before the meeting tonight. You look really tired." And he left, giving Dirk a concerned look over his shoulder, even as his own step had new spring in it as he moved through the door, closing it quietly behind him.

After Crow had gone Dirk leaned far back in the comfortable office chair, stretching his arms high above his head, pulling at the sore muscles of his back that too much inaction produced. He fully intended to take Crows' heartfelt advice about getting some rest.

If he were lucky, and had no other interruptions, he might actually get a couple of hours of sleep before it was time to begin preparing for the meeting tonight.

"Good luck to that wishful thought." He mused half aloud to himself.

Chabov and Osov, Routes Out

About the same time as Dirk was finishing his conversation with John Crow, some three thousand miles away two high ranking Russian officers, from different parts of the military, were also engaged in a conversation.

They were using cellular telephones that had been supplied by Dirks' envoy, Yuri Garov. That conversation was being held in calm, but urgent tones, the men speaking in short sentences that said much more than the words uttered.

"Yes Dimetri, I'm getting the same feeling every time I have to talk to Moscow. I don't know how much longer I can put off going into headquarters there. The brass there are acting very strange, asking questions about staff grade officers. Almost like they did in sixty eight, during the purge of the colonels! I think that it will be time to go soon, don't you?"

"Da, I believe that you're right Peotre! I'm sending you a young lieutenant with all of the paperwork. The routes and methods are very good ones. Please send the lieutenant on as quickly as possible to check them, as I think the weather will soon be getting much worse! Much sooner than we had anticipated for this exercise we had planned."

"I will do as you ask, Dimetri. There are a lot of troops going on this exercise, so I will move the timetable up on this end. I assume you will do the same, Da."

"absolutely Peotre! Having advance warning of the weather to come is a distinct benefit. Get your key people moving right away, and I'll do the same here. I'll contact you again when we are on the way. And Peotre, good luck to you!"

"The same to you my friend. Tovarisch!"

Thus began the exodus of some of the most talented people the old Soviet Union had ever produced.

Just a few short weeks prior to this exodus these men had received notice that their planned exit routes were to be the 'Beta", or Canadian routes. This would make border entry and travel to their destinations much easier, due to the relaxed entry requirements.

This drew a large sigh of relief from both men.

Dirk and TuLan, Conversations

In the method that had been agreed upon Dirk directed a thought-feeling-mind touch query towards the mind of his symbiotic partner TuLan, who was a temporary co-habitant within his body. That small alien body had been with Dirk, it seemed almost like a part of himself, for a little more than fifteen months now. *TuLan. Are you free to speak with me?*

The response was, when it came, as this form of communication always was, almost instantaneous. *I am always free to talk with you my friend.* TuLans' now familiar mind voice came.

There are many things that we need to discuss my friend! And, at this point in time, I don't think some of them can be put off for any length of time before they become serious problems! Dirk said in a heavy and weary mental tone, a tone that was even more expressive when sent telepathically.

As I have told you before Dirk, you must project your thoughts directly to/ at my mind for me to get the full meaning of what you are thinking! Your species seems to have a natural barrier that keeps your thoughts from broadcasting openly. This is quite rare, as most other races do not have that block, or barrier, and they are usually broadcasting their thoughts constantly. TuLan sent plaintively.

Dirk was well aware of this, but kept that knowledge well below the level of his surface thoughts. Something that had served Dirk very well over many years, especially for those who served in the intelligence field and were considered to be 'pros', was a well developed memory. Dirks' memory was nearly capable of total recall or 'eidetic', and he remembered everything that TuLan had ever told him about himself, his race, and the 'Union of Races' his people belonged to.

Because of this Dirk had been pondering several things TuLan had told him, things that might become problematic when the men of Earth ventured out to the stars. And that day was coming very soon!

Dirk continued, these previous thoughts having taken only a long seconds time to review, *Some months ago we had a long conversation about the 'Drel', after we had discovered them attached to those humans in my old service unit. What you told me then has been proven to be true and very accurate! Since that time we have developed some methods for detecting who those humans are that have been taken over.*

After a short thoughtful pause he went on, *those methods are good, but they are only about eighty percent accurate! And that is just not good enough to enable us to fight them effectively! My people are far too diverse in both appearance and demeanor, and that alone makes the job harder to do. We need better methods for identifying those who have been taken over by the enemy!*

TuLans' response, when it came this time, was considered and thoughtful, *The only really effective method I have, or know of at this point, is my reaction to them. And the only way that I can describe that reaction is to say that it is a mental recognition of the others presence that causes an acute physical and mental discomfort response. Because my race evolved as telepaths early on we are aware of many mental emanations on a subliminal level, and our response to the Drels emanations I can only liken to one of your shudders at certain things you find distasteful!* TuLan said, one of those shudders going through his mind at the mere thought of the Drel being near, or even worse, capturing Dirk!

Although TuLan wasn't aware of it, Dirk felt that shudder as it reverberated in his companions mind. It wasn't strong, but he felt it none the less! He was, the more he interacted with him, becoming more and more able to detect such things without TuLans being aware of it. 'He really must give this more thought' he mused to himself. He said, *TuLan, can you contact your people from earth, mentally?*

No. I truly wish that were possible for me to do! TuLan stated wistfully.

What about your ship? Can any of the communications equipment on it reach them?

Not unless they were within one light year of this planet, and my ship was in orbit far enough out to breach the solar distortions caused by your sun!

OK, we can come back to this later. But contacting them is becoming more important by the day!

You are quite right about that my friend. They must know about this new incursion as soon as we are able to do so! TuLan said with feeling.

The next question," Dirk started slowly, almost hesitantly, *"is in conjunction with your being able to contact your people. I want to discuss with you a possible alliance between our two races!"* he hesitated, then *"But,*

That is most good news!" interrupted TuLan, *"When can a meeting be set up between your leaders and myself?*

That!, Dirk broke into TuLans flow of thought words, *is what the 'but' was that I started to say! You are not familiar with our governing systems. Our political leaders are not known for their ability to get things done quickly, or well!*

Dirk paused, and TuLan said, *I would have thought otherwise, based on what you have accomplished over the last few months.*

What has been accomplished has been done by my team and myself, with very little help from them! And yes, to answer your unasked question, there are some very capable individuals who also happen to be politicians. But, sadly, they are the exception! Not the rule. Dirk paused, ordering his thoughts, holding up his mental hand to forestall comment.

He then said, *At this point in time our planet is governed by many different governing bodies that control geographic areas called 'countries' or nations. We have been moving towards a unified global governing body for the last fifty years, but there are still many differences to be settled before that can happen*

I see. Said TuLan, *Yes, I now see that I did not have a good enough grasp of your political situation. Please go on Dirk.*

Because of that situation my people and I will retain control of whatever negotiations that are to be done concerning earth, and the war I see looming. Politicians, as they presently see themselves, will only muck up and delay any decisions that need to be made quickly!

Too, politicians are not known for their ability to keep anything secret. Nor do most of them have any real idea of what war, real war, is about!

So, for the foreseeable future, all decisions pertaining to any or all negotiations and alliances will remain within the purview of the infrastructure that My team and I have been building. Which leads me back to the question of a possible alliance with your people? Dirk finished, still a question in his statements

Thoughtfully, slowly, TuLan began to speak, *I believe that we would be able to deal with whatever body that represented itself as the legitimate speaker for your planet. You and your group are, to the best of my knowledge, the only ones to be actively resisting the Drel, and you have done more in a short time than I would have believed possible if I had not witnessed it at first hand! So I don't see a major problem for my people to deal with you as that representative.*

TuLan, several things have come to bear fruit since we last had a chance to discuss matters in depth. The most important of which bears directly upon my question about an alliance with your race. You and I, because of our unique association, know and understand just how deadly the threat posed by the Drel really is! And thanks to your help, and the access to your technology, we will have a fighting chance to save my planet and my people!

Because I was able, through you, to become aware of this threat early in its formation I have been able to begin a viable and committed resistance movement. That movement now has many good people, and a cohesive command and control base cadre to guide it. And soon we will have the means, again thanks to you, to take the fight to the enemy.

You are aware of almost all of our efforts to create this resistance movement and the progress we've been able to make so far. He paused for a second, hoping that as he went on that TuLan would not take offense at what had been withheld from him until now, *what you do not know is that within the next six to eight months we expect to have a working interstellar space ship! Built and ready to test fly.*

Dirk heard, almost as if it were aloud, TuLans mental gasp, *but how? Where?—!!*

TuLan, Dirk interrupted his mental sputtering, *Please hold your questions for a few minutes and I will tell you as much as I am sure of. That should also answer many of the questions you will have.*

Yes, please go on! TuLan almost pleaded shakily.

First, you should know that much of our success is due to your teaching machine, and our computers. They are a lot faster and more versatile than yours, you know. Over the last several months my people were able to reverse engineer that unit, and rebuild it so that we could use it safely! It contained a lot of information about your starships, and their drive and hyperlight unit repairs. That gave us the nudge in the right direction we needed. It also showed us that some of the requirements needed to build such a ship paralleled some of the research we were already doing.

But the real breakthrough came when we realized that your fusion reactor principles had a flaw in them. It came when we were modeling the energy output specifications from your fusion reactor energy converters that powered the trans-light vortex portal generators. What it all came down to was that my people found an anomaly in the vortex stabilizers, something to do with balancing the harmonic build up in them.

From what they tell me about your trans-light flight system you must jump in and out of trans-light flight about every thirty hours to let them recalibrate themselves. They say they can eliminate that requirement by including a harmonic sequencing controller in parallel with the vortex stabilizer!

Dirk paused here for a second, mentally and physically rubbing his temples, then went on, *anyway, talking, let alone thinking about this stuff, gives me a headache. Suffice it to say that our scientists tell me that they think our ships will be able to stay in trans-light transit from point 'A' to point 'B' without dropping out!*

From that we quickly went on to design a working ship that utilized the principles of both our technologies. Once the basic design was done we computer modeled it to test our concepts. Those models told us that our ships, with the increased outputs from better computer speeds and capacity for greater energy management, will be able to cruise at sub light speeds of one eighth light year per day.

If TuLan had had a human type mouth it would have been hanging open in stunned surprise. He stuttered, if one can do that telepathically, *how are you able to do so much in so short a period of time? But! But that is half again as fast as our fastest ships can travel! When? How?* And he faltered to a stop, apparently at a loss for further words.

We owe a good deal to you for our success! Because you let us pick your ship apart we were able to reverse engineer most of the systems and adapt them to our faster computers.

We're not positive of that speed yet, but based on the output ratios given for your ship at optimum performance levels our computer models showed the performance for our ship as I stated it!

Part of the improvement in performance is due to the higher operating speeds and control our computers give us in engine control and navigational plotting reaction time. Another part is due to, in large degree, some of the improvements we made to your engine design! Dirk paused for a mental breath, and to let what he had told the being sharing his body sink in.

Then continued, saying, *The thing that gave us the most trouble was the force field that your engineers use for containment in the mass reaction chamber. We didn't like the fact that there was no backup redundancy built into that operating system. So we had to devise a secondary power source that was strong enough to generate enough power for that redundancy, and make sure that it was independent of the main engine system.*

We did this by rebuilding your power storage system. First, we replaced your storage cells with our own high capacity storage cells. They're much smaller than yours and have a higher output. Then we will supply power to them from one of our mini nuclear reactors, like the ones we use on our submarines. The upshot of all of that is that our first ships will be twice the size of the one in the canyon, have three times the usable interior space, and will be, unlike that one, capable of interstellar flight.

Dirk paused again, knowing that he was giving TuLan a lot of information all at once. It was not that he though TuLan couldn't handle it, it was because TuLan had little experience with beings who he had initially thought of as not very advanced. But he was finding out very fast that he was dealing with beings who could absorb his own technology, and adapt that technology to their own needs and uses very quickly.

Continuing, Dirk said, *we also made a few other changes and improvements we thought might be useful. We noticed that your object sensor array system was very similar to our own 'radar' system, though yours' has a longer range than ours. When we asked you about it you said that the Drel system was very similar to your own, as far as you knew.*

So, keeping that in mind, our ships will be coated with a compound that we use on our atmospheric fighter planes. That coating makes them virtually invisible to our own radar systems, and, I'm happy to say, invisible to your systems as well! This should give us some small advantage when we try to sneak past the ship we think is hiding behind our moon!

Dirk! Dirk! Wait! Do you mean to tell me that you have aircraft that are invisible to my scanners? TuLan gasped, somewhat like a fish out of water.

Yes. We do. Oh! I forgot. You do very little optical scanning. I would have thought that you would have at least picked up the heat signatures when they operated at extreme altitudes!

Your thermal imaging systems are very good! Much better than ours, Dirk said a little ruefully, not liking that loophole one little bit!

All I can say, Said TuLan in a very disturbed tone, *is that I'm very glad we were able to become friends! I think your race would be a terrible enemy to face!*

Your people, he continued slowly, *under very restrictive conditions, have accomplished more in a little over a solar rotation, a year you call it, than most of the technical races we know of could in ten solar rotations! Where? How, will you build these ships? And why?*

Where. Well, we've just acquired access to a very large tract of land in the far northern part of this continent, in very mountainous terrain, and it has a series of huge caverns located in them. The location is also in an area that we call a blind spot. This is an effect of our gravity well, and solar interference with electronic spying devices. We will build the ships there.

As to the how. Over the last few months, thanks to the individual known as 'Chickie' Martinez, we have been able to acquire several small computer and electronics manufacturing companies, and a small steel mill with manufacturing capabilities. We have also acquired a scientist who has just perfected a new process for combining steel and glass. That process is done by spinning hair fine fibers of both and combining them in a woven sheet, and then fusing them together. The end product of that process is extremely strong and flexible, and very malleable to shaping. And it is only half the weight of our strongest light weight steel. This product will be used to make the hull and engine housings. Most of the ship fabrications, electronics, and other material and equipment will be prefabricated and sent north to be assembled at our new site.

As to why. We are virtually defenseless from space! We have at this moment only your ship, which is damaged and not capable of extended flight until it is repaired. The parts and equipment for which, by the way, are being fabricated as we speak and should be ready to install in a few weeks from now. And, most importantly, we must have a means to resist in space or to flee from this planet so that we can fight on later if the latter should become necessary. Which I think it will! Dirk said sadly.

One last thing you should know now TuLan! We are planning, as soon as the first ship is finished and test flown, to visit several of the star systems on your charts that you said would support our life forms! We will be doing so for two reasons. One will be to have a place to go to should it become necessary to flee from earth. The other will be to establish bases that can be used for manufacturing and the staging of our resistance forces.

Those bases will sustain us, and be much more secure than anything here on earth will be if we cannot stop the Drel from gaining a foothold that they cant be driven off from with the forces our world has! But, from what I've already learned, I don't think that is something that we will be able to do! Dirk stopped, the heaviness of his tone evidence of the bleakness of his thoughts.

Unfortunately, said TuLan, his own tone matching the heaviness of Dirks' *I think that you are right about that! But, I also think that the Drel will end up paying a heavy price for whatever advances they may make on you world.* A hesitant pause, then, *Dirk, there is something I'd like to ask you about?*

Ask. You know that I will tell you anything you need to know! Dirk said quizzically.

Very hesitantly now TuLan began, *since we have been together, except for the period when you were in such pain from the injuries caused by your fall from the rim of the canyon, and during your recovery, I have noticed that your mind is closed to me at times when I am trying to contact you! Do you know why this is?*

Taking a moment to think, which is a long time mentally or during telepathic conversation, Dirk responded with a question of his own, *does this happen all of the time, or are there specific times when it occurs?*

Wondering where this was going, and knowing that Dirk had an extremely analytical mind, TuLan responded slowly himself, *it is generally prevalent, but seems to disappear when you are thinking about me or about something that has to do with me.*

Dirk, several months ago, had become aware of his ability to block TuLans' access to his conscious thoughts, and had been working very hard behind his mental wall to enhance this ability. It was not that he distrusted TuLan, for he had given Dirk no reason to do so, but thought that this thing might be an innate thing within himself that caused him to hold things back from him.

After all, how many people carried around a softball sized alien being inside their bodies. A being that had the ability to talk directly with their minds. One that is possibly able to read their innermost thoughts, all protestations to the contrary aside that this was never done for ethical and moral reasons.

It would seem to me, he replied, *that this blockage is a combination of factors. First: it seems likely that it may be a natural occurrence, because it is something that I am completely unaware of doing. Second: It might be a racial trait, something that our makeup as humans has built into our DNA. Lastly: it may be some form of a subliminal self defense mechanism that has developed unknown to me because of the newness of having someone who has so much direct access to me and my mind!*

Too, Dirk went on slowly, *and in conjunction with the last, we humans have just begun to study what we call paranormal abilities, which includes telepathic communication along with some interesting potential abilities.*

Thank you for trying to answer my question. TuLan said slowly, realizing that he had just learned something new about Dirk and these humans. Learned that he was beginning to understand that he could be told the truth, without being told the whole truth!

Dirk and TuLan,
Conversations for the Long Term

A few days after their last long conversation Dirk and TuLan were again about to speak at length. Taking a deep mental breath Dirk said *TuLan, there is something very important that I want you to think about for me!*

It must be very important indeed, for you are seldom so formal in your approach to a subject. But, having said that, you know that I will always do what I can to help. What is it that you would like me to think about?

Being perfectly honest with you," he began slowly, thoughtfully *"I don't think that this fight that is shaping up with Drel is going to go well for us at all in the beginning, and I'm certain it's not going to be a short one! As a matter of fact, I think that the sooner we start thinking in and planning in terms of decades, even centuries, the better off we will be in the long run. That is the reason my planning has begun to concentrate on the long view as much as the near term.*

He paused briefly to reorder some of his thoughts, *because of this, and some of the things you have told me about what my life span might be thanks to your intervention, I would like you to consider two things that may well be very important to the future of both our races, both near and long term!*

He paused again, girding himself because he had come to a conclusion and made a decision based on inadequate information, something he very seldom did.

Shaking himself mentally he plunged on, *first, I would take it as a great honor if you would consider staying with me for the duration of the coming war with the Drel!*

'There, I've done it!' he thought to himself, as a sense of relief flooded through him.

There is much that I need to learn about the other races in our galaxy, and you have been a most capable teacher and friend. After contacting your people I will need your friendship even more, as someone who understands them and the other races, to guide me and keep me from blundering too badly in dealing with them. What do you think of this?

TuLan was quiet for a long time before answering. When he began it was slowly, as if feeling his way in the darkness, *I too have grown most fond of you Dirk! And, to tell the truth, for the short time that we have been together I have felt much more alive and interested in the many things going on around me! For the first time in a long while I have been giving thought to things other than my work!*

Still taking his time TuLan went on, *my race is used to taking much longer to think things through before we decide to act. You are, however, a most invigorating race. Watching and participating in the way you think and plan is almost breathtaking in its speed and agility!*

If for no other reason than this I would like to stay to see more of this process you call intuitive reasoning!

It is a thing that is most rare in most of the other races. Most, like my own tend to be more sedate, plodding if you will, in their approach to new thoughts and concepts.

To answer your question, yes, I believe that I would like to remain with you for, as you call it, 'the duration'. But you did mention a couple of things. What else would you like to know?

I am very happy at your choice," Dirk said warmly, *and I believe that our association will be a long and interesting one, for many reasons! But, before I continue, let me digress for a moment. TuLan, do you think that your people will join us in this fight?*

That is, if I may say so, a complex question looking for a simple answer, and a place to park it! TuLan quipped. Startled at what he had just done, TuLan mentally rubbed his non existent chin with a non existent forefinger, thinking to himself that these earth beings sense of humor was beginning to seriously affect him.

My race, he harrunphed mentally. *As I have said on several occasions is generally given over to taking much time to answer questions as complex as that one. Too, you will remember the devastation suffered by all of the races in the last war fought with the Drel. And the centuries it took to recover from it! That result will remain a factor in any decision they make!*

At the same time there are the alternate possibilities to consider if they do not fight! Those are not ones that I, or they I think, will want to take too much time to consider because I believe the Drel will be even more inimical than the last time they invaded this galaxy! So, the short answer to your question is that, yes, I believe they will join you. If for no other reason than that of survival!

That too is very good to hear, for I have a dilemma that very much needs your assistance in solving it! Here is the dilemma. But it was a long moment before he began to describe the dilemma because this would take careful wording on his part.

He began cautiously; *here is the crux of the dilemma. The people that I have been assembling to form the core of our resistance to the Drel are all highly trained and skilled, and for the most part all have some combat experience. Those that don't have that experience have technical or technological skills that are just as important. We are, by your standard life spans, a very short lived species who are facing a conflict that may, if we don't survive the first major assault, end us as a viable race. Or a conflict that may last for decades or centuries if we do survive that first major assault!*

The real basis of my dilemma is that I must be able to keep these tried and trusted core people alive and with me long enough to win that first major assault, or to ensure that we will be able to establish a strong enough position to fight on against the Drel if we only survive it!

I think that before that happens we will lose most, or all, of the earth to Drel control! With that terrible admission made to himself, and to his symbiotic companion, Dirk paused to take a shuddering breath that was as much mental as it was physical.

So, he said, gaining control of himself, *this is what I need to know. Do you know of several members of your race, ones who might be similar to yourself in their thought manner, who might be interested in, no!, willing to, partner with a number of my own people?* he finished in a rush.

Still slowly, still thoughtfully TuLan answered, *This question is both easier, and harder, to answer than your other question.*

More sure of his reasoning TuLan quickened the pace of his answer, *Our meeting and joining was circumstantial, and of necessity a choice made for survival by both of us. Not withstanding that we have come to accept each other and, I believe, like each other.*

Now he paused briefly, knowing that what he was about to say could well be misconstrued, *you Dirk, and your people, are downright scary on several levels. Your people have a penchant for scientific study and developing new technologies. If it is a technology that you did not develop yourselves your innovative ability is amazing in the way you absorb and utilize it for your own ends.*

Your people show a depth of philosophical thought that is rare for a species as young as is yours', yet you consider mortal combat in a manner that is almost nonchalant! You are generally honorable, from what I have learned, and loyal almost to a fault to your friends. But you can be, and often are, viciously terrible in your reprisals if that loyalty is ever perceived to have been abused or compromised! And you will continue to fight for a cause, even knowing you cannot win that fight! TuLan finished this with a shudder of his own

Do not misunderstand me; traits such as yours are not entirely unique to your species. The difference is that few of the races in the 'Union' having similar traits will go to the extremes that I know yours is capable of.

I say these things to you only because you should be prepared for what you will be confronted with when you come up against the reasoning of the 'Union

Counsel' to present your case. This is something you will eventually have to do if you expect to make alliances!

Picturing a palm held out TuLan let Dirk know there was more. ***But that aside, yes, I believe that I know of several members of my race that might be induced to join us! But, if they agree, they will have to be pre prepared for a race such as yours. For none of them, and I include myself here, has ever come across a race that is such an anomaly as yours is before this!*** Now TuLan stopped, wondering what his honesty would bring.

CHAPTER FOURTEEN
The New Core Group

Ingathering

"This is a step in the process that I'd much rather eliminate, but here in St Louis and the hole in the world, the name given to their base in the Canadian Rockies, are the only two places we can effectively set up the agitator to scan large groups of people." Said an angry Tony Ebbets to Jimmy Lester.

The agitator was a new device that caused a Drel attached to a human to squirm about in a manner that made them easily seen. This was a tremendous improvement over strip searching everyone, and could be set up in a very unobtrusive manner.

This last had allowed them to capture two of the Drel mounted humans alive as they tried to penetrate the resistance movements smaller facilities while it was being tested. Their capture had quickly been disguised by planting a story in the local papers about two men with their names being killed in an auto accident.

"You're preaching to the choir." Jimmy said placatingly, "If there were anywhere else we could process all of these people as fast as we can here I'd be much happier myself! The only real benefit from doing it here is the direct access we have to the river port that we control, and the size of our complex hides the extra traffic. But I agree with you, and would like to see the processing done somewhere away from our main operations center"

"It's amazing," said the somewhat mollified head of security for a resistance movement that nearly no one else in the world knew existed, "Do you know that we have transported in, processed, and transported out of here almost thirty eight hundred people in a little under five months, and that number looks like it will double next month! I just don't know how much longer we can continue handling that kind of volume without being noticed, and the wrong kind of questions begin to be asked about this location." Tony ended, a worry frown creasing his forehead.

"Dirk knows that you're upset, and that this has put a lot of extra pressure on you, so here's some news hot off the presses! There is only one more big contingent supposed to go through here. It's a mixed bag of 'Spetsnaz', and Russian space agency personnel! He said that you are to be very nice to a Captain Valsovic. She is to be the operational commander of a new unit of space marines we are putting together."

"He also said that you're to land rout these new arrivals to a ranch that Carmella bought up near the Canadian border. Don't ask me how he did it, but Dirk got the Canadians to pull all of their RCMP out of the area bordering the ranch! The routing info is in this brief." Jimmy finished. Handing Tony a fat manila envelop.

"Well, that's some good news anyway. Give me a couple of hours to study this, and I'll get back to you if I have any questions, OK?" So saying, he rose from the table in the cafeteria in the operations control building where they had been having coffee, and left.

Jimmy wasn't offended by Tony's abrupt departure because he knew that Tony Ebbets was a man with a lot on his plate, and that everything he did was done as right as it was humanly possible to do it!

Just before speaking to Tony Jimmy had been in contact with Ron Colefax, Tony's counterpart at the new mining operation, which was a front for their new space ship construction facilities in Canada, to check on any problems he might be having with the volume of incoming people being redirected there. Thankfully there had been none at that end. That was due in large part to Dirks' contacts with the RCMP, who also oversaw immigration and Guest worker permits. That could have been a real sticking point but apparently there were enough Canadians being brought in to mollify the powers that be were in charge there.

The real problem they were facing, as far as people were concerned, was that the amount of information coming in now was that it was becoming near to impossible to process it all and get it to the core people who needed it to do their jobs well. What they needed as badly now as the technicians and military types were analysis specialists who could sift and process that information quickly, and get it to the people who needed it in a hurry.

Dirk had said that that situation was being addressed. He hoped so, because those now handling it were already being pushed to their limits, and that was not a good sign so early in the game! Well, jimmy thought to himself, if Dirk said not to worry, he wouldn't worry about it, because Dirk was one of the few people in the world that Jimmy 'Bad Boy' Lester trusted without reservation.

"I'd better get moving myself!" Jimmy chided himself, as he got up and left the cafeteria. He went to his own small office to begin plans for the first full meeting of the core group in six months. People would be coming in from wherever they were, and there was a lot to be done to prepare for this meeting.

That was another bone to throw on Tony Ebbets plate because security would have to be extraordinarily tight for this meeting! Other than that it would be great to see the whole gang together again.

"Well, I guess I could give Tony at least one more day before hitting him with this." He thought to himself. "After all, the meeting isn't for another two weeks yet."

Crux Meeting

For many of the members of the core group it had been a long and arduous journey. These were the newly appointed members, many of them from Russia, the Middle East, and Asia. Some, their journeys still not over were still en route, their journeys made longer by the routes taken to retain the covertness of their movements.

This was something that was becoming more necessary as time fled this fledgling resistance movement, for nothing had ever been attempted on a total worldwide scale like this before!

In part some portions of the journey's were imposed as security measures by Dirks' people, wanting to make sure that the last leg of the trip that led to the box canyon where TuLans' ship still lay was as secure as it could be made to be.

They had already caught two of 'The Others', the new term being applied to those humans who had been taken over by the Drel, trying to penetrate one of the small airfields the group had acquired, and was using as a transfer point for those on the last leg of their journey. That field had already been sold to one of the groups' offshore companies, and unless it was a dire emergency no more traffic from the group would pass through there.

The meeting was being held at the original ship site for a very good reason. Many of the new members had never seen the ship, only photographs of it. Nor had they ever seen a human who had been taken over as a Drel steed! Again they had only seen photos, albeit very graphic ones, they were still only photographs!

Dirk, and the rest of the original group, had agreed that this was the best way to imprint on them not only the reality of the threat they faced, but that they did in fact have off world allies! The first part was basic and simple. Let their eyes and hands do the final, total convincing by showing them the human with the Drel attached to his back that they had preserved in cold storage at the ship.

The second part was much easier, because the ship was of obvious alien manufacture. These things should be more than enough to convince even the most hardened skeptics. It would have to be! This meeting was crucial to the continued existence of the resistance movement Dirk had begun. After a long and soul searching bout of self doubt Dirk had come to the conclusions he would present to the whole group, less a few members who, for security reasons, could or would not attend this meeting.

It had taken an additional nine days past the original date set but all of the members who could attend were here at the box canyon site. Tony Ebbets had security set up so tight that a fart couldn't pass without clearance! All in all though, every one was on good behavior and doing their best to cooperate. Some were, like the head of the Russian space program Admiral Dimetri Chabov, after touring the ship, ecstatically enthusiastic. Often having to be rounded up from his explorations and escorted back to his cabin to get some rest.

Others, many of them already hardened men and women, were somewhat less pragmatic after seeing the human body with its' Drel rider in the cold storage compartment. They were very quiet and pensive, going back for second and third viewings, their expressions growing grimmer, their conviction hardening to diamond hardness with each trip!

Still others, mostly the younger ones like Lt. Valasovic, were too dumbfounded to grasp the whole of the situation. They often looked to the older members for guidance most of whom had attained high rank and had been blooded enough in real combat to be able to understand how to deal with something so much outside their experience. Even so, it was hard enough for all concerned to assimilate!

Dirk gave them three days to come to grips with this very new and unforgiving reality. The meeting would come to order at eight AM on the morning of the fourth day.

On the morning before the start of the meeting Dirk called all of his original; core people in for a few words. "I just want you all to know how much you all mean to me," he began once they had all found seats, "and to thank each of you in front of all the rest in acknowledgement of all your individual efforts. That is something that is all too easy to forget to do in the heat of things for those who are working just as hard as you are working! Thank you all!" he finished with real warmth in his voice

Then, with a mischievous grin on his face, said "And I hope that you are all ready for the shit to hit the fan tomorrow!

The Meeting Begins

When the last of the attendees had found their seats, in the largest hold of the ship where the meeting had been set up, Dirk stood up and began to speak, "I want to thank all of you for coming, many of you at high personal risk, to this meeting. Over the last three days you've seen and learned a lot of new things, and I'm sure you're still trying to digest much of it. I have no doubt you will succeed for you are, all of you, among the best this world could produce!"

Dirk paused briefly, knowing the value a small amount of drama could have, "And you are about to become members of the largest clandestine resistance movement this world has ever seen! But we will not be joining each other to fight an abusively repressive government, or a disease that threatens a large portion of our populace. As you all have seen, we will be fighting for the survival of our world, and mankind as a species!"

Now Dirks' voice was cold, hard, "We are here to make sure that 'Those Others', who have come from the deeps of space to steal our world and our people, do not succeed! And to make them wish they had never come!"

"We don't know much about them yet, but we will learn what we need to know. It's not going to be easy, but then what ever is in our trades. It will, I believe, be a very hard, and long, fight."

Looking at their grim faces, Dirk finished his preamble, "We will take the fight to the enemy when we can, and we will run and hide when we can't, so that we can come back and fight again. The one thing that we cannot, will not, do is give up! This is our world, and our people! And we intend to keep both of them! No matter how long it may take us!" He finished, as these normally staid men and women stood and showed their approval by applauding his words.

When this had died down he went on, "OK. I'm going to read the role of those in attendance at this meeting, which will also act as an impromptu means of introduction for those who just arrived, and those who have not had a chance to introduce themselves all around."

Most of the people here knew each other by sight or by reputation. Those few very young members attending were still too overawed by the stellar group that they had been lucky enough to be included in to say much of anything, unless asked by one of those demigod like personalities for an answer to some question. Their heads swung back and forth, like they were on swivels, trying to catch every word uttered by the legends most of these attendees were!

"If you would be kind enough to," Dirk went on, "stand when I call your name, and give us a brief description of your background specialty I, and the rest, would appreciate it." Dirk finished and then began to read of the list from the papers in his hands. The list went;

Jimmy 'Bad Boy' Lester. Surveillance, electronic countermeasures, and black ops penetrations and extractions. Major William 'Bill' Tate. DIA, black ops security specialist. Colonel Yuri Garov. KGB, military counter insurgency tactics, black ops operations coordinator and tactical analyst.

Gerry 'G. Whiz' Burke. IRA commander, explosives expert, electronics and computer sciences technology specialist. Ron Colefax. CIA, Counter intelligence and black ops operative, internal operations security specialist. Rick Davis, CIA Operations security and counter measures specialist.

Tony Ebbets. DIA, Counter intelligence and operational field security specialist. Wet work specialist. Brevet Colonel Katarina Valasovic. Spetsnaz, Commander of special troop training, executive commander of First battalion-Earth Expeditionary space Marines.

At the mention of her name the pretty blond and blue eyed woman, sitting next to a distinguished looking man from the Russian group, jumped to her feet. As dirk read on a look of utter disbelief, and stunned delight, was warring on her very attractive features for dominance! As she looked down at that man, he in turn was looking up at her with an open smile of approval.

He said to her, "You will not let my recommendation and faith in you come to dishonor, will you colonel? You are one of the very best we have ever produced!" he finished, his smile grave now. It could be seen that honor was very important to this man.

As she sat back down she replied, "No Sir! You can, as the Americans say, take that to the bank!"

"I'm sure I will be proud of you." he said, rising as his own name was called. Admiral Dimetri Chabov. Commander of Strategic Rocket Forces. Director of Space Operations for the New Democratic Republic of Russia.

Chow Fan Lau. Professor of physics, specializing in electro-magnetics, PHDs in physics and Computer Sciences. Dr. Mark Belzer. Ph.D. in Bio-genetics, associate director of the human genome sequencing and mapping study project, Specializing in human improvement through genetic preferencing studies.

Mr. & Mrs., and Drs. David and Sheila Hull. Ph.D.s in Physics and Engineering. they both specialize in physics and engineering for space based applications.

Seeing that this method was going to take much too long to complete Dirk said as much, and "I will read the names and attributes of the rest of the attendees to speed things up a little."

He began to read, "Mr. Felix Ortiz. Mr. Ortiz is an 'entrepreneur extraordinair'. He specializes in innovative technology applications and implementation, and is probably one of the two best expediters in the world. Or so says the Wall Street Journal! General Richard Potter. General Potter is the commanding general of the joint military procurement and logistics office, and is perhaps the finest officer to hold that post in the last hundred years. If you need it and he can't get it for you, it doesn't exist!"

'General Peotre Osov. General Osov is the commander of the Fast Reaction Forces for the New Democratic Republic of Russia. He also holds masters degrees in Military tactics and Strategy from the Frunz Military Academy. He also wrote their manual on speedy troop insertion and withdrawal, and, I might add, that that manual has been adopted as the most insightful treatise on that subject in the last fifty years."

"Admiral Timothy Berg. Vice Chairman, Joint Chiefs of Staff. The admiral has recently retired to join us! General Carl Miles, Ret. General Miles was the commander of the Third Infantry Division. He was also scheduled to become a member of the Joint chiefs but was RIFed out by the last administration. He was held over by the present administration, but was forced to retire due to mandatory age requirements. Gen. Miles almost single handedly revamped the Third ID into one of the best fighting units in the U.S. Army."

The list went on to cover many of the members who could not, for various reasons, attend and many more of those who were present. When he had finished reading the list Dirk paused to give those here an opportunity to absorb the implications of the total number, quality, and talent of those who had joined the movement so far.

"All Right!" he said loudly enough to cut through the buzz of conversation that developed. "I'm sure you're all curious to know why you're here at this time and place, beside the information you've already been given."

Pausing briefly to make sure he had all of their attention, he continued, "All of you have been involved in this movement in various ways and for various periods of time! There are two truths that you're all going to have to accept, and you will have to do so quickly!"

Again he paused briefly to let his words sink in, then "The first truth is that you can't go back to your previous lives and positions for two good reasons. First: we desperately need your talents and help! Second: because of your previous positions or talents you are marked for takeover by the enemy we've shown and told you about! The very reason you agreed to come here and find out what we were going on about! I believe we have given you ample proof of what we have been telling you in that respect."

"But, there is more proof for the real die hard skeptics if you need it. From your reactions over the last few days I doubt that will be necessary now. You are all here because you were chosen by us and we requested your presence, or you were referred by someone we trust implicitly, after checking to see if you had been compromised by the enemy."

He went on swiftly now, saying, "You are the best there are and we want you to become a part of the governing body of the 'Earth Resistance Movement Alliance! You are here to defend your planet and your species from becoming what you saw stored in that cold storage room!"

Dirk waited now, letting everything sink in. Knowing that there would be many questions, knowing that he had answers for not nearly as many questions as he could think of himself. He would do his best to put things in forward momentum, and keep it moving in that direction. And, hope that his instincts and the quality of the people he had gathered so far, and was still gathering, would be enough. He had made a good start, and had been very lucky so far, but good starts were not the things that won wars. Good intelligence and perseverance were!

He now had a group of some of the most intelligent, innovative, and hard headed people ever to come together to face an enemy. And he was sure, deep in his gut, that this enemy was not at all prepared for what they would find when Mankind started to fight back!

Dirk was a deeply committed patriot, believing fervently in the principles upon which his country had been founded. And he was sure that most of the others present felt similarly about their own countries.

But there was one thing that he was absolutely certain of. He was certain that those principles, and the form of government they stood for, would not survive the coming conflict. There would be little enough time for politicians or debating on anything, because war demanded strong, decisive leadership.

His one deeply seated worry was that he might destroy those beliefs, for a time, to do what he knew must be done to help man survive as a species in this coming conflagration. It was going to be a long, hard fight. He knew this as instinctively as he knew that water was good when you were thirsty.

Brass Tacks and Hard Facts

Dirk had called a break after the roll call and his closing comments to the group, and had had coffee, tea, and other refreshments brought in on trolleys. This was to let these men and women continue the process of absorbing and pondering their dilemma. They were the cream of the crop of what the world had to offer, yet he knew that some would find what he still had to say objectionable for various reasons. It did not matter! This was a fight for species survival. Something they all would have to accept. And sooner than later!

A half hour later he said, "Ladies and gentlemen, would you please return to your seats so we can continue."

A couple of minutes later, everyone having seated themselves, he began, "First off there are some hard facts that have to be dealt with immediately!" he paused looking around to be sure he had everyone's attention.

Then, seeing that he did he plunged on, saying, "You all understood the rules before coming here. We would prove our claims, or you could leave with our blessing thinking we were mad. I believe that we have proven our claims beyond a shadow of a doubt! If there is anyone here that doesn't believe that please get up and leave now!" Dirk stopped and looked at them. No one moved.

"I take it by your silence that you agree, and that you understand that past this point there is no way out of this short of death! And that death would be preferable to being taken for the uses the others have planned for us!" he finished, voice hard and flat. Now he said, his voice not as flat but just as hard, "So, that having been said, and according to the results of conversations we've had with each of you prior to this meeting, this is how things are going to be from this point on."

'Due to the nature of the enemy we are facing, and the very new theaters we will have to learn to operate in, it has been decided that the only way we can operate effectively is by the formation of what we will call the ERMA Prime Governing Council. That council will be formed from the core people who started this movement, and will be filled out with the addition of several of you here in this room, and several other leaders from around the globe."

"In addition, there will be several other councils formed to facilitate the requirements of the prime council. All of you here will be members of one or more of those councils, along with several others who could not attend this meeting. Each of you has been given a printout of what and who, so please take a moment to peruse them. Then I will go on with the rest of what you will need to know." Dirk stopped as they began opening the packets each had been given upon entering.

After ten minutes Dirk tapped his coffee cup with a spoon to signal that he was ready to continue.

"Item one:" he began, "Prime has determined that politics, politicians, and political factions are, with the exception of what may be necessary to negotiate treaties with potential allies, are a dead issue, and are suspended for the duration of this conflict! However long that may be!"

"Item two; Governance, for the duration, will be based on that of military rule. The only exceptions will be such rules as the prime council shall deem it necessary to make under wartime conditions.

Any and all infractions will be dealt with according to the UCMJUS, or the Uniform Code of Military Justice of the United States. It's not perfect, but it's the best we have for the present!" Dirk paused, looking at some of the startled looks on some of their faces.

"It's not all bleak news," smiling to ease the sting of his previous words. "Because, besides what most of you have already seen, there have been some striking advances made by those who worked so hard to get you all here, as some of you have already found out!"

"Thanks in great part to our first extra terrestrial allies, the Chai, we are not entirely defenseless!" he paused to gauge their reaction.

"Nor are we any longer bound to our own solar system!" he finished with a wide smile, as he lay this bombshell on his unsuspecting audience. He was gratified to hear the many gasps of surprise, for he had kept the knowledge that the ships they were trying to design were actually ready to be built.

"Ahem." He coughed, clearing his throat to get their attention. And they quieted at once, eager to hear more from this amazing man who was still an unknown factor to many of them. "I am really pleased to tell you all that we will, within the next thirty days, begin construction on the first eight ships of the new ERMA Space Navy! There will be five light cruisers and two freighter/troop transports. They will be built at a new secret base we have been building for the last few months!"

This second bombshell was met at first with looks of stunned amazement on their faces, and silence so thick you could hear stilled lungs begin to draw breath again. These men and women, just a moment ago, had been looking at a bleak, hard future of secretive effort before anything this spectacular might have been achieved.

Then, by ones and twos, they began to rise from their seats and applaud his extremely welcome news. Their faces were now, as he had prayed they would be, showing the two things totally necessary if they were to even stand a reasonable chance against an enemy that had untold resources it could bring to bear against their planet and its' people.

Those faces, to a person, were set in chiseled lines of determination to face whatever was to come. More importantly their eyes were now, unlike a few moments ago, shining with the light of hope! Hope that they could, would, make the difference that would mean a future for mankind.

"A couple more things people!" he said loudly to be heard over the buzz of new conversation, "In conjunction with the news of our pending new ships, which by the way, will be three times the size of this one, I would like to announce that Admiral Berg will be the first commanding officer of the ERMA Space Navy, and Chairman of the ERMA Joint Military Operations Council."

"Also," Dirk said, holding up his hand to stay comments, "General Miles will be the Vice Chairman of that Council, and advisor to the new Command Operations Council."

"And," He went on, Still holding up his hand, "there are a few more announcements so please bear with me for a couple of minutes. Admiral Dimetri Chabov will be the Director of Space Flight operations Development, and Vice Chairman of the COC. Colonel, Now General Yuri Garov will be director of Strategic Planning, and Chairman of the COC.

Seeing that they were ready to burst with excitement at these revelations of forward planning Dirk rushed on. "There are many more appointments, which are outlined in your handouts, but there are two that I want to make now. Colonel, now General Peotre Osov will be the commanding general of the ERMA Space Marines, and the other Vice Chairman of the JMOC."

"And finally Captain, now Colonel Katrina Valasovic will be the commanding officer of the First Battalion, ERMA Space Marines. She will also be the Director of training regimens for all space based non naval fighting forces, and councilor to the JMOC. Both of these fine officers looked on with pride on their faces, and the beginnings of slightly haunted looks in their eyes at the thought of the daunting jobs ahead of them.

"Lastly," Dirk said loudly again to keep their attention, "I have of course saved the best for last. Thanks again to our 'Chai' allies we will, within the next eight months, launch the first ERMA exploratory expedition to two star systems that are purported to have planets capable of sustaining life for human beings! This mission is, if possible, to secure those planets for bases for our operations, manufacturing, and training centers."

Dirk waited out several more gasps at this last bombshell he had let go, and then gave them his last one. The one he knew they would not want to hear.

"I am, because of additional information I have recently received," this a small lie he felt necessary to tell so he wouldn't have to reveal the true nature of their 'Chai' allies, "convinced that we must move our main bases of earth if we are to survive the coming battles and go on to victory! There, I've said all I had to say at last. Still, there is much work and planning to do before we can move to our new base. If the people I just noted will meet me in the main lounge in thirty minutes I would appreciate it.

With that he stepped down from the makeshift podium and left the storage hanger for his own quarters to have a precious minutes alone before beginning another grueling planning session.

CHAPTER FIFTEEN
Incidents

The Incident, Russia

Dirk lay on the sleeping pad in his compartment, his eyes closed and his arms folded across his head, his body trying to relax in a yoga exercise he had learned many years before that was designed to relax the mind and relieve stress. Most of the stress built up before and during the just past meeting was gone, but he was having a very hard time relaxing his mind. There was just too much to think about!

He finally sat up, giving in to the prodding of his internal sense of time elapsed and slipped his feet back into the shoes he had kicked off before laying down. Finished straightening his clothes now, he ran his fingers through his unruly hair to straighten it somewhat, and left his cubical for the next meeting of the day.

Seven thousand miles away, in the headquarters building of the 'Spetsnaz' special training facilities in northern Russia, Major Vasily Kukov was finishing up the last of the days training progress reports. There came a sharp rap at his office door and it opened abruptly as two burly men in Ill fitting suits marched in. The lead man, a particularly ugly individual with flat dark eyes, said, "Major Kukov, you are needed at central command headquarters in Moscow. You will come with us immediately!"

Kukov, sitting rigidly upright at his desk snapped, "Who are you, and how did you get in here?"

"We are military intelligence." Said both men, almost in perfect unison, flipping open leather wallets taken from the inner pockets of their shabby suits. Returning them the one who had spoken upon entering said, "You are to notify only your second in command of your departure. You will return in two days time. Quickly now, we still have another stop to make!"

Realizing he had little choice he picked up the phone from its cradle and dialed his adjutants number.

They were now six hours into the trip, and three additional officers had been picked up from sites that Kukov would have considered to be strategic locations. The 'Zil' limousine they were traveling in was cramped with the seven big men in it. The two who had picked up Kukov also had a driver waiting for them, bigger than the first two had been. It was hot and cramped because the heater was turned up to its' highest position.

An hour after the last pick up they pulled through the gates of a small military airfield and drove straight out to a transport waiting on the verge to the ramp leading to the main runway.

They were unceremoniously herded into the waiting plane, which took off almost before they could fasten themselves into their seats. It was at this point that Kukov began to worry about what was really going on. Even though he had had several run ins with the KGB over his many years in the army, he had never before had the cold feeling in the pit of his stomach he was feeling now.

Although he couldn't quite put his finger on it there was something odd, wrong, about the way these three were behaving! Almost as if they were automatons, being directed by an unseen puppet master!

The flight was uneventful and boring. But his suspicions were re-aroused and heightened when, after landing at the military section of Sheremetyevo Airport in Moscow, they were hustled into a closed, windowless van that sped away as soon as the doors had been closed securely.

The drive to military headquarters was, for those enclosed in the back of the van, an hour of jerking and swaying punctuated by the loud blaring of the horn and the sudden application of the brakes several times as some Muscovite had the temerity to place himself in front of the speeding van.

The van stopped briefly, Kukov being able to tell that they had reached their destination from the shouted challenge and reply from the driver. It then moved slowly ahead as it passed through the gates facing the former Lenin Prospect.

The van stopped, and a moment later the rear doors were flung open, the sudden brightness from the late afternoon sun temporarily blinding them, as they were ordered out. They were then told to follow the designated officer standing nearby into the building. Kukov was becoming increasingly worried because this type of treatment was usually given to criminals and traitors, not to officers in good standing.

They were led down long dimly lit corridors, and down several flights of stairs, into the bowels of the huge complex that was Moscow's central command headquarters. Their journey ended in a large bare room, devoid of furniture except for two long, scarred wooden benches that looked to be very uncomfortable. They were peremptorily told to sit and wait to be called. Kukov could see the fear building in the eyes of the officers who had made the trip with him.

Fifteen minutes later one of the officers name, another major, was called from the next room. That worthy, a short bull of a man, rose with much trepidation. Squaring his shoulders, and pulling at his uniform to straighten it, marched to the door and passed within. Thereafter a morose silence fell over the three remaining officers waiting to be called. About an hour and a half later another name was called, a captain this time, and the previous scene replayed itself.

About the same time period had elapsed when Kukovs' name was called. He rose, brushing now at his own wrinkled uniform, doing what he could to straighten it. Done, and unable to delay longer, he strode to the door displaying a confidence he really didn't feel.

Inside the room was a single table and chair with a full colonel seated behind it. Laying open in front of him was a folder with a blue stripe running diagonally across it. It was, Kukov could see clearly, his service file. The officer brusquely asked him several questions intended to verify his identity. When done the colonel gave him a cold smile and told him to go into the next room where he would be briefed.

Puzzled more than worried now Kukov saluted briskly and moved to do as he had been instructed. This next room was the complete opposite of the previous one. It was painted bright white, even the floor, and was very brightly lit. It was also very warm, the temperature probably close to eighty five degrees. There were several white uniformed people in the room, all with short sleeves, and a table in the center of it that looked suspiciously like an operating table. At the sight of this his steps faltered.

Seeing this one of the people, a doctor he thought, was quick to reassure him, "Come in major, and do not look so worried. There are a few tests that must be completed before you can be briefed, that is all. All quite normal, I assure you. Just samples of your blood, a tissue sample, and a check of you heart rate and respiratory system. If you would, please strip to the waist and sit on the table there." That worthy said placatingly.

The cold diaphragm of the stethoscope touching his upper back caused him to flinch away from it. "Please relax and breath normally," the man said, "That's it. In and out, deeply."

That feeling of queasiness had returned to his stomach with a vengeance now. It had always been a warning of danger to him in the past, and it had seldom been wrong. It was almost a physical pain now, causing his stomach muscles to clench painfully.

"Now for the blood sample. "The man said brusquely as he tied a rubber hose around his upper left arm. "Please flex your fist several times to raise the vein." The needle was pushed into his vein quickly, almost callously, and his blood began to fill the ampoule.

When that was done he said, "I'm going to anesthetize a small area of your upper arm because there will be some small degree of pain when I take the tissue sample." That feeling was now raging in Kukovs' stomach, but it was too late. Before he could protest a syringe was plunged into his arm, causing it to begin going numb almost immediately.

Then, without warning, Kukovs' eyes rolled up into his head and he toppled backwards to sprawl arms akimbo on the examining table. The drug was so powerful and fast acting that he didn't even realize that he was out! There was only blackness. Some time later, he didn't know or care how long it had been, his eyes flickered open.

Then it came! A tearing, searing agony of pain, like someone was using a blow torch all up and down his spine!

Kukov tried to role away from that pain, to crawl away from that searing hell, but he could not! His body refused to obey him! That superb body that he had conditioned to respond instantly to any threat would not respond to his frantic commands to move. Commands that were now almost pleas! And that searing, tearing pain went on and on, causing his eyes to see nothing but the red haze of his agony.

Then, suddenly, there was something else! Something so utterly strange that he was frozen in shock. A shock so strong it momentarily blocked that awful pain. That didn't last, as the pain came back with a vengeance! What was so utterly shocking to him was the voice he was hearing. The voice inside of his head! And it wasn't a reflection of his own thoughts! It was cold, harsh, demanding! It was saying *Get up! Stand up! Do it now!*

There was a short pause during which the essence of the being that was Vasily Kukov, a being that was a superb fighting machine in both mind and body, found itself scurrying to find a dark place to retreat to. He knew, with the certainty of a man that had faced many crises in and out of battle situations, that this new battle field was going to be on a landscape like no other he had ever fought on, yet it was a landscape he knew very well. That landscape was his mind! Still, he retreated into himself! Stammering as he did so. *Who? What? Where are you?* Demanding, pleading to know who or what it was he faced.

The disembodied voice inside his head said coldly, *I am of the Drel, and your new master! You will obey my every command without hesitation. If you perform well you will be rewarded, if you do not there will be pain! More pain than that you have just experienced. Now, stand upright as is normal for your species. Quickly now! Do not try my patience.* That cold voice hissed in his head.

To the almost gibbering thing that Vasily Kukov had so suddenly been reduced to in his own mind there were very few things, if any under his present circumstances that might have rallied him to resist as quickly as did those coldly spoken words from within his own mind! Without understanding exactly what he was doing, or even how he was doing it, he struck out at this thing that was obviously his enemy. He struck violently, desperately!

He sensed some kind of weakness now that he, in his initial pain and fear, had not noticed. He grasped desperately at it, and held onto it like a terrier does a rat. He shook and tore at it viciously, his own pent up fear and anger lending him new strength!

What that Drel, that self assumed master and rider of a race it thought would soon be a subjugated one to do its' bidding as well as being a potential food source, did not know would be its' doom.

What that Drel and the untold numbers still in transit to earth did not know, did not even suspect, was that unlike the many other species it had subjugated this one would fight back! It would fight back, striking out even in the face of its' own death to damage or kill its' enemy!

This Drel did not know this, had never been warned about this, even as a remote possibility, by the overlord spearheading the expeditionary forces of this invasion.

It was too late to warn it now, for the panicked attack by this steed had sent a massive surge of mental energy that burned out all of its' mental circuits, much like an uncontrolled surge of electricity will burn out the circuits of a computer.

Unfortunately for this Drel, this assumed master and rider, this being from another planet and galaxy that gained its' ascendancy from the theft of the free will of its' victim, this parasite, it was too late! It was dead before it knew that its' death was imminent! Unfortunately for the steed, Major Vasily Kukov, it was also too late. He was also dead. His body just had not stopped kicking yet!

The Drel had already, seeing yet not understanding its' own doom as the first wave of that massive mental energy began to wash over it, clenched the talon like penetrators it used to insert its' micro fine tendrils into the steeds spinal column and brain stem. This caused a complete shutdown of all communication between its' steeds brain and its' body.

Major Vasily Kukov was aware of his own death In those final seconds. But, unlike the thing on his back that had tried to make his life into that of a slave, he took some solace in knowing that he had struck a mortal blow to it, and that it would do this to no one else.

And, without understanding how he had done it, he knew that this thing that had called itself his master was dead or dying!

Major Vasily Kukov died as he had lived. Proudly!

As the warrior he was!

The Incident, U.S.A.

Dateline November fifth, St. Louis Herald;

The surprise attack on the small, privately owned, airfield fifteen miles north and west of Cape Girado, Missouri, near the town of Ashton woke every inhabitant within a three mile radius. It happened on Tuesday in the pre dawn hours of a brisk fall morning.

The attackers struck viciously and without warning, employing automatic small arms, killing two and wounding one other of the airfields security people!

When asked, the airfields Chief of Security stated that he did not know why the airfield had been attacked, but surmised that the attackers might have been after one of the high value, high risk, cargo loads the company specialized in transporting. He also expressed his condolences to the families of the two men killed in the attack, at the same time stating that he was very proud of his men and the way they had acted to defend their clients property!

When asked if the attack might have been drug related the chief of security scoffed at the idea, stating that his company had always been very careful to make sure that that type of thing did not happen. They had very careful screening procedures in place to prevent such abuses of their services, and that those things would never be a factor in their operations.

He also stated very emphatically that any further such speculations would be 'pure tom foolery'!

When contacted this afternoon the corporate offices for the small airline that owns and operates the airfield stated that they were contacting the families of the men who were lost and would help them in whatever way they could.

They also stated that they would increase the security for the airfield, but were considering not sending much of their high value cargo load transfers through there for a while due to this incident. They might even, after further study, shut that facility down.

Upon further questioning they would make no other statements concerning the attack, saying that additional questions should be directed to the local police.

Story by Susan Magill

When he had finished reading the copy of the story from the newspaper Dirk raised his eyes questioningly. Looking back at him, his own eyes troubled, jimmy Lester said "we don't know how they found out about that place yet."

"We do know that the two of them who were killed were steeds because the bodies were checked on the spot, as per policy, after the battle! But the rest of them we think, were nothing but hired guns."

After pausing reflectively for a moment Jimmy then went on thoughtfully, "We've either got a leak, which I personally doubt, or we have to revamp our traffic patterns. You know that we're moving a lot more people around than we should! Especially the non English speaking foreigners who stick out like red on a white background!"

"I think you're right about the traffic patterns," said Dirk tiredly, "but I think that will slow down some now that we have the new base underway. Be that as it may, check it out just the same, will you?"

"Ron's on it already! What do you want to do with the field, close it down?" Jimmy asked quietly.

"No! Keep it open, but operate it at absolute minimum use. If we close it down they'll know for sure that it was one of ours. We'll keep it operational, but in reserve, as an emergency out."

"What if it was a leak? How far do you want Tony to go if it was?" jimmy asked, already knowing the answer before asking it but not liking it one bit.

With an exasperated look that was intended to wilt, Dirk said, "I don't like the idea any more than you do, but you know what will have to be done!" he snapped.

"I know that Dirk," Jimmy snapped right back, "but it's different when your dropping one of those you thought were your own!"

Looking at his friend steadily for a long moment, deciding that this wasn't worth creating a rift over Dirk said, quietly now "I really didn't mean to snap at you like that. But I made you number two in this thing because I believed that you would make the hard decisions when they were necessary!"

Dirk paused thoughtfully, then, "Jimmy, we've been friends for a long time now, but more important than that is the fact that you are one of the best men in this business and I respect your talents! This thing we're involved in now is going to get much bigger than I think you have allowed yourself to think about yet, and the time will come when those decisions will have to be made when you are the only one there to make and have them enforced on everyone else. Don't let that time sneak up on you and catch you unprepared!" Dirk finished softly.

"You're right, pushing that back on you was wrong on my part. It will never happen again!" Jimmy said contritely, knowing that his perception of his own virginity, and all other refuges, were lost forever now.

The Incident, North Central Africa

The almost inaudible click from the radio bud in his ear told the man, as per the pre arrange signal they had made, that his partner was going to move into position a little closer to the new log compound that had been constructed in the shallow valley below. The one they had been looking for, for two days now!

It was a big compound as these temporary structures went, covering nearly a full acre of ground in its' enclosure. It contained several thatched roof structures, mostly open sided, and their uses were easily discernable as eating and sleeping huts. But there was one large hut, near the back wall, that had full walls and a door. This was the object of their interest!

Almost in the exact center of that compound was a large corral like structure, with woven mat wall that were a little more than seven feet high. Inside this were being held about forty men who had been captured from the local tribes inhabiting this area.

The two men had been observing the compound since dawn, and it was now late afternoon. About every hour and a half one of the men in the pen was dragged out and frog marched to the structure against the back wall and thrust inside. An hour later, almost like clockwork, muffled screams could be heard coming from that structure.

Shortly thereafter the man who had been taken in came out, staggering stiff jointedly, almost as if he were unsure of his equilibrium. He was quickly joined by one of those who had come out previously and had regained his balance, and led to one of the open huts to eat or sleep.

Done with that the one who had most recently been led waited for another to come out, while the one who had waited for him went to a hut and sat down with those who had gone before him. It was almost a factory like operation.

The man who had just moved in closer to the compound, and had been observing this process, lay at the edge of a rise about a thousand yards from the compound. He was concealed by the dense brush and tall grass that both surrounded and covered the rise. The rise was about forty feet high, giving him an unobstructed view inside the compound.

Slowly he raised the pair of camouflaged and deeply shaded binoculars to his eyes, sweeping them back and forth across the valley the compound was hidden in. He then lifted them slowly upwards, to the low hills that formed the opposite side of the valley, giving that rim a slow careful scrutiny.

These two were expatriates of the former country of South Africa. They were decent men who had been willing to give the new regime a chance, but left when it became plain that those now in power were completely inept and would be able to do nothing but destroy what had taken so long and so much sweat and blood to build.

They had been part of an elite military unit that was formed to fight in the bush country in and around their homeland. Now they were freelance operators, and had signed on with the only black man that they both completely respected. One who knew his trade and wasn't afraid to get down in the mud with them.

They didn't hate black men, but having not been more than a few hundred miles in any direction from their own country they had little experience with any other than the shallow, opportunistic despots who seized power and pillaged the newly founded countries surrounding them. And because they were generally better educated than their black countrymen, and had enjoyed a better lifestyle for the most part, they found it hard to understand the deep rift and bitter resentment that existed between them.

But what they had been watching disturbed them deeply. Those men down there were being turned into slaves by something neither could see, but they understood what was happening instinctively. Both of these men had come from families that had had forebears who had been indentured servants at one time, and remembered the stories told of those times. Both men hated the thought of slavery, no matter what a mans color was!

Clicking open a channel on his headset VHF radio he spoke quietly into the microphone extended from his headset, "Your clear two. I can't see any part of you. You can move up about twenty five meters."

Then, suddenly, as he swung his glasses back to the compound, he whispered urgently "Wait one! Two, there's a patrol coming out of the gate." He paused for a few seconds, then "Oh Shit! Go to ground two! There're coming right up the side of your hill. Out."

"Copy." was the curt reply. Then there was nothing as two shut off his radio, making sure there would be no noise at all.

The four man patrol moved up the ridgeline, moving almost in lockstep, seemingly heading right for his partners hiding place. The patrol walked right past the place where his partner had said he would be, and One let out a relieved breath he had forgotten he was holding.

One waited several more minutes after the patrol passed two's position before opening a channel on his radio, "Two. Wait about twenty more minutes, then ex-filtrate to the alternate meet site. I think we have enough to report in with" "Roger that." Was the quiet reply.

Four hours later they were on a 'Huey' helicopter, flying close to treetop level, and getting, as someone important had once said, 'The hell outta Dodge!'

The Incident, Bulgaria, South Eastern Europe

The two people the team was trying to extract were frightened almost to the point of panic! They were a man in his mid forties and a pretty woman in her early to mid thirties, both top flight metallurgists. They were holding their fright in by main force, but that couldn't go on much longer before it broke.

That fright was evidenced by the paleness of their normally dark olive complexions, and the constant darting of their overly rounded eyes. Rick Davis knew he had to get them to cover soon or they wouldn't last long enough to make it to the extraction point!

Rick also knew that he shouldn't have come on this extraction; it wasn't what he did best. But they had been so short handed, had been since they began the big move to the northern base in Canada, that there hadn't really been anyone else to send. Even with the limited personnel they had they were still moving close to twelve thousand people a month into, and through, St. Louis to Canada and some of the smaller sites they had.

Besides, they told him that these two were really needed because they were the ones that had invented and perfected the process for combining glass and steel by spinning and weaving it into flexible sheets that could be laminated onto any type of framework. It was supposed to be stronger, more flexible, and more durable than even the best tungsten aluminum alloy being used today. This stuff was needed for the new ships, and so were they!

The safe house they were using was about two blocks away, but getting them there might be a problem unless they could create some kind of diversion. Ricks' team was comprised of the two men he had brought with him, and two local recruits, their names given to him by Jimmy Lester who knew the city of Sofia very well. Rick had already decided to take them out with him when they reached the extraction point.

Clicking his whisper phone radio once he said quietly into it, "Bates, how many do you make it?"

"Looks to be six, or seven. If we don't move soon they're going to have us boxed boss!"

"I know. Ask Lemos if there is some place they can be led off to, some place you can exit safely and lose them."

"He says there is, but we'll have to move real soon. They're almost on top of us right now!"

"OK. Here's the new drill." Rick said, thinking fast, "You and Smith stay with Lemos and lead them away. Tell Stosh to join me here as soon as they pass. Once you dump them get to the safe house pronto! We'll extract from the safe house roof instead of making a run for the extraction point. The chopper can come in on stealth mode to get us, and we'll make a run for the Italian border! It's only twenty minutes away. And Bates, tell them that we're taking them both out with us!"

"Roger that Boss!" His man Bates said, approval evident in his voice, "I'm sure they'll both be glad to hear it. Will do. Out."

About a minute later Rick saw, as he peered around the corner of the building they were hiding behind, three of his men break from cover and ran down the street in the opposite direction from his hiding place. All of a sudden five or six men broke from their own cover and went chasing after them. Rick waited for three minutes, getting impatient, but there was still no sign of Stosh, his other recruit.

Rick was about to backtrack, to see what was wrong, when he heard the unmistakable sound of a silenced weapon fire twice! He knew he wouldn't have heard it if he hadn't been listening so hard. He quickly pulled himself back into his cover, and turning his head back to his two charges, made the universally understood sign for silence. Then, mouthing, "Stay here." He drew his own silenced weapon from under his coat and peered around the corner again, and was almost run over by Stosh as he whipped around the corner. He whispered urgently, "Come, we must go! There may be others coming!" and without waiting stepped off up the alley they were in.

Motioning the man and the woman to follow quickly, Rick ran the few steps needed to catch up with his man, who was moving quickly but carefully along the alleyway.

"What happened?" Rick asked quietly as they moved along, dividing the chore of scanning the front, rear, and side openings along the alley.

In broken English Stosh told him, his eyes never ceasing their constant search for danger, "After Lemos and the others run, and those others follow them, I know that one did not. I see him go to cover, but he not come out! I climb up fire escape and wait for him to come out. He come out careful like; move real slow with gun out. I let him pass, then shoot him in back like you tell us to do!"

The man visibly shuddered, but went on, "It was very bad, very ugly. His back move all around under his coat, then go still! It was terrible thing to see! Ugh!! Then I run to catch you up." Stosh paused for a breath, then finished with, "I know place Lemos will take others. Will take him two hours to get there and back to safe house again. Tell me, you really take us out with you when you go?"

"Yes. You are good men, and I don't want to lose you so soon!" Rick said simply, smiling.

"Good! Thank you! Let us get to safe house and get out of sight. Others will come in over roof tops when they come. I will wait for them there and keep watch." Done speaking, he moved ahead to take the point position, leaving Rick to herd their charges along.

They got out without further mishap.

The Incident, Bar Al Said, Jordan

The two men were moving quickly but cautiously through the crowded marketplace of the small but bustling town. The taller of the two, Jamal Asanni, was a native Jordanian. But his companion, though very darkly tanned under his kafia, on closer inspection was obviously of European decent. He was Czech and Russian. They were hoping to lose the two Somalians that had been following them on and off for the last week in the crowded marketplace.

They had to lose them, and quickly, because they had something of great value to trade to the man from the west. These two men were freelance intelligence operatives that had been RIFed from their respective services and had turned their acquired skills to a more capitalistic approach. They had become information brokers and bounty hunters.

The man from the west had given them ten thousand U.S. dollars, and promised them forty thousand dollars more, for the delivery of a live specimen of one of the Somalians with the grotesque black growth on its' spine. The terms had been simple. The specimen must be alive and in reasonably good health. Now all they had to do was get the one they had captured to Rhiad.

If they could keep the distance they had gained they would be able to pick up the new Land Rover they had purchased this morning and be gone before those two behind them knew it.

They were certain now that there were only two of them following, so they agreed to split up and meet at the Land Rover. Then they would go to the house they had rented on the outskirts of town and pick up their package.

Jamal told his partner that he would stop and call the westerner to tell him to expect them within four or five days time.

The Incident, Kuwait City, Kuwait

The westerner that Jamal had just finished speaking to was also a freelance agent, one who was well known to both Dirk and Jimmy 'Bad Boy' Lester. His specialty was finding things that were hard to find. Because of the economic incentives involved he had expanded his operations to include delivering them to those who were looking for them.

The word had come to him, through the inevitable grapevine, that his services were needed. When he made contact he had been surprised and pleased to learn who it was seeking his services.

When he had been informed as to what was wanted and part of the reason why, he had almost balked, thinking that there was some deeper reason and he was being left out of the loop. He was not one to work in the dark! But he knew these people, and they had insisted that he personally escort the package to them for delivery. He would be told more at that point! He made up his mind to take on the contract because they had always dealt straight with him in the past.

The number he had given his men for Rhiad was set up on a call forwarding system to Kuwait City, so he had much to do in preparation for a pick up in Rhiad and transport back here to Kuwait City. Then to the U.S. He dialed the number he had been given using his scrambled secure line in his small office. When the call was answered he heard, "Please hold for secure interface verification."

Then he heard the warbling and clicking that said the unit on that end was matching frequencies. Then, "Miller Technologies. How can I help you?" a pleasant female voice asked. He said, "This is Zircon Specialty Acquisitions. Connect me with the special requisitions office please."

He waited for several seconds as the line hummed and clicked, then "This is the SR office. What order are you referencing please?" He checked the code he had been given, then said, "Deep space backpacks for ERMA2."

There was a pregnant silence, and a series of clicks that lasted a few seconds, then, "Phil?" said the familiar voice of Jimmy Lester, "I didn't expect to hear from you so soon! Do you have that new model ready for us so soon?"

"I expect to have it ready for shipment in six or seven days. How would you like me to set up transportation for it?" Philip Myers asked with satisfaction in his calm voice.

We'll handle all transportation requirements at this end; just give me the pick up time and location." The now excited voice came back to him.

"Eight days from now at my shipping facilities at the Kuwait City Airport would be best for me." He said.

That was how the ERMA forces got its' first Drel prisoner for study and interrogation.

CHAPTER SIXTEEN
Reunions and New Friends

Balor's Vigil

The huge golden eyes looking out from within the darkness of the inner cave were the color of molten gold in the smelting pot, and the irises seemed to swirl with a slightly deeper red gold color. The slitted black pupils were open wide to catch the least nuances of the remaining light from the dying day. Those eyes were scanning vast areas of wilderness for that which he had been waiting for almost five months now. Their owner was waiting for two of its' siblings, a male and a female, to join him. And they had been traveling hard all this time to reach him.

They had come from a long way away. Come from the northwestern mountain regions near the borders of Iraq and Turkey. They had traveled around the Bosporus and Adriatic Seas, sneaking like ghosts onto boats for rides when necessary. Then across the southern Adriatic countries to the southern borders of Russia.

Then they had gone across that countries southern plains and up into the Urals. They followed them north, then down into the northern Steppes and on into the far northern wastes and out onto and across the Bearing Straights to Alaska. They were now somewhere in the western Canadian Rockies. They were close now. He could feel them almost constantly now if he opened his receptors wide.

Those two were coming to join him at the behest of the council of elders after that body had digested all of the information he had passed on to them. The council had been both excited, and cautious at the same time, upon hearing of the landing of the off world ship!

They had relayed to him that some mention of this race had been made in the long memories, but little was known of them. They had been mentioned because the 'Brethren' had said that they had been involved in a very long war with a species from another galaxy. But since the brethren were also from another galaxy, and they were from the far side of this one, little or no contact had been made at the time of the stranding on this planet. They were sending Balors' siblings, they had told him, to both add perspective to his findings and to enable him to boost his sending directly to the council.

Balor knew, of course, why they had been sent. He was still, by his races standards, very young! Only some two and a half thousand of this planets revolutions about its' sun. The eldest of the elders was now some eight thousand earth years old, and could not move very far from their enclave without very good reason. There were only a bit less than fifty thousand of Balors people left now on this planet, the youngest having been born only a hundred or so earth years ago.

They had ceased aligning themselves with these twolegs since the big migrations from the great countries of north central Africa about three thousand years ago because of the weapons they had begun to develop. And had started to use against the people, taking a great toll on them. But things, Balor thought, were about to change soon. There had been very few like his brother Dirk and his friends since the time of the great Egyptian kings. The people had been guides and councilors to the early ones, holding places of reverence among them. The latter ones had destroyed themselves in self aggrandizement, taking whole peoples into slavery and forcing them to build great useless monuments in their honor.

For the last couple of thousand revolutions the people had kept mostly to themselves, keeping mostly to the high places and the deepest forest areas of the planet.

Several things were beginning to cause Balor to worry about what was happening outside of his retreat area. Chief among them was his sense of his brother Dirk, that he was much closer now. Since he had bonded with Dirk, a thing his people very rarely did anymore, he always had a sense of him, even as Dirk was always aware of him. That bond had deepened as they had become more respectful of each other as individuals, and he saw the respect demanded by Dirk of others for his brother Balor. This was a thing he would always remember. He could even feel the 'Tate' one occasionally.

Balor liked the Tate one, as he thought he was liked in return, even if Balor did tease him a lot! He too was a warrior like Dirk, as were many of the others he had been introduced to, but Dirk was the greatest of those warriors. The only one of them who might be Dirks equal was the one called 'Crow'. Those two were the descendants of the ones who had originally been the inhabitants of this land. Those who had been the last one Balor had befriended three centuries ago.

The questing tendril of thought broke into Balors reminiscing, snapping his head around to face the direction from which it had come. The touch came again, this time with his name picture attached to it. *I await you with a glad heart!* He sent, and *I have prepared a safe lair, with soft bows and leaves for your resting.* He sent, pushing his thoughts outward forcefully, for they were still a far distance away.

We are still five suns hard travel from you, Came the thoughts of his true sibling, the male, *but it will be six full suns before we arrive.* Came the thoughts of his female half sibling, *for we must stop to rest and hunt.*

On the day of your arrival I shall hunt and have a fresh kill waiting for you in welcome. He sent back.

That will be most welcome to us, as will being again with our sib be. That thought couched in a feeling of warmth.

I await your coming eagerly! he sent back with the same warmth.

Then, *but do not tarry long, for there is still much to tell you that I could not send with the long thoughts!* And then, more somberly, *there is a great evil come to this world, and I fear for all of us!*

We will not tarry brother, any more than is truly necessary. Until then fare you well. And the already tenuous connection was gone.

With that Balors thoughts turned to those others which he had spoken of to his siblings. His first encounter with them had been a total surprise to him! And his reaction to them had been unlike anything he had experienced in a very long life. It was as if he had become a complete and total stranger to himself, reacting with a combination of utter revulsion and unreasoning fury towards them.

Balor had, over his many long years, encountered many of the two legs who had caused him to inflict terrible pain and injury on them because of their thoughtless cruelty, but he had never been driven to the point of instant hatred and absolute desire to maim and kill that those that attached themselves to the two legs invoked.

Without his friend/brother Dirk to help him regain some semblance of sanity he would have instantly killed the others they had found, after that first one so many months ago. He would have done so without ever questioning the 'what' or the 'why' of them. He doubted that he would ever have found out that they were not of this world, only that something totally inimical to himself and his kind had been slain.

This thought brought other thoughts coursing through his mind. Balors people were true sentient beings who, in the dimness of the origins of their development, had been forced to reason out that by banding and working together they could face down some of the truly daunting killing machines that had shared their world then.

They quickly learned to reach out with their minds to warn the others of their kind of the carnivorous thoughts that were always present when one of their kind was being hunted. This began the process of being able to think and express ever more complex concepts to others. Soon picture thoughts were not enough and they were forced to begin developing a real language to express ever more complex ideas and convey them to others. This whole process had led them, like these two legs, from unreasoned reaction to reasoned response, and eventually to the concept of future intent.

With an effort, Balor pulled his thoughts back to the present, and his concerns about those others. He had been gone for a little over five months now and he desperately wanted to know what was going on with Dirk and his friends. Suddenly, as if he had been reading his thoughts, he felt Dirks' unique touch in his mind. He was far away, but the sending was surprisingly strong. That did not matter now, his brother was seeking him out!

Balor, my brother, can you hear me?" the thought came, and Balor could tell that his abilities had improved much!

Balor mentally gathered his strength and pushed his thought reply out, concentrating on the familiar patterns of Dirks' mind, and the direction the mental energy output said the thought had come from. *I hear you my brother. Your sending is stronger this time. Our bond is strengthening your abilities.* These thoughts were surrounded by feelings of warmth and welcome. Balor also saw that there was a longing there to be near Dirk again.

Dirks thought came again, stronger now, as if dirk had homed right in on balors position. They were also surrounded by the same sense of warmth and welcome, as had Balors'. *I miss you greatly Balor. Why have you stayed away so long? Will you return soon? Can you tell me where you are? Are you well? Do you need help?* Dirks' questions pelted him, his obvious concern evident.

I am well my brother and I too miss being with you! Much has happened that I must tell you of. I am in the high mountains far north of our first meeting place, and I plan to start my return trip within six turnings of the sun. Yet I sense that you are even further north than am I. Will you return soon, for I too am eager to see you. Balor sent, sure now that his sense of Dirks direction was right.

Balor, this is very odd! I too can sense that you are far south of where I am. Dirk sent with some wonder, *Let me ask you this. Can we find each other using this sense?*

Yes my brother. The closer we get the stronger it will become. This thing happens when two beings form a close bond. Why do you ask? Balor asked, puzzled now.

Just this, Dirks thoughts were excited now, *in seven days time I want you to begin seeking me, and I will do the same for you. I am coming to get you in one of the flying machines we call helicopters. It will save you much travel and time. Will you do this thing for me?*

Yes. I would like that. But I must warn you that I will have company. Two of my siblings will be with me. Will they be welcome among your friends? Balor asked, somewhat tentatively. For he had just made a snap decision to introduce them to Dirk sooner than later.

My brother, you and yours will always be welcome among me and mine as long as I live. Why, even Bill Tate has been walking around here mumbling to himself that he misses you, even if you do tease him a lot. Dirk sent, the sense of a smile coloring his thoughts.

Then, more soberly, *have no fear my brother, they will be under my personal protection! Not that I think they will need it! Balor, this form of sending is new to me, and I am tiring quickly. I will come for you in seven days time. Fare you well my brother!* And Dirks thoughts began to fade.

I will be waiting! Fare you well! Balor sent quickly before dirk faded completely.

Reunion

It was a week later now, seven days to be exact, and the night before Dirk had asked George Casey to fly the pontoon equipped 'Huey' helicopter personally for him the next day. When Casey had asked where they were going so he would know how the chopper should be outfitted he was told 'Into the mountains', snow country. "We're going to pick up a friend." Casey hadn't asked any more questions, just said, "OK. I'll be ready to go at six AM tomorrow morning."

That same night he had asked Bill Tate and Jimmy Lester to accompany him the next day, again saying only that they were picking up a friend. Bill Tate was left wondering at the mischievous grin Dirk was having a hard time hiding.

Bill and Jimmy, riding In the back, could hear Dirk saying over the headphones they all wore, "A little more south, and into that big valley just beyond those two peaks there." Dirk was pointing as he said this, and George banked the big bird over to the left and down. Dirk said then, still pointing, "The other side there, about midway along that ridge with the big stand of pines on it."

Casey flared the Big 'Huey', tilting its' nose up to kill much of it's speed as Dirk said "OK George, slow us down a little more now and swing around the trees to the right. Find us a place to set her down."

Casey found a fairly flat spot about thirty yards away from the edge of the trees and set the big chopper down. After the swirling snow kicked up from the prop wash settled down Dirk went to the rear compartment and, pulling the door open, jumped to the ground, followed by Bill and Jimmy.

Dirk walked out, bending low to get past the now slowly turning rotor blades, to within fifteen yards of the tree line, Bill and Jimmy joining him there as they all hunkered down facing the trees to wait. A couple of minutes later Bill asked, "Just who are we waiting for out here in the middle of nowhere, Dirk?" Jimmy, on his other side, didn't ask but the question was in his look.

Suddenly the snow almost directly in front of Bill shifted and a large midnight black head lifted from it, a pair of huge golden eyes staring out at bill from the head. *I greet you little brother. It is good to be in your presence again.* Bill heard in his head.

Bill flew up and backwards from his crouching position to land on his out stretched hands and backside, shouting "Jesus, Balor! I wish you wouldn't do that!" But there was no real rancor in his words.

Just as Bill was lifting himself into an upright position the snow next to him heaved and a slightly smaller version of Balor lifted itself up, only this one was a beautiful sable brown. The deep chocolate brown only found in seal or mink fur. Its' eyes were, he saw as he fell off balance again, ice blue. And, like Balors', they were mesmerizing. He heard in his mind, as he made contact with the ground again, *I also greet you, little brother to Balor!*

"GAWD DAMMIT, Balor," Bill shouted, wildly looking between the two apparitions, "You could have warned me about this!" But Bill was now looking at this new member of Balors' kin with awe, for with the words that had come in his head he had felt a sincere feeling of welcome.

By this time both Dirk and Jimmy were sprawled on their respective backsides, laughing so hard that tears were beginning to leak from their eyes. George Casey, seeing the two apparitions appear from the snow, was out of his seat and half out of the cockpit with a pistol in his hand when he saw Dirk waving him back.

Jimmy Lester was on his hands and knees now, still laughing as he began to get to his feet when the snow right in front of him shifted, and a huge pair of emerald green eyes blinked at him! At the same time he heard it the others did too, *I too give greetings to our brother's, brothers.*

Jimmy fell flat on his face, realizing as he did so that this perfect version of Balor had been laying right beside him all along with her face in the snow to keep from showing her pink nose. He knew it was a she, because nothing so beautiful and graceful, he could see as she rose completely up out of the snow that so closely matched the color of her glistening fur as she moved join the other two, could never have been misconstrued as a male.

Mesmerized, his eyes followed her movements as they drank in the beauty of this splendid being, as did they all. As she moved her gaze took in all before her, seeming to each of the men that her look was for him alone, and the sun reflected green fire from her eyes like the finest emeralds nature had ever produced.

Getting a hold on himself he continued to raise himself from his former face down position, when his head suddenly snapped back around to stare at this beautiful creature again, his mouth gaping open as he heard, *your thoughts are most kind and complimentary to a stranger, brother of my brother's, brothers.* She said in a voice, just as beautiful as she was, that was directed only at Jimmy.

Dirk, more sensitive than the rest heard all of this interchange, as he knelt in front of the trio. He looked deeply into Balors' eyes and speaking mind to mind said, *well met my brother. We have been apart far too long.*

In turn, Balor replied *You too are well met my brother. It has been far too long.* And there were reams of unspoken meaning in those simple words between the two!

Dirk sensed it when Balor changed the level, on which he had been sending, one he could also hear, and said, *and well met to TuLan, my friend from the stars!*

On that same level Dirk felt TuLan come forward to that portion of his mind that they used for communication to say, *well met Balor. I am glad of your safe return. I sense that you have brought others of your kind. This is most interesting!*

Balor said, *my siblings will find it hard to speak on this high of a band/level.* And sent an almost warbling mental tone, indicating that all could participate on that level.

Dirk did not miss the startled half thought that passed between the other two, and was hidden before it was completely formed.

By this time George Casey was standing a few feet away, staring in fascination at the tableau before him, not understanding what was going on. He did of course know about Balor, but because of a near miss head wound he was deaf to the mental interplay taking place. Bill Tate, not taking his eyes of the three now sitting in front of Dirk said in an aside, "These are some of Balors' relatives."

Sending now so that all could hear, except George, Balor said, *these are my siblings, Daleel and Jamat.* Each of them again expressed 'well met' greetings.

Kneeling beside Dirk now Bill carefully reached out with both hands, so as not to startle those beautiful creatures, and placed one on each of their shoulders. They flinched slightly, no more than a ripple of the skin where his hand touched them, but they did not pull away. Bill formed the words slowly in his mind, still unsure of this manner of communicating and said slowly but distinctly, *Balor is always scaring the bejesus out of me like that! But if you're kin to him you're welcome with us!*

Those two, their ice blue and emerald green eyes looking directly, mesmerizingly, into his own accepted his welcome because the warmth of his

349

tone belied the complaint in his words. The silent chuckle he heard, so like that of Balors', brought a wide smile to his face.

As Bill moved back Jimmy moved forward to take his place beside Dirk, reaching out as had Bill to place a hand on each of their shoulders. He had fewer occasions to speak with Balor than Bill had but was determined not to miss this chance, saying without realizing that he had heard the exchange between Bill and them, *I too welcome those who are Balors' friends or kin!*

Did you know Mr. Bad Boy, came the crystaline tones of Daleels mental voice, settling on Jimmys' awareness like snowflakes, *that you have much of the talent of mind speak!*

We agree! came the combined voices of Balor and Jamat. Stunned, Jimmy sat down hard on his backside again, to stare at the trio with a look of utter wonder in his eyes!

On that same wavelength Daleel and Jamat said in unison, *We also welcome the unseen one from the stars. Our brother has told us of his great service to him. For this we thank him.*

TuLan replied soberly, not quite sure about, or comfortable with, having so many know of his existence in such a hostile environment, *you, being members of Balors' race, and family, are most welcome among us. I hope to get to know you better as time allows.*

This was the reason Dirk had thought to bring Bill and Jimmy, for they both knew of TuLans' existence, and where he resided.

In an aside to Balor Dirk said *let's not leave George out of this!* and so saying turned to him and said, "George, come over here and say hello to Balor and his kin."

Startled, George hesitantly came over and knelt down next to the rest of them, asking, "what do I do?"

"Just put your hand on his shoulder and think hello to him and his kin." Dirk said.

Casey was a brave man, but it took all of his courage and will power to reach out and place his hand on the huge cats shoulder, but he did it anyway. Screwing up his courage he thought, *you guys are scary as hell, but you're beautiful too. If Dirk says you're friends, that's good enough for me!*

To his utter amazement a long red tongue reached out and rasped on his whiskered cheek!

"Well I'll be damned!" a very pleased George Casey muttered, his leathery, lined, face splitting in a wide grin!

In an aside to Dirk, and on a level that he was sure none of the others could pick up on, Balor said, *my brother. There is much I have to tell you that is of great import! We must take time as soon as is possible to discuss many matters, for I have learned much on my sojourn here.*

It will be as you say, replied Dirk on the same level, surprising himself yet again that he did this so effortlessly. *We will take time as soon as we have returned to our new base far to the north of here. It is a place I think you will like!*

Dirk, Balor said hesitantly *do you think there will be any problem with my siblings coming among so many of your kind? I worry for them also, because they are not used to being among so many two legs at one time!*

No my friend, I do not think there will be any problems. Look at George, he cannot hear you at all, and doesn't know if you hear him. But he accepted my word, and was pleased beyond words at you generous response to those he tried to send to you. As for the others just look at Jimmy. He may be the first human to fall in love with an alien the way he's fawning all over Daleel. No, if there is a problem it will be that too many will want to be in their company!

But I did hear him! It was faint, but I heard him none the less! Balor said to a surprised Dirk.

Deciding to give Balor a surprise of his own dirk said, *Besides, I happen to know that you, and the others, can hear the surface thoughts of others who are thinking about you!*

Balor said nothing, just gave Dirk that molten golden stare.

Home to Main Base One

Dirk broke that tableau, both speaking aloud and sending to Balor, *we must be getting back to our base now if we are to get there before darkness falls. Balor, please ask you siblings to join us on the helicopter for the trip back as it will save them many days travel.* So saying he got up and started moving towards the big 'Huey'.

Balor sprang to his side, even as the others began to move towards it also. Daleel and Jamat sprang to either side of the group with effortless bounds, as if they were taking protective flanking positions.

All Now aboard the helicopter, the big side doors closed against the cold mountain air, Casey lifted the big bird off that ridge effortlessly, banking back and upwards, to head back in the direction from which they had come. He climbed and gained speed quickly, all now anxious to be back at, or see, their new mountain base.

Dirk had settled himself in the flight cabin bulkhead seat. Bill Tate and Jimmy Lester had settled themselves on the aft bulkhead bench seat. Once their flight had leveled out Balor, Daleel and Jamat got up from the crouched positions they had taken on the floor of the passenger compartment and seated themselves in a semi circle facing Dirk.

Dirk was now looking deeply into Balors' eyes, but at the same time he was very aware of the presence of both Daleel and Jamat on the edges of his mind. He still marveled at the deep bond that he had formed in such a short time with this beautiful black creature. No, being! For that is exactly what he was, no matter what his appearance.

Dirk was one of those individuals who did not make friends or form close attachments easily or quickly, but once he had they were, for him, life long and deep. Dirk thought that it might have something to do in the case of Balor, with their form of communication where so much more could be, and was, said and expressed in a much shorter period of time. But that wasn't all of it either, for as different as Balor was from him physically, he felt a sameness of spirit, of personal honesty and honor, as well as a reservation of self that held all in judgement of those standards. In amazement Dirk thought to himself that Balor was his counterpart in another form.

Dirk let that line of thought go, and said instead, *my friend, you return at a good time, for much has occurred that I must tell you about. But first I Must ask you a question that may have bearing on what is happening on our world.*

Ask my brother, and if I know the answer I will tell you. Balor replied calmly

Actually there are a couple of things I would know! But first, it would please me if your siblings would join our conversation.

Suddenly Dirk felt as if he were in a room, with three separate individuals. He knew this was only an impression, but it seemed to be real none the less. *We are most grateful and pleased that you would include us* Daleel and Jamat said together, yet their individual voices were quite distinct to Dirk.

Letting as much of the warmth he felt towards Balor overflow to include them he said *You are kindred to my true brother! How could I not include you in what will most likely have a direct impact on you?*

Dirk started to ask something as he was looking at these two but saw that those huge eyes seemed to be radiating something that he was totally unprepared for. They were radiating a sense of belonging! A sense that said that they now belonged to him, as he now belonged to them! It happened that fast. Dirk had just become a member of Balors' family, and he now had something he had not had for a long, long time. A family.

He changed his mind about the question he had been about to ask. It was not the time or place for that. He asked instead, *Balor, it is evident by your siblings here that you have an extended family. Just how many of you are there?*

It took so long for Balor to answer that Dirk thought he might not answer at all. Then, reluctantly, Balor said, *there are only about fifty thousand of us left.*

You two legs have not been kind to us over these many years! the rebuke in his statement, though not directed at Dirk personally, was plain.

Somewhat taken aback, but knowing that complete honesty was of utmost importance now, Dirk said slowly, carefully, *It is true! We humans have not always dealt fairly with those who share this planet with us.*

Dirk paused, then went on expressing himself in terms learned from his grandfather on those rare occasions when he had accompanied him to the tribal meetings and witnessed solemn oaths being given or taken, *but from this day on, you, and all of your kind shall be welcome as equals among all of those that I hold sway over. This I swear upon my life!*

Having said this he was a little amazed, because he knew to the deepest fiber of his being that he meant every syllable!

Jimmy Lester and Bill Tate quite suddenly sat upright from the relaxed slouches they had been sitting in on the rear bench seat. Alarm was starting in their eyes and rigid posture as a deep rumbling, almost a muted roar, began to issue from deep in the chests of the three beautiful creatures sitting in front of Dirk!

Jimmy and Bill relaxed now as they watched in astonishment! They were witnessing a sight that had not been seen by mankind for nearly three thousand years. All three of the beautiful feline creatures were now butting their heads, and pushing and rubbing themselves against Dirk. And that deep rumbling, they now realized, was the sound of those creatures purring with pleasure! Whatever Dirk had said to them they were very pleased about it, the two were thinking. Without warning the two new cat things came over and sat in front of Bill and Jimmy. Dirk said to them "Please put your hands on their shoulders!"

To their immense surprise they, after touching the cats, heard Dirks voice in their heads. *I have just sworn an oath of brotherhood and equality to Balor and his kind! And that no one connected with us will ever raise hand or weapon against them on pain of death!*

Dirk looked long and thoughtfully at his two friends, wondering if what he was about to ask of them was the right thing to ask them bind themselves to personally. Then, coming to his decision, he went on, *will you two, as my closest friends, also swear to this oath. I know I'm asking a lot of you, but not only is this important, it is the right thing to do!* And, to the surprise of both of those hard men, they both swore to the oath without hesitation!

Now the rumbling purring started anew, as the two beautiful creatures pushed and rubbed themselves against the two men. Those two were now completely bemused, and would remember that sense of closeness and oneness for the rest of what would be, for them, long, long lives.

It would also help to console them during the times of stress and loss that were ahead of them.

CHAPTER SEVENTEEN
Ships and Consolidations

Consolidations Considered

Dirk had been back at the new main base for three days now, and was still a little upset with himself for a couple of reasons. First because he had waffled on asking Balor if his people, for that is exactly what he thought of them as, were earth natives. He was pretty sure of the answer, but wanted it confirmed anyway. And, for some reason he wasn't quite sure of yet, he felt the answer was going to be important to the future of all of them.

The second thing that was upsetting him was his impending meeting this afternoon with Samuel McCarthy, the president of the USA. That situation was really two minor problems in one.

The biggest part of the problem was that McCarthys' secret service detail would be aware of the location of this new base, and in turn some of what was going on here! His own security people were very upset with him, asking why the meeting couldn't be held somewhere else instead. The answer to that part was basically simple. McCarthy had been, and was still pivotal in gaining them direct, preferential, access to the key materials and personnel that they needed, now and in the near future. And those avenues had to be well established before he tendered his resignation for health reasons, as he and the resistance had agreed he should do. To do this without arousing alarm he would claim that the stress was adversely affecting his ability to do the job he was elected to do properly, and that was something no one but he could determine.

This meeting was both a respectful courtesy because he had come into this early on, and had provided both access to large sums of money and presidential clearances for many of Dirks' people. And the meeting was also a necessary confrontation! The confrontation itself was necessary because the man was a forceful personality who was used to wielding a great deal of power and authority, and he had to be shown that this game was a whole new ball of wax.

In this game you didn't lose political points or position, you lost lives. McCarthy was a good and responsible man, but he had no experience with death up close and personal, and if you were going to order men and women to die you had better know what you were asking of them.

He was also not stupid or pig headed. But he did have to be convinced that the form of governance he was used to administering had to be put aside for a time for one that was more direct. One that was not a dictatorship, but something very close to it! He would have to accept a form of governance that would be overseen by a ruling council formed from the resistance's working parts. And accept that he would no longer be governing a whole country. He would be governing Earth's first off world colony and would be responsible for a whole world!

Dirk had discussed this whole matter with his core group at length and they had decided that McCarthy would be the ideal choice to head up their first off world base planet. They had agreed on him not only because he was a strong political leader, but because he had also been, before entering politics, an adept and very successful businessman who was known for his ability for getting things done. And done right the first time!

Ships

As Dirk was sitting at his desk, thinking these thoughts, there was a light tapping at his door. It opened to reveal Felix Ortiz, backing into the room, his arms full of computer printouts.

Turning to face Dirk, with a very serious look on his face, he said, "We've got a couple of wrinkles we've got to iron out if we're going to be able to keep to the schedule you set up for us!"

Then he smiled, "But there's some good news to report on our progress too!"

"That's what I like about you Felix," Dirk said smiling himself, "you always bring me some good news to soften the bad with!"

"Actually," said Felix, his smile slipping only a little "the wrinkles aren't really that bad for a change. But I suggest that we do something about them before they become problems. Serious ones!"

"OK, what's got your drawers all bunched up Felix?" Dirk asked, not really intending it to be funny, but smiling just the same.

"The situation is threefold," said Felix, going into his 'Felix the entrepreneur' mode, "and it shakes out like this. First, we need another construction crew to help with the living quarters being built in the upper galleries of the fourth of the main caverns. We need the living quarters because we need another batch of tech's, about two hundred I'm told."

He paused briefly to let the import of that be absorbed, then hurried on, "That is if you want those five well armed light cruisers you asked for built on time!" he finished, as a broad smile again broke across his features.

"Well armed light cruisers" Dirk asked, his curiosity quickly aroused.

"Damn Right!" Felix blurted, "You didn't expect us to send our guys out there defenseless did you?" But seeing the consternation on dirks face he quickly went on, "Geez Dirk, I'm sorry! I thought that Yuri and Dr. Hull had already spoken to you about them. They said they would." And at that very moment there was another tapping at the door, and it opened.

"Speaking of the devils." Dirk said as Yuri Garov and Dr. David Hull maneuvered their way into the room, their arms laden with large rolls of engineering drawings. "Hullo Dirk." Said Yuri by way of greeting sounding more British than Russian, something he was constantly being ribbed about.

Then he said, "We've got something very interesting to show you." And David Hull said, "And we think you're really going to like it!"

"Hi fellas. Have a seat. But I think I should warn you that Felix here has already blown your surprise." He said chuckling, "But I'd like to hear it anyway."

"That's OK Dirk. He couldn't have told you everything because we didn't tell him everything!" Dr. Hull said smirking in self satisfaction.

Garov let a rumbling chuckle escape from his deep barrel of a chest. He was used to these two now, and knew that this was only fun teasing between them. As a matter of fact, he thought to himself, these two worked better together than any two people he had ever met, and they had only been working together for a little over a year now!

"OK fellas, lay it on me quickly because I haven't got a lot of time today. I've got Sam McCarthy coming in for a meeting a little after one p.m. today." Dirk said a little more tiredly now.

"Da." Said Yuri soberly. "Knowing what you have to say to him I don't envy you your job now. Will he balk, do you think, at what we will propose?"

"No." Dirk said thoughtfully, "he's a much better man than most politicians, and he understands what we're up against. He will do whatever needs to be done, and won't let us go down without a fight! Besides, don't envy me too much. You're going to be right here with me for this one!" Dirk said, smiling sardonically.

"Spaciba." Garov said with a pained look on his face, "I need this like I need warm vodka on a hot summer night!"

"OK Dirk." Dr. Hull said as he started unrolling several sheets of engineering drawings across his desk. With a big self satisfied grin he began to describe what they had done that was different from the original plans, "Yuri, Felix, and I were grousing about sending these beautiful ships out there with nothing but a couple of twin thirty seven millimeter cannons mounted for and aft."

"So, after a couple of hard scull sessions, and considering we have no real idea what we'll be up against out there, we decided that the first five ships should be light war cruisers! So, in that vein we made a few minor modifications based on the theory that the others won't know what to expect from us either."

"What all that boils down to is this is what we came up with based on what you got from the 'Chai', and what we could learn from the teaching machine."

Looking at Dirks expression he said quickly, "I know, I know. This is a little long winded. But if you don't see how we got there you won't see why we made the choices we did."

At dirks' understanding nod he hurried on, "Based on that we think most of the weapons we might be facing will be in the form of big lasers and smaller pulse beam weapons that are hard to aim unless they're shooting at a slow moving or standing target. Neither of which we intend to be!"

Getting into his subject now he took a deep breath and hurried on, "Those thirty sevens are ok for anything our size, and we can stand off a little bit and pot shoot, but we need something with a much higher cyclic rate of fire if they have anything like fighters!"

"So we modified several of the chain guns they use for defense on our big carriers. And we solved the problem of air loss in a vacuum from explosive expansion by adding a gel sealant during the crimping process. That actually gave us a higher muzzle velocity too."

Holding up a hand, as he saw the questions forming on Dirk s face, to forestall interruptions now that he was on a roll, he rushed on. "The really big surprise for anyone we run into that is too big to mess with close in will be the auto loading triple rail gun system built into the bow behind retractable doors. They will fire depleted uranium rods about a foot long at a velocity of around twenty five hundred miles per second. At fifty thousand miles that's twenty seconds to target!"

He took a gulp of air and rushed on, really getting into his subject now, "And, unless they have a lot better detection systems than we think they do they will never see them coming. On top of that their kinetic energy on impact will destroy up to eight hundred times their own mass!" he said, almost panting now.

He gulped more air now then hurried to finish, "Just a little more to tell now. Each ship will also have several medium range lasers spotted around the hull on retractable turrets. We got the general design from the teaching machine. Turns out we made a good match. Their power output is higher, but our optics and computer guidance systems are faster and more accurate!"

"Well, that's about it for now for me, but Yuri has something else to go over with you. Phew, I'm done in for now!" he said as he plopped himself down heavily into one of the chairs by the desk.

Dirk just sat there for a minute, looking at the three of them with admiration, knowing that he could never have done nearly as much without them.

Garov cleared his throat and gave Dirk one of his rare 'cat that ate the bird' grins, as he unrolled another set of drawings over the ones already on the desk. Done with that he began to speak, "Those of us tasked with building our new ships had a long discussion after the last meeting, and we all came to the conclusion that it would be a total waste of time using the cruisers as cargo transports too. So we decided to build two large cargo ships as part of our new fleet! Do you see the wisdom in this Dirk?"

Dirk already had an idea what was coming but wanted to see just where his chief strategist was going with it. He nodded, saying, "Go on Yuri, please."

Seeing Dirks look he said, "I see you're already with me on this, so I'll lay out the preliminary plan outlines we developed. "First, one of the fully armed cruisers must always be available on or near earth for whatever needs may arise."

"Second, two of the fully armed cruisers should be set up as exploration and first phase base set up ships, carrying a mixed complement of troops, construction workers, and technical people for setting up preliminary base headquarters and staff support facilities when suitable sites are found."

Yuri paused to order this thoughts then continued, "Once a preliminary base is established one of our cargo transports can be sent out with most of the equipment necessary to begin producing the raw materials necessary to begin building the factories to produce the other machines and equipment necessary to making those bases self sufficient."

"Jesus Yuri," Felix broke in, quipping good naturedly "how long did you have to practice that one to get it all out in one piece?"

Ignoring him, but smiling just the same, Yuri went on, "During our planning on this methodology we have found out how to pack almost a complete miniature factory, along with a fair amount of spare parts, into one of the standardized containers used for ocean shipping. And that by packing one ship with only equipment and the other only with personnel, we can have a base up and producing within the span of two complete trips!"

"This method," he continued, "is riskier than spreading things out among the ships, but we think that risk is worth the reward. The time frame we are looking at is six months from the site location to the deployment and implementation of the equipment and personnel from the second shipload." Yuri Paused, knowing there would be questions now.

But he held up his hand to forestall comment for a moment, and hurried on, "The big question we have is 'How will humans react to FTL travel? It is a question we haven't considered as yet, have we?" This time he paused to let that one sink in.

Seeing the considering looks this question evoked he proceeded more slowly now, "That is information you will have to get from the chai, if possible. Also, the examination of the being you said was called a Trine indicates that its' physiology was similar to our own and should pose no ill, or permanent, side effects on us. This is also indicated from the design of the command chairs from the original ship."

He paused again briefly, looking around the circle of faces and taking in their thoughtful looks, "If that is the case, the second cargo vessel can be fitted out as a troop transport that can easily carry several hundred people per trip! Now Yuri stopped to let Dirk ask questions.

Dirk said, shaking his head and smiling "I knew there was a good reason for pulling you out of Russia! Alright! Assuming all of this works as you've set it out the real question becomes, how do we get these big cargo vessels off earth? They're going to be massive, aren't they?"

"That's the real beauty of it!" said Felix and David Hull almost in one voice. Felix waved his hand at Dr. Hull to proceed.

"Two things make this possible." He began in a measured voice, "First, we have been able to completely integrate our stealth technology with our new fabrication process for making the plating for the ships hulls!"

"And unless they have some technology the Chai know nothing about we should be completely invisible to them! Second, And this is the big one that I was saving for a grand slam to lay on you! Because of that teaching machine we were able to re-engineer and build, we can now build anti gravity repulesor engines that will lift our ships right up and out of the atmosphere! And with little, or no, worry about heat friction buildup!"

"Now comes the really good part!" he hurried on, relishing what he was about to say, "Amazingly enough, the FTL drive engines are quite small in relation to the mass of the ships. Actually, calling them engines is a misnomer because they really don't drive the ships! What they really do is create a hole in space for the ships to fall through!"

"Suffice it to say, the most complex parts on any of the ships will be the navigational computers that control the 'insertion' and 'emergence' timing for the FTL Drives." He finished happily.

"But what about the regular drive engines for the ships?" Dirk asked, very impressed with the amount of knowledge they had been able to extract from the Chai ship and its' teaching machine.

Smiling broadly himself now, Felix picked up the narrative, "They are basically very simple. They are mass conversion fusion drive engines, something we were very close to developing ourselves. Actually, we were able to improve on the designs we found in the maintenance and service manuals in the teaching machine!"

Smiling even more broadly now, if possible, Felix finished with, "And we were able to increase the output of those engines by almost fifty percent in the computer simulations we ran!"

This question and answer session went on for another full hour and a half. Finally Dirk called a halt to it, saying, "OK. It sounds like you guys have everything we can think of well in hand, so go ahead with your plans. I have to meet president McCarthy in twenty minutes."

As the three were getting their things together to leave Dirk said, "Felix, come back in about forty minutes, and bring your drawings with you. OK?" At Felixs' nod he turned to Garov, "Yuri, are you really going to try and sneak out of here like that?" he asked, smiling maliciously. Then, more soberly "I really would like you to be here for this."

Garov gave him a quizzical look, but all he got in return was one of Dirks big 'Cheshire' grins as he got up and crossed to the ever present coffee pot, and poured two cups. He came back and sat down at his desk, then reached down and opened his bottom drawer and removed a bottle of brandy from which he poured a health dollop into each cup. Accepting the cup Dirk proffered Yuri said, "What gives, as you Americans like to say?"

After taking a sip from his cup Dirk said, "McCarthy will be here in a few minutes. After he comes in, just keep your famous grim face on.

Consolidating McCarthy

A few minutes later there was a light knock and the door to Dirks' office was opened by one of the security detail that had escorted the president there through the vast cavern complex. They overheard him telling the head of his own security detail that they would have to remain outside during this meeting. As the man entered the large room cut into the side of one of the smaller tunnels off the main complex he smiled and strode across the room, his hand outstretched, "Dirk, and Mr. Garov I see, it's good to see both of you. Boy, you guys have really changed things around here!"

"Good to see you too, Sam. Yes, we've put the money you gave us to good use." Dirk said, smiling and shaking the mans hand.

"Well, I didn't really see that much on the way in, but what I did see was impressive!" McCarthy said taking the seat Dirk indicated, a comfortable narrow backed wing chair next to the coffee table now laden with sandwiches, coffee, and a bottle of brandy.

Directing his attention to the Dark complexioned and dark eyed man sitting on the sofa across from him Dirk said, "Sam, let me introduce you to Yuri Garov, the former Director of Counter Intelligence for the KGB. He has very kindly volunteered his services to us. He is now our Director of Strategic Planning." Dirk finished, smiling at the look developing on the mans craggy featured face.

Hesitantly McCarthy stretched his hand across the coffee table. Saying "You're that Yuri Garov!" he blurted, "From the reports I've read you practically single handedly stonewalled our intelligence efforts for years! Christ Almighty Dirk, I don't know how you did it but I damn glad he's on our side now!" the man finished fervently

Taking the mans hand, Garov, playing the part Dirk had asked him to, his face and voice dour said, "Da. Is good to see you also."

Then, deciding to forget his role, Yuri said more diplomatically, "It really is a pleasure to meet you Mr. President. I think it only fair to tell you that our file on you said that we would be having a much harder time doing so if you were elected. That prediction proved to be all too true!" Garov finished with a lopsided grin lighting up his normally dour expression.

"I didn't know I was so highly regarded by your people." he said, grinning himself now.

"Sam," Dirk said to redirect his attention, "you're going to find that we have many people with us now that were, before this ugly beast reared its' head, from places that were formerly thought of as enemy states. The one real advantage we have is that most of us in the intelligence game were members of a very small community."

"And the members of that community either knew or knew about each other, and about the reputations of each of our opposites.

When we put our offers out, and to break out the proof we have to back up those offers, the end result would be totally incontrovertible. It also helps knowing who to talk to because, as you well know, it can open many doors."

Samuel McCarthy, President of the United States, was now sitting back in his seat holding the cup of coffee that had been handed to him, watching and listening to these two men with rapt attention. Looking directly into that mans eyes now, Dirk went on in a thoughtful voice, "We have reached out far and wide to bring together many of the most respected and talented people this world has ever produced. All of them came here setting aside philosophies that were often disparate with our own! Many of them you will get to meet on the tour we have planned for you later today. But they all came in the hope that we, all of us, can save our planet! And our Species!"

Looking at the mans expression now, Dirk quickly added "I really don't mean to preach, Sam."

McCarthy, his own smile somber now, replied "Preach away, but you'll be preaching to the choir. I meant it when I said, at out first meeting, that I was in!"

"Well Sam, that's part of the reason you're here today. To make sure that your commitment is steadfast. The other reason I'll go into after we finish bringing you up to date on what we have been able to accomplish so far." Dirk and Yuri then proceeded to give him as thorough a briefing as he had ever been given in his life.

"That's absolutely remarkable!" The man was saying some time later, "And you say that you will have five space faring light cruisers and two cargo ships ready for deployment within the next six months?" He asked his wonderment obvious in his voice and on his face.

"That's right Sam. Listen, we've been at this for almost two and a half hours now. Let's take a break and have some dinner before going on to the next thing."

"Yuri, would you ask security team two to take Sams' security team to the cafeteria for some dinner. And ask them to send someone back with dinner for four, Felix will be joining us in a little while."

Felix returned for the second time as the food arrived. His first trip had been brief, coming back as Dirk had asked with the drawings they had quickly gone over them and he had been asked to update them and return, which he was doing now. The four of them relaxed for an hour with a nice roast beef and potatoes dinner, then coffee and brandy afterwards. Only after the dinner cart and dishes had been removed did they begin serious conversation again. After refreshing the coffee, sans the brandy this time, Dirk cleared his throat to signal that he was ready to begin.

Consolidating Governance

Posing his words thoughtfully, carefully, Dirk began to speak "Sam, you are probably one of the most honest, hardworking, and down to earth politicians it has been my good fortune to know, so I hope that what I'm about to tell you won't be taken in the wrong way. He paused checking, and seeing, that he now had the mans' complete undivided attention.

He reflected for a few seconds, his fingers thoughtfully rubbing his chin, "I guess the simplest, and best way to say this is bluntly, so here goes. Those of us that form the core governing group for this newly formed ERMA have discussed, for several months now, how we are going to manage governing our actions. Because we're not even sure that we'll be able to hang onto the earth for the short term we decided the best way was to use a military model! That model will be based on the UCMJ Law and will be comprised of an Operations Command Council that will have total authority over everything and everyone that is involved in this resistance movement!"

As he watched one of the most powerful men in the world digest this Dirk was prepared for questions or arguments, not the simple response he got from him, "Please go on."

"OK. This is war, make no mistake about it! We have never had to face an enemy that could turn much of our own population against us like this one will eventually do! Because this will be a war unlike any other we have ever had to fight, and an enemy we know far, far too little about, using the forms and methods of government we are familiar with will do us more harm than good!"

He paused for a breath and hurried on, "We just can't afford the time for politics the way they are! As far as personal rights and justice are concerned we will, as I said, depend on the UCMJ. The council will issue orders based on the best information available, but giving orders without the real authority to eliminate those who are derelict or incompetent is worse than useless! We just won't have the time, or luxury, of debating issues endlessly. Can you see why we came to this decision, Sam?"

Again the McCarthy's composure and quick mind reinforced Dirks initial assessment of the man, as he again replied simply, "Yes."

Smiling now Dirk continued, "Would you be willing to accept a seat on that council Sam?"

Seeing the man about to answer he held up his hand, saying quickly, "It's a little more complicated than that, so please wait before you answer. Sam, time is a factor here, and from the indications we're getting now there may not be much of it left! With that in mind, and if you decide to accept, It will be necessary for you to resign the rest of your term as president! You have just over a year left, don't you?"

From President to Governor

Again the mans' coolness made Dirk glad he had made Carl Miles take him to meet the man, as he asked "I know this is leading somewhere Dirk, why?"

"Because Sam, we're going to need you, in about six or seven months, to become the governor of Earth's first colony planet!" he said, smiling broadly now.

"Well I'll be damned!" The man said in open amazement, "I take a big demotion to get a major promotion!" he said, laughing softly to himself, clearly enthralled with the idea. "What excuse could I give that would be plausible enough for resigning?"

"This is your second term, and your doctor has been after you to slow down before job related stress aggravates your heart murmur." Dirk said smugly, knowing that that bit of information was supposed to be a closely guarded secret.

"How did you—?" he started, then, "Never mind. Information is your stock in trade, isn't it? He said, smiling ruefully. "Ok Dirk, I can see the why for. Now, what, and where, is this planet I'm to be governor of?" he finished, excitement creeping into his words.

"It's a planet the Chai told me about. It's about thirteen or fourteen hundred light years out past Bernards star. It is very earthlike, and has no indigenous species occupying it! We intend to make it a troop training/transfer and manufacturing base. Our first one!"

"How long will it take to get there?" McCarthy asked.

"Felix here will explain all of that to you a little later. I take it from your response that your answer is yes?"

"My wife said she wanted a change of scenery. Well, this should keep her from nagging me about it for a while!" He said, laughing aloud now. "The answer is definitely yes!"

"Alright! Here's where we are Sam, and here's what we need. In about two and a half months our first cruiser will come off the line. Immediately thereafter we are going to test the hell out of it on the ground, then a quick run out into the void. Providing everything works as well as my people say it will we'll leave for an exploration run to verify the info on your planet!"

"I'm told the trip will take from two to four weeks each way, and about two or three weeks for site exploration. Figuring on the high side that's about three months, give or take a week. That's our time frame."

"Wow, that's fast! But why do I have to wait six months?" the man asked in puzzlement.

"Because the cargo vessels won't be ready until then! Nor will we have the machinery, spare parts, and supplies ready until then either. We won't send you out there on a shoestring. We're going to give you every advantage we possibly can to get you started right!" Dirk said very seriously. What he didn't say however, was that if everything went wrong here there would at least be one outpost of humanity left!

"Can you be ready in six months, Sam? I mean ready to leave Earth?" Dirk asked just as seriously.

At the mans slow nod Dirk went on, slower now, making the man look at him more attentively, "OK, Here is what we need. As I said, indications tell me that time will become a problem all too soon. So, instead of building just two cargo and troop transport vessels in the next six months I want to build eight in the next year! To do that I'll need access to another ten billion dollars. Can you help us with that?"

"It may take a month or two, but yes, I think it can be arranged." Sam said slowly.

At that answer Dirk said, to finish up this part, "And I want them to be bigger than the first two. I think that we're going to have to move a lot of people and material very quickly, and if we have to leave here in a hurry I don't want to leave much behind! My gut is really beating me up on this score! One last thing before we stop, Sam. Your security detail, how well do you know them? And do you trust all of them without reservation?" He finished fervently.

The reply, when it came, was terse and to the point "Yes! Why?" The mans' look said, and asked, volumes.

Smiling to lessen the mans' worry, and ire, Dirk said calmly "Because I want you to ask the ones you're sure of to retire with you. There's no sense in having to break in a whole new team."

Seeing him relax a little Dirk said soberly, "Even so, we will want to vet them! I'm sure you understand why. So speak to them soon, and let us know through the channel we set up for you. As soon as they are cleared we'll brief them. All right?"

"I'll speak to them by the end of the week, and get you a list before the end of the week after."

"Good. I think you still have a couple of hours before you have to leave, so let Felix here give you the five cent tour."

There was a tickle at the edge of Dirks' mind, then *we are here my brother.* At the same time there was a knock at the door, and it opened immediately as Balor and his siblings entered. Almost as if on cue they arranged themselves to either side of Dirk, and in a half circle facing Sam McCarthy, their large, luminous eyes locking on the man.

Surprise Introductions

Not having seen or heard of them before McCarthy was transfixed for several moments. Finally he said in a hushed voice, "They're beautiful, but what are they? I can see that they're a lot more than just big cats."

"Sam, I'd like to introduce you to three friends of ours. The big black fellow here is Balor. The brown one is called Jamat. And the white beauty is known as Daleel. Balor here is the reason we found out so early about the others. The others being the Drel. He took an instant, and lethal, dislike to them. The first one he met didn't survive that meeting!"

"Are you telling me that they're intelligent?" he exclaimed, this while still transfixed by those captivating eyes.

Standing, Dirk stepped around the coffee table, Balor moving at his side, to stop in front of McCarthy. He reached down, took the mans' hand, and placed it gently on the big, beautiful, black cats' shoulder, saying, "Just relax Sam, and listen with your mind!" For a moment there was nothing, and then a look of wonder came across his features as he heard *we welcome you, friend of our brother Dirk.*

Sam McCarthy was, for the first time in his life, left totally speechless and nonplussed! It wasn't that he had never heard of the possibility of telepathy before, he just hadn't expected to experience it himself! And from something that looked like a cat. And on top of that he was surprised, surprised at a level that in itself was surprising, considering everything else that was going on here.

Dirk, keeping his own council on his first meeting with Balor said, "We met quite by accident out in the woods. Believe me; I was as surprised as you are when I first found out." In the meantime Balor had gone back to sit with his sibs.

"There are not many of Balors' people left, for there is no other way of thinking of them, because mankind has not been kind to them over the centuries. There is one thing you have to know about them and their relationship with us! And you must make this absolutely clear to your men! They are our FRIENDS! They have helped us, and will continue to do so. They have free run of everything, everywhere, and come and go as they please. But the most important thing you need to know is this! Anyone who harms or even attempts to harm, one of them will be shot out of hand!" Dirk finished, deadly intent in his voice.

Looking at Dirk Sam McCarthy felt a chill run up his spine, for here in front of him now was the deadly man he had heard about. And there was no doubt in his mind that he meant exactly what he had just said!

Smiling gently now, Dirk said "They, more than anything else, are the real reason your men were disarmed before they were allowed to enter."

CHAPTER EIGHTEEN
Lessons and Space Fleets

Lessons

The man in the brush moved almost silently. He was dressed in camouflage fatigues, with bits of rags and small branches stuck or tied into the pieces of fishnet sewn over parts of them, put there to help break up his silhouette. The exposed skin of his hands and face were coated with mottled blotches and stripes of greens, blacks, and brown camouflage grease paint making them, and him almost invisible in this heavily wooded area.

His weapons, like himself, were also camouflaged to blend in. His movements were slow and careful. His attention was centered on his intended target, but his senses were attuned to almost everything about him. He dropped to the ground before proceeding on to the lip of the low ridge that topped the shallow ravine where he believed his intended target was holed up.

He pulled himself carefully to the lip, peered over it with one eye, then slid silently back away from the edge. He let out an inaudible sigh of satisfaction on proving his instincts right, as he glided like a wraith into a small stand of pines a few yards to his left. Still staying close to the ground he slid in under the low branches and crawled back to a position just under the lip of the ridge top, and there lowered himself to a sitting position against the bole of one of the trees to consider his next moves.

He didn't see or hear the movement of the arm and hand, with the knife in, it that dropped down silently from the branches above him as he craned his neck to peer over the lip of the rim. The arm, hand, and knife pivoted above his head, then plunged down, then up and back, leaving a bright red line across his jugular vein and larynx!

There was a surprised expulsion of breath from the mans' lungs, followed by the disgusted expletive "SHIT!"

Then, in the earbud piece of his whisper phone he heard, "You were doing fine Sargent Jenkins, until you ignored your directives! Do you remember your training directives Sargent Jenkins?" came the soft feminine voice that cut like a razor.

"yes ma'am." Was Jenkins pained reply.

"And what, Sgt. Jenkins, is the training directive you believe I am referring to?" The velvety soft voice asked.

"never move more than ten meters in any direction away from your partner. Ma'am."

"Please finish the directive, Sgt." The soft voice coaxed.

Painfully embarrassed, Jenkins finished it, "And never, ever, move out of sight of you partner unless it is completely unavoidable. Ma'am."

"Thank you Sgt. You will now return to base camp, where you will wait at the trail head and stand in review of your squadron mates. You will explain to them, if asked, what you did wrong as they reform from today's exercise." The soft voice finished quietly in his ear.

Dejectedly Sgt. first class Alvin Jenkins got to his feet and began the long trip, made longer by this incident, back to the training base camp. He was furious with himself because he hated being made a fool of. But he hated even more making a fool of himself! Ruefully he touched the now dry line of indelible red ink there. He would take his punishment, and he would damn well learn his lesson!

Sgt. Jenkins was an eleven year veteran of the 'Rangers' and 'Green Berets', with a chest full of fruit salad that read like a book of the actions he had participated in. And several more he had earned that would never see the light of day. He would be double damned if he would let himself flunk out of this new unit!

From what he had seen since he had arrived, those being sent here were the absolute best of the best! And they were from military units from all over the world. That first day here, wherever here was, had been a real eye opener. The commanding officer was a Russian Colonel, and a woman to boot! What had really gotten his attention right away had been her very simple welcome. It went something like this—;

She had said, "I welcome you all to this new unit being formed here. You are all here because you are among the very best fighting men and women that the earth has to offer! If you survive your training here you will be among the very first members of the 'Earth resistance movement Alliance' fighting forces. That is something you can, and should, be very proud of."

"Look around you! You will see members from many different places. You will notice that I did not say 'Countries'. That is over with as of now! It is over because we don't have time for those distinctions any more! It is over because we only have 'EARTH' to think of now!"

"I know you are all wondering what I'm talking about, so I will tell you what I know. Our planet, and Mankind, are being threatened by an alien race that is in the process of invading our planet. They are insidious, and have already established a foothold on earth! Who, and what, they are will be shown and explained to you during your training. You are here to become the Earth's first, and perhaps last, line of defense! You are here to become Earth's first 'Space Marines'!"

"You will learn and know as much as we do, as fast as we learn it, about this enemy and the ways we have already found to fight and kill it! Let me make this very clear to you all. This is a fight for our very existence, and those around you are now your brothers and sisters in arms! You don't know or love them yet, but believe me you will! You will because they will be the only thing standing beside you as we fight for our very lives!"

"Yes, you will come to respect and love each other as brothers and sisters! Or you will be dead! So, if there are any among you who cannot let go of the past step out of ranks, and a place will be found for you elsewhere."

"One last item. Some of you who complete this training successfully will be offered immediate promotions to officers rank. Some of you will not make it, but all of you who finish successfully will eventually be promoted to the rank of lieutenant or captain to take command of new companies as they are trained. I wish you all the very best of luck. If you have not left yet you are now my men and women, and I am already very proud of you. And I will try very hard to make you proud of me. Dismissed!"

Within a few short days Jenkins was sure that everything he had been told was true, because within two days they were testing everything he had ever learned about combat. Then had come the new training methods, the first of which was the buddy system. An old and well tested concept, but with some new twists.

First they were formed into ten man squads of five two man teams. The twist was that each teammate was trained to operate as an alternate teammate to another team or squad. Teammates lived, ate, slept, and washed their backsides together, as well as trained together.

They were also required to learn the skillsets of their teammates and of their alternates. They were trained to think like their teammates and their alternates so that under combat conditions they would always know what to expect from them. This method worked so well that they quickly began working very well as teams and squads.

Then a monkey wrench was thrown into the mix. The original teams and squads were broken up and everyone was sent to join other teams and squads from separate sections of the training facility, and then all were sent out to exercises. What surprised them was how well they quickly meshed with their new teams and how well they worked together.

What they learned was that they now had counterparts in at least five other squads, and that they knew what to expect from them when something was needed by either one. They were all quickly, much more quickly than they had expected, becoming part of the whole.

Then the training changed again! Spacesuits!? Now thermally warmed lightweight snowsuits. Now they had to wear light body armor of something they called glassteel. It was half the weight of the old kevlar and was supposed to be ten times better! It was becoming a challenge to guess what was coming next, and a small pool was started with evening meal deserts as the prize for those who guessed right, which was not often.

But the best part was that they were not only learning many new things, and retaining more of it, they were beginning to see the challenges as something to look forward to! And even better than that, they had completely forgotten that their squad and teammates were often from somewhere they once thought they hated!

All of this was going through Jenkins mind as he wove his way through the trees and brush towards base camp. He didn't even think about the way he was moving, almost soundlessly like a wraith, through the woods. But, unbeknownst to Jenkins, he was being observed every step of the way, and the looks and thoughts of those who watched as he passed were approving, for they knew that if they had not known the paths he would take they would not have known of his passing.

What each one of those watchers did not, could not, know was that they in turn were being observed, and their positions marked by the man following Jenkins some twenty five meters behind at five o'clock to his direction of travel.

Now, all that really remained was to see how this one handled his punishment. For all of those observers, to a man, thought that this one would make a fine officer.

Jenkins wove his way through the perimeter security like a ghost, moving so softly and quietly that not even some of the grass he stepped on in passing was sure he had been there.

Shortly thereafter he presented himself, at rigid attention, in front of the commandants tent. That soft voice of velvet covered steel asked from inside it, "Where is your teammate sergeant?"

Right at this moment Ma'am, he is on the ridge to the north with the flap of your tent in his crosshairs!" Jenkins replied confidently. At the double click in his earphone he was assured that that was the case.

"Very well sergeant. You will present yourself at the trailhead to answer any questions the returning teams may care to ask concerning your error. How much detail you give in your responses is up to you. Dismissed!"

"Yes Ma'am!" And Jenkins left to accept his punishment, and accept what was another learning experience. He would do it, and do it well, he told himself as he went to the trailhead. That was all, except for the lesson already learned.

Looking over at her adjutant sitting on the other side of her field desk Colonel Katrina Valasovic said with a wide smile softening her features, "He learns fast, and does not forget, Thomas. That one we will promote to major, and make him a brigade executive commander!"

"I agree Trina. When do you want me to make the orders effective?" he asked, already knowing the answer.

"Tomorrow morning of course. He must still have the lesson embedded by his own admission of the error!" And she nodded for emphasis. She had spent many agonizing hours and days with her staff developing this units training methods, and now those methods were not only proving her right, they were turning out fighting men and women the likes of which this world had never seen before.

"What do you think of them overall?" he asked her for the hundredth time.

Instead of he usual 'They're all good' she said, surprising him, "They are much better than I had hoped for. And the Americans are better than our intelligence even suspected!"

Knowing that time was fleeing on swift feet, she had discussed the promotions she had in mind with her command superiors two days ago, and had been given a green light on all of them. She had also been told that in the future her judgements about any and all promotions would be deemed as automatic unless they concerned a rank higher than major.

The New Earth Space Fleet

This conference had been called on short notice, and there were now about thirty people standing or sitting around the hastily set up tables that formed a large u shape in the room. The man seated at the center of the u now stood and tapped the table with the bowl of his unlit pipe, saying loudly enough to be heard over the buzz of conversation in the room, "Please take your seats, this meeting is now in order!"

Those standing quickly found their seats, and the room became quiet as the hum of conversation died away, all faces were now turned to the man expectantly.

"Thank you all for coming so quickly. I know that you are all very busy, and involved in multiple tasks that demand every minute of your precious time. But there are changes about to be made, and other very important information you all need to have." The man paused to let his words sink in, as he stood rubbing his stubbled square chin.

"Many of you know me, but for those of you who do not, my name is Dimetri Chabov. And the first thing you need to know, and as most of you have guessed, is that we are about to launch Earth's first space Navy!" There were a few whistles and some applause at this but it died quickly.

"The second thing you need to know is that I have been appointed the rank of 'Admiral of the Fleet'. That means that under our ERMA organization I take my orders from the 'Command Operations Council', and the newly formed naval forces take their orders from me!" He took a breath and then said, "Admiral Berg?"

"Yes Sir!" came the crisp reply from the man sitting three seats to the left of Chabov.

"You are hereby promoted to Vice Admiral of the Fleet, and commander of ERMA naval forces operations. You will also act as vice chairman of the recently formed 'Joint Military Operations Council'. Congratulations Timothy!" he said to his new friend.

He went on briskly now, "General Carl Miles. You are hereby re— commissioned and promoted to full General. You are appointed as Commander of Army Ground Forces Operations, and Chairman of the Joint Military Operations Council. Congratulations Carl."

"Colonel Peotre Osov?" he called, and that man answered promptly "Sir."

"You have been promoted to the rank of Major General and are to command the ERMA Space Marines, two brigades of which are being formed now. You have my congratulations Peotre, you have earned this! And Peotre, please inform brevet colonel Valasovic that her rank has been made permanent. You will also sit as a member of the Joint Military Operations Council."

"One last thing general, colonel Valasovic is to retain command of the first brigade, and we would appreciate it if you would approve her recommendation that Sgt. Jenkins be promoted to the rank of major! He is to be her new adjutant, and her existing adjutant is promoted to the rank of colonel and will command the second brigade."

"Yes Sir. Consider it done. Thank you sir." The man who had slipped out of Russia with him said.

And, as the meeting went on more appointments were made, more promotions were given, operating outlines were established, and the operational chain of command was set.

After four arduous hours Chabov called the meeting to a close, asking Messers Berg, Miles, Osov, and a small handful of others to remain for a few moments. After the room had cleared they gathered in seats close around the new fleet admiral. Looking thoughtfully at the group he said, "All of you, in addition to your regular assigned duties, will act as advisors to the Command Operations Council."

"That Council," he continued slowly, "will be the supreme authority from which we will all take our orders and guidance for the duration of this war." He paused to let this sink in before continuing.

"Gentlemen, and Mrs. Hull, you may have noticed that although our efforts have been moving along quickly there have been some signs of bottle necking on certain projects. This meeting was held to establish some very clear lines of authority which we hope will stop those trends. Under these conditions your authority is nearly absolute, so please make all of your decisions considered ones!"

He looked at them, seeing their nods of understanding, and the weight of their authority settling on their shoulders. "I expect there will be some errors, but you are all top quality professionals, so we don't expect many of them!"

He looked at them all again, letting the warning sink in also! Then said, "Thank you all for your attention and courtesy, and Good luck to us all. Good evening." He finished, and standing up abruptly, he saluted them smartly. Then left the room.

CHAPTER NINETEEN
New Ways for the Elonee

Alor, the Council of Elders Concedes

The three beautiful catlike creatures sat facing each other near the top of the mountain that hid the vast cavern complex below its' tree shrouded shoulders. They were sitting just inside the tree line, and the bright moonlight was casting their shadows intermittently as its' light fell through the fast scudding clouds above them.

If one were to look closely the hair fine tendrils at the tips of their ears could be seen to be straining towards each of the others as they sat in a close circle, and that their large luminous eyes seemed to be glowing from some light source from within, as their concentration on each other deepened to the point of the exclusion of all else around them.

Each of them was a strong telepath in their own right, but linked together as they now were, they could send and receive thoughts half way around the world without going into the trace like state that had been necessary for Balor to use when sending long distances alone. The link to the enclave was now complete, and the council of elders had gathered to hear them.

Jamat has told me of the spread of "the others" in the vicinity of the home enclave. How bad is it?" Balor asked, the concern clear in his thought.

The infestation spreads outward like the ripples from a stone thrown into a still pond, and at an alarming rate now! It is within a ten-day of overrunning the area of the enclave! Elder Tagon, third eldest of the council members said, his thoughts cold with the fury and detestation all of the clan members seemed to feel instinctively towards the Drel.

Then the enclave must be moved, and quickly! Balors' thought came bluntly, foregoing the normal protocols of polite speech.

Gladly would we do so, were there a place to move it to! came the succinct thought in reply, *there are many elder clan members to think of now, and too little time available to locate another suitable site!* the tired, almost resigned, reply came to the three on the mountain top almost a half world away.

As Balor sent his reply there was an undercurrent of excitement coloring the tone of his thoughts that caused the elders to perk up and pay closer attention to what this youngling had to say.

We have found a new sanctuary with those I spoke of, when last I far spoke the council. You can gather all of the clan members and bring them here to this continent. And all will be welcome here, for it has been sworn to by my brother among the twolegs!

Does this twolegs command such power then, that he can protect all of the people? Tagon asked skeptically.

Not over the whole world, Elder. But among those who follow him his word is law. He has welcomed myself, Daleel, and Jamat into his clan, as they will attest, and has sworn a death oath to any who raise weapon or hand in harm to us! And further, he swore this oath to me and mine! He is astute and very honorable, and knew that he promised to protect all of my people. This one is very different from most of the twolegs we have known! Balor finished, proud of his relationship with Dirk.

Elder Tagon asked for, and received, a confirmation from Balors' siblings, and also asked for their impressions of this twolegs. Both Jamat and Daleel stated that they had looked into the mind of Balors' brother, and even though they could not go too deep, because of some kind of block they had not encountered before in the twolegs, what they had seen told them that this one could be trusted. And Balor chimed in with, *you asked, elder, if this one commands so much power? My brother, Dirk is how he is called, is a great warrior who is descended from those who first walked in the lands of this continent. He has called for war on the detested ones, and leaders of nation states, and their war leaders, generals they are called, come quickly at his call! Even the leader of the largest nation state on this continent has accepted my brothers leadership!* Balor stopped, knowing that his thoughts were beginning to run together.

And, to all of their consternation's, a strong masculine thought broke into the conversation. Balor, Jamat, and Daleel all tried to break the link at their end, and elder Tagon tried to let it go from his end as well. This was unheard of! No one had ever broken into one of the peoples' telepathic conversations before! But it was useless! The link remained intact as they all heard the vibrant masculine thoughts.

Elder Tagon, my brother gives me much credit, perhaps more than I deserve. Relief and alarm flooded through Balor in the second that it took him to realize that the interloper was his brother Dirk! The alarm was because he had had no idea that Dirk was such a strong telepath. He had known that he was strong, and different from most twolegs, but this strength amazed him!

Dirk sent again, *I don't know exactly where you are, or what your number is, but I have given my oath to my brother! Since you are directly, or indirectly, related to my brother I extend my oath to include you and all of yours! And so that you shall understand what My oath means I shall give it again. No man or woman under my control shall ever raise hand to, or harm any of your people, on pain of death from my hand! Of this all have been informed. You and yours' are welcome in our lairs!* These thoughts tolled formally into the minds of Tagon and the other elders. It was a declaration that left no shadows in the wake of its' passing.

There was a long pregnant silence in the telepathic link that Dirk was now holding open by the force of his will alone. And this was not lost on those others! Then came Tagons' thoughtful reply, *truly are you different from the few twolegs that we have let know of us.* Then Tagon, one of the strongest telepaths ever to develop among the people, sent a strong probe streaking back along the link that was being maintained by Dirk alone. It was stopped, and shattered, as if it had struck against cold mountain stone!

Tagon, Dirks' mental voice was now iron hard, and totally, coldly, uncompromising in his rebuke to the elder, yet eloquently simple, as he said *If you truly wanted to see that which is myself, you had but to ask to do so!*

Balor, Daleel, Jamat, and most of all Tagon, were shocked, for no one in known memory had ever resisted, let alone stopped, one of Tagons' mental probes!

Tagon, elder and leader of his people, the strongest telepath ever to have developed among his people here on this planet, now shocked and abashed, did something none could have thought of him doing. His words were, as he said them, contrite and formal, *I am shamed before he who offers me and mine the warmth and safety of his lair. I ask you then, as he who is responsible for his people, to see the truth of he who offers so much.*

Balor had been deep inside of Dirks' mind, by invitation, many times over the nearly two years since they had met, but this time he and the others were excluded as Dirk opened his mind to Tagon.

Balor understood the reason for this, for it was a ritual between two very strong leaders, and something that must be if there was to be total trust between two such strong wills. And, seconds or minutes, or perhaps even hours later, the three were fully back in the link! *I am humbled,* Said Tagon very quietly and respectfully, *and ask that you accept the allegiance of the people! We will come, and quickly!*

The three sitting just inside the tree line on top of that mountain in northern Canada were, for the moment, dumbfounded! Only once before in memory had the allegiance of the people ever been promised, and that was long before any who were now alive. That single previous time had been to the 'ancient ones'.

Getting his mind to think coherently again, after that last shock, Balor came back to the conversation in progress. He heard Dirk saying, very formally *honored One, I do not know why you feel humbled, for it is I who should now feel so, considering the trek you are about to undertake! But We can help!*

After a short thoughtful pause he continued, *I will send Daleel and Jamat, if they will leave Balor, with food and transportation! But I am afraid that they can only meet you at the halfway point. That is the best I can do for now.*

It is more than we expected, and therefore doubly appreciated! came Tagons fervent reply.

Then please make any further arrangements with Balor. Balors' little brother, Tate, will come with those two, for he is well aware of your uniqueness. There was the slightest pause, then Dirk went on, *I must go now, for I am tiring quickly because I am not used to holding onto a link like this one. Fare you and your people well Tagon!* and just as quickly as he had entered it he was gone from the link.

Again Balors' thoughts wandered, for his heart was pounding, but this time it was in pride for his brother Dirk. He had given the people, the Elonee, lair rights in his clan! And he did so from a position of strength that he leavened with compassion and respect! Balor felt closer to Dirk now than he ever had, and he knew without asking that Jamat and Daleel felt as he did. They knew that they would do virtually anything this human asked of them now.

But Balors' thoughts were abruptly snapped back to the present with Dirks sudden departure.

Tagon's Wisdom

The three of them scrambled to retain the link as it was suddenly deprived of the strength Dirk had been lending it by himself. Even Tagon had to act quickly to keep it open at his end. Fairly stammering, Balor asked, *Did I hear you correctly, Elder? You gave the oath of the people?*

Still somewhat daunted by what he had found in the humans mind, Tagon said very quietly in response, *listen well younglings, and remember what I tell you! We have been on this planet for nearly twenty eight thousand of its revolutions around its' sun. These humans call those revolutions years, and I have been alive for almost nine thousand of those. I have knowledge, that is passed only from eldest to elder, that bears upon my decision. There is that in this human, that you name brother and give clan status to, which is very close to that which was in the Ancient Ones!*

But! Balor started to interrupt.

Be quiet and listen! Tagon said fiercely! *Your brother, Dirk, knows that we are not from this planet! Has suspected it since his first meeting with you! This one is very attuned to his world. He also has very strong telepathic abilities, as you have witnessed! He is stronger even than he suspects. I say he has the attributes of the 'Ancient Ones' because he has accepted us as "People". He understands that we think, and try to maintain a society! He also understands that we are in trouble, and asking for nothing, has opened his lair and clan to us!* Tagon paused for seconds, thinking, wanting these bright younglings to understand completely his reasoning, *there is a war coming quickly! He knows this. He is also not sure that he can win it, but he will fight it anyway! I have looked into this one and found him to be honorable, and a keeper of his oaths.*

He paused again, looking into their minds. These were the future of the remnants of the people, the Elonee, on this world. And he approved of what he saw there. He continued very slowly and clearly now, for this was the crux of what he wanted them to know and understand about their time and this human.

He said clearly, *we are stuck here on this world for the foreseeable future and the war that is coming, is really already here, will engulf this entire planet. And we will have to fight it ourselves at some point. So I gave our trust and allegiance to one who might not only be able to win that war, but to one that will not squander or abuse that which was given!*

And, most importantly, I think that this is the one who will make it possible for us to go home! He finished, the weight of these thoughts plain for all to see.

Lessons and Alliances

Dirk felt that strange, almost tickling, feeling in that part of his mind where he recognized Balors' mind touch and thought that his four limbed friend might be trying to contact him. He opened a receptive channel in his mind, as he had been shown how to do, and Balor was there. But he was not there either!

Dirk could feel his distinct presence, but he was not trying to speak to Dirk. This had never happened before! Curious, Dirk pushed outward with his mind, trying to capture that elusive thread. He didn't think he was intruding because Balor would block him out if he didn't want Dirk there.

As Dirks mind reached outward, seeking the source of what had first caught his attention his mind suddenly came up against something that felt like a large energy bubble, round and smooth. It seemed to also have what appeared to be a slender filament leading off from it far into the etheric distance. Not knowing exactly how he was doing it he began to follow the filament, feeling as he did so that his mind was rushing at great speed along it.

Soon enough he saw that the filament ran into a much larger energy bubble. One that glowed and pulsed with what he could only describe as life force. Floating just outside that large glowing bubble Dirk carefully extended part of his mind to touch its' surface. As his mind gingerly touched that glowing orb he was completely taken by surprise as it parted for him, letting him see and hear what was inside of it!

What he saw inside that bubble surprised him even more! Inside was a scene that might have been the inside of a large cavern, with many small alcoves indenting its' walls. On a clean smooth floor in the center of the cavern sat several older versions of Balor and his siblings.

They were sitting in a semi circle, facing a much older version of Balor himself. This one, dirk could see, was concentrating very deeply. And Dirk could hear the words the old one was speaking as they formed in his mind.

He was saying, *does this two legs command such power then, Balor, that he can protect all of the people?* The ancient one, whose name Dirk could now see was Tagon, asked.

Now, eerily, Dirk heard the response that came from Balor, *not over the entire world, Elder. But among those who follow him his word is law. He has welcomed myself, Daleel, and Jamat into his clan and given us lair rights, as they will attest, and sworn a death oath against any who might raise a hand against or harm any of us. Further still, he swore this oath to me or mine!*

Dirk withdrew his mind from the energy sphere carefully, slowly, so that he left no indication of his presence, and swiftly followed the filament back to its' source. Once back at the smaller energy bubble he ever so gently pushed his mind into it, with the same results as with the larger one.

He saw, as he expected to, Balor, Daleel, and Jamat, sitting in a circle just inside of the tree line at the top of the mountain that held his own cavern complex and new base.

Again he withdrew silently. He needed to think about this, for during his excursions several things had become clear to him. The most important of which was that he was a much stronger telepath than he had thought it possible for him to be. Also, he was developing abilities he was completely unaware of possessing!

He hadn't really known how to penetrate what he now understood to be mental energy spheres, he only knew that what he was doing felt right to him.

He hadn't known that he could keep his presence from being detected either!

On impulse Dirk extended his mind again, reaching out with mental hands fashioned a very large energy sphere and engulfed Balors' within it. Then, as he had done once before, he opened Balors' globe, inserting his own presence within it also.

At the same time he reached out with his mind instinctively, reinforcing the filament that connected to the elders energy sphere. Once that was done he created another sphere to englobe that of the elders, and inserted a portion of his presence there also, so that now he controlled the whole connection.

Projecting his thoughts throughout the entire connection he said, *Elder Tagon, my brother gives me much credit, perhaps more than I deserve.*

There was immediate shock and apprehension, and an effort on both their parts to sever the connecting filament. This was all to no avail. Dirk was now firmly in control of the connection, maintaining it by main force alone.

The rest is part of the little known history of how Dirk forged the first, and strongest, alliance with an alien race during the beginning of the Earth—Drel wars!

CHAPTER TWENTY
Interludes

Downturns, Somalia

The three men and two women of team twelve were very good at what they did. They had to be, because they were mercenaries! They were not just fighters. No! They were more than that. They were a well trained team of intelligence operatives whose skills were highly prized and paid for.

When they had heard that one of the real pros in the business was looking for seasoned people they jumped at the chance, by contacting him immediately.

There was no haggling, they were hired on the spot. But when what they were up against was explained to them, and shown by photo, they almost balked.

They stayed because they had worked with Jimmy 'Bad Boy' Lester before, and he had never lied to them. Nor had he ever let things get to the point where they might have to be left 'out in the cold', a phrase that meant abandoned due to circumstances. So they stayed on.

Jimmy paid them very well indeed, with a fair sized up front lump sum advance. He told them he needed two things from them. After showing them how to recognize the enemy, he wanted, he said, head counts with names, and approximate sizes of areas under their control. The second thing he wanted was for them to make contacts from lists he would send, and for them to set up extraction routes for those on the lists who were successfully contacted.

Over the last ten months they had done very well by him, getting nearly eight hundred people out through the routes they had set up. Most of those were technicians of one sort or another, but there were also a good mix of business people, tradesmen, and soldiers in the mix. But on their last sortie something had gone very wrong!

Now, it seemed, the opposition had begun to hire local bandits to circumvent their operations. It was definitely time to get the hell outta dodge! However, when they tried to get out of the area of Baghdad, where they had been headquartering, they found their northern routes of escape were blocked. So they had begun making a run for it southward, thinking that East would be an unexpected move on their part. They were right. And wrong!

They had been caught in an ambush as they were crossing into Somalia. The initial contact killed the two women, and one of the men!

The last two fought their way clear of that one, but were caught in another ambush ten miles further on. They did not survive that one!

Turkey

The captain of the platoon of border security guards hit the man being held by two of those troopers another ringing blow to the head. That mans face and mouth were streaming blood and one eye was swollen shut, with the other one not far behind it!

"Where are the people you helped cross into Iran heading? If you answer your death will be a quick one!" the captain snarled, yanking the mans' head back by his long sweat dampened hair. "Who else was helping you?" the captain fairly yelled into the mans face.

The man groaned, barely conscious now. The captain slapped the man again, backhanded this time, completely closing the other eye. "Speak dog! My patience wears thin!" The man slumped, his weight now fully on the arms of the troopers holding him.

"Throw a bucket of water on him!" the captain snapped at one of the troopers standing nearby. Even the newest troopers in the unit noticed that the captain had changed. He had always been a hard man, but he had also been a fair one. He was now a cold stranger, even to those who had served with him for several years. And the change had come on him very quickly, from one week to the next.

The men had also heard stories of similar behavior about the colonel commanding their battalion, as well as about several other officers. Some of the men had heard some much stranger stories! What really scared many of them was that many of the men they had heard those stories from in the beginning were now missing.

There was a change coming over the battalion that was not good at all, and not a few of the men had already deserted. It wouldn't surprise most of these men if some of those men were among the group that had crossed the border just ahead of this platoon.

This man they were now holding had been a straggler, or a rear guard, and had been wounded and captured before he could get across the border.

The sergeant standing next to the man put his fingers to the mans throat, at the carotid artery, for a few seconds. When he took them away he looked at the captain and said simply, "Sir. This man cannot be revived. He is dead."

The captain looked at the prisoner coldly for a few seconds than said, "Throw him in the drainage ditch. We will continue our patrol."

Kazakhstan

The major commanding the three companies of security troops for this section of the border for this relatively new republic was not the same man that the three company commanders had known. He had changed drastically since his recent trip to the capitol. He was now very pale, and seemed to have the shakes when he was angry, as he was now.

He had been gone for a little over a week, and since his return everything was in turmoil. He had come back very short tempered, and quick to accuse. For many of the noncoms and officers who had stood with him during their country's bid for independence, and knew him well, he now seemed supercilious, as if he were looking down on them! Yes, he was now a very different man from the tough but even handed man they had known.

Speaking now to the assembled officers and noncoms his words seemed to be being spit at them, "I don't care how long you have to maintain your patrols, you will put a stop the traffic in smuggled people. By our governments estimates there are close to three or four hundred of them passing through and crossing our border every week. And the worst part of that is that at least half are deserting Russian military, wanted by the Russian government!" he stopped, spittle gathering at the corners of his mouth.

"You will put a stop to this traffic or you yourselves will pay a penalty!" he screeched. He stood there now, almost panting, as if it had been a fight to get those last words out. Then he fairly shouted now, "Get out there and do your jobs! Dismissed!"

The captain and the lieutenant standing directly in front of him saw something none of the others did.

As he had spoken those last words there had been a pained, almost panicked, look in the mans eyes, which he shut for a second when he noticed their looks.

What those good men could not know was that their previously well liked and known commander had become a 'Drel steed'!

They also could not know that he was a valiant man who was fighting a progressively losing battle to retain his own personality!

Smolensk, Russia

The man now coding the message into the high speed burst transmitter was very afraid. The fact that he felt this fear was important, because this man was not generally given over to fear of any kind.

A short time earlier he had barely escaped a trap being set up to snare him! It had only been chance that he had recognized the face of a man in the passing foot traffic as he was making his way to one of his regular drops.

This drop point would have a message from one of his best contacts, with information he wanted very much. But that face, so close to the drop point, meant that it had been compromised! He backtracked immediately, getting away from there as quickly as he could without drawing any attention to himself.

This also meant that his fifth, and last agent, had been compromised too, and that his safe house would probably no longer be safe for much longer either. He would complete this report, send the message, then destroy the transmitter and hide it. Once that was done he would check the area carefully, then leave for the one place he had left that he thought he would be secure enough for him to hole up in for a few days. Then he would make his way out of the country.

Finished with the coding he calibrated the transmitter for the frequency for today. Then he climbed up the ladder to the trap door leading to the roof. Pushing it open halfway he extended his hand with the very compact handheld transmitter just far enough out to clear any obstacles.

Satisfied now, he pressed the transmit key. There was a short, high pitched warble from the transmitter, then the green LED light on its' face lit up indicating the transmission had been completed. With a deep relieved sigh he pulled the radio transmitter back in and began to lower the trap door back into place.

He was still balancing on the ladder when there came a loud pounding on the apartment door, startling him almost to the point of falling.

At that same moment the roof heaved, and splinters of wood and shards of tin that had covered the trap door rocketed downward at him, lacerating his hands, neck, and face as the trap door blew inwards.

He was thrown to the floor with the violence of the blast, the hand that had held the radio was almost severed from his wrist!

He didn't even have time to think to himself 'OH SHIT!, as another grenade dropped through the now open roof to land beside him where he lay on the floor.

Reports

Jimmy 'Bad Boy' Lester was fast becoming a worried man, and that was a situation he didn't like in the least! He had been the one to call this meeting between himself, Dirk, Dimetri Chabov, yuri Garov, the Drs. Hull, and their newest acquisition, General Richard Potter. And he wasn't going to be giving them any good news either! He had been getting reports in from Russia, the Baltic's, and most of the northern portion of Africa, and the news was not good at all, in any of those locations!

The characteristics of the invasion, and the amount of the area now under nominal enemy control, was beginning to spread faster than had been anticipated by anyone on his staff.

The enemies strategy was a good one. First they had established a primary beachhead nexus in a sparsely populated area, then they had sent out units to establish mini beachhead nexus points. This was done in a manner that overlapped all previous ones, like tossing pebbles into a still pond. The ripples soon began to intersect each other as the whole expanded ever outward.

The only reason Dirk and company had caught on so quickly was due to the one Balor had caught and killed, and the warning TuLan had given Dirk a few short days prior to that incident. Oddly enough those two occurrences had happened nearly simultaneously. It was also true that if those incidents had not occurred the Earthmen would have had no warning at all!

Jimmy was now very nervous, and getting more so with every passing day, because he didn't like not knowing what was going on. In fact Jimmy's' report would tell that he had lost, or lost contact with, close to fifty percent of his operatives in the last six months.

The last one, one of his best contractors, had been in Smolensk Russia. He was now presumed compromised or dead, because Jimmy had not gotten the confirmation from his last communiqué. The confirmation was a simple method of confirming the operatives identity, and that all was well.

Jimmy was rearranging some of the reports, and checking the statistics he had derived from them, as the individuals he had summoned began to filter into the meeting room.

No! His report would not be bringing good news to those who needed to know in the resistance movement. Not good news at all!

CHAPTER TWENTY-ONE
The Calling

Tagon

Tagon the Elder, and nominal leader of the remaining Elonee here on Earth, was tired to his bones, and this incursion by the 'detested ones' had only added weight to that tiredness.

The number of Elonee on earth had been shrinking for the last few hundred revolutions of this planet about its' sun. The main reason for that attrition had been due to the twolegs, hunting them like animals!

This situation had only become serious since the twolegs had begun to become technologically advanced. The advent of the explosive black powder had initially caused many losses, but more insidious was the fall in the birth rate. Unfortunately that circumstance had been partially self inflicted, the result of fighting off the terrible possibilities that inbreeding might bring!

There had only been ten younglings brought forth in the last fifty estrus cycles, which only occurred annually for the Elonee. Even worse, there had only been two pregnancies in the last ten cycles, and those were recent. The Elonee had long gestation period, and carried their young to live birth over a two cycle period that was equivalent to two earth standard years, and giving birth in the twenty fifth month.

Lately the birthings seemed to be getting longer, and harder on the females, more often than not leaving them near cripples for the last quarter of the gestation period. And of late they had to be kept in the enclave to be watched and fed until they gave birth.

Tagon missed the energetic Balor! Missed his optimism, and daring willingness to venture into the areas closely held by the twolegs. The clan sorely needed his spirit to help stave off the slowly creeping feelings of moroseness that threatened to overtake them all.

Now! Now, Balor brought great hope to Tagon and the clan! He had been sent out to check on a mind call that had been heard during one of the telepathic sweeps the council of elders made of this solar system on a regular basis.

That call had been heard nearly a cycle and a half ago. It had been faint, and seemed to have come from the central part of the continental area that he liked to roam. The only reason the elders had heard that faint call was that they still, after all these millennia, sent their minds out seeking in the fading hope of finding some trace of the 'Ancient Ones' they had traveled the star paths with.

A half cycle after he had been asked to seek that calls source out he had sent a message to the council, promising startling and wondrous news. That message had been weak because he had not been in his own lair, and was unable to trance himself for a full sending. Perforce the message had needed to be boosted along by those roamers nearest to him. The Elonee were strong telepaths, and Balor one of their stronger ones, but distance was a factor that affected even the strongest, especially here on this planet.

Only after he had made the long trek to his far northern lair, and its' beneficial location that seemed to enhance his sending while in trance state did the council get some detail of that adventure.

Even then he had insisted that his siblings, Jamat and Daleel, be sent to join him so that they could make a joining so that they could send strongly, and also to see and verify what he had found.

Reluctantly Tagon had acceded to this request, for that was a long and dangerous journey for them to undertake. That journey had taken the two of them nearly three quarters of a cycle to complete. Then the call had come from the joined three, with news that there was a good chance for an ally among the humans. A twolegs who had sworn a death oath upon his own kind to any who would harm or kill any of the three or their kin. This had not been heard of since the time of those rulers to the east of the enclave who called themselves 'Pharaohs'.

Then the astounding had happened! A twolegs had broken into the mental forcefield the Elonee used to create channels for sending and receiving communications over long distances.

He was a tremendously powerful telepath, not even aware of his own strength, Tagon was sure. Tagon could feel a rightness about this one, a sense that he was much alike to the 'Ancient Ones'.

And, this one had done something that had not been heard of in more than fifty thousand cycles! He, like the 'Ancient Ones' the clan had traveled the star paths with, had offered the Elonee sanctuary and lair rights. More importantly he had claimed the Elonee as clan kin! As 'Brothers'! Yes! Now Tagon could again begin to feel hope for the future!

Hope for the future because this one, he was sure, would be the one to take the Elonee home!

Ingathering

As leader Tagon had made a decision, and a commitment that bound the clan, but he was also a diplomat. He courteously laid out for the rest of the council of elders what had transpired, what he surmised about this twolegs Dirk, and what courses of action he planned to implement. The council, to a being, agreed with him. Especially considering the rapidly expanding encroachment of the others, the 'detested ones'.

With that behind him he sent out a mental summons to all clan members within a weeks easy travel of the enclave. The urgency of the summons convinced all who heard it that something momentous had occurred, and they began heading for the enclave as quickly as it was safely possible to do.

With that done he next gathered the strongest of the younglings still at the enclave to himself and formed a large out sending circle, so he could reach out to those much further away. This would be a long and tedious task, so he bade the younglings to eat and perform whatever bodily functions were necessary beforehand.

Having taken care of these immediate tasks Tagon tried to relax for a space of time while he thought of the many other steps to be taken before such a momentous undertaking could begin in earnest.

First he must assign scouts to seek out the best routes for the clans' line of march. But they must also range far enough ahead to hunt and leave provisions for the clan as it followed on, for there would be no game if the clan tried to hunt as it moved as a group. Also, the route must be accessible for the older clan members, but far enough from prying eyes to not cause comment of its' passing.

Not in several hundred cycles had the clan moved in such great numbers at one time, there would be close to fourteen thousand in the main body at the beginning of this journey, and as quiet and elusive as the clan had leaned to be, such large numbers could cause unnecessary attention to be drawn to it from the twolegs.

The rest of the clan, spread out as they were, would gather in several smaller groups as their lines of march converged. Those groups would converge with still more groups along the lines of march until all met at a point he would give them that would bring all together at about three quarters of the total length of the journey.

Tagons' greatest fear was that the clan might be caught in the middle of the spring melt while crossing the great northern peninsula between continents. It would be a disaster for the clan if that were to happen. He knew that route, for he had crossed it twice as a youngling and nearly lost his life on the second crossing.

Of all the places on this planet that one was one of the most dangerous there were to be when the ice began to melt.

Another consideration was the route itself, which meant that most of the trail would be over snow covered terrain. This meant that as soon as the main group entered the upper reaches of their track they had to stop, and all must force the change that caused their fur to emulate the predominant color of their surroundings.

This ability was a survival mechanism that the Elonee had learned from the 'Ancient Ones'. It was a skill that only the elders still knew how to effect, and they would have to show the rest of the clan how to do it at that time. This would take several risings of the sun to accomplish under those conditions.

Yes, Tagon ruefully thought to himself that the elders had been, of late, remiss in their duties of passing on the knowledge of the clan to the younger members, ***there was still much knowledge that must be passed on once we are resettled!***

The younglings returned in twos and threes until there were a full dozen assembled. Tagon could see that they were nervous, for never in their memories had such a large number been assembled for a sending. Tagon sent out calming and comforting thoughts, along with instructions on what he wanted them to do, and how he wanted them to do it.

He showed some of them how to form and maintain a large mental energy bubble, others how to add their strength to his own as he sent out questing thought patterns, and the remaining few how to build and hold an energy reserve he could tap as he needed to.

The call went out! It ranged far and wide, touching minds spread out over much of the earth. Some of those minds were very surprised, some were startled, by this summoning. But all of the clan members heeded the call for the 'Ingathering'!

Many were given task to perform necessary to the coming trek. All obeyed!

Although the clan was rather loose knit in the manner of its' day to day living habits there was not the least bit of looseness in the way they all responded to their societal responsibilities. They all knew that that was the mainstay of their ability to survive here, or anywhere else for that matter!

CHAPTER TWENTY-TWO
The Trek

Visions in Passing

The old man had been hunting in these mountains and woods for slightly over sixty five years now and never, it seemed, had the game ever been so scarce as it was this season. It was as if something had scared it all away, or had killed so much of it off that there was very little of it left to find.

The old man, nearly eighty five years old now, and since the death of his father at the age of one hundred seven years of age, was the patriarch of a family that eked out a meager existence on several hard scrabble farms that existed several hundred feet below the tree line on this mountain range.

The last of the two frozen cows slaughtered early in the fall were gone, along with the three pigs slaughtered just after the first big snowfall of the winter.

The snow was now several feet deep, even below the tree line where it usually only got to be two, or three, feet at the most. It had been a hard winter, snowing almost every week, and it was already well past the normal start of the spring thaw.

Last month he had been very lucky. He had brought down two skinny upper range deer. That had helped tremendously, but there were twelve mouths to feed on the four poor farms, and the deer meat was near gone now! Hunger was a gnawing reminder of just how hard life could be here in the upper mountain farms, but they dared not kill the milk cows or the sows. To do so would mean the end of them all!

He had been up here on the mountain, just inside the upper tree line, for two days, and had bagged only two thin 'Coney' rabbits and a skinny white fox. That would only last a couple of days at most, even as a thin soup with the last of the turnips and a few dried onions.

Even the young ones had to be put on starvation rations. He had to get more game! He had to skin and eat the fox roasted over a meager fire last night just to keep his strength up, but even so he was so cold he could just barely feel his fingers.

He knew these mountains like few men could, and he was a good hunter. He was well concealed in a snow covered brush blind just inside the tree line, and had positioned himself at the deepest part of a huge u formed between the tree lines that outlined a mile wide saddle between two towering peaks, and had been scanning those trees to either side for any sign of game for several hours now.

Finished scanning the right side tree line, his eyes aching now from the strain of his searching and snow glare, swung to the left side tree line.

As his eyes passed over the bare center of the saddle between the peaks his attention was caught by what appeared to be a rippling movement of the fresh snow cover there.

He thought at first that his eyes were playing tricks on him, because no game would move so openly up here. Rubbing his eyes, he looked again.

Sure enough, the snow seemed to be rippling in a wave that was moving directly towards him. He had no idea what could cause the snow to act in this way!

Removing one thick mitten he slid trembling, near frozen, fingers inside his dirty white greatcoat and pulled out a pair of ancient brass bound binoculars. Putting them to his eyes his stiff fingers fumbled with the brass wheel between the barrels that adjusted the focus on the antiquated lenses.

As the center of the saddle came into focus a gasp he was unaware of making escaped from his throat! The gasp turned slowly into a low moan as he stared, unable to move now, at the sight of what was boiling up and over the saddle. And it was coming straight at him!

The old man, Boris Borisovitch kolinsky was his name, was not faint of heart. He was an ex-soldier of the Russian Army, who had survived the invasion of the German Army, and the madness that was the bloody siege of Stalingrad! But the sight before him had frozen his body to stone, as his mind brought forth the tales related down from his father, his grandfather, and his great grandfather! Tales that now, from the sight before, him left him barely able to breath!

Coming straight at him, leaping, bounding, and boiling through the new top snow in the center of the saddle, were what appeared to be hundreds of white and off white mountain lions! They moved with long loping strides, their powerful hindquarters driving them forward at incredible speed! They came at him like an unstoppable white wave that would roll right over him, and leave no trace whatsoever of his existence!

Yet, as that wave reached the trees and brush concealing him, it parted and flowed around him to either side, melting into the forest, as if they had never been there at all, and this had been a waking dream.

Several minutes passed, and nothing else happened. There was utter silence in the forest now. He could hear his breath rasping in and out of his throat raggedly, each breath sounding as loud as gunshots to his ears. Boris shuddered, virtually from the top of his fur trimmed hat to the tips of his heavy boots. Then he began to shake uncontrollably.

Slowly, after pushing himself up onto his hand and feet, he sank back onto his buttocks, his arms splayed out behind him to keep himself from falling over backwards completely. Finally he took in one, two, deep shuddering breaths, giving his old oxygen starved lungs new life!

Turning over onto his hands and knees, so he could push himself upright to a standing position, Boris suddenly froze to stone again, for he was now looking at two dirty white paws. And they were very large!

They were nearly a hands breadth across, with razor sharp claws that were agitatedly sliding in and out of their sheaths. Frozen in that position Boris dared not look up, yet at the same time he dared not, not look up either.

Still in his awkward position Boris forced himself to raise his head and eyes. There, not six inches from his nose was the muzzle of one of the creatures! It was one of the most terrifying moments of his long life. And the creature was one of the most beautiful things he had ever dreamt of ever seeing! The creatures muzzle was wide, and he could see that it had fangs that were meant for tearing meat from its' preys carcass. Oddly enough that muzzle seemed almost to be smiling at him.

Raising his eyes further Boris saw that the head was large and, unlike any mountain lion he had ever seen, round. It had long tapering ears, with fine hair like tendrils that seemed to wave and weave of their own accord, coming out of the tips. But most arresting were the eyes!

They were huge, yet fit perfectly with the creatures head, and they were orange. The color of orange that was a setting sun on a late August summers eve. The orange was flecked with gold, and they were all, iris and pupil, one color because the pupils were slitted so closely from snow glare. That gold flecked orange felt like fire in his minds eye.

And, those eyes glowed with what he could only describe as intelligent wisdom, the kind of wisdom that only came from a long life of hard lessons!

The color seemed to swirl in them, like gold in the smelting pot. Boris could not move. Would not have been able to move or look away if his life were to end at that moment!

Boris was completely mesmerized! His thoughts, those that seemed coherent, were chasing each other round and round the inside of his now spinning head.

Slowly, slowly the magnificent creature raised one of its' large paws, and gently placed it on Boris' shoulder.

Then Boris heard the words. Heard them inside of his head! Boris' mind began to quail, and gibber in fear! Surely he must be dead, for animals could not speak! Could they?

Then the gibbering and fear retreated, and a calmness cascaded across his mind, soothing his terror. Then he heard *be still old one! Do not fear. You shall not be harmed by the people.*

Boris now felt a calmness he had never known before. He felt almost as if he were floating just off the surface of the snow.

The creature turned its' head on a long sinuous neck, and Boris knew that it summoned another that was out of his line of sight.

The creature then turned back to him, its eyes glowing brightly, and he heard *Nor shall you recall our passing!*

When Boris woke some time later he found a small roebuck laying next to him, and for some reason, felt a longing for something important he could not remember.

Into the Wastes

Tagon, Elder of the Clan Of The Far Seekers, and its' leader, stood on a small rise that looked out over the nearly flat expanse of the beginning of the 'Northern Crossing'. That part of this world covered in snow and ice the twolegs called The Bearing Straits. A barely noticeable shudder passed across his shoulders as he gazed out over the seemingly endless snow and ice. Looking back over his shoulder he scanned the declivity where his people were digging sleeping alcoves in the sides of snow banks.

There were nearly eighteen thousand five hundred of the clan here now, their numbers bolstered by the last group of one hundred or so, to join up with the main group three days ago. That group, one of the smallest to converge with them was comprised of many who had been away from the enclave for several years.

So far the clan had been very fortunate, for until two days ago the hunting had been scarce but adequate. But now the group was so large that Tagon was having to send his hunters further and further afield to provide enough food for all. The one true advantage the Elonee had was that they were omnivorous. Though they preferred meat as a staple they could live on anything a human could. They had also been fortunate in that they had only lost two clan members on this forced march.

One of those lost was an elder from one of the groups that had joined the march in its first few weeks of travel. That one had been lost when jumping an eight foot chasm and landing on an unsuspected piece of loose rock, falling to his death. That had been on the path down out of the mountains three weeks ago.

The other one had been an inexperienced youngling. He had fallen into an old bear pit that had still been lined with sharpened stakes. Thankfully he had not suffered. He had died instantly when one of the stakes had gone through his heart.

The group had come a bit over eleven thousand miles in a little under five months, averaging somewhat over seventy three miles per day. The Elonee were superb runners, and when well fed could average a good eighty to ninety miles a day, with their ground eating lope, without pushing themselves too hard.

But Tagon had been pushing them very hard for the last five months, knowing that he raced both time, weather, and the punishment put on the oldest and youngest members of the clan. Their once well fed, and sleek bodies, were now starting to show the thinness of short rations and hard travel. It would get much worse, Tagon knew, on the push across the near barren ice floes.

Tagon tried not to let these worrisome thoughts bleed over into the instructions for distributing the food they had, as he also went about setting out guard patrols to thwart any of the very large bears that were native to this region. They were very formidable creatures, and could do great damage if not spotted early. He decided that the group would rest here for a couple of days, giving his hunters enough time to gather as much food as possible before attempting to cross this wasteland.

Three days later the news was a lot worse than he wanted to hear. The hunters had only been able to bring in eight dozen of the creatures called seals, and four huge ungainly creatures the twolegs called a walrus. They were so big that it had taken ten each of the clans' strongest to drag them close enough to eat. They had also caught five of the creatures called sea lions.

Even on starvation rations, and with all of the frozen meat that had been carried with the clan as it traveled, this would not be enough food to make the trip across the wastes, even with extra kills along the way. Also, the weather was taking a turn for the worse. It was beginning to snow. If the clan got caught out in the open on the ice floes during one of the blizzards normal to this time of year all of them might perish. The crossing was a long trip, fraught with perils, and the clan was tired from the long run to get here before the ice broke up.

Tagon was trying to decide whether to reach out to Balor when he felt the slight tingling in that part of his mind that he used to communicate with. Someone was trying to farspeak him! He gathered several of the younglings about him and set them to building an energy bubble. Then, opening his mind to its' fullest receptive capacity, Tagon sent it reaching out for that touch. Suddenly warmth spread over his mind as he felt Dirks' thoughts of welcome embrace him. ***Elder, I sensed your distress. How may I help the clan?***

Warmed beyond measure by this offer, but startled at the same time by the fact that this twolegs could sense his troubled thoughts, Tagon replied cautiously, *How did you know I was troubled, brother Dirk? But that aside, it is good to hear you.* He finished, not forgetting courtesy.

Dirks' reply was guilelessly simple and to the point, *I was doing as my brother Balor instructed. I was reaching out and seeking my remembrance of how your mind felt when last we spoke. When I found you I felt a sense of worry.*

Accepting this explanation, not wanting to seek other answers at this time, Tagon went on to state their predicament, *we are near the beginning of the place you call the Bearing Straits, at the eastern edge of the continental mass you call Russia. The hunting has not been as good as could be hoped for, and the weather has taken a turn for the worse, bringing much snow.* He went on thoughtfully, *Although we have gathered enough food to last us for a couple of weeks, if we stretch it, the crossing is extremely dangerous at this time of year.*

Now Tagon rushed to finish what had to be said. *I do not want to be caught out on the ice floes in the middle of one of the frequent blizzards common at this time of year! Nor do I want to be caught out there without enough food to make the crossing in a weakened state.* Tagon finished, His mind was now sending a picture of the clan trapped in the middle of the crossing, weak from hunger and unable to make the leaps from floe to floe should the ice begin to break up.

Dirks' answer was slow in coming. When it did it was a question, *I see, how many of the clan are gathered there with you now?*

Our number is near to nineteen thousand! Tagon stated proudly. Then, sensing Dirks surprise, he went on, *"And another fifty five hundred or so more that are on your continent, and nine thousand more on the one to the south of yours! There are also near to fifteen thousand more spread out on other parts of the world that will not be able to make this ingathering in time. Those that can make it are coming to meet us at the place you and Balor designated.* Then, at Dirks surprise he said with chagrin, *you seem surprised. Is our number to great for you to accommodate in your lairs?"* he finished with some small trepidation at that thought.

I am surprised! Dirk said thoughtfully, *But only because I thought there would be more of you!*

He paused, and Tagon could almost feel him thinking furiously, then he went on slowly *Tagon. Elder, please wait in the place you are for six days time. At the end of that time period I will have arranged for some help for you and the clan! I will contact you again at that time.*

Tagon was surprised at this request, wondering what this twolegs might be able to do from so far away for the clan. He chided himself silently for this kind of thinking, for he had had little congress with the twolegs for far too long to be judging this one by knowledge that was so out of date.

Tagons' response to dirks request was thoughtful and courteous, for he had pledged himself to the clan. And had he not pledged the clan to him also? *I will do as you ask, brother Dirk. In six days time my mind shall be looking for your questing. It should be easier for you to find me this time for we are becoming attuned to each other.*

He paused for just a second, then said warmly *Fare you well brother Dirk. Fare you well elder Tagon.* And the link was broken.

As Tagon informed the other elders of their change in plans he saw some relief in their minds, for none looked forward to the crossing. And the rest would be most welcome to many of them.

As he went about getting the clan settled in for the wait he wondered to himself what kind of help the clans new brother could provide, and how he might provide it.

Oh well, he thought to himself, *it will do no good to surmise, and there was still much to attend to!*

As he went about these tasks there was still the niggling feeling at the back of his mind that he could not completely shut out of his mind.

He had been alive for a long time, and there had been many twolegs who had tried to use the people for their own ends over those long years, and there had been precious few of the twolegs who had ever kept their oaths to the people.

Even with all he had learned of this twolegs, who was even now called brother by members of the clan, doubt still held on. As much as he wanted to believe that this one would be different, he could not erase that small itching doubt completely. But he would try, for the clan desperately needed this twolegs to be what he represented himself to be.

He would try because he himself wanted the twolegs to be what he represented himself to be!

A Promise Kept

The wind had come howling out of the north with a vengeance, and had been blowing for nearly five straight days now. The wind drove the snow that had come with it at an almost horizontal angle that made sight and movement nearly impossible!

Many of the younger clan members, and not a few of the elder ones, were angry with Tagon for bringing them here. The food was all but gone now, and it had been pure luck that the hunters had stumbled on a small herd of seals three days ago. Even then they had only been able to take several score of them before the rest had escaped. The only other food taken had been another two of those walrus', taken on their arrival here. Their food would be gone in another two days! The clan now would be in some serious trouble if its new twolegs brother could not send the help promised, and soon!

Tagon, like the rest of the clan, was well aware of the technological marvels these twolegs had achieved, but weather like this could quite possibly surpass anything that these marvels might be capable of handling.

He had heard the death calls many times from the minds of those who challenged the elements, like those that were beating at his people now.

Many of the clan were now becoming weak, especially the elder members, from loss of body heat, even grouped together as they were in the snow caves they had dug. The constant wind and the fifty degree temperature drop seemed to suck the heat out of even those normally warm chambers.

It was now early afternoon of the sixth day, as far as Tagon could determine it since he had spoken to the twolegs Dirk, and there had been no word from him since then. The snow had all but stopped, but the temperature had dropped another ten degrees. He was even more worried now because the three females in late gestation were becoming much to weak from body heat loss. If the temperature dropped much further and they lost their kittens it would be devastating to the clan and himself personally.

Even though the snow had stopped, the sky was still filled with clouds that shouted the portent of more snow to come. The daylight, such as it was, was already beginning to fade, and the bone aching cold of the coming night was beginning to reach its' icy fingers further into the sleeping chambers.

Tagon himself was beginning to succumb to the cold, but forced himself to rouse himself from the relative warmth of his chamber and go outside to make the rounds, checking on the others and seeing that the pregnant females and the very young, or old, got what was left of the remaining food. As he was moving from one shelter chamber to the next Dirks mental voice crashed into his tired mind! *Elder Tagon! Please form a sending circle and send out a homing signal that we can follow! We come!*

Tagon, flooded with relief now, expanded his awareness. He sent his mind out seeking that bright bubble that he would recognize as Dirks mind. As he found it he was surprised at its' closeness. He pushed out a thought towards that bubble *Right away Dirk! Where are you now?*

The answer was swift, strong. *From the strength of your sending we are very close I would guess. But I need a steady signal to home in on to find you.*

Sending an imperative call to several of the still strong younglings to meet him at the center of the encampment he moved in that direction himself with renewed vigor. He quickly set up the circle and began to broadcast a steady mental tone that would make it easy for someone to find its location.

About ten minutes later there came to his ears a muted buzzing sound that quickly became a loud roar as a huge aircraft raced directly over the encampment and the circle, and was quickly followed by nineteen more. The huge aircraft flew far out over the ice covered bay before it dropped one wing and began to turn back towards them, the others following closely.

As it finished its' turn blindingly bright lights came on along the wings and fuselage, lighting the area in front of it nearly as bright as a clear day. The big plane seemed to drop like a stone as it sped back over the ice towards them, dropping huge wheel carriages from its' belly and from under its' wings. It was followed by the others of its' kind as they emulated the maneuvers of the first one in line.

The monster plane touched the surface almost, it seemed, at the edge of the ice where it met the water, sending up high sprays of snow where the wheels plowed through it. The huge plane slowed rapidly for something of its size, but still it seemed to be coming towards them at breakneck speed, the others close on its' heels!

Then, its' massive bulk shuddering as the pilot applied reverse thrust to the engines, the plane slowed almost to a fast walk, then to a full stop not more than a hundred feet from the clans shelters. The engines roared for a moment, nearly deafening Tagon and the circle, then began to spool down to silence, the others pulling up in a line beside and behind it.

A portal in the side of the massive body of the first plane opened and light from the interior spilled out, outlining in silhouette the form of a tall twolegs. He jumped to the snow and ran about half the distance to the circle before stopping. Then Tagon felt the strong warm words in his mind, *Elder, I have brought fresh meat, and water, to ease the hunger of the clan.*

Tagon felt gladness and relief flood through him at these words, but did not miss the almost ritualistic manner in which they were spoken. Truly this twolegs was of a far different caliber than most of his kind. He responded, his words also couched in ritualistic cant, *you are well met, Dirk, brother to the clan of the far seekers.*

The man now came forward and stopped in front of Tagon and, kneeling to make their heights more equal, reaching out slowly placed his hand gently on his shoulder. It had been nearly five thousand revolutionary cycles since a twolegs had touched him, but Tagon felt only a strong sense of warmth and welcome from this one.

Into Tagons' mind came the calm cool thoughts of a being that felt nearly like one of the people. *Elder, please restrain the younger bucks, for my men must first unload and then unpack the supplies we brought before they can be eaten. Although they are familiar with Balor and his siblings I'm not sure how they will react to being confronted with so many of the clan at one time! They are still very new to understanding what goes on now!*

It will be as you ask, brother Dirk. Is there ought else that I need to know?

As soon as you have distributed the food and water, and all have eaten, you must make haste to get all of the clan loaded aboard the planes. This break in the weather will not last much longer, so we must take off again in three to four hours. Can this be done?

It will be as you say! The meat is most welcome, and will go far to raise both our spirits and our body temperatures! Tagon spoke with true warmth in his tone.

This is as Balor informed me. The clan will be warm shortly as the interior of the cargo holds are heated. But know this! It is a long trip back to the new refuge, so please ask that the clan take care of any necessary bodily functions before boarding for it will be close and crowded inside.

Dirk paused, a large smile breaking across his face, and his mind, as he said the next words, *you and the rest of the clan will be in your new home soon, and, I would like to welcome you, and the clan, as members of my own clan!*

With that the big man dropped his hand from the old, but still big and beautiful cat things shoulder. The man did not get to his feet right away though. He strayed kneeling in front of Tagon, staring into his beautiful eyes. After a moment he nodded slowly, as if doing so to both Tagon and to himself. Then he rose, and turning, began to shout orders to those still in the planes.

Three and a half hours later the engines were roaring, as if the monster planes chaffed to be gone into the air, as the pilots stood on the brakes to hold them back, building the power needed to lift their huge bulks into the air. Then, after the brakes were released, the planes shuddered along their entire lengths and began to roll forward slowly.

Then they began to move forward faster and faster until the wings bit deeply into the air to lift them slowly but majestically into their true element. they lifted themselves higher and higher into the air until they were lost in the new snow that had begun to fall again on the now empty encampment of the clan.

A New Life

The elders of the Clan of the Far Seekers was well pleased with the description of their new home and enclave! It was in truth, they were told, twenty times as large as the one they had left. It would also have, to the clans' delight, several hundred small to medium sized galleries within and just off the main cavern section that had been set aside for them as their new home. Dirk told this to Tagon as they waited for the clan members to load aboard the planes.

The flight off the ice floes, and back to the main base would be a very interesting event for both the clan and the human crew. Dirk would remain in mental contact with Tagon for most of the flight back because most of the clan had never been in, let alone flown in, an airplane before.

When it came time for the clan to board the monstrous aircraft Tagon had had to invoke council authority on some few of the clan members to make them enter the aircraft. Most, as they cautiously entered, sniffed at the oil and metal smell of the craft with distaste, but enter they all did! In the end they were packed in like sardines in a can, so many of them that there was no need to turn the heat up higher than it already was!

Many, Dirk could see, were sorely afraid of these huge machines, but they stoically held their fear in check. When the engines coughed to life, one by one, he saw a startled ripple run through every last one of them! Then, as the behemoths taxied around for liftoff, and the engines began to roar with purpose as they strove to lift themselves into the blowing snow they huddled down close to each other with the fear of not knowing what was to come next spilling over mentally. At that point Dirk did something completely unprecedented in the clans history!

From his already established contact with Tagon he reached out, working instinctively with his mind, and encompassed all of the clan aboard the planes. He sent calming thoughts to all, telling them to sleep if they could, for the flight to their new home would only take a few hours, instead of the two months it would have taken had they crossed the ice on foot!

There was much surprise at this,, even some cautious delight that this twolegs could speak to them directly. The elders of the clan were the cautious ones, understanding of the impact of what had just happened not lost on them. They knew how rare it was for a twolegs to speak directly to the Elonee mind to mind, a thing that had happened only rarely during their long tenure here on this planet. And the power of this one was something extraordinary, only hinted at in the tales of their great forebears about the 'Ancient Ones'. Keeping their own council, they thought that this was something that needed much thought!

Because of the stress imposed by this plunge into the unknown two of the three pregnant dams went into early labor. Tagon informed him, after being asked, that birthing for the Elonee was something that was normally a long and hard process. He also let it slip, without being aware of it, that too many of the birthings of late had ended up as stillbirths, something that was very painful for the whole clan because they were telepaths.

Dirk, after telling Tagon to slow the labor as much as possible, went forward to the pilots cabin and radioed ahead to have several top flight veterinarians on hand at the airfield when the planes landed, to assist however possible. This caused a bit of consternation at the base, but he was assured that all would be ready when he landed.

Dirk came back and informed Tagon that the best medical help available would be waiting for them when they arrived, and again asked him to do everything possible to delay the births. The rest of the flight was basically smooth, even a little boring, and the clan members settled down, some of them even managing periods of fitful sleep in the very cramped quarters.

The huge aircraft came lumbering in out of the night sky, dropping it seemed, like a big ungainly rocks. That impression however was very deceptive because the planes touched down on the runway as lightly as a dropped feather, for the pilots had been informed of the events about to take place in the cargo bay.

Dirk was informed that four of the huge hangers had been prepared as temporary quarters for his cargo, and that the vets had set up a field hospital in one corner of the first one. As soon as the big rear doors of the planes were open wide enough the Elonee began streaming out and off. Dirk felt the familiar touch of Balors' mind, and knew that the exiting Elonee would be guided into the hangers quickly.

Using a hand held radio Dirk called for men, and two stretchers, to carry the dams to the field hospital, as their labor was becoming quite active again. The men and stretchers came quickly, and the two were coaxed by Tagon to let themselves be carried inside. Dirk was asked to accompany them as he seemed to be the only one who seemed to know what was going on.

With the help of the vets the first kitten was brought forth quickly, and because of that help almost painlessly for the dam! It was not to be that easy for the other dam though. That dam was older, and the hard trek had had caused severe complications!

That kitten, a beautiful deep black in color, had presented itself in the breach position. After the vets had gotten it turned around they could see that the umbilical cord was wrapped tightly around its' tiny neck! When they had it removed from the dam, and had suctioned the mucous from its' little throat, they placed it by the dam. But there was no response from the tiny thing.

When the first kitten had come forth and started to breath on its own a low deep throated purring sound had ensued.

Now though there began a low half growl, half plaintive mewling. It came from those throats with a true sense of loss and sorrow that the humans present could not interpret for anything else. It began to grow in volume!

Trying to ignore the sound, the vets worked feverishly over the still form of the tiny creature. Dirk watched sadly, understanding completely without knowing how he did so, feeling to the marrow of his bones that great sense of loss from the clan.

The vets were slowing their efforts, shaking their heads negatively when Dirk whispered fiercely "Keep going, there's a spark of life there!" Stunned, the vets looked at him, then turned back, renewing their efforts even more feverishly than before on the tiny being! They, like almost all who came in contact with these beautiful creatures, were very taken with them.

They would not give up the fight for this tiny life while there was the remotest hope for its survival! These doctors had seen much in their time, but oddly enough they believed this man with the fierce eyes! They didn't know why, but they did.

Without knowing when it had happened the hanger was now so quiet that a butterfly in flight would have been making a racket!

Suddenly there was a small cough! Then a ragged first tiny breath that could be heard in that absolute silence.

Then, to all of those waiting with breath that seemed to have been pent up in constricted throats forever, there came a tiny mewling cry! There was a tumultuous mental and physical release of breath, and hope realized, as that cry cane again, stronger this time!

There were nearly fifty of Tony Ebbets' security men in the big hanger distributing meat and warmed water to the exhausted clan members when Dirk came out from the curtained off medical area with two men carrying the very tired dam on her stretcher.

As tired as she was the dams' attention was all for Dirk, her large bright eyes shining with approval as he held up the tiny kitten in his cupped hands for the clan to see. And amazingly the kitten too, eyes still glued shut, had its' head turned on its' wobbly neck towards him.

Dirk stopped in the middle of the big hanger, and turned in a complete circle very slowly so that every member of the clan might see its' newest member, as he gazed down at the tiny kitten in his cupped hands with a fond smile. Balor appeared as if by magic to sit beside him, pride and joy warring for supremacy in his glowing golden eyes.

Then occurred a scene that no one present would forget for the rest of their lives.

As Dirk stood there with the tiny kitten cupped gently in his hands, the clan began to move in their silent manner. They came, surrounding him, yet still leaving a small space around him and Balor. They moved in as close as it was possible to each other for so many of them, while still maintaining that small space.

Then every single one of them lay down facing him.

Then it began! To the last being, every single one of them began to purr in that deep throated manner they had. The sound began as a low throbbing rumble, deep in their throats and chests. Then it grew, and grew more and more in volume. The sound of their purring grew until nothing else existed but that sound!

He was being told that he was one of their own! Told that wherever there were Elonee he would never again be alone!

He was being welcomed home to the clan of the far seekers!

Home

Tagon was pleased with, but still a little leery of, this arrangement for the new enclave for his people. There were more twolegs living within this huge cavern complex than had been living within the entire region of the old enclave. And this complex of cavern was truly gigantic!

There were seven caverns in the complex that were at least three miles in overall length, and two that were a mile or more wide. Two had ceiling heights in excess of two hundred fifty feet. The only reason these caverns were not famous was that they had just recently been discovered by members of the property owners family.

The reason Tagon was so pleased was that the cavern that had been set aside for the Elonee was twenty times as large as the one they had left behind at the old enclave. It was easily a mile and a half long, and their cavern was the smallest of the seven under these mountains. The roof of their cavern was about a hundred fifty feet high at its' highest and both sides were lined with hundreds of alcoves and small galleries leading off from the main cavern. Yes, the clan would do well here!

Twolegs or not, the one called Dirk was now considered a member of the clan, and he walked among its' members freely. His unsuspected telepathic abilities made him that much more acceptable and welcome among the people of the clan.

His abilities, Tagon mused to himself, far outstripped what most of the clan were capable of, and that left Tagon wondering just how much more they might develop, because he could feel the strength growing in him every time they made contact. But much more importantly, the clan owed Dirk a great debt of gratitude, for he had given them back a life that had been presumed lost. Even Tagon, strongest telepath among the people, had not been able to detect that tiny spark of life still glowing! That would not, could not, be forgotten! Even with his own reservations, Tagon was now ready to agree with Balor that this Dirk was very different from those known before by the clan.

Through the ages those who had found out that they could speak to the Elonee had eventually ended up trying to use that knowledge to gain personal power over their own kind. Usually to the detriment of the Elonee! No, this twolegs was very different. He had gone to great lengths to keep a promise made to those he hardly knew, and though he hardly knew them he also accepted them as a people! And he had given the clan back a life it could ill afford to lose! Too, Tagon had glimpsed parts of this ones mind, finding much there that was very similar to himself.

It was hard for a being that had seen as many years as Tagon had to let go of so much ill he had seen in these people, but this one was giving him back hope that they were better than they seemed. He sincerely wanted them to be!

The clan, after he had sensed life in the stillborn kitten when no other had, had paid homage to him. They honored him as no other twolegs in the memory of the clan had ever been honored. They had surrounded him, claiming him as one of their own, making him a member of the clan at that very moment.

Dirk had just done something else that had endeared him to the elders and the females of the clan. He had delivered to the entrance of the cavern hundreds of wonderfully warm sleeping mats the twolegs called wool blankets, enough for every member to have one. They really weren't necessary, as the Elonee had fur coats that kept them warm or cool as needed, but they did make sleeping a lot more comfortable.

There had also been the gift of fifty or so frozen carcasses of one of the domesticated food animals the twolegs ate. This gift had also been very welcome even though the people preferred their meat fresh killed. They did not require large mounts of meat, as their bodies converted what they consumed very efficiently, thus they seldom depleted an area of game.

Yes, this would be a very good new home for the Elonee. There was also an unexpected benefit here as well! It seemed that this was one of those rare spots on this planet that enhanced telepathic abilities. Just the other day Tagon reached out with his mind seeking one of the groups still enroute, making its' way north to the new enclave from the continent to the south of this one, and had reached them without the need of a sending circle.

Tagons' worry about how the Elonee would be accepted by those of Dirks' clan had been, for the most part, out of proportion to the idea of the possible problem itself. For the most part those who had had contact with the people were more curious than anything else. After finding that the Elonee were friendly to them if they did not move to fast at first, they seemed to accept their presence without many questions.

Many of the more timid ones actually had to be coaxed by the clan members to come close, those clan members having to act like kittens to get them to come close enough to make contact. But all in all they were fast becoming an accepted part of the scenery around the base.

Dirk had asked only one thing in return for all that had been provided to the clan. That the clan help patrol the area surrounding the base and provide warning against the others, the detested ones, should they come looking around. This was very little indeed to ask for so much that had been received.

What had truly shocked Tagon was what the twolegs were doing in these caverns. What he would never have guessed them capable of doing at this point in their development. They were building space ships! Ships capable of reaching the stars!

The one thing Tagon dared not let himself think about was the possibility of starfaring again, even though Balor assured him that they would go with Dirk. He must not think of this, for there was far too much knowledge in his mind that might be discovered. About the Elonee, and about the 'Ancient Ones'!

CHAPTER TWENTY-THREE
The Ships

First Ship, The Shrike

The little ship was little only by galactic standards! She was four hundred twenty five feet in length from her sleek prow to her blunt, powerful, stern. This was nearly half the length of one of the larger ocean going aircraft carriers of earth. She was nearly flat on her bottom side, one hundred ten feet from side to side at her widest point, and almost eighty feet high on her landing skids. Still she was a lightweight, weighing in at only one hundred seventy tons. So they classified her as a light cruiser.

She was beautiful in a morbid sense of the word, for she had clearly been designed as a war ship! She was a hunter/killer, and a bringer of death and destruction to those who dared to attack her. The humans who had designed her had had only one thought in mind when they built her. She must have the ability to engage an enemy, and survive that engagement while her enemy, hopefully, did not!

The little ship had a name. Though any name would generally do, a great deal of thought had gone into choosing one for her. The people who had built her were still young enough as a race to retain some superstitions, and believed that a name went a long way in instilling pride in those serving aboard her, as well as making a statement of the ships intended purpose.

She was called the 'Shrike', and like her namesake she was designed to swoop in on an enemy and inflict great damage to its' prey. Then fly quickly out of harms way, only to return and strike again!

She was truly a bird of prey! Her lines were sleek and clean, indicating great speed, which she had plenty of. Her engines were big and powerful, capable of driving her at speeds of up to twenty five hundred miles per hour in earth normal atmosphere. In normal deep space those engines could build up her speed to ten light days per hour of constant thrust, and at maximum, to two hundred ten light days per constant thrust hour in hyperspace. These speed potentials had only two purposes. The ability to run away from an overwhelming enemy force very, very fast. Or to attack in the same manner.

These speeds, Dirk was told, were only possible due to the newly designed inertial gravity dampers. They were something only the Drs. Hull and a very few others truly understood well at all. Suffice it to say that they worked well in principle! It would soon be time to put those principles to the test.

This bird was also armed to the teeth! Besides the two much larger versions of TuLans' plasma pulse rifles that were mounted in tandem below the nose, and just forward of the main battle bridge, she had several weapons of purely earth design.

Those included four turret mounted twin twenty millimeter cannons whose shells had been modified for deep space firing. There were two mounted topside just behind the bridge hump and one topside at her midsection, with another one on her downside at the midsection.

She also had three turret mounted single thirty seven millimeter cannons mounted, one on each of her bridge wings, and one downside on her centerline, just forward of the engine exhaust faring. This aft gun was mainly to discourage pursuit.

She also carried a very nasty surprise for any potential enemy ship much larger than she was that she could not get away from. She had, concealed behind retractable doors just below the nose of the ship, two auto loading, auto firing rail guns that were powered by a byproduct that was in abundant supply.

That source was the steam from the nuclear power reactor that supplied the ships independent internal power. The steam could be bled off the reactors cooling system to power these weapons that were purely of earth design. They fired ten pound depleted uranium slugs that were like mini asteroids that had been aimed at something. They were so small that they could be upon their target virtually before it knew it was a target! And they were also almost undetectable when loading and firing because there were no electronic power source buildups prior to firing such as there was with the plasma rifles.

And, last but not least, she carried eight modified patriot missiles in two four unit firing racks. One facing forward, and one to the rear for easier targeting. These missiles were programmable, and had target acquisition mass detectors built into their targeting systems. There was only one problem left to be solved. She had to fly as well as she was armed!

But when all was said and done, the improbable had been accomplished. Dirk and his people had designed and built the little ship called the 'Shrike' in slightly less than two years, and with less people than it normally took to launch the space shuttle 'Columbia' for its' orbital flights! If you had asked this group of people two years ago if this ship could be built in that amount of time they would have laughed quietly and walked away shaking their heads sadly at your naivete. But then they wouldn't have had the same incentive to do so either!

That was before they learned that they were about to lose their planet and way of life to an invading alien race. Before they knew that they would have some help from another alien race that had agreed to ally itself with these humans. But these humans also had a very apt saying for this type of situation! 'That was then. This is now!'

There was just too much to say about the innovations, and sometimes pure brilliance, that had made this ship a reality. It could only be said now, that it was, and it is!

It was now ready for its' maiden voyage!

Star Light, Star Bright

The little ship sat on its' landing skids, backed into a man made recess that had been cut into the side of the mountain, and was all but invisible there. It gave anyone looking at it the feeling that it was indeed a great bird of prey. It was! And it was waiting to stretch its' invisible wings, to leap into the sky, and fly away.

Its' seeming invisibility came from the final coating of the carbon and glass fiber fusion coating that had been applied just before it had left the assembly and testing center in the main cavern. This coating reflected no light, seemed to absorb it almost! And it reflected no electronic or laser or other reflective guided signals directed at it. It had also been equipped with an earth made version of the Chai cloaking device, but was not using it at the moment.

The little ship was waiting to take off on her maiden test flight and also her first voyage. She wouldn't have to wait much longer. Everything that could be tested on the ground had been tested, and retested.

She was now as ready to go as her builders could make her. She needed to perform successfully on her first flight because she was needed very badly by the people who had made her. Her sister ships were sitting in pieces in the assembly cavern waiting to be made into likeness' of her based on how well she did on this trial.

Her sister ships were also needed very badly. The planet of those who had made her was under attack, and their makers were not sure they could hold that enemy back for much longer. She and her sisters were needed to help her makers flee to some point of safety so that they could regroup and continue to fight on.

She was ready! You could see it in every line of her, as if she strained to be free of this place and fly!

Now there were several sets of shielded lights coming towards her from the direction of the main entrance to the cavern complex hidden below these mountains. Her crew was coming! Within minutes several military type 'Hummers' and canvas covered troop transport trucks pulled up in line beside her, as several figures in black fatigue uniforms detached themselves from the vehicles and ran to a personnel lift platform that was waiting near the base of one of the landing struts.

They climbed on and were quickly lifted into the belly of the ship. A few minutes later two cargo bay doors dropped open in the aft section of the belly and two huge cargo lifts lowered themselves to ground level. The waiting vehicles quickly drove onto them and they were whisked into the belly of the ship.

Just as the lifts returned to ground level several more 'Hummers' and covered trucks pulled up. They too were quickly whisked away into the ship. The big cargo doors whined closed, and all was dark and quiet again.

The silence after this spate of noise and activity was almost deafening, yet there was now a palpable sense of waiting. The wait was not long, as the silence was replaced with high pitched whining. But that too died down quickly to an almost inaudible humming. Then it began! The little ship seemed to tremble all over. There was a sense of it straining at the invisible bonds of gravity holding her to the earth.

Creaks and groans began to be heard as if some great weight were being eased from the earth where the ship sat, and the stress were being relieved from metal that had been compressed by great weight was lifted from it.

The sense of straining increased, then slowly, majestically, the little ship broke free from its' bonds and began to lift itself from the earth.

With ever increasing speed she rose higher and higher into the dark night sky. She was reaching for those bright lights in the dark sky that were the stars. She was going into her true element!

High, high up in the dark night sky two bright pinpoints of light suddenly appeared close together, then flared into brilliant life as the twin ion fusion engines were bought on line. That brilliant flare died away quickly and the twin points of light became steady pulsating glows.

Then the ship was gone, as if it had never existed. Gone into the darkness. Into the void.

The not so little ship was spreading her invisible wings in her true element. She was flying!

Flight, The Beginning

The operations bridge of the Shrike was a marvel of engineering, and rough beauty! It was laid out in three tiered ovals, with the arc of the ovals towards the rear. Centered in the forward bulkhead was a mammoth LCD display screen twelve feet high and twenty feet wide. That screen itself was composed of twelve individual screens, each four feet high and five feet wide. These were networked together to be able to give one panoramic display or several individual displays as needed.

To either side were two additional screens set at fifteen degree angles to the forward bulkhead. The big center screen gave a forward view to one hundred degrees, or fifty degrees to either side of the ships forward centerline. The side screens were divided in the middle lengthwise, the top half giving a side view of one hundred ten degrees to either side for a full one hundred sixty degrees of view from the forward centerline. The bottom screens gave an eighty degree view to either side of centerline, or one hundred sixty degrees down view. The big center screen could also be split to show a one hundred twenty degree rear view from centerline, or sixty degrees from center to either side.

The lowest tier had fifteen work stations that controlled internal power management, ships maintenance, and damage control. The second tier also had fifteen work stations. These controlled long and short range detection scanning sensors, electronic countermeasures, communications, and weapons fire control. The highest tier was the command and control center, with ten work stations and the captains control chair dais. It was from here that the ship was really flown and fought.

The captain for this shakedown flight was also the man who had designed most of the ship and her operational capacities. His name was 'Blackjack' Jones. Jones was a former astronaut who had never gotten the chance to make it into space. If they could only see him now, he thought too himself, they would all be green with envy!

Jones had graduated in the top five percent of his class at MIT, and held both doctorates and masters degrees in aeronautical space ship engineering, and a masters in physics. After the last big shuttle accident had nearly shut down the space program in the late nineties he had retired from the NASA space program and started his own business. His firm did conceptual design and special applications testing, mostly for NASA and other companies and countries that needed his expertise.

When approached by Dirks' group he had been very leery, only acceding to take time from his busy schedule because he knew, or knew of, who some of these people were who had come to see him. The letter from the president hadn't hurt matters either. Once he had been taken to see the ship in the box canyon he had practically badgered them into letting him take the project on, making only one demand in return for his services. That he be allowed to do the shake down flights for whatever he designed and built!

The deal was not all one sided by a long shot, for he gained much knowledge and understanding of principles and systems far in advance of anything NASA or any of the other space going entities had. It could now be said that he was the leading authority on spacecraft on earth!

He was, perhaps, the single driving force in designing and building this ship, and the seven waiting to be assembled, for the fledgling ERMA forces. He drove everyone very hard but drove himself hardest of all, often working twenty hour days. He, and those under him, had built earth's first deep space going ship capable of faster than light speeds, and they had done it in a little less than two years where it would have taken ten under normal circumstances. Blackjack Jones was now a legend, and—living his dream!

In a little over three hours the ship was out past the orbit of Mars, something that three years ago would have been thought of as highly improbable, and the engines were performing at a perfectly pitched muted roar. They had been cruising since leaving the 'L point' just off earth at a leisurely one quarter throttle. The ship was doing everything he asked of her, and before this was over he would be asking a lot more from her.

"Bring her to one third throttle, Mr. Blain, and Maintain your course at zero degrees galactic north please." Jones said to his second in command.

"Very good Sir." And, "Force shields are at fifty percent and show no anomalies, Sir." Mr. Blain replied smartly.

"Very good, Mr. Blain. We'll take her out past Uranus, about ten PDs (planetary diameters)I think, then you can bring her to a course of two two six point one by one niner three point nine two degrees galactic relative north, towards Bernard's Star, and open her up to three quarters throttle for two hours twenty minutes to get some distance between us and earth."

Now that he knew his bird could at least get off of earth Jones smiled in both relief and pleasure. He said in afterthought, "Oh! And please make sure the Nav.-Con. Recorder is on at all times! Wouldn't want to lose our bearings out here would we Mr. Blain?"

"Aye, Aye Sir. No Sir!" said Mr. Blain, bending over his console to enter his captains instructions into the bridge computer log.

"All right people!" the captain said some time later, raising his voice over the hum of conversation and computer keys being tapped, "The jump coordinates have been set and the jump generator has been primed and is ready! Take your stations and strap in."

Then, pressing the ship wide intercom button, he said, "All hands, this is the captain speaking, attention to orders! Batten down for Jump. I repeat, batten down for jump! Jump will commence in two minutes. I repeat, jump will commence in two minutes from my mark."

Still with the intercom key open, he looked over at his first officer and said, "All right Mr. Blain, on my mark begin your countdown. Mark!"

Mr. Blain depressed the key that started the digital counter that showed the countdown on one corner of the big screen, and gave an audio count to the rest of the ship.

The digital counter came down to zero. There came a high pitched whine that quickly went to a low throbbing hum as the jump sequence vortex generator kicked in. The hum increased to a low growl as full power was fed to the generator. This quickly died to a sub audible whine that couldn't be heard, but was felt like a low charge static electricity discharge over any exposed skin.

A couple of thousand miles in front of the ship an area of space seemed to be distorting, turning blacker than the space around it, and rippling like the skin of some gigantic amoebae that had been irritated.

Suddenly there was a loud 'Wham', and everyone was thrown back against their seat cushions as the main drive engines went to full power. It pressed them back harder and harder, then there was a moment of utter darkness and disorientation!

When the main engines went to full power the small ship sped like an arrow released from some gods bow, straight at that distortion of space in front of it. The only thing fully aware at that moment were the computers regulating the vortex generators, the main drive engines, and the duration run time counters. It was as if all animate life aboard was frozen into one blink of time.

Within minutes of kicking in the vortex generators shut down with a loud bang. The little ship was once again surrounded by normal space in a star filled galaxy. It was speeding towards a bright yellow red sun, with one planet and two planetoid sized bodies orbiting around it.

With a loud thump doors in the front of the engine nacelles opened, and the drive engines whined loudly as they spooled down, only to whine loudly again as they went into reverse, slowing the small ship rapidly.

She came to a near stop, then coasted ahead sedately at a mere crawl by cosmic standards. Her crew, now completely aware, were madly going over their instruments, making sure all was as it should be.

"Verify our coordinates Mr. Blain. And stand the bridge crew to. All sensor personnel to their stations and scan out to five Pds, if you please Mr. Blain. And

Mr. Blain, weapons to ready standby just on the off chance!" the captain issued his orders coolly as his eyes looked on with approval at the seemingly chaotic, but very controlled, actions of his crew.

On the big screen was something no living human on earth had ever seen before up close. Another planet swinging sedately around its' sun in another solar system. Man was now truly spaceborn.

There was a supernumerary crew of eleven aboard the Shrike for this trip, and they had all spent the trip in the auxiliary bridge compartment three decks below the main bridge control room.

That complement consisted of Dirk, Jimmy Lester, the Drs. Hull, G. 'Whiz' Burke, Felix Ortiz, Bill Tate, and General Carl Miles. There were also three others there. Three of the Elonee. Balor, Tagon the elder, and the kitten named Blade, who was now a foot high at the shoulder. The reason Blade was there was that he was seldom if ever seen far from Dirks' or Balors' side. Dirk called him nuisance most of the time, but very fondly.

Most of the others had tried to argue Dirk out of coming on this first flight, saying that if he were lost the whole resistance movement might collapse. He poo-pooed that, calling it nonsense. The truth was that he could no more stop himself from coming on this historic flight than any of the others could.

Dirk picked up the intercom handset and said into it, "Blackjack?" And after an affirmative answer said, "Let's just take a quick look around, then, now that we know it works the way you designed it, punch in that set of coordinates I gave you before we left. OK?"

Putting the handset back he turned and said to the others, "As soon as we take a quick look see we're going to jump to the planetary system that we plan to set up our first off planet base on!" The others just sat where they were and looked at him for a moment, stunned! They hadn't any idea of what Dirk had planned. Then happy smiles broke out on all of their faces as the knowledge that they would not be immediately returning to earth sank in.

Dirk coughed, and held up his hand for their attention, and the group fell silent quickly. "We are going there because all of the Intel we are getting, and my gut instinct, says that we may not have much more time before we see open fighting. And it won't be just in Africa and Europe either. I'm afraid we'll see a fair amount right in our own backyard!

He paused for a few seconds, ordering his thoughts, "Sam McCarthy said he didn't feel it was wise to hold off informing Congress, indirectly, about the invasion much longer."

"He also said that he needed to get some open resistance moving so that he could divert as much money and material, as many men, and much equipment, to us as he could before he announced his forced retirement."

Another short pause, then "I know that some of you think we should have said something sooner to the proper authorities, but you all, in the end, agreed with the course we took!"

"Let me tell you that we did try, carefully, to drop the right hints for them to follow. They didn't, and went on in their normal fashion, and would have played their political games right up to the point where it would have been too late to get done what we have. We made the right decision!"

"Anyway, we both believe that the end result will be that we will be pushed off of earth. Don't get me wrong! We'll fight like madmen to hold it, but the real problem is that we'll end up fighting against a lot of people we might have known and liked, or loved!"

"We may well have to in the end, when we come back, anyway! It's going to be very hard, and bad, anyway we do it! So, we decided that if the ship worked as well as we hoped it would we'd use the time to our advantage and check out the first two systems, and their planets, for our base sites now."

He paused for a long minute, looking at them all for the effects his words were having, then went on slowly "All of you have been working too hard for too many hours a day, and have been too close to our problems for too long now. So, the next few weeks will be the last vacation any of you will get for a long, long time to come. Use it well, to get rested, and relaxed enough to go back and face the problems you all know we'll find when we get home!"

Finished at last, he sat down in the command chair, the look on his face telling them all not to bother him for a while.

Blade, sitting next to the command chair, as young as he was, was nearly as attuned to Dirk as Balor was. He pushed his head against the hand Dirk had dropped to his knee, and without realizing it Dirks somber look lightened as his hand searched for the cats neck and began to scratch it gently.

Balor came over silently and lay down in front of him, the look in his glowing golden eyes plainly telling the others not to bother Dirk for a while.

Tagon, sitting across the room, silently took all of this in.

CHAPTER TWENTY-FOUR
Interlude

TuLan's Introspection

TuLan had learned a great deal about his hosts' species, and his host in particular. He had been with this host for almost two and a half cycles now, and in the vernacular of that species, 'it had been a hell of a ride!'

This species had seemed unique to him from his first real study of them nearly two century's ago. After deciding to return to see how much they had advanced a century later he had been dumbstruck at their technological advancement. That was when he had returned to the council to seek his observation platform. He had returned seventy five cycles ago and had not been able to quell his amazement for the entire period up to the accident that had placed him on this planet.

Now, being forced by circumstances to be fully embroiled in the happenings on this planet, he was terrified! Terrified for these people, because he knew from history what would happen to them once the invasion got fully under way, or when they succumbed.

He was also terrified of these people! They were unlike any species he had ever run across before. They were technological quick studies, and even brilliant in their own right.

Giving them open access to his interplanetary runabout was one thing, but he was not so sure that he should have given them open access to the teaching machine, and the ships library. All runabouts were classified as life ships and came equipped with the standard library, which contained all of the technical manuals for the various drive systems used by the different types of ships still in use. This species, with the help of the library and what appeared to be very limited resources, had produced a working deep space vehicle in a little under two and a half cycles. This was something that it might have taken many other advanced species with unlimited resources twenty five to fifty cycles to accomplish.

To top it all off they weren't just building one ship, they were building eight of them! What was even more spectacular was that those ships were Trans lightspeed capable! When TuLan had found this out he had withdrawn from all contact with Dirk for a full two months because he had been so rattled.

Then there was the other thing! With the exception of Dirk, many of those he had met were fledgling telepaths. Dirk himself was an anomaly. He was such a strong telepath that he could block TuLan from any part of his mind that he wanted to, something that was not easily done. TuLan was of two minds about this for true telepathic races were, in a very large galaxy, still a rare occurrence.

Then there was Balor and the Elonee, another anomaly! Digging deep into his memory TuLan seemed to recall some mention of another catlike species that was telepathic, but the references were shrouded in history from ages ago. Those reports had been sketchy, stating that they had traveled the starways with a race that might have been even older than the Chai.

This, even more than the anomalies that Dirks' species presented to him, bothered TuLan. Why were they here on this planet with this species? How had they gotten here? Why had Balor been there just at the location where he had crashed? Why had Balor formed such a strong bond with Dirk? There were just too many questions and not enough answers!

Then there was Dirk the human. He was intelligent and very resourceful, with a good education and a plethora of hard learned experiences that he employed with the precision of a surgeon.

And, like so many others of this species, he had the innate ability to take random bits of information and form them into a cohesive hypotheses that was more often right than wrong. There was, also, one other thing about his host. Like many others of his species, many of whom TuLan had met vicariously through Dirks surface memories of them, and his day to day dealings, he was a member of a warrior class.

TuLan, in his very long life, had known several species that had warrior or military classes as part of their societal makeup. These were, for the most part, beings that fought for survival or territorial dominance. They fought passionately, sometimes berserkly, but when the disputes were settled they let that passion go.

These Earthmen, especially those like Dirk, had evolved a very different type of warrior. They were called professional soldiers or sometimes mercenaries. And they could all kill another being, without compunction or passion, when they thought it necessary!

Then there was a type in a class all by itself. The very elite of this breed! Those who were the deadliest of those warriors. They were the ones of above average intelligence, able to adapt to changing environments and situations quickly. They were the deadliest, most efficient, killers of them all! They were this because they could kill another being coldly, dispassionately! But they were not wanton in their acts of violence. They just did what they thought was necessary, and little more. They did this as part of their profession! This frightened TuLan, because he had not come across this behavioral pattern before. TuLan also understood survival instincts. Most of the species he knew of, when faced with the certainty of death, accepted the inevitable and let it take them.

Not this species! Even when death was close to certain and there was no hope of escape, they fought on with a defiance and determination that was both awe inspiring and terrifying in its' intensity.

TuLans' species, in their hundreds of thousands of years of history and exploration, had never come across a race like this before. He was now terribly worried because they were about to be loosed upon the galaxy!

Even as well as he knew his host there was that much more that he didn't know about him, and his race, so he was most worried because he had no real idea of what to expect from them! And he was the one who had let them loose!

TuLan personally did not think that they could stand against the Drel, but even if they fought them to a standstill they would pay a terrible price. If they could stop the Drel it would be because their greatest weapon would be their total determination to resist unto death in the face of insurmountable odds.

The Drel, history reminded him, had been relentless, and even harsher taskmasters to those they conquered. Raping their planets of their raw materials, and using those populations as steeds to transport the Drel about and fight their battles for them, and forcing them to fight those of their own kind that resisted them.

Even worse, the Drel often used subjugated species as a food source, saving the strongest as steeds and sending the rest back in stasis to their already overpopulated planets to be slaughtered like these humans did their domesticated cattle. The difference being that the cattle were not an intelligent species.

TuLan was of two minds about these Earthmen. They were a hardy species, intelligent and inventive. They were frighteningly intuitive, and nearly without peer as innovators. They were compassionate to a fault at times, and utterly merciless to any enemy who threatened their survival. It was this last that frightened TuLan the most, for he knew that many of the races in the council could be obstinate and obtuse at times, including his own!

This fear was well founded, he thought. Just look at what they had done with just a little of the information that they had retrieved from the ships library. Look at how they had modified the very complicated teaching machine, something that was still beyond many races that were supposedly more advanced than this one. The thought of what these beings might be able to do with what could be found in the wide galaxy was truly daunting to him!

Yes, any dealings and negotiations with this race must be done with a care not to threaten their survival as a race. Even though TuLan had agreed to intercede with the council on their behalf he knew the council and the races on it. They might not be induced to fight this coming war until it was in their respective faces.

Well, for better or worse, the Earthmen now had access to the galaxy, and they would bring good or ill as fate dictated! The thing TuLan truly dreaded, if the latter were the case, was that his name would bring bile to the throats of those who could bring themselves to utter it, for his name would forever be linked to the advent of the Earthmen into the galaxy.

CHAPTER TWENTY-FIVE
Outward

Void

The little ship was barreling along at nearly one hundred fifty light days per hour of constant thrust in hyperspace, or nine point eight six light years per Earth standard day, about three fifths of her maximum speed in hyperspace, yet she didn't seem to be moving at all to those inside of her. She didn't seem to be doing much of anything at all, but it would have been foolish to believe ones physical senses out here! She was actually moving faster and farther than anyone connected to Earth's space programs would have dreamed possible to do for at least another hundred years.

There had been very little activity on he bridge for the last six days, as it had been manned by a skeleton crew for the last five of them. All of that was different now! People bustled about, going back and forth between duty stations where last minute equipment diagnostics were being run. Many lights were blinking, and machines were talking to each other as the ship was prepared for the transition from hyper to normal space.

"Mr. Blain," said her captain, Blackjack Jones "call the bridge to attention please."

"Aye, Aye Captain." His first officer responded smartly. Then "All hands on the bridge! Attention to general orders!" This was repeated once more and the hubbub of conversation and general noise died down to only the low hum from the equipment.

When all was quiet, and all heads that could look away from their equipment were turned to him, the captain said clearly, "On my mark it will be twenty two minutes to breakout." He paused, looking at his watch, the others looking at theirs to make sure they matched on his mark. "Mark. Mark. Mark!" The hubbub returned as the crew performed very last minute checks, and tweaked their equipment.

Blackjack Jones was very proud of this crew. They had drilled almost ceaselessly for months prior to lift off, and had done so without any real complaints other than the normal grumbling of a crew that was becoming part of a working team. They wouldn't, for each one of them had worked hard to get their position to be one of the first humans to visit another star system. Well it had all paid off handsomely so far, but the next half hour would be the proof of the pudding!

The ship was sailing in a place all of their sensors told them didn't exist! But it had to! They were here weren't they? Not knowing if the place you were in really existed was a very scary feeling! But they were all managing that fear very well. They would. They all wanted to be out here more than they feared being here!

Twenty minutes later he said "Mr. Blain, start the normal space reentry sequence on my mark, if you please." Saying this just loud enough to be heard by his first officer.

"Aye, aye captain." Came the prompt reply. Then it came "Mark. Mark. Mark!"

The little ship hummed and thrummed as her reactors generated the tremendous power necessary to create the vortex portals for entry to and exit from hyper space. Suddenly where there had been only the black nothingness they had been traveling in, lines of power reached out and grasped that medium and tore a hole in it, creating a passageway back into normal space.

About two hundred million miles out from the sun called Barnards Star, in space devoid of most solar system debris the Earth ship Shrike flashed back into existence in normal space! This was a momentous occasion for those aboard this ship, for they were the very first humans to visit another star system. There was a short period of jubilation for them before their captain called them back to their duty.

Barnards star had one planet and two planetary satellites. The planet was one third again the size of earth, and its' primary satellite was slightly smaller than earth's moon. Its second satellite was no more than a large asteroid that had somehow attached itself to the gravity field of that moon.

The sun itself was a class four Sol type, but larger and younger than Sol, with more orange in its' color spectrum. The planet itself would be found, at a later date, to have an oxygen/nitrogen atmosphere of point zero seven one earth normal, only slightly higher than that of sol systems Mars.

It had two small seas near each of its' polar ice caps that were very shallow, and frozen solid. The planet swung in an elliptical orbit about one hundred five million miles out from its' sun. The only forms of life that would be discovered on it would be forms of algae, frozen in its' seas.

"Take us in at one third power to about two Pds Mr. Blain. Let's take a quick look at it shall we?"

As the ship moved in towards the planet, its sun sent hydrogen flares of orange fire shooting twenty million miles out into space towards the planet and its' very thin atmosphere. This would not be a place for humans to live.

Its' sun was still to young and unstable for that, had not burned off enough of its' mass to settle down and burn steadily for human type life to exist there.

The little earth ship did not stay long.

Star-10310 @ 294.494.61 by 735.692.11 Galactic North from Earth Standards

The Shrike had stayed in orbit around the planet at Barnards Star for only one earth standard day, taking photographs and running whatever other tests could be done from space. Then it had headed back out to the point where it had entered normal space, traveling at minimal speed while its' navigator plotted its' new destination course.

After the appropriate commands were given the ship picked up speed quickly, its' vortex generators hummed loudly as they built up the power needed to tear a hole in normal space for the ship to disappear through.

Again beams of power reached out in front of the ship, grasping and rending the fabric of the space in front of it until a hole filled with black nothingness appeared. Seconds later the ship flashed out of existence from normal space near Barnards Star. The small earth ship known as the Shrike was now on its' way to a new destination.

Ninety four days, and nine hundred twenty six point eight four light years distance later, the Shrike flashed into existence three hundred eighty million miles out from a huge yellow white sun, nearly half again the size of Sol.

No sooner had the Shrike entered normal space than every proximity and collision alarm klaxon on the ship began sounding at once! Completely startled the bridge crew scanned their instruments seeking the culprit that had set them all off. They didn't have to look far. The culprit was staring at them from the main view screen directly in front of them! They had come out of hyperspace practically on top of the outermost planet of this system!

"Bring us hard to port Mr. Blain! Cut power to the port main engine and give me a three second full power burn to the starboard main engine and the forward starboard up maneuvering thruster! Full power to the forward force field screens also if you please Mr. Blain." Blackjack Jones ordered calmly, even though his own heart was racing madly!

The captain had seen it as soon as the view screen had picked up the image, thinking OH SHIT! But the next instant his mind was very busy extrapolating the moves that would be necessary to avoid the collision that would end his career far too soon. "Don't lose it now Blackjack!" he chided himself in a low tone as he began issuing orders in a voice intended to keep the rest of the crew calm and at their jobs.

The issuance of those order, in that calm and controlled voice saved the Shrike, the two hundred five humans, the three Elonee, and the unknown Chai passenger on board. It also saved Blackjack Jones' newly realized career!

The Shrike, pulling sixteen Gravities as it fought the huge planets gravity well, bounced off the uppermost layer of its' methane atmosphere. Slowly, one by one, the alarms and klaxons began to go silent as the ship retreated from that near fatal encounter.

"Mr. Blain," Captain Jones said in a quiet aside to his first officer, "If you would, please, send my compliments to the crew with a very well done to all." He hesitated for a moment, then, "And Mr. Blain," he said, causing that worthy to turn back to face him "your excellent performance will be noted in the ships log. Your captaincy will not be long in coming if I have ought to say about it!"

Slightly abashed at this praise from a man that he had come to respect very deeply, all commander Victor Blain could do was humbly say, "Thank you Sir. That's very kind of you to say."

"OK Victor," Blackjack Jones said, using Blains' first name for the first time since he had been assigned as his first officer, "my info says that this system has fifteen planets and a gaggle of moons, with some decent sized asteroids thrown in for good measure. The one that we want is fourth out from the sun. Pick the best course you can to bring us in to pass most of them close enough for a look see. Bring her about and go in at one eighth power, and if that's too fast slow her to one sixteenth."

"Aye, aye Sir!" Blain said smartly, and turned to issue orders to the navigation crew.

As they cruised slowly in towards the fourth planet in the system, Blackjack asked "Victor, do our star charts show a name for this sun other than the coordinates we were given?"

Looking in a reference on his console Blain looked up in some surprise as he said, "Yes Sir, it does. Its called Fenris, after the Norse god!"

"Then Victor, as is my right as captain, and considering the fact that we soon expect to have the wolves at our backs, I shall name our target planet. I think that I'll name it Wolfsbane! Yes, that's what it will be called, Wolfsbane."

Fenris was truly one of the galaxy's giants, nearly two hundred fifty thousand miles in diameter it would later be found out, almost two and a half times the size of Sol. It had fifteen planets and some twenty three moons and moonlets circling about it. Five of those planets were gas giants. The one furthest out, the one that had nearly brought an end to the Shrike, was in a wobbly orbit nearly nine hundred seventy nine million miles out from its' primary. Two, the closest in, were molten balls of super heated magma. The third planet out was an arid, waterless, ball with two moons swinging about it in erratic orbits.

Wolfsbane, the fourth planet, was nearly twice the distance from its primary as earth was from Sol, about one hundred sixty five million miles out and half again as large as Earth. What made it unique was that it had an oxygen nitrogen atmosphere that was within .001 percentage points of Earth normal Oddly enough its orbit around Fenris was also nearly identical to that of Earth about Sol. Its two moons were slightly larger than Luna, one having a thin atmosphere and pale green vegetation that showed phosphorescently when seen from Wolfsbane at night

The next four planets were spaced out almost evenly at fifty to one hundred million mile intervals going outward, almost as if some godlike hand had placed them that way. They would provide spectacular views to those who first came to set up the bases, and eventually settled on Wolfsbane.

All of those had mostly mountainous terrain's, the one next out from Wolfsbane showing a promising atmosphere and many lakes and rivers that flowed into small but deep seas. Another had a shallow atmosphere that looked like it had been bleeding off for a long time. One had a dirty yellow atmosphere that swirled madly about its mountain peaks, and the last one had a shallow but dense atmosphere with dark gray-green vegetation that grew very close to the ground. It looked very cold there. These four planets had captured a total of nine moons.

The ninth and tenth planets out were small in comparison to the rest in this system. They were also a binary pair, dancing an erratic path about each other as they circled Fenris. They had dense cloud filled atmospheres that showed the angry red glare of many active volcanoes dotting their surfaces.

This was the Fenris system, a veritable hodge-podge of what was possible in a very big galaxy. There was one planet in that system that would become a human stronghold, a first step in mans attempt to retake his home from the Drel invaders. The captain of the first human space ship to visit it had named it, and had done so with great mirth in mind. It was called Wolfsbane.

Wolfsbane, by all possible human standards, was physically and literally beautiful! Almost pristine to those looking at it through the view ports and view screens of the Shrike.

Almost pristine because the planet below them did have some indigenous life forms. That was plain to see as the first unmanned high altitude exploration and surveillance drones were sent into its upper atmosphere to test and sample, listen and photograph, with the myriad tools that their technology had put at their disposal.

Wolfsbane was beautiful. It had a diameter of thirty four thousand miles, and a gravity of one point zero one zero Earth normal. It had eight continental sized land masses divided by deep green oceans that lightened to blue green along the long continental shore lines.

Three of the continents virtually circled the globe, and were joined by archipelagos whose islands were covered by lush blue-green plant life. It also had polar ice caps, but much larger than those of Earth. It also had two continents about one and a half times the size of Australia in the temperate zone of the northern hemisphere, and a string of large islands that stretched across the southern most, and largest, ocean. The largest island, at the center of the chain, was about the size of the state of Texas, twice over.

The larger equatorial continents had both huge mountain ranges and large areas of rolling plains of green and golden grasses and grains that were divided by wide deep rivers, and vast tracts of deep green and brown forestlands.

The surveillance drones photographed vast herds of grazing herbivores, the smallest of which looked to be the size of elephants. This meant that there would be predators, some possibly very large indeed.

There was marine life also. Some with forms that had huge dorsal fins that spread like sails, pushing their owners through the water at a fair clip, and others whose dorsal fins cut wakes through the water that told of both great size and speed of their submerged owners.

The samples brought back by the first drones showed that Wolfsbane had an atmosphere with a richer oxygen and slightly higher nitrogen content, along with several other types of innocuous particulate matter, but it was completely breathable by humans.

The water samples picked up from the atmosphere, and from remote dipping from several rivers, also proved to be entirely drinkable for humans, so it was time to put an exploration team of scientists and other technicians, along with a platoon of space marines, on the ground to do more extensive sampling and study.

After two weeks, and after all things considered that could possibly be considered in that compressed time span, nothing was found that would be inimical to mankind other than some rather toothy predators who fed on the large herbivores.

This was not to say that nothing was there to be found, it was that the teams worked on the principal of 'Murphy's First Law on How Things Worked'. You know the one. It went—If something could go wrong, it would! But as far as

Wolfsbane was concerned right now, it seemed as if Mr. Murphy had taken a vacation. Still, the technicians took samples of everything they could pull, cut, or pick up, knowing that Murphy never stayed away from anywhere for long!

Everything would be checked, and rechecked, on the trip home to verify or disprove their initial findings.

During this period Dirk and Jimmy had unloaded the small, collapsible, two man helicopter that had been brought down on the second landing lighter, and were flying it in ever widening circles out from the base camp. They were doing double duty as they flew this pattern, collecting samples of anything that looked different from what could be picked up within a few hours walk from the base, and photo-mapping the area as they flew over it.

During these trips they spotted several varieties of grazers, and a couple of carnivores that were a little bigger than the large Kodiac bears of Earth. There were also several types of avian life, some quite large, but those stayed well away from the area the noisy helicopter was in. The only real surprise they had was when Jimmy was attacked by a small rodent no bigger than a ground squirrel, when he stepped to close to the entrance to its' burrow.

All in all, the prospects for Wolfsbane becoming one of Earth's first colonies was looking very promising indeed. But during the bull sessions after the evening meals Dirk warned them that Murphy could come back from vacation at any time! So they shouldn't get too comfortable with what they were finding.

The ship had not been idle during this period either. It had mapped this solar system and photographed most of its' planets.

Outward Again

Everyone and everything was back from the surface of the planet, had been decontaminated, and stowed in its proper place. The crew had made whatever minor adjustments or repairs that had been necessary. They were ready to go on with their historic journey. It had been decided that before leaving they would take a closer look at Wolfsbane's two moons on the way out of the system.

The first one they looked at was the smaller of the two, and the first to rise in Wolfsbane's night sky. They had named that one 'Pup'. It was very much like Luna, earth's moon, only a bit smaller, and like that moon it was airless and pock marked with craters from meteor strikes.

When they came to the second moon, a quarter again as big as Luna, they found a completely different story. It had a shallow but dense atmosphere, full of dark gray clouds that swirled with titanic storms, and gray seas that rolled and thundered against massive rocky shorelines. In several spots under those gray seas could be seen the angry red glow of active volcanoes that caused the seas around them to boil and froth. Looking down into that roiling maelstrom someone commented that it looked like the mother of all bitches. That's how 'The Bitch' got its' name.

It was time to leave, but before doing so Blackjack Jones called Dirk to the bridge, asking him to bring Jimmy with him. When they arrived he told them what was on his mind, "Dirk, since our being able to be out here is mainly due to your efforts we think that you should be the one to rename this solar system if you want to."

Dirk was surprised and pleased that they would think of him for this, but he asked instead "It already has a name doesn't it?" knowing the answer before he asked it. When told the star chart name already given to it he stood looking at the huge golden red sun for a couple of minutes.

"I think it already has a good name, and like the Norse God it's named after I think that this is a fitting place to begin the Drel's decent into their long, long winter! They'll wish they had never thought of trying to take Earth from us before this is over!

It seemed that everyone and everything on the bridge went silent for a few seconds when Dirk finished speaking, then wild pandemonium broke out as the entire crew began to applaud and whistle their approval.

Jimmy just stood there looking at his friend, knowing that those few simple words spoken by him had created a true moment in history. Knowing also that Dirk had galvanized this crew, and that this story would be told and retold until it became a legend that would not stop. Balor, sitting unnoticed a few paces behind Dirk, flashed a thought to Tagon and Blade, ***Do you begin to understand the strength that is in our new clan brother?***

Because he was grooming Mr. Blain for his captaincy Blackjack Jones, just a few minutes before they were scheduled to enter what everyone was now calling hyperspace, got up from the captains dais and said brusquely to him "You have the con and the bridge Mr. Blain!" and promptly left.

Blackjack had had his choice of several officers when it was being decided who would crew the bridge of the Shrike, but he had been singularly impressed by this young officer. As were all of the candidates, he was very smart. Blain held two degrees. One in aerospace engineering, and the other in celestial navigation. It had been the second one, Blackjack thought that had tipped the scales in his favor.

But it was more than that. He was personable, getting along well with officers and subordinates alike. He tended, after being chosen, to drive the crew hard when running drills for this or that contingency, at the same time praising them lavishly when they did well.

When it came to dressing someone down he never, ever, did it in front of the others but found a way to get the culprit alone somewhere for a few private and choice words. When all was said and done, Blackjack thought to himself, young Mr. Blain seemed to be in his natural element out here. In other words he was a natural born spaceman.

Blackjack also had another reason. He had learned a great deal on this flight, and no doubt he would learn a good bit more before it was over. He was the head of space ship design and development for the resistance and would have to replace himself at the end of this trip to put what he had learned into practical use.

Mr. Blains performance had far exceeded his expectations, and he liked that a lot! When he did replace himself he had to have someone he knew and trusted, someone he would be able to talk to and bring him honest appraisals of performances, or shortfalls, between trips.

Dirk and admiral Chabov had left the choice of a new captain up to him, and he believed he had already found him!

The transition to hyperspace went without a hitch, as he knew it would so he did not return to the bridge for nearly three hours, spending the time made by his act discussing his thoughts with Dirk.

The star system they were heading for now was twice the distance from Earth as Fenris was, and about fifteen degrees further in towards the center of the galaxy. The small advantage they had now was that this part of the trip could be done in about half the time it took to get to Fenris, because they were approaching their destination from a tangent instead of a straight line flight, as they had from Bernards star. The trip would take, at the speeds they had proved this beautiful little ship could maintain, a little under two months in subjective time. That star system, according to the coordinates they had been given, was almost fourteen hundred twenty light years away from Earth.

Blackjack entered the bridge quietly, shushing the master at arms stationed by the hatchway as he entered, but Blain spotted him immediately, and got up from the command chair saying in a normal tone of voice that carried to the crew without interrupting their duties, "The captain is on the bridge. Do you want the con Sir?"

"I have the con, Mr. Blain." Blackjack said formally, then "At ease Mr. Blain."

Seating himself he looked proudly out over the ship he had designed and helped to build, and the hard working crew that manned her.

"Excuse me Sir," Blain said in the same tone and pitch he had used to announce his entry to the bridge, "but I have to report that there was a slight error made in the jump coordinates. When it was discovered, it was to late to correct it as we had already entered hyperspace. I took it upon myself not to drop back out to correct it because it will only cost us one extra days travel once we come out!"

Blain looked at Blackjack directly, steeled himself, and went on "The error was in the plotting software Sir! I neglected to adjust for point zero zero five two five degrees of galactic drift when I entered the coordinates. I believe that that is why we came out so close to that gas giant at Fenris!"

He paused for only a couple of seconds this time, then rushed on "It's my fault Sir. I should have checked that program before we left the Fenris system!" he finished, placing the blame on himself.

"What makes you think that the same thing won't happen when we reach our new destination?" Blackjack snapped.

"Because Sir, we had plotted for the same emergence point we did for Fenris. Our target system has only three planets and four satellites Sir, and it's quite unlikely our repeating that on this one!" Blain said, some small relief entering his tone at his solid reasoning.

Wanting to let Blain know that he trusted him completely, and lighten the mood at the same time Blackjack said while trying to hide his growing smile, "Mr. Blain, if you cause me to place skid marks on these nice new drawers, like got placed on my only other pair the last time, you'll be cleaning the scuppers all the way home!" he finished, smiling openly now.

"Yes Sir." Blain said, smiling in recognition of the effort to lighten the mood on the bridge. As Blain turned away Blackjack heard him muttering to himself, "This ship doesn't have scuppers! Does it?"

Blackjack saw several surreptitious smiles on the faces of crew members who were fighting a losing battle to hide them.

They broke out of hyperspace exactly where Mr. Blain said they would come out. The transition to normal space went flawlessly for both the ship and the her crew. It was a good sign. They jumped back right away to make up the difference from the faulty navigation program and came out where they were supposed to be a second time.

The crew went competently about securing the ship for interplanetary flying, setting sensors and forcefield screens, scanning for any other objects that might be floating or flying in the vicinity. When all was ready Mr. Blain turned to his captain and said "We're ready to proceed insystem on your orders Sir."

Deciding that this was the right time for it Blackjack said, with a wide grin on his face, "This will be your ship soon Mr. Blain! Take her in as you please!"

Standing and giving him a very smart salute Blackjack said so the entire bridge crew could hear him plainly, "She's my ship until we get back to Earth Mr. Blain, But it would please me if you would take command for a while now!" and he stepped down from the captains dais and chair.

The Shrike swung into orbit around the second planet in the system about a thousand miles out and prepared to launch her surveillance drones for close in observation. The drones would establish decaying orbits at one hundred miles out, one equatorial and one polar, about the planet below. These would stabilize when they reached a height of twenty miles out. This would give the technicians two days of live video feed, and telescopic photography shots of feedback, to work with while the drones mapped an accurate depiction of the surface. That mapping would give them a forty degree swath around the polar and equatorial belts. Even this far out the planet below looked to be a very promising place.

Two days later the Shrike dropped down and scooped up her drones. They were refitted and prepared for a one day trip down into the lower levels of the atmosphere at five thousand feet. They would now fly at forty five degree tangents to their original courses, and make two passes each around the planet. They would then drop down to sea level, where possible, and scoop up containers of atmosphere along with whatever particulates and water vapor were in it for testing. This would be a very trying and busy time for the remote operators who must fly the drones at these low altitudes.

All of the remote testing went without a hitch, and nearly every test on the materials retrieved tested out to within plus or minus one percent of ninety eight point seven percent Earth normal! It was time for a manned landing!

Fifty miles above the planets surface the big belly doors of the Shrike opened and a miniature version of the Shrike dropped away from its' mother and down towards the planets surface.

This tiny eighty foot long copy of the Shrike was called the 'Raptor'. It had a miniature version of its' parents gravity repulsor system, and retractable wings for in atmosphere high speed flight. It also had two twin turret mounted fifty caliber machine guns and two single turret mounted twenty millimeter cannons. The motto when building her had been, 'Better to not need what you have than need what you don't!'.

They had been on the surface for a week now, and the worst thing that had happened was a couple of cases of the runs due to particulates in the water.

One of the Tec's, while speaking to Dirk who was still on the ship, was telling him about a site located some ninety miles to the west of base camp. "It's perfect for the glassteel mill setup. If you'll check the map I sent up you'll see the spot I'm talking about!" She said excitedly. Then, "It's a low mountain range showing high iron content, and there's a large sandy desert just on the other side of the range."

"That's great news," Dirk said encouragingly, "keep up the good work Cindy."

It was looking like this planet was too good to be true. They were right! Unbeknownst to the people on the Shrike there were those on the planet that thought it belonged to them!

Chimera

Its' eyes were fiery red, and seemed to glow from within. They had large black vertical slits for pupils, that could open so wide they almost hid the red of the eyes when it hunted at night. Those eyes had near telescopic capabilities when needed and could pick out a tiny nit at fifty feet if the creature desired to find it.

The eyes were deep set behind a large overbearing brow ridge, in a head that could only be described as canine. It had a long canine like snout that ended in a flexible nose, and dewlap lips that, when drawn back in a snarl exposed long upper and lower fangs that were meant for only one thing. Tearing the flesh from its' preys body!

It had a long torso that was covered predominantly with coarse black hair that had red highlights when seen in the sunlight. Here and there on its body it had irregular patches of white, gray, or light tan that helped it stay hidden in the shadows of the trees. The torso was set on two short but powerful hind quarters that ended in feet with four taloned and flexible toes each.

Its' head was set on a short but flexible neck. The torso had no discernable shoulders but sloped down so radically that it gave the neck the appearance of being much longer than it was.

At the midpoint of its torso the creature had four long, whip like, appendages with two gripping digits at the end of each. These were more like tentacles than arms because they had no wrists or elbows. They were composed of long muscles and tendons, and were tremendously strong. They enabled the creature to move through the trees, its' natural habitat, much faster than it could on the ground.

This creature was, all in all, a formidable predator! It was by natural instincts a carnivore, and there were only a few other creatures on this planet that it feared, but right now the creature was terrified!

With all of its' many formidable natural weapons this creature had one major flaw! That flaw was in its hearing, for it had no external aural appendages to directionalize sound for it. It had only two small aural openings set far back on its' canine head. That is why it hadn't heard or seen the large flying thing until it was almost on top of him. That flying thing was what was terrifying it so, for it had never seen anything like it in its' entire existence. It was very, very different from any of the flyers it knew of, and it was huge! It also flew in a manner that was very strange.

It could hover in one place in the air, making an angry thwopping sound when it did so. It could also move forward and backward at will, and from side to side without banking as most of the flyers it had seen must do. It was something so big, and so strange, that there was no other reasonable reaction but fear for the creature.

Right now it was hovering over the creatures hiding place in a thickly leafed section of trees making that strange thwopping sound, which was much louder now with it right overhead. The creature was terrified that the strange flying thing had spotted him and would soon swoop down and pluck him from his hiding place.

Slowly, ever so slowly, the angry thwopping sound moved away, and the creature screwed up its courage enough to raise itself above the leafy cover of its' hiding place to see where it had gone to.

There, yes there! Towards the clear place in the forest. It was landing there! But what prey had it found to strike at there, the shivering creature asked itself?

Though more frightened than it had ever been in its' life the creature made its way towards the clear space in the forest, moving from branch to limb to tree bole, its' four arms working in perfect unison as they pulled or swung the creature forward. As it neared the clear space it began to slow its forward movement, for its' fear of just moments ago was still fresh with it.

This creature did know what fear was, but was normally unaccustomed to experiencing it, for there were few creatures in its' world that it had found to fear. Until now it had been used to being the feared one as it passed through its' hunting territory. Its' kind were normally solitary, gathering in groups only during the mating season. That was a time of fierce competition, often bloody, when the young males vied for the privilege of impregnating one of the females in estrus.

The females of his species were, when nursing young ones, much fiercer than the males, occasionally killing one of the males who got too close to her litter. The females often carried the seeds of several different males to term sequentially, thereby insuring a healthy population. Approaching a female with young ones was one of the kinds of fear the creature knew and understood completely.

Moving very cautiously now it parted two of the branches screening it from the flying thing now sitting in the middle of the clear space in the forest. The watching creature rubbed its' eyes, thinking something had gotten into them and was affecting its' vision. But the strange flying thing was still doing what the creature had first seen it doing. It was emitting creatures very much like itself from an opening in its' side!

They were about the same size as the creature was, perhaps a bit smaller, and had only two arms! They had funny round shaped heads with flat muzzles, and very long hind quarters as well! They were covered in some kind of multi colored skin that, had they been in the forest, would have made them very hard to see well at all. Also, they seemed to be carrying long pieces of sticks in their paws. They were spreading out from the flying creature and making strange sounds at each other, looking at the ground and the surrounding trees.

They were invading his hunting territory! This thought exploded into its' awareness!

This should not be! The creature began to shake with anger, forgetting the fear of only moments before. It released one set of muscles that controlled the opening of a sphincter located just above its' penile recess. It clenched another set of muscles causing the sphincter to collapse explosively, and a stream of decidedly foul smelling liquid shot forth from the sphincter opening. To emphasize this warning it began a low gargling growl from deep in its' throat that quickly built up in volume to a challenging roar!

The creature, from the flying thing nearest it, staggered backwards and threw up one of its' appendages to cover its flat muzzle. At the same time it gesticulated wildly, with the stick it held, at his hiding place in the low leafy branches. Others of its' kind came rushing towards the one who had staggered backwards, raising the sticks they carried and pointing them towards his hiding place.

They were challenging him for his territory! This he understood, and would never allow to happen. The creature flung itself forward from its' hiding place, and hit the ground moving speedily towards its challengers, roaring its own challenge fiercely back at them now.

It rushed forward, the creature from the flying thing trying to point the stick it held at him, but he was upon it now! Using its hind quarters and two of its arms to slow its' forward momentum and balance itself it reached out with the other two arms and gripped the challenger about the head and torso. It heaved mightily, pulling the head and torso in opposite directions.

Two things occurred simultaneously! The creature it was holding emitted a high pitched sound from an orifice in its flat muzzle At the same time the head the creature from this planet was pulling on separated from the torso!

The red eyed creature stood there snarling in triumph as it waved the severed parts of the now limp creature at the others in warning, the body fluids from them spraying out in a wide arc, hoping they would now leave his territory.

But now another came from the body of the flying thing, heading not away from but towards him, and it was pointing one of those sticks they all carried towards him too. The others, with the newcomer, formed a half circle in front of him, making odd noises from those openings in their flat muzzles.

He roared louder, flinging the torso and head of the one who had challenged him at their feet! It fell just short of them.

They began to retreat, but at something barked from the one come recently from the flying thing they stopped. Then, as one, they began to move towards him slowly.

He roared again, preparing to take on the next challenger. Then, suddenly, there were flashes like small lightenings coming from the ends of those sticks they pointed at him, and what at first felt like gnat bites. This went on for a very few seconds, then he looked down at his body for those stings were beginning to burn.

The creature could not understand what it saw, because its' life fluids were now leaking from his body, and that burning was now roaring pain as each new sting was now tearing gobbets of flesh from its' body!

Real pain broke through its anger, and it staggered. Then real fear began to take hold of it again, for in its' final moments it understood that these things did not belong here! They were too different, and they could reach out and strike him without touching him.

This once proud predator, and master of its' own territory, this member of this planets dominant species at the top of its food chain, was dead! It just wasn't aware of that fact yet. And it hadn't fallen down yet!

When the creature finally did fall down an auto mechanism, that was part of this species survival pattern, kicked in. It let out a high piercing whistle that carried for miles and miles in all directions. That whistle was the one thing that all of its' kind could hear without trouble, and it told others of its kind much about these newcomers.

Unfortunately for them what was told in that message was mostly wrong, because his revelations were clouded with the agony of his final moments!

In the end what that whistle told of was of the most important thing that had happened. It told all of its' kind of its' passing.

What saved a fair number of them from extinction was not their cunning, nor was it their prowess as fighters. Nor was it their ability to run and conceal themselves from these creatures from another star.

No, the thing that saved them from extinction was chance. A chance encounter with a smallish feline creature that was also not of this planet, or even of this star system.

What saved them was the Elonee!

That Elonee's name was Tagon.

Chimera, Base One

"Base one, chopper one, copy?" came the clear radio signal, for there was nothing on this planet to interfere with it.

"Chopper one, base one kay." The commo operator replied promptly to the call.

"Base one, we're about thirty klicks out, south west your position. Lotsa forest with intermittent grassy plains in this direction. Spotted some big grazers but they scattered when we flew over em. Copy my last?"

"Copy that chopper one. You didn't spot anything else out there did you?"

"negative base. Funny thing though, we thought we saw some kind of movement through the trees a couple of times but couldn't find anything when we went to look see. Whatever it was it was about man sized, and was movin through the upper parts of the trees. Copy that base?"

"Roger that chopper one. Copy you five by five. Chopper one, you have about three and a half hours of daylight left. Say your intentions. Over."

"Base, we spotted a fair sized clearing about two klicks north of our present position. We intend to proceed there and put down to stretch our legs and look around a bit on the ground. I say again. Our intention to proceed two klicks north to clearing and put down to for look see. Will notify you when we are dirtside. Copy last base?"

"Roger that chopper one. Your intention is to proceed to clearing two klicks north your present, your intention to put down for look see. Is that a roger chopper one?"

"Roger that base. Chopper one out."

A little over an hour after chopper one notified base one that it was dirtside and the pilot had just checked in to tell them that nothing had been found, and they were going to lift off in ten minutes to return to base, when there was the sound of gulping in the base one operators earphones. Then "Holy Shit! What the hell is that?"

The commo operator sat up straight in his field chair, adjusted his headphones with one hand while slapping the switch that lit a red light to get the attention of the duty officer, then said into his microphone in a calm voice, "Chopper one say again!" He waited ten long seconds, then said "Chopper one, base one. Say your situation please!"

The others in the command and communications tent, alerted by the now flashing red light over his work station, and the tenseness of his body position, turned in their seats to see what was going on as he said again, "Chopper one, base one. I repeat, say your situation!?"

At that moment the duty officer came running into the tent, alerted by the twin of the flashing red light over the work station by the one mounted on the tent pole outside. A little breathlessly he asked "What's up sparks?"

That worthy, not turning away from his work station, held up one hand for silence, while with the other he fiddled with his headphones, as if that would help get him a response. He reached up with the hand he had just held up for silence and flipped on the switch for the radios open intercom while he repeated his last call.

Just then the speakers crackled and they heard, "Bates just staggered backwards with his arm across his face. He's coughing somethi——." And the transmission stopped in mid sentence!

Just as the base one operator was about to speak into his microphone again the speakers crackled again as the pilot said, "Holy Shit! Something just jumped out of the trees and ran right at Bates! OH NO——!" The pilots transmission stopped again.

Those in the tent heard a faint scream come from the speakers, then "OH GOD AMIGHTY! That thing just tore Bates' head right off his shoulders! I've got to get out there!"

A minute went by, then those gathered about the radio operator heard what sounded like a roar and challenging scream all rolled into one come from the speakers.

Then they heard the unmistakable staccato sound of several automatic rifles firing.

Then a loud piercing whistling scream that chilled them all to the bones.

Then silence!

The radio operators voice shattered the silence now in the tent as he spoke urgently into his microphone, "Chopper one, base one. Come in please. Say your situation! I repeat, say your situation!"

Another tense two minutes of silence ensued over the open channel. Then the speaker came to life as the now subdued voice of the pilot said, "Base, this is chopper one."

The pilots shaken voice came as if it were being forced out of the mans throat "The thing that killed Bates is dead! We're bringing them both in. I can't talk right now. ETA to base is estimated to be forty five minutes. Chopper one out!"

The duty officer, a lieutenant in the newly formed space marines, said to the radio operator, "Get me the Shrike! Captain Jones. ASAP!"

The conference twenty hours later, after all of the tests, the debriefing of the pilot and marines, and all of the information collected and gone over, was held in the shipboard conference cabin.

The full complement of the supernumerary crew was present as well as Captain Jones and his first officer. This also included the three Elonee on board.

"Well, according to what we've been able to put together," Dr. David Hull was saying, "they appear to be only semi intelligent at the most, and from the way the pilot and his marines describe its' actions it was just protecting its' territory. From its' appearance"

"Also," he went on, "from its' physical appearance, and the conclusions those attributes lead us to, it was at or near the top of the food chain here. I might add that our actions, and the creatures response, were an oversight on our part in dealing with unknown planets, and unknown species. I can assure you that it will not happen again due to a lack of training of a representative to accompany explorers on new planets."

A short, thoughtful pause and he finished his presentation "This is something that we have made a priority consideration for all future ships who conduct search and exploration duties."

"Although it has legs," Dr. Sheila Hull picked up the narrative of the creatures physical description, "they seem to be secondary appendages. Its general appearance suggests that it is basically arboreal and spends most of its' time in the trees."

"That's probably the reason that they haven't been spotted before this." Dirk said.

Wanting to bring this meeting to a close Dirk went on quickly, saying "All of this is very interesting, but we're going to use this planet just the same! We need it too much not to!"

He looked around at the faces about him, at their looks torn between the possible discovery of a new species and their own needs. He said "I'll do what I can to see that they're protected, but mark my words, they better learn quickly to stay out of our way!"

This statement had a definite impact on one of the Elonee. Tagon!

Wanting to change the subject he looked thoughtfully at them for a few seconds, then said "I've decided on a name for this new planet. We'll call it Chimera!"

At first they all looked at him with startled expressions, then heads started to nod in understanding and appreciation. Colony world two was about to become an Earth outpost!

"All right people, Blackjack, call every one up from the surface. It's time to head for home. Time is beginning to run in short supply!"

In an aside to Jimmy Lester Dirk said, "Jimmy, as soon as we get back I want this ship re-provisioned, and then your going to take it right back out! I have the coordinates for three more solar systems I want you to take a look at ASAP."

At the look on Jimmy's face dirk smiled and said, "Don't give me that look Jimmy. I told you this was going to happen, and now it's time."

"Victor Blain will be your captain, and your second in command. Blackjack says he's very good, so, other than overall command decisions I want you to give him free reign in running the ship."

Unnoticed by Dirk, or anyone else, the patriarch of the Elonee was sitting to one side by himself, apparently in very deep thought.

The results of those thoughts would, in the not too distant future a very nasty element to the fighting forces of the resistance movement!

Because he had recognized the potential for their intelligence, as limited as it was at this time, Tagon had made up his mind to intervene on their part as soon as he could do so with a well thought out proposition to put on the table for Dirk and his council.

He knew he would need one that was well thought out, because he understood very well the urgency these people felt about establishing these bases they were exploring for. And he knew, without a doubt, that they would let nothing stand in their way of getting what they needed. Not unless they could be shown what they would gain by the changes he would suggest in the way they approached colonizing this planet.

Yes, he would intercede on the behalf of the Chimerans!

CHAPTER TWENTY-SIX
Interludes

Paul Denton

The cell phone that he had carried for over seven months now had never rung. Not even for a wrong number! It had been a part of the second package that he and his boss had received after their turbulent meeting with the president. That meeting had lasted for nearly six hours, and as hard nosed as both he and his boss were they had come away convinced. His boss had commented as they were leaving the White House that it was really a matter of wanting to be convinced that had made them demand so much convincing!

Since that time they had been asked to do some odd things. Things like putting pressure on certain officials to approve the purchase of restricted materials to small firms with new security clearances.

Like arranging for the transfer of highly classified research materials from pentagon research and development programs. Even to, on a couple of occasions, threatening certain congressmen and senators with outright blackmail if they didn't back off of certain avenues of investigation they were beginning.

In all that time that phone had not rung once. Not until this moment that is. Its ring startled him so much that it actually caused him to flinch slightly! "Get a grip on yourself, Paul!" he muttered, chiding himself as he reached for the instrument. Pulling it from the inside jacket pocket where it had been for those seven months he answered it as he would any other call, "Denton here."

Without preamble the voice on the other end said, "The president will resign in three days time! Contact your boss and pass along the information now waiting for you with your secretary. She received a package about an hour ago. Execute plan 'C' in those documents, that is very important! Have you got all of this so far?"

After affirming that he had, the voice went on, "You and your boss can make arrangements for up to six people each, who you think are either important enough or are personally attached to you to accompany you to the destination designated in the plan. But under no circumstances are you to inform them unless you clear them using the number supplied in the document to do so!

There was a short pause, then, "This last is extremely important! Do not, I repeat, do not use any of your agency phones or cell phones, or any other form of communications from your agency or home, to contact those people or us! They have all been compromised! You will find four new cell phones for each of you in that package. Use them! Good luck. Goodbye!"

If the truth were told Denton had been dreading that call, for it meant that everything he had been told was true without question! It also meant that he would now have to look at his world with very different eyes.

It wasn't so much that he didn't believe. It was just that he had, deep down inside himself somewhere, been holding out hope that it might be wrong, or that it might not be as bad as it appeared to be.

But Denton was, if nothing else, flexible by the nature of his personality and his training. Using his agency cell phone he called his secretary and asked her to track down his boss, and to ask him to join Denton for lunch because he had a personal matter he wanted to talk to him about. If he could make it he would meet him at their usual spot. After she assured him she would do her best he hung up.

The term usual spot was code for an alternate location they had agreed on several months ago. The term personal matter was also code which meant that the meeting was of utmost importance to their present situation.

That meeting, three hours later, was both hard and easy for the both of them. The easy part was in knowing that the waiting was now over with, and it was now time to get out. The hard part was in deciding on who they would be taking with them!

Neither man had any close family left, nor did either of them maintain any close personal relationships of the amorous kind, because those often got in the way of their work, which both men were dedicated to. So they both decided to ask their secretaries to come with them.

Both women were widows who did not have close relationships going on at the moment, as far as they knew, and losing them would be real blows to both men! Each of them knew how valuable those women were to them, and how much easier each of them had made a hard job to do. The rest, if any, would have to be thought about until the next morning, at the very least, and until they could examine the package and plan 'C'!

Dentons' boss, looking very troubled, asked him "You say they told you that all of the agency communications, as well as our personal ones, have been compromised?" At Dentons nod he said that he personally found that hard to believe, but that they would also take no chances on them being right, so they would do as instructed.

They discussed several things concerning methods and means personally developed by them as potential backup contingencies to whatever the arrangements in plan 'C' laid out, but would not use them unless it was absolutely necessary. None the less, the message had been clear. And it had come from people that they knew were as professional as they were, and who seemed to have better sources than they did right now.

Yes, the message was very clear. It was now time to get out of Dodge! And not waste any time in doing so either!

Dateline 24 May, 2008
Reuters News Service

Reuters news, Cairo, Egypt

After a lengthy secret conference, and nearly eight long months of very bloody fighting, it was announced late last night that seven of the north African countries of the Mid East have come to an agreement to form a new alliance, and a cessation of all hostilities!

The north African mid east countries of Egypt, Iraq, Syria, Jordan, Yemen, Kuwait, and Iran, in a joint announcement last night, said that the fighting between the Pan Arab Muslim Movement and the governments of the countries listed above had reached an accord. It was also alluded to that Sudan and several other north central African states would be joining them soon.

When contacted, and asked about this potentially explosive situation, the newly inaugurated president of the United States, George Atkins, responded that they were keeping a close eye on the situation, and that the US would not interfere in the formation of the alliance unless provoked.

Observers on the scene have stated that the situation is still very tense, and that there are also pockets of fighting going on inside the new alliance. But on the surface open hostilities have ceased.

On a strange note it has been found out that several of the most ardent of the former officials, from several of the former governments, have done a complete one eighty in their opposition to the new alliance after attending private meetings with the new alliances leaders!

This reporter is most puzzled by this development because he has maintained close, and mostly cordial, ties with many of those officials and individuals for some time. Those ties were severed peremptorily a few days ago, just prior to those private meetings with the new alliance leaders.

If this reporter had just a few more facts to go on he would conclude that there was an outside influence at work here.

Byline by James Cole, Reuters News

Reuters News, Cairo Egypt

Reuters News reporter James Cole was killed late this afternoon in a freak accident. The accident happened when a delivery truck lost its' brakes and couldn't stop before it crashed into Coles' vehicle, which was just pulling away from his parking spot in front of the Reuters New Service building in Cairo, Egypt.

Cole was crushed to death in the accident. He was pronounced dead on the scene by the paramedics who arrived on the scene very quickly. Mr. Cole was an excellent reporter, and he will be missed.

Dateline 26 May, 2008
AP Wire News

AP Wire News, Jerusalem, Israel

In a move that stunned everyone Saudi Arabia and Israel announced today that they had just signed a non aggression and mutual protection agreement.

This move came after Israeli intelligence informed members of the Saudi ruling family about elements in the Saudi military that were actively plotting their overthrow.

Spokesmen from the Knesset and the Royal family, in a joint statement, announced today that from this day forward any person, or group, found to be plotting against either the Royal Family or the State of Israel will be summarily shot! Both spokesmen said that this policy change will take effect immediately.

As testament to this new policy, and the seriousness of their joint intent a spokesman from the Royal Family stated that over one hundred known members from groups ranging from the PLO to Alcaida have been rounded up and were executed early this morning, along with the thirty eight members of the Saudi military found to be guilty of plotting against the Royal family!

Story by Calvin Ostroffsky, AP Wire News

AP Wire News, Jerusalem, Israel

In a related story the long time leader of the PLO, Yasser Rafata, was arrested earlier today and shot in a coup staged by dissident members of that organization!

The leader of that faction, Abdul Kazani, stated that they were tired of Mr. Rafata, and his policy of having the Palestinian youth waste their lives on a battle that was already lost, and could have been peacefully settled twenty five years ago, continue to do so.

Also, in a surprise move, Mr. Kazani stated that the ruling council would be willing to sign a non aggression and mutual protection pact with both the governments of Israel and Saudi Arabia as long as those governments would be willing to cede the city of Jerusalem as an open city to be ruled by a coalition government from both Israel and Palestine.

Mr. Kazani stated that his council felt that there was so much blood on the ground of both countries that he could no longer distinguish which was which, and that they just wanted to live in peace from now on.

A spokesman from the Israeli government said that this was a day that all could call historic, and that they were looking forward to working hand in hand with the Palestinian governing council to rebuild that country.

Story by Ibrihim Ben Yousef, AP Wire News

Dateline 10 June, 2008
London Times

Several extra terrestrial space ships have appeared and taken up stationary positions over many of the major cities of the European Union over the last few days, including Paris, Bonn, Rome, and Madrid.

Today more ships have appeared over Mexico City, Buenos Aires, Moscow, Cairo, and Baghdad. These ships are somewhat larger than an aircraft carrier, they are in geo-synchronous orbit over these cities, and are maintaining an altitude of approximately eighty five thousand feet. As of this writing no overt hostile gestures have been made by these visitors, but their number and positioning are somewhat ominous!

Up to this point they have made no attempts at communication with the governments of the countries those cities are located in, although those governments have been trying feverishly to contact them. Their silence, some say, is not a good sign.

Prime minister Jean Paul Marceau of France, in an early interview today, stated that calm and patience was the best policy to follow at this time, but when asked about French troop movements having been sighted he stated that France's military had been put on ready standby only, and that France would not be the first to make any overt hostile gestures at the presence of these mysterious visitors.

This reporter did find it odd that none of these ships have appeared over any of the major cities of the United Kingdom, or those of the United States!

When contacted, spokespersons for those governments stated that their military's had been brought to a 'Defcon two' readiness status with their long range missile batteries standing by in a 'Triggers Free' mode until the intentions of these visitors have been clarified.

The same spokesperson said that neither the US or England would make the first move, but that they preferred to be ready for one should it become necessary.

As a personal observation this reporter is a student of history, and is reminded of the fiascoes of the 'Chamberlain' era by the lax attitude being displayed by the bulk of the EU countries.

It would seem to this reporter that it would be much easier to make a diplomatic apology if one's suspicions were wrong than to not be prudently defensive, and be put in a position where that apology was necessary.

England and the United States, this reporter thinks, will not be put into such a position as Chamberlain found himself boxed into with the Axis in nineteen thirty nine. Their motto seems to be one of 'talk softly, and have a big missile ready'!

Rocky Mountains Base, Canada

"I know that Dimetri!" Dirk said heatedly, "but we've gotten over two million nine hundred thousand people off Earth in the last year! That's something I didn't think would be possible for us to do. To tell you the truth I was thinking that if we got half that many away we would have been doing very well. But it's time to get out now! There may be another eighty or ninety thousand we can get out if we pack them in like sardines on the last three trips out. But right now planning even that far ahead is risky at this point!" he finished tiredly.

"I know Dirk, but we must try to save them!" Chabov said fiercely, but also tiredly.

"I know, I know. But I want you and Yuri out on the next ship bound for Wolfsbane. We can't afford to lose you or Yuri at this point. I mean we really can't afford to lose you two at any point, but especially not right now! Damn It! It doesn't matter how I say it, it doesn't come out right!" Dirk ended plaintively.

He, like the rest of the command council, had been working twenty hour days for the last two months, and the dark circles under his eyes only underscored this.

"It's OK Dirk. I understand what you mean." Chabov said, smiling tiredly himself, "But I think what must be done is to set a deadline for final departure. Those who make it will go, those who do not will have to fend for themselves until we can return in force!" he said, the iron back in his voice now.

Changing the subject Dirk asked, "Have we gotten anything more, or new, on that big mother of a ship that was spotted about forty five light days out beyond Uranus yet Dimetri?"

"No. Captain Blain didn't want to get too close to it, and give away his position. The long range photos he sent by burst transmission were a little fuzzy, and this one is very different from any of their other ships. And your right, it is one big mother of a ship! The photos also show some kind of weapons placements mounted on the outer hull!"

Is he still shadowing it?"

"Yah, but he's staying at max sensor range to be safe. He did say that this one definitely looks like a war ship though. He's not sure, but says that his gut is telling him this one is some kind of carrier and there's a good chance there's some kind of fighters on board. That thing is really big, about four thousand feet long he estimates." Chabov finished, the worry lines deepening on his face.

"OK. Tell him to stay well back from it for now. Damn it, I wish we had one of those communications satellites left! That really hurt us when they knocked down that last one when all of those ships came in and parked over all those cities.

"I'll tell you one thing I did completely right though, that was changing my mind at the last minute and sending the alternate captain in line out with Jimmy instead of Blain! He has been a source of pure inspiration when it comes to finding and shadowing them out there, and he's been responsible more than once in drawing off the two ships they kept out near the moon to try and find out who we are. Without him out there I doubt we would be able to get our ships in and out as easily as we do?"

"Da! I will second that praise. It is very well deserved!" Chabov agreed readily.

"Anyway, I do have some good news for you Dimetri. McCarthy sent these back on the last transport that came in." Dirk said as he began unrolling the sheaf of papers he had been holding.

"Those men are amazing! Between him and Ortiz they have designed and have under construction a mini carrier for us and the fighters to go with her. She will carry four fighters that have three man crews. they got the idea for the fighters from those 'Foxbats' you sent along to him for refitting. It's amazing how much they can pack into those ships, because their cargo capacity is near half again as much as we first thought!"

"Back to the new ships. The crews will be the navigator, weapons, and the pilot. They can't go hyperspace yet, but they will have an effective combat range of ten light days at max power! He says he can have the first one, including the fighters, ready for us in about three months! That's why he needs this last shipment of machinery and parts so badly."

"That is very good news! And Yes, I think that Yuri and I will go with the next ships. The last cruiser will be done in a day or so and we can pack up all of the equipment from the production area and take it with us to Wolfsbane. Those ships will give us a total of fifteen cruisers and ten cargo transports. If we can hold out here for another three weeks we'll have a fighting chance out there!" Chabov smiled in surrender to Dirks concerns about him and Garov.

"We'll hold out! We have to!" Dirk said forcefully. "Chickie Martinez is on her way in with eight simi trailer loads of computers, parts and chips for new ones. She said she got out just ahead of the border shutdown! She said things are getting really bad in the 'States' now, with open fighting everywhere!"

"Yah, is what my reports are saying also. Is why I want to wait as long as we can. To give our outlying people a chance to come in, although I think we will lose many of them." Chabov said sadly.

"I don't think they stand much of a chance! Those ships brought a lot more of the Drel with them, and now there is another fleet coming. They worked a lot faster than we thought they could!"

Dirk paused for a second, then said, "We sent several messages to what's left of the organized government troops, telling them to go to ground until we can get back here. McCarthy signed the letters personally so they wouldn't ignore them completely." He finished, his tired eyes looking somewhere into the future.

Transitions

Dirks' people weren't panicking! Not yet anyway. But if things got much worse they thought they might give it some serious consideration. The recall had come four days ago, and the message had been simple and to the point. 'Close up shop and head home with any baggage you now have!'

The message meant that they were to bypass St. Louis and cross the border using the ranch route through Montana. 'That's going to be some trick.' Rick Davis thought to himself. He was herding nearly a hundred machinists and metal fabricators, the last ones to get through the New Orleans transfer point.

They had almost been caught there, but had slipped through the net the Drel controlled NOPD had set up when they had grabbed the wrong container from the ship they were using! The one they had grabbed had been full of Mexicans trying to flee the chaos going on in that country.

Things were falling apart everywhere! There was even open warfare going on in the streets of New York City, Washinton DC, and Chicago. It was also close to breaking out in many of the major southern cities now, and as far as Rick knew California was now completely under Drel control!

He was also aware that Chickie Martinez had pulled out of St. Louis three days ago, and as far as he knew she hadn't even left a paper clip laying about for them to find.

A real smart girl that Chickie was! She didn't miss much. He knew, also, that there were six to eight other groups making their way towards the ranch crossing. His, and their groups, were about the last ones to leave their pickup points, trying to get these desperately needed people to the Canadian complex so they could be shipped off Earth.

Every group had not made it out of the metropolitan pickup centers. The resistance had already lost contact with more than five groups so far, and all Rick could do was hope for the best for them.

If they had been taken their loss would hurt the resistance, but it wouldn't stop them. Thanks to Dirk they had had enough warning to get a good start and had built a serious organization with very good people in a relatively short time.

"Oh well," Rick said to himself, "it's time to get this gaggle of geese moving." He loaded them all into two busses and gave each driver a route to follow, and an alternate one to use if they got separated or were stopped for any reason.

Then he jumped into his car and it sped out ahead of the busses to make sure that those routes were still clear.

Desperation

A bullet spanged off the concrete abutment he was hiding behind, just above his head! The soldier, one of a five man special forces team, tried to scrunch further down into the shallow depression he was laying in as another bullet whizzed by just over his head! The trouble was that it was his turn in the barrel. This last was vernacular, meaning that it was his turn to draw fire to make those chasing his unit reveal their positions.

His team had been on the run for the better part of the last three months and they were now very low on food, ammunition, and most of all medical supplies. And it would seem that they were fast running out of places to hide and the time to find them.

The only read on that was that they hadn't found out what was going on up here because they had been on a mission in Central America. Things were bad down there, very bad, and the team had barely completed their mission and gotten out.

When they had gotten back to their base in southern Texas they had immediately been disarmed and placed in semi confinement quarters to await, they were told, a full debriefing. That had been a mistake on the part of the enemy. The team leader had quickly jimmied the loch and they were out and overpowering the single guard almost before the squad that had brought them there had cleared the building.

The team didn't know what was going on but they weren't going to stop and question their leader right then and there either. One thing in his favor at that minute was that their treatment was so out of character that they weren't even ready to question his actions.

Overpowering the guard had been their first real contact with the enemy, and that had been a real eye opener for them. There wasn't much need for thought after that. They rearmed themselves, commandeered a vehicle which they loaded with everything they could cram into it, and slipped off the base using the skills they had been taught.

Squirming a little to his left to check his line of retreat he drew another shot that went wide to his right. Just then his cover mans silenced rifle coughed once and there was a clatter as the possessed soldier who had been shooting at him let his rifle fall from his dead fingers.

There was a single click in the earpiece of his whisperphone, then the quiet, calm voice of his partner said softly into his ear, "OK Ben, you're clear to move back towards me, but do it fast cause there's a whole platoon movin up fast behind that scout! If you hadn't drawn that one out they would have overrun us in no time. Get a move on now, I've got your six."

Sgt. Ben Teller didn't waste any more time. He was up and running within a second of his partners last word. He made straight for the tree line of the woods they had let themselves be backed up against. He dove the last four feet and landed in a body roll that brought him up against the bole of a tree six feet into the woods, facing the way he had come.

His partner fired two well placed shots at the now advancing platoon of Drel ridden men, causing them to scatter and scramble for cover. Ben Teller slapped his partners booted foot, and as he looked around at him Teller said quietly, off the radio "Come on. We've got to cut and run! The others found a deer track and marked it for us to follow. Let's put some distance between us and them while we can."

They rose, and moving in a crouching run moved deeper into the woods, following the faintly marked trail.

About five minutes and a half mile later their earphones clicked once, and their leaders quiet voice said urgently "We think they're using thermal imagers to track us, so find someplace with good cover and go to ground fast. Then cover yourselves with your moon blankets!

The trick seemed to work because the platoon moved off to the south and west. The team moved due north, heading for Tennessee border and the mountains there. Teller had some family in there, and knew the area like the back of his hand.

Two days later they were breaking out of the deeper woods they had been moving through and into a wide valley they had to cross. They scanned the area for a full hour before heading out into the open at a fast trail trot to cross it.

They were almost half way across the valley when a 'laws' rocket arched out of the woods behind them and landed not twenty feet behind the fast moving team. Their forward momentum and the overpressure from the blast saved them from serious injury as it knocked them down to sprawl in the deep grass. They recovered quickly turning, as they sought whatever cover was available, to face the threat.

It was a full platoon and they were moving forward from the tree line at a run, firing sporadically as they came. The team formed a defensive line and began to return fire. They had to make every round count because there wasn't any more to be had out here.

All of a sudden the man on the end of the line said loudly, "Shit!" then, "There's another group coming at us at our four o'clock. It looks like another platoon!"

It looked to the men of the team that their number was finally up, but they weren't going without taking a lot of them with them! They looked at each other and seeing the same thing in each others eyes pulled the few grenades left between them and the remaining ammo clips.

Taking quick stock of what they had, they divided it evenly and got down to the business of killing their enemies. It was a losing fight, but that didn't matter to them now. All that mattered was that they take as many of them with them as they could.

All of a sudden there was a crackle in the earpieces of their headsets that startled them. Then an unfamiliar voice said, "Been followin you boys for the last three days now. Looks like you could use a bit of help. We're at your six o'clock and comin fast, so get your heads down!"

The team was astonished, but very battle savvy, and all five men immediately threw themselves flat to the ground and tried to become part of it.

There was the sound of a large swarm of angry bees about ten feet over their heads, and the first group that had attacked them began to literally disintegrate before their eyes. Body parts and blood flew in all directions as that swarm tore into them!

The sound of angry bees stopped and there was near silence for precious seconds after the carnage stopped. Then there was a louder buzzing that was fast coming towards them.

The buzzing very quickly grew to the distinctive thwopping sound that only a big 'Huey' helicopter could make. The sound grew louder and louder until the 'Huey flew right over their heads at a height of only twenty feet above the ground.

The big 'Huey' flew over the killing ground then swung back towards the team. It was a military job, and it had two seven point six two millimeter mini guns slung on swivel mounts below its armor plated body.

It flew right back over their heads and then banked sharply towards the second platoon.

It began firing with the same devastating effect, then turned back towards the teams position again.

The big 'Huey came back towards them flying slower now. When it reached their position it came to a hover about forty five feet up, and their radios crackled again, We'd give you boys a lift but we just ain't got the room. But we're gonna drop you boys a care package cause we know you're short on supplies."

There was a short pause, and then a large bundle was lowered on a line out the side door. When it was about five feet from the ground it was let go to fall a few feet away, and as it landed the radio crackled again, "There's food, ammo, some jackets and long johns and a couple of first aid kits too. You'll find a map and some instructions in there too"

There was another short pause, then the man continued "If you wanna keep fightin just follow them instructions with the map. If you don't just divvy up that stuff and scatter. We know you guys can be discreet, so if you decide not to come and join us we'd advise you to do just that."

Looking up at the chopper the team saw that the man speaking, and looking down at them, looked like a grizzled marine drill instructor. Now he smiled at them as he went on, "The fight ain't over yet boys! We just got to cool our jets for a while until the resistance comes back!"

The big 'Huey banked backwards and up, turning north towards the same mountains the team had been heading for. The words they heard as it departed were, "See you boys in those hills yonder!"

Losing Ground

These men were called sweepers. Their role was to go in after a base, safe house, or some other type of installation was shut down and sterilize it. This meant cleaning every inch of it to the point that nothing of it's former occupants could be determined. They also very often planted certain materials and items that were meant to misinform and misdirect anyone who might be looking for the former occupants.

This group of sweepers were part of a much bigger team that covered a large geographical area. The problem was lately that they were being hard pressed to do their jobs well, for they were being called on nearly every day for a new sweeping job. Each call, it seemed, had the same message. It was a priority job! The message was always the same, 'this or that installation was being closed down, please make sure it was sanitized ASAP'.

These men and women didn't really mind too much because they understood just how important their work was. They were all trained field agents but this was what they did best. Without their efforts there would be a trail to follow, and they wouldn't allow that unless they were misdirecting someone.

The men and women of section 'B', team one, could see the writing on the wall. The resistance was losing ground steadily. It wasn't as if they hadn't known it was coming either, they had been told to expect it. Even so, they didn't have to like it! No sir, not one little bit!

Section 'B' was a good unit but they were so short handed that they didn't have any regular field spotters with them today, that's why they didn't catch onto the watchers who were waiting for them at this location, one of the safe transfer houses used by the hundreds of resistance personnel being sent to one place or another.

In the end it wouldn't really have mattered if they had spotted them because they were outnumbered, and the only backup was at least an hour away. They wouldn't have gotten there in time to help! When the Drel watchers closed in they made two major mistakes! The first mistake they made was in trying to take these people alive so they could wring as much information from them as possible. The second mistake was their intention to make these people into Drel steeds!

The members of section 'B' may not have been full time field agents, but they were fighters! And they weren't having any part of what the Drel had in mind for them!

They killed seven of the ten Drel watchers before the last member of section 'B' died!

CHAPTER TWENTY-SEVEN
Drel

Drel An Vass

An Vass! An Vass was a ship! But what a ship! From stern to prow she was a more than three quarters of a mile long. Her main control room and flying bridge stood on columns above the main hull almost a half mile above her keel line, and she was nearly a thousand feet wide beam to beam! This huge ship was An Vass Drel, the mother ship of the Drel fleet that was slowly approaching the small blue white planet in the nine planet solar system ahead.

The flotilla, what was left of it, was comprised of nineteen ships, eighteen in the main flotilla and one scout about a light day ahead of the main body. The nearest in size to the An Vass were two that would be described as heavy cruisers and stand off gun platforms, a mere half mile in length from stem to stern. They were the An Vass' escort. Eight of the ships could be called light cruisers, and acted as scouts and flankers. The last seven were big ungainly transports. They were big fat things, and old, very old.

Their like had not been seen in this galaxy for nearly half a million years. The Drel had found them parked in geo synchronous orbit around their planet when they had taken over a hapless explorer some four thousand years ago and gone back into space. Two of these ships carried supplies necessary to the Drel. The last five, as far as the Drel were concerned, were the real prizes in the flotilla.

They were the ships that had been converted to stasis carriers, and were loaded to the gun whales with thousands upon thousands of their brethren who were being maintained in that deathlike condition called stasis. Nearly one million of them! These ships were designed to do one thing. Carry Drel to newly conquered planets and begin the process of shipping the spoils of that planet back to the Drel home system!

The Drel had already conquered almost their entire sparsely populated galaxy, some one hundred thirty or so species falling to their onslaught as they expanded ever outward. They were profligate breeders, and their early successes caused their population to explode and expand rapidly to the point where they could no longer control it. All they could do was expand the sphere of their conquests to keep the ships full of food and spoils moving back towards their home system to feed the ever widening mouth of their growing population.

The reason that they had come back to this galaxy was twofold. The first being the pressure of their population and its' ever expanding demands for more of everything.

The second was that they had only been able to find bits and scraps of information about their last foray into this galaxy and had interpreted what they had found to mean that the last incursion had failed due to some great natural calamity, and ignored any who advised caution.

The truth was that they had come here nearly half a million years ago and found something that they had never believed they would find.

They found resistance, totally implacable resistance! They had not been ready for this kind of resistance, thinking that their numbers and the methods they used to conquer would work here as well as it had in their home galaxy.

Two things had led to their downfall on their last attempt at expanding into this galaxy. The first had been ignorance and arrogance. As stated, they had never run into any serious resistance prior to entering this galaxy, so they had not been prepared to encounter species that would fight desperately to keep what they had!

That had been a very sobering experience for them! Not only had those races fought them individually, they had banded together and created a force that first equaled, then surpassed that of the Drel. Those forces had not only stopped the Drel advance, they had caused their forces to collapse back in upon itself and retreat back into its' own galaxy in total disarray. Once they had been forced back the Drel had begun to fight among themselves for control of what was left in their own galaxy.

Once that happened the hegemony they had built began to fall apart quickly, and the remaining pockets of resistance they had not managed to clean out in their own galaxy began to recover and take an additional toll on what was left of their empire.

The factor that clinched their defeat happened at the very outset of their venture into this galaxy, and was the undoing of them. The very first species they encountered just happened to be telepathic, and much stronger ones than they were. They had never encountered another telepathic species before and had always used their abilities to their advantage. Their true intentions were soon discovered and the end result was their utter defeat.

If that contended version of their history were at all true they were determined that that history would not repeat itself this time. The Drel had brought An Vass, the mother ship, and there were five more fleets under construction and near completion even as they were leaving the home system and galaxy for this one.

The story of the An Vass was a strange one. The An Vass was a relic that had been discovered in the last system in their galaxy to be conquered. It was being used by the race populating that system as a museum. Apparently that race had at one time been very warlike and had set out on their own program of conquest, but the scarcity of populated systems and their own dwindling resources had caused them to turn to other, and more peaceful endeavors.

The Drel had conquered them in their turn, and at the same time had found a spark of that warlike nature still existing in them. They became, if not willing partners, a good source of their front line shock troops for any major confrontations they might encounter as they ventured further afield.

That race turned out to be good fighters, and they were good scientists. Their conquest had been the deciding factor in the Drel decision to return to this galaxy.

The only real problem the fleet commander and captain of the An Vass was having was in understanding why it was taking so long in subduing and bringing to heel a basically primitive race and planet. The reports he had been getting were spotty, telling of pockets of fierce resistance.

Then there was the recent report from the An Vass' scanning tech that made the commander sit up and pay serious attention. Their long range detectors had been getting intermittent hits on a ship, or ships, that appeared to be shadowing his fleet.

There was nothing positive as yet, but enough to warrant serious attention on his part. This was odd because this race was not supposed to have craft capable of deep space flight. And whoever that ship or ships belonged to they were very elusive.

The commander of the fleet and captain of the An Vass, properly referred to as Drel Gol An Vass, was at present a rather perturbed being. One of the lesser, but still bothersome, of his worries was that his steed was wearing out.

This, as far as it could, saddened the Drel for it had been a good steed. It had been a strong and pliable one when he had first taken it, but it was old now and in poor health. It would be a shame to lose this one but he would soon have to go to the corral and choose another one, and send this one to the food processing vats.

That problem was really secondary at the moment, what was really bothering him was a compound list of things. The most aggravating of which was the number of problems that had occurred during the crossing, and the bulk of those concerned the An Vass. Those problems had caused the An Vass to drop out of hyper dive several times during the crossing between galaxies.

Not that he wasn't pleased with this great vessel, he was very pleased with it. It was the biggest and best ship in the Drel fleet right now, and without its' navigational systems and hyperdrive vortex generators this crossing wouldn't have been possible at all.

Why, right now five more ships just like it were being built by the klin Tal on their home world where the Drel had found this one. The An Vass had still been operational but the Klin Tal had been using it as a museum when the Drel had come.

The commander jerked his thoughts back to the present! This wandering of thoughts was just another sign that this steed was getting too old.

The original Fleet had started out with thirty ships. When they had reached the edge of their own galaxy eleven of those ship had then left the main fleet and leap ahead to their target system in the next galaxy.

First had gone a heavy cruiser designed for infiltration and foothold operations on the target planet. Then had followed ten light cruisers. These were the foothold consolidation and resistance suppression forces. Fourteen Earth standard months later the rest of the fleet began the crossing.

This ship was so big and powerful that they had had to bring the rest of the smaller ships in close to it and attach tractor beams to them to hold them inside its' protective force screens when jumping into hyperspace.

In the first jump they had lost one of the cargo haulers to one of the outermost planets of their galaxy by not doing so. Once in normal space again they could make way under their own power.

But even then the commander had to hold the An Vass at only the highest speed of the slowest ship for fear of losing another one.

That was not so much of a problem now that their target system was discernable in the navigation scopes so he had ordered increased speed and pulled far out ahead of the rest of the fleet. He'd had little fear of the An Vass being attacked when he had first issued those orders, but now he was not so sure of that still being the case.

The information sent back with their advanced forces scout had been very clear. Their intended target had very limited space operations capabilities and no weapons systems the Drel could not overcome. Even though their report was over three solar revolutions old now he felt confident that little would have occurred to have changed it.

At least he had felt that way until they had started getting those intermittent hits on their long range scanners! He preferred to remain on the safe side of such questions, but how to do so?

To answer such questions without more information led to only two logical possibilities. Either the race on the target planet had made some radical advances in their space technology, or they were being observed by the remnants of the races that had fought the Drel to a standstill.

Either way, neither of these were possibilities he wanted to give credence to by thinking about too much. No, for him the real problem right now was that the scanners could not get a lock on whatever was out there shadowing the An Vass. He would have to push the scientific types to solve this problem with their equipment.

To this end the commander decided to put his decision on a wait and see holding pattern. That decision, or indecision, would cost him and the Drel one third of this fleet and substantial damage to the An Vass.

The An Vass was now only about one quarter of a solar revolution, three local months, out from its' intended parking orbit when one of the Klin Tal steed technicians approached in a hurry and reported that three small vessels had just taken off from the planet and were heading to the galactic north at great speed towards the center of this galaxy.

Now the commander began to worry openly and ordered a reduction in the An Vass' speed. Then he sent a message to the follow on fleet, telling them to increase their own speed and close up on the An Vass' position immediately.

The commander paced the deck of his bridge, trying to fathom the impact of this news, and why it gave him a queasy feeling. His final conclusion was that it was not a good thing at all. He was very right!

The fleet had come up and closed on the An Vass, and were taking up positions around her four days later when the first objects came out of nowhere and began ripping holes in them!

Fangs

The first vessel to go in that onslaught was one of the slower stasis transports that was still trying to get itself into its' assigned fleet position. The strike against the Drel fleet, it was later determined, came in from a tangent to its' flight path. During the three minutes the attack on the fleet lasted the first minute caused eighty percent of the total damage to it.

Within one minute of the first strike five of the nineteen ships still with the main fleet were holed and seriously damaged! As said, the first vessel to be destroyed was one of the stasis transports. The loss of that vessel cost the Drel ninety thousand Drel soldiers who were being shipped in stasis, and the crew of sixty one Drel and steeds.

That loss would eventually cost the Drel an extra year in their campaign to generally subjugate the Earth. It would also cost them an additional twenty years of fighting and a large portion of one of the perpetually snow covered polar continents that they could not dislodge the remnants of the resisting Earthmen from.

They finally gave up and cordoned off that entire area to try and starve them out. That didn't work either, for they seemed to have a hidden source of food and weapons.

One of the equipment and stores transports and another of the stasis transports were holed and seriously damaged, the second stasis transport now barely able to make headway. The second ship to be destroyed was the big stand off gun platform, the heavy cruiser, with its' six huge plasma cannons. These were used in troop support to bombard hardened planetary targets in areas of strong resistance. It blew up when one of the, for many long crucial years unknown, projectiles tore through one of its' main drive engines. That cost them another two thousand Drel and steeds!

Even the An Vass took serious damage before its' gunners could figure out where the attack had come from and were able to open up with every weapon still able to fire. When they did open fire it was a real fourth of July fireworks display as the big and small plasma projectors sent streams of deadly fire into the void where they supposed the enemy to be.

The big bore lasers on the huge An Vass sent fierce beams of fiery light stabbing out for tens of thousands of miles seeking to boil away the hulls and destroy any ship they touched. Any ship without very heavy shielding would have been instantaneously incinerated when touched by those beams.

The problem was that their unknown enemy was totally elusive, leaving only questionable telltales on the fleets long and short range detection scanner screens. The commander tried to launch his short range fighters, to both screen the fleet and to engage the enemy, but could get only half of them launched. One of those terrible projectiles had holed the second launch bay, destroying or damaging half of those fighters and setting fires that they were still trying to put out.

Damage Assessment

All of this effort was to no avail. The elusive enemy was gone! In the aftermath the commander was also trying to deal with his own shock! But recriminations would have to wait! From the looks of things he would have plenty of time on his manipulators later to give consideration to them.

Right now the commander of what was left of the Drel fleet had far too many things on his mind to think about what could or should have been done differently. But one thought kept creeping back to bother him. That thought was that it had been far too long since the Drel had had to face an enemy that could fight back effectively.

He pushed that thought away viciously, and went on with the painful job of assessing the total damage to his once proud fleet. The picture that was being painted by the river of reports coming in was not one to bring any light to his ocular receptors. Two ships had been totally destroyed, and three more had taken serious damage, including the An Vass.

The An Vass had lost four of the ten short range fighters on launch bay two, and the use of that bay for at least one quarter of a cycle. Another two fighters would not be able to fly for as long also. Worse yet was the loss of three of their pilots and sixty trained service crew members.

Two other ships had been lost completely. One blowing up when its' main engines took a direct hit, and the other to explosive decompression. A second ship almost went the same way, but the crew managed to isolate the area before that happened.

The fifth ship had lost one of its' main drive engines and the harmonics on the other were now unbalanced, so that it was now only able to hobble along at one half light day per week. The commander dared not leave it out here alone to make its way for fear that the raiders would return to find it easy prey, so the rest of the fleet was held to its' best speed.

The commander avowed he would have some choice words for the on planet commander for not getting a warning to him. As it was he would be three local months late in his scheduled arrival.

The commander went on with his gory task of reconfiguring and reassigning crew and repair priorities. This was a task that kept him busy until he and his steed were ready to drop from exhaustion.

But even in his exhaustion that nagging thought managed to intrude itself again. We have not had to face an enemy who would fight back effectively for far too long!

The commander had the feeling that this fact was going to cost the Drel dearly before this was all over!

He could have no idea how right he was!

CHAPTER TWENTY-EIGHT
The Elonee

Perceptions of Change

When they returned from the exploratory flight the three of them had no peace until the whole story had been told and retold to the clan several times over. Blade the kitten, now nearly a foot and a half tall at the shoulder, found all of the attention very flattering at first but soon found himself seeking ways to sneak away so he could be near Dirk.

In the course of these events Tagon had called for a full council meeting in which Balor was to be elevated to council member. This meant that he would most likely be accepted, but Balor must attend whether he was elevated or not. The subject matter of the meeting was to define just how far the clan pledge to Dirk was to go.

A discussion of this nature required a full council, therefore Balor was nominated to fill the place of the council elder lost on the trek. When Balor found out what the meeting topic was to be about he was furious, and would have attended the meeting with or without permission.

When Tagon tried to tell Balor that there were many things he did not know or understand yet he had replied acidly that the one thing that he did know was that he would not start acting like the worst of the twolegs! A thing, he went on, that Tagon seemed willing to consider doing.

He would not, he finished angrily, become what the Elonee said they detested most about the twolegs, a being who set levels of degree of meaning on their word of honor!

Just because Dirk might not know exactly what the pledge meant to the Elonee it was no reason for the Elonee not to see that the pledge was honored to the full by and for themselves!

Tagon pleaded with him to attend and be inducted into the council, then just listen to what must be discussed before making any rash decisions, for the sake of honor and the clan.

Balor, now somewhat mollified, agreed to do this but said that he would not agree to anything that would impugn his word. Tagon accepted this as the best that he would get from him now.

Tagon had known that he should have breached this subject with Balor much sooner than this, but there had been so much going on recently that he had not been able to do so. He had intended, too, to tell him of his intention to raise his name for council status the last time he had been in the old enclave.

But again there had been other more pressing things that needed his attention. Now he wished he had made the time to do so when he'd had the chance.

With the knowledge Balor would have been given upon being raised to the status of council member Tagon did not think he would be reacting so strongly. In this Tagon would have been dead wrong!

After so many millennia on this planet Balor, and most of the other younger clan members, had taken the teachings of the clan elders completely to heart and used them to form the foundation and reason for their existence here.

By contrast to those teachings the twolegs had, for far too many years, proven themselves to be mostly unworthy of the friendship of the Elonee!

But again, by contrast to past experience, this new twolegs Dirk had proven himself to be the opposite of all that the Elonee found to be distasteful in them!

Though civilized for countless millennia the Elonee were born warriors who believed in and lived by a very strict code of ethics, especially the younger clan members! Finding one such as Dirk among the twolegs would be a natural magnet for any young Elonee warrior.

Yet again, this in itself was not the problem. For, since coming to this new place that was their new home, the Elonee had been treated with the utmost respect and honor from nearly all in Dirks' clan. Even to witnessing the harsh punishment meted out to the one twolegs who had, inadvertently it seemed to Tagon, raised a hand threateningly to one of the Elonee.

Three of the Elonee had even, after eons, been able to briefly return to space with these twolegs. Most surprisingly of all were the type of people these twolegs of Dirks' clan were!

They all were all of a type to their leader Dirk, as far as the clan elders could determine without breaking their own cannons, sharing his sense of honor and warrior ethos.

Tagon was having a very hard time rectifying his own past experiences with his recent ones with Dirk's clan. The people of his own clan had taken Dirk into their hearts and accepted him as one of their own, and Tagon had learned long ago not to try fighting such a thing as that.

What Tagons' real problem was he could not put his paw on specifically, yet he was sure that it had a great deal to do with Dirk! And for all of the Elonee here on this planet!

Even more so was his deep rooted feeling that those very changes might reach out and affect the Elonee home world, if that long lost place could be found.

Then there was Dirk himself! He had already wrought great change upon the Elonee in a very short time span. Tagon had great respect for this twolegs, for he had not only given a precious life back to the clan he had proven himself to be a keeper of his word.

Tagon had, over his very long lifetime, learned much about the twolegs that was not to be admired. But, if he were to be completely honest with himself, there was also much that could be admired too! What he did not let himself visit often was an even more deeply rooted feeling that the fate and future of his people were inextricably tied to that of the twolegs.

He did not know how, or understand why he felt this so strongly, he only knew that this feeling had gotten much stronger since Dirk had come into the lives of the clan!

The Council Meets

The council of elders were laying facing each other in a large circle on the floor of an adjunct cavern they had discovered the entrance to behind a large boulder at the end of one of the passageways off their main cavern.

At the center of this circle stood Balor. He turned slowly, facing each member of the council in turn and lowered his head respectfully to each as he did so. This was an intaking ceremony, and Balor was the candidate who had been proposed to take the place of the elder member who had died in an attempt to jump a wide ravine on the trek to this new home.

Finished acknowledging all of the members properly he lay down in the center of the circle, waiting. Presently the elder laying next to Tagon rose and paced to the center. He faced Balor squarely and looked deeply into his eyes for a long moment, then slowly reached out with a paw and rested it lightly on Balors head. This gesture was a sign, made for all present to see, that this elder had chosen to accept Balor as a council member. Had he placed it on Balors shoulder it would have been a sign of rejection.

The rule was that fifteen of the members present must vote to accept him into the seat now empty. If accepted he would be the twentieth member, and the council would once again be full and ready to govern the clan. The count was eighteen in favor, the council leader abstaining as the one ritualistic dissenting vote.

Now all of the council members rose and moved in close to Balor, gently butting heads with him and purring in welcome. They then all returned to their places, but now there was an empty place between two of them. The purring rose in volume until Balor rose and went to lay down in the empty spot. He was now a member of the Elonee ruling council on Earth.

Twenty hours later Balor had been shown and told many things, some that he had guessed at or suspected for quite some time. Some that surprised him greatly, and some that shook him to the very core of his being! Henceforth he was not, could never again be, the Balor he was before entering the circle of councilors. Too, he would never again be referred to as the youngling Balor!

Balor, even for an Elonee, was a very strong and adept telepath, and unbeknownst to the council or Tagon Dirk had taught him how to erect a mind shield around certain parts of his mind that he didn't want other to have access to at any time. So, after all of this very often disturbing information had been passed on to him by the council the meeting was called for a break. It would give Balor some time to digest much of what he had learned, and give them all a chance to take care of bodily functions, and also get some rest.

The council would reconvene in another twenty hours. As Balor came out of the council chamber he spotted Blade sitting in a small alcove, nearly invisible except for his bright eyes. Reaching out with his mind he asked him if he knew of Dirks whereabouts at this time. The younglings response nearly stopped Balor in his tracks, for it was stated so simply, as if it was common knowledge *I am never out of contact with my twolegs father.*

You can actually reach him from this far down in the caverns, through all of this rock? he asked, quickly getting his surprise under full control.

I can. Do you wish me to convey something to him, elder brother? Again the reply and question were stated simply. *No Blade, but I would like you to accompany me for a while if you would little brother. By the way, how is your Dam? I remember that she was still having some ill aftereffects from your birthing? It was so, but when Dirk found out about it he sent his clansmen to get her and bring her to a place they called an infirmary. They kept her in that place for two of their weeks, and when she returned she was in good health and spirits. She told me then that she has an interest in learning more about this thing the twolegs call medicine.*

They went up to the main cavern, ate something, then went outside for a walk on the mountain and some conversation. Balor learned many things that day especially that Blade, young as he was, was a much stronger telepath than he was. Maybe even as strong as Dirk was! Surprising him completely again Blade said to him, *I doubt that very much. I do not think the ten strongest of the Elonee are as strong as my twolegs father!*

When Balor prompted him to explain further, but he would say no more about it. Instead, he changed the subject. What he said next shocked Balor well beyond what he thought was possible. ***Balor, you are my elder brother, and also first friend to my twolegs father. You are now a council member and very well regarded by the entire clan. Tagon respects your wisdom and will listen to your voice. I think it would be a terrible thing if the council foreswore any part of their oath of allegiance to Dirk and his clan! There will never again be another advocate so strong for the Elonee, and I, nor you I believe, want to face the shame on our honor such an act would bring!***

As he was saying this he had turned to face Balor squarely and looked directly into his eyes. He apparently saw something there that he approved of for he said, ***forgive my lack of respect in speaking so, for this is a matter that is very close to me, and I am still very young.***

Balor asked spontaneously, ***Blade, why do you always put yourself with me when you're not with Dirk?***

Blade thought about this for a moment, as if he were deciding how much to say, then said, ***you, my Dam, and Dirk are my true family,*** and, as he spoke, he looked directly into Balors' eyes, ***and Dirk told me that you are very wise. He said that I must learn all that I can from you, for you will someday be the leader of all of the Elonee people!***

He paused just for a couple of seconds then finished with, ***He also said that someday in the far future I would follow in your paw prints!***

Dirk told you these things? Balor asked, stunned again in spite of his efforts at self control.

He told me also that Tagon will have much trouble dealing with what is coming in the near future. You will have to aid him greatly during the coming conflicts for it will soon be necessary for the people to choose to separate among the Humans in order that they may be together again at the end of it.

Blade paused, and looked away as if what he was about to say shamed him, then he shook himself, and plunged on ***Dirk has great and deep respect for Tagon, and knows that he has been a strong and just leader. But he fears that Tagon will not have the strength to give the orders necessary in the coming fight. Dirk is well aware of the cannons of the Elonee, but this enemy does not, nor would they care one wit for them. Dirk says that you must convince the council that what we all face is a fight for our very existence!***

Another short pause then Blade looked him in the eye and said. ***This Dirk said I must say to you in this manner. Balor, this will be the hardest thing you will ever have to do, for in this matter you will have to do whatever is necessary for the good of your people. In the end I will trust in your good judgement and our friendship.***

Now Blade was watching Balor closely, and noted the pained and far away look in his eyes. He felt parts of Balors mind close themselves off from him as his thoughts sought after answers he did not really want to know, but sought them anyway. Blade was at first surprised that Balor could do this, but quickly realized why Dirk wanted him to be with Balor. He had much to learn from him!

Blade touched Balors' mind politely to get his attention back, then went on *Dirk said that there is light at the end of this dark tunnel we all must travel. He said to tell you that Tagon and most of the rest of the clan will live to see the home world. He does not know why this is so but he says this feeling is very strong in him.*

With that statement still tolling in Balors' mind like a bell, Blade got up and left. His parting thought was *Dirk says he will meet you in his quarters in three hours time, if that is all right with you?* Balor was having trouble getting his mind around all that had been revealed to him, first by the council and then by Blade, and indirectly by Dirk. But he did manage to get out *That will be fine Blade.*

Balor knew that he would need every minute of those three hours to assimilate all of these things. What began to bother him was that Dirk seemed to know him better than he knew himself. If the things conveyed to him via Blade were even half true, and he had no reason to give them any serious doubt, he would have to give dirk and what he appeared to be developing into some very hard thought.

Some little time later Balor was just reaching out for Dirks' mind when he felt Dirks mind brush warmly against his own. Then his as yet unasked questions were answered in Dirks' inimitable fashion, unvarnished and to the point, *yes my brother, I told Blade those many things. As I see it you are the one that must guide the present as well as the future we know is rushing at us all too fast, and Blade is the future that can be! He will need strong guidance from both of us for he can be willful at times as you well know.*

Dirk gave him a few seconds to absorb this then went on, *I recognized his strength at the moment of his birth because I touched his tiny mind, and even then he bespoke me! I had to call him back for he had already begun to seek the dark. I asked him to fight, and come forth, for there is a great need for all of us. And there are far too few of us as it is to do what is needed!*

Dirks thoughts paused for a few beats, then he went on *I thought that you might want to talk but I see that you are still trying to straighten out the many things you have learned. Let us delay this conversation until after the council meeting, and until after you have gotten some much needed rest. OH, by the way, congratulations on your appointment to the council. I think they have shown wisdom in their choice of you. I am very proud of you my brother!* And he too was gone, leaving Balor to mull his thoughts alone.

Balor desperately needed time to think, and to rest. So he reached out for Tagons' mind, and when he answered begged for another ten hours before the resumption of the meeting.

Tagon could feel the turmoil surrounding Balors' thoughts but thought it was due first to the intaking, and then to the long period of revelation part of the meeting that followed. He too was tired beyond normal and readily agreed to this request. Then he told Balor that he would notify the rest of the council of the change.

Yes, he too was tired beyond his own understanding. Too much had occurred in a very short period of time, and the exhilaration of the recent trip into space was wearing off to be replaced by the tired exhaustion such sustained excitement leaves in its' wake. He also realized, sadly, that he was not making the decisions and choices he was expected to make with the clarity that was expected of him as leader of the clan, and he should begin to think about his own replacement as leader. For this Balor was the logical choice because he was at the hub of much that was happening now, and had a better grasp of what the future implications might be for the clan. Yes, he too had much to think about, and was sure the rest of the council members would feel the same. The extra ten hours would be appreciated by all! He had better get busy and notify the rest of the council members of the change in plans.

The Council Reconvenes

The reconvened council meeting was a much more solemn affair now, for all there felt the weight of the decisions they must make this day. What surprised Balor was that he now felt that most of the council members felt the same as he did about the clans pledge to Dirk and the clans honor in adhering to it.

Tagon had told Balor many things after the intaking ceremony, some of which he had already suspected. But there was one thing he had told him that Balor dared not even think about openly now. As a matter of fact it had shaken Balor so much that he had buried that secret in the deepest recesses of his mind and erected the strongest shields around it that he knew how to devise.

After thinking about it at length while he rested he now thought he understood what Dirk meant when he said that the clan must separate to remain together. After going over it once again to be sure he was fairly certain of Dirks reasoning he reached out and touched Dirks' mind gently to get his attention. Dirk confirmed his suppositions and fleshed out his own thoughts on the matter for him. Balor then told him that he would put it before the council when it reconvened.

Tagons thought query intruded on Balors' introspection, *I asked, Balor, if there was anything you wished to put before the council at this time?* he repeated himself testily.

There is elder but I would beg your indulgence for a few more minutes while I put my thoughts in order, for what I have to say is both weighty and lengthy. Balor replied formally but politely.

Very well, Said Tagon *If none disagree we will break for one hour to attend to personal needs before continuing."* Hearing no dissent he then said, *so be it.*

When the meeting had once again reconvened all eyes and minds waited attentively for Balor to begin presenting what he had to say. Balor looked upon and around at the faces of his fellow councilors and clan members, and steeled himself for the storm he knew was sure would come after he spoke.

Clan and fellow council members, he began slowly, being careful to present this first part formally and properly, *my brother, and our fellow clan member, Dirk has asked me to place the following before you for your knowing.*

After only the briefest pause Balor plunged on *Dirk as a clan member says this, for I repeat his word thoughts as he gave them to me.* Balor then opened a memory portion in his mind to the council. It played out in the following manner.

I am deeply honored to have been accepted as a member of the Clan of the Far Seekers. But I also understand that with that great honor comes a great obligation to the clan. In accepting the honor of clan status I also accept the obligation it places on me and will continue to do so to my dying breath, for it is not a thing to be taken lightly!

It has come to my knowledge that the Elonee are not originally of this world, and yet they are very much a part of it, as I one day hope to be a part of the Elonee home world!

There was a short pause in the memory, then it went on *as I see it fate and good fortune have conspired to bring us together for purposes of their own. Yet whatever those purposes may be I have only two purposes that consume me now. One of those purposes is to aid my clan in finding the home world and returning them to that place they have been away from for so long.!*

To do this is a promise I made to my brother Balor, and I now make the same promise to the full council! I shall not rest until my clan has been returned to its' home world.

I have said that I have two purposes that consume me, and so there are. The second purpose, and just as important to me, is to reclaim my own home world and defend my people from the threat that has come from outside our galaxy and overtaken it. In this quest I ask of my clan its help.

Here dirks' narrative paused just long enough to let the council absorb what had been said so far, then it went on *To give this help the clan must break itself up into small groups, as we ourselves are doing, and accompany its' twolegs brothers to many different places. From these places we will build our strength and then take back what is rightfully ours!*

Our Elonee brothers and sisters can be of great help in this by being our partners and silent sentinels on our bases and on our ships. I am sure that the enemy does not suspect your existence as yet so they will not be prepared to combat what you can add to our forces. Your contribution to us will be to fight this enemy in ways you are much better at that are we. You will fight by recognizing and exposing the enemy as they are found, before they can do damage to us. I, Dirk of the Clan of the Far Seekers, and leader of the clan of the twolegs called Earthmen, ask this of you!

Some hours later Dirk was awakened from the light trance he had put himself into by a persistent tickle in his mind. When he acknowledged it he was drawn mentally to that deep cavern where the full council of the Elonee met.

Then came slowly, almost ponderously, the combined voices of the full council *the council has pondered your thoughts deeply, and for the first time in thousands of revolutions have we nearly come to 'Elashu' (Ritual combat) because of such deliberations. Consensus was reached through our heritage and 'Lashna'a' (Bonds of Honor) for we were and are of a warrior race. We do not abandon our own nor those we call friend. You are both!*

We have reached our decision, and now the full voice of the Council of the Clan of the Far Seekers speaks as one! SO BE IT! Then Dirk was enveloped in a sense of warmth and belonging nearly as strong as his welcome to the clan.

CHAPTER TWENTY-NINE
Ghost Brigade

Ghost Brigade

"Davis," The quiet voice said into the earpiece of the mans' headset as he moved forward stealthily towards his target, "the flanks of your two follow on men are exposed." Finished the voice of the commander of the very elite unit that had become known as 'Crows' Ghosts'.

"I know that Sir." Davis said just as quietly himself, as he moved forward another few feet. "We're trying to get them to expose their position. I have a six man fast reaction team flanking those men, three to either side." He finished calmly.

"I stand corrected Mr. Davis. My apologies." The cool voice returned, only a little chagrined.

"None needed Sir. My fast reaction team is very good at what they do. If you had spotted them I would have reamed them a new one!" Captain Davis said, a smile in his words.

The meeting after the exercise was standard procedure, but at this one John Crow intended to overtly reward the men who had performed their duty extraordinarily well. Crow was a very hard taskmaster who hated losing men in combat because they were not properly trained, but he was also a commander who believed in rewarding efforts that well exceeded what was normally expected, or asked, of them.

The eight full platoons, two full companies of men and women, were lined up in front of their mess places in the mess tent standing at rest. Chow formation almost never had the full compliment assembled at one time, so the rank and file knew that something important was up. They just couldn't figure out what it was. It was rumored that the 'Ghost' commander, John Crow would be in attendance for this meal. That would really be something because he was supposed to be the most elusive man alive with the exception of John Dirk, and many said that that contest would end in a tie.

"Attention in the hall!" came the barked order, and every body there came to rigid, quivering attention. Military protocol was nothing new and was well understood by these men and women, but was seldom used here, for they were the 'First ERMA Special Operations Group'. The first ERMA unit to be comprised of men and women from every conceivable branch of service and from nearly every country on Earth.

"Take seats! Be at ease!" the barked command came at last. Every one took their seats with a sigh of relief, for they had now been standing there at attention for fifteen minutes and it had been a very long day already.

The mess tent was laid out in the standard military manner with the rank and file tables running parallel to the length of the tent and the officers table set at a ninety degree right angle to these at one end.

There, the adjutant commander rose from his seat and began tapping his tin field cup with his marine k-bar knife.

All conversation and noise came to an abrupt halt as he said in his slightly stilted Rumanian accented English, "Our 'Kammandant' has requested permission to speak to his troops. Shall ve velkom him to our meal?"

There was a loud cacophony of noise as all of the tin cups in the mess were pounded on the table tops in approval. These men and women really appreciated being asked for their permission for anyone to interrupt any portion of their very limited and precious free time!

"Then komrads, I vould like to introduce you to your very elusive commanding officer. The floor is yours Sir!" With that the adjutant sat back down in his seat with a very large 'Cheshire' smile on his ruggedly handsome face.

The men and women there began to look at each other expectantly because the seat at the center of the officers table was empty. Then a man that many there knew as Sgt. Muller rose from his place among them and paced slowly up the center aisle to the officers mess table, and then around it to come to a halt standing behind the empty chair.

He stood there for a few seconds looking out at the group seated in the tent, then he came to rigid attention and brought his hand up in a very proper salute to all assembled there. The adjutant stood quickly and barked "Atten-hut!" Every one in the tent scrambled to their feet and stood at quivering attention. The command "Present arms!" was given and three hundred and ninety hands snapped smartly to just above their right eye.

Sgt. Muller released his salute and said, "Order arms. At ease, and please be seated." But he remained standing behind the empty chair.

After letting the expectant silence drag on for a full minute he said "As you have guessed by now I'm not a Sergeant. My name is Lieutenant general John Crow, and I have the very distinct pleasure of being your commanding officer."

He paused as a slight smile curved his lips briefly, then continued. "I want you to know right now that you are the finest men and women that I have ever served with! You're hard working. You're intelligent. And you're very resourceful people. You are also the end result of an elimination process that very few were expected to make the grade in. So I guess that makes you the nastiest, meanest, the most dirty trick playing, and the best fighting force this world has ever put in the field!" he said with a big approving smile on his face now.

Crow stopped for a few seconds to turn slightly and nod at a lieutenant standing a few feet away near the exit. That worthy nodded and stepped through the tent flaps, only to return immediately with a large piece of poster board in his hands. This he kept turned away from those seated and came to stand beside and slightly behind Crow.

Crow waited a little longer, looking out over the faces assembled there as he examined them.

He saw some that had the harsh features of seasoned combat veterans and many more of them had deceptively boyish and girlish features, but they all had one thing in common. They all had the eyes of trained killers! They had gone through a grueling three month training and elimination period, which only the hardest working most dedicated ones had survived. A little over fifteen hundred had been sent to him. Only four hundred of them remained!

Crow resumed speaking, every eye and ear following his every gesture and word, "I have a surprise all for you. As of this moment all of you have graduated this training period, and each and every one of you has earned the right to be called one of 'Crows Ghosts'!" he finished, smiling openly at them now.

The tent erupted in applause, whistles, and the banging of tin cups on table tops. They were applauding both their elusive commander and themselves, for they had been winnowed down to only the very best of the best. They had excelled and worked very hard to achieve the standards set by him, and had a right to be proud of themselves, for he was very proud of them!

When the noise died down he raised his hand to let them know there was more to come. They went almost instantly silent, and he said "You are the first but not the last of us, for those that follow you will have very large shoes to fill! So, with that in mind, I have taken the liberty of having a unit emblem designed for you."

He turned to the waiting lieutenant and nodded. That worthy promptly turned the board he had been holding to face the tables and held it high for all to see. There was a hushed silence as four hundred pairs of eyes took in what would become the sigil of the most feared unit the Drel and their minions would ever have the misfortune of facing. Even Valasovics' vaunted space marines would give due respect to those who wore this patch!

The patch itself was a spear shaped four pointed shield that was colored blood red. Inside the field of this was a smaller three pointed shield that was all black. In the center of that shield was an upright gold and silver sword with blood dripping down half the length of its' blade. In an arc cross the top of the black shield were printed three words. Havoc and Death.

After setting the poster board on an easel so that all could continue to see it easily the lieutenant motioned to several men waiting at the rear of the tent. They nodded, picked up boxes sitting at their feet, and began passing out to each man and woman in the tent berets with patches already sewn on them, and patches to be sewn onto their uniforms later. During this Crow watched his troops noting their reactions.

Now, in a deep voice that stilled every other sound in the tent, he said, "I have two questions for you. The first is who are you?"

During this whole proceeding there had been a palpable undercurrent running through the tent that could almost be touched, and could definitely be felt. At that roared question the undercurrent burst forth as every voice there roared back at him, "We're the 'Ghost Brigade', Sir!"

"And what will you bring to the enemy?" he roared back at them.

"We bring fear!" they roared right back, caught up completely now as they finished the process of melding into a whole as a unit.

"Will they see you coming?" he shot at them.

"They will never see us coming!" their response came back at him like a rolling wave.

"What will they know when you make your presence known?" Crow roared again.

"Havoc and death!" they roared back. Even the officers were caught up in the melding now, for their voices were just as loud as the rest.

"Will they know when you've left?" he snapped at them.

"You can't see a ghost leave, Sir." They came right back at him.

"Who are you?" Crows' voice fairly shook the fabric of the tent now with its volume.

"We are Crows' Ghost Brigade Sir!" They roared back at him as every body there surged to its' feet.

"What do you bring, and what do you leave?" This last was said in a voice so low and so cold that many of them actually shivered.

"We will bring fear to the enemy, and in our wake we shall leave Havoc and Death!" their reply this time was just as low and just as cold with meaning.

"See that you Do! Now, sit down and finish your meal." Crow finished, a cold smile of satisfaction on his face.

Forty five minutes later Crow pushed back his chair and stood up, clearing his throat loudly as he did so. Quiet descended on the mess tent abruptly, all eyes now on him.

"I have some additional information for you. Two days from now you are going to infiltrate the Rocky Mountain base in Canada and take control of the command center and the production facilities in that mountain base!" he stated flatly.

If this brigade had wanted something to challenge what they had been taught they couldn't have been given a harder task. They were beginning to look at each other when Crow spoke again.

"There are three things you need to know. First: you will operate in five and ten man teams as you have been taught. Second: they do not know you are coming!"

"Third:," and here Crow paused with a malicious smile on his face, "Any team caught by anyone other than one of the Elonee will stand in review for one week and explain to anyone who asks them how and why they were caught!"

He paused for a full thirty seconds to let that sink in, then said in a very quiet voice that left no doubt whatsoever about the meaning of what he said, "This will be your only dry run. After this if you get caught you get dead!"

Looking out over them now the looks of dismay at another drill were gone, replaced by one look only. Determination!

"Your team leaders will be issued whatever information is appropriate at the morning mess call. Good hunting people."

As the men and women there began to rise from their seats, and quiet conversations were begun about what they had learned, Crow once again cleared his throat loudly.

Again all noise ceased abruptly as they returned their attention to him.

"Oh, I almost forgot," he began with an impish smile now in place, "I know that all of you have heard a lot of tales about the Elonee. Most of those stories are pure BS, so I'll set you straight about them here and now!"

"First: the Elonee are telepaths. That is true! But they cannot communicate with every one. About two thirds of the twolegs, as they call us, have no telepathic abilities at all."

"Second: they do not go around reading every ones mind! That is false! They will not attempt to do so without your express permission! To do so is strictly taboo to them, and there are very, very few reasons that will allow them to break that taboo!"

"Lastly: during the course of this exercise they, the Elonee, will be making choices as to who they will work with in this brigade. That is a choice only they can or will make. If one of the Elonee confronts you kneel down in front of it.

Then, carefully and slowly, place a hand on its' shoulder. The rest will work itself out." He looked out at the attentive faces for a few seconds, then said "Do you understand what you have just been told?"

One slightly grizzled master sergeant in the front rank looked around at the rest, then turned back to face him with a mischievous smile of his own on his face as he replied for the rest, "Yes Sir! Don't screw around with the cat people unless they let us know otherwise!"

Even though he appreciated the gesture he wanted these people to understand what could happen to them if they messed up.

He said to that worthy, "That's right sergeant. I would hate to be the one who made the mistake of underestimating them! I've seen what the one who is always with Dirk did to a couple of the Drel he caught! Keep that in mind! That's all for now men. Again, good hunting."

One of the men overheard Crow say to his adjutant as he was passing by on his way to the exit, "Well Vinosh, we've taught them to maim, kill, and destroy.

I just hope we will have a chance to teach them to live!"

CHAPTER THIRTY
Interludes

Blade and Dirk

Dirk was sitting on a thinly wooded rocky outcrop high up on the western side of the mountain overlooking the base. He had been sitting there for a couple of hours now. He came here for two reasons. The first was that it was quiet and he could think clearly and freely without the normal multitude of interruptions and distractions that took up so much of his very long work day. The second reason was that he could practice his mental exercises unhindered by the constant press of other minds. They often felt so close that they began to intrude on his conscious thought processes. Not that he was actually reading anyone's mind.

He couldn't do that without expending a great deal of energy, and even then he only got the surface thought that person was thinking. And, generally, the other person had to have some real degree of telepathic ability, and then it was only when that person was thinking about him, or something that had something to do with him. It was like some external pressure that pushed at him, at his mind, even when he was alone.

TuLan had told him about this effect, explaining that he would have to practice erecting a basic block to keep out the unwanted mind noise. When asked how he put up with the constant pressure TuLan had said that erecting his own block was so automatic that he didn't even think about doing it any more. He also told Dirk that he would learn how to attune himself to know when someone was trying to contact him directly through that block.

As he sat there trying to make decisions about what to do about some of the more troubling things that were happening to some of his people still out in the field he heard the faint but distinct sound of a twig cracking as weight was put on it. Even as the muscles in his legs and shoulders began to tense for some required action, he was pushing his mental awareness out to encompass his surroundings.

His awareness touched a familiar mind. It's owner was thinking of itself as crafty and skillfully quiet. Dirk smiled to himself, then sent a warm thought

473

directed at the young mind. ***Blade, why don't you come up here and join me instead of trying to sneak up on me?***

Completely unabashed Blade replied succinctly, *as always, my two legs father, you are ever aware and set high standards for this one to reach for.*

No Blade, I doubt very much if I could hear you coming if you did not intend me to do so. Dirk replied warmly.

You are much to lenient with a mischievous youngling. Came the warm, almost purring, reply.

Changing the subject of this good natured give and take Dirk asked a bit more seriously, ***Blade, why do you always refer to me as your twolegs father?***

You have but to look into this ones mind to know the answer to this. Came the simple reply.

You know I would not break the 'cannons' of the clan! Dirk responded in a sharp tone.

Please forgive this youngling, for I meant no disrespect. Blade said almost contritely, although Dirk felt a mischievous smile hiding somewhere behind the contriteness. Then, *"I meant only that my mind is always open to you."*

There was a short pause, then the young Elonee went on *the clan has claimed you as one of its' own. Balor claims you as his near brother. My sire was lost on the Trek here, and at the time of my birthing there were many complications for my Dam and all forsook the tiny life within her as lost! But only you saw the life that all accepted as lost, and gave it back to me! So, I claim you as my near sire. Or father, as your clansmen call it.* He finished, no trace of a smile in his mental voice now.

Then, without the slightest remorse, he said with a bright smile and a hearty chuckle transforming his tone, *you just happen to be a twolegs.*

Then, more pensively, he went on, *there is also a bond between us, so strong that it is hard to understand. It calls to me when we are apart. I sometimes think that it is very important that I be near you to learn many things of import, that you are somehow very important to my future, and that of the clans.*

Those are very deep thoughts for a youngling. Dirk chided him good naturedly, but Blades' statements had struck a chord within him. Blades next words pulled that chord taught!

I have a memory of a mind of great strength, seeking and finding that thing that is myself, and the feeling of great joy in that strong presence when contact was made. That presence called me forth saying that my life was important, and that I was needed! Were it not for that firm guidance, and the strength to fight for this life lent to me by that presence, I might have easily let go of it!

Blade took a mental breath, then went on, *the strange thing is that now, at this very moment, I understand that you left a part of yourself with me at that moment of choice. So, in truth, you are as much my sire as any in the clan might be!*

Dirk now acknowledged to himself why he so often felt at odds with himself when Blade was not around, admitting the reality of that bond. But he said only, *then, in all truth, a sire could ask for little more than a youngling like you.*

Blade didn't say anything else. He just came and lay down next to Dirk, resting his big beautiful head on his knee. This gesture said volumes without the necessity of poor words. They stayed that way for a some time, each enjoying the silent company of the other.

On a plane, well above what Blade could sense, Dirk sent a questing thought, *Balor my brother, I need your council!*

Paul Denton and His Boss

Dentons' boss had brought a daughter, that Denton had not known he had, and her husband. In the beginning those two had pestered them with questions and complaints at all of the restrictions placed upon them. His boss had quickly tired of this, and told them in no uncertain terms to shut up and do as they were told if they wanted to live! Life was no longer 'things as usual'. The daughter knew her father, and knew what he did for a living, so after that she took her husband aside and had a few words with him. After that there were no more complaints.

Denton, like his boss, brought his secretary. She in turn brought her unmarried daughter and her married son, along with his wife and single child. The son and daughter knew of their mothers' position, and did everything they were asked to do.

Though the three week trip to the Canadian base was rough, and a little scary at times, the group was treated with respect and some little deference. After only three days at the base they were hustled, eyes all agoggle, into an amazing space ship. Once settled in the cramped quarters they were allotted they were made to wait for a full day. "Just like the army," his boss groused, "hurry up and wait."

Early in the morning of the fourth day they were awakened to the feeling of the ship moving. Within minutes the intercom in their rooms came to life and they heard "All passenger not in their bunks please return to them immediately! Planetary departure in five minutes. I repeat. All passengers return to your bunks, departure in five minutes." Five days later they heard another terse message. "all passengers, attention! Return to your bunks immediately! Hyperspace jump will commence in ten minutes."

It had been twenty days since those events and the group was beginning to get on each others nerves from a lack of things to do. It did not seem anything at all like what any of them thought space travel would be like. Then had come the call over the intercoms and loudspeakers, "All hands, breakout from hyperspace in ten minutes from my mark. All hands not at duty stations strap down. All passengers return to your bunks now!" This message was repeated once more, and at the end of it they heard "Five-four-three-two-one-mark!"

Ten minutes later there was the same gut wrenching feeling that they had felt when they had entered hyperspace. Twenty minutes later the speakers came to life again and they heard "All hands and passengers. Successful reentry. Welcome to the Fenris System, and to Wolfsbane, your new home!"

Then the speaker went on, "We will make planetfall in three days time. All passengers stow and have your gear ready for debarkation. Also, in one hours time, we will start letting passengers in groups of twenty visit the main crew lounge to view your new home on the holo-screen there. You will be allowed one half hour in the lounge. Please be prompt when you are called, and leave promptly when you are asked to! Thank you for your co-operation."

Suffice it to say that, other than the fact that they were actually in another star system, the half hour spent in the lounge was the high point of the whole trip out. They were in for many more surprises.

The ships landing was anti climatic. As a matter of fact, other than the announcement, they hardly noticed the landing at all. But as they boarded the huge cargo elevators with the single duffel bags they had been allowed to bring they were met by a muted roar of sound that rose in volume as they neared the ground. As the elevator dropped away from the belly of the ship the bustle of activity around it at ground level was stunning to say the least. They had not expected anything at all like what that panorama unfolded for them.

That cacophony of sound and activity arrested them as the elevator touched the ground. Having somehow expected some half developed town of jerrybuilt buildings and open spaces they were dumbfounded by what they saw.

Instead they were greeted by the sight of a bustling small city. One with many well built homes and larger buildings that could only be factories, and streets that radiated out from the spaceport. Yes, a spaceport, for they could see now that it was a truly huge, concrete, area that had been designed with rapid expansion in mind. There were also three other space ships sitting on pads loading or unloading cargo's of people or materials. As the group stepped off the elevator, trying to absorb what they saw, a man in a neat black and silver uniform stepped forward and asked their identities. Once assured he had the right party he said quite politely, "If you would follow me please, there is transportation waiting for you. Governor McCarthy would like to see you as soon as possible!"

"What about our charges here?" Denton and his boss asked the man almost simultaneously.

"You will all be put up at the governors residence until quarters can be arranged for you. Please follow me." He said, and without further ado he turned and walked quickly towards a large truck-like vehicle parked about forty yards away. The truck was actually an oversized humvee that was designed to transport full squads of soldiers, and as could be expected, the ride to the governors residence was a bumpy one. The governors residence was a large three story wood and stone structure built in the shape of an 'H'. One entire wing, and most of all three floors of the central hall were used for government business. The ground floor of the last wing and half of its' second story were used as the governors residence. The balance of the second story and the top floor were used for guests, and temporary quarters for newly arrived upper rank ERMA members waiting for permanent quarters assignment.

They drove up to the building via its' long 'U' shaped driveway and were deposited at the front entrance. One of the governors aides came over and took charge of them. Calling one of the sentry's over that man told him to have the group led to the visitors guest quarters, and to get some help with their bags. He turned to Denton and his boss and said to those two that the governor would like to see them immediately if they didn't mind, and that their bags would be taken care of for them. In an aside he said in an undertone that governor McCarthy had been asking them if the new arrivals had landed every ten minutes for the last hour.

He led the two up the walk to the main entrance and, once inside, up two flights of steps to an office that encompassed the entire top floor. There must have been fifty computer terminal work stations set up in there, and every one of them was manned by someone busily entering or checking data. They were led across this room to a hall that led to the front left wing of the building, and down that to a large door that the aide tapped on and opened for them to enter. His boss went right in, with Denton close on his heels.

Sam McCarthy got up from the large, comfortable looking, chair behind his desk and came forward smiling warmly, his large beefy hand outstretched in greeting as he said, "Percival, I'm so glad you finally got here.", and "And you too, Mr. Denton." He said turning to face Paul, extending his hand, still smiling.

"Bit of an adventurous trip, but we're here as promised." Pauls' boss said, then, "But what's so all fired important that we couldn't get whatever passes for coffee around her before you put us to work?" he finished, but there was a warm smile creasing his face as he said it. "It's good to see that you're still in one piece Sam."

"It's just like you to think of the really important things first Percy. Come on over here and sit down on the sofa and I'll get you both a cup of the god awful stuff myself." He said affably. The sofa was across the large room, facing a large picture window that looked out over the bustling small city they had just traveled through to get here. It was a panoramic view of what can happen when the right man is put in charge of things that have to be done fast and right the first time.

The small city they now looked out over was laid out with large boulevards in concentric circles, and many thoroughfares cutting it into large pie shaped wedges. So far there were three main circular roadways, with two more of them now under construction. And everywhere one looked people and vehicles scurried hither and thither on unknown but obviously important errands.

As the two men seated themselves it was hard for them to take their eyes from that view. It was also obvious that neither man had expected to see anything the size or scope of what they were looking at. Percival Whitney, Pauls' boss asked McCarthy, as he handed each of them a cup full of a very dark brown liquid, "How did you manage to do all of this in such a short period of time, Sam?"

"It's much easier than you might think, Percy, especially when you don't have to deal with unions and damn fool bureaucracies. And it helps a lot that where and how you eat and sleep depends only on how much you're willing to work for it!" he finished, a sardonic smile flitting across the features that both men could now see showed signs of deep tiredness.

"Ugh! This stuff is really terrible." Whitney said, his face screwed up to show his distaste, "Don't you have any real coffee in this place yet Sam?"

"You'll get five pounds of coffee and two hundred tea bags issued to you when your quarters are assigned. It will have to last you for four local months before you get another issue. The good news is that there is some local barter for it going on with those who don't drink coffee. Anyway, that stuff is something local we found to help extend the coffee. You'll get used to it pretty quickly. I'd really recommend that you do so because our supply of coffee will be gone within a year if we don't get another shipment soon." McCarthy finished ruefully.

Not one to let politeness get in the way of getting things done, Whitney said abruptly, "OK Sam, you got us here. Now what can we do to help you out?"

"I'm glad you haven't changed much Percy. OK, I got you out here because I want you to be my Lieutenant Governor! That's Planetary Lieutenant Governor to be exact, Percy!" he said, smiling at the look on his long time friends face.

All Percival Whitney could think of to say was "Well, you always could throw a hell of a good surprise party, Sam!"

A couple of hours later, after getting a very concise but thorough briefing about what had been done to date, and what would be expected of him, Whitman accepted the job. After a handshake to cement things McCarthy asked him, "That leaves me with one post yet to fill. What do you think Percy, would young Mr. Denton be the right man to put in charge of planetary security?"

Without hesitation Whitney said "It would be hard to find a better qualified man Sam! I know. I trained him myself."

"Then that's taken care of." McCarthy said, a genuine smile of relief breaking out on his face. "Your office is right next door to mine Percy. Paul, your office is right under mine on the second floor. Mr. Carter, my aide, will introduce you two to your staffs and get you and your people set up with quarters in the residential wing until permanent quarters can be assigned to you."

"Percy, I have an excellent idea. Why don't you promote your secretary to your chief of staff position. I happen to know that she is very capable."

"Paul, one of Dirks' top men is here on planet. He's waiting to bring you up to date on what we've learned about the Drel, and some other very interesting things as well."

"Oh," McCarthy said almost as if in afterthought, "there is one last and very important thing you have to know about, and tell those who came in with you about this also!" He paused with the hint of a smile playing at the corners of his mouth as if he were about to enjoy startling them with something he knew they were going to have to learn to deal with.

McCarthys' smile was open now, in anticipation of what he was about to say to the men before him, "You will, during your wanderings around here, encounter several large cats, I mean nearly 'Panther' sized, walking freely about this building and many of the production facilities! Now, understand this very clearly! They are never to be molested or interfered with under any circumstances what so ever! It's not that I'm too worried about them being hurt by one of you, it's the other way around. And, if they didn't kill you Dirk probably would!"

He paused at the looks on their faces, remembering his own consternation when he had first learned of the Elonee, then went on quickly, "They are sentient beings, and our allies! You, Paul, will most likely be working very closely with them in the future! There is an awful lot you don't know yet, but everything will be explained to you fully starting tomorrow morning. I'll see you then."

Paul Denton and Percy Whitman looked at each other, their eyes asking each other the question they were both thinking at the same time. 'what have we gotten ourselves mixed up in?' Then, almost as if one man, they both gave themselves a mental shake, accepting the fact that they were now involved.

Both Paul Denton and Percy Whitman would have occasion to have very close ties to the Elonee in the future. Paul Denton would even be chosen as a partner by one of them.

Too, Paul Denton had no idea that he was a very strong telepath that was just waiting to happen!

Jimmy Lester and Daleel

Jimmy Lester was busy making plans for his immediate return to space with the Shrike when he felt the tickle at the edge of his mind. He was still not that comfortable with his newly discovered telepathic abilities so he was slow to respond to the polite touch at his mind. It came again, a little more insistent this time. He visualized a pathway, as Balor had shown him how to do, and sent a query thought along it. *Who?*

Suddenly his mind, at least that part that he had opened the pathway in, was suffused with an intense warmth. Right behind that warmth came the thought, *I greet you twolegs Jimmy Lester.*

Jimmy jumped up from the small desk he had been working at in his small alcove living and work space, and almost tripped as he hurried to open the door. He pulled the door open, at the same time he pushed a thought along that still rude pathway in his mind, *you are most welcome here Daleel! Will you share my space for a while?* he said, stumbling a little over the manner of the Elonee formal greeting. As the beautiful feline being, known as Daleel of the Elonee, padded into his quarters she playfully sent back, *were you an Elonee your invitation would have been a proposal of mating!* This was sent with another, stronger, sense of warmth and a hint of mirth. Jimmy was a little flustered at this, but came back with, *were I Elonee it would have been, for you are very special in my thoughts!* This seemed to catch the normally very cool Daleel by surprise, for Jimmy was sure he sensed what would pass for a blush in her thoughts. Daleel was very fast to recover, and shot right back at him, *were you Elonee I might even have considered accepting!* But this time Jimmy was sure he felt an almost wistful coloration to her thoughts. He said contritely, *my apologies Daleel. I meant no disrespect to you. Please call me Jimmy.*

She turned her lambent gaze on him and looked searchingly into his eyes for a few ageless seconds before saying, *I was taking your comments as what you twolegs call a compliment, so your apology is not needed by this one.*

Changing the subject abruptly she said, *I bring a message from Dirk, through Balor. Do you wish to hear it now?*

It didn't matter that she was an alien! The beauty of this being nearly drove Jimmy, who was normally very reserved, to distraction, and he almost stammered as he said, *yes, of course, please go ahead.*

Jimmy was distracted again, but this time it was because it was almost as if Dirk were speaking directly to him in his minds eye. This was one of the hardest things about telepathic communication to get used to, for the Elonee could project the entire message, with pictures, and through as many intermediaries as it took to get a message to the right person.

Jimmy saw Dirks' head and shoulders as he spoke. The message went, *Balor, would you get a message to Jimmy Lester right away for me? Good! Please tell him that there has been a change in plans. He will not be taking the Shrike out, he will be taking the Griffin out instead. It will be ready in two days time. Jimmy is to see Captain Miller and introduce himself. Captain Miller already has his orders, so Jimmy is to make all arrangements with him. Thanks Balor.* The message ended and the images faded from his mind. *Thank you Daleel, and thank Balor for me will you?*

Daleel said reproachfully *you could thank him yourself if you but tried a little harder to master what is already in you!*

I know but I have so many responsibilities, and I have no one to practice them with. Jimmy said, hoping to dodge that bullet.

This was strange for Jimmy was not known for dodging things.

Jimmy, she said almost diffidently, *I would ask something of you, if you wouldn't mind.*

Sensing her diffidence Jimmy said quite honestly, *Daleel, you are the one being in this crazy galaxy who can ask me anything!* he said with real feeling.

Thank you Jimmy, you know of the choosing that is beginning to take place among the Elonee?

I do, he said simply, *but I don't know much about how it works.*

It is a thing that first began when our people first began going into space with the ancient ones. We, as a people, do not make things, but we are very good scouts, seekers, and communicators. We had a deep yen to learn about and visit other stars, so we partnered with other space faring races to do so. When we partnered it was called a choosing. This was never done lightly for we learned very quickly that there were those who would use our abilities for ill. Do you understand now? she said intently.

Yes, I think I do. Thank you for telling me. But why do you ask?

She seemed to take a deep, shuddering, breath both physically and mentally. Then, *would it please you if I were to choose you?*

Jimmy was stunned, but remembering his sense of her diffidence said to her with deep feeling, *Daleel, there is nothing in the world that would please me more than that. But could you not sense this in me?*

Now she spoke with a great sense of relief in her tone, *this is still very new to me, also, and I would not want to place myself where I was not wanted. But now I make my choosing!*

Jimmy felt her open her mind on many channels as she sent out a strong thought pattern. Daleel sent her message out on many channels and levels. Her thoughts reached out to touch her people as she stated firmly *I have chosen! I will partner with our twolegs brother Jimmy Lester. I have spoken as custom requires!* Jimmy looked at this wonderful being with new eyes now, for he understood very well that this would not be a short term relationship. This Elonee had just committed herself to him. That was the reason for the formality and the manner of the announcement.

With the exception of Dirk and a couple of others, Jimmy had seldom allowed himself the luxury friendships where it was possible to trust that friend with his innermost thoughts, and this one, he was positive, would be one of those. He wondered what this would be like for the both of them.

He did know that Dirk and Balor had become very close over the last three and a half years. And because he had just begun to understand the real implications that a telepathic relationship could have he was still very unsure of himself.

Because he was who he was, and had been doing what he had been doing for so many years, Jimmy had naturally been drawn to people like Dirk and the rest of those stalwarts who were now involved at the core of the resistance movement. They were all men and women who had come to prize two things above all else. Honor and real friendship! Those were the things that were the hardest to maintain or give, for honor was a thing that was constantly challenged and tested, and friendship a thing that was often used as a weapon used against you. This made them all the more rare, and all the more valued. But, of one thing Jimmy was very sure. Daleels' decision had made him very happy! Then he realized that Daleel was waiting for something. It hit him then that he had been uncharacteristically wool gathering and he acted quickly to right this omission.

He sent out his thoughts in open sending, as strongly as he knew how to do, *I am Jimmy Lester of the twolegs, and I have been chosen! I say that I accept this choosing!*

Jamat and Bill Tate

Why do you not try, Tate? Jamat of the Elonee asked of the man sitting with his back propped against the landing skid of the newest ship off the production line, located in the main cavern of the Earth Resistance Movements main base.

It's no use Jamat! Balor said that I didn't have any telepathic ability. Bill Tate said plaintively. He really liked Jamat, and tried to talk to him at every opportunity. Maybe it was because Jamat always took pains to let Bill see him coming when he was around, and Jamat was just as quiet as any of the Elonee when he moved. *Besides, we get along OK this way.*

We do not! I tell you this because I feel in you the ability. It is faint and lies deep, but it is there. Do not forget that I have come to know you somewhat better than Balor does, for we have spent much time together these last several moon phases. This makes a difference between what Balor, and what I, can sense in you! If you will make the effort again I will attempt to guide you. He finished hopefully.

You are my friend Jamat. In three short years my life has changed in more ways than I would have dreamed possible. And I have a big, beautiful cat that I talk to as a friend! Just tell me what I must do! Bill finished almost desperately.

Before we begin I should tell you that there is one thing that I might try. I believe that your talent is being interfered with by a mind shield that you created unconsciously, and you are not able to penetrate it by yourself. To help you I must first find, then break, the shield. But to do so I will need your willing help, and permission! Will you do this with me Tate? Jamat said, excitement now coloring his thought tone, for he felt in this that he was right. All of the little telltales had crystallized, finally, into the right pathway to follow for him.

Thinking furiously Bill went through all of his previous efforts to try, and bring forth, any talent he had, but to no avail so far. Without really understanding all of the reasons yet, Bill came to the conclusion that this was something that he really wanted for himself. He steeled himself, with that new understanding, to do whatever would help him achieve it. He said, *I trust you nearly as much as I do Dirk! Do what must be done Jamat.*

This conversation had gone on as usual, with Bill resting one hand lightly on the big cats shoulder, direct contact the only way he could carry on any lengthy conversation with Jamat. Now Jamat said, *my friend Tate, you must place both of your paws on my shoulders, and your head close against my own, for the closer our contact the easier it will be to join minds with you.*

Bill woke up several hours later. He was in his own bed, and he had the mother of all headaches throbbing in hammer strokes behind his eyes. Then he felt a slight tickle in his mind, and he heard Jamats' voice clearly although he was nowhere in sight. *We did well together Friend Tate. It is done, and you are free to learn how to use your talent now!*

CHAPTER THIRTY-ONE
Rear Guard Actions

Ghost Actions

"Wait one!" was the prompt reply. Then there was only the quiet hissing of the open carrier wave for an eternity of seconds. When the next words broke the silence in the mans earbud the quiet words almost sounded, to the man, like thunder in his ears. The quality of the mans nerves and training proved themselves, as he barely twitched in response. "Can you penetrate the inner security ring?" The quiet voice asked.

"The problem is not in getting in," the man in the camouflage battle gear said very quietly into the tiny boom microphone slung in front of his mouth, "the problem will be in getting out again!" He was silent for about five seconds, then said hopefully "About four or five hellfire missiles and a couple of fast choppers would sure make a difference in how this comes out. If they could be gotten to lift off and chase a couple of those fast helicopters they would be caught in the air when the charges go off."

"Hold your position! I'll get back to you in five to let you know what can be done." The disembodied voice said crisply in his ear, and was gone again.

As he waited, the night sounds around him and his ten man team seemed to become louder, more pronounced, unavoidably drawing their attention to each new sound. Each man in the team knew that the smallest thing could give them away, and that if they were taken alive they faced certain death or worse. But their training was the best there was to be had, and they had learned well what they had been taught so they hunkered down thinking of themselves as part of their surroundings. And they became so! There was a whisper of crackle in the mans whisperphone earpiece, then he heard "Penetrator two, Charlie Bravo Delta is six minutes out your position, and will parallel your track eight hundred meters forward your position at twelve o'clock. Also penetrator five has been diverted your position and will be in place in five from my mark. Mark. You have your diversion. Good luck. Control out."

"Roger that." Was his short reply. Then he turned to the man nearest him so he could be seen clearly, and giving hand-speak signals, told him of the change in their approach and timing, which that man would pass along to the next man, and so on. Almost five minutes exactly from the mark he had been given there was a double click in his earphone bud. The other team was now in position. He scratched a small stone lightly, almost silently, with his fingernail to get his mans attention, then notified him to pass the word to keep down and be ready to move. The fireworks were about to start. Within thirty seconds of this his earphone earbud crackled, and he heard, "Hope you boys found some deep spots. Incoming!"

Close to the near horizon behind their position four blossoms of orange and red fire came to life. Then, with incredible speed, those blossoms turned into hurled spears of fire as the four 'Hellfire' missiles released by an 'Apache' helicopter sped past overhead towards the opposite side of the airfield from their position. He only had time to snap out "Protect your eyes!" before those missiles hit a company of revetted tanks placed there to protect the Drels' newly arrived atmospheric ships, which were their targets.

Almost before the missiles had finished detonating into huge rising balls of orange and red fire that threw parts of the exploding tanks and bloody tatters of their hapless crews almost a thousand yards away from their points of impact he heard the sounds of small arms fire and rifle launched grenades going off. The other team was giving a good performance of a major raid. As he raised his head higher he could see from the flickering backlighting of the burning tanks and support vehicles more vehicles loaded with men rushing to reinforce that quadrant.

The team leader whispered urgently into his tiny boom mike, "Heads up! Two charges per ship, ten minute timers. Then scatter and regroup at rendezvous Alpha three. Go!" The men began to slip, ghostlike, across the landscape lit up intermittently by the flickering flames of the burning tanks. After taking one last look to see that all were moving towards their assigned targets the team leader jumped up and ran in a half crouch towards his own. Then, as a thought struck him he switched his radio to his second in commands private channel. Gasping a little from running so far in a crouched over position he said, "Tommy, meet me about a hundred yards to the backside of the operations center, after you've set your charges. We'll give the other team a little help while they're disengaging by creating a small diversion. Three grenades each and one full clip each, then get outta dodge! K?"

"Roger that." Was the quiet reply he got, as he was thinking that it wouldn't take the base personnel long to bring enough fire power to bear to force them to start retreating. He also knew that it wouldn't take them long to realize that the ordinance that had hit the tanks had been air launched. He just hoped his people were as fast in real time as they had been in practice. This was a very important mission for two reasons. It was very important to make the enemy believe that the resistance could hit them anywhere, and the other reason was to turn them away from their present line of march towards the Canadian base!

The members of the team flitted from one dark spot to another, shadows among many other shadows and all but invisible. They made no noise as they worked their way towards the new Drel atmospheric ships that were their targets. The guards could have, should have, been much more alert but they were looking off towards the sounds of firing. It really didn't matter that much now because they were all dead men before they could realize anything was wrong. Six and one half minutes later the team leader heard four very distinct clicks in his earbud. The team had finished setting their charges and were exfiltrating. They left no sign of being there. They had hidden the guards bodies which would not be found for several days, which would only cause additional fear when they were found.

The team leader waited near the perimeter fence, hidden behind several parked vehicles. He heard a double click in his earbud and several seconds later, Tommy, his second in command slid in beside him. In almost sub vocal whispers they finalized how they would place themselves and fire their grenades and clips of ammunition, then melt away to join the rest of the team and make their way to their pickup point.

They launched four well placed grenades each that were aimed at the windows of various buildings so that the explosions would create the most damage and confusion both inside and outside. They each fired six five round bursts from their automatic rifles as they retreated in a large x pattern that would give the impression of there being many more men firing than there were. The ruse worked because they could hear men screaming into their radios that the headquarters was under attack by a large force. They also heard the Drel atmospheric flyers begin taking off from their pads as they retreated.

They wouldn't get very far. That was the whole point of this mission, to cripple or destroy their air superiority in this quadrant so that those who were still trying to get to the big northern base would have a reasonable chance of doing so without being spotted from the air, and troops landed in front of them to cut them off.

The explosive charges attached to the airframes had been set with detonators that began their countdowns when the craft began to vibrate as they took off. The ships climbed quickly to three hundred feet and began to search for their attackers, but the ships were new to their pilots and it took nearly seven or eight minutes for them to organize themselves into a reasonable search and cover pattern. That was their undoing!

A minute or so later the first craft exploded in a ball of flame and flying pieces of steel and alloys. There was consternation and confusion as they now broke their search formation and began to look for attacking aircraft! What else could it be? There had been no rocket engine flares or exhaust trails from the ground! The pilots searched frantically, by instrument and by eye, for their attackers. As the craft after craft exploded in mid air those pilots and their crews died wondering how it was being done, for they could find nothing. They were being attacked by ghosts!

As the two men made their way to the point where they would meet up with their other team members they spoke softly to each other in short, clipped, sentences. "We were really lucky tonight, Tommy! They had no idea we would come at them like this. They won't be caught sleeping next time." The team leader said, grief and anger coloring his words because he hated the idea of killing men who had no control over their actions.

"I know, Phil, and it's going to get a lot worse before it's over!" There was silence for a few seconds as they checked their surroundings, then Tommy went on, "I've been thinking about what the general said at the graduation dinner, and he was right. We're going to have to think up some very interesting ways to make them fear us! I think that one way to do that is to never, ever, leave anyone behind. Dead or alive! It's awful hard to fight something you can't find!"

"That's a very good point, Tommy. I'll bring it up at the after action debriefing. I think that one will get you your own team! Let's pick up the pace a little, we're running a little late now. I don't want to get shot by one of our own people after such a successful raid!"

"I don't really want a team of my own, Phil. We work real well together cause we know what the other is thinking and will do in most situations." He said softly, thinking that he didn't know how well he would handle giving the orders that would eventually cost men their lives.

"That's exactly why you'll get one, Tommy! I don't trust anyone who is looking for that job! That type is usually out to make a name for themselves, and they make mistakes that usually get one of their team members killed uselessly!" Phil whispered vehemently.

"But I don't have enough experience yet." Tommy whispered, alarm in his tone.

"You have as much experience as I do, Tommy. Don't crap out on me buddy, I know you better than that." Phil whispered with finality. There wasn't a lot of talk after that because they needed all of their wind to keep up the mile eating pace they were now maintaining. It was hard going, and Phil was thinking that they really had to do something about getting rid of some of this extraneous gear they were lugging about. He would write a note to the general suggesting that gear be picked to fit the mission from now on. He wrote the note, and it got him a promotion to staff rank. Phil was a planner and very attentive to detail, and he would go on to plan some of the most successful missions the 'Ghost Brigade' ever pulled off. Tommy was also promoted, and took over in Phils' place. His thinking was also right that night. His idea was made part of the 'Ghosts' operating procedures.

The Drel would come to fear the 'Ghosts' more than anything they had ever run into. Mainly because they had never run into an angry 'Human' before!

Team Six

"You don't have to take this mission captain. It is strictly a volunteer operation!" said colonel Vinosh, the new commanding officer of the 'Ghost Brigade'.

The previous commander, John Crow, had been promoted again from Brigadier General to Major General. Vinosh had been promoted from Lieutenant Colonel to full colonel and Crow was still his CO, but Crow was now very busy putting together two new support brigades to aid the operations of the 'Ghosts'. Something that both knew would be necessary, but the 'Ghosts' had been so successful that it was necessary to move that timetable up drastically.

At the moment Crow was sitting quietly in the corner of Vinoshs' office listening to the conversation. "Yes I do, Sir." The captain said simply, his tone of voice speaking eloquent volumes.

"All right captain, the job is yours'. You already know how dangerous it's going to be so let me explain what we hope to accomplish by doing it!" Vinosh said wearily, hating this part of the job because it was such a high risk mission.

"Before we start would it be possible to bring my exec in on this so that I won't have to repeat everything to her?" The captain asked deprecatingly, a small smile playing at the corners of his mouth now.

"I told you this was an all volunteer mission, captain! Did she also volunteer for this?" Vinosh asked almost peevishly.

"Sir, my entire company, all ten teams to a man, volunteered for this mission! Sir, if you'll check, my exec should be speaking to your adjutant as we speak." The captain said, smiling openly now. So was John Crow, sitting in the corner.

After First Lieutenant Mary Pitman had joined them, colonel Vinosh said to them bluntly, "Do either of you know what we expect your loss percentage to be is?"

"We have a good idea, Sir." They said almost in unison.

After giving them a hard stare for several seconds Vinosh said quietly, forcefully "Eighty percent!"

Captain Zelinski looked at his exec briefly. She nodded after a couple of thoughtful seconds and he turned to the colonel, saying "Actually, we think your estimate is high by about sixty percentage points, Sir!" he said, face deadpan.

"And just why do you think that?" The colonel barked.

"Because we're the best that Earth has ever produced, and the enemy just has no idea what they have let themselves in for on this one, Sir!" The captain said in an even tone of voice.

There was a bark of laughter from the corner, and John Crow said as he rose to his feet "I told you he was the right choice, colonel Vinosh!" He started for the door, saying as he went "Join me for a drink after you're done here, Jacob." He finished, smiling and shaking his head as he went out the door.

Colonel Jacob Vinosh turned back to his two junior officers with a pained smile on his craggy features. He looked at them thoughtfully for a couple of long moments, then nodded to himself, as if he had come to some conclusion. He said, "All right, here's the why and the wherefore of it. I'll leave the how of it up to you!"

He began speaking in earnest now, "The raid we pulled of on their northwestern base was more successful than we could have hoped for by magnitudes of desire. That base is now in total disarray and confusion that will take them some time to recover from. They lost over a hundred ground troops, twelve of their new atmospheric flyer gunships, and nearly three dozen pilots and crew. That was a major loss to them because all of the pilots and crew were carriers!"

He paused thoughtfully, then went on more slowly, "We caught them off guard, and totally by surprise that time, but they'll be looking for us in the future. You can bet your bottom dollar on that! We had all of the luck going for us on that one, but luck doesn't like to hang around in one place very long so we'll just have to start making our own. This is what we want to do!"

He looked at them as a smile began to build on his rugged featured face that bode ill for the Drel as he said, "We're going right back at them, even harder this time, and we're going to put the fear of the 'Ghost Brigade' into them so bad that whatever they might think of as hell will look very inviting to them after that!"

His smile was in full bloom, and nasty now, as he went on, "One of the men on the last mission was a prankster, and he left a stylized ghost emblem in the pocket of one of the guards they took down. Our intel is telling us that this thing is driving them batty now, so I've taken the liberty of having a few hundred of those things made up." He finished, holding up a small cloth strip with the features of a ghost printed on it.

The stylized cloth ghost was attached to a safety type pin that would allow it to be attached to almost anything. "This," he said with inimical glee in his tone of voice, "is our calling card, and the day will come when the thought of finding one of them will send shivers of terror through them!"

"So," he continued more calmly now, the nasty smile replaced by a look of concerned concentration, "what this mission is supposed to accomplish is to begin to teach them to fear us. Your team, composed of ten teams and a support platoon, comprises our concept of the new light attack company and will have the designation of 'Team Six'."

He looked at the two speculatively for a few seconds then went on, the nasty smile returning once more to his craggy features, "Your mission will be to infiltrate right into their headquarters on this continent and bring 'Havoc and Death' to it! If you are successful, as I believe you will be, you will accomplish two things at once. First, you will take a lot more pressure off our base here. Second, you will teach the enemy that he is definitely not safe in his own house!" he finished grimly.

"What kind of equipment can we draw on for this one, Sir?" lieutenant Pitman asked, speaking for the first time.

"You can have anything we have, short of a space ship!" The colonel said, and, "Plan well because you will have very limited support once you've embarked on this."

"Yes Sir. If you will excuse me I'd like to get with our supply and tech weenies to see what kind of things they'd like to include on a wish list. I'd better include the ordinance people too, just to be fair. Captain, I'll be waiting for you in our company HQ when your finished here. Good night Colonel." She said, saluting smartly before she left, closing the door quietly behind herself as she left.

The colonel and the captain went over many issues over the next three hours, at the end of which the colonel said "All right captain, you know what is wanted, and what is needed. Go do your wicked thing. And god speed to all of you!" He said smiling warmly now, and "Now I have to go and let the general gloat for a while. He told me that you would be the right choice for this. I admit it when I'm wrong. I now think you are too!" With that he shook the captains' hand and opened the door for him, saying as he left "Again, god speed to all of you!"

As the colonel shut off the lights to his office and prepared to meet John Crow he was saying a silent prayer to himself, while at the same time thinking to himself that he had met some of the finest young people he had ever known in his life in the last few months. Sadly he thought to himself that it took something like losing your planet to an alien species to bring the fractious people of this beautiful planet together.

The prayer he was saying was simple, and called on the generous and forgiving god of his childhood. He asked that deity to bend the unforgiving rules of war a little and show leniency to these proud and brave young people who went to fight for their home.

Things That Go Bump in the Night

"Freeze Position!" came from his whisperphone earbud, and the man in the shadows froze in position, breathing silently through his open mouth. Very slowly, quietly, he brought the ten inch combat knife up to guard position, from which he could either attack or defend, the wickedly serrated edge of the blade facing away from himself.

"OK, now move three meters to your left. That will put you in position for his next pass." Came the soft voice of his team partner, who was acting as his spotter on this mission. His voice had a slight gobbling sound to it because he was sub vocalizing. He was doing this because he was laying on a cross member of one of the hastily erected guard towers the 'others', the term now used to describe the Drel, had put up to defend their positions. He was laying right below the guard pacing around the platform above him!

This team was one of the new, elite, special operations teams of the 'Ghost Brigade'. Their sole purpose was to strike randomly and silently, leaving terror in their wake as they did so. Unlike the small cloth emblems the regular 'brigade' members left these men had a small ink stamp with the image of a ghost holding a scythe dripping blood with which they left an imprint in the center of their victims foreheads.

But they didn't always kill their victims! Sometimes, with the help of some very effective gases that rendered the victim almost instantaneously unconscious, they stripped the victim naked and left him or her with the imprints in prominent places on the bodies as warnings of what could have happened! That gas had been developed at main base one in the Canadian Rockies, and was one of the new arsenal of weapons the teams were using to very good effect.

The victims were left for the others to find, the message clear for all to see. Leave Earth or Die! And the team might come back a day, a week, or even a month later to finish the job! What the 'others' did not know was that a tiny transponder was injected just under the skin of the armpits of the victims so they could be found again later. The teams' unerring ability to find those victims again was doing exactly what it had been intended to do in the first place. It was causing 'Havoc' among the regular carrier troops, and the officer cadre carriers too!

When one of those who had been marked and tagged was found dead at some later time it caused great fear in the others who were known as steeds, for they were invariably chosen for this particular form of psychological warfare!

The Drel would not learn for many, many years how the ghosts could determine who was a steed for they had no idea that the Elonee, who could detect a Drel from fifty yards away, existed. And it was having a telling effect on the Drel, especially those of the lower cadre ranks. Those trod in fear as far from anything that cast a shadow as it was possible to do so!

These teams had been in operation for only six months but they had slowed the Drel advance nearly to a standstill from the fear they caused.

Only one team member had been killed since the start of their operations. The four guards placed around the body had been found by their relief a half hour later. Two were unconscious, stripped naked, and marked front and back with the ghost sigil.

The other two were in sitting positions, their heads down upon arms crossed over their knees as if asleep. That is until an officer, shouting foully, kicked him. The body toppled over but the head rolled several feet until it came to a stop at one of the guards booted feet. The team members body was gone!

"He'll be out of sight of the other guard for about ten seconds as soon as he comes around the side of the atmospheric flyer Bobby. Do it———Now!" the voice gobbled in his ear.

The man standing silently, nearly invisible in the shadow of the big flyer, raised a thin eight inch tube to his mouth and, as the guard rounded the back of the machine, he blew strongly into it.

There was a near inaudible phht, and the guard almost got his hand up to block the almost invisible cloud of gas that englobed his head, before he crumpled bonelessly to the ground.

The man sped to the body and, turning it over, slashed diagonally across its' back where the cloth began to wriggle furiously as the Drel attached there tried to detach itself. There was an almost inaudible shriek as the serrated blade sliced through fabric and cartilage. The writhing stopped!

The man rolled the body back over and stamped the middle of its' forehead, then quickly and quietly left, flitting from shadow to shadow. The Drel, in its' death throes, severed its' steeds spinal column as its' tendrils spasmed mightily one last time. The steed was dead almost before the Drel.

A Patriot Made

William J. Nash knew that he was in very serious trouble. He knew it because the three men who were still chasing him had already killed two of his friends, and captured eight others. William J. Nash was known to his friends as BJ, and BJ was the last member of the senior class first string football players that was still free.

It had all started two days ago when he had noticed that all of the players had been rounded up in the gym and were being handcuffed together!

The only reason he had not been taken then was that he had been late to practice. BJ was one of the quiet, studious members of the team who always had good grades. He had stayed late in the library to finish a history paper due in the morning, and as he came into the locker room from the outside door he heard loud shouting in the gym. Curious, he stuck his head around the locker room door to see what was up in the gym. He was just in time to see one of the assistant coaches slap one of the players hard across the face. That boy was in the front rank of the three the players were lined up in.

As BJ looked further around the gym he noticed several strange men in there also. He didn't know what was happening but realized how serious it was when those men started to handcuff the players together. One of the boys broke ranks and ran towards the exit doors. One of those men stepped back from handcuffing the boys, drew a pistol from under his coat, and shot the running boy in the back. The bullet ripped through the boys spine and came out his chest, spraying blood in a fountain in front of him as he arched backwards from the impact of the bullet. The boy sprawled to the floor in the middle of the blood that had sprayed out in front of him.

BJ was so shocked that he almost cried out, but the fact that his throat was so constricted in that shock prevented him from doing so and saved his life right then and there. BJ was a very intelligent young man and the situation, and his own very real danger, hit him like a bulldozer running over him. He backed into the locker room and walked quietly but swiftly back to the outside door. He slipped through the door and very softly closed it behind himself as he left.

BJs' first thought was to get home and call his father at the airbase some twenty five miles away, and tell him what he had seen. BJ had a great relationship with his father and knew that he would believe him. BJ had not lied to him since he was five years old, even when it meant a spanking or the loss of his privileges for a period of time, so he knew his father would know how to help him.

As BJ ran around the back of the school building to cut across the playing field he saw several of the first string players already out on the practice field, about a hundred fifty yards from the rear exit of the gym building. He poured on speed as he ran towards them, waving his arms but not yelling at them. One of them spotted him and called to the others, and they al began to trot towards him. BJ frantically waved them back. Panting, he finally reached them.

Gulping words out between gasps for breath he told them what he had seen, but from their expressions it was clear that they didn't believe him. He was just about to plead with them to run away from the school area when four of the men from the gym came out through the players door leading some of the manacled boys towards a truck parked near the building. A truck that BJ hadn't noticed before.

One of the manacled boys saw them and yelled clearly "Run! Run!" One of the men leading them cuffed the boy back handed, knocking him to the ground to land in a limp heap. Another one of the men raised what looked like a walkie-talkie to his mouth, pointed to the boys on the practice field, then spoke into it. He then spoke to one of the men with him. That one started moving towards them, trotting.

There was no doubt BJs' friends believed him now. They turned, almost as one and ran in the opposite direction, scattering as they went. Within seconds, it seemed, several men were closing in on the fleeing boys from many different directions. BJ was lucky, he was close to the low fence that separated the playing field from the woods that ran into the foothills behind the school. He vaulted the low fence and hit the ground running full tilt into the woods.

There was only one problem with this, these woods ran in the opposite direction from his house. Panting for breath again Bj slowed his pace to a trot, then slowed once again to a fast walk. He heard someone crashing through the brush about a hundred yards away and his heart flipped upward in his chest like it would lodge in his throat. Then he heard one of his friends calling his name.

BJ, still fearful, called out in a low voice. His friend called out again, this time in a lower voice himself. The two boys came together a few minutes later. Then, in typical teenage fashion, they asked each other what the hell was going on. Then expressed the fact, in the same manner, that they were both scared shitless! BJ finally suggested that they try and locate some of the others.

Calico was a very small, semi isolated, town located in the upper foothills of the Cascade mountains in Oregon. It was about fifty five miles from the pacific coast. The only reason it still had a population of thirty nine hundred souls was the small air base located twenty five miles nearer the coast. The base was a leftover from the old early warning response system, put there during the cold war. They were now slowly shutting the base down. That was why BJs' dad was there. He was the security officer in charge of dismantling the old missiles still in their silos there.

The boys had worked their way back through the woods towards town and were about to emerge near the old train station when BJ grabbed his friends arm and pulled him back into the woods, putting his finger to his lips for silence. Then BJ pointed, there, about two hundred yards away near the main road to town, there were two of the men from the school. They were standing near the road with eight of their friends trussed and seated on the ground in front of them. The men were openly holding rifles in their hands now!

The boys eased their way further back into the woods, then knelt down and placed their heads close so they could whisper together. Both boys were shaking now, thoroughly frightened! Finally BJ asked his friend if he still had his cell phone with him since he hadn't gotten dressed for practice either. Surprised, his friend patted himself, then a large smile broke across his features as he pulled it from a jacket pocket and handed it to BJ. BJ promptly flipped it open and dialed his fathers cell phone number.

The phone at the other end rang eight times before it was answered. The voice that spoke was full of pain, and gunfire could be heard in the background. "Nash here." Was the curt response.

"Dad! What's going on there? I hear gunfire! Are you all right?" BJ said all in a rush.

"BJ? Thank God!!" his fathers' voice said painfully, then "Where are you?"

BJ blurted his story out in a rush, then he asked again "Dad, what's going on there? I still hear gunfire in the background!"

There was a long pregnant pause before his father answered. When he spoke his voice, both sad and pain filled, said in that harsh/kind tone he used when he had something very important to tell BJ said, "BJ. Listen to me very carefully! I want you to go to our hunting cabin. If any of the other boys are there take them along with you, but make it clear to them that you are in charge!"

There was a short pause, and BJ could hear his father breathing painfully when he went on, "There is some kind of insurgency going on all over the country! We are badly outnumbered here, and I don't think I'm going to make it out!"

At this BJ blurted "But Dad—"

His father interrupted harshly, "BJ, Shut up and listen! I don't have a lot of time here!"

Completely chastened now, and more frightened than ever BJ said, "OK dad, I'm listening."

When his father continued it was in a softer, kinder voice, "There is a chest under my bed at the cabin. It's full of books. I want you to read them all! They are about survival and guerilla fighting tactics. I had hoped that you would never have to learn about those things, and that's why I kept them there instead of at the house. Now they may save your life, and give you a fighting chance to survive!"

His father paused to take several pain filled breaths, then went on slowly and carefully, trying to make sure his son was taking in what he was telling him, "You're going to have to become a man very fast now, and you're also going to have to fight for your survival and whatever may be left of our way of life! Gather people around you that you can trust, but make them earn your trust first. Soon you'll have to start making hard choices, and even harsher decisions. I've tried to raise you to handle both, and I believe in you completely. Always remember that I love you. And never forget that you were born a free man!"

There was a short pause again as his father tried to control a bout of pain wracked coughing, then he went on, "There are three rifles and ammo for them in the gun case. Don't hesitate to use them to protect yourself! If you can get to the house there is a case there in the basement with several more rifles and handguns in it along with the ammo for them! There are also some books on military structure and tactics in it. Try to get them, but be careful doing it!"

Just then BJ heard a loud burst of gunfire, then another one. Then all he could hear was the open carrier wave.

"Dad! Dad!" BJ shouted into the phone. But he knew already that it was to late. His father was gone. NO! He wasn't gone. He was dead BJ told himself harshly! In those next few moments that he allowed himself to grieve in front of anyone else, the last time he ever did so again, BJ promised himself that those who had killed his father, and shattered and stolen his life, would pay and continue to pay for as long as he lived!

BJ told his friend what his father had said to him, and that he had heard him die. He also told him his intentions were. "I want you to circle all the way around by the saw mill and go into town from there. Gather up all the older boys and girls you can find and bring them to the falls near the river before dark. Can you do that without getting caught?" he finished, looking at his buddy hard.

That young man, the fright obvious in his eyes, nodded slowly. Then more vigorously at BJs' stern look! Then, at BJs' nod, he got to his feet and moved off in the direction of the sawmill. He was careful to stay well within the trees as he went.

BJ slipped quietly back towards the train station, being careful to make as little noise as possible as the hunting skills his father had taught him kicked in. At the edge of the woods he carefully peered through some bushes seeking the whereabouts of the men and his other friends, but they were nowhere to be seen.

Even more cautiously now he moved towards the station building, and without volition the thought of the water fountain inside the station popped into his mind. And with that came the thought of how thirsty he was!

He was sorely tempted to throw caution to the wind and make a dash for the fountain inside. What stopped that reversion to his former self was the picture of his former friend who had been shot by one of those men. And the way his manacled hands had flown up as he arched backwards in mid stride, then flew forward as if he had been slammed with a full body tackle.

The difference was that his friend would never get up again

A Patriot Made II

BJ Nash didn't understand the process he was going through at that time, at that place. He only understood the anger that drove him now. It would be many months later, after learning and beginning to hone those skills that would keep him alive and help him to become one of the fiercest and most successful resistance fighters in Earth's' history, before he began to know the things his father had bequeathed to him.

The core of his ability to plan and carry out raids against the Drel would begin to develop in him a few short weeks later after he had a chance to go over his fathers last words to him time and again, seeking the wisdom that the father had known existed within the son.

The knowledge and skill would begin to manifest itself as he absorbed the information contained in the books he had told him to read, and this he did as if they were the very essence of life itself. To his fathers' great credit one of those books had been 'Sun Szu's—The Art of War'. It greatly shaped the way in which he thought and planned.

The friend he had sent to gather others of their peer group was never heard from again. It was by chance alone that on a bright day two weeks after the incident that he was out hunting for his dinner when he came across a troop of Eagle Scouts returning from a month long field trip in the mountains. He stopped them and told them of the horrors he had seen, but of course they refused to believe him. They did, however, agree to send one of the group ahead into town to check things out on the off chance he was telling the truth.

The next day that individual came back to the pre-arranged meeting place they had set, riding pell-mell on a bike he had found laying in the road. He told a tale of horror that far exceeded the one told by BJ. One of bodies laying openly in the streets, and the sight of what must have been a terrific battle put up by the adults after they had found that their children were being kidnapped.

That youth was pale and thoroughly shaken, very close to the brink of tears because his parents had been among those bodies. BJ, heeding his fathers words, quickly took charge of that group and led them back to his hunting cabin. He knew he must begin planning, for there simply wasn't enough of anything to go around. These were generally self reliant youths, but they were also used to being led. He would become their leader!

That was how it started for BJ Nash and his freedom fighters. Over the years BJ and his group caused the Drel terrible losses and delays in their efforts to pacify planet Earth.

It also sparked both a legend and a rallying point for those who refused to submit and would fight on for their planet and their freedom.

CHAPTER THIRTY-TWO
Transition Points

Drel Gol Am Vass

He was two years behind schedule now, and he was furious! His anger stemmed from several sources, problems that had plagued his fleet since it had left the home galaxy for this one. Not the least of his problems was the unknown species that attacked his fleet a half light year out from their first target system in this galaxy, Sol the natives called the star.

Those attacks by this unknown species had caused his fleet grave damage and slowed their progress measurably. That first attack had nearly crippled the Am Vass, his flag ship, and the rest of the fleet. It had also cost him two cruisers, and several stasis freighters as well, damaged or destroyed.

The repairs to the Am Vass and the other damaged ships had been laboriously performed, taking nearly a local year to complete before the fleet was able to get under way again at cruise speed. Another reason the repairs had taken so long was because several of the under officers had understated the real extent of the damages. Those cretins were now in the food vats!

Expecting another attack their progress had been slowed even more due to the necessity of having his remaining cruisers, and the Am Vass' fighter wings, patrol the space ahead and on the flanks of the now crawling fleet before it could move through it. When no further attacks came for several diurns the patrols were pulled back in closer and the fleet was able to make better headway.

Gol Am Vass was not comfortable with this situation but he had to make a choice between being late, or being the reason for the defeat of the advance forces! The fleet had gotten back up to a speed of twenty light hours per local planetary rotation, the period called a day by the locals in the target system, when the fleet was attacked again!

They had a little more warning because the anomalous readings on the sensor scopes were closer this time, and the fleet sensor officer called a warning that sent the fleet into a pre arranged scattering pattern. Even so the same hanger deck that been so severely damaged before, and was now almost completely repaired, was hit yet again!

This time those wraithlike ships came in much closer, firing lance like energy weapons that cut into the hulls of his ships wherever they touched them. They also fired spreads of small missiles that were hellishly explosive, creating havoc with the fighters because they seemed able to follow them, and came in so fast. Even in the face of all of this his screening ships managed to take the brunt of this latest attack and minimize the overall damage.

Then those ghostlike ships were gone. But, Gol surmised, their intent had been accomplished. He now thought this, because there was no other logical reason for those ships to attack him, unless they were somehow connected to the target world! He swore mightily, something that was a rarity for a Drel, because it would now take another three diurns, three months local time, to re-assemble his now far flung fleet and get it under way again.

With more time on his pads now Gol was reminded that this new steed was still awkward, and a little hard to control. That would change with time, but the way things were going he had serious doubts about how much of that commodity he might have left! He tried to reassure himself, but bitterly acknowledged not having that time as a possibility!

The bridge officer honked to get his attention, a tone on the ships communicator that was his personal call note, and notified him that there was a high speed message pod coming in from the direction of the follow-on fleet broadcasting a high priority signal. The pod was captured quickly by one of the cruisers and delivered to the Am Vass. When the recorded message was played Gol wondered if all things in this universe were conspiring against him. The message went—

From—Commander, Drel Main Fleet

To—Commander, Am Vass Expeditionary Fleet

The Council of Officers and Administrators has received word from our advance scouts in sector Glan Ack that there is an early stage mechanically adept species on one of the planetary systems they are scouting. They have also sent word that that system is rich with vast deposits of much needed metal and energy producing ores.

It has therefore been decided that the main fleet will divert from its' present course and proceed to this new system and capture this plunder for obvious reasons, not the least of which is our ever increasing need for such.

You are therefore ordered to continue on to your assigned objective and complete the subjugation started by the advance expeditionary force. Any additional delays in your timetable will not be favorable to your advancement to council status!

Content by order of the Council of Officers and Administrators

End of recorded message

Gol, for a Drel, was a patient being, but this message sent angry flashes coursing through his mind, causing his new steed to flail its' manipulatory appendages wildly and throw its' body into uncontrolled fits of shaking that threatened to dislodge Gol. It took many ganidil (minutes) to bring the poor creature under control again.

Hardly had he gotten his steed calmed down, and begun to think about the ramifications that this message posed, when his personal communicator honked again. At his barked response the subdued voice of his executive officer said that another message pod was coming in. Only this time it was from the planetary system they were headed for.

The message, when it was captured and brought aboard, was terse and foreboding in its' content! It read;

From; Commander, Advance expeditionary Forces

To; Commander, Am Vass Expeditionary Fleet

Have established strong footprint as per standard procedures. At this time our forces control most of landing site continental land mass and we are in the process of taking control of leaders of other significant land masses.

Unfortunately we have run into serious resistance on the second largest continental land mass

We also have serious need of soldiers now in transit via your fleet as we have sustained some heavy losses on that continent. Please advise as to your earliest anticipated arrival date.

Message Ends

But there was a postscript in code that only Gol could decipher. He got out his decoding book and began the task of decoding this portion of the message. When he had finished it caused him to make the three legged steed lean so far back that it almost toppled over before he could right it. That portion of the message read;

Strongly suspect extra-solar aid and intervention here! Advise you use utmost caution your approach to this system! Have also sensed otherness that is not common to this species, and have encountered weapons not thought possible for their level of technology. Use Caution Gol!!!

Message Ends.

Gol Swore vehemently, for the second time in a very short span of time, and the vitriol coming from his speech orifice would have put a drunken earth sailor to shame! He roared for his executive officer and told that worthy to make all haste in re-aligning the fleet for getting underway again.

He then went about the laborious task of determining approximately how long it would take to put the fleet over the target planet. This done he set about coding a message to the Advance Forces Commander, and having it sent ahead via high speed message pod.

After much haranguing, and many threats of consignment to the food vats, to the inept seeming officers, Gol brought the fleet into orbit above the target planet, all be it the arrival was two and one half years later than the council had originally anticipated. Gol didn't care much about that at this point, he was just grateful that he had gotten most of the fleet here at all!

He set in motion the process of reanimating the soldier Drel in stasis, and began shipping them down to the surface of the planet as quickly as they were able to be moved.

This was a laborious and highly time consuming process, and the time it took was all time taken away from that which he needed to make his damaged ships completely space worthy again. He chaffed at the delays that seemed to plague his every attempt to come back onto his original schedule. As soon as that process was well underway and running smoothly he sent one of his remaining cruisers down to land on the surface at the original landing site to begin building a permanent, fortified, base there.

If there were truly, as he already suspected there was, assistance coming to this system from extra-solar sources he wanted to have a base of operations that was a real stronghold, with all of the firepower that the cruiser would afford it.

Gol didn't know it at the time, for he had very little hard information about the planet below him, that the Drel would never completely subjugate that planet. There were sections on its' surface that were just too cold for the Drel to operate there, even using the natives as steeds. All too often this species were recalcitrant, even at times being able to reject the Drel riders. After reviewing the reports sent up to him by the advance forces commander Gol had to admit that that one had run into some serious problems of a singular nature.

As he kept reading he began to get the feeling that there was much about this species he should know personally. As he read on he made a gesture that for a human would be a puzzled shaking of the head.

This species were ferocious fighters who were, it seemed at times, even gleeful in their attacks on those of their own species who were steeds of the Drel. They seemed to take a perverse pleasure in killing them in manners that would cause the most pain to both steed and rider.

Their tactics were innovative, always using the terrain of the planet to its' fullest advantage, and more often than not leaving more Drel dead or injured than themselves. And there was a specific group of them who were causing many problems of morale for the forces. Their tactics were insidious because they were using an emblem that was fast instilling terror in the Drel ranks because they came and went almost like ghosts!

They would enter a site and kill or mark a soldier for later killing by marking him with that emblem, and no matter if the emblem were washed away those marked were always found and killed at a later time!

Also, they never left any of their dead or wounded to be captured and studied. The one time that one had been killed and put under four guards they had come back and killed two of the guards and marked the other two for death. Those two were still recovering from that trauma!

And no matter how hard they worked or what strategy the Drel employed, they could not catch the elusive ships that Gol knew were landing on the planet periodically!

Gol was distinctly getting the feeling that they may have chosen the wrong species as prey!

The Message

It had been nearly six months since the cavern base in the Canadian Rockies had been closed and sealed. A small but well armed detachment of the newly formed space marines were all that were left there now. They were there mainly to pick up any stragglers who finally made it there and send them on to safe pick up points that were being maintained at great risk to the pilots of the small ships slipping stealthily back onto the planet.

The corporal and the sergeant sitting in the well hidden blind about thirty feet above the sealed cavern entrance were bored because there had been no activity for nearly a month now. They were doing a standard hour on/hour off routine and the corporal, on duty now, was slowly panning his seven by fifty binoculars across the wide expanse of the cleared area that led from the wooded slopes in the near distance up to the entrance of the cavern below them.

He grunted in surprise as he pulled his view back a few yards, fiddling with the focus wheel as he did so. He spent another moment studying the area of interest, then gently poked the sergeant in the ribs with his toe. That worthy, who had been dozing lightly, came fully awake and alert, looking at the corporal questioningly as he lifted his weapon into a ready position.

The corporal, not saying a word aloud, used hand sign to let his partner know that he should take a look through his binoculars. The sergeant took the glasses and following his partners pointing finger began to scan that area.

Sure enough, just at the edge of the tree line there was furtive movement. Now he could see them more clearly, two men moving very, very cautiously towards the open ground leading to the small buildings a short distance in front of the caverns entrance. Both men were armed with semi automatic rifles and pistols. They were dressed in camouflage fatigues and carried packs on their backs.

The man in the lead made a stay back motion with one hand as he moved to the edge of the trees. There he dropped down at the base of some low shrubs and reached into a leg pocket, bringing out a small pair of binoculars. He put them to his eyes and began a slow and careful scan of the entire area.

Seeing this the sergeant used hand signals himself to tell his partner to radio this in to their small HQ, set up in a small cave about six hundred yards to the left and a little lower down than their position. He made the signs for two men, their location, and that they were armed. The sergeant asked for a flanking team to be sent out.

The corporal gave his partner the OK sign and began to speak softly into his whisperphone. That finished the two watchers now settled down to watch the two cautiously advancing men, and wait for their teammates to get into position.

The two men moved out of the tree line cautiously, using a leap frogging movement that allowed them to give each other the maximum amount of coverage as they moved forward. They were good at it and it was quickly obvious that they had worked with each other for some time. They made it to the old wooden mine office and disappeared as they went to cover.

The corporal put his finger to his earbud for a few seconds, then tapped his partner lightly on the shoulder. The sergeant lowered the glasses he was scanning the area of the buildings with and turning his head towards his partner raised one eyebrow in question. The corporal indicated in sign talk that the team had now moved into position behind the two men and were waiting for instructions. The sergeant pulled a small hand held radio from a sleeve pocket and began to speak softly into it.

Down near the buildings where the two had gone to cover his voice crackled from another hand held radio hung on a nail next to the mine office door. "Who are you two? And what are you doing here?"

Almost to fast to see a hand reached up and snatched the radio off of the nail, pulling it down near the base of the building and out of sight of the two marines watching from above. A moment later the sergeants handset crackled and a voice said, "Who are you?" The man must have been holding the transmit key down because the two marines could hear a whispered conversation. That stopped, then, "We're looking for someone that goes by the name of 'Bad Boy'. Do you know him?"

The sergeant smiled, then spoke into his radio, "Yeah, we know him. OK, sling your rifles over your backs and come out into the open. No funny business now! You're covered from all sides. We'll meet you about fifty yards straight ahead of where you are now. We'll even come out first if it will make you feel any easier!"

"OK. We'll come out. Keep your hands empty too!" came the curt reply as the sergeant smiled mirthlessly, thinking that he already liked these two.

He and the corporal made their way down their hidden path to the level area in front of the cavern entrance and proceeded to walk slowly to a point about half way between the cavern entrance and the mine office building.

As expected only one of the men came forward into the open, rifle slung over his shoulder, barrel pointing downward. He moved forward slowly, and slightly off center of the building he had just left the cover of. The sergeant was sure that the mans' partner had the corporal and himself lined up in his sights right now.

They met at the agreed spot and stood looking at each other for a long moment before the sergeant asked why they were looking for 'Bad Boy'. "Got a message for him." Came the terse reply, and "So, where is he?" The sergeant said he wasn't here right now, but that he would forward the message to him for them.

"I dunno," the man said phlegmatically, "I was supposed to give it to him personal like. How do I know you really know him, or can get a message to him?" as he looked at the two marines with a flat eyed stare.

Then he said, "Ifn you really do know him you got some kind of password, or sumethin, that will let me know your on the up an up? The people sent this message said there might be." The mans eyes went hard, as his hand dropped surreptitiously towards his holstered pistol.

The sergeant smiled openly now and said "EFO." Then the smile left his face as he waited for the countersign.

The man, eyes still hard and flat, looked at the sergeant for a few long seconds. Finally he said simply, "FALAIT." as he let his hand swing past the pistol butt.

The smile returned to the sergeants' face, this time reaching his eyes as well, as he said warmly "Welcome brother!" Then sergeant stuck out his hand, and as the other hesitantly took it, shook it warmly. Looking over his shoulder he said to the corporal "Tell them it's ok to come in. These two are on the up and up."

Turning back to the man he said "Tell your man he can join us now. We'll all go back to our HQ and set up a burst message to Jimmy. It may take a while to get an answer so there's no reason for you two to stay out here. By the way, how long has it been since you two had any hot grub?"

It took nearly two weeks for that answer to get back to them. It was short and to the point when it got there. It read 'Verify personally! We'll be standing off the back side of the moon thirty days from now waiting for your answer.'

While they were waiting for the answer the sergeant and the corporal had gotten fairly friendly with the two messengers. The captain in charge of the marine unit assigned them to go back with the two messengers to verify the info.

Since it would take them nearly three weeks to get to a point where they could meet up with the resistance fighters who were taking care of the people who had sent that message he gave them a portable burst transmitter that could reach the captain here. Timetables and codes were set, and the four left the next morning.

The trip was long and hard, nearly three hundred miles through very rugged and wild country. They could have used the roads but they wanted to attract as little attention as possible.

With this in mind the captain also gave them two of the units ATV's and ten gallons of gas for each besides their full tanks. It was very important that they verify the message ASAP, that was the wording of the reply to the message.

The long and short of the message was that a group of scientists working with the resistance, but unable to make it to the last ship out from the mountain base, had found a way to remove a Drel from a human without killing the human while doing so. The process had something to do with an anesthetic compound that knocked the Drel out, and a chemical compound that caused it to retract all of its' tendrils from the host body.

It seemed that they had done this several times successfully, and wanted to get to someplace where they could perfect the technique without worrying about having to move every couple of days.

What to do with all of the people who had been taken over after the war was won had been one of the sore spots for the resistance. For, short of killing them all, they had had no solutions up to this point.

They had no doubts about winning, that's what the password and countersign meant. EFO stood for 'Earth Fights ON', and FALAIT stood for 'for As Long As It Takes'!

Now there was at least the hope of an answer!

That answer would come in the form of Jimmy 'Bad Boy' Lester in person, for that was how important the leaders felt that information was.

The Rescue

The small ship sitting in close geo-stationary orbit, just inside the shadow of the dark side of the moon, was one of the newest ones in production on the resistance controlled planet 'Wolfsbane'. It had come off the production line only two months before, and it was especially built for this kind of work.

She was nearly invisible to all known types of detection devices, and she was fast. Very fast! Almost a third of her two hundred twenty feet of length was taken up with her engines, which gave her an all out, pedal to the metal, speed of nearly forty light days per minute hour of thrust. She couldn't maintain that speed for long, but that speed could get her out of some tight spots in a hurry when needed!

She was only lightly armed, carrying four modified tomahawk missiles. Two eight round batteries of souped up and modified for space use stinger air to air missiles. She also had two ten giga-watt lasers and one mini rail gun. She wasn't a cruiser, but she definitely had fangs!

Her real job was to be like one of the Elonee in the night, moving silently and unseen through space. She had been built expressly for use on clandestine operations, and Jimmy Lester had fought long and hard in the council to get just two of these silent and nearly invisible little beauties built. This would be the litmus test of her abilities.

She had been sitting here for two days now, her antennas searching the ultra high frequencies for a message from earth. But all she had found was the silence of the space around her, and the almost incomprehensible code of the others that she picked up intermittently. Her captain knew how important the message had been. He also knew that there was now a Drel fleet moving towards earth, and that it had just passed the orbit of Uranus. He couldn't stay here much longer!

Suddenly the speaker in the armrest of his command chair came to life "Con, this is 'sparks'. We have incoming mail sir!" The captain grunted in surprise, then said "OK sparks, I'll be right down." As he rose from his seat he said, "Take the con number one.", and, "I'll be in the radio room." This last as he swung himself through the down hatch.

As he came through the hatchway to the radio room 'Sparks', the head communications tech said, "It'll be out of the decoder in about fifteen seconds sir." As they waited for that machine to do its' work it seemed more like fifteen minutes to the waiting man and woman. Then there was a click, a couple of beeps, another click, and paper began to issue from the machine into a receiving tray.

The captain began reading the text as the paper came out. The message read: 'Situation verified. Repeat, situation verified. Eight pigeons in the coup. Recommend retrieval soonest! Repeat, soonest! Please advise your intentions. Message Ends.' There were a few seconds of breathless silence as the captain reread the text a second, then a third time, then looked at his comm. tech. He said softly, "Sparks, get a message torp ready right away, and code this message into its' sending unit "Message Verified! Message verified! Chickens in the coup. Will attempt to extract soonest, repeat soonest. Message ends"

After another moments thought the captain said "Belay that last! Send this back by burst transmission, and by torp. Will retrieve birds! Say time and place, and any special needs. Respond soonest as time is a factor!" As the captain was leaving to begin setting up things for a pickup with his exec. and his supercargo, Jimmy Lester, he said, "keep me posted on this sparks."

Twenty four hours later the ships lander slid down into the earth's atmosphere, using the blind spot created by the north poles' magnetic field, and began its' southward journey to the co-ordinates designated for its' clandestine meeting place with the resistance fighters. It flew nap of the earth almost all the way to the American border to avoid detection. No one knew it was there, or saw its' passing, except for some yearling wolves who were staring at the moon as it, and the lander, slid silently by overhead.

The lander was a boxy affair built to handle large cargo's and people as efficiently as possible. And, like its' mother ship, her engines took up nearly a third of her available space because they were a combination of jet engine and anti gravity repulsors. The jets were there mainly for maneuvering use in the vacuum of outer space where a short burn would give it tremendous boost of momentum, but they were also there to add forward speed in atmospheric conditions when necessary.

The anti gravity repulsor plates on the bottom of its' hull could be angled for forward, reverse, and side to side movement as well as vertical lift and decent in a planets atmosphere. The vehicles speed was controlled by the angle of the repeller plates in relation to the ground and the total amount of power being fed into them. The way in which the anti gravity unit was shielded and insulated within the landers' hull made its' passage nearly silent.

The lander bored on through the night, bearing down on the location where they were to make the pick up. The co-pilot/navigator said, "Twenty five minutes to target site, boss." Then, a few seconds later, "How many are we supposed to pick up this trip? I hope it's not more than a dozen, cause we'll be packin them in like sardines until we drop those supplies to the unit at the old base!"

"Only twelve as far as I know. Eight science types, and two resistance fighters who are going along to make a personal report to the big wigs back on Wolfsbane. The two marines with them are hitching a ride back to the old base. We're supposed to drop them off about five miles away from it with those supplies and their equipment. Don't worry, we'll squeeze them in." the pilot said confidently. Then he said, "You better reach out and touch base with them on the tac. radio to let them know we're right on time." He finished as he banked sharply to follow the contours of the valley they were flying through.

The co-pilot did as he was asked, reaching out to flip the switches that would set the radio from intercom to the pre selected channel they were supposed to use for contacting the resistance fighters. He spoke softly into his throat mike, "Trojan two one, this is skip dancer. Do you copy? Over."

The reply came instantly. "Skip Dancer, this is Trojan two one. Copy you five by five. Over." But the voice was terse, strained!

"Trojan, we are now fifteen out from pick up point." And, thinking about how that voice had sounded, he asked, "Trojan, you sound a little wound up! Say your situation!?"

The reply, again, was immediate. And there was no doubt this time that the man on the other end was nervous as he said, "Skip Dancer, we may have a problem here! Someone has been following us for the last twenty minutes or so. We've tried a couple of shaking tactics, but they've hung on to us so far. We're about twelve minutes out from the pick up site now. Can you provide cover for us if we can't shake them off our tail?"

The pilot and the co-pilot looked at each other for a pregnant few seconds before the pilot told his man to tell them to wait one. The pilot keyed his own radio and called the ship, explained the situation tersely, and waited for a reply. It was another thirty seconds before they were told to do whatever it took to get those people off planet. Hearing the answer the co-pilot spoke into his own mike, saying, "Will do Trojan. Please say your intentions and needs!"

"Skip Dancer—," The reply came, and then a few seconds of near silence before the other went on, "There's a pretty deep, and wide, gully right next to the pick up site. Drop down in there and we'll pull up right next to it. Then you can do a pop-up on them if necessary. We're now about eight minutes out and about to head cross country on my mark! Mark! Can Do?"

"Roger that, Trojan. Can do!" the co-pilot pulled his night vision goggles from the side of his headrest and put them on. He then said "I've got it." As he grasped the control yolk so the pilot could put his own set on. As soon as the pilot had donned his the co-pilot relinquished the controls to him again, and began to warm up the twin two giga-watt lasers mounted just below the nose of the lander.

Seven minutes later two full sized military humvees broke through the line of trees and brush that surrounded a fair sized meadow that was cut nearly in half by a wide, deep, gully. They roared out of the trees and raced, bouncing and jouncing, across the uneven ground of the meadow towards the gully, then slued to a stop at the very lip of the gully, just as two more humvee's broke through the trees at the edge of the meadow behind them.

Those two braked to a stop about eighty yards from the first two, and began disgorging men armed with automatic rifles, which they pointed at the first two humvees as they did so. One of them, apparently an officer, raised a bullhorn to his mouth and told those in the first two vehicles to come out with their hands in the air. And that, if they acted promptly, none would be harmed! As he spoke those in the first two humvees were quietly slipping out the side away from the fast deploying armed men. As soon as they were out they flattened themselves to the ground behind their vehicle. Seeing this the man with the bullhorn motioned his men forward.

As those men advanced there came a deep humming sound from the center of the meadow, near the gully. Then, without any further warning, the lander popped up from the gully and opened fire from the twin lasers mounted below its' nose. The men, their leader, and their humvee were sliced to boiling ribbons where those twin beams of light touched. They were dead before the pieces that were left of them hit the ground! It was all over in a matter of seconds.

The lander lowered itself to the ground fifty feet away from the humvee at the edge of the gully. A moment later a doorway opened in the body of the lander near its' midsection, and a flight suited figure jumped the two feet to the ground from it. He ran to the now smoking bodies near the now burning humvees at the tree line, keeping the weapon he carried pointed at them as he did so. He came to the body of the man with the bullhorn and kicked him hard in the shoulder, When he got no response he toed the man over onto his stomach. He stood looking down at him for a moment, then drew a knife from his shoulder sheath and, bending down, he slit the mans tunic open along the spine. He stepped back quickly, looked at the body for a few seconds, then fired several shots into it at the place where its' spine was. Satisfied, he walked back to the group now assembled at the door he had come out of.

Introductions were made, information traded, and the group began to climb into the hold of the lander. The two resistance fighters went back to the humvee to get their weapons and some personal gear. As they came back two of the scientists ran back to the humvee and pulled two heavy metal cases from it and ran back to the lander, each heaving their burden into the hold door as they returned.

One of the marines had just reached down to give his hand to one of the two who had run back for the cases, a woman, when several shots rang out from the edge of the tree line. The two resistance men standing by the door waiting for the two scientists to get in went down, mortally wounded, and the woman, who had just taken the marines hand, went limp as a large red stain blossomed in her back.

The marine, realizing she was dead, but pulling her aboard anyway, yelled for her companion to jump into the hold. Before he cold take two steps the side of his head disappeared in a spray of blood and bone. The marine dropped to the floor of the cargo hold and as he rolled away from the door, kicked it shut. As he was doing this he was also yelling at the pilot to take off!

The pilot, seeing the flashes from the tree line, wasted no time. He threw his levers into position for full vertical lift and punched for full power to the repulsor panels. The lander virtually jumped into the air, flattening those in the cargo bay to crumple to the floor and causing them many cuts and bruises. And one to break his wrist.

At full power the lander rose nearly a thousand feet before the pilot regained control of his emergency take off. That day the lander proved out what its' designers had hoped for. It was fast and fleet as her power plant hummed happily, taking her cargo to safety.

Once aloft the pilot struggled to fight the effects of the emergency lift. As he regained control of his movements he began throwing switches and moving levers, and the lander sped away to the west, dropping back to nap of the earth flying. Once control was regained the co-pilot spoke to the marine who had closed the hatch and was informed that the two resistance fighters, and the two scientists still on the ground were dead. That worthy was mentally, and vocally, berating himself for not expecting a third vehicle full of men, and they had been caught flat footed in that field.

It would be only a short time later that they would learn that the two scientists that had been lost were the two who had developed the Drel removal process. They would also learn that much of the knowledge about that process had been lost with them because they had not had enough time to get all of their findings down on paper or CD.

The only good thing to come of the incident was that those two had thrown the cases they had retrieved into the lander. It would take the remaining six scientists nearly fifty years to rediscover the exact process that had been developed by those two. The problem was that the actual ingredients used in the formula were not to be found anywhere but on earth. Those six dedicated men and women would endure brain wracking trial and error work for many years before the truth of the situation finally dawned on them.

The answer to their frustrations would be so simple that it would drive them to many sleepless nights, and one of them to near suicide, before it was revealed to one of them while she was going over the notes that had been saved that fateful afternoon. When she realized that she had the answer they had been searching for, for so long, she let out a whoop of joy so loud it brought the others running to her office. When she realized how simple the answer was it reduced her to abject tears she could not stop for several days.

But they finally succeeded, giving mankind still on the earth a chance for hope of saving his humanity!

Balor and the Council

For Balor, this summons from the council was not unexpected. He and Dirk had discussed the matter now before the council at great length, and at last they felt they now had a workable solution to it. Balor acknowledge the call with an affirmative thought and began preening himself so that he would be presentable when he arrived.

When he arrived at the new council chamber, on the planet which had become their temporary new home, he saw that nearly two thirds of the council members had already arrived before him. He could see that many of those present were still uncomfortable in this new space, mainly because this was the third new council chamber they had know in less than that many years. Another part of the problem was that the planet didn't even have a name as yet.

The planet itself was ideal for the Elonee. It had three major and one minor continents that were very much like those of earth. It had large areas of grassland prairies, but were mostly mountain ranges that were covered in lush forests. The climate was temperate to cool. The planet had been found nearly a year before, but its' location had been kept secret. It had been decided at the time to use it for the ERMA ruling councils new headquarters.

I bid you welcome. Came Tagons' thought as he entered. He responded in kind and took his place in the circle. The others already there acknowledged him politely also as he settled himself. Within the next five minutes the remaining members of the council arrived and the formalities of exchanging polite greetings was dispensed with as they took their places.

Tagon wasted little more time with formalities and brought the subject for the meeting right to the fore. *We are called together to consider a proposal put before the council by our clan mate Dirk. The full council is required because the proposal affects the Clan of the Far Seekers as a whole. Balor is most familiar with the proposal so I will let him present it to you.* With that Tagon nodded mentally to Balor, bidding him to take over the meeting.

Balor acknowledged the whole council formally, then began to speak. His thoughts were presented to them in sharp, concise, streams. He neither hurried nor went slowly, but established an easy cadence that all could follow easily. His presentation went like this—

Because of the menace that came to the only home any of us here has ever known we find ourselves once again in the vast reaches of space, a place many of us had forsaken as lost to us forever. And because of that menace we find ourselves in alliance with the twolegs who were the real natives of that home, another thing that very few of us ever thought to be possible.

He let a few seconds pass for them to accept this, then went on. *Also because of that menace we have claimed one of those twolegs as one of our own, a thing that has never, ever, been done in the long history of the Clan of the Far Seekers! There is much that has changed for our clan in but the blink of an eye as time goes for us!*

He paused again, briefly, at the soft mental murmurs of ascent to the truth of the words of his opening statement, then continued, *this twolegs has become very precious to us for he has done a things unheard of before this by any twolegs! First he took me as his near brother, seeing no difference between us in our physical appearance as sentient beings. Then, even before the clan claimed him as one of their own, he gave succor to us by taking our entire clan into his own, and under his protection, even to the point of giving us clan rights within his own clan!*

Balor paused just long enough to breath deeply, and to make his next thoughts hard and crystal clear as he sent them, *even as he did this he proclaimed death to any who would do harm to even the least of us! And, above all else, he has made blood oath that he, or his heirs, will assist the Clan of the Far Seekers in finding our lost Elonee homeworld!"*

There was a short period of loud purring at the end of these thoughts, for there was not a one of those present who had not felt the truth of those statements directly from Dirks' mind. For those gathered there now, Dirk had become the rock upon which the fulfillment of their long held dreams of returning to their home planet were so precariously perched in these times of turmoil.

Having gotten their full attention now, Balor went to the heart of what he had come here to say to them. *My brother, and our clan mate, has made the clan an offer. One that will give the Clan of the Far Seekers full status as a member of the Alliance he has formed to fight this menace that has come to take what it will by force from those who have it. By accepting this offer we will be recognized openly as a member of the alliance. It will also afford us the status of being the first race to join the Earthmen in this alliance!*

There were pleased murmurs of thought at this, for there were those on the council who longed for such recognition, who would like to be accepted as equals with the twolegs and any others, like the Chai, who might join the alliance. Most of the council knew about the Chai at this point, as it was something that could not be hidden from them for any length of time.

Therefore, Balor interrupted the pleased murmurs from their minds, knowing that he must maintain his rhythm in this to get it across to them in a manner that they could, would, accept, *to present this to the council my brother must speak as the leader of his people, foregoing his status as a clan member. Remember this as I continue for he would not have you mislead at such times as he must act in this capacity!* Balor scanned the minds around him, making sure that all were attentive to what would follow. *There is a cost in this proposal to the clan, as there is for everything in life! But that cost, in this case, will be little enough indeed.*

As stated before we left the Earth, and agreed to by the council, he needs our help in his fight to reclaim his planet from that menace that has recently forced him, and ourselves, from it. He is now formally asking us to join his alliance and fight alongside him by using our natural skills as telepaths to aid him.

How can our abilities as telepaths aid in this fight? It is a fight that is rich in that which they call technology! Our physical makeup is poorly designed for such as that! Came an interruption from one of the eldest there.

That is where you are wrong, respected elder, Balor interjected quickly, placatingly, reclaiming control of the meeting before more such questions and statements could throw it into discussion before he was ready to do so. *On Earth we were strong telepaths, capable of communicating over very long distances. Here, in open space, we are capable of far speaking over vast distances because there is not the anomaly of the planetary gravity well to interfere with our sendings and receivings!*

This statement caused looks of introspection to appear in the eyes of most of the councilors, so Balor hurried on to complete Dirks' offer. *Our brother has asked, in return for the status that will be bestowed upon us, for one or two Elonee to ride upon each of the alliance ships as far speakers. Their mechanical means of communicating take time, often precious time, to reach from ship to ship or from ships to persons on planetary surfaces. With our help communications within the alliance will become very near to being instantaneous, even were it necessary to use relays of Elonee to get messages from one point to another.*

Balor, thanks to the tutelage of Tagon, was becoming quite the statesbeing, as could be seen from the prideful glow in that worthy beings eyes, as he looked on approvingly. The council would now reflect on the offer. But acceptance, in this case, was a foregone conclusion!

This was how the Elonee became the very first race to formally join the Earth Resistance Movement Alliance.

It wasn't as hard a decision for them to make as might be thought. They had been on the Earth for nearly as long as mankind, and although all of them held the dream of finding the Elonee homeworld, they had also become a part of Earth.

It was the only home any of them had ever known!

They would do their part to get it back!

Balor and Blade

It was now several weeks after the council had voted to accept Dirks' offer, and make the Elonee the first extraterrestrial race to join the Earth Alliance as a full working partners with the Earthmen, and Balor was working very hard to work out the assignments of which Elonee would go on what Earth space ships, and eventually those of whatever other races might join the alliance. He had to also make assignments for those that would accompany military units.

As it stood now he had many more volunteers than he had assignments for, but that would change, he knew, in time. He had two basic problems to solve to get things going along smoothly. The first problem was that even though the Elonee were superb telepaths distance was still a factor.

So he solved that problem by pairing Elonee who were the strongest with those who were only slightly less capable. These pairings, who usually ended up being mated pairs, he placed on the ships that fared the furthest from the headquarters planet. This was, on the whole, a good solution to the problem in general.

Balors' main problem was much more complex, and needed to be dealt with sooner rather than later if it were to be kept from getting completely out of control. This problem concerned Blade, and his refusal to leave Dirks' side for any reason whatsoever!

Balor understood that, in large part, the problem stemmed from Blades' immaturity. He had watched him transform rapidly over the last three and a half years maturing, physically, much to fast while his tutelage in many other areas lagged due to the conditions that existed because of the war. His own maturity had been a long time in coming. But that coming had been leavened with first, the lore and knowledge of his people, and a hard won knowledge of the people his own people shared a planet with. Learning to understand both knowledge bases had very quickly brought the way he looked at, and dealt with, things more in line with his age. Now he had to help his clan mate learn what he had had the time to learn in a much shorter time span.

Blade barely had three and a half full seasons on him, and a great deal had transpired in that short span of time. Also, it didn't help matters a lot that Blade was early on recognized a an extremely powerful telepath, that now rivaled his own and Tagons strength. Dirk was the only one whose strength surpassed Blades', and Dirk was the only one Blade would submit to without question!

Balor and Dirk had discussed this growing problem several times over the last few months, and both of them had believed it was a thing that would pass as Blade began to understand all that was transpiring about him. This had not become the case however, and the problem had come to a head when Balor had learned that Blade had enlisted several other younglings who now called themselves Dirks' 'First Protectors'.

Blade, having no natural living sire, and as was his right, had claimed Dirk as his near sire, or father was now developing along a tangent that was decidedly unhealthy. He had forged a deep and abiding link with Dirk which could become physically and mentally painful if they were to be separated for to long a span of time.

Balor also understood this situation for he had, when he was very young, forged such a bond with his mentor, Tagon. Unlike now, there had been time then to let time itself be the agent that would overcome that attachment.

What Blade did not, would not, understand right now was that Balor and Dirk had formed a bond that transcended the one between Blade and Dirk by whole orders of magnitude! It wasn't that their bond was stronger, it wasn't. The difference was the depth of their bond. Theirs' was a bond of many facets that was encompassed the sum of their knowledge and personal experience.

Theirs' was a bond based on a mutual respect and liking for each other, and on experiences, both shared and individual, that brought perspective to their relationship. And within that perspective they had come to trust each others judgement. They had also come to the point where each others' personal goals could abide with their shared ones!

Balor and Dirk would always be closely tied and attuned to each other, no matter whether they were together or separated by vast distances of space or time. Balor could imagine that it would be much the same, in time, for Blade and Dirk, for there was an undeniably strong bond formed between them already. The only real difference in the manner of those bonds was the level of maturity that cemented them together.

Having thought all of these thoughts many times over Balor came to the sad conclusion that there must be a confrontation with Blade. One in which he must convince Blade that he must bow, in great part, to the will of the councils' authority. And Blade must do so in a manner that would not cause the other younglings to rebel.

It was also necessary that Blades' capitulation to the councils overall authority include reprimand for actions unsanctioned by the council. But a reprimand that could be attributed to his youth and inexperience. A reprimand that would let him save face with his peers, and he could still accept as being rightly imposed!

His reasoning about the problem and the conclusions he had reached accepted as valid, Balor reached out for that bright spot in space that was his bond brothers mind. As he touched that point he felt the instant recognition and warmth as Dirk completed the link between them. ***Balor, my brother, it's good to hear from you. How goes our project?***

The project goes very well, and as always it is good to speak with my brother. He paused slightly, knowing that Dirk would pick up on his hesitation.

Sure enough, Dirk asked quickly. ***What bothers you my brother? Is it something I can help you with?***

Before he could answer Blade broke in, saying ***Balor, Elder, it is good to sense your thought pattern!***

Uncharacteristically Balor snapped, ***youngling, remove yourself! This is a private conversation!*** then erected a shield around himself and Dirk.

Surprised Dirk said quickly, as he reinforced Balors' shield with one of his own, ***"This must be serious indeed! Talk to me my brother."***

So Balor went through all that he had been wrestling with, all the while expecting Dirk to try and lessen his own alarm at the growing situation as he saw it.

When he had finished Dirk was silent for an eternity of seconds, then he dropped his and Balors' shields. When he spoke it was to Blade, and his tone was very stern! ***Blade! You have been summoned before the council of elders. Immediately upon landing you will take yourself, and the other younglings with you, and present yourself to the council!***

All blade could do was splutter. ***But Dirk, Sire, who will be there if you have need—***

Dirks' response was quick and sharp! ***Be quiet youngling! I will not defy the council in this. Balor is both your accuser, and your defender, in this matter. Be respectful to all, and think clearly before making any answers.***

Dirk paused slightly, then concluded with, ***make no stain upon our honor, and represent yourself in a manner that gives confidence to my pride in you!*** he ended, giving Blade that morsel of pride to hold onto from Dirks' rebuke.

I will do as you, and the council, command. Blade said meekly, for never had Dirk, nor Balor for that matter, ever spoken to him so sternly before this.

Dirk erected the shield around himself and Balor once again, then said quietly, thoughtfully, ***my brother, I did not like doing that. But as you said, it is a thing that must be attended to, sooner than later. It's just a shame that present circumstances will force our younglings, both yours and ours, to face adulthood at such an early age. Please keep me apprised of the council's decisions in this matter.***

It will be as you ask, my brother. Before I depart there are a few other things I would like to go over with you. Do you have the time now? Balor said, pride in Dirks' immediate understanding of the situation and the decisive way he had dealt with it coming through in his thoughts.

Dirk knew that Balor took his new responsibilities as a council member, even forced into it as he had been, as seriously as he took his own and he would do anything in his power to help this being that had become such an integral part of his own life and himself! He said *for you, my brother, there is always the time.*

Blade presented himself to the council as he had been instructed to, and Balor did act as both accuser of, and defender for, him.

During the following two days that it took the ship to approach the planet and land, Blade kept pretty much to himself, and did a great deal of thinking about all that had happened to him.

In the council chambers he had kept silent unless spoken to. His answers had been concise and well thought out.

In the end he accepted, if not quite graciously, the reprimand from the council and whatever penance they prescribed.

Also during that period his thinking patterns changed, and he matured by leaps and bounds!

Upon his return to Dirk he was somewhat hesitant, but Dirk smiled at him, saying, *you are a son that would make any sire proud of him. Especially this one!* And life, as it was in those times, went on.

Intelligence School

This meeting was one that Dirk had hoped he would not have to call, but Dirk was above all else a man who had been trained to face and deal with hard facts, and the hard facts in this case were inescapable. As good as the people they had been able to get off Earth were, there were just not enough of them to do the job properly! That job was the gathering and analyzing of intelligence.

The quality of the people he, Jimmy Lester, and Yuri Garov had put together were at the apex of their trade, but they were getting bogged down with the amount of intel coming in as each one tried to wear three hats at once. His own work was beginning to be hampered by this fact as well. Therefore this meeting of the core group of the resistance movement. They had to find more people and train them. And quickly!

The people gathered in the low ceilinged cavern conference room all knew each other. Most of them had gotten to know each other very well in the nearly three years since the evacuation from Earth. They all knew the reason for the meeting, and had been asked to come with suggestions ready for airing.

The heavy doors were closed and bolted shut, and Dirk rose from his seat at the final sound of the bolt slamming home. All conversation stopped, for every one of those men and women were professionals who knew the value of time to those who had very little of it to spare! Dirks' opening remark hit that nail squarely on the head as he said, "I hope all of you came here loaded for bear, because time is a factor that none of us has much of to spare!"

He looked around the big table at those expectant faces, knowing that without them IRMA would never have been born, and Earth's last hope would have been gone forever. He felt that it was important to say something to them to let them know how he felt about all of them. "Before we start on the subject at hand for this meeting though," He started slowly, seeking the words he knew were there, "I wanted to say thank you to each and every one of you! Not for doing what was right for Earth, but for the way in which you all have done it. Each of you have given up all or parts of your belief systems, your homes, your friends, and some of you have even given up you families! And once you knew what we were facing you gave up what you had to without question! Thank you."

There was no applause at this, but there were many far away looks in many pairs of eyes, even some abashed looks from men or women who had been national leaders. These were people who, to the last one, had come to respect this man. And too, to depend on his drive to resist when their own flagged. No. There was no applause, just polite nods in his recognition of their efforts and sacrifices.

"I also have a formal announcement to make!" This statement brought all heads up as all eyes riveted on him again.

"I would like to introduce you to the representative of the first race to join the Earth Resistance Movement Alliance! His name is Tagon of the Clan of the Far Seekers. He is Eldest of the Elonee on Earth, and leader of the Elonee Council." Dirk turned to the large cat sitting on a cushioned platform at the table next to him, and bowed slightly from the waist.

There were quite a few murmurs from the group, for most of them knew of the Elonee's existence but little else about them other than then fact that they were supposed to be telepathic. Holding up his hand for silence, Dirk went on, "The Elonee have been on Earth for thousands of years. They have watched us develop as a race, and have suffered much harm from us in the past! Yet they have, and it's a mystery to me why, elected to fight along side of us in this fight. Be that as it may, they have elected to do so on their own."

Dirk paused just long enough to see the bright looks of interest on all of those faces before going on. "Those of you who have not been privy to much information about the Elonee should know that they are a telepathic race, and they bring something to this table which we sorely need. That need being a means to communicate securely over truly vast distances in space! They have agreed to man our ships in pairs as our principal communicators. That is their contribution to this fight. Please welcome them as our equals."

J. A. DI SPADA

Every individual at the table rose and applauded, facing the old cat politely. Then Dirk said, "Tagon has requested that he be allowed to address you. For him to do so you must all sit quietly and try to relax you bodies and your minds. Try thinking of opening your minds to him, or of thinking of your minds as a radio receiver. Most of you, and I'm sure you will be surprised at this, have some degree of telepathic ability. For those of you who don't you will receive a transcript of what is said over your laptops."

The group settled back into their seats and tried to comply with Dirks' instructions. Soon you could have heard a dropped pin hit the floor in that large room. Startled looks began to appear on nearly all of their faces, then slow smiles began to appear as the elders words started filtering slowly into their minds. *I have been sending a repetitious message so that you might find the manner of receiving it. I see that nearly all here have been able to do so with little trouble.* The elder said, pausing briefly to verify the truth of his thoughts.

Seeing the looks on almost all of their faces he went on, *The Elonee have been here on this Earth, living beside mankind, for many, many, thousands of years! We were stranded here when the ship we traveled on was damaged and forced to land on your planet, never to rise again.*

There was a deep note of sadness in his thoughts in this telling, but he went on firmly. *We, the Elonee, have lived side by side with the twolegs, mankind, for many ages. Sometimes as friends, but most often not. But now that history has little meaning for we find ourselves adrift in the same boat with you! Some on our council said that we should stay separate, and find our own way. We argued, in truth, that this could not be, because for those of us alive now, like you, the Earth was the only home that we had ever known!*

He felt the rapt attention of those minds on every word he spoke as he went on, more slowly now, *yes, we are originally from another star system and planet, but the Earth has been the home that has succored us these many, many ages. We shall not let it be taken from us, or you, lightly! So we stretch out our paws, claws sheathed in brotherhood, to fight this evil that has come from the dark of space and befallen our shared home. We have become as we are now. Clan brothers of the twolegs!* And with that he lay back down and regally looked out over the assembled group.

There was a complete, nearly stunned, silence for nearly a full minute after he had stopped sending his thoughts to them. Then, slowly, almost ponderously, Yuri Garov got to his feet and faced the old, grizzled, but still regal Elonee. After looking at that being for a full thirty seconds he bowed deeply from the waist. This was followed by a hasty scraping of chairs on the rock floor, as in ones and twos the rest got to their feet and followed suit. In their way these people were showing Tagon, and his people, great respect. He felt this as well, and was deeply

520

affected by it because other than Dirk, who he both respected deeply and feared, he knew very little about the rest of this group.

When they had all reseated themselves dirk rose once again and as before silence fell quickly. "Thank you all for welcoming our new ally so warmly." He said with a smile, then more soberly, "Now, on to the matter for this meeting. I have let you know my thoughts on this some while ago, but there are a few more things you should consider and factor into your conclusions."

He paused very briefly to marshal his thoughts, then dove into his subject. "First, this galaxy is nowhere as empty as we might have liked to think a few short years ago. It is full of intelligent races, and we're going to have to deal with them individually or jointly. Many of them have had star travel for a long time, and are generally more technologically advanced than we are. But, from what I have learned from another race we are currently seeking to open negotiations with, the Chai, most of them are equivalent to us or are, technologically speaking, more advanced than we are."

He paused just long enough to let that sink in, then said, "The situation itself remains the same. Whether those races are friendly or not we will need intelligence on and about them as much as we do the Drel, so that we can deal with them in an intelligent manner. Right now we lack that capability, and our resources on Earth, and resources here are stretched to the limit! We desperately need more assets for intelligence gathering, and analyzing what we gather. First for Earth, then for whatever we find out here."

There were many nods of agreement to his assessment of the situation, especially in light of his information about so many new races that might have to be dealt with. Dirk waited patiently for the low buzz of conversation around the table to die down before going on.

"I have two suggestions in this regard," Dirk finally broke into that buzz, "that I hope will make sense to you all. The first is that we establish an intelligence school, and staff it by rotating our best trained field and analytical agents through it as instructors. That will have two major benefits that I can see immediately. It will give the new trainees the best, first hand, practical knowledge there is to be had, and it will give those agents a well deserved break from their harrowing and nerve wracking work."

He took a quick breath and continued, "For our Earth operations we can cull some of the students from those we have already brought out, but the vast majority of them will have to come directly from those we had to leave on Earth. Those will become our most valued assets because they will be the survivors, the ones who have learned to deal with the situation as it exists on Earth today."

He paused briefly again, this time to let that sink in, then, "The second suggestion I have is that we find a planet similar to the one we are now using and establish this school on it. Also on that planet will be our central analytical processing, vetting, and redistribution center, which will be designed to handle the massive amounts of information that will start pouring into it. As the school grows, so too will the number of personnel we will have to man that center. Also, having an entire planet will give us much more flexibility in the manner in which we are able to train the agents from many of those races I spoke of earlier."

He stopped speaking and looked around the table for a few seconds before saying in closing, "I have something that I must attend to personally, so I will leave you in the very capable hands of Yuri Garov for a while. I will return for the afternoon session. Thank you all for your attention." And he quickly walked out of the meeting, the interior guards unbolting the door as he came towards them. Unbeknownst to the majority of those there this was the one move that had been preplanned. He had wanted them to work on this without any undue influence his presence there might have caused.

As he left the meeting TuLans' thought came to him, *I perceive that you got what you wanted from that meeting. Even though the concept of the school is, in and of itself, still fascinating to me I find it even more fascination in the manner in which you introduced two new races to them, and the idea of a whole galaxy full of intelligent races that they would have to start dealing with! You continue to surprise me my friend Dirk.*

Thank you TuLan. Dirk replied modestly, *we have a method of dealing with the unknown, and that method is all in the manner of preparing to deal with it.*

When the time comes there will be a great deal of novelty in the actual doing, but the normal fear of the unknown will be replaced by the knowledge that there is just one more thing that must be prepared for dealing with. Dirk finished softly.

TuLan Chai

TuLan, being the scholar he was, had been thinking a lot of late about the many twists and turns that had befallen himself over the last four and a half years since his crash on earth. Never in his wildest fantasies had he dreamed that so much could happen in such a short period of time.

He had had three hosts, all of them of different species, and had come to both admire and fear his present one, the Earthling. That fear was in great part due to the fact that he had been forced, by existing conditions, to accept the fact that he was now more of an observer than he was an initiator. But the bulk of his fear came from a growing certainty that he may have unwittingly loosed on the galaxy a species that could either be the most benevolent, or the most terrifying, that it might ever encounter!

TuLan was still quite young by his own races standards but very old by the standards of most of the Union races. His race, among those many varied races that formed the Union, was venerated because of their age, generally peaceful nature, and their willingness to share the knowledge they garnered from their constant studies. His penchant, and that of his races', had led him to be in the position he found himself in now. And it was becoming more complicated by the cycle!

Therein lay the dilemma he now sought to come to terms with. His present host, one of the indigenes from the planet he had been observing when his observation platform had been holed by that stray meteorite, was much more than he could have possibly anticipated. Had he known as much about this species as he had thought he did he might have accepted entropy willingly at the point of choice.

This species, these humans as they called themselves, were a complete anomaly! They were barbarians! Yet they were philosophers of deeply penetrating thought. They were warriors, savage and merciless in their battle lusts. Yet when those battles were over they were more often than not giving care and comfort to those they had so recently been trying to kill with great abandon. And they had a penchant for technological brilliance that far and away outstripped anything TuLan had ever seen or heard of!

And above all else they had a fear of entropy, death they called it, that was to his way of thinking nearly manic. And in that too they were totally contrarian, for they might flee to avoid it, or run to meet it!

TuLan had never heard of a species, any species that would do this in a like manner. It was a totally unheard of thing for a species to fight and scrabble to its' last breath to survive, but under circumstances that it considered to be right, turn and rush to meet its' own demise with great glee. And to top all else off, TuLan had discovered something he had not even suspected.

These Humans, or a large portion of them, were latent and very powerful natural telepaths! He had found this out, to his own chagrin, when he had discovered another alien species living on the same planet with, but unknown to, the humans. That species called itself the Elonee. They were quadrapedal felines of high intelligence. And they were natural telepaths of a very high order!

The Chai, within the bounds of their hosts, were normally the dominant species. Not so with these Humans! The Chai were also very powerful short range telepaths. Again, not so with these Humans! Even worse both his human, and the Elonee seemed able to communicate on a bandwidth that was unreachable by TuLan!

Now TuLan, after four and a half years, was learning at first hand just how complex the minds of these humans were. They seemed able to think and plan on several levels simultaneously, and utilized something they called intuitive thought to reach the correct solutions to very complex questions or problems, doing so with the scantiest amount of relevant information.

Even more amazing, they seemed able to do this with bits of seemingly unrelated information. Then there was an aspect to their minds that they referred to as the sub conscious. This they relegated problems to that were not immediately solvable, saying that they could call up the information at will to see what progress had been made on reaching a viable solution.

If this sub conscious function was what TuLan thought it was, this race was tapping a portion of the mind that most other races must go through a long series of preparations just to make it possible to open a pathway capable of reaching it. Yes, this race was potentially a very dangerous one!

And yet TuLan liked being with this host. He had learned a great deal from him, and in the coming years he was sure he would learn a great deal more, too. TuLans' dilemma was that not only had he cast his lot with that of his host and his people, but that deep within himself he knew that he had wanted to do so.

So, when it came right down to it, and if he were being completely honest with himself, he would have to admit that he was just beginning to learn about who the being known as TuLan of the Chai really was!

Intelligence School Too

While waiting for Yuri Garov, Chabov, Osov, Tim Berg, Carl Miles, John Crow, and a number of other members of his core group, to join him for a special meeting Dirk had been conversing with TuLan. Balor was stretched out on a sofa against the far wall, languidly following their conversations twists and turns. TuLan was now saying, *but I don't understand why you would want to spy on the other races of the Union. They are not your enemies!*

Let me try to clarify this for you TuLan, because it is very important that you are clear on the reasons and ramifications of these matters if we are going to be able to work together as closely as we must in the coming years. Dirk said in a pensive voice, not wishing to express himself in any manner that might cause divisiveness between them.

Dirk, ordering his thoughts, began slowly, *all of the governments on Earth, even those on the friendliest of terms, keep a close watch on each other. This is done for one basic purpose, that being that when one of those governments is planning for its' future there will be less likelihood of it being caught by some surprise move by one, or more, of the others.*

Taking a deep mental breath Dirk plunged on with his explanation. *All of those governments know that the others are watching them, and as long as that scrutiny does not become too intrusive they generally turn a blind eye towards those efforts. In the case of those governments who may become confrontatious the efforts by the others become more active, and clandestine in nature. Information gained in this manner is most often used to bring the confrontatious one to the bargaining table by discretely letting them know that their secrets are known by the others. This has more often than not made it possible for disputing parties to work out their differences in a manner much less destructive than open warfare.*

Dirk paused briefly to see how TuLan was absorbing this, but at the others urging he continued, *Too, if the disagreement becomes one of irreconcilable differences, and degenerates into open warfare spying, or espionage, is at its' highest levels. The side that has perfected their information gathering techniques is usually the one to come out on top in any such conflict.*

Quite simply, having information about someone else advancements or intended actions allows you to take whatever countermeasures you are capable of in a timely manner, or at the very least to take actions that will minimize the expected impact from those advancements or intended actions!

A case in point was your own surveillance of our planet. You were gathering information that would put your race, or the Union, into a position of being able to make an informed decision as to what, if any, response might be made to any possible adverse actions that the Drel, or we, might be making that would have a deleterious impact on you.

Or, as you correctly surmised, put yourselves into a position to set in motion counteractive measures based on information coming to light about a Drel re-incursion into this galaxy, something you seemed to have some reason to suspect. The next part was at the core of what Dirk wanted to get across to TuLan, so he now proceeded at a slower pace. *Even though one governing body may be working in alliance with one or more other governing bodies, it might make a decision that it deems to be right for itself, yet as right as that decision may seem to be for the one, it could at the same time be vastly counter productive to the efforts of the group as a whole.*

Having some, or full, foreknowledge of that decision would give its recipients a wide range of options to choose from to put in place a reasoned response to it. Then again, if the governing body making that decision had foreknowledge of what the response to such a decision would be, it might well forgo making that decision in the first place! The gathering of information about your allies and their situations is not only prudent, it is the only sensible thing to do.

It is in how that information is used that is the important thing. In the case of friends, or allies, it is important to know how they will, or might, react to certain things. In the case of gaining that information about an enemy, it is doubly important to know how they might react to any given set of circumstances, and be able to use whatever is gained against them!

Dirks' faith in his symbiotic partners ability to grasp things quickly was much reinforced when he responded after a moments deep thought with, *so in essence what you are saying is that it could be just as dangerous not having a good idea of how your friends might react, or what they might do as it is not knowing what your enemy will or can do!* TuLan finished thoughtfully.

As I thought you would you have grasped the concept completely. Dirk said, a mental sigh of relief escaping him. *That is why it is essential that I enlist your aid in this next phase of our war with the Drel! You, and I, both know that the Drel will not stop with the conquest of Earth, and not knowing how the Union will, or may, react when they are told of the extent of the incursion so far can be just as dangerous for us. Our planning must be based on a knowledge of how our potential friends will react, as well as what we know about our enemy! This is why I am seeking your aid in enlisting potential agents who might be able to see the danger we see. And why!*

Encouraged by TuLans' Thoughtful silence Dirk went on, *Not only do we need agents, we will need those willing to teach those agents as well, for a good agent must be educated in a well rounded manner in his or her general knowledge to be able to interpret, to a degree, the value and the importance of the information they are gathering. Quite often the most important information comes from an agent who was able to connect the dots on seemingly unrelated bits of information because their knowledge base let them see the relationship, although obscured, of the subjects!*

What you're saying is both very interesting, and novel to me, for it makes me view this concept of intelligence gathering in the manner you describe as both sensible and necessary! TuLan said slowly.

Then, releasing a mental sigh, he went on thoughtfully once again. *If I view this in the manner you suggest, it makes me think that because the Union has had no major conflicts between Union or non Union species in many thousands of your years it may be falling well short of its obligations to its' members by not knowing what is going on in those members back yards, to coin one of your sayings, as well as the back yards of the areas not under their immediate influence.*

TuLan paused here momentarily, as he gave reign to his private thoughts about these Earthmen. After Dirks' explanation he knew without doubt that the Unions' intelligence apparatus would fall woefully short in its' abilities to gather the information necessary for its' own survival. The Union, as it was now, was very old, and had become unwieldy in the manner of its' operation, given over to much debate about every detail on every matter. Given this, TuLan could see plainly how dangerous these Earthmen would be were they to become adversaries of the Union. TuLan knew how important information was to accomplishing anything that needed doing, but now thanks to Dirk, he had been made to realize just how important it could be under any condition of conflict. And, because of this last five years spent with Dirk, he knew without doubt that conflict was coming to visit his galaxy. And it was coming with a vengeance!

TuLan had been over much of these things in his mind several times, but with the addition of this latest it changed the whole complexion and manner of the way he viewed them. Yes, these Earthmen could be very dangerous, but not to the Union unless they were directly threatened by it. The Drel on the other manipulator, if left unchecked, were a much greater threat. One that would not wait to be debated with. After being with Dirk for a little under five earth years now, TuLan felt that he knew him, and his motivations, well enough to place a great deal of trust in his stated intentions. And he had also come to the conclusion now, albeit sadly, that this tough, resilient, species might well be the salvation of the Union itself.

With these thought going round and round in his mind he did something that was totally atypical of his own species. He acted solely on instinct when he said to Dirk, *What you have told me, and shown me, has brought many troubling thoughts to my mind. The Union has enjoyed a very long period of peace and prosperity, with very little in the way of conflict to mar that history. But in the end analysis I believe that you will be proven right. So, I will work with you to compile a list of races, and the beings I know among them, who might be of use to you in this school. And as potential agents! I believe that my doing so will also, in the end, greatly benefit the Union!*

This admission and agreement was made in a rush of thought that TuLan slowed with great effort as he went on, *What you and your people have accomplished in a little under five and a half short years is near miraculous. With the limited information you gained from my outdated planetary runabout you have built ships capable of interplanetary and interstellar capabilities. You are now building ships that can rival, or even surpass, the capabilities of those that it has taken the Union thousands of years to develop!*

TuLan rushed on, both to finish his admission of wonderment of these people as a species, and to complete his personal agreement, *With fewer people than would populate one of the Union planets medium sized cities you have set up colonies on four worlds, and made them into thriving and self sufficient entities!* TuLan paused for a mental breath, then went on a little more slowly as he tried to contain the combination feelings of dread and excitement that were now coursing through him as the true realization of the enormous personal commitment he had just made hit him.

Speaking more slowly now he said, *On top of everything else you have accomplished you have begun fighting a war against an enemy it took the Union, at the height of its' power, nearly three hundred thousand of your years to win the last time the Drel made an incursion into this galaxy!* Now TuLan seemed to force himself to say the last of what he had been thinking. *I am in awe of what you may attempt next!* His outburst of revelation about the way he had been thinking about his hosts' species completed TuLan sighed mentally, and waited for Dirk to respond.

Dirk was quiet for so long that TuLan began to mentally fidget, for the admission of his personal views of the Unions' state of readiness, and his commitment to aid Dirks cause, had taxed his personal reserves greatly. That commitment had caused him to cross the lines of species loyalty into uncharted territory, a place his people ventured very cautiously indeed. He felt, in the least amount, justifiably impatient for a response in recognition of this monumental commitment.

As TuLan was about to prompt him for his reply Dirk spoke as he sent TuLan a picture of himself peering at TuLan, a thing he had recently learned to do.

With a benign expression on the face of that mental image he said, *we have to go back to the Earth and get another five million people off the planet for our colonies!*

CHAPTER THIRTY-THREE
Transition Points Too

Data Potentials

This meeting, planned for six months ago, was now viewed as a dangerous thing to have happen at this time. The resistance had struck the Drel four times now, and they were mad as hornets whose nest was being stirred with a stick. There had been much debate between the members of both councils about whether all of the members should be together in one place at the same time.

In the end it had been Dimetri Chabov who had clinched the need for it to take place, when he had sent messages to all of the members of both councils. It had been a simple and straight forward message that went to the heart of many questions. It read;

My fellow Earthmen, and esteemed Alliance members

Although secrecy is an essential tool, especially during conditions of wartime such as we find ourselves in now, it also has its' downside. That downside was one of the major reasons that led to the dissolution of my own countries position in the scheme of our world. Secrecy, by its' very nature, will take on a life of its' own, and it's use, and the need for its' use, will grow to the point where the left hand will never know what the right hand is doing. Such was the case in my own country.

If we are to survive this conflict we must have trust in each other, and in the good judgement of each other. We must use secrecy as a tool, not let it grow to the point where it will end up being the tool that used its' makers!

It is particularly important that we meet, face to face, to discuss the subjects that are most likely to affect the Alliance, so that essential information can be channeled where it will do the most good! Even though the Elonee have given us a tremendous advantage by joining us, and acting as our long range communicators, there is still no substitute for the understanding one gains when discussing matters across the table from one another.

I thank you all kindly for your immediate attention to this matter.

This message broke the deadlock between those who believed that the knowledge of the existence and location of the headquarters planet should be kept completely secret, and those who argued that the location was already known to too many for so many of the Alliance leaders to meet in one place, at one time, because their loss would mean the end of the resistance and the Alliance.

The solution that was reached and agreed upon was that regular meetings would be held, but only half of each council would meet jointly at any one time. It would then be the duty of the attending councilors to inform the balance of their respective councils members as to of the results of those meetings.

It was also made clear that, although the existence of the headquarters planet was known to many, its' location was known to only a very few. It was also now understood that should some incident befall those few individuals, the information disclosing its' location was to be kept in a safe place which was known to only a very few scattered individuals in the Alliance. These individuals would bring forth the location should some disaster occur. So the meeting was set, attendees chosen, and timing and transportation details worked out.

The main agenda for the meeting was a report to the councilors about three key subjects that had become critical to the survival of the fledgling Alliance. Two of these were to be presented by Carmella 'Chickie' Martinez on the subjects of computer manufacturing and the establishment of a viable economic system for the new Alliance worlds. The other was to establish a plan to get more people off Earth to fill the needs of those worlds.

It had taken nearly a month to get those chosen to attend together, and transported, but they were finally all here and the meetings were begun in earnest. After the amenities were attended to and the agendas manner of presentation explained 'Chickie' Martinez was introduced to those who had not met her as yet. Those were the ones who knew only that most of what they had to work with were the results of her terrific efforts. Those who knew her welcomed her warmly, knowing full well how much her contributions meant.

Her introduction was brief, and she got to the point of her first presentation quickly. "As most of you are aware, one of the biggest advantages we have right now, besides the Elonee, is our superior computer technology. For whatever reason it far outstrips what we have found in the alien technology that has been made available to us so far. That advantage has allowed us to interface with, and in most cases, vastly improve on the performance of that technology."

She paused to see what impact, if any, her statements had made before dropping her bombshells on them. "I have some very good news, and some not so very good news to report to you! I will speak to the not so good news first, as it impacts directly on the third topic for this conference. That news is that we are desperately short of computer technicians, or tech weenies as most of us call them! We are short of all three types of these people. They are the hardware designers and producers, the software developers and producers, and as important as those two categories are the third category, those who can teach the rest of us how to use them, are very few in number within our ranks. If we are to maintain the level of our advantage, let alone expand upon it, we need more people from Earth!"

This time her pause was to assess how the murmured comments to her statements were being expressed. Then she went on to give the brighter side of her report. "On the other hand, our first efforts are about to pay off very handsomely for us! It was recognized very early on that at some time we would have to become self sufficient, and to that end we began to recruit the very best and brightest from the chip and computer producers on Earth. We listened very carefully to them, and brought as many, and as much, of their products as we could get our hands on, and crammed them into our cargo holds until there wasn't a square millimeter of space unused in them!"

"But," She hurried on, "more importantly, we bought and brought as much of the machinery that made the production machinery as we could get our hands on. To top that off we got the top designers from both 'Pentium' and 'AMD' to join us in this fight for our home!" This news brought a ripple of approval from the group. Now she would give them the reason to implement Dirks' plan for a mass extraction of people from Earth.

"We have," She said a bit loudly to stop the side conversations that had started, "within the last six months, found a planet with every resource necessary to begin the production of our own computers and peripherals! We have already set up first and second stage production facilities there, and are about to begin construction on a plant for integrated production of finished units for both standard and demand design type computers! This is why it is critical for us to have more people to man these facilities without striping them from jobs already being done!"

Their reaction was all that she had hoped it would be as she saw them nodding somberly in agreement with her points. All of them knew of the increasing demand for all types of computers and replacement components that were used in their fields of control, and the slowly increasing waiting period for fulfillment that they faced.

Many of those there had been privy to the first exposure to much of the alien technology that had made it possible for them to be here now, and had witnessed the ingeniousness of the improvements made to that technology by melding it to the superiority of Earth's computer technology.

They also knew that most of that technology would be useless to the Earthmen without their computers to provide a venue for transitioning it into its' present use.

That technology had had millennia to be developed by the aliens, but the Earthmen did not have that luxury of time to assimilate it for their own use!

These council members had not only been chosen for their knowledge and previous experiences, they had also been chosen for their ability to apply hard headed common sense to solving tough problems.

They would see the need here, and they would act upon it.

Necessary Evils

After a one hour break for coffee and light sandwiches, and a little time to digest what Carmella had already laid out for them, the council reconvened. Carmella was already at the podium going over some last minute notes she had been jotting down during her last presentation as the council members began drifting back in. From his seat at the round conference table Dimetri Chabov banged his gavel once, loudly, then spoke the words that brought the meeting back into session.

As silence once more descended on the room Carmella began speaking in a quiet and metered voice that commanded attention to her words because it would be easy to miss something important. This woman had a reputation that many of those in attendance openly admired, and secretly envied.

She was saying, "Ladies and gentlemen. No matter how far we travel, or where we go, or how hard we try to shake it, there is a necessary evil that follows us! It is the same evil we all contended with, in one way or another, on earth. I am, of course, speaking of money." At this there were some open guffaws, and many sadly smiling and nodding heads.

"Many of you sitting at this table had, before disaster struck our home world, a fair share of it to a greater or lesser degree. And, at this point, none of us has any of it will do us much good out here now! Most of us, because of the situation we find ourselves in, don't miss it or think that there is much need for it. Well I'm here to tell you that nothing could be further from the truth!"

As she had expected this last was met by many of the members with looks of mild consternation. But on the faces of a few of them she saw thoughtful looks, and slow grudging nods.

"Let me explain." she said quickly as she saw several of them about to protest. "If our new fledgling society has no hard value medium of exchange system, other than the barter methods we have been forced to depend on so far, we will fail before we can even get a really good start! History, if we care to look at it realistically, has taught us several lessons about this topic. Among them are the following;

No society can long exist without a fair value trade exchange system.

No military organization can function well under stress conditions for any length of time without a civilian base to draw support from.

Direct barter, as a medium of exchange, becomes less and less effective the more complex the society using it becomes. And becomes even less effective over long distances and periods as that society expands outward.

She paused briefly to look at her audience again, seeing many more faces with thoughtful looks on them now. She hurried on again, warming to a subject that was dear to her, "And no matter how just our cause we are just as surely doomed to failure if we continue to operate only as a military unit and not as a reflection of the society and value structure that drove us to be in the position we find ourselves in now!"

She looked grimly about her as she went on, "Our people will lose heart without something more than the fight ahead of us to look forward to. Both civilian and military alike need something that reflects what they left behind, even if only a microcosm of it, to know that they fight for that to come home to!"

She took a deep breath, and plunged on, "Our civilian population, in this case, is fighting a twofold battle. On the one hand they have been uprooted from what is familiar, and have been transferred to somewhere that is almost familiar. On the other hand they, out of natural instinct, are trying to recreate as much as they can of what was lost to fight that feeling of displacement, and to give themselves an anchoring point so that they can go on with the fight they came here for in the first place."

Another deep breath and she hurried on again, "The military arm has it a bit easier in this respect because they are more used to being displaced as a matter of course in their duties. Even so, they need the civilian effort, and the anchoring point that they create, as an anchoring point of their own that creates a place to come home to. A place to blow off some of the tensions that they build up in the course of their duties, and as a place of respite from those duties themselves."

Now the room was completely silent as the members absorbed her words, and their implicit import. Gratified she proceeded more slowly now, speaking carefully, "A society, even the microcosm of the one we are trying to recreate from what we knew, needs two value systems in place for it to flourish. The first is a moral value system that treats both factions, civilian and military, firmly but justly with laws that govern their actions jointly, and other laws that are specifically separate to each. We are near to accomplishing this first."

"The second is a material value system that allows for incentive. One that is separate, but relative to, and cohesive with, the moral one. The acquisition and accumulation of a trade medium that has a base value, money, is necessary for healthy interaction between the two primary forces of our fledgling society. And as a means of valuation for trade with whatever other races we may come to deal with! Our people must have a means of exchanging perceived value for both giving and receiving goods and services, and as a means of incentive for both."

"All of this," she went on thoughtfully now, "is leading to the absolute necessity of establishing a monetary system, and that least liked of all systems, a taxation and collection authority to pay for the management of both."

Carmella smiled at the groans that escaped from many of the members, then went on slowly, "Working with Governor McCarthy, since he now has a population that exceeds three million, we believe that we have been able to come up with a viable system."

Now her face went deadpan as she said, "Taking into consideration that we must have a competitive market system that will drive incentive for both accumulation and spending, we have decided upon a taxation system that will not stifle entrepreneurial spirit and effort, nor will it overly penalize those who are willing to work that little bit harder to accumulate a little more!"

Here she took a deep breath to steady herself before finishing. This next was crucial to the resistance movement as a governing entity. Still with that deadpan look she continued, "We believe we have simplified our plan to the point where it will be understandable by any seventh grade student. Our proposal is for a tax base that starts with a rate of five percent on all earned income at the lowest level of income, and rises incrementally to peak at twenty five percent for those who earn over seven hundred fifty thousand EADs. (Earth Alliance Dollars). Business' will be taxed on the basis of their profits, also incrementally, to peak at fifteen percent over a total of two million EADs per annum. We also suggest that there be a two percent VAT (value added tax) tax imposed on all non essential items sold."

"The benefit to the individual and the business is that they will know exactly how much tax is due at the end of each tax year. They will pay their taxes on a quarterly basis. It has not been decided as yet whether the employer will withhold and pay the withheld taxes for their employees on that basis, but we favor that method."

"The benefit to the government will be that they will have an excellent idea of what they can expect, because there will be no personal deductions for income. And no deductions for business other than the cost of materials and labor. There may be some minor adjustment necessary to this proposal, but not much, because keeping it simple will keep it simple."

"As for planetary governments we are suggesting a matching two percent VAT tax on non essential goods, and a three percent gross income tax should suffice to cover their operating expenses. This may have to be adjusted at some point in the future but at present those governments are really extensions of the Alliance government, and other than local policing and adjudication they have few other expenses to deal with that the Alliance does not cover. We firmly believe that governance should not exceed what is truly necessary. These taxing measures are the simplest and fairest that we can reasonably recommend."

Now her smile was less grim as she went on, "The establishment of a standardized currency is an absolute must, and I am recommending that it be based on the American dollar system, a ten point decimal system. And, as I mentioned before, they should be called EADs, or Earth Alliance Dollars. If you will open the packages placed next to each of your water glasses you will find samples of both paper and coinage we propose to use. The paper currency is made from a paper that only we make, and we control all of it. The ink used to print it is a specially made product that has a magnetic residue in it that only we know the correct formula for. It will be very hard to counterfeit."

"The coinage is in denominations from ten cents to ten dollars. Because gold and silver has been found to be so plentiful out here we have made the coins from a combination of gold, silver, and platinum. This both makes the coins durable and gives them their value from the platinum content."

"We have given this as much time and effort as we have because it has become one of the lynchpins of our potential success. We believe that what we are offering is the best that can be done at this time, under the circumstances that rule us now."

"We also hope that what we have presented will meet with your approval. If there are any questions about this please set them aside for a few more minutes so I can finish."

Holding up her hand to forestall any comments she looked around the large table, marking each face with a name. Then, choosing her words carefully, she began speak slowly, forcefully, "We now have, after nearly three and a half years out here, four settled planets, two more in the process of being settled, and three more of them after that scheduled for settlement. We now have a viable population of nearly five and a half million souls, and we expect that number to double within the next three years with our climbing birth rate, and the continuing influx of refugees from earth."

"In view of this, and the need for the systems I have just described to you to be instituted, and in place and operating, in a very short period of time there are two laws that we feel must be put in place!"

Now she looked at each one of them directly, seeking their eyes, telling them that this part was as important as what had gone before. "The first one is that anyone convicted of tax cheating must forfeit any and all of their accumulated wealth, and start over again from the bottom! The details on how this can be implemented I must leave in your hands, but that penalty must be severe."

"The second law has a penalty even more severe. Anyone who is caught, and convicted, of the crime of counterfeiting should be put to death! And It should be done publicly! This because that one crime could very easily, and very quickly, destabilize us to the point of complete failure!"

"Please review the materials in your presentation packages. Also, a voice record of my comments here today will be available within a half hour for your deliberations. I will be available in the morning for a Q&A session after you have had some time to think."

Now she said, with a warm smile as she made contact with each pair of eyes around the table, "I want to thank you very much for your time and consideration on these matters I have placed before you."

She quickly gathered her notes and left the council chamber as Dirk had instructed her to do.

Realities

The council members were somewhat surprised when they began to assemble for reconvening the afternoon session, after a hurried lunch, as aides started bringing in another two dozen chairs which they began to place around the large conference table. That surprise didn't last long as they saw many of their military counterparts file in and begin to seat themselves about the table.

When they were all seated Dirk walked in followed by two aides pushing a large trolley laden with stacks of bound reports. He came to his seat at the head of the table, but remained standing behind it, his hands resting lightly on the headrest. He surveyed the group with a grim expression as he instructed the aids to begin passing out those reports, then leave after they were finished.

When they were done he began speaking, his tone as grim as his expression. He began by saying, "I hope those seats have good padding on them, because you're going to need it before we're done here today!"

There were a few smiles at this comment but they didn't last long when his grim visage didn't change one iota. His meaning was clear now, this was to be one of those long, hard, sessions.

"As some of you are aware," he began, speaking slowly and clearly, making an effort to be sure that there would be no doubt about the import of what he was about to tell them got across to them, "I was going to push for a stepped up extraction program for getting more people off Earth before the enemy got too strong for us to operate safely. And I was using the term safely as a euphemism!"

Now there was the ghost of a smile playing at the corners of his mouth as he said, "That is no longer the case! As you will see, when you've had a chance to go over the reports just handed out to you, it is now imperative that we devise and execute a plan for a massive extraction program to bring out another four to six million of our brothers and sisters! And it is equally important that we do so as soon as it is humanly possible to do it!"

He stood there for a full minute after he stopped speaking, looking at them to see if the full impact of what he had just said to them was hitting home. It was! Their expressions were turning as grim as his own was. They all knew the dangers in what he proposed were, but for Dirk to have proposed it in this manner meant that it was very important indeed!

"I know that we are stretched thin right now," he began again, speaking slowly, "but that is exactly my point! In the five and a half years since this thing began we have established four colony worlds and two more that are about to be colonized. The current census report will show you that over the last three years we have been able to extract nearly four and a half million people from our planet."

"Add to that nearly three hundred fifty thousand births and we now number almost five million Earthmen. And already we are beginning to be stretched thin!"

What these fine dedicated people he had gathered from all over the Earth had done in so short a period of time was near miraculous, but he couldn't let them rest on those laurels for more than a minute! "By best estimates," he went on, "we believe we have between five and six more years before the enemy's hold, and strength, on the Earth will make it all but impossible to get anything bigger than one of our smallest stealth ship anywhere near Earth. If we don't do this we will end up being nothing more than a thorn in the enemy's side!"

At the look of the grim expressions on those faces he knew that he had to say it all now, "I need your combined brain power to come up with a workable plan to extract those people from the Earth within the next year!"

He waited now for the stunned expressions to leave their faces. He didn't have to wait long, as looks of thoughtful contemplation began to appear in place of their previous frowns.

As that reality was sinking in he began to speak again in a normal tone of voice, "If the numbers I've already given you hold true, and I'm sure they will, we've brought out from Earth between four and a half and five million of our brothers and sisters, and close to fifty thousand Elonee. This total, along with the displaced children we were able to bring out total nearly five and a quarter million souls all total!"

He paused again for a few seconds to let those numbers sink in. Then, in a slightly firmer command tone, he went on, "That, my friends, is only half the number we need to start and guarantee the next generation of free humans!" He paused again, looking at their rapt faces, seeing in many of them that this was something that they had perforce given little thought to."

He continued to look searchingly at their faces for another long moment, wondering if they saw what was already beginning to give him nightmares that woke him in the middle of the night with cold sweats! With a deep mental sigh he plunged on, saying what had to be said, "It will take only one serious setback my friends, and humanity as we know it may well cease to exist as a viable species! I will not let that happen!!" He ended forcefully!

"Think about this as you deliberate," He now said so quietly they all had to strain to hear him, "We must propagate our species! With as few of us as there are still free now, we, Mankind, could conceivably become just a footnote in the history of this galaxy!" he finished very somberly. There were instant shouts of protest at this, but those shouting the loudest knew the truth of his words!

"The outline for this rescue and extraction of our brethren from Earth contained in those folders in front of you I have named, aptly I think, operation 'Phoenix'. And, like that mythical bird, it is designed to make it possible for us to rise up out of our ashes and strike our enemy to his very heart!" He stated this as forcefully as he was capable of doing, using the power of his command trained voice, projecting his own determination to make what he planned happen successfully.

"This time," He continued in that riveting tone, wanting to keep them centered on what he needed them to know, "we must bring out farmers and ranchers, teachers and craftsmen of every sort, miners and mid level managers, the whole gamut of those who make it possible for an advanced society to exist and flourish! And we will need more men and women for our military, but in this instance that will be secondary. All of the types we will need are in that report in front of you."

"Then," He said, as he continued in that same command tone to keep them focused on his line of reasoning, "while this operation is being carried out the governing council must debate and establish a basic set of laws that will be the guidelines for our settlement planets to follow while they generally govern themselves, for each will have its' own unique problems and requirements to deal with."

Now he grated out the next words, "Overall, those laws must be fair, but they must also be inviolate, for there is no room for any final authority but the ERMA council under these circumstances! This task must be set to as soon as the extraction plan is finalized and set in motion, because, as has already been established, everything and everyone is beginning to be stretched a little thin,"

As he paused for a breath, he looked out over those faces that were looking back at him intently. He let a small smile begin to play at the corners of his mouth as he said, "I know that this is a lot to add to your already loaded plates right now, but hell, we've already done what anyone in their right mind would have said was impossible already!"

He now saw the intent and worried looks on those faces begin to be replaced by smiles and new looks of determination. Now, Dirk knew, now they were ready to scoff at the devil again!

Now he went on in a normal tone, saying, "You will also find my ideas concerning several of the things said here in your folders. Please take the rest of the afternoon to read it, and we'll reconvene after the evening meal for some Q&A on those subjects."

Then, almost as if stating an afterthought, "Bring some pointed questions to that session because I'm sure that I missed a lot in my rush to get that report done in time for this meeting. I'll see you all this evening then." He turned and nodded to the guards to open the doors as he walked towards them. As he left the room the buzz of conversation began in real earnest.

TuLans' thoughts came drifting into his consciousness as he walked out, *I did not believe that you could convince them that your plan was feasible, yet as I speak they are already thinking of ways to make it happen!* he said, wonder and puzzlement warring for dominance in the tone of his thoughts.

Then, *is there nothing your species will not attempt in the face of adversity?*

Dirks' answer was curt, yet held worlds of meaning that would eventually dawn upon his symbiotic partner, *Nothing!*

And on another level of his mind, one that TuLan was not able to reach, there came a familiar chuckle, and, *Well done my brother!*

Important News

Balors' thought touched Dirks' mind as he walked down one of the corridors in the cave complex on the headquarters planet and, unlike his normally polite touch, this one was tinged with a sense of urgency, *My brother, there is news of import being brought in on the ship bound here from Wolfsbane! Together I think we could reach the communicator on board her. Will you join me in your quarters?*

I'll be there in five minutes. Thank you Balor. Dirk sent. not missing a word said to him by Yuri Garov. who was walking with him.

"Well," that worthy said as he turned into an adjacent corridor, "I'd better get back to the meeting. After five days they are beginning to make some very good progress."

"OK Yuri," Dirk said, reaching out to take his friends hand in a warm grip. "thanks for the heads up on this."

As he walked on down the hall he heard Yuri Garov let out a loud guffaw which he quickly tried to stifle as passersby turned to look at him. Dirk turned into the door of his quarters and saw Balor stretched out on his sofa, the one piece of furniture that he had that was not strictly utilitarian in nature, and sent to him, *I see that you two are still telling each other off color jokes since you taught him to mindspeak. Then Dirk guffawed himself as Balor sent him the gist of what had passed between the two of them in picture form.*

Balor stood up on the sofa and, arching his back as he stretched, turned a couple of times before resettling himself. Dirk went straight to his well padded desk chair, which he let himself down into with a sigh. The two reached out to each other, meshing their minds in an effortless manner that had become almost second nature after a good deal of practice together.

As one now they reached out together with their minds, these two beings that were almost as one now, reaching for the small ship that was speeding on its' way here from Wolfsbane. As they pushed their thoughts out they formed a query-welcome which they held at the fore of that thought bubble they pushed towards the ships Elonee communicator, Lannoc by name.

Since the Elonee had started riding the ships the councils had a much better grasp of matters within the sphere of the Earth Alliance and the new territories it now controlled. And the Elonee had a new spark in their demeanor, a new sense of purpose that showed as a sense of belonging. This made the interaction between them and their human partners much easier on both species.

Even though the little ship was still two light days out from the headquarters planet they were able to establish a link with Lannoc fairly quickly.

Lannoc was one of those among the group that comprised the Elonee's best and strongest telepaths, and she truly seemed to enjoy her new duties, as tiring as they could be at times. Tiring because 'farspeaking' required the expenditure of tremendous amounts of personal energy. This was why it had been decided to pair the Elonee on the ships.

Well met clanswoman. Dirk and Balor sent as one, and, *your previous sending said you had news of great import for us?*

Well met clansmen. Came her warm reply, *Indeed it is so! The captain,* and at the mention of that worthy her tone became even warmer, *"has said that this news was of the degree of importance that he was told not to spare any of his horses!*

She paused as her thought stream turned questioning, then said in a puzzled tone, *but it is very strange, for as hard as I have looked I cannot find any horses on our ship?*

Dirk sent the image of what was a warm smile for the Elonee, saying to her, *Lannoc, that was a figure of speech meaning that he was to go, and make great haste in doing so! Did your new friend, the captain, tell you of the news that was of such great import?*

He did clansman. If you are ready I will begin sending to you those messages. There are two of them. One from Wolfsbane, and the other one is from Chimera."

We are ready Lannoc. Please begin as you will. Dirk said as he and Balor reached out further to lessen the burden of sending on her.

Well enough. She said, and began to stream thoughts at them, *The first message was farspoken over many Elonee contacts, and it reads as follows; 'The biologists sent to work on Chimera have perfected a drug that effectively and safely slows the human metabolic rate by ninety to ninety five percent. This knowledge was sought in conjunction with the request you made nearly a year ago. They have already begun to produce this drug in very large quantities there, and will have the first full batch ready for shipment within the next sixty rotations of that planet! By our closest calculations that message was sent some twelve of your local rotations ago.*

Dirk was stunned, for this was the kind of good news he wouldn't have dared to hope for. Balor felt Dirks' elation and said to him in an aside, *this is good news Dirk?*

Indeed it is my brother! Indeed it is! Remembering the strain being imposed on Lannoc he said quickly to her, *please continue Lannoc.*

The second message is from the one called 'Felix', at the shipyards on Wolfsbane. It reads; In conjunction with the news from Chimera we have designed and begun building space worthy modular containers for shipping large numbers of human beings under the influence of the new drug they are now producing. Once loaded those containers can maintain life support for up to fifteen months loaded with up to ten thousand adult humans or up to twelve thousand human children age twelve years or younger."

Dirk felt Lannocs' strength flag slightly, so he pushed out even more to help her as much as possible. She sent a sense of warmth towards him for this effort and went on, *More importantly those containers can be joined together and transported 'in train' while in vacuum, and guided by one of our large cargo ships. Right now we are working out the bugs on installing anti-grav units that will make it possible to land them on the planet to be loaded. We will send more info as it develops. Felix.*

Now Lannocs' sending was weakening rapidly, so Dirk and Balor thanked her profusely for her efforts and broke the link.

If Dirk had felt stunned by the news from the first message he now felt as if he had been felled by a blind side roundhouse punch. Two messages, originating from tremendous distances apart, and both bearing good news of vast import at the same time. It was really incredible the way some things worked out!

He said to Balor, as they slipped back into their more familiar personal mode of speaking to each other, *this changes the face on everything!"* he said with new excitement in his voice. *What I thought to be a task of near improbable proportions is now in the realm of the merely hard to do! I must get this new information to the council right away. Please excuse me while I write a report to the council leaders about this.*

An hour later Yuri Garov, Dimetri Chabov, and admiral Timothy Berg were startled by a very loud pounding on the council room doors. Had they not left instructions that they were not to be disturbed until those doors were opened from within? Angry frowns beginning they nodded to the guards just within the doors to open them.

They were even more startled when they were summarily called from the council chambers by a harried messenger who was being escorted by two armed guards. The three of them rose from their seats and headed for the door, the frowns on their faces deepening the lines already there.

The three men were gone for somewhat more than twenty minutes. When they returned their backs were straighter, and there was a new spring in their steps. And their smiles were so broad it seemed as if they were being escorted by a bright sunrise, the careworn lines of just a few moments before completely gone now.

They said to the assembled council members who, to a being, had turned to look at the three as they came back through the doors, "let us tell you all what we have just learned—."

"That is what is contained in the report, sent to us by Dirk, that we just finished reading." Yuri Garov said through the smile that still transformed his normally dour features.

CHAPTER THIRTY-FOUR
Transition

Discussions on Basics

After ten days of intense discussions the council called itself, and Dirk, back into session. They also made it a point to invite the Elonee representative, Tagon, to this meeting for they had learned a valuable lesson from the regal old Elonee.

Over the last ten days he had helped the council immeasurably by making it possible to smooth frayed tempers. He had provided a means of showing exactly what one council member who was having trouble expressing his thoughts on a subject to the other members. This was done by letting all the members see that members thoughts just as he or she did. Although this wasn't done very often it did help to break several deadlocks log jamming their progress.

It had been decided, the council spokesman told Dirk after all the members had arrived and seated themselves, that there must be a body above the governing council itself for the duration of the war. Thus the council had created the ERMA Prime Council. This council will have final authority on any and all matters concerning the war, and in addition it will act as an arbitrator on such occasions that the governing council might become deadlocked on any matter of general governance. Lastly, Dirk had been unanimously elected to be the president of that council.

Dirk accepted this new position, pending several reservations he had that he would like to think about and get back to the council with. They agreed to this readily enough and the spokesman continued with what the council had come up with.

The council had decided that during these extreme times extreme measures were called for, so for the duration of the war the following rules would be applied as laws in the human parts of the alliance. Too, because they knew so little about any other species that might join the alliance they would reserve certain of those laws to be negotiated into any alliance agreements

As a final result of this council meeting two things occurred that were very beneficial to the fledgling alliance. The first was that they had recognized a potential shortcoming, and had taken steps to ameliorate it before it could become serious. The second thing seemed inconsequential at the time but would prove to be the one deciding factor in cementing their relations with their first non human ally.

By including the Elonee representative in these major discussions so he could see at first hand how they intended to handle the problems of a growing colonization program, and its' people, they did the one thing that that being had never expected from them. They proved, conclusively, that his input had real value to them!

They had heeded Dirks' warning about having to deal with other species, so they had asked Tagon a great many questions about how the Elonee dealt with those who were breakers of the law. Using what they had learned from Tagon they fashioned a methodology for dealing with interspecies law breakers that surprised him in its' simple but effective fairness.

Dirk could see as the spokesman went on that the council had been thorough. The mechanism for dealing with interspecies lawbreakers was that the local ruling council would appoint a representative, and also select another representative from the species of the lawbreaker. They, in turn, would select a third representative to act as an arbitrator in the event that a deadlock might occur on reaching an agreement as to the form of punishment the lawbreaker should receive if he or she were found guilty. This methodology would apply as soon as the next species joined the alliance, for Tagon had assured them that the Elonee were comfortable with the councils assurances of fairness.

There were only two instances where the council was totally adamant about the penalties to be imposed. Those were murder and treason. Tagon, in the beginning had some small difficulty understanding the differences between killing and murder, but once the distinctions were explained he tended to agree with the council.

Because of the early history of the Elonee, and their narrow escape from extinction, the killing of any sentient being was a very serious matter. As the council became aware of this fact they were more than willing to show Tagon their reasons for those distinctions.

All in all, Tagon came away from those council sessions with a much better understanding of the Elonee's new twolegs allies, and a new respect for them as well. He knew that there were bound to be some problems as time went on, but he no longer felt that separation was the right path for his people to travel.

In its' turn the council gained much respect for this being, that walked on four feet instead of two, that would greatly help it in its' future dealings with the new species it was soon to encounter.

The advantage they gained in dealing at first hand with a species that was not human in form went leagues to reinforce in them that the quality of a mind had very little to do with the appearance of a being. They were good people who learned lessons quickly.

New Life, New Laws

The Alliance Governing Council had spent ten grueling days, often for eighteen hours a day, hammering out a set rules that could be used as directive laws. Laws that would insure the basic freedom of all alliance members and still leave the Alliance Governing Council, the planetary governors, and the military councils the tools and authority for waging this war for survival.

What they had come up with was far from perfect, and the council footnoted, in its' meeting notes their understanding that they expected to revisit these subjects many times to amend and perfect them as time went by, or permitted.

What it did do was establish a workable foundation that could be built upon as needed. There was a good deal of preliminary outline work that dealt with the ground rules for establishing a basis of understanding in interspecies interactions and relationships.

They also took into consideration the necessity of the military being able to supercede or suspend parts, or all, of their operating directive for periods in the case of emergency situations. But on the whole they set a basis that let the local and planetary governance authorities deal with local issues as long as they did not try to supercede the tenets established by the council.

The following is a snapshot view of the basic rules set forth by the council, that were designed to act as guidelines for local governance in establishing their own local laws. In general they went as follows;

Article One

1.1) All human males and females over the age of seventeen earth years are now obligated to serve in the alliance Armed Forced for a period of five Earth years, unless they are in a profession that is deemed to be 'essential' to the war effort.

1.2) Once that obligation has been met that individual will have earned full voting rights in all Alliance electoral matters other than active Alliance military decisions concerning the war.

(Note 1) Pending certain modifications that may become necessary at times, any species determining that it will join the Alliance as full Alliance members, other than as military allies only, shall be subject to this rule within the boundaries of any treaties made at the time of their induction into the Alliance.

(Note 2) Under certain circumstances individuals who perform certain essential services or trades may be exempted from active military service if that service or trade is put under military jurisdictional control. In such cases those who perform those trades or services honorably shall be deemed to have fulfilled their obligation of service.

1.3) All beings who serve honorably in the Alliance Military for a period of five Earth years will become full alliance citizens, with whatever rights and privileges status may convey.

(Note 3) For those who may be physically unable to serve in the active military but desire to attain full Alliance citizenship status they may do so by serving as non combatants for a period of ten years in military related services such as military hospitals, essential support services, etc. These services will be paid at whatever military rate is current. *It is important to note that the length of this form of service must be served in a concurrent manner.

Article Two 2.

1)All Alliance Citizens shall have the right to keep and bear arms for the purpose of the protection of their persons, their families, their personal property, and the defense of their planet against any and all enemy aggressors.

Article Three

3.1) Any Alliance citizen, or legal resident, convicted of the crime of murdering another being, the only exception being killing as a proven act of self defense concurrent with the aforementioned, shall upon conviction be held liable for the material well being of the decedents immediate family, if any. If no immediate family is involved the duly authorized court for that jurisdiction shall impose such a sentence as it deems proper.

3.1)Conviction of such a crime will include the forfeiture of any and all, if any, of the perpetrators personal property for the purpose of covering the cost of the court and the support of the family. In addition, should the perpetrators personal assets not be adequate to cover these costs, he or she may incur a period of indenture not to exceed the time the youngest child of the decedent reaching the age of seventeen Earth years of age.

3.2)Refusal to perform such indentured services will be grounds for immediate public execution. There will be one appeal allowed to the perpetrator if such becomes the case.

3.3)Local courts shall retain the right to make determinations with regards to special circumstances, but they shall not use that right to circumvent the spirit of this law.

(Note 1) The Alliance Governing Council settled on this method of punishment more as a method of dissuasion to individuals from letting things go so far as committing an act of murder than as an end result punishment for that crime.

They did so hoping that it would be a real deterrent when realization that the sentence could put the potential perpetrator into a virtual state of slavery for a lengthy period of time. They also wanted to put all citizens and other individuals on notice that the penalties would be high and punishment swift!

The council also took this tack because it simply did not have the resources, or staff, to administer prolonged support for victims from the public trough for extended periods of time. It would be much easier to control the perpetrators and make them pay those costs while giving them some hope of a normal life after their debt had been paid.

Article Four

4.1)Treason against the Alliance, or any of its' Allies, will be punishable by public execution. If any individual is convicted of this crime there will be no exceptions to this sentence.

4.2)Agreement and adherence to the penalty for treason will be one of primary points for entry into the alliance for all species.

Article Five

5.1)Any being convicted of breaking local laws shall pay the penalty prescribed by that locality for the specific law broken, which may include fines or a period of incarceration or both.

5.2.1)The sentence for any being convicted of a crime within the territorial borders of the alliance will also carry a mandatory period of community service to the community in which that offense was committed.

5.2.2The period of such services will be commensurate with the crime committed, such service being a means to offset the cost of administering the laws.

Article Six

6.1)Planetary and local governing bodies shall make all such laws as are beneficial for the operation of those bodies and their communities, and shall set the penalties for the violations of those laws. But in all cases those laws shall not exceed, nor supercede, these directives

6.2)In cases where local laws and these directives overlap the local jurisdiction may adjudicate based on the severity of the overlapping violations.

6.3)In cases where there is a clear violation of these directives there will be imposed a mandatory sentence of a minimum of one years service and a maximum of fifteen years service based on the severity of the violation. The exception to this shall be the mandatory penalty set for treason which is death by public execution.

Article seven

7.1)With the exception of the office of planetary governors all members of regional and local governing bodies shall be elected by their populations. Elections shall be held at a minimum of every five years, and the rules governing those elections and the duties of those elected to office shall be set by a committee chosen by the electorate.

7.2)These rules shall be revalidated every second election by the electorate and a copy of those rules sent to the Alliance Prime Council to be validated for compliance with the general rules for elections established by that council.

7.3)Planetary governors shall be selected by the Prime Council and be approved or disapproved by the Alliance Ruling Council for as long as a state of war exists with the Drel or any of their allies.

7.4)Because of the distances involved each planetary governor shall randomly select five civilian members from each planetary body to monitor and report to that planets communities the intended actions of the Alliance Ruling Council, and to act as representatives to argue to the council if their actions may seem deleterious to that planets population.

These representatives shall be selected every three years, and may not serve as representatives for more than one term in any nine year period.

Article Eight

8.1)In cases where active military personnel are charged with a violation of local laws, or of a major crime, that individual shall be brought before a military tribunal for adjudication.

In all such cases a representative from the local charging authority shall be present to represent that body. If the individual charged is found to be guilty Punishment will be swift and commensurate to the offense.

8.2)Local governing bodies should take note of the following. If the charges brought are found to be frivolous or false severe penalties will be imposed on the body bringing such charges.

(Note 1)This caveat was included because the council was well aware that there had been many cases where communities saw the military as convenient sources of revenue to be gained from the imposition of frivolous misdemeanor statues directed at them and the inflated fines that were imposed for violation of them. They also knew that the military could be quite overbearing at times itself so they sought a fair middle road to follow by a policy of control by inclusion.

This was a small sampling of the work of the council. They well knew that without a supportive civilian population they would not be able to fight what was more and more looking like a very long and drawn out war.

They set, and agreed upon, these basic directives and laws with the understanding that most of them would have to be revisited and refined as circumstances dictated from planet to planet, and sector to sector.

They also established rules for governance, elections, and also general law to govern interplanetary trade within the fledgling Alliance. Within that framework they worked out an outline for the advent of interspecies trade that they knew would impact them all too soon. They did all of this by taking from the best of the methods Earth had developed, and completely eliminating the worst of them.

Much of what they did was derived from the application of simple common sense that applied to the circumstances that existed around them. And, above all else, by making the individual, as much as possible, responsible for his or her own actions and choices.

For the most part these, and many of the following laws rewarded honesty and hard work, and tried very hard to make sloth and dishonesty a very expensive proposition to those who would try to circumvent those laws.

The great majority of those who were brought out from Earth were dedicated to winning this war. They were hard workers who often played as hard as they worked, and would work even harder if they saw that there was something they could do that would better their own and their compatriots situations.

Simply put most of these people were willing to do whatever was necessary to win this war. But they were also, the greatest majority of them, tired of the stifling and petty laws that tended towards the self interest of the majority on Earth who weren't willing to work and strive for what they wanted. Most, when the findings of the council were posted, found that they readily agreed with those findings and directives.

It would take a long time but the people who would survive this were up to the challenges. They had few illusions about what lay ahead of them, nor what failure would bring!

CHAPTER THIRTY-FIVE
Interludes

Virus

The small, dark, ship came out of hyperdrive well out from the three suns that resembled a triangle set like a huge travelers beacon in normal space. The little ship had been following a fleet of eight much larger ships for nearly six months now. The only reason they had been able to do so was the other ships drive signature would blink out every time they dropped out of hyperdrive into normal space.

The little ships sensors, very powerful ones, could pick up the other's ships in hyperdrive and in normal space but not from one to the other. The people running the little ship had set up an auto sequence that allowed them to drop out of hyperdrive within minutes after their quarry did, so that they would not lose them, or even worse, overshoot them and give themselves away by exposing their own drive signature.

The dark little ship was feeling her way cautiously forward, using only the minimal power necessary to operate her long range sensors as she neared one of the three suns. That sun had a family of five planets and seven planetoid sized satellites, three of which were moons circling the second planet out from this sun. The sun itself was a reddish yellow orange, its' carona reaching only a hundred thousand miles or so out from the main body. It was also a bit bigger than Earth's star, Sol, and a bit more stable but of lower intensity and much older. The planet was also a bit bigger than Earth, much of its' surface area shrouded with cloud cover.

But where there were breaks in that cover it could be seen to be covered by vast gray oceans that hurled huge rolling waves that broke against shorelines that were mostly high craggy stone cliffs, sending spray and streamers as much as two hundred feet or more into the air.

The land masses were comprised of eight continent sized islands, the smallest the size of Australia and the largest the size of the United states on Earth, along with ten or so other islands the size of the state of Texas or smaller.

Those land masses were covered with yellow-green vegetation that looked like it tended to be jungle in their lowlands, and vegetation that was a darker green to green-black in their upper altitudes, much like Earth's vegetation.

Most of the islands were very mountainous, some with vast areas of snow and ice covered peaks jutting through the cloud cover at their highest points. Many also had savanna-like areas that covered huge sections.

All had large, deep rivers, many of which emptied into lakes the size of the great lakes in North America. Many others ran to the vast gray ocean, spilling themselves over falls that were truly a breathtaking sight as they plunged hundreds of feet to the oceans tumultuous grasp.

The small ship was now hiding itself in what might be this systems version of Earth's Van Allen Belt. There was debris here that looked like the detritus of an exploded planet, which made an excellent place to hide.

The ship was now gathering information. Information about both the fleet it was following and the system it was now in. It was getting most of that information from an 'RSV', or 'Remote Surveillance Vehicle' that it had launched before hiding itself in this belt of debris.

The RSV was so small, only fourteen inches long by eight inches high by ten inches wide, that it was almost totally invisible. But its' size was very deceiving for it was packed with some of the most advanced micro and nano technology electronics ever devised by Earthmen.

The RSV had been sent in to a position that was within only five pds. (planetary diameters) of both the planet and the eight ships that were now in close orbit around it, and it was now sending back both digital and optical telemetry for those on the ship to analyze. And what they were now seeing was making those aboard the ship both angry and sick with sympathy!

The eight Drel ships they had been following were now spread out in an englobing formation around the planet and, after only a couple of days, there was now a steady stream of small landing vessels shuttling back and forth between the ships and the planet. The largest of those ships had taken up a geo-stationery orbit over the largest of the planets' island land masses, and the stream of landers to and from it was very heavy. Those on the small ship couldn't see exactly what the Drel were doing, but they knew. They knew!

The planet was populated. This could be seen when there were breaks in the cloud cover for there were large areas of twinkling lights that could only be cities as seen from high altitude at night. The shape or form of those inhabiting the planet was unknown to the watchers but the fact of their intelligence was obvious.

The fact that the Drel were taking the planet over by force was made plain when one of those areas of bright lights was suddenly surrounded and then inundated by bright flashes of light that could only be large explosions.

Thereafter there were only far spaced single lights to be seen from that area of the large island at night. There were several more examples of this on the other islands, and the results were the same, near total darkness in those areas thereafter. The only places that that seemed to be immune to these attacks were those islands that formed the polar points of the planet.

There were far fewer points of light from these, but they remained undisturbed for now. Those watching made special note of this. Then, after only a few short weeks, those on the small ship were caught by surprise when three of the ships around the planet broke orbit and headed for the second sun that formed one of the corners of the triangle constellation. That one was a red dwarf with only three planets. The watchers were in a quandary as to whether they should follow the three ships or not. In the end they did so, and witnessed a repeat of what had happened on the first planet.

The small ship withdrew to a safe distance and reentered hyperspace, heading back the way they had come, and marking the triangle constellation as dangerous territory on their star maps!

The Drel menace was beginning to spread like the flu!

Insertion Points

Two messages came into the council almost simultaneously. One bringing very good news. The other bringing frown lines to the faces of those on the council with the need to know what that one said.

It had been almost fourteen months to the day since the council had approved the plan to rescue more men, women, and children in vast numbers from Earth, and the mines on Carona and the shipyards on Wolfsbane had been working around the clock since that word had been given to them.

On Carona, the sister planet of Wolfsbane, it had been discovered that there were vast deposits of iron, nickel, copper, and all the other ores that were required to build space ships. But the discovery that had completely blown everyone's mind though, had been a huge deposit of fibrous carbon, nearly eight billion tons of the extremely rare substance. It was so rare that the largest deposit ever found on Earth had only been ten tons. This find took three full steps out of producing the stealth coating used on the resistance movements ships, enabling the shipyards to produce forty percent more ships every month.

The Alliance now had nearly a million men and women in uniform in the combined space navy and ground assault troops it was able to field. They also had twenty frigate class fighting ships in operation, twenty eight of the swift and deadly little heavy cruisers and fifty two of the light cruisers.

They also had nearly eighty of the small scout ships that were near invisible to every kind of sensor except those that registered drive signatures, and with the new engine baffles installed on them the only time they could be spotted was when they had to run at speed to make a jump into hyperspace. And to top everything off they now had seventy five of the huge cargo ships that could double as troop transports.

And to date they had produced almost twenty five hundred of the special human cargo modular transports.

All of this was very good news to the Prime and Military Councils. But all of that paled before the news that Balor brought to Dirk this day. The tension lines around Dirks' mouth and eyes seemed to retreat visibly as he listened to the tape that Balor had insisted on carrying to him personally.

The message went;

From: Forward Command Base, Calysto
To: Military Command Council
Att.: Admiral T. Berg
Due to the stealth coating on the transport modules we have been able to insert and place a total of two thousand two hundred modules on earth in their pre selected locations.

This command fully expects to have the final six hundred modules inserted and in place within the next ninety days.

Phase two has already been initiated and six hundred fifty five of the modules are now ready to lift.

I am very happy to inform you that the hibernation formula is working at a ninety seven point nine percent positive ratio, and the med teams are working at capacity. We could use more med teams!

The hoppers you provided with the chameleon devices are allowing our med teams to move from site to site almost totally unhindered.

Our scout teams and the on ground resistance fighters are raising hell with the enemy strong points, keeping their attention diverted from our extraction efforts.

Thanks to the Elonee working with our gathering teams we caught and killed twenty three Drel and steeds who were trying to infiltrate our underground people trains.

We have field promoted sergeant Misha Galenko to the rank of First Lieutenant for his idea of linking the modules on the ground and slaving their controls to one of the lift vehicles, and his efforts in making that idea work. This has freed up hundreds of pilots and thousands of crew personal, which we had no trouble finding other work for them that needed doing.

By P-day we anticipate lifting four and a half to five million of our brothers, sisters, and their children from our beleaguered home, God Willing, to aid us in our fight to retake it from the Drel.

Commanders Note: The planning and execution notes provided with the overall plan outline far exceeded what we had expected to have to work with. Also, the ready access to fuel, munitions, and other supplies has made our job that much more doable, and every member of this command sends their heartfelt thanks to you and the council.

For security reasons I have sent this report in both a video format and a digitally written copy on computer discs, each by separate courier.

—End Message—   C.R. Jenkins Maj. ERMA Forces

The members of the councils printed and passed around copies of the written report, gathering in small groups to discuss certain points of it and then moving on to other members to discuss still other facets of the report. This was the best news they had received in many months.

Like everything else in war it is seldom that good news is not followed by some bad news.

Bad News

The bad news came in the form of one of the oldest of the scout ships. It had broken out of hyperspace nearly on top of one of the freighters traveling the now heavily trafficked route between Carona and Wolfsbane. It had come so close that the captain of that ship had called for help in a panic, thinking he was under attack. This prompted a near panic and the callout of several heavy frigates that were on picket duty near the outer edges of the system.

The little ship had barely enough engine power left to bring its' breakneck speed under some semblance of control, and avoid several more possible collisions, turning them into near misses. After that she lost the engines as they burned out completely, and she began coasting through the system in uncontrolled flight.

It took the work of several heavy space tugs, using powerful magnetic grapples to bring her to a stop and keep her from coasting right out the other side of the system and into empty space.

When she was finally boarded it was found that most of the crew were near death or dead! Most had succumbed to burns or other wounds when the port side engine nacelle had exploded and fire had ravaged most of the crew area. A good number of those still alive were in terrible shape from the effects of dehydration and near starvation.

The rescuers found her captain, Mr. Blain, her first officer lieutenant Sheila McKenzie, and a couple of ratings in a state of near total delirium from their tribulations. Each of them were also suffering from multiple wounds that had begun to suppurate from infection.

When the team securing the little ship came to report to their chief that worthy was shaking his head in wonder muttering to himself that he just didn't believe what was before his eyes. He said to his second in command that he didn't know how they managed to break back into normal space, let alone get into hyper space in the first place! That starboard engine was fried before they jumped!

"Just look at this," he said in awe, "they spliced an emergency control repair cable into the port engine control board and ran it out a pressure release vent to the external maintenance control panel, then rerouted that to the main control board. And all of that had to have been done outside the hull!" Several days later the council got most of the story from the fast recovering first officer, lieutenant McKenzie, who had sustained the least amount of damage to her body and mind.

When the importance of her report was realized by the governor of Wolfsbane, who was in attendance for her first debriefing, he immediately had her and the surviving crew sequestered. He then sent an emergency message to Prime Council Headquarters because he wanted several additional bodies from that council present who could make the kind of decisions now necessary present to hear the whole report.

In just six days, Dirk, Yuri Garov, Admiral Berg, and Dimetri Chabov showed up at the hospital. When the now fast recovering survivors were finally brought to the largest conference room that could be arranged, and still maintain the security the governor felt was necessary, the story was finally told in full detail.

When the young lieutenant McKenzie began the story, for captain Blain was still in intensive care, it was a little hesitantly because she was a bit intimidated at being debriefed by two of the legends of the resistance movement. Her hesitancy didn't last long as both men smiled and encouraged her to go on. Her words were soon flowing out in a rush.

"As per our orders we were backtracking the direction from which the Drel fleet now in orbit around Earth had come in from. Initially we were taking it in short jumps from the last star cluster that we were using as a reference point, just to stay on the safe side of error, but each jump just put us out further into that area of space known as the Magellan Deeps."

She gulped a breath, then, "It was after the eighth jump that Captain Blain told the navigator to plot a six day jump that he thought should bring us out about a day or so from a fringe system that had an old, nearly dark, red star. And sure enough it brought us out within a couple of light days of that dying old red giant."

She paused just long enough to take a sip from the water glass in front of her, then went on, "We had realigned the ship to the course we were backtracking, and the captain and Nav. were shooting some last minute long range instrument sightings, when the sensors operator called for the captains attention. When the captain went over to him he said he was getting some very feint long range drive signature readings from out near the edge of the galactic gulf, but he wasn't even sure they were true readings."

She paused to take a couple of deep breaths, then hurried on, "Because of the anomalous nature of those readings, and the fact that we had found, nor seen, absolutely nothing since we started out, the Captain decided, since those readings had come from the general direction we were heading for, to make another long jump."

"We jumped into hyper at three quarters speed and stayed there for three weeks when the Captain decided that we should come out for a look see. Well, we broke out into normal space and there was nothing. I mean absolutely nothing! We were right on the fringe of the galactic gulf!"

Dirk and Garov had both noticed the other crew members present nodding at times during her narration. She took another sip from her glass and prepared to continue, and as she began both men notice the slight pinching around the corners of her eyes, and the eyes of the others as well. "Sir, when I say nothing, I mean we couldn't get a reading in any direction, even from our longest range sensors."

"We sat out there for a full two days checking over the ship, and preparing to jump back the way we had come. Nav. had just laid in the direction-duration coordinate settings, and locked them in, when the skipper, I mean the Captain, told us all to stand down for a four hour rest break before we began our return journey."

Now she went on more slowly, a haunted look coming into her and the others eyes as she spoke. "The watch had just been set, and most of those not on duty were heading for their quarters, when every alarm klaxon, bell, and whistle on the ship went off all at once!"

The haunted look became a fixed stare as those memories began to replay themselves! She shook herself, then went on with her story in a voice that trembled only slightly, "Thank god we were only a few short steps from the bridge when everything cut loose. As I stepped back through the bridge hatch I was right on the captains heels, then we stopped to look at the forward monitor."

She gulped air, then continued, "It showed ships breaking out into normal space. We checked the port, aft, and starboard monitors and they showed the same thing. There were hundreds ships breaking out all around us! One really huge ship broke out nearly on top of us. It was so close we could feel the vibrations from its' engines through the hull!"

She took a deep breath and went on, her voice shaking with the emotion of her memories as she spoke, "Funny thing is, they didn't seem to know we were there! The Captain grabbed me and pulled me close, saying quietly in my ear 'go to stealth mode, no noise. Pass it on'. Seeing the look on his face I told the third officer very quietly to shut down the alarms, fast, and to go to stealth mode. No noise! And I made sure he understood by telling him to pass it on very quietly."

"Well Sir, That was the fastest and quietest we had ever done that! And within the next minute everything that wasn't absolutely necessary was shut down. Then the skipper told sensors to get a count. We were up to two hundred forty nine when sensors sang out that we had just been hit a glancing sweep with one of their sensors!"

She gulped a deep breath, and rushed on, her voice trembling with both the horror and excitement of those moments. "The Captain didn't waste a second, sir! His orders came in rapid fire as he called for full emergency power—one jump warning for a jump in fifteen seconds. Then he said to weapons that he wanted a full spectrum firing spread in all direction on his mark. He waited five seconds then said 'mark, mark, fire all weapons!'"

"The ship shuddered as we cut loose with every weapon we had all at once. And it was a good thing we did or else we would never have gotten out of there, because sensors was yelling that we were being painted. The jump warning sounded and right on its' heels the captain said 'Emergency jump, Now!' Just before we went hyper we saw one of our Tomahawks hit one of that big ships engine nacelles. Unfortunately for us a laser beam hit our starboard engine nacelle as we entered hyperspace!"

The haunted look was back now, in all of their eyes, as she forced herself to relive that period. "We shut that engine down because we were getting a lot of red light on the warning panel. Five days later we dropped back to normal to reset our jump coordinates, and to see what could be done for that engine. We patched it up the best we could but the captain told nav. to plot the whole time/direction factor into the nav computer because he didn't think we'd get more than one more jump out of that engine!"

She paused now for a long couple of moments, a shudder wracking her body as she remembered what was coming. The shudder continued in her voice when she began to speak again, slowly now, "We got that one jump push from that starboard engine, but before we could shut it down once we were in hyperspace it exploded, killing near half the crew and injuring another quarter of them from fire, explosions, and decompression before we could get everything under control again."

"We spent nearly nine weeks in hyperdrive," she said quietly as a couple of tears spilled from her now brimming eyes. When she realized she was crying she scrubbed at her eyes angrily, as if they had betrayed her. She swallowed once as she finished the sentence she had started. "trying to salvage what we could of the ship. And those left alive!"

She went on hoarsely now, "Captain Blain, because the flight controls were nearly useless now, went out-ship while we were in hyper, and jury rigged an external bypass for what was left of the flight controls so we could shut her down when we came out of hyperspace." She finished with the kind admiration in her voice that can only be earned.

That admiration colored her words as she went on, looking right at Dirk now as she spoke, "Sir, the Captain wouldn't let anyone else go out with him while we were in hyperspace. He said he didn't know what the effects might be, and put me in command of the ship."

Her words were now almost awe struck as she went on, "When he came back in he didn't seem to know where he was, so I put him in the bridge cabin. We cared for him and the others the best we could with what we had left, and waited out the duration of the jump. You pretty much know what the rest of it is from the time we dropped out of hyperdrive into normal in this system." She ended with a sigh.

TuLan said in Dirks' mind, *that is totally amazing! I don't know of any other race of beings who would have tried what these brave people did! Your race is truly an amazing one!*

Those thoughts were echoed by Balor, who was laying on the sofa across from the young lieutenant, his eyes glowing brightly as he watched her.

"Sir," lieutenant McKenzie said almost diffidently, "Just before we jumped I looked in the aft monitor, and those ships were still dropping out of hyperspace when we jumped the first time."

"So," said Dirk somberly, "they're coming in force now. I guess we'll just have to have some kind of welcome set up for them when they get here."

"'Phoenix's' time frame will have to moved up now Dirk." Yuri Garov said quietly.

"I don't think so Yuri. I think I have the beginnings of an idea that will create a very nasty welcome for our unwelcome visitors!"

After thanking the lieutenant and the crew members for their valiant efforts Dirk asked Yuri come with him for a private conference.

Three and a half hours later Yuri Garovs' wolfish grin was just as big and mean looking as the one on Dirks' face as he said, "Now I understand why you were such a good foe. You are truly a very nasty man Dirk!"

"Pity those poor people that 'Phoenix' is going to try and lift out if what we are planning to attempt does not work the way we think it will for us!" Dirk replied sourly.

But then in a lighter and more cheerful voice he said, "But, like the ant and the rubber tree Yuri, I have very high hopes!"

Heads Up

It had been nearly five and a half months since the badly damaged scout ship had limped into the Wolfsbane system, its' crew decimated and more than half of them dead. But it had not been idle time for the ERMA forces now inhabiting the newly settled planets there and in other systems, for they were very busy getting ready to stage one of the most spectacular rescue efforts ever made by anyone on or off Earth.

Back on Earth, the man occupying Dirks' old office in the base located in the Canadian Rocky mountains was the highest ranking ERMA officer left on the planet. At present he was sitting in front of the radio and speaking to several other officers scattered all over the Earth.

That radio was one of the new ones that operated on oscillating ultra high frequency bands, and it was one of his most prized possessions and tools. It had also been one of his most effective weapons for the last few months, because the small computer it was hooked up to oscillated the frequency fifty time a second, and only another radio set up in the same way could pick up its' signal or broad cast to it!

The man sitting at the radio was a full general and he was conferencing with fourteen full colonels, five lieutenant colonels, seven majors, and four captains of the ERMA forces who were part of 'Operation Phoenix' here on Earth. His voice, as were most of the others, was a little hoarse and showed the strain and tiredness of the last few months of effort as he responded to the last question put to him by one of the full colonels.

"All I can tell you, colonel, is that I was contacted at three AM this morning, and told to issue orders for all units to go on full standby alert as of midnight GMT on the fifth of June. That gives everyone nearly ninety six hours notice. That also means that that you are to have every single launch vehicle manned and ready to launch on sixty seconds notice! Anyone not processed and loaded aboard the transports by nine PM of the fifth are to be sent to one of the alternate safe sites. Is that clear, colonel?"

"But Sir!" said the voice of the colonel from the largest site in the Ural Mountains, his English accented by his Russian background "I still have almost eight thousand people to process because I've been taking the over load from three other smaller launch locations. My med tech's are sleeping on their feet as it is, trying to keep up with that load!"

Another voice, her English heavily accented by her Polish ethnicity, broke in saying, "I can help you there, Boris, if you can send those six stealthed Hinds of yours to me. We are finished processing and I can send you my one hundred fifty med tech's to help out. We are only two hundred or so kilometers from your site as the crow flies. All I ask is that you guarantee them births at lift off!"

"I can send you another fifty, and the balance of our sleep juice. We are only five hundred kilometers from you. Same request!" came another voice.

"I can send fifty also. We are further away but we have our own transports. Just give us your security transponder codes, and where you want us to set down. Same request here."

"Da, spaceba.' Yes! Thank you all! I think that would make the difference! All my people need is four hours of uninterrupted rest and they will be able to complete the processing. Does that meet with your approval general?"

"It does Boris. Make your arrangements. Are there any other questions, or comments? No. Good!"

The general's tired voice broke in a cough as he started to speak again. He cleared his throat and when he continued there was a new spark in his tone as he went on again, "This is the 'Heads UP' we've all been waiting for! Remember, shut down all processing at nine PM sharp on the fifth and go to standby alert status!"

He paused for a few pregnant seconds then concluded with, "Good luck and God speed to us all my friends!"

Then, with a weary sigh, he reached out and flipped the switch that ended his transmission.

The weary sigh was because he knew that he and his people had at least eighteen hours more hard work left to do.

And then the nerve wracking tension of waiting for the launch signal to come would begin!

In Motion

"We know, without a doubt, that they will bring their fleet of atmospheric flyers down to cover such a threat!" stated general Osov emphatically, his hard eyes seeking those of the others at the table as he continued. "We have been giving them a very hard time at almost all of their biggest intaking centers, and the only reason they have not been able to crack down harder is because we have been effectively hitting and running faster than they could react to our raids. We stand to lose a very large portion of our effective numbers of ground insurgency forces by conducting a raid of that size and scale!"

The look in his eyes was bitter, as his agile mind kept going over what was being asked of him. He had placed many of his most trusted officers on the ground to help train and develop those insurgency forces, and he knew that if this raid went forward many of them would surely be lost! But Osov was a product of the old Russian Army, and a real pragmatist, so he knew that he must go forward.

He held up his hand to forestall comment until he had finished, saying, "I do not like to waste good people, but I do see the twofold benefit of such a raid if it were successful. Just the fact of destroying, or seriously damaging, one of the few main line ships they have put down on the planet would set their 'steed' transformation efforts back by as much as two years! And, I do not forget that tying up so many of those atmospheric fighters in one place, that far from most of the launch sites, would improve our chances dramatically!"

He looked again at those gathered around the big map, and report strewn conference table. His eyes were the thoughtful ones of an experienced combat commander. But they were also cold, and as hard as steel plate, as he continued, "Yet still, gentlemen, there is the other side of that coin to consider. That is the very real possibility that not enough of those fliers will be destroyed, or damaged, before the launch signal is given!"

He paused again, very briefly, then finished, "For the most part I agree with this phase of the plan, because I know how much we stand to loose if it is not put into play. You all know my concerns. I've stated them often enough over the last ten hours! But yes, I support the overall plan as it has been laid out here." He sat down abruptly, the weariness that was beginning to affect all of them seeming to grab at him harder.

At a nod from Dirk, Yuri Garov got to his feet and, looking around the table, let a huge grin break out across his normally dour features as he began speaking, "Comrades, my friends, it was important that you accept the plan as set forth, but there have been occurrences that we believe will eliminate those atmospheric fliers from the equation!"

At the surprised, almost joyous, look in his friends eyes Yuri hurried on to explain, "Because of information just recently received we are changing the off Earth tactical approach we will make. Actually there are two pieces of news that impact our actions henceforth!" At the clamor of questions he saw building in the eyes and faces around the table he quickly said, "Wait, wait! I will explain all to you!"

As those around the table settled themselves, he began to speak, "First, the recall order went out two and a half months ago to every ship that could conceivably make one of two rendezvous points by a certain date, to do so. We expect, from the responses we've been able to get so far, and thanks in the most part to our Elonee allies, that as we reach our jump off date we will be able to field nearly one hundred ships for this operation!"

At the startled looks around the table he hurried on, "We did not bring this up before now because, until a few minutes ago, we were not positive of this information, but it has been confirmed. Too, there is icing to go on this cake! That icing is that our first destroyer class ship has just completed her shakedown cruise. And it has come through it with flying colors. This ship is five times the size of our biggest heavy cruiser, and has eight times the fire power!" he finished, his smile getting even wider now as he saw the looks on the faces of those around the table.

"The second bit of news is not nearly so pleasing! A fleet has just entered the outer reaches of our galaxy from the direction of the first Drel fleet. It numbers between six and seven hundred ships from what information we have." he went on in a much more somber voice, "but we intend to make use of it in ways that they never intended!" he finished, as the smile he wore turned completely feral!

The men and women around the table began to speak, throwing questions at him, and each other. The stunned looks on their faces, and in their eyes, was that of hope and fear warring for dominance. Then those looks began to change slowly to ones of anger. Anger that these aliens were coming in force to take the rest of all that they held dear, as if it were their natural right.

Yuri Garov smiled grimly now as he looked on with satisfaction at their anger. They would need it to get through the balance of this planning meeting.

He harumphed loudly now, then said "Shall we get back to work then?"

In Motion Too

Within a few short hours of the completion of the planning conference one of the newest and fastest of the scouts went into hyperspace, heading for a point near the edge of this galaxy. That ship, Felicity, had entered hyperspace at maximum speed. Fifteen days later she dropped out of hyperspace, and began casting about for the ship she was sent to meet.

Within three hours Felicity was sitting off the bow of the heavy cruiser, Agamemnon, and the two captains were in conference with each other via their Elonee communicators. Felicity had been chosen specifically because her captain, like the captain of the Agamemnon, was capable of linking telepathically with his Elonee communicator, thus making their communication completely safe from any known Drel detection.

"So," the captain of Felicity was saying, "the council wants you to match jumps and speeds with this fleet until you think you have determined speed, flight path, jump duration times, and normal space intervals. Dearborn is due to arrive within the next three hours, and will stay with you until you have made those determinations."

"As soon as you think you have them you are to transfer that information to Dearborn, and send her ahead to the coordinates she has in her safe. Then you are to break off and head for the coordinates in the packet in your own safe. Once there you are to await orders from Shrike. Is all of that clear to you captain?"

"Yes sir. Very clear sir. Came the swift response.

"Good." Then, "This is what we have been working so hard at for the last eighteen months, Jim. Good luck,, and God speed."

Then the link was broken, and shortly thereafter Felicity's engines flared brightly to life again. She maneuvered away from Agamemnon and sped away, her engines flaring once again as she kicked herself into hyperspace once again.

Two and a half days later Dearborn dropped into normal space some three to four light hours from Agamemnon. Her engines flared several times as she matched speed and course with the bigger ship.

Information was exchanged, tactics agreed upon, and the two linked ships began the waiting that was so often part of the deadly game of cat and mouse.

CHAPTER THIRTY-SIX
Waking the Dragon

The Dragon Stirs

"I got the idea," Dirk was saying to Admiral Timothy Berg and Yuri Garov, as they sat on the bridge of the G.W. Bush, the newest of the ships to join the ERMA space forces, "from part of a conversation I once had with TuLan Chai. He was telling me about the accident that caused him to have to force land his small planetary runabout ship on Earth. The one you first saw in the box canyon, and gave us the knowledge we are using on every ship we now have in space! It only took one little piece of space debris the size of a dime to destroy his entire space station observatory!"

He looked at them, his smile feral now as he said, "So, I asked myself, what kind of damage would several hundred thousand of them do if they were fired from our rail guns? Fired from a good distance away from a hyperspace exit point? Fired at a fleet of ships that has no idea whatsoever of what they are flying into? Especially if they were fired at a fleet as big as the one that is coming at us now!

"What about their deflector shields?" Tim Berg asked. And, "won't they deflect or stop most of them?"

"Tim, those shields are designed to operate at low to medium power during flight in normal space, and to stop things from microscopic to about a sixteenth of an inch in size at that power. To stop something a half to three quarters of an inch and the mass of the depleted uranium we're using they would have to operate their shields at full power. If they did that they would have to fly blind because their sensors, like our own, won't penetrate those shields at full power more than a thousand yards.

Dirk paused for a few seconds before going on, his smile looking totally wolfish now. "That's the whole point of attacking them in this manner in the first place! Also, besides the amount of damage I believe we'll be able to inflict in the first attack, I want to force them to blind themselves by throwing up their shields at full power so that they won't see the much heavier stuff that will be coming at them in the second wave of our attack!"

"Da! It is a good plan Dirk! It will work." Yuri Garov said fiercely, and to Timothy Berg, "My friend Timoty, we have only a hundred, possibly a hundred twenty, ships we can use for this operation without stripping all of our defenses bare to the bone. We can only send sixty five of them to confront this giant that is coming. Of the flotilla we can send against them we will have only twenty five scouts, thirty nine light and heavy cruisers, and our new destroyer! Of these numbers you are well aware, for they are the ones you gave me."

Yuri paused for a second, then said "You are a very good tactician my friend, but in this Dirk has the right of it."

With that said he pulled a scrap of paper from his pocket, and looked down at it for a few seconds. Looking at it was unnecessary for he knew exactly what it said. Now, as Yuri went on, his voice turned somber. "I got this relay message from Agamemnon a few minutes before I came up here. It says that they counted five hundred eighty nine ships before they had to stop, because the fleet was jumping again. It also says that they estimate that there are possibly another hundred to hundred fifty more!"

Dirk picked up the conversation from there, saying, "I know you're coming into this cold Tim, and I'm sorry to have to saddle you with this as well as everything else on your plate. Besides the fact that both Yuri and I have to leave on the Shrike to direct operations near Earth, you're about the best fleet tactical planner and executer we have! That's because you've got the kind of devious mind that makes you a damned good strategist. And you can think and act on your feet! That's why we need you in command out there!"

Dirk paused for a breath before finishing, "We need you to follow the general plan as closely as you can, adding the embellishments you think necessary, to accomplish two purposes. First, you've got to hurt them, and hurt them badly, destroying and damaging as many ships as possible in the first two stages of the assault we've laid out. The third stage is to make them so mad they will chase you blindly! If you can do that we will have another very nasty surprise waiting for them when they are about half way to Earth!" Dirk finished, the look on his face so feral that Tim Berg sat just a little back from him.

"You know that I'll do whatever I can Dirk." Admiral Timothy Berg said, his voice firmer now that he had a better understanding of what was being asked of him.

"Good!" Dirk said, reaching out to shake his hand warmly. And Yuri Garov reached across the table to shake his hand warmly also.

As they rose from their seats Dirk said, "The captain of the Bush has been informed that you will be taking command."

Now Dirk smiled at him warmly as a friend, not as a superior, and said with real warmth in his voice too, "Give em hell Tim. God speed!"

Then the two turned and left for the Shrike, and a return to the front they were setting up near Earth for operation Phoenix.

The Dragon Awakening

The G.W. Bush, along with thirty nine light and heavy cruisers, and twenty six scout/fighters, was floating some forty degrees above the estimated flight route direction of the oncoming Drel fleet. Twenty five heavily armed scout/fighter ships were lined up at thirty degrees to either side of that route, at twenty degrees below the estimated line of the flight path.

Each group of ships was stationed approximately five million miles from the point where they believed the Drel fleet would transition from hyperspace to normal space. The commander of the small ERMA fleet was using a tactic from the infantry manual on ambushes. He had modified it to his own needs, for space warfare, by creating a transversing field of fire from multiple directions and angles, or enfilading fire for space warfare. This fire was designed to rake the incoming fleet from front, sides, and bottom to back.

Admiral Berg, the ERMA fleet commander, estimated that by reversing course, and retreating eight light hours back, after firing his first and second salvos the incoming fleet's sensor detectors would pick up their retreat, and the trap would be well sprung. He believed that the Drel, seeing his much smaller fleets drive signatures in full retreat from them would embolden them to move forward in attack mode.

He expected his first salvo of depleted uranium ball bearing sized slugs to completely escape their sensors notice, and rake nearly three quarters of the oncoming fleet as it intersected his fire pattern. Compound that with the crisscrossing fire from both above and below their flight path, the damage and destruction should be quite extensive. The first salvo was really intended to do two things. Cause serious damage, and also cause it to begin evasive maneuvers!

The second salvo was intended to do the real damage though. That salvo would be comprised of hundreds of missiles, fired in spreading patterns to cover a much larger area. The big Tomahawk missiles, converted for space warfare, carried both mass and motion detectors to guide them to their targets. They also carried more fuel for their redesigned engines that drove them almost to half the speed of light at their targets. There were nearly two hundred fifty of these that would be fired at the oncoming fleet.

The smaller, modified for space, Sparrow and Aegis missiles, almost five hundred of them, were equipped with heat seeking guidance systems to guide them to their targets. Their purpose was to damage further, or destroy, ships already damaged by the first salvo.

The fleet coming at them was huge, nearly seven hundred ships. Admiral berg understood that if he destroyed and damaged only one quarter of that fleet, he would have done his job well. He also understood that if he got them so angry that they would chase him in a blind rage, he would have done his job completely.

That's why his third attack would be so dangerous! He had to turn his small fleet back and attack them as soon as his first salvo hit!

The Dragon Awake

The Drel fleet began dropping into normal space in clusters of ten and fifteen ships at a time. They were strung out in wide, loose, formations to avoid collisions, but once in normal space again they very quickly began to tighten their formation into a huge globular one. The first hundred ships formed themselves into the vast convex forward wall of that formation. The following ships expanding the globe and filling in the center.

To see this process taking place most beings might have thought that the coming of the fleet was never going to end, because the ships just kept coming! There was a certain beauty to the dance the ships performed as they both positioned themselves, and began to move forward as a single unit.

It was nearly forty standard hours later that the flow of ships dropping into normal space slowed to a trickle of stragglers, and the huge globe formation began to move forward with a purpose toward the next jump transit point in their march into this galaxy.

On a truly gigantic ship, that could only be described as a combination battle ship and aircraft carrier, or a battle carrier, which was flying in the third inner ring of the globe formation, the commander of this fleet was sitting astride a couch like console seat on the top tier of the command control portion of this ships bridge. He was overseeing the preparations of the bridge crew for the next jump sequence of his fleet.

His rank was Councilor Prime, and he was a member of that elite group of 'One Thousand' prime councilors who were the second tier of the ruling class of the Drel Empire. His name was Zega An Drel, and he was not, like so many others of his rank, a member of one of the old lines. He had clawed and scratched his way to his present rank, over the bodies of many of those pampered nitwits.

Zega was very uncomfortable in any portion of normal space that was not totally under Drel control, and this fact showed itself quite clearly in the manner in which he kept prompting his officers to verify the coordinates for the next jump point. He felt justified in this for, after all, had not most of his senior commanders read the message left in the communications buoy at the outermost reaches of this galaxy? And the warning it had contained!

Several factors from that message were making him very uneasy, chief among them the damage reports of the main expeditionary fleet that had preceded them. Those reports spoke of a heretofore unsuspected enemy of some capability, about which very little was known at this point.

Zega had no desire to meet this enemy unprepared, hence his use of the globe formation which put many layers of ships between the four battle carriers, and the outermost ring of ships protecting them. Those outer rings also protected the hundred frozen sleep transports that were carrying close to ten million of his race to their first conquered planet in this galaxy.

It was a small backward place, in a system far out on one of this galaxy's spiral arms. The indigenes quaintly called it Earth, or Dirt.

The fleet had just completed the first phase of it's speed buildup for their next jump, when his chief detection officer called out that they had found multiple drive signature telltales, moving away from the fleet along its' line of flight. There appeared to be nearly seven 'stani' (tens) of them, and they were building speed very quickly!

Councilor Zega was a seasoned war leader, and he quite correctly decided that seven stani of ships, seventy ships, was far to many for a group of scouts. "What distance?" He snapped.

"They are at approximately three and a half light hours sir, and building acceleration quickly! They will be out of our detector range very soon, at our present speed." That officer responded smartly.

Thinking quickly, Zega snapped, "Have the fleet increase speed to pre jump speed now! And have the outer sphere increase shield power to full!" he almost shouted, a terrible feeling of dread suddenly overcoming him. But it was already too late!

He knew this even as he spoke those last words, his eyes confirming his foreboding, and the tightening of his anal orifice, as he swung about to face the forward viewscreens! There, far ahead, near the outer ring of the sphere, a scene rebroadcast from a repeater drone was beginning to unfold that told of his, and the fleets' overconfidence in their superiority.

Zega, and his bridge crew, watched in horror as ships in the outer sphere began to explode in balls of brilliant actinic fire! Other ships were dying, in large clouds of vapor, as they and their crews explosively decompressed. Still other ships were beginning to tumble out of control, having been raked by weapons they could not see, crashing into still more ships as they tumbled erratically! Ships in the third innermost ring were beginning to maneuver frantically, trying to avoid colliding with the dead or dying ships from the two outer rings.

"Tell the third ring to go to full shields now!" Zega near screamed, jarring his bridge crew loose from their transfixion on the scene in the monitors. Even as he screamed those orders he was unable to move or to pull his eyes from the scene of carnage before them.

Before he could bring himself to act further, ships in the second sphere ring began to explode, and began the same erratic dance as those in the outer ring, as they tried to avoid both the unseen weapons destroying them and the now rolling and tumbling ships that were already dead!

With every erg of his considerable mental strength Zega broke the hold of that spellbinding scene of horror on his forward monitors. Physically shaking himself he roared out, "Attention to orders! Dog shut all hatched connecting compartments! Damage control crews stand by for action!" Issuing those orders acted as a catharsis that completely broke his transfixion.

Ships in the third innermost sphere ring began to explode or decompress, but with less frequency now. He could see, even as the last dregs of shock were being forced from his mind, that the damage had been terrible to his fleet. Just doing a quick visual estimate told him that they had lost nearly two hundred ships, destroyed or damaged!

He shook himself again as he felt the shock trying to reassert itself. He didn't have time for that! He had to do what was necessary to save the rest of his fleet. He began issuing orders again.

"Have what's left of the second ring move up to reinforce the outer ring, and make sure they raise shields to full. Also, put some scouts forward to keep an eye on that retreating fleet! They caught us off guard once! Let's not let them do it again." But, again, even as the remainder of the second ring ships began to move up to reinforce the outer ring his orders were scant seconds too late.

By some miracle that forward repeater drone had escaped undamaged and was still transmitting visual and data telemetry. His eyes had barely registered this fact when there was a shout from his detector operator. "Incoming missiles!"

"Of course! Oh, by the gods of my ancestors, of course! They forced us to blind ourselves!" Zegas' mind berated him as, before his horrified ocular members, hundreds and hundreds of bright spots appeared before and among the ships of the combined second and outer rings of his fleet formation, that was trying desperately to reform itself.

There were now so many of the bright spots, that indicated missile engines, that he couldn't begin to count them! And once again death and destruction was meted out to what was once thought to be an invincible fleet.

Sickened, Zega watched those missiles find targets, and destroy them as that swarm slammed into his injured fleet. Proving the iron will that had raised him above so many of his peers Zega shouted, above the pandemonium that was starting on his bridge, to have all ships execute the emergency dispersal plan!

It was a testament to those Drel commanders that they were able to execute that order, as ships blew up or spun out of control all about them. But they did it!

With the huge globe formation now dispersed the destruction and damage to his ships fell off precipitously. Zega strained mightily, with all that had befallen his fleet, forcing his commanders to reform into some form of a defensive formation.

And it was fortunate that they did so for on the heels of all the foregoing he heard an oath, again from his chief detector officer. "By the egg of my great ancestor!" Then that worthy shouted, "That fleet has changed direction and is now coming straight at us!"

Their unknown foe now came straight at his much decimated fleet. He could see flares as more missiles were launched, and the glare as powerful lasers reached out for them with tongues of actinic blue white light that would boil into nothingness anything they touched.

All of a sudden their massed formation broke apart into smaller groups that began to come at his fleet from several tangents at once. Through all of the ensuing turmoil, what amazed and stayed with Zega was the precision with witch those maneuvers were executed!

His efforts to get his decimated fleet into a defensive posture now paid off for Zega. The attack took only twenty additional ships, and cost the enemy nearly as many!

Now a rage such as he had never known took hold of Zega, and he ordered his much diminished fleet to attack their attackers, who were now running to make jump speed. He told his detection officer that if he lost that fleet it would mean his, and his whole lines', death!

Chasing the Dragon

Zega An Drel had never in his long life known such fury as he was experiencing now! This enemy, this tiny fleet of small ships, had destroyed, or damaged beyond repair without the services of a dry-dock facilities, three hundred and ten of his ships. That was nearly forty percent of his fleet! He was still trying to understand how this had happened.

One of those destroyed, the 'Golgolan', was one of his new super battle carriers the Drel, up to now, had thought to be impregnable! And the Issim, another battle carrier, had been hit by three of those damnable missiles, and had lost a third of his crew, and four of his six fighter launch decks! That left him with only three of his original five battle carriers fully effective!

The fury ate at him as his fleet stayed hard on the heels of the fleeing smaller enemy fleet. They had jumped into and out of hyperspace three times now, and his astrogator confirmed to him that they were heading in the same direction as his fleet's original destination.

His fleet had so far dodged two more missile attacks, and lost one more ship to those damnably accurate weapons. Thank the powers that were that the enemy was running, and seemed to be running short of those missiles, because there had only been those two hit and run attacks since this chase had begun.

"They are breaking out into normal space again, sir." The detection officer called across the bridge.

"All right, order the scouts and flankers out, and prepare for breakout to normal space." He ordered the captain of his flag ship, then "Shields at half power, man all gun batteries. And have one squadron standing by on the launch deck in case they decide to turn and fight!" Zega barked sharply. He listened closely as different officers relayed his orders, hoping fervently that this enemy would turn and fight.

The huge engines thrummed, sending vibrations throughout the titanic ship, as he prepared to drop out of hyperspace. There was that internal wrenching that felt like it was trying to turn you inside out, and they were once again in normal space.

Officers gave orders. Answers came. And more orders were issued, Finally the ships captain turned to him and said, "All secure, sir. They seem to be running at full speed towards their next jump point. We are increasing speed to three quarters and should pick up half a light day by jump point."

Meeting the Dragon

Zega had complimented the captain of his flagship, for they actually had picked up the estimated three quarters of a light day on the fleeing enemy ships. It had been only two 'pleci'(days) since his fleet had entered hyperspace again, when the detection sensors operator called out very smartly, "They're dropping into normal space again sir!"

'This is too soon' Zega thought to himself! Thinking furiously, as he began to issue orders, he said, "Bring us out right on top of them this time captain, and pass the word for all ships to stand to battle stations!" As these orders were being relayed he turned to other officers and issued more orders, which were relayed to those concerned immediately.

As his flag ship began its' preparations to reenter normal space he sat astride his command couch, again thinking furiously to make sure he had covered all that needed to be done. 'This time,' he thought to himself, 'his fleet would come out completely ready for battle!'

By the time his flagship dropped into normal space there was already a full scale battle developing, and he noted with satisfaction that his hunch had been right. The small fleet they had been chasing had now been joined by another somewhat larger one, bringing the total number ships his fleet faced up to about one hundred twenty or so. "Still, they are outnumbered and out gunned by three and a half to one. Why then," He pondered aloud, "do they stand and fight now? Here? I'm missing something?!"

Looking at the developing battle on his viewscreens he felt a small shudder go through him! He turned abruptly to his captain and said in a hoarse voice, "Bring up Yassek and Eskul, and have them join with us to form a massed fire front. This is another trap!"

That officer immediately relayed his orders, and within twenty minutes the three gargantuan ships had arrayed themselves abreast. They now presented a truly terrifying firepower potential to the enemy!

"Sir, the two fleets are breaking off and are running for jump point! Shall we pursue them?" The detection officer queried.

"Yes, but keep the forward shields at three quarters power, and have all three battle carriers prepare to salvo in unison when we exit hyperspace this time. Let's see how they like it this time!"

They jumped into hyperspace. This time it was only two hours later when he was notified that the enemy fleets were dropping out again. "Stay on top of them captain," Zega ordered, and, "And be ready to fire your salvos immediately!"

The leading elements of the Drel fleet dropped into normal space already formed into a huge bowl shape, the three battle carriers at the deepest part of that bowl. The sensor operator called out, "Sir, those two fleet are breaking away to either side."

Then there was a full three second pause, then there was the sound of the detection sensor operators breath hissing inward loudly! Then he blurted out "Oh, by the power of my ancestors egg! Sir! There is another fleet dropping into normal space dead ahead, and there is a battle carrier sized dreadnought leading them!"

Zega was trying to absorb this new factor when the operator screamed shrilly, "They're opening fire!!!"

"Fire in salvos! All ships fire!" Zega shouted above the sensor operators wail. The captain slammed his upper body manipulator down on the button that sent that pre arranged signal to the other ships, shouting to his own fire control people at the same time, "Fire. Fire. Fire!"

Now Zega felt the fury that he had been keeping in check with such effort for the last weeks break free of his control, as he shouted loudly to no one and everyone on the bridge, "Blast every last one of them out of space!!!"

The three colossal ships opened fire! The dark of space was turned nearly as bright as a sun springing to full life as missiles by the hundreds were launched at the new comers. Laser beams fully sixteen feet across reached out towards the new intruders, slicing neatly through the smaller of the new ships, then seeking new targets. Plasma pulse cannons sent salvo after salvo into the dreadnought coming at them.

It was not all one sided, for the new fleet had opened fire as soon as it had dropped into normal space, and seen the Drel fleet before it. Several of the escort ships around the three titans exploded as the missiles from that volley penetrated their shields.

But in the end the new fleet began to disintegrate before the vastly superior Drel fleet. The flag ship of that new fleet fought valiantly but could not stand up to that massed firepower. He died when one of the pulse cannon rounds penetrated his shields and exploded one of his main drive engines, tearing huge holes in him.

That ship died just as Zega screamed in horror, "Cease fire! Cease fire!" for he had had time now to see, and recognize, that dreadnoughts' profile. It was the brother battle carrier of his own carriers, sent with the expeditionary force to this galaxy! They had just destroyed nearly seventy of their own ships! And the other ships they had been chasing were gone, disappeared! All that was left were the very few ships of the Drel Expeditionary fleet that had not been destroyed.

Now there grew in Zega an anger so deep, so consuming, that it was like a physical blow that caused him to collapse onto his command couch. Through that anger drifted a saying so old that its' origins were lost in the mists of his races history. That saying was a warning to him, demanding caution of his future actions. It was saying to him, 'The being who chases the Dragon is very likely to meet him!'

Zega shuddered. He had now he realized, ruefully and shamefully, that he been chasing the dragon. And he had met him!

CHAPTER THIRTY-SEVEN
Operation Phoenix

The Phoenix Stirring

The Drel Expeditionary Fleet that had limped into orbit, around the small blue-green planet the locals called Earth, had remained unmolested and unchallenged for the two and a half local years since doing so, and the revival and transportation of Drel cadre from the sleeper ships had gone very well for the last year and a half.

The most excitement experienced by anyone in the fleet had been the very real argument between the planetary administrator and the commander of the expeditionary fleet.

That argument had concerned whether the revival process priorities of the planets new administration personnel or the bulk of the military cadre should be processed first. The military commander lost this argument for two reasons. First, the planetary administrator had made a very good argument for his case.

And second, he just happened to be the fifth egg offspring of the new over councilor for this sector!

The administrators argument had been that without fully staffed transfer centers that were set up to operate properly it wouldn't make the slightest difference whatsoever how many soldiers were awakened, because there would not be enough steeds to transfer them into. It was an argument that the commander could find little leverage against.

And, though it left too many of his ships undermanned, the commander capitulated. After some weeks the commander had had to admit that things were going smoothly for a change, and other than some pockets of rather stubborn resistance there had been no new threats to the Drel fleet. But, just the fact of this resistance existing worried the fleet commander for, as limited as it was, it was fierce. It bothered the commander so much that the planetary administrator finally agreed to revive a battalion of combat ready troops, and process them on the next rotation of the planets' moon.

The only other thing that seriously perturbed the commander, over the next eighteen lunar rotations, was that his sensor operators were constantly making reports of ghost sightings on their detection instrument screens.

The chief sensor operations officer, a very capable being, had become so frustrated with his tech's, and his own, inability to resolve these sightings that he was tearing apart those units on each ship, and rebuilding them from scratch.

It had now been nearly a full lunar rotation since the last report of a ghost sighting, and his sensors officer was no longer moving from station to station mumbling dire imprecations to his equipment.

The commander was, as was his custom, sitting astride his command couch standing first watch with his bridge crew when that very officer called up from the sensor ranging pit. "Sir!" This was unusual because he did not use the command intercom!

"More of your ghost sightings?" The commander called back in the same manner, his tone laced with suppressed amusement.

"Yes sir, but we're getting multiple readings now! And they are not like the other ones that came from the close in areas of this planet. These are coming from an out-system direction!"

The commander sat upright and, all amusement gone from his voice now, snapped, "Get me a better direction on them, and tell signals to send to the fleet, 'Stand by for battle stations'! This is not a drill!"

Within bare minutes every ship in the fleet was tensed to have every able bodied crew member man his battle stations. And those ships engines, which were never shut down completely, except for dry-dock repairs, were brought up to ready standby status. All officers made haste to be at their ready or standby stations.

This was not due so much to training, which all of the crews complained there was too much of, as it was to the devastation their previous laxity had visited upon them when they had encountered an enemy force in this galaxy. False alarm or not they would be ready for such an encounter this time!

"Sir! I'm beginning to get hard drive signature readings now! We have one 'stani' (ten) of signatures, and there are more coming up every few seconds!" the sensors officer called, his voice cracking a little now with nervousness.

"Sound 'Battle Stations', all ships! And bring our forward shields up to half power!"

The commander forced calm into his voice to reassure his bridge crew, and to mask the excitement of pending battle that was trying to creep into it as he continued to give orders, "Pilot, bring us up and out of orbit to face the threat. Signals have the heavy cruisers Ziks and Simsa, along with five scouts, stand to and take up a screening position ahead of us! Code Glek!"

These orders were rattled off calmly, the commander pausing only seconds to assure himself that each officer had heard him correctly. He turned to look over into the sensors pit and said to that officer even more calmly, to make sure that that worthy was settled down, "keep me apprised of your count Sensors."

The calmness of the commanders voice seemed to have helped, as that worthy replied in a steadier voice, "We now count eighteen separate drive signatures sir, and more are breaking out of hyperspace further out." Then he paused just slightly before saying, "Sir, if you raise the shield power much more I'll lose track of them!"

"As a last resort Sensors. Keep me informed." Then the commander turned and said, "Signals, have the other three battle cruisers move up and take up support positions around us. Also, have two wings of fighters launch for close in support." He then turned full forward to check his forward and lateral external monitors.

Since the huge battlecarrier had now swung himself up and out of close orbit around the planet, he was facing the impending threat head on. As the commander surveyed the scene before him he asked, "Are you still counting, Sensors?" To which that officer responded promptly, "Thirty four hard signatures and still counting sir!"

This is getting very serious the commander thought to himself, as he said, "Pilot. Tell the rest of the fleet that we are moving above the systems solar rotational plane to be on an even footing with our visitors."

Turning his head towards the communications officer he asked dourly, "Do we have anything to indicate that they are not hostiles, Signals?"

At the negative reply he turned his eyes back to his forward monitors, as he said crisply, "I want two more fighter wings ready to go on the forward launch bays, and two more on ready standby!"

"Weapons!" He snapped. And at that officers prompt reply he said grimly, "You are now weapons free!"

As the Drel fleet lifted itself above the solar rotational plane the commander was now well into the rhythm of combat management as he shifted his attention from station to station, getting information from one source and issuing orders to others, and feeling the ships crew meshing into that rhythm with him. He called out, "Sensors. Are we still counting?"

Sensors replied that he had a count of thirty-eight hard signatures, but no new ones in the last five lal (minutes).

"I told you to keep me apprised, Sensors!" he snapped, then "Stay on your ambulatory digits!" More calmly he said, "Just keep it timely, Sensors."

The commander sat astride his command couch for a long moment thinking, then, expressing his one real concern, asked, "Do you read any heavy signatures in that group sensors?" At the negative reply from the sensors officer he heaved a mental sigh of relief.

As he watched his monitors for any change in posture from the intruders he was thinking half aloud, "Well, we outnumber them by about two dozen ships, and outgun them to boot or they would have already made some move on us.

Still, thirty-eight ships was nothing to take lightly. Especially if they were, as he surmised from their daring entry into this space, the same species that had attacked his fleet on its' way into this galaxy."

"No," he continued to mutter to himself, "it was much more prudent to take no chances at all, where those beings were concerned! They were aggressive, daring, and tricky! That was a combination that was very, very, dangerous, and he would not be caught out a second time!"

Making up his mind he called out, "Pilot. Make towards the intruders fleet at one tenth speed." And, "Signals. Tell the other captains to keep the formation tight!" Then, "Power management. Make sure you hold our forward defensive shields at one half power, but be ready to go to full power instantly!"

The huge ship shuddered as his main thrust engines spooled up higher, propelling him ponderously forward, increasing his speed from his normal in system one thirty second potential to a clear space slow cruising speed of one eighth potential.

The monster ship bristled with the barrels of laser rifles and plasma pulse projector cannons, and the flattened oblong box turrets with big round openings that were his missile launchers.

His fighters had launched, and his bay doors were wide open, ready to launch ten times more than the number already flying close support. Those deadly little close in fighters could cause ships a hundred times their size serious damage.

The Drel battlecarrier, combined with the three heavy battle cruisers and escorts, made a truly intimidating sight!

Even with all of that impressive firepower at his command, the fleets' commander was not a fool. He knew that this enemy had a vicious sting, one that he had experienced at first hand, so caution was the watchword now!

As his fleet moved slowly out past the planets satellite moon the commander surveyed his fleet and his preparations, and was wondering what else he could do, when his sensors officer called out, "The other fleet is moving further out into open space, and appears to be matching our speed."

The commander thought again about all he had done. Then he thought about what the intruders actions might mean.

He really saw only two possibilities for them. They were tempting him to follow them into a trap they had set, or they want a fight, and are moving further out for more maneuvering room. He was inclined to believe the first possibility.

The two fleets moved further and further out of the system, neither one making an overt offensive move, other than their current flight paths, for the time being.

His sensors officer called out suddenly, breaking the commanders searching introspection, "Sir. I think they are starting to spread out their formation, but they are not increasing their speed, they're slowing down!"

"Thank you sensors." Then, "Pilot. Match their speed. Signals. All ships hold our formation."

The commander thought to himself, "Could I be wrong? Do they really want to take us on? That's what it's beginning to look like, but am I missing something?"

The commander wasn't wrong at all!

And he only made one mistake!

His mistake was in not looking in his rear view mirror!

Subterfuge

The seventy five ships of the Drel Expeditionary Fleet moved steadily, ponderously, forward. The commander of that fleet doing everything he could think of to keep from falling into the trap, he now firmly believed, they were trying to lead him into. He had his fleet advance inexorably on the other fleet, making for open space where there was only openness, and nowhere to hide an ambush.

Now, the only thing he could think of that they might try to do was engage him and keep him busy while others of their fleet dropped out of hyperspace around him, and try to overwhelm his forces.

But in open space he had the distinct advantage, didn't he? He was a good tactician, and had been very careful in his preparations. Or so he thought! His only mistake was that he completely forgot to look over his shoulder!

"Sir," his chief sensors operator called, "they're slowing their retreat and beginning to spread their formation out!"

"So, they are going to fight us after all! Good." After a short but thoughtful pause the commander ordered, "Have five of the medium, and five of the light cruisers, from the main body maintain this position. The rest of the fleet is to move forward with us, matching their present speed." He ordered the captain of his flag ship. He turned back and asked, "Anything new sensors?"

"Sir, they're still retreating, maintaining course and speed."

"Good enough. Lets see what they're made of, shall we?" The Drel fleet was now about eight hundred thousand miles out past, and above, the planet's rotational orbit, and moving into relatively open space. The Drel commander had fallen into the very trap he had been trying so hard to see and avoid.

The Drel fleet was well out and away from the moon now, and it was also swinging away from the moon's orbital path, so they didn't see the fifteen ships that rose silently from the deepest craters and fissures on its' surface. Didn't see them swing out of sight again to the side of the moon away from their direction of flight.

Five of those ships held themselves close to the moons surface, staying out of sight behind it. The other ten pushed themselves approximately a hundred seventy thousand miles out and away from the moon, but still hidden by its' body. Then they flipped themselves over one hundred eighty degrees to reverse their direction of flight, their engines flaring brightly as they applied full power and drove back towards it.

They had calculated their flight path so that they could use the moons gravity, weak as it was, as a slingshot to propel them at the rear of the Drel fleet at a third again their best normal speed. They were in a tight globular formation as they shot around the moon, using that airless mass to gain every erg of energy they could to drive them at the rear of the Drel fleet.

As they catapulted away from the moon, towards the rear of the Drel fleet, their formation changed. It flattening itself out into a flat disc. As soon as the formation change was complete they began to fire at the rear of the Drel fleet with their rail guns. Those had been loaded with canisters, each containing thousands and thousands of three quarter inch depleted uranium ball bearings. Those canisters had been designed to disintegrate by the use of time delay explosive devices after leaving the rail gun track. Those explosive devices were designed to be directional, adding more forward impetus that spread those tiny killing slugs out even more as they sped towards their targets.

These ships were about a hundred thousand miles behind the ten ships the Drel commander had left behind as a reserve when they fired their deadly swarm. Those ten ships had no warning whatsoever, because they were all watching what was about to happen in front of them, as that hailstorm of death ripped through them.

Eight of those ships disintegrated in bright flaring balls of light, the energy released from their engines eating all matter as they were riddled with those super heavy plugs of speeding metal death. The other two spun off, their crews all dead from explosive decompression. The ten ships sped on towards the rear of the unsuspecting main Drel fleet.

Five minutes later, and only two hundred fifteen thousand miles ahead now, the Drel fleet was just beginning to become aware that something was wrong, as the ten ships fired two more salvos of their deadly canisters from their rail guns.

And, as good as he was, the Drel commander, now aware of his peril, couldn't warn all of his ships to go to full shield power fast enough to save some of them.

He lost five more ships, one of them one of his heavy battle cruisers, and three more badly damaged, to that sleeting hail of death. The fact that their shields were already at half power, and took less than fifteen seconds to run them up to full power, is what saved the rest of them.

At the same time that the Drel fleet was reacting to the attack from their rear, the fleet in front of them let loose with a volley of missiles that did some more damage, but very little in comparison to the attack that had come from their rear. The Drel commander deduced correctly, some time later when they were in hot pursuit of the other fleet, that that salvo had been a diversionary tactic designed to give them a chance to run.

And run they did! But his sensors officer had, in a daring move ordered the shields dropped to three quarters power, and had a fix on them before they could all slip away into hyperspace. Direction and speed had been noted, and the chase began.

He had been wounded, and wounded badly again, but this time he would exact a heavy penalty for that wounding!

By his great ancestors egg, he would!

The Trap

As the resistance fleet turned and ran from Earth, the Drel fleet hard on its' heels, two things happened near simultaneously. Three of the resistance ships slowed their entry into hyperspace just enough to make sure the Drel sensors operators would get a good fix on speed and direction, and that fleets flagship increased its' speed to its' maximum.

The resistance fleet flagship would make one very long jump to a predetermined point and, once there, await a resistance ship coming from the opposite direction. The balance of the fleet would make short jumps in and out of hyperspace, ostensibly trying to shake off the following Drel expeditionary fleet. The direction and duration of those jumps were also predetermined, to bring them to a meeting point with the flagship again.

On the bridge of that flagship, having dropped out of hyperspace some five hours earlier at the appointed place, its' sensors operator and Elonee communicator both reacted at the same time to the awaited arrival. The sensors operator sang out that a ship had just dropped into normal space about three light hours distant. The Elonee communicator Dimon, 'Big Ears' as he had been affectionately dubbed by the crew because of his very small ears and his very big ability at farspeaking, sent his message telepathically to the incoming ships commander, *Admiral Berg has arrived Admiral Chabov. He will meet with you within four hours time, if that is acceptable?*

Thank you very much, Dimon. Admiral Dimetri Chabov sent back, his telepathic sending much improved after his long practice sessions with Dimon. Then he sent *Please relay to Granthis,* Admiral Bergs Elonee communicator, *that that will be fine.*

Three and a half hours later the two ships were floating in space side by side, a long, flexible, transfer tube attaching the two ships. Since the G.W. Bush, Bergs' flagship, was nearly five times bigger than Chabovs' Gargarin, the meeting was held aboard the Bush. It was the first time he had even seen the Bush, and he swelled with pride at what his fellow Earthmen had been able to accomplish in so short a time. The two men greeted each other warmly, then headed for the main conference room behind the bridge.

After the normal pleasantries the two men got down to work quickly. "I've lost eight ships that I know of, probably more." Tim Berg said sadly to Chabov. Then with a feral grin he said "But we hurt them, and hurt them badly! I think we destroyed, or badly damaged, near half their fleet!" He paused, thinking for a moment before saying, "Dirk was right you know. They just don't seem to understand the rail guns. I think they're too simple for them to grasp their real potential. But they certainly understand their lethality!" He finished wolfishly.

He held up his hand as he took a breath, letting Chabov know there was a little more. Tim Berg then said, "The missile barrage did its' work too. You tell G. whiz that his idea of piggy backing the heat seekers on the Tomahawks worked great. But the only thing we have left for our rail guns now are the solid sabots. We have to be in pretty close for them to work because they can see them coming because of their mass. But tell me, how did your end go?" he finally finished.

"First, that's really good news Tim! That fleet commander must be madder than a nest of stick poked hornets now! Chabov congratulated him. Then he went on to describe the results of his own action, saying, "That commander at Earth was pretty good! I didn't think he was going to take the bait for a while there, but we finally got him far enough outside the system to make our move. As soon as we were far enough out we slowed down and made like we wanted to fight."

Chabov paused, his eyebrow rising significantly, then went on, "He didn't charge right at us, just kept coming at us steady, being real cautious. But we knew we had him when he dropped off ten ships for a ready reserve, and brought his big battle cruisers up around that monster battlecarrier of his. Damn, but that thing is big!"

Now Chabov paused for a breath before continuing. "Anyway, as soon as we saw this move, our Elonee sent the word to our ships hidden on the moon. We took out fifteen of his ships with that tactic, including one of those heavy battle cruisers. In the end we took out two of our own ships as we jumped out. They got hit by our own salvos fired by the ships from the moon. They were damaged too much to keep jumping so I told them to slip away after the second jump, but I don't think they'll make it. They were pretty chewed up!" Dimetri Chabov finished somberly. Neither man spent much time mourning their losses openly. They were the kind of men that did that kind of thing privately.

The two men then got down to trading the strategic information that fluxed as combat was met. When that was exhausted Chabov asked, "Do you think that you will be where you estimated, and on the same timeline?"

"I believe so." Tim Berg said hesitantly, then said more firmly, "We're pushing the envelope on speed, but yes, we'll be where I said we'd be at the appointed time Dimetri!"

"Good! Then we are two jumps and nine days apart. Just before we make our last jump we're going to turn and scrap with that feisty commander, and make him so mad he'll come out of his last hyperspace jump shooting!" Dimetri Chabov said, wearing a feral grin of his own this time. "One of our fastest ships will then do an in and out jump, then scoot back to Earth to give the go." He finished.

Tim Berg turned to one of the cabinets along the wall and pulled open a door. He removed two glasses from a rack and a bottle from its' swing cradle, bringing both back to the table where he filled both glasses. He handed one glass to his friend, and touching the rim of his own glass to it said "To the Phoenix!" He raised the glass to his mouth and downed it in one swallow.

"To the Phoenix!" Responded Dimetri Chabov, and threw back his own drink.

The two men solemnly shook hands. Then each went back to war!

The Trap Sprung

The Drel Expeditionary Fleet dropped out of hyperspace almost all together. They had gotten much better at pre jump staging so that their formations stayed together in formation when they emerged from hyperspace, especially since this long chase had begun.

This time, when they dropped out of hyperspace, the sensors operator called out almost immediately "Sir, the enemy fleet isn't running." Then in an alarmed voice "Missiles! I have multiple missiles inbound, sir!"

"Sneaky bastards!" the commander muttered to himself angrily. Then he growled "Shields up full! Fire a return salvo weapons." Then he said to no one in particular "Their shields are not as strong as ours so we'll see who gets hurt this time!" he finished, his oral orifice splitting vertically in, what for him was, a wolfish grin.

Only one or two of the enemies missiles got through during that exchange, to explode almost harmlessly against the powerful Drel shields. The one that exploded near the front of the battlecarrier's prow only rattled some loose equipment on the bridge. At that the commander commented, "Those missiles are small, but powerful. I'd like to know how they're made." Then, after the first exchange, "Shields to half power. Give us a look sensors."

As soon as the shields had lowered enough the sensors officer said with satisfaction "They're running again sir. But I've got course and speed!"

"Enough of this nonsense!" the commander grated. "Increase speed to three quarters, and make sure you catch them when they drop back to normal space! He glared around the bridge, then, "Navigation, sensors," he said hoarsely, "if you want to keep your exalted positions you'd better bring us out right on top of them because, we're coming out shooting this time. We'll see how they like their own medicine!"

Two rotational periods (days)and five hours later the sensors operator, his ocular protrusions itching in irritation from staring at his instrument scopes for almost four hours straight without a break, was startled when he saw the distinctive halos begin to form around the sparks on his scopes that were drive signature indicators. This indicated that those ships were dropping back into normal space.

After checking twice to be sure, he called out loudly, startling the rest of the tired bridge crew, "Sir! The enemy is dropping back to normal; space again, and we're right behind them. Only thirty light lal (light minutes) at most!" he finished triumphantly.

The commander, who had been dozing lightly in his command couch, snapped to alertness. Then, with a snarl, he snapped, "Sound battle stations for all ships! All ships are to follow these directives! All missile batteries are to fire three salvos on our exit. Then I want full braking retro's, and all shields to go to full power."

He paused for a few seconds to make sure his orders were being relayed properly, then began issuing more orders, "Signals, make sure the rest of the fleet acknowledges confirmation of those orders! And have two fighter wings launch, ready to clean up any damaged ships. We're going to wipe that fleet out this time!" he snarled angrily.

The commander was leaning forward in his command couch as his huge ship made the transition from hyper to normal space. As soon as he felt the familiar wrench of that transition, and the black of normal space fill his forward monitors he yelled, as all of his pent up anger took complete control of him, "Fire! Fire all missile batteries! Plasma pulse cannon and laser rifle batteries, stand by."

As the first rush of his released pent up anger ebbed slightly, he glued his ocular protrusions to the scene unfolding on his forward monitors so he could thoroughly enjoy the spectacle of his surprise for his enemy.

His anticipation was so intense, so deep, so desirous of seeing the destruction of his tormentors, that it took a few seconds for his brain to translate the picture in his monitor.

The picture became clear, and he gasped for air as he saw the huge fleet of ships coming at him, five of them battlecarriers as big as his own!

And they, and the hundreds of ships around them in that fleet were firing every weapon they had right at his fleet! Too late he realized that this was the real trap he had feared from the very beginning of this debacle! The action back at the solar system had been the bait!

And far, far too late was it that he realized the nature of the trap he had been led into. That he had been enticed, from the first salvos fired at him back near that miserable little planet, to come out at this point in space firing on his own kind. For those huge battlecarriers were the brother ships to his own.

And also, it was far, far, too late for him to have more than mere minutes to admire the fiendish cunning of this enemy.

The only thing that he did have time for was to realize that he and his fleet were dead!

Phoenix Watch

The small black scout ship dropped into normal space a hundred fifty thousand miles out beyond the orbit of Pluto. She aligned herself with her attitude thrusters, then her powerful engines flared brightly as she drove in-system towards Jupiter's moons. Ten hours later she flipped herself over one hundred eighty degrees and her engines flared brightly again as she braked hard to slow her in-system rush.

Charley Jenkins was sitting at his small desk, which was actually a rock shelf cut into the wall of this dead end tunnel he used as his combination office and quarters. The tunnel was part of the complex of caves that had been discovered on the moon Calysto, and had adapted them for the use of the ERMA forces using them as a base.

He was leaning back precariously, on the three legged plastic stool that passed for a chair, with his feet propped on the edge of the shelf. His hands were locked behind his head with the fingers interlaced, and he was thoroughly enjoying the fact that for the last six hours he had not had to do anything but routine housekeeping on the base here.

Ten days ago he had sent everyone but the four man crew of the small scout ship hidden under a big rock overhang on the surface, and the three men he had kept to finish shutting down the base, when the word came back from Wolfsbane on the last supply ship. The only other being on the base was the Elonee communicator, and his friend, Jax.

Jax was sprawled in his usual place on the foot of his bunk, his big head resting on his paws, which were crossed in front of him. His huge emerald green eyes were half lidded, as he also enjoyed having little to do, for normally his powerful mind would be busy questing in the ether, seeking messages for this base, or those to be passed on by him to others on or near the Earth.

Charley Jenkins was marveling at the last four years of his life, and especially the last three of them. Four years ago the call had discretely come down to his unit for volunteers, and had come in a manner that had let anyone thinking of volunteering know that this one would be extremely dangerous. And so secret that he couldn't discuss even the possibility of volunteering for it with others he knew for certain were also considering doing so.

The only thing that those making the offer would say about it was that he would get to do something totally new. At the time the call had come he was a master sergeant in the special forces, with ten years in the service and four years combat experience under his belt.

As he sat there thinking about that period in his life, he unconsciously shook his head. Four years ago he had been Master Sergeant Charles K. Jenkins, a tactics and weapons implementation specialist in the U.S. Army.

Three years ago he had been breveted to the rank of Major, after completing the special combat techniques course that everyone who had been accepted in the new units being formed, had had to attend as part of their new duties. That sudden rise in rank had come from a most unexpected direction too.

It had come from the recommendation of a female Russian Spetsnaz colonel who had been in charge of the course. He had very quickly learned to respect both her, and her judgement in matters military related. He had learned early on that criticism could be a positive learning tool that would help him rise through the ranks if it were accepted as such, and he had.

In Colonel Valasovic he had recognized a born leader, and he had tried hard, possibly a little harder than he might normally have, to earn her respect. Apparently he had done so, for upon completing that course he had been breveted to the rank of Major, and a month later his new rank had been made permanent. Now, and for the last two years, he was Major C.K. Jenkins, ERMA Space Marines of Earth.

He had always been a man dedicated to the service of his country. Now he was a man passionately dedicated to the survival of his home planet, his species, and their allies.

Charley Jenkins was a man who did not make friends easily, but those he let get close enough to become friends were friends for life. What he had never, even in his wildest dreams, expected was that the one who would become his closest friend would be a being from some place far away in the universe.

There had been many changes and surprises in his life over the last four years, but the most important and rewarding was his bond of friendship with the Elonee, Jax.

He had, like all of the other officers and non commissioned officers, been tested for any telepathic ability, and had been told that his was marginal at best. Other than complete surprise that he even had any portion of such an ability, he did not let his lack of it deter him from performing his duties on a higher than average level. Then Jax had come into his life, and everything had changed!

What was different, and telling, about Jax was that unlike most of the other Elonee who paired with officers and non-coms., he was considered to be an elder, as opposed to most of the other Elonee he had met being called 'younglings' or adults, among his people. And the first thought words he had heard inside of his head when he had first met him! Jax had said, as if he had known that they would become closer than brothers, *I have chosen you to partner with! Therefore, if we are to work well together, we must develop a bond of trust between us! I will work hard to earn yours. Will you do as much? Will you bond friendship to me?*

Charley Jenkins did not understand at that time what made him say yes, but what he understood instinctively was that this was to be one of the most important choices he would ever make! He and Jax had been virtually inseparable since that moment three years ago, and neither one of them had ever looked back.

Jenkins dropped his feet to the stone floor and sat forward, turning his head to look at his friend, unnecessarily, and asked for what must have been the umpteenth thousandth time in the last few days, *Any word yet Jax?*

Jax just raised one eyelid, his bright emerald green eye giving him the same answer he had last spoken several hundred repetitions of the same question ago. *As I will be the first, you will be the second to know when the word comes!*

The eyelid dropped back to that half asleep look it normally showed, and Jenkins felt the chuckle floating in his friends mind that told him Jax was not irritated by this show of impatience on his part.

Two hours later Jax abruptly lifted his head from his forepaws, his eyes gleaming. He sat with his head canted at what could only be described as listening position. Then he sent to Jenkins, *a ship has just entered normal space near Pluto's outer orbit, and is heading insystem at speed.*

Jenkins spun around on his stool to face Jax, his face tight with the expectation of anticipated action, and Jax continued to send to him *The Elonee aboard, Barca, is sending this message! It is time for the Phoenix to rise!*

His anticipation of action rewarded, Jenkins asked Jax, *Will you need to link with Barca to push the message all the way to Earth?* knowing how tiring waiting could be.

Jax actually snorted with contempt as he sent to Jenkins *I do not need that weak youngling to reach them! I will send the message on, be assured!*

Jenkins had not realized that he had stood up in his excitement. He sat back down at the desk and reached out to flip the intercom switch on, but did not press the talk key as Jax continued, *the ship will brake near the moon so that we can join them for the trip insystem. They are about ten hours out from us, but are coming in fast.*

Then, typical of Jax, he laid his head back down on his forepaws, eyes half lidded again.

Jenkins now depressed the talk key and notified his men to get their gear together, and to start the final close down procedures for the base. He then called the scouts crew and told them to get the ship ready to lift.

'This was it' he thought to himself. This was the culmination of all the hard work he, and Jax, and the sixty odd men who had spent the last eighteen months on this moon, had worked so hard to make happen!

The Phoenix was about to rise!

Phoenix Rising

The pilot, and his gunner/co-pilot, had been sitting in the seats of their modified planetary shuttle craft for the last four hours of their eight hour shift, just like the other six hundred or so pilot standby crews all over the world. And, like most of the others, this pair was bored. The smart ones slept as much as possible, or read to relax themselves. Others ran checks on their instruments for the hundredth time. Still others moved about their craft inspecting details they knew so well they could now draw them in their sleep. After all, ready standby meant you were able to lift ship in sixty seconds or less!

There were a little more than twelve hundred crews alternating on eight hours on, eight hours off, shifts. Those crews not sitting in their cockpits were confined to a bunk, a chair, or a couch in the ready room only steps from their ships.

They had been doing this for eight straight days now, and they grumbled and groused continuously. But none of that grumbling or grousing was in the least bit serious, for they knew that when the word came they would strike a mighty blow at their enemy. And in striking that blow they knew that no matter what else happened on Earth after that, there would be representatives of mankind out there to carry the fight for Earth on. That was the reason that most of these men and women had volunteered for this very dangerous mission!

The pilot was just in the act of shifting around in his seat, trying to find a more comfortable position in the cramped pilots chair, when the radio let out a loud squawk on the ready band, sending both crewmen upright in their seats! Both crewmen sat breathless, listening to the open carrier hum that came from the radio, knowing that some kind of orders were coming very soon.

Then the speaker coughed raucously once more, and the message came! The person getting ready to speak cleared his throat once before announcing, "'Operation Phoenix' is a go! I repeat, Operation Phoenix is a go!' We received this message one hour ago and received verification of it three minutes ago. The original message we received was 'The Phoenix must Rise', which was the code phrase for a go on our mission."

There was a five second pause before the speaker continued by saying the words all had been waiting to hear. "Attention all flight crews! Lift of will commence in two hours from my mark. Mark, Mark, Mark! Good luck boys and girls, and God speed!" And that was that! The waiting was over. But the real waiting was just beginning now, for the next two hours would be the longest any of these dedicated people would ever spend.

Now all of the pre-flight checking began again in real earnest this time, as the pilots and co-pilots went over every instrument minutely to assure themselves they were operating properly.

And the standby crews, because they now knew they would not be the active flight crews, came out of their ready rooms to begin checking the control linkages between the lifting craft and the transport modules, going over them twice to make sure that all was in order before entering their craft and strapping themselves into the bunks located in the tiny cabins behind the flight control decks. They were now the relief crews.

The medical technicians continued to process as many men, women, and children as they possibly could for another hour after the notice came, then hurriedly packed their equipment and stowed it safely aboard the transport modules in secure compartments.

They then sealed themselves into specially constructed sections of their transport modules, that were designed to maintain full life support during the trip. They would have to check those in slow sleep during their time in hyperspace, even though their life support requirements were minimal.

It was now thirty minutes before the Phoenix was to rise, and the five ships that had remained behind began to stir from their hidden positions on the surface of the moon away from earth. They rose from the moons' surface and moved silently around that body towards the Earth. As hey picked up speed they spaced themselves out, and twenty minutes later they had taken up orbits around the Earth that let them see, both visually and by instruments, the entire surface of the planet.

They would be joined in minutes by the two ships now streaking in from the base on Calysto, and the three ships that had been hidden on the surface of the Earth. Their job was to suppress any attempts by the Drel ships, or their atmospheric flyers still on the planet, from interfering with the rising of the Phoenix from the Earth. Too many good men and women had died to make 'Operation Phoenix' possible, and those aboard these ships would not fail them, or their sacrifice. The Phoenix would rise!

Twenty five, twenty four, twenty three! Pilots and co-pilots began taking deep breaths to aid in relaxing their bodies as they leaned back in their flight control couches all over the planet as the powerful engines under them flared to life, blowing away the light camouflage that had hidden them and the human packed cargo modules they would lift into space.

Nineteen, eighteen, seventeen! Three ships lifted with a roar from the surface of the Earth, streaking to join their comrades in orbit around the planet. All of them were nearly invisible to the Drel because of their stealth coatings. All of them were heavily armed as well.

Two were light cruisers, one an oversized scout ship. They rose from the United States, Russia, and Australia. They rose swiftly, and before there was any reaction from the Drel ships still on the planet they had taken up their assigned stations with the other ships already there.

Twelve, eleven, ten! The two ships coming in from the Calysto base arrived and took up their positions. All of these ships had every square inch of their exterior surfaces coated with the stealthing material that made them nearly invisible to the Drel. And each of them had an Elonee communicator aboard to make sure their communications could not be jammed or overheard, because this was the second most important part of 'Operation Phoenix.

The first had been luring the expeditionary fleet away from orbit about the Earth! If any of the Drel ships that had landed on the Earth, or any of the atmospheric flyers that were capable of stratospheric flight and stationed on the planet, got aloft and above the rising cargo lifters and their payloads the 'Phoenix' would fall back to its' surface in flames and death. This would not happen! Four, three, two.

One! Those hundreds of idling powerful lift engines, that powered both the oversized anti gravity lifters and the ships, were quickly spooled up to full lift capacity as they waited for that one word.

At the same time, all over the planet, troops of different armies still in cohesive units, and groups of underground resistance fighters, began attacking Drel strong points.

They did this, even though they knew before hand that they could not do much real damage to the already well entrenched Drel positions, to create a diversion that might give those lifting ships that one bit of extra help to get away. They knew they couldn't hurt the Drel much in this way, but they did it anyway!

Humans were strange that way! They would fight even in the face of certain defeat. But they would fight even harder if they believed that the sacrifice they were making would make the slightest iota of real difference!

Suddenly the word came. Go! Go! Go! And all over the globe hundreds of small but very powerful interplanetary shuttles began to rise up into the Earth's atmosphere, towing their cargo's of specially constructed and linked modules.

Each of those modules had small, but powerful, anti gravity booster engine built into it along with its regular lift engine, and as soon as the shuttles pulling them reached sixty thousand feet, and began to strain for more altitude with their loads, Sergeant Galenkos' genius went to work.

The booster engines and directional controls of the modules slaved to those of the lifting shuttles roared to life, both engines and antigravity lifters adding their power to that of the shuttles, lifting all up and into space.

Those hundreds of shuttles with their loads of sleeping humanity, that could mean the virtual survival of humanity, rose higher and higher into the atmosphere until they finally broke free of the Earth's gravity and entered space.

To those on the ships in orbit around the planet it almost seemed that the planet were sprouting a head of hair as the shuttles, and then their modules engines, left vapor trails as they rose through the atmosphere from the surface.

Two of the Drel light cruisers, and several of the atmospheric flyers, did get aloft, but they were blown apart before they could get into the upper atmosphere above the rising shuttles.

The Drel units on the ground could not react in time, because they were too busy fighting an enemy they had thought, in their arrogance, had ceased to exist!

Five of the shuttles were lost to ground fire, but the rest made it into outer space where they were rounded up and escorted to a rendezvous point, their precious cargo's in tow.

Soon many more ships began to flash into existence around them, which they were then linked to. Engines again flared brightly, and they all disappeared into hyperspace.

The Phoenix had risen!

Epilogue

The Drel Fleet

The Drel fleet commander of the follow-on occupation and expansion forces was to tired, for even his raging anger at an enemy he didn't even know, to do more than stop where he was and lick his wounds, even if for no longer than a couple of Drel normal turns. He had to assess his losses and the damage to what was left of his once magnificent fleet.

He and his fleet had been mauled, and mauled terribly, by an enemy he had not known. One that he had virtually never seen close enough to identify if he ran into them again. The only thing he knew for certain was that they were smart, tricky, and extremely dangerous. And he had never seen a fleet of ships move together with such precision, especially under combat conditions!

One thing he was totally sure of was that this kind of debacle would never happen to him again, not in the way it had! His anger was no longer the hot boiling thing it had been. It was now a slow seething thing that ate away slowly at his psyche, marking it with scars that would never leave him in peace.

His anger was also a teacher, for it had forcibly made him remember the hard lessons he had learned on his way up to his present rank. It made him remember that underestimating an enemy because of his apparent size or strength was a tool that could, and most likely would as it just had, be used against him. Forgetting that early lesson had cost him nearly half of his once proud fleet and set the Drel expansion into this galaxy back months, if not years!

He would also remember just how devious this enemy was, for it had cost him the entire Drel Expeditionary fleet, including its' commander who was one of the very few beings Zega had ever dared to call friend. The dagger of recrimination went even deeper because Zega had been the one to appoint his friend as commander of that fleet.

Nor had he fully understood what had happened until it was too late to stop when his three battle carriers had opened fire on the fleet dropping into normal space in front of him firing, at his fleet he had thought. Had not realized that they had been firing, as the fleet he had been chasing began breaking to either side in front of him, his own oncoming one.

591

Yes, this new enemy was devious. And they were good tacticians too! They also used weapons that he had never encountered before, weapons that struck with little or no warning! Their missiles, too, were very powerful and acted in ways that were unfamiliar to him. He believed he understood the principle of their behavior but would have to capture one of their ships intact to be certain of his guesses.

But all of this was for a time when his seething anger could be turned to better use, a time when his thoughts could be applied rationally. For now he would lick his wounds, then limp on to his original destination.

Drel Expeditionary Occupation Force

The captain, of the Drel defense forces for the main transformation center on this continent, looked out over the large compound that was his area of responsibility. He was standing on a metal platform that circled the topmost portion of a stone tower that was part of the main structures stone walled enclosure.

It was a huge facility, inside the walls, with many large buildings containing several levels of small, metal barred pen-like enclosures, and an outer area three times the size of the stone walled enclosure that was enclosed by high, open latticed, metal mesh fencing. It was called a prison by the local inhabitants, he had learned, from rifling through his steeds memories, and it was a perfect place to operate the transformation center from.

The center had processed close to ten thousand of the locals into steeds since it had become fully operational, but right now the dregmas (captain) was feeling very uneasy. All too many of the signs that things were not right were there for those who would look, to see.

There had been several raids against the center, but none of them had done any real damage so far, but the feeling of uneasiness would not go away. He was muttering to himself that all of the signs were there, he could feel the tension building, and knew that another raid was coming very soon! He quietly notified his adjutant to start getting the men ready for it.

In one way he was grateful for the earlier raids, for they had convinced the consul to process two full companies of his soldiers instead of the three platoons he had initially processed. Although they had been little better than drones for the first couple of weeks it had taken to acclimate to and break in their new steeds, they were now operating as well trained units. These steed were quite well suited for his soldiers needs.

They were strong and agile, and when treated properly they had great stamina. But they were also very recalcitrant when first taken over, taking several days, instead of the one or two it normally took for the other species they had conquered.

Still, he was well pleased with the ten officers and thirty mid ranks he had received, for they had been actively trained before entering cold sleep. Their control of this new steed species manifested itself very quickly once acclimation was achieved.

But the common soldiers training was bred into them, and it took a good deal longer for that training to kick in and take control of these steeds.

Four hours later nothing had occurred, but his feeling of an impending raid persisted unabated.

As a matter of fact, the hair that grew at the base of his steeds neck, he was one of the strongest and best to have been processed so far, was rising as if attracted by static electricity. This, he knew, was a sign of nervousness or worry in this species, and that only increased his own feeling of uneasiness!

After another four hours, and still nothing untoward had happened, the captains feeling of uneasiness had only increased to the point where it was almost a palpable thing. Also, he'd had to start using more control because his steed had begun acting in a disquieting manner the locals described as fidgeting.

The captain had been on this planet for three local years now, and he knew that this species was very devious, and they were also vicious fighters. He didn't know why nothing had happened yet, unless this was a new tactic they were using. Still, even with the confidence he had in his troops, and his own capabilities, he could not shake his sense of imminent danger!

Suddenly the captain snapped his head up to look at the night sky as he caught first a glow, then a bright flare, out of the corner of his steeds ocular organ. As he stared upward several more flares occurred, then those flaring lights began to move across the night sky. The ships of the Expeditionary fleet in orbit above the planet were beginning to move out of orbit and away from it. 'What now,' he thought to himself as he continued to watch the night sky.

It had now been seven of the planets rotations, and absolutely nothing had happened that had threatened the center since he had begun feeling this way, and yet his feeling of unease only kept intensifying as nothing out of the ordinary happened. Maybe it was the fact that nothing had happened yet that was driving that feeling? He did not know. He only knew that the feeling kept growing stronger!

He moved from guard post to guard post, making sure that his men stayed alert. But, without realizing it, his movements over the last eight days had become less brisk, his posture less harsh when finding a guard leaning against a building in a relaxed manner. Or when he came upon two steeds standing facing each other, two sets of hair fine antennae waving idly from either side of their necks as they communicated with each other in the close range telepathic manner natural to the Drel.

Most Drel, even the lowest ranks of soldiers and laborers, preferred this manner of communicating, even though this species had a richly descriptive language the Drel could use.

His steps were a little slower on this eighth evening, after watching the fleet break orbit and leave for the dark of deep space. His awareness not quite as acute as it normally was, while he walked between guard posts on this moon bright starry night. Suddenly, from the near distance, he heard the distinct rumble of a space ships engines starting up. Then, from a good distance further off, he heard the echo of another one.

From some distance off he saw the tail of bright actinic light that could only be a space ship taking off. Then from further off still, from the area where he thought he had heard the second engine noise, he saw another one rising into the night sky.

With a rush, awareness of his surroundings and duty began returning to him, as he realized that the Drel had no ships that he knew of in those areas. Perhaps that is why, as that awareness rushed back to him, he didn't notice the three or four grenades that arched out of the darkness, and over the top of the compound fence, to land near the guard commanders shack with dull thumps.

The only reason the captain wasn't killed right then and there was that the duty communications tech came running out of the guard commanders shack yelling, and sending telepathically at the same time, placing him between the grenades and himself.

The captain heard him through his steeds aural cavities, and just barely received his thoughts because he was at the very limit of his sending capabilities, about twenty five yards. "Sir, there are ships taking off from all over the planet, and the Consul won't send up any of our ships because our fleet is gone, and he believes that there are enemy ships in orbit above us right now! He said to try to knock them down with our missile batter—"

And that was as far as he got when the grenades went off, blowing him into several pieces and knocking the captain totally unconscious!

When he awakened three and a half days later, he found he had a very serious head wound, and more than three quarters of the company on duty was dead. And all but six of the remaining troops were down with serious wounds.

He learned that the steel portals to the main facility inside the stone walled enclosure had been breached, and the transition center almost totally destroyed.

The steed evaluation and preparation equipment was now useless tangles of metal, glass, and wires, and the technicians that were on duty had been killed to a being. In addition, all of the steeds that were in the process of being prepared had been freed from their holding pens.

They would not be processing steeds from this center for many local months, if ever again! Thanks to the remarkable recovery capabilities of his steed he was up and about soon again.

The rebels had finally been driven off when the other two companies had counterattacked, but not before all of this damage had been done.

The captain was to learn, as time passed, that nearly every other center on the planet had suffered similar attacks. The damage to those centers had paralleled that done to his own, to larger or lesser degrees.

The damage to the centers themselves could be repaired, but the loss of technicians and their specialized equipment, and the thousands and thousands of already selected and prepared steeds, would set the takeover of this back water planet back by an incalculable amount of time.

Several weeks later they began to find mass grave sites containing the bodies of the missing steeds. The odd thing was that only those steeds who had received the implants that prepared their minds for immediate takeover were found in those graves.

In the end the captain came to three hard and fast conclusions. One was that he would never underestimate the species on this planet again, for they were very good tacticians and exceedingly devious in their planning. They had to be just to execute the planet wide raids as they had.

And the second was that he would always pay attention to his intuition in the future.

The third was that they would pay for the havoc they had caused!

ERMA Planetary Resistance Forces

Worldwide, on the day that the mythical Phoenix rose symbolically for humanity, some forty nine thousand six hundred and fifty three men and women who were part of regular military units still intact, or were partisan resistance fighters, died or were seriously wounded, to make sure that someone would be left to avenge Earth and Humanity in the future.

Those men and women had spent those lives well, and cost the enemy dearly, taking nearly two and a half times their number of the enemy Drel and their steeds with them.

Few of those who had had to be left behind on the Earth felt any bitterness at their lot, or their losses, even though their numbers had been close to halved, for the Phoenix had risen!

It had risen gloriously as ships all over the world had risen into space pulling their specially constructed, humanity packed, cargo modules! Yes, against all of the odds stacked against it, the Phoenix had risen and taken better than five million souls out of the reach of an insidious enemy! An enemy that had come sneaking out of the dark of space to steal Mankind's home. But they had come not only to steal his home, they had come to steal his humanity too!

But they had not counted on the tenacity of this species, nor its' willingness to fight on even in the face of certain defeat! This enemy from another galaxy who had come in their arrogance to take what was not theirs' would learn that they could not buy this small backwater planet, nor its' people, cheaply!

Now, from the ashes of their dead, and the pain of the souls lost to those taken over as steeds for the Drel, had risen the means for mankind to reclaim his home and his humanity. And the destruction of the Drel as a species loose in this galaxy.

And what of the fate of those left behind? Most of them would fight on as hard as they could, for as long as they could. After all, that was the only free choice left to them!

But make no mistake. They were not to be counted out of this fight soon, for they had been made stronger by these trials set upon them.

And they had learned a great deal about their enemy in their encounters, and would use every scrap of what they had learned to fight him!

The Drel had made several mistakes in coming to Earth to take what they wanted from the planet and its' people, but the biggest mistake they had made was that they had really pissed them off!

The Phoenix Risen

To the men and women in the ERMA ships floating in space around the Earth, guarding the rising of the Phoenix against pursuit from the planet below, or from attack from above, the scene was one that would be a never forgotten spectacle. Over the coming centuries the stories would be told and retold until they would become something nearing mythology.

Centuries later the final story would tell the story of Mankind and his struggle to not only survive, but to rise and become the dominant species on his planet. And it would tell of his decent from that height by the coming of the Drel! And his near extinction!

It would also tell of his rising from the ashes of what he had once been, like the mythical Phoenix from his races' fables, in one last mighty effort to preserve his species. But more importantly it would tell of his efforts to reclaim his heritage, and his natural home.

But none of this had happened as yet! There was only the majestic sight of hundreds of small space ships rising from the earth's surface, on brilliantly flaring engines that had already begun to strain, as they pulled thousands of specially designed cargo modules packed with millions of sleep induced human beings to safety.

Once above the sixty thousand foot level necessary, the booster engines built into those twenty five hundred modules, their controls slaved to the ships pulling them, came to life and added their thrust to that of the ships straining to lift them away from the pull of the earth's gravity, and relieved much of the strain on those ships. Now there were nearly twenty six hundred bright stars lifting away from the planets surface, reaching for the blackness of space and freedom!

And come away they did, losing only one ship and the four modules it was towing to ground fire belatedly suppressed!

It took the ships in orbit around the Earth nearly two weeks to round up, and get those ships and modules into a convoy formation. As the last ones were being herded into the formation, nearly thirty ships began dropping into normal space some little distance from them. Once all of these new ships had entered normal space they quickly formed themselves into a tight formation around the convoy.

Very soon communications lasers started reaching out to all of the smaller ships from the new larger ones and their controls were now slaved to those of the new fleet via computers controlling those beams. In turn the new ships slaved their flight controls to those of the fleet flagship. Now the whole combined fleet could move as one.

Each of those ships in the new fleet had been positioned in such a way that their hyperspace generators would create an overlapping field that would envelop the entire fleet, in effect treating the whole fleet as a single ship, and allow it to enter hyperspace as one unit.

This had only been done once or twice before successfully, and with much smaller groupings of ships! But it was a risk that had to be taken, because they would never have gotten away from the Sol system in time to avoid the remnants of the oncoming Drel fleet.

The planners of this move had spent many days of running trials and simulations, trying to perfect what they believed should work, and many more sleepless nights worrying about what they might have missed in their planning.

But in the end they agreed that they had done all that it was humanly possible to do to ensure that it would work, and sent the planning details ahead to the fleet to implement.

It worked much better than they had dared to hope, and without the loss of, or damage to, a single ship or module.

Now, like that great mythical bird, this Phoenix flew away to safety so that the precious cargo it carried would someday be able to come back to fight another day.

Their cargo would not be able to do this, but their great, great grand children would be the ones to help make that return possible.

For those watching from the planets surface there was a long period where a bright grouping of sparks of light could be seen in the night sky, then there was a brighter flash where those sparks had been.

And they were gone!

Dirk and Yuri Garov

"I cannot believe it! Nearly half of that monstrous fleet destroyed! And we lost only twenty three ships!" Yuri Garov said, awe in his voice, "Yet it must be true! Timothy is not one to embellish things. You have an American saying for such occasions I believe?"

"Da, yes," He went on, his normally dour features now transformed by a huge grin. "I believe it is 'Holy Shit'!"

Dirks' grin matched Yuris' but his tone was serious, almost somber, as he spoke. "Yes Yuri, that phrase is most apropos in this case. But the unparalleled success of Operation Phoenix has much deeper ramifications for us in all of this."

"Da. But I will enjoy the fruits of our labor for a few more minutes, if you don't mind." Yuri said, his tone and smile softening his rebuke.

"I don't mind in the least. The lord knows you've worked harder than anyone else to make this plan work!" Dirk said, warmth and respect for this man who had once been his enemy, but was now one of his closest friends, in his voice. Dirk honestly didn't know if he could have accomplished half as much as they had without this mans help!

Somewhat sobered himself now, Yuri said, "We all do what we can in this thing. But you are the glue, the inspiration that holds us together and makes us believe that that we can do the things we have. And to keep trying when it looks like we can't!"

"No," He held up his hand to forestall dirks' impending protest, "do not sell yourself short my friend. I do not know of anyone else who could have pulled such a disparate group together in such a short time, and make us believe we could do the things we have!"

"Enough Yuri." Dirk protested. "Getting back to what I wanted to say about Phoenix. I know you understand how much we needed this success, for, as much as we have been able to do in the last five years, there has been that one flaw in all of our accomplishments. That flaw was that, until now, we have never taken any real part of the fight to the enemy! But now Yuri, we have! And our people see and believe, really believe, that we can!"

"Da. I agree that this has been so. It has worried me also." Garov said solemnly. But the grin refused to leave his face completely.

"There are three things," Dirk went on soberly, earnestly, "that we must make sure we do. The first thing is to continue to take the fight to the enemy whenever, wherever, and however we can, because even the smallest victories now will produce large dividends in boosted morale for us! And, our people will need those dividends, especially those that we just brought out. They will need them more than the rest because they haven't played any part in what we have done so far."

"Da. It is as you say. Even though the lives we have given them back will be hard, they will feel like outsiders until their contributions are able to show some tangible results in this war."

Dirk started to speak but waited because he saw that Yuri was trying to frame a thought into words. Nodding his thanks, Yuri thought for a few seconds more, then began to speak. "This topic has a relationship to conversations you and I have had in the past, and I think there is a way to improve both situations. We both know that the enemy is not likely to leave any sort of threat unchallenged for any length of time, and that they will eventually discover where some of our bases and planets are."

"Yes, they will, eventually. And even with the numbers we brought out with 'Phoenix', we are going to be stretched very thin for a long time to come yet." Dirk interjected, thinking he might know where Yuri was going with this.

"Just so!" Yuri said, picking up his train of thought again. "So, we must begin to promote two things right away. First, we must encourage pregnancies, and also encourage the use of drugs and procedures that will result in multiple fetuses, so that we may increase our numbers as quickly as possible."

"Second, we must make every person on every planet a part of an active militia, make them an active part of their own self defense. Thus they will become closer to each other, no matter what planet they end up on in the end, and closer to the whole resistance collectively." He finished

"I think your right, Yuri," Dirk said thoughtfully, "and your idea ties right into my second point! That being that we must make every single person understand that this is going to be a long fight. A very long fight! And we must do so in a way that will give them heart, not cause them to lose it! This, I think, will be one of our hardest chores!"

"Nyet! No!" Yuri said forcefully. "I am supposed to be the great pessimist in our group. Dirk, sometimes I do not see how you manage to keep the schedule you do on only three hours sleep a night. But, occasionally as now, it seems to affect your reasoning!"

He softened this LAST with another smile as he went on, "You have had less time than even I to look about this new mankind we are trying so hard to save, and I can tell you that I, Yuri Garov, who was born a real Russian pessimist, have seen a change in nearly all the people about us!"

"The greatest majority of them no longer seek, or see, ethnic differences in each other. No longer see the color of ones skin as something that sets that person on a higher or lower level than another's. What I have seen, and heard, is that they are now thinking of themselves as a single race. As human beings!"

Garov stopped for a few seconds, because this was something that had penetrated his self defenses, and had affected him deeply, brought him closer than he had ever been to belonging to something he wanted desperately to be a part of. He looked at Dirk sharply before ending with, "Even I am becoming a convert!"

Dirk could think of nothing else but to reach out and clasp his friends' shoulder warmly, for without knowing it Yuri had given Dirk renewal in his own beliefs and aims.

Dirk realized with sudden clarity that he must get out among the people more often, because his single minded drive to fight the Drel and win this war was making him a stranger to the very things he was fighting it for. The fight for the survival of humanity, and the reclamation his home was truly beginning to put a rift between himself, and those he was so committed to helping.

Finally, letting go of Yuris' shoulders, Dirk said simply, "Thank you my friend." Then, smiling ruefully, he said, "You're right. I have been losing touch lately, and that is something I'm going to change."

"Still," He said, his tone sobering, "the second thing we must do is make sure they understand that this war could go on for a hundred fifty years, even two hundred years." He ended, a trace of the anger, and fear, that that thought engendered in his voice.

Now, almost musingly, he went on, "The trouble is that we humans are too prone to thinking of things in the short term, whereas most of the aliens species seem to think of things in the much longer term. And that's mainly due to the fact that most of them live a good deal longer than we do!"

He paused briefly, thoughtfully, before going on. "That may well end up being one of our biggest problems in dealing with them, because their longevity has developed in them a 'manyana' complex. They may not understand that they just don't have the time to think overly long about things that are happening now."

Shaking himself, both physically and mentally, Dirk continued, "The third, and possibly the most important, thing we must do is make sure that they never lose sight of what it is we are fighting for, that they never forget." Dirk paused to order his thoughts.

Yuri interjected "I do not think they will forget, Dirk."

"No Yuri!" Dirk ground out harshly, angered now that he was having trouble expressing in the right way what he felt in his very soul. But he went on anyway, "They must never forget that Earth belongs to us Yuri! It is our home! And we, they, want it back!"

Dirk took a deep shuddering breath, "And just as important, possibly even more important, they must never, ever, forget all of those who volunteered to stay on Earth, to fight on or die there, hoping and praying for the day of our return! What will we say to them a hundred years from now?"

At the look on Yuris' face Dirk was quick to apologize, saying "I'm sorry my friend, I know how much you care. I'm just blowing off some of my own frustration at being able to do so little. We will win this war, and reclaim what is rightfully ours. This I swear!"

Dirk's warning about the possibility of the war lasting as long as a hundred fifty to two hundred years was well founded. It would last much, much more than two hundred years!

Dirk and Balor

Balors' familiar thought pattern touched Dirk's mind while the ship he was on was still well out from the solar system that held the ERMA ruling council's secret headquarters. *We shall be well met soon again my brother, for I have been gone from your side for far too long this time.*

I too, have sorely missed my brothers presence, and his wisdom. How long will it take for your ship to get in? Dirks' thoughts went out to Balor, his feelings of warmth and friendship carried in their overtones, laving his friends mind with the intensity of his feelings.

It will be two more of the planetary local days the captain says. Tell me, has Blade been behaving himself as he promised? Balor asked, a smile in his tone.

He has been a perfect gentleman. Dirk sent back. And right on the heels of Dirk's thoughts came Blade's.

I do not break my promises! Blade shot back at Balor sleepily. Then, relenting, he sent *"But you will be well met by this one also, uncle. In truth this one has missed your presence sorely!* Then he dropped out of the link and was gone just as quickly as he had entered it.

Tell that one that, Balor sent back, chuckling in that manner the Elonee had, *"even though I suspect he still impolitely listens, that he is also missed and shall be well met.*

There was the feeling of a sort of echoing emptiness in the link after that, and both Balor and Dirk knew that Blade had truly dropped out of the link this time. Now Balors' thoughts came on a band so high and tight that both he and Dirk believed no one else could hear them while they were using it. *There is much that I have to tell you brother!* Balor stopped, leaving the statement hanging.

Dirk sent back immediately, the tone of his thoughts guarded even on this level. *We will discuss what you learned at length, when you are here with me brother! Just give me the gist of what you found now.*

Now Balors' tone came to him with suppressed excitement. *It is as you suspected brother. There are many species that have never been visited by the Chai, or the other species of the Union! Two that we were able to approach discreetly are bipedal like your own.*

Then the suppressed excitement broke through as Balor went on hurriedly, *And one of them is telepathic. The telepathic one's are low level telepaths about on the level of the Tate one, but could be very valuable allies even as such. That species also uses an audible speech mode, and do, I believe, prefer a combination of both when communicating. We managed to make contact with a being of that species, and it would like to have further contact with us, because it was able to grasp quickly the danger coming from the Drel.*

You and the captain did very well Balor, and I thank you. But there is news that is not so good, isn't there? Dirk asked.

Now Balor raised a shield about his mind, and reached out to match it with the one Dirk was also raising about his own mind. Their thought projections met and meshed, then Balor began to send again.

His thoughts now came flatly, all business in their tone. *It appears that our friend, the Chai, has not been completely forthright in his description of the Union's technological capabilities. We came across two separate ships that belonged to one of the Union races, and we shadowed each of them for quite some time.*

Balor paused here, letting Dirk absorb this, then went on, *We found in each case that their technology is on a par with what you found on TuLans' small ship, and much of it not as good as what we have developed since meeting that being. It should also be noted, with importance, that they at no time even suspected our presence. However, some of their defensive/offensive screens and weaponry do seem to exceed that which you are now employing. There is a good bit more that we found out, but that I will discuss with you in person after I arrive.*

Well enough brother, and thank you again. My lair will once again be made brighter when you are again by my side. Until then, Balor. Dirk sent, ending both the conversation and the link.

Balor had brought potentially good news, and news that on the surface of it was quite disturbing. Dirk wanted to chew over what Balor had told him, and do it undisturbed, so he asked the leader of the current guard detail to make sure he was not bothered for at least the next four hours.

The disturbing news gave him pause, and made him want to rethink and reweigh the benefits versus costs possibilities of forming an alliance with the Union, or at least the manner of such an alliance.

Too, once he had a chance to speak with Balor at some length, he would have to speak at length with TuLan, and then put whatever he found in front of Yuri Garov and the rest of the council to be worried like a bone before a final policy could be laid out.

Yes, he would have to discuss this with TuLan at some length very soon.

Dirk and TuLan

I want to thank you for letting me so closely follow all that occurred during your 'Operation Phoenix'. What you and your people did was a thing that, had I not seen it through your mind and eyes at first hand, I would have said was an utter impossibility for them at this stage of your development! was the comment TuLan made in opening this conversation.

Dirk kept his thoughts private for a moment before answering TuLan, wanting to, needing to, say many things to this being who had brought and wrought so much change to his life. Then, nodding to himself mentally as he came to a conclusion, he began sending his thoughts to his symbiotic partner.

He began by saying, *There are many things I must tell you, and many more things that we must discuss. But first let me start by saying that you're welcome, and also to say thank you to you.*

I do not understand why it is that you are thanking me? TuLan said in puzzlement.

I am thanking you for several reasons, and I suppose I should also be thanking fate or whatever it was that brought you to me and my people when it did. But no matter what the circumstances for your being here, you have played a major role in our ability to fight the Drel! Had you not come when you did, we would not have known our peril until it was far too late to do anything meaningful about it! Dirk said succinctly.

I did not do that much, and much that I did do was initially motivated by my instinct and desire to survive. Said TuLan honestly, for he now felt that this conversation was to be another of those turning points in their relationship.

You did only what any being would have done, and I don't fault you in any way for that." Dirk said simply, and, *"Were it not for the technology you gave us access to, none of what we have so far achieved would have been remotely possible for us. The difference was in the boost your knowledge gave us. The leg up, as it were!*

No Dirk. You made far better use of the technology we had than ever we did! And your people made advances and strides of improvement to that knowledge in ways we hadn't even considered! Again a completely honest answer, even though it said much, and nothing new at the same time.

Let us stop fencing TuLan. By your actions you have shown me that not only can we serve each other in this relationship, you have shown me that you are the kind of being that I would like to have as a friend! Right now, at this point in time, you and I are at the juncture of being here, and having to get there! And it is vitally important that you understand where my species was when you were forced to join us!

Have we not covered much of this in previous conversations? TuLan asked, somewhat perplexed now.

We have, but still I do not think that you have grasped the essence of what it is that makes my species what it is!

Dirk paused for a significant few seconds, as his thoughts coalesced into the meaning he wanted to convey to this being from elsewhere, then he began to speak in measured a tone, *To the best of our knowledge, my species began to develop into what we are presently about a half million to a million years ago, we're not sure of the true length of time yet, and on the way we passed through many stages. What is important about this is that all throughout our early history every other species that was contending for primacy was bigger, faster, stronger, or had natural weapons that far outstripped what we had developed with!*

But what we did have, what gave us that little bit of an edge to be able to compete, was a combination of three things. We had a mind developing that sought reason over instinct. An innate sense of curiosity, and indomitable will to survive. What that combination has finally made of us is the species at the top of the food chain on our planet.

Dirk paused, giving TuLan a mental look that left little doubt as to the real importance of what he was about to say as he continued, *We were at a point in our mental and technological development where we no longer sought to immediately kill what frightened us. A point where we were just beginning to appreciate the true immensity of what was out there in space, and the potential of the diversity it had to offer us. Because of our innate sense of curiosity we had actually begun to honestly ask ourselves 'what if', and were looking forward to those answers. Our minds were at the point of being ready to take the first real steps outward, and to meet whatever the universe and the stars held for us.*

Now, as he went on, there was a tinge of sadness to his words as he said, *Now, even though we now have the means to visit those stars, the veils of wonder have been torn from our eyes, and we find that we must still fight for our survival against those who would arbitrarily take from us what is ours. And even though we have been fortunate enough to save a large portion of our people, thanks in large part to you, we find that our home is lost to us, for how long we do not know!*

As he went on speaking the tenor of Dirks words changed from a tone of sadness to one of pure savagery, *But mark you this TuLan, and mark it well on what I am about to tell you! Earth is my home, my species home, and we are going to take it back! We are going to take it back even if we have to kill every Drel, or any other species, that thinks they can take it from us, in both of these galaxies!*

The pure, utter, savagery in the meaning of those words caused TuLan to involuntarily shudder, physically and mentally, inside of Dirk! The suffusion of raw, red, emotion contained in those words hummed and vibrated through TuLans' mind, leaving no doubt whatsoever that his host, and his species, was perfectly capable of doing just such a thing.

No, TuLan did not doubt this, for Dirk had just given him a look into the darker side of his species through his mind.

Seeing TuLan's reaction Dirk relented, grasping his surging emotions by the main force of his mind, bringing them back under his rigid control as he continued, *There TuLan, you see the other side of us, the part even we are wise enough to fear! This is the part of us that you must come to understand and accept about us if we are to be able to continue with each other. The part of us that will, no matter what else happens, never let us lose sight of or forgo the goal we have stated.*

If, after seeing that side of us, and understanding what it means, you can accept that until our home is once more our own, our primary aims will be directed to achieving that goal. If you and your race can accept this, you will gain a friend that will willingly shed its' own blood to make sure that your own race remains as free beings, and your own systems remain free of such a threats!

If this can be, I swear the following on my life! As soon as it is humanly possible we, the ruling council, will draft a treaty of mutual protection between your people and our own.

TuLan thought for several long minutes before responding, then started to speak almost hesitantly, holding himself to the strict truth, *I cannot speak for my entire species, for I am not, as you are, its' leader. But this I can tell you without question. There are many of my species who are very dissatisfied with things as they are now. My species, and the Union too for that matter, have become static, satisfied with the status quo. There has been little that is really new in our science, nor have we explored the galaxy as we once did, in many centuries!*

The innovations you have made and applied to the science you gleaned from my ship has far exceeded everything new the Union has accomplished in the last two or three centuries. And your computer sciences outstrip anything that exists in the entire Union.

TuLan took a deep mental breath, relieved now not to have to continue to hide these truths from these very astute beings. He went on with more confidence, and more comfortably now, as he said, *I believe that a majority of my species will accept what you have shown me in all honesty, especially when they are shown the truth of the peril that is coming at them now. Yes, I believe that I can speak with confidence in that!*

Good! Dirk responded, *I can accept that. As soon as we can get the people we brought out settled, and can plan our near term strategy for defending our new planets, we will begin planning for a trip to your home system so that you can speak to those you think you must.*

After thinking for a few seconds Dirk said, *there is another thing, one of great importance that we must speak of.*

TuLan started to become a little apprehensive again, but was soon relieved by Dirks' words.

I have grown very fond of you as a being, gaining much respect for your intelligence and ethics. So, if you are willing, I would very much like our relationship to evolve beyond what it is to one of mutual trust and friendship! Now Dirk radiated a feeling of warmth at his small companion as he said, *It is past time for this, for fate has seen to it that we are bonded and bound to each other, with still a great deal to learn from each other.*

With simplicity, and uncharacteristic short windedness, TuLan said, *I believe that I would really like that!*

One last thing that we must speak of, Dirk said slowly, concerns a conversation we had some time ago. Do you recall our speaking about the possibility of there being a number of your species who might be willing to pair with a number of my own?

Indeed I do! Said TuLan, his interest rising quickly.

Would they be willing, do you think, to do so with the understanding that for the foreseeable future that partnership would put them in the position of being the observer rather than the controlling factor?

Why do you ask that in just that manner, Dirk? TuLan asked, his suspicion and curiosity warring for dominance in his tone.

Because, Dirk spoke slowly, choosing his words carefully, *as I think you would agree with me, we both know that this war is going to be a long one. There are those among my people whom I trust implicitly, and I would sorely miss their talents and council were they to die of old age. You know my species is comparatively short lived, and those I have in mind would gain that which you have given me in such relationships. The real benefit to them being that of longevity.*

Dirk smiled mentally for TuLan as he went on, saying, *But do not misinterpret me. For those relationships would be reciprocal to your people in the transfer of knowledge, and a chance to study at first hand, as you have so often opined, our unique perspective in the way we approach problems and situations. And the ride would be for them I think, at the very least, a very interesting one!*

Speaking of unique perspectives! TuLan muttered to himself. Then, *It will most likely take a unique perspective on my part to explain what is desired of them. But the answer to your question is yes. I believe there are those who could be persuaded, if there was an understanding that the relationship could be reviewed periodically for renewal or dissolution. Uh, how many did you have in mind?*

That is entirely acceptable! Dirk said without any hesitation whatsoever, completely sidestepping TuLan's last question.

Now, with his most pressing concerns about humanity's relationship with the Chai out of the way Dirk said in a much more relaxed tone.

Now, my friend, let us discuss matters more mundane, though still important, while we return to Wolfsbane.

TuLan, who did not completely understand this concept of friendship in the manner these humans meant it, was wondering where the future was about to lead him.

Then he recalled a phrase he had come across while studying these people, and it seemed completely apropos to his present situation.

It was quaint, but fit in perfectly with the turmoil of his thoughts. It went something like the following, as close as he could remember it.

'In for a penny, in for a pound!'

Transition

The revival, and placement, of the last of the refugees from 'Operation Phoenix' was done and over with for six months now. The doctors and medical technicians had diligently worked wonders in their revival processes, yet still, twelve thousand of those precious lives had been lost to unsuspected ailments and complications, or recovery shock.

Dirk knew that that number was minute compared to the total number saved, but still he felt their loss. He was sitting in his office, located on the hidden headquarters planet of the ERMA ruling council, staring longingly at a three dimensional holograph of the Earth, and the way it pulled at him was a physical thing that would not be denied.

He would reclaim his home, he promised himself silently, and nothing in this universe was going to stop him. No matter how long it took him to do so, or what the cost!

Elsewhere, on the newly colonized planets of the Earth Resistance Movement Alliance the refugee humans and their Elonee allies had been sent to, they were busy trying to build, or rebuild, as much of their society as they could amidst the chaos of a war they had not sought, but had sworn a blood oath to win.

All things considered, the fledgling Alliance forces had done more than most observers, had there been any besides the single Chai and the last of the Elonee who had been stranded on Earth ages ago, would have thought to be even remotely possible for them to do.

They had escaped the finality of the Drel takeover of their planet, fought the Drel, even if it was only temporarily, to virtual a standstill in space, and with little more than ten million human beings and fifty two thousand Elonee, colonized seven new planets in just under six years Earth standard time.

Three of those planets were already booming industrial centers that were now able to produce everything from potato peelers to space ships that could travel faster than the speed of light.

One of those planet was the secret headquarters that housed the military, and other councils, that governed these humans. It was the heartbeat of the Earth Resistance Movement Alliance, and its' location was so secret that only those who had to be there knew its' exact location.

Three more of those planets were agricultural planets, with rich soils and oceans plentiful in their bounty of sea life. Already they were burgeoning with crops and food animals that would soon be exported to the other worlds of the alliance.

Not only were the plants and animals native to the Earth doing well on those planets, several new species of plants and animals native to them had been found to be non harmful, and very tasty and beneficial, to humans and Elonee alike.

In addition to the one large mining operation on Wolfsbane's moon there were four newly discovered planets, that had been found to have tremendous deposits of the ores and minerals necessary for the Alliance to survive and flourish, that were in the process of being prepared for colonization.

Dirk had risen from his desk, and begun to pace about the room as he thought about all that still had to be done to ensure the survival of his people. And not just them, for he, in mankind's name, had made commitments to their Elonee and the Chai allies.

There were also the people discovered and contacted by Balor who must be re-contacted and negotiated with to join their alliance, and possibly to open trade with.

There was also the new dreadnought that Blackjack Jones had designed and was ready to start building to think about. That would be a major project that would drain a lot of resources, but it was something that was totally necessary to do if they were to be able to stand up to those battle carriers of the Drel!

Actually he needed two of them, because he needed one of them to take to the Chai homeworld, both to impress those beings, and so that TuLan could open negotiations with his people, and also begin work on his and Dirks' most secret project. But thoughts on that subject must wait for a while longer.

Dirk also needed two more battle cruisers, ships big enough and strong enough to defend themselves under most circumstances that must be sent out to do covert exploration.

The Alliance desperately needed more, and better, intelligence about the other races that they were likely to meet out here! And they also needed to be able to keep a close eye on the Drel! They had already started another planetary takeover, and were looking at several other planets in this galaxy to take over in the near future.

Then there was the situation on Chimera. He needed that planet as a base station, but the local beings there were pathologically opposed to anything that even seemed to be taking, or making a challenge to, any part of their hunting territories. There Tagon, and several of the Elonee elders, had volunteered to take on solving the problem.

Neither he nor Dirk wanted to be any part of anything that even seemed to be racial genocide, especially not after what has just happened to Earth. But many of those indigenes would die if something were not worked out with them.

They would die because they were right in the path of the Drel advance, and Dirk's planned lines of defense. They were truly caught between a rock and a hard place!

Dirk stopped his pacing and walked back to his desk. Putting all of those things and concerns aside for the moment he took one more long look at his hologram of Earth, then started gathering the papers he would need and putting them into a folder.

He hurried now because he had only two minutes left to get to the full meeting of the council he himself had scheduled.

As he rushed out the door his thoughts were leaping forward again to the seemingly endless list of things that still had to be done, started, or finished.

But as much as he, and they, still had to do, he felt optimistic!

Because today they would start planning on how they were going to take their home back.

And take the war to the Drel!

The Drel had made a terrible mistake in their plans for conquest! They had made an even bigger mistake in choosing the first planet, and people, in that conquest!

They had awakened the Dragon!

Now they must feed it!!!!!!!

This is the end of *Waking The Dragon*, book one of *The Earth-Chai Saga*. Book Two of this saga, *Whispering into the Dragon's Ear*, is expected to be completed by the spring of 2007. Here is a look at how book two begins.

Foreword

Dirk hurried now because he had only two minutes to get to the meeting of the full military council that he himself had scheduled.

As he rushed out of the door his thoughts were already leaping ahead to the seemingly endless list of things still to be begun, completed, or started anew.

Even with as much as he, and they, still had to do he felt buoyantly optimistic. Optimistic because this was the day, the day when they would start the real planning on how they would begin to take their home back!

This was also the day when the Alliance would begin to take the war to the Drel!

The Drel had made a terrible mistake in their plans for conquest! They had made an even bigger mistake in choosing the first planet, and people, in that conquest!

They had awakened the Dragon!

Now they must feed it!!!!!!!!

Yes, he thought grimly, they had had to abandon the Earth for the time being. Also, in the aftermath of doing so, they had done what many would have said was impossible to do.

They had formed a real resistance movement, one with strength enough to fight back effectively. Effectively enough to save ten million of their fellow Earthmen from the horror that would be the end result of the Drel invasion and takeover of their planet!

They had built Earth's first spacecraft capable of faster than light space flight! They had then gone on to build nearly a hundred of those craft capable of carrying on the war with the Drel. Then had hurt the Drel badly, letting them know that their prize would not come cheaply!

Since leaving the Earth they had found and colonized seven planets with thriving communities on them. Made alliances with two alien species that had pledged to help fight the Drel, and they were about to begin making contact with some of the many others they had found out inhabited their galaxy.

Yes, Dirk had cause to feel optimistic, but he would have given much for that optimism not to be so grim in nature!

But, in the end, he need not have hurried so much, for time would end up being both his friend, and a bane that would take much from him!

As he hurried to the meeting his thoughts worried about time. Even with his greatly expanded life expectancy he felt that precious commodity slipping through his grasp, for the things that must be done by yesterday were fast approaching the limits of today in the order of their urgency!

Taking a firm grip on his sense of time fleeing his grasp he entered the conference room.

Prologue
Whispering into the Dragon's Ear

The two ships were dead black in color, making them nearly invisible to the naked eye, and they bristled with turrets and tubes that stated they were warships. As they began to move slowly and carefully towards the asteroid belt, their engine signatures were hidden by baffles that helped to make them hard to spot with sensor arrays designed for that purpose.

The black color on their outer surfaces was not just to make them hard to see in the deeps of space. This also was another method of stealthing! It caused search impulses sent out by other ships to slide harmlessly of them as if they were not there if someone, or something, were actively looking for them.

The two stealthed ships picked a group of four of the largest pieces of blasted rock, each about the size of the state of Rhode Island on Earth, that were flying in close formation together. Those huge pieces were accompanied by lots of smaller debris that acted as a natural screen to hide themselves within. Then the smaller of the two ships moved itself cautiously into a position where it could observe the second planet in the system.

The Earthmen aboard her began the laborious task of charting the positions of the much larger Drel ships in orbit about that hapless planet. Two days later the smaller ship moved back to join its' larger companion, where they joined and extended connecting tubes to allow members of the smaller ships crew to transfer to one of the larger ships.

Hours after the collected information had been scrutinized, and analyzed, a conference began between the captains and certain officers of both crews. The expedition commander, one Jimmy 'Bad Boy' Lester, called the meeting to order. He opened it by asking a question of the big, burly, man in camouflage fatigues, "Alvin, do you think you can get the lander down there to drop you off without it being spotted?"

"Yeah, we can do it, but they're gonna have to drop me real close to the ground and scoot the hell outta Dodge real fast so's none o them Drel can get a fix on where they dropped me!" Lieutenant Alvin Ofstroffsky said in an affected Tennessee Drawl.

"OK, I'll take your word on that part. What kind of equipment do you want to take in with you?" Jimmy said, smiling at the affectation because he knew the man held a Masters degree in English.

"Not much Jimmy. Just my usual weapons and gear, and the new commo pack those guys back on Wolfsbane rigged up. The only special item I think I'll need is a pair of those floater attachments for my boots. That area where I agreed to meet that native is all bog and marsh land." The big man said with a frown on his rugged face, telling volumes about how he felt about going into an area that he knew nothing at all about.

"Your sure Alvin? You know how important making contact with your native buddy has become! I'd suggest you take at least three weeks worth of rations with you just in case he is late, or can't make the meet."

"OK. That sounds smart. Don't call me for at least two weeks though, cause those little guys are kind of skittish, and you never know if the Drel have figured out how to tap our signals. I expect to call you in about that time though, so keep your sensors peeled.

"Will do Alvin. If those guys have any kind of resistance set up we're going to bring them a lot of help, including a 'Ghost Team' to show them some nasty new tricks to play on the Others." Jimmy said with a nasty smile on his face.

Then he said in a serious tone, "Dirk said that making allies of these people would be a big help to us when we try to make contact with a few of those 'Union' races. It'll go a long ways towards showing them that we're strong enough to help someone besides ourselves."

After a short, thoughtful, pause he went on, "I think he's right on this one, cause playing from a position of strength is always a good idea!" Jimmy finished earnestly .

"I'll do what's necessary, Jimmy. If that's all I'd like to get started."

Just as Alvin was turning to go there was a barely audible chirp from Jimmy's' earpiece. He raised his hand and tapped the tiny button on it, turning on the transmit/receive mode, and said "yes Conley."

He listened for a moment, then a slow smile began to spread across his wide mouth. After a few more seconds of listening he said, "Thank you Conley, and send my thanks to captain Ritter along with a well done."

Looking at the small group of officers at the table he said, "Captain Ritter has just sent word that he has found a nice, big, hole in the Drel's planetary coverage. One where you can drop down to the surface with little chance of being spotted!"

Smiles broke out on all the faces at the table as one of the officers said, with admiration in his voice, "Leave it to Ritter to find a door nobody is watching!"

The rest nodded their admiring agreement to the mans' obvious talent for finding holes in the enemies defenses. Jimmy said "OK Alvin, you've got your entry point! Now, how long before you depart?"

"Most of my gear's already packed, but I need about another hour to add a couple o things I just thought about."

"Alright, I'll have the lander crew standing by in one hour. Get going, and good luck!" Jimmy said, gripping the other mans hand warmly before he left.

CHAPTER ONE
Interstice

Conversation One

"Do you think we should open a link to our subject?" The female asked, already knowing the answer by the look on the males' craggy features.

"Nooo, I don't think that would be a wise thing to do at this point in time." The male said in a thoughtful manner.

"But," she said argumentatively, "you see the strength that one is developing as a telepath! He may, if he gets any stronger, begin to pick up some of our sendings!"

"Not if we continue to take the extra care these new developments on his part demand, he won't!" The male said, giving her a glare that said she had better not forget.

With a sigh she let that part of the conversations subject matter drop for the time being. She hadn't given up, she just knew her partner.

The male also knew, with a solemn certainty, she would not let the matter of the subject lay fallow for long before she broached it again. He also had to admit to himself, that the subject had been a complete surprise to him!

The two Watchers had long been aware of the alien feline race that occupied the planet, along with the subject's species. They had taken great care to shield their own thoughts because that species were natural telepaths, and very strong ones too!

That was why they had been so surprised when they felt the new presence! It was a very, very, strong one, and completely different from the feline races thought pattern. What surprised the two watchers, and drawn their immediate attention, was the seemingly effortless manner in which the new presence had penetrated a very strong mind shield. One set up by a group of the felines as they met in one of their council meetings. It took great strength, and dexterity, to break into one of their shields.

Even more startling was the strength of the shield the subject had penetrated! The watchers had not been able to penetrate it, and had tried no harder to do so after their first effort for fear of alerting them that they were being observed, and of letting the subject know of their presence.

The two Watchers had conferred at length after that, and had agreed that a thought bubble, outlining this occurrence, should be sent into the void in the direction the Others had left specific instructions about with the elders. They would take no chance that the Others would be disappointed with them. Even though there had been no contact with them in the eight thousand years the Watchers had been watching the development of this species, on this backwater planet. The male often wondered why the Others had taken so much interest in a species that had not even shown a strong potential of surviving its' infancy. But this species had survived, and flourished!

The two Watchers had been sent to this backwater planet for two reasons. The first, and most important reason, was the 'Compact' with the Others. That compact had been established nearly a million local years ago. It had come about when the Others had first come across the Watchers species who, had at the time, been in the throws of a galaxy spanning war that had been going on for ten thousand years!

The Watchers species were on the point of annihilating each other to the point of extinction! That was when the Others had intervened! The Watcher race, both factions of it, turned on the Others and attacked them in a blind fury!

The Others had stopped them dead in their tracks, and literally spanked them like the children they were acting like, by showing them the meaning of real power! That lesson had nearly ended the Watchers as a species!

The Watcher race had been, by all prevailing standards, a very advanced race technologically. They had controlled their own galaxy, which was on the other side of the universe from this one, and a large portion of an adjacent one. They thought they controlled vast power, and thought they knew much about life, and what constituted it. As so often happens, a disagreement between two competing factions occurred. It escalated into open conflict, then escalated again into open warfare, dividing the watcher race!

The real reason for the war had been completely forgotten. Only the fury survived, and the killing of their own kind. That was when the Others had intervened, and put a stop to it!

The lesson had been a harsh one, and had been imprinted on the psyche of the Watcher race indelibly! The Watcher race would never, could never, forget that lesson. They had been shown, in their ignorant arrogance, just how frail they really were! They had literally been scared into using some common sense, and they took that lesson to heart!

The Others had stayed long enough to help the Watchers regain a sense of equilibrium, and had shown them a new path to follow, if they chose to. The

Watcher race was a very intelligent one, and saw the value of the gift they had been given, so they listened carefully when the others asked one thing of them. They Others asked that some portion of the Watcher race become 'Watchers' for them, to keep an eye on budding new species, and certain parts of other galaxies that they had some interest in. But, if they did so, they must decide to do so willingly!

So was formed the 'Compact' between the Watchers and the Others. That had been a little over a million local years ago now, and the Watcher race had learned much, and had flourished greatly since then. The Others had continued on their journey, leaving instructions for contacting them should something of import come about concerning those things that they had asked to be watched

The Watchers often did not understand why they were asked to watch and report on certain species or parts of other galaxies. They only knew that it was of great import to the Others, so they did it diligently and willingly.

The second reason the two Watchers were here, at this backwater solar system and planet that was part of this sparsely populated galaxy, was because they had pulled a prank. They had mischievously altered information about the timing of an impending super nova that was to occur in a galaxy on the other side of the universe from this one. They thought the surprise that would be experienced by their elders would be entertaining, and interesting to see. They were right! They were also very wrong!

Their elders had been very surprised. They had also been very angry because a budding aquatic species had nearly perished because of their thoughtlessness! Their reprimand had been swift and painful, and included being sent here to relieve the Watcher team who had been stationed here for the last twenty thousand local years!

The male said placatingly to the female, "There is to much going on here since the incursion from the next galaxy. And, there seems to be a great deal of advancement going on with our subjects race at the present time. We don't know how long, or even if, the Others may take to respond. I suggest we make another detailed report and send it along as well. The Others deem this species important to them, so I expect we will hear something from them in time." He finished, knowing that he didn't know what the Others deemed to be important.

The female knew this also, and decided not to enlarge on what they didn't know. She also knew that both of them had begun to become fascinated with this species as they watched it begin to develop technologically by leaps and bounds. This species had an innate curiosity that drove them mercilessly to delve into everything.

She kept a quiet silence for so long that the male was about to say something to her, when she said abruptly, "I know that we must adhere to, and stay strictly within, the rules of non interference as watchers. I also think it would be very enlightening if we were to go and take a look at the planets our subject has populated with the people he took off his planet!" she finished thoughtfully, hopefully.

The male gave her a long, hard look, saying, "I'm not so sure that would be a good idea."

Smiling, because she knew she had him now, she said "Did you not just say that we should forward a full report on things as they stand now?" Seeing a look of uncertainty in his eyes she rushed on, "How can such a report be complete without that part of the picture included?"

The male smiled warmly at her, acknowledging that he had been foxed, and nodded. Besides, truth to be told, he wanted to do the same thing himself.

They rose together from the table in front of the little sidewalk cafe they had been sitting at during their conversation. She absentmindedly began smoothing the pretty print dress that clung so revealingly to her voluptuous figure, he straightening the tan sports coat that pronounced his broad, well muscled, shoulders.

They would go to the building they owned in this city, the one that concealed the very advanced spacecraft they used, and begin their preparations for departure!

Printed in the United States
74151LV00003B/2